THE SPEAR OF ATLANTIS

By Andy McDermott and available from Headline

Featuring Nina Wilde and Eddie Chase

The Hunt for Atlantis
The Tomb of Hercules
The Secret of Excalibur
The Covenant of Genesis
The Cult of Osiris
The Sacred Vault
Empire of Gold
Temple of the Gods
The Valhalla Prophecy
Kingdom of Darkness
The Last Survivor (A Digital Short Story)
The Revelation Code
The Midas Legacy
King Solomon's Curse
The Spear of Atlantis

The Persona Protocol

ANDY McDERMOTT
THE SPEAR OF ATLANTIS

HEADLINE

First published in 2018 by
HEADLINE PUBLISHING GROUP

1

Cataloguing in Publication Data is available from the British Library

Hardback ISBN 978 1 4722 3689 0
Trade paperback ISBN 978 1 4722 3690 6

Typeset in Aldine 401BT by Avon DataSet Ltd,
Bidford-on-Avon, Warwickshire

Printed and bound in Great Britain by Clays Ltd, Elcograf S.p.A.

Headline's policy is to use papers that are natural, renewable and recyclable
products and made from wood grown in well-managed forests and other
controlled sources. The logging and manufacturing processes are expected to
conform to the environmental regulations of the country of origin.

HEADLINE PUBLISHING GROUP
An Hachette UK Company
Carmelite House
50 Victoria Embankment
London EC4Y 0DZ

www.headline.co.uk
www.hachette.co.uk

For Kat and Sebastian
making life an adventure

Prologue

The Islands of Thera

1627 BC

'We shouldn't be here,' said Kora nervously.

Lunos gave his companion a mocking look. The heavyset youth was useful as a strong pack mule, but his cowardice was becoming tiresome. Once they returned to the mainland, it might be time to strike out alone again.

But for now, there would still be a lot to carry. 'Second thoughts, my boy?' he said. 'A little late for that.' He surveyed their sun-baked surroundings. The isle of Kameni sat in the centre of the ring-like Theran archipelago, the blue Aegean shimmering beyond the distant cliffs. Higher up was the town of Intiri, squat buildings clinging to the gnarled slopes.

And it was completely deserted.

Kameni's highest peak was a fire mountain, home to the gods beneath the earth – and a few days earlier they had made their presence felt, shaking the islands as they spat out smoke and ash. Such occurrences were not rare, but this eruption had been particularly fierce, waves pounding the surrounding shores. The leaders of Akrotiri, Iathis and other Theran cities had taken it as a bad omen and ordered an evacuation. Everyone had fled . . .

Leaving their homes ripe for the picking.

1

Lunos reasoned that the closer a place was to the fire mountain, the more likely its fearful inhabitants were to have left valuables behind. And nowhere was closer than Intiri. Another earthquake the previous day had almost changed his mind, but though smoke was still rising from the mountaintop, the gods were, for now, minding their own business.

It did not take long to reach the town. Lunos stopped in the shade of an olive tree and looked around. Nobody was in sight, no smoke rising from kilns or ovens. 'I think everyone's gone.'

They approached a small house. The two men exchanged wary looks, then entered. 'I don't think we'll find anything worth much here,' said Kora, disappointed, as he took in the simple wooden plates on a low table.

'Maybe not, but I was right that they'd leave in a hurry, wasn't I?' Lunos countered. 'They didn't even finish their food.' Flies were making the most of an abandoned meal.

A quick search turned up nothing of value beyond a necklace. 'Might get a couple of coins for it,' said the older man, clicking his fingers for Kora to open a sack. 'Not much, but money is money.'

They emerged back into the morning sun. The fire mountain rose behind the town: it was not tall, but the pillar of smoke from its peak made it much more imposing. Lunos tried to judge if the dark plume had thickened. It seemed unchanged. Reassured, he was about to move on when . . .

Kora saw it too. 'What's that?'

'I don't know.' Lunos squinted. The unexpected sight was near the top of the mountain's highest foothill. A point of reflected light, the sun glinting off metal . . .

'There isn't a temple up there, is there?'

'There isn't *anything* that close to the mountain.'

'Maybe the gods left it. Maybe it *is* one of the gods!'

'Only if the gods are made of gold.' Whatever it was, thought

Lunos, the colour was unmistakable. It was bigger than a man – much bigger. It would be worth a fortune! 'Come on, we need to see.'

He set off, but Kora hesitated. 'The mountain, Lunos! If we get too close . . .'

'We're already too close, boy,' Lunos pointed out. 'If it starts spitting out fire and ash, we won't outrun it anywhere on this island. Trust me, though. There are always earthquakes before that happens, and there hasn't been once since yesterday. We're safe.'

Conflicted, Kora scurried after him.

The trek took longer than Lunos had expected. The harsh rocky landscape was dusted in recently fallen ash, and debris spilled by landslides slowed their progress still further. 'Gods' balls,' he muttered as he slipped.

Kora cringed. 'Don't say things like that! Not here.'

'If the gods were going to strike me down, they would have done it years ago.' Lunos scrabbled to the top of a small ridge.

They were not far below the hilltop, giving a clear view of the mysterious object lying amidst rubble. Lunos still had no idea what it actually *was*, though. A slightly squashed sphere, made of metal – and *big*, almost the size of the plundered house. It wasn't pure gold, however, the tint too red. A shame – so much gold would have made him the richest man in the Minoan Empire!

Kora pointed. 'It must have come from there.'

Higher up was a ragged hole in the hilltop. There was no ash on the sphere itself, so the landslip had exposed it after the fire mountain's most recent outburst. 'Must have been buried,' Lunos said.

'Who buried it?'

'I don't know.' He had never seen any smith or sculptor make anything so large. Maybe it really was of the gods . . .

3

Despite his concerns, he went to it, spitting on his fingers to wipe the metal. 'It *is* gold,' he said with rising excitement. It might not be pure, but any impurities could be separated when it was melted down. 'There must be tons of it! Tons of gold – and it's mine! Ours,' he hastily corrected as Kora moved past him.

The younger man wasn't listening, though. 'Lunos, look! There's a door!'

Lunos followed and saw that his companion was right. The sphere was hollow. He bustled to reach the door first. The foot-thick curved slab of gold was buckled, almost wrenched off its hinges when the fall smashed it open.

A flickering glow lit the interior. But it wasn't a fire. The light was a strange, unearthly cyan. 'What is that?' he said, moving closer.

Kora put a hand on his arm. 'I don't think you should go in there.'

Lunos regarded him sternly. 'You telling me what to do now, boy?'

'Look at it! This is the gods' work, I tell you. Or . . . the Old Ones.'

'The Old Ones are just a story,' Lunos replied. Gods he could understand, but he had little time for the local legend of a great and powerful ancient empire that had vanished without trace. If they were so great and powerful, why weren't they still around? The Minoan Empire certainly wasn't going to disappear and be forgotten.

Kora was not convinced. 'Then it *must* be the gods. And we're so close to their home!' He shot a worried look at the peak. 'Please, let's just go, while we still can.'

'If the gods had made it, it'd take more than a landslide to break it.' Lunos thumped a balled fist against the mangled door. '*Men* made this. Which means men can take it. Men like us. Or like me,' he added, with meaning.

Kora's anguish as he struggled to choose between riches and survival was plain. 'Are you *sure* it wasn't made by the gods?'

'Of course I'm sure. And I'm sure about something else: nobody knows it was here. It was buried, for who knows how long? We're the first people to find it. So whatever's inside belongs to the two of us. We'll be rich, my boy. Rich!'

Avarice finally overcame fear. 'All right,' Kora said. 'But you'd better be right.'

'I'm always right,' said Lunos smugly. He turned back to the doorway.

The sphere had come to rest at an angle, the floor inside sloping steeply away from him. Whatever was casting the light was against its lowest edge. He climbed cautiously over the threshold. The chamber he entered was circular, strange angular writing on the walls between crystalline pillars. A shiver crept up his spine. The room somehow felt unimaginably *ancient*. Maybe there was something to the tales of the Old Ones after all . . .

At its centre was an altar, a column of dark purple stone. Its top was hollow, forming a basin. More text was inscribed around it. He peered into it, but the bowl was empty.

He could now see the source of the light, though. On the floor was something extraordinary. A jewel, or crystal, but larger than any he had ever seen, about the length of his forearm. In shape, it resembled a double-ended spearhead. It glowed white from within, with brilliant flashes of blue and purple and red. The basin in the altar's top was the right size to contain it.

'What is it?' Kora whispered, awe and fear in his voice.

'I don't know. A diamond?' Lunos moved closer, one hand holding the altar for support. He flinched at a vibration through his fingers. An earthquake? No – this was too constant, unchanging.

'What's wrong?'

'Nothing,' he hurriedly replied, letting go. He held out his hand. The strange fire inside the jewel was not giving out any heat. Warily, he touched it.

The spearhead was the cause of the vibration, the crystal *trembling*. He squinted into the pulsating points of light. They were whirling around the gemstone's very heart . . .

'What is it?' the youth repeated.

'It's ours,' said Lunos, giving Kora a grin. 'That's what it is – *ours*! Look at it, boy! A diamond from the gods!'

'But you said men built this place.'

'Men who are long dead. It's a vault, where they hid their greatest treasure. But it's not hidden any more.' He took hold of the jewel with both hands.

Kora recoiled. 'Are you sure we should do that?'

'Yes, I'm sure,' Lunos snapped, increasingly irritated by his companion's fearful whining. 'Come on then! Either help me or get out of the way.'

'What are you going to do with it?' asked Kora.

'Take it back to the boat, of course. When everyone returns to Thera, I'll find a buyer.' He climbed back out through the opening. 'I know a jewel-cutter in Triakas who can turn it into smaller stones. If they all shine like this one, we can name our price. Kings and queens will want them!'

'But if you break it, the gods will be angry!'

'The gods are *always* angry. Now, are you going to carry this?'

Kora reluctantly took the spearhead. 'It's like . . . there are little earthquakes inside it.'

'As long as they *stay* inside it, we won't have anything to worry about.' Lunos regarded the sphere. 'We'll come back later. We might be able to get this door loose. Then we'll have gold as well as diamonds!'

He began to retrace his steps downhill towards Intiri. Kora followed, holding the gemstone at arm's length.

Lunos's daydreams of his impending fortune were cut short

after a few minutes when the younger man called out. 'The diamond! It's – something's happening!'

Lunos turned impatiently . . . to see Kora was right. Even under the glaring sun, the lights were visibly brighter than before – and more violent, seething inside their crystalline prison.

'It's shaking more,' Kora added. 'And it's making a noise – listen!'

Over the rustle of wind, Lunos heard a deep rumble, like endless thunder. But this was not far in the distance. It was coming from the gem.

'I think,' he said hesitantly, 'we should put it back. Yes, you should put it back.'

'You took it out!' Kora protested. 'You put it back!' The flashes from the spearhead grew brighter still, forcing him to look away. 'Oh gods! It's shaking, it – it feels like something's kicking inside it!'

The thunder grew louder, peals pounding in time with each new burst of light. Kora's resolve finally broke and he threw the jewel to the ground. Lunos gasped, terrified that it would shatter, but it stayed intact.

Yet the noise did not stop, nor did the searing pulses of light. Both men ran, Kora quickly outpacing the older thief. 'No, wait!' Lunos cried, afraid now that his erstwhile partner would reach the boat first and leave him behind. 'You shit, you whoreson! Stop!'

The crack of a thunderbolt split the air behind him. He glanced back in fear . . .

Another flash, so intense that the Minoan's eyes seared in their sockets – then he, Kora, the golden sphere and the island of Kameni ceased to exist.

An explosion utterly annihilated everything within two miles, a fireball a thousand times brighter than the sun flashing the sea into steam. The volcano's peak was blown away . . .

Unleashing a still more powerful force.

Deep beneath Kameni was a vast magma chamber, the isle merely the visible tip of a much bigger massif beneath the sea. The sudden release of pressure as its cap was ripped open triggered a colossal volcanic eruption. Ash and toxic smoke and lava blasted skywards, waves over a hundred metres high pounding the island chain and obliterating all traces of human settlement along the inner coastline.

Even greater waves raced outwards from the ring's far side, sweeping north through the Aegean to hammer the shores of Greece and Turkey, and south across the Mediterranean to swamp the mouth of the Nile. But it was the island of Crete, home to the Minoan civilisation, that was doomed to suffer the most damage. The entire northern coast was drowned by a tsunami, a wall of water destroying everything for miles inland.

Those who survived the deluge suffered a slower but no less terrible fate. The sheer amount of airborne ash blotted out the sun for days and affected temperatures worldwide for years afterwards, winters that were normally hard turning lethal. The remaining Minoans lived on, absorbed into other civilisations as refugees, but as a powerful seagoing empire, their time was over.

The evacuation of the Theran islands meant there was nobody to serve as witness. Without anyone to hand down the story, the eruption passed into myth with surprising swiftness. A record of flooding in Egypt, tales of earthquakes in Greece, accounts of failed crops from as far away as China would be all that remained. Even those few settlements on Thera that survived the tidal waves were buried by falling ash, reduced to silent, empty time capsules that would remain lost for millennia.

Forgotten . . . like the strange vault buried on the hill, and its deadly secret.

And the knowledge that it was not the only one.

1

The Mediterranean Sea

Present Day

'That,' said Eddie Chase, 'is a bloody big boat.'

His wife, Nina Wilde, gazed from the descending helicopter's window. 'You are absolutely not kidding.'

What lay before them was less a vessel, more a floating city. The cruise liner *Atlantia* was a great white-and-gold block of steel and glass, dwarfing the other ships Nina had seen during their flight from Malaga in southern Spain.

Their daughter, Macy, pressed her face excitedly against her own window. 'Wow, Mom! It's massive! Are we really going to land on it?'

'Bit of a wasted journey if we aren't,' said Eddie. He got an eye roll in return; even at seven years old, Macy was well used to the bald Englishman's drily sarcastic sense of humour.

The remaining passenger was Nina's grandmother, Olivia Garde. 'The helipad looks rather small. I hope that's just because the ship is so big.'

'Don't worry, Mrs Garde,' said the pilot. 'We do these landings all the time – I flew another VIP in earlier today, actually. And the pad's more than big enough for this bird.'

He hovered the Airbus H155 above the ship's bow, lowering

the landing gear and easing it on to the helipad. Macy squealed as it bumped to a stop. Crewmen hurried over, ducking beneath the whirling rotor blades to secure steel cables to the aircraft. The lines were quickly ratcheted tight, locking the helicopter firmly in place.

Nina looked across at the superstructure's sloping front. More people waited in a doorway. 'Looks like we've got a reception committee.'

'I would certainly hope so,' said Olivia. 'You are the guest of honour, after all.'

'They're probably only here for Nina,' Eddie retorted. 'The rest of us have to go in through steerage. Still, at least we'll be able to do some dancing.'

The red-haired New Yorker wagged a finger at her husband. 'Remember what we said about *Titanic* jokes?'

'What, "don't tell any"?'

'Yep.'

'Come on, we're right at the front! I've at least got to go "I'm the king of the woooorld!"'

'No, you don't. You really, really don't.'

'If I can't do *Titanic* jokes, I'm going to do *Speed 2* ones instead,' the Yorkshireman muttered. Outside, two men in crisp white uniforms jogged to the helicopter. 'Ay up, here they come.'

The new arrivals opened the doors and helped the passengers out. 'Welcome to the *Atlantia*, Dr Wilde,' said the older man, an imposing, craggy-faced American with white hair. 'I'm Arnold Snowcock, the captain.'

'Thank you,' Nina replied. 'I wasn't expecting the captain to meet us right off our flight!'

'You're a very special guest.' He shook her hand, then greeted the others.

'Nice boat you've got here,' said Eddie.

'Thank you. Although it's a ship, not a boat.' Snowcock's brow revealed a faint furrow of impatience, suggesting he was very particular about correct nautical terminology. 'If you'll come inside, Mr Moretti and his men will bring in your baggage.'

The visitors quickly made their way to the open door. Snowcock offered to assist Olivia, the nonagenarian walking with a cane, but she waved him away.

They entered the ship, a sign telling them they were on Deck 8. The reception area resembled that of a top-end hotel, the liner's owner wanting to create a splendid first impression. Nina found the gilded decor too gaudy for her tastes, but she kept this to herself, since said owner was there to greet her.

The Emir of Dhajan, ruler of a small but wealthy emirate in the Persian Gulf, had invited her personally to join the *Atlantia*'s maiden voyage. He was surrounded by an entourage, standing out from his traditionally robed male companions by being the only one wearing a suit. He was several years younger than Nina, she knew, in his mid thirties, but in the half-decade since taking the throne had thrown his country full-speed into a programme of modernisation that had transformed it from an oil-rich backwater into a hub for tourism and finance with aspirations to rival Dubai and Bahrain.

'Dr Wilde!' he said with a broad white smile. 'Welcome aboard the *Atlantia*. I am delighted to meet you.' His English was perfect, with undertones of an expensive Western education.

Snowcock handled the introductions. 'Dr Wilde, Mr Chase, Mrs Garde . . . and Ms Wilde Chase,' he added, winking at Macy, 'this is His Majesty Sheikh Fadil bin A'zam, the Emir of Dhajan – and the *Atlantia*'s owner, so also my boss.' He chuckled, the Emir giving a little laugh in return. 'Your Majesty, your guest of honour, Dr Nina Wilde.'

Nina shook the Emir's hand. 'It's an honour to meet you.'

'The honour is all mine,' he replied. 'To meet the discoverer of Atlantis, the Pyramid of Osiris, the Ark of the Covenant . . . incredible finds. And I am sure you will find many more such wonders.'

'Maybe,' she said. 'But I've got other priorities now.'

He raised an eyebrow, then turned his attention to Eddie. 'And Mr Chase – the saviour of Mecca.'

'Just doing my job,' said Eddie, shaking hands. Several years earlier, he had prevented a deadly chemical attack on the Hajj, the very centre of the Islamic faith in Saudi Arabia.

'There is no need to be modest. Every Muslim owes you a great debt.'

There was one woman amongst the Emir's companions, wearing a long dress of royal-blue silk and a matching headscarf covering her hair. 'You also saved your own country,' she observed. 'Even if you did not save Big Ben.'

Nina saw her husband hide his discomfort at the reminder of what he still considered a failure on his part. The couple had two years previously uncovered a plot by a rogue MI6 agent to bring about a coup in Britain by destroying Parliament; though their actions exposed the conspirators and warned of the impending attack in time to save many lives, Eddie had been unable to stop it from being carried out – and as a result, the iconic London clock tower had collapsed, killing hundreds.

'Been doing your research, have you?' he said.

'His Majesty's security is my responsibility,' the woman replied. 'Nobody meets him without having been thoroughly checked.'

The Emir quickly smoothed the awkward moment. 'This is my sister, Her Royal Highness the Sheikha Alula bint A'zam, princess of Dhajan.'

'Your sister?' said Nina. She had assumed the woman was his wife, but now realised they had very similar features. Twins?

'And also my minister of state security. A position I assure you she gained through merit, not nepotism. I believe in equality for all, men and women – before I took the throne, women in my country were not even allowed to hold political office – but also I believe in fairness to all. A person should prove they are the best for the job before they take it, no?'

From the fleeting look Alula gave her brother, Nina guessed that no such requirements were placed on the job of emir. But there was no time to reflect on the emirate's internal politics as its leader pressed on with the introductions. The redhead responded in kind. 'This is my grandmother, Olivia Garde, and my daughter, Macy.'

The Emir crouched to greet Macy. 'Hello! And how are you?'

'I'm very well, thank you,' she replied politely. 'I made you a present.'

'You did?' he said, with exaggerated surprise. 'Why, thank you! What is it?'

She produced a small gift-wrapped object. The Emir took it. Alula watched with wary disapproval – handing unvetted items to the monarch was doubtless a security breach, Nina thought – but Fadil himself was unconcerned, peeling away the paper. 'This is beautiful,' he exclaimed. It was a little photo album, thick covers protecting photographs pasted to the card pages.

'These are pictures of the best places to visit in America,' Macy explained.

The Emir smiled, leafing through it. 'The Statue of Liberty, the Empire State Building . . . are they all in New York?'

'Well, it *is* the best place in America!' she said proudly.

He straightened, slipping the book inside his jacket pocket. 'Then I shall make sure I visit. Thank you, Macy. I'm certain I will find this very useful.'

'My mom helped me make it,' Macy added proudly.

'We've been practising crafting,' said Nina, smiling.

'You have taught her very well,' said Fadil.

Macy looked around. 'Is this whole ship yours? You must be really rich!'

'Macy,' her mother chided.

The Emir laughed, unconcerned. 'My country is rich, Macy. I merely decide where the money is spent. We built this ship, and its sister, the *Pacifia*, to encourage tourists to come to Dhajan. We want to give them a very warm welcome, and show them a good time. Which,' he continued, 'I will do when I give you a tour. But first, I will have you shown to your cabins. You have the VIP suites, the best on the ship.'

Snowcock signalled to a woman in a white jacket. 'This is your personal steward, Ana,' he said. 'She'll attend to absolutely anything you need. You'll all get special wristbands with a call button. Wherever you are on the ship, if you press the button, Ana or one of the other stewards will be with you as soon as they can.'

'I'm here to help,' said Ana. She was in her mid thirties, olive-skinned with short black hair, and Nina placed her accent as Brazilian. A name tag on her lapel gave her surname as *Rijo*. 'If you'll follow me, I'll get your wristbands and take you to your suites.'

'VIP suites?' said Eddie. 'Sounds good. Definitely a cut above steer—'

'No *Titanic* jokes,' Nina interjected.

'Tchah! Well, so long as there isn't a bloke with a bath full of leeches next door, I'll be happy.'

'What?'

'*Speed 2*.'

'What's *Speed 2*, Mom?' asked Macy.

'A bad old movie that nobody but your father remembers,' Nina told her. 'Thank you so much for inviting us aboard, Your Majesty.'

'As I said, it is my honour,' Fadil replied. 'I look forward to your lecture. Perhaps you would give me a private viewing of the Atlantis exhibition beforehand?'

'I'd love to,' she said.

He bowed his head. 'Then I shall see you again once you are settled.'

'Please, follow me,' said Ana.

She led the way to the exit. Nina took Macy's hand, Eddie and Olivia behind as they headed into the vast vessel.

'Look at this!' Macy whooped, leaping on to the huge double bed. 'It's bigger than my whole room!'

'I don't think it's *quite* that big,' said Nina. Their suite was far larger than she had expected, though, VIPs aboard the *Atlantia* being given the luxury of space. 'And stop jumping on our bed! You've got the single, over there.'

'Aw, *Mom!*'

'The balcony's a decent size an' all,' said Eddie, opening a sliding glass door. A stiff breeze hit him; the ship had resumed its course, heading west. The suite was on the starboard side, overlooking the Spanish coast. Stepping out, he found that the curved balcony extended out from the superstructure's vertical side, giving him a panoramic view of both the coast and the ship itself. He looked down. They were ten decks up, the sea a good hundred feet below.

Nina joined him. 'Ooh. Long drop.'

'Yeah. Let's hope we don't need those.' He pointed astern. Five levels down, large orange lifeboats were lined up within a recess in the ship's hull.

The starboard wing bridge jutted out several decks above, but the view ahead was otherwise unbroken. Off in the distance he could see the Rock of Gibraltar, a great dark hump at the end of a peninsula. Beyond it was Tarifa, at the southernmost tip of mainland Spain, and past that the Gulf of Cadiz, the entrance to the Atlantic – where Nina had first discovered the submerged remains of the lost civilisation of Atlantis. 'Can't bloody stay away, can we?' he said.

Nina gave him a quizzical look. 'Hmm?'

'Atlantis. How many times have we been back there now?'

'I kinda lost count,' she said, amused. 'Don't worry, though – at least we don't have to dive eight hundred feet down this time.'

'Good. I'm getting too old for that.'

'Forty-seven is the new twenty-seven, or so I heard,' she said brightly. He made an appalled face. She grinned and went back inside, Eddie following. Their steward, who at Nina's request had attended to Olivia in the neighbouring cabin first, was now unpacking their belongings. 'Oh, Ana. I said you don't need to do that.'

'That's okay, it's my job,' Ana replied with a smile. 'You're a VIP passenger. You don't have to lift a finger while you're aboard.'

'If we need you, we'll call you with this,' Nina insisted, indicating the gold plastic wristband she was now wearing. She knew from a demonstration when they had first been logged into the ship's computers as guests that pressing a button on the band pinpointed her location to within a few feet.

'She just doesn't want you going through her pants,' said Eddie. 'Especially not the sexy ones.'

The redhead was not amused. 'Eddie! I *will* throw you overboard if I have to.'

Ana tried to hide a smile. 'Whatever you say. But remember, if you *do* need me . . .'

'We'll call you, don't worry,' said Nina. 'Thank you anyway.'

The Brazilian nodded, then exited. Nina followed her into the lounge, then knocked on the door to the adjoining suite. 'Olivia! Everything okay in there?'

Her grandmother opened it. 'Oh, yes. I've been on liners

16

before – proper ocean liners, mind, not these floating vacation resorts – and this is by far the biggest cabin I've ever had. There are definite advantages to being a VIP guest of the ship's owner.'

A telephone by Eddie and Nina's bed rang. Eddie picked it up and had a brief exchange with the caller before joining the two women. 'That was Captain Snowcock – Snowcock, what kind of a name is that?'

'The kind you're not going to make fun of in front of him. Or Macy,' said Nina.

'As if! Anyway, the Emir wants to give us a tour of the ship in an hour, before we have dinner.'

Nina put on a faux-Valley Girl voice. 'But I have to do my *haaaair*!' She reached up and pulled a hairband from her ponytail, letting her red locks fall below her shoulders. 'Okay, done.'

'Me too.' Eddie rubbed a hand over his shaved head.

'In that case,' said Olivia, 'I'll see you in fifty-nine minutes.' She closed the door.

'So,' said Nina, 'what do we wear for dinner with a king?'

2

'Wow,' Nina said to Eddie, smiling. 'You're almost present-able.'

The Yorkshireman had exchanged his leather jacket and jeans for a suit, but despite looking smart, he was not comfortable. 'Too much starch in this shirt,' he complained, fingering his collar. 'Like being back in bloody uniform.'

'You'll be fine,' she assured him. Her own outfit was a stylish black dress rather than her usual trousers. 'Now, do I wear heels or slip-ons? We're about to do a lot of walking . . .'

'Wear the heels and bring the other pair just in case,' Eddie suggested. 'Or call Ana to bring 'em if your feet start hurting.'

'I still don't feel comfortable about having someone jump every time I call. I guess I'm not cut out to be a queen.'

'I'd like to be a queen,' Macy proclaimed, striding into the room in a dress of her own. 'I'd have a crown, and a sceptre, and . . .' She tried to think of another royal accoutrement. 'And a special crown for weekends,' she decided.

'This is what we get for letting her watch all those Disney princess shows,' said Eddie.

'Better than those movies based on us,' Nina complained. 'I *still* can't believe you let her see them. They're PG-13, and she's seven!'

'Yeah, but PG stands for "parental guidance", right? I'm her parent, and I was guidancing. I did tell her to look away when the bad guy got thrown into the mummification machine and had all his blood sucked out.'

Nina folded her arms. 'And did she?'

'She's seven, what do you think?'

A sigh. 'We are the world's worst parents. And by we, I mean *you.*'

Eddie shrugged. 'She's smart, she knows it's not real. Don't you, love? You've been on set, you know it's all just actors and special effects.'

Macy nodded. 'The director let me hold Osiris's skull!'

'Did he now,' said her mother disapprovingly, before shaking her head. 'And it still bugs me that they're ignoring what actually happened and making up whatever nonsense they like. They brought the supernatural into the last one, for God's sake. I wish *I* had magic powers from being descended from the Atlanteans, but I don't.'

'You *were* able to use Excalibur to cut stuff like a lightsaber,' said Eddie, reminding her of a past adventure when they discovered the legendary sword of King Arthur. 'And you've got the,' he tapped his temple, 'brainy thing.'

'Being able to do complex math in my head isn't a magical power!'

A knock on the connecting door ended the discussion. Nina let her grandmother in. 'You look nice.'

'Thank you,' Olivia replied. She too was wearing a dress, though hers was more traditionally formal. 'I may be ninety-three, but that doesn't mean I don't enjoy dressing up.' She looked at her watch. 'Fifty-nine minutes on the dot. Now, let's see how punctual that girl is.'

'She's a grown woman, not a girl,' Nina chided. 'And don't treat her like a serving maid, either!'

Another knock, this from the main door. Macy skipped to open it. 'It's Ana!'

'Hello,' said the Brazilian. 'I've been asked to bring you to the Emir.'

'We're all ready,' Nina told her.

'Okay.' She turned to Olivia. 'Mrs Garde, the *Atlantia* is a very big ship. Would you like a mobility scooter?'

Olivia bristled. 'Absolutely not. I'm perfectly capable of walking, thank you.'

'Thank you for offering, though,' Nina said to Ana, who nodded appreciatively. 'Shall we go?'

Ana brought them to a VIP lounge overlooking the bow. Waiting were the Emir and a smaller contingent of his entourage, including his sister and Captain Snowcock. 'Hello again,' said Fadil. 'I'm delighted that you could join us.'

'We're looking forward to the tour,' Nina replied.

'Good, good. I will show you around the *Atlantia* personally – I am very proud of her!'

The tour began, the Emir reeling off facts and figures as they took a lift to the uppermost deck. 'The world's largest, most luxurious and most ecologically friendly passenger liner,' he said. 'Over two billion dollars to build, two hundred and fifty-six thousand gross tonnes, four hundred and two metres long – bigger than the largest American aircraft carrier. But it produces under a quarter of the pollution of its nearest rival.'

'That's quite an improvement,' said Nina.

He nodded. 'Normal liners burn marine diesel for fuel – filthy stuff, and the largest burn *twelve tonnes* of it per hour. That is as much pollution as a million cars. But *Atlantia* uses liquefied natural gas, and its engines are hybrids – almost an entire deck below is full of batteries. Our ultimate goal is to make an entirely electric propulsion system, but for now, anything that reduces the use of oil is an improvement.'

'I thought Dhajan was a big oil producer,' said Eddie. 'Aren't you putting yourself out of business?'

'Dhajan *was* a big oil producer, yes. But we are only a small

20

country, and we do not have the same reserves as our neighbours – Saudi Arabia, Qatar, Bahrain and the other emirates.'

'Our regional rivals,' said Alula, with an undertone of hostility.

'Since I took the throne, I have diversified our economy. When demand for oil falls, which it will as more cars become electric, we will have other means of support.'

They emerged from the lift. The front of the liner's top deck was sheltered by a large geodesic dome, a streamlined glass shell housing a bar and sun lounge. The Emir led them aft, however. The deck divided a quarter of the way down the vessel's length, broad wings housing cabins on either side of a twelve-storey atrium running along the centreline. Shouts and squeals came from one of its main attractions: a giant zip-line to starboard, the cable running beneath bridges and cross-decks down to the centre of the stern. A hanging cage was descending, the legs of its dozen shrieking passengers dangling as they swept away from its launch platform.

Macy ran to the railing to watch. 'Oh, cool! Can we have a go?'

'Maybe later, love,' Eddie told her.

'Just one of the many entertainments,' said the Emir. 'All kinds of pools and water sports, climbing walls – even a jungle bio-dome. Then we have shops, restaurants, bars, casinos, cinemas, live shows, go-karts – electric, of course!'

'Of course,' Nina said with a smile. Alula, however, had revealed a flicker of distaste at the mention of the bars and casinos, suggesting she was more conservative than her brother – though the redhead suspected she was not a fan of the colossal floating pleasure palace as a whole.

'Then there is dancing,' the Emir continued, 'cookery lessons, exhibitions, boats and jetskis – but I'm giving everything away!' he said with a laugh.

He led them down the promenade's starboard leg. Several passengers recognised the Dhajani ruler, phones coming up to take photos. But he was not the only celebrity in the group; Nina saw a couple of people snapping pictures of her. 'Ay up,' said Eddie. 'You've got fans. Must've seen your TV show.'

'Or read my book,' she replied, hoping it was the latter. While her time as the presenter of a television documentary series had brought her additional fame beyond what she already had as the world's best-known archaeologist – 'non-fictional', she would qualify whenever anyone mentioned Indiana Jones or Lara Croft – it had also led to repercussions she preferred not to dwell upon.

'The *Atlantia*'s hull is seventy metres across,' the Emir continued. 'Two hundred and . . . twenty feet, I believe?'

Snowcock was about to give the exact size, but Nina had already made the conversion in her head. 'Twenty-nine.'

'Ah! Excellent, even bigger. Its nearest rival is only sixty-five metres. We could have used that extra width to squeeze in more cabins, but they would have been very small. I come from a small country – I appreciate space.'

'It's crowded enough as it is down there,' said Eddie, regarding the packed atrium. 'How many people can it take?'

'Seven thousand and fifty-three passengers at maximum capacity,' Snowcock told him. 'This voyage, it's just over five and a half thousand pax. Plus almost three thousand crew.'

'When *Pacifia* sets out on her maiden voyage from Dhajan next week,' said Fadil, 'she will have, I believe, six thousand eight hundred passengers.'

The Yorkshireman was about to say more, but was taken aback when his phone rang. 'Sorry,' he said. 'Didn't think I'd get reception in the middle of the sea.'

The Emir pointed out two large communications dishes flanking the glass carapace at the front of the superstructure. 'The ship has satellite links and its own cell masts. Just because you are on a cruise doesn't mean you should be out of touch! All included in the price. I do not like to . . . what is the English slang? "Gouge", to gouge my guests. Please, take your call.'

Eddie did so. 'Hi, Gerry. No, I'll call you later. I'm on a boat . . . No, I haven't turned into a salty seaman, you cheeky sod. Yeah, talk to you soon.' He disconnected. 'Business associate. Sorry.'

'It is no problem,' the Emir assured him. 'As I was saying, our competitors gouge their guests; they will charge thirty dollars to use the gym, twenty dollars a day for Wi-Fi, five dollars for a Coca-Cola. We ask for a little more up front, but most things are included in the price.'

They reached the largest of the cross-bridges over the atrium. This housed a bar and restaurant complex, resembling a UFO that had landed on the liner's back. Rather than enter, the Emir brought them to a bank of glass elevators. 'I will take you to the shopping decks. They are where we make back our money!' he added with a wink.

Ana had already called a lift, holding the doors open. 'Thanks,' Nina told her, before turning to Olivia. 'You okay?'

'I'm not an invalid, Nina,' her grandmother told her. 'I may use a cane, but I'm perfectly capable of walking.'

'Grams got frostbite and had to have two of her toes chopped off!' Macy announced excitedly.

'Thanks for telling everyone that, darling,' said Nina with a fixed smile.

The lift descended, giving its occupants a better view of the atrium before stopping on the level below. To Nina, it seemed they had gone from a ship to an expensive mall. A boulevard wound along its length, carefully designed to funnel passengers to clusters of shops. They sold designer clothing, shoes, cosmetics – nothing that couldn't be bought on shore, and probably for half the price, but none were having trouble attracting customers.

'Mom, look! Mom!' Macy cried, tugging at her arm. 'It's you and Dad!'

Nina looked to see what she meant, only for her heart to sink. 'It's not really us,' she explained to her quizzical hosts. 'They're from the movies based on my books. Very, *very* loosely based.' Nearby was a toy shop, featuring in its windows a selection of merchandise from the most recent film in the series, *The Pyramid of Doom*.

'Oh, these I must see!' proclaimed Fadil, giving Macy a conspiratorial grin.

'No, we don't have to . . . Ugh, fine,' Nina sighed as her daughter tugged him into the store.

'There they are!' said Macy, pointing out a display of action figures.

'I'm afraid,' said the Emir apologetically, 'they are not a very good likeness.'

'They're not *us* us,' said Eddie. 'That's Jason Mach; he's based on me, but he's played by Grant Thorn.'

'Ah, yes. The star of the car movies? And one about a baby in the White House?'

'Afraid so,' said Nina, shaking her head. *First Baby*, starring their Hollywood A-list friend, had been as terrible as she'd expected after first hearing Grant's pitch, yet somehow had earned hundreds of millions of dollars. 'And that's Eden Crest, who's . . . well, she's based on me insofar as she's an archaeologist, but that's pretty much where any similarities end. And they didn't even keep the same actress for the newest film, they recast her!' she added, offended. 'I guess they thought nobody would notice. 'Cause, y'know, women are interchangeable.' Alula seemed to share her disapproval. 'I mean, they couldn't even get the colour of my hair right. I've been a redhead my whole life, never a brunette.'

Macy was not interested in debating Hollywood sexism,

instead jabbing a finger at another toy. 'And look! They've got a trikan.'

'You've already got one, love,' Eddie said.

'But this one lights up!'

The Emir peered at the item. 'What is it?'

'A trikan? It's an Atlantean weapon,' said Nina. The toy was a palm-sized disc with three curved blade-like arms spiralling outwards, connected by a string to a plastic handgrip. 'There's actually a real-life example in the exhibition on this ship. The movie version, though? It's . . . well, a cross between a boom-erang and a yo-yo, only magic. It's all very silly. Unfortunately, I don't get to cut things I don't like out of the script.'

'If you did, there'd be nothing left,' her husband pointed out.

'I will buy it for you, Macy,' said the Emir. 'If your parents will allow me?'

'Uh . . . sure,' said Nina reluctantly, not seeing how she could refuse.

He spoke to the man at the counter, who hurriedly fetched him one of the toys. 'Thank you!' cried Macy, delighted, as Fadil presented it to her.

'Glad we let *him* buy it,' Eddie whispered to Nina. 'It was fifty bloody dollars! No wonder he said they make back their money down here. Bet it'd be about twenty at Walmart.'

'Give it six months, it'll be three bucks fifty in the discount aisle,' she replied.

They continued through the mall. A melange of expensive scents wafted out from a perfume store, the glint of gaudy gold jewellery twinkling from its neighbour. Deciding that none of the shops offered anything of the remotest interest to her, Nina turned her attention back to the ship itself. Despite the *Atlantia*'s size, she had been unable to shake a constant feeling of vague claustrophobia. The corridors serving the cabins were narrow, barely half as wide as in a hotel on land, and even in the spacious mall everything was just a little bit *low*, the heavy crystal chandeliers oppressively close. She was glad of the brief respite when they passed a set of escalators, daylight from above piercing the artificial glow.

The group continued back towards the bow. 'We should have brought our bikes,' Eddie joked. Macy had become fast enough on a bicycle to make it impossible for her parents to keep up without their own.

'It's a big ship, sure, but it's not Central Park,' said Nina. 'Although you don't get sea views from there . . .' She trailed off, realising that what she had thought was a huge panoramic window actually had a shop entrance behind it. 'Wow, is that a TV screen? I honestly thought it was a real window.'

Eddie peered at it. 'It looks 3-D.'

'It is,' said the Emir proudly. 'The very latest. No need for glasses!' As he spoke, the view changed to an angle over the bow, with Africa to port and Europe starboard, the helicopter at the bottom of the frame. 'We have many of them, to show the passengers what is happening outside. Why be on a ship if you cannot see the sea?'

They reached the mall's forward end, Snowcock leading the way to another elevator bank, twin staircases curving around it. The group took one lift to Deck 16. 'If you'll come this way, I'll show you the bridge,' he said, emerging on a broad landing.

Macy bustled to the front of the pack. 'Wow, cool! Can I drive the ship?'

'We will see,' the Emir told her, smiling.

Snowcock brought them to an anonymous metal door, holding up a card on a lanyard around his neck to a rectangular panel of black glass beside it. It was a screen, a green circle appearing as the ship's security systems confirmed his ID. He opened the door and ushered them through.

A short passage led into the *Atlantia*'s spacious bridge. It ran the liner's full width, doors leading to the wing bridges that extended out over the water far below. The entire front wall was glazed, floor-to-ceiling windows raking backwards to match the streamlined slope of the ship's forward superstructure. The exception was at the centreline, where the glass tilted forwards around a pulpit-like extension housing a small wheel. Large sections of the softly lit room's rear wall were taken up by video screens displaying live feeds from the ship's numerous CCTV cameras.

'Very futuristic,' said Olivia, impressed.

'Like being on the Starship *Enterprise*,' Eddie agreed. 'You must have to shout if you want to talk to someone on the far side, though.'

'We get by,' Snowcock told him with a chuckle. He greeted the other officers present, who had all straightened respectfully at the Emir's arrival. 'So, welcome to the *Atlantia*'s bridge,' he told his guests. 'We can control every aspect of the ship's operations from here with just five bridge crew – although,' he gestured at his eight officers, 'we usually have more on duty for safety. With so many people aboard, there's a lot to keep an eye on.'

'Suppose you've got to watch out for hackers trying to crash you into oil tankers too,' said Eddie. Snowcock gave him a bemused, slightly concerned look. 'Like in *Speed 2*?' The look intensified.

'I told you, nobody remembers *Speed 2*,' Nina sighed. 'You'll have to forgive my husband. His cultural references are about twenty-five years out of date.'

'Tchah.' Eddie walked to the front of the bridge. Macy joined him. The purpose of the glazed pulpit immediately became apparent; the windows' rearward rake made it difficult for any-one to get a clear view down at the bow without hitting their head on the sloping glass. 'So you can drive the whole ship with this little wheel?'

'Here, or from either of the wing bridges,' Snowcock told him. 'But that wheel's really only used for slow manoeuvres in port. We normally use the azipod controls.'

'What are they?' Macy asked.

'Come and see,' said the Emir, going to a large central console. She hurried around it, Nina joining her.

'The *Atlantia* doesn't have traditional propellers or rudders,' Snowcock explained, pointing to a trio of black spherical controls on squat joysticks, chromed throttle levers curling over them. 'It has three azipods – electrically powered thrusters that can rotate three hundred and sixty degrees. By turning them in different directions, we can literally spin the ship around in its own length. We won't try that right now, though,' he added with another chuckle. 'At this speed, it would send everyone flying.'

Macy nodded, resisting the temptation to twist one of the controls. 'How fast can the ship go?' she asked instead.

The captain glanced at a digital display. 'We're currently doing twenty-two knots. That's twenty-five miles per hour. Our full cruising speed is twenty-five knots – about twenty-nine m.p.h.'

A sly smile crept across Fadil's face. 'But we can go faster,' he whispered to Macy. 'Would you like to see?'

She grinned. 'Yeah!'

'Then watch this.' He reached for a black glass panel amongst the controls, then hesitated as Macy struggled to peer over the helm console's edge. 'Dr Wilde, could you pick her up so she can see?'

'Sure,' Nina said. She lifted her daughter.

'Now, look at this,' said the Emir. The panel lit up as his hand neared it, displaying a keypad. Nina watched as he carefully tapped in a six-digit code: 0-3-2-0-1-5. March 2015? She wondered if it was an important date to him. It certainly was to her; it was the month Macy was born.

The keypad flashed in acceptance, then disappeared. A new window popped up, Arabic text followed by its equivalent in English – *Owner's Code Accepted*.

The Emir brought up a new window. A tap at a digital toggle switch, and a message appeared: *Speed Limiter Disengaged*. His grin broadened. 'Now,' he said, 'Captain, if you would take us to . . . thirty knots?'

Snowcock looked surprised by the command, but took the azipod controls and pushed the throttles forward. 'Twenty-four knots, twenty-five . . . twenty-six?' He glanced at the Dhajani leader, who nodded to tell him to continue.

'It's not meant to go that fast?' asked Nina.

'It would appear this ship has some tricks even I didn't know about.' The captain sounded unsettled by the discovery.

'Well, we've just hit thirty knots,' Eddie noted.

'Shall we go faster?' the Emir asked Macy. Her reply was inevitably in the affirmative.

'Your Majesty, I'd advise against it,' said Snowcock, obviously deeply uncomfortable. 'We're in a major shipping lane—'

'Just for one minute, Captain,' the Emir told him. Despite the lightness of his tone, it was unmistakably a command. 'We are not in danger of a collision, are we?'

Snowcock glanced towards an officer at a radar screen, who shook his head. 'No, sir.'

'Then let us see what she can do.'

The captain's lips tightened, but he pushed the throttles further open. The speed display rose, thirty-two knots, thirty-three, thirty-four . . .

'There is a trophy,' said the Emir, 'the Blue Riband, given to the fastest liner to cross the Atlantic. It has not been challenged for seventy years, but the last ship to win it, an American vessel, managed an average speed of thirty-five knots. I would very much like to claim that prize for Dhajan!'

'I don't think you'll have any trouble,' said Nina. The display approached forty knots.

'Your Majesty,' said Snowcock firmly, his eyes on another screen showing coloured bars – several of which were creeping upwards, shifting from green through yellow towards orange. 'I *strongly* recommend that we return to normal cruising speed. We don't want to risk redlining the drive systems, certainly not on our maiden voyage.'

'Oh . . . very well,' said the Emir, disappointed.

Snowcock immediately pulled the throttle back, the speed indicator and the bars falling. The Arab re-entered his code. A new message popped up: *Owner Logged Out.* 'I guess being ruler of a whole country has its perks,' said Nina.

'I never have to wait at traffic lights in Dhajan either,' the Emir said. 'So, Macy, were you impressed by how fast we can go?'

Macy glanced at her mother before answering, as if worried about giving offence. 'It . . . didn't feel any different.'

He laughed. 'Then the ship is very well designed! Now,' he said, turning to his visitors, 'our meal will soon be ready. I have some business I must attend to first, but Ana will escort you to the royal dining room. I shall meet you there.' He gave his guests a small bow, his expression boyishly proud. 'I hope the *Atlantia* met your expectations.'

'It's very impressive, yes,' Nina assured him.

'Like a five-star hotel, except on water,' Eddie added.

'Only five stars? We must work harder. Perhaps dinner will win us an extra star!' The Emir addressed Macy. 'And did you like my ship?'

She nodded. 'I did. It's very cool. And very huge.'

'And what part of it did you like the most?'

Her eyes flicked to the box she was holding. 'The toy shop?'

'Sorry,' said Nina, wincing.

He straightened, amused. 'There is no need to apologise. Often, when dealing with the ruler of a nation, people can be . . . circuitous. But children let you know their true feelings.'

'Do you have children yourself?'

He shook his head. 'Not yet. I hope to. But bringing an entire country into the future is all-consuming. I have not even had the chance to find a wife, never mind devote the time I would need to a child. I could have married for political convenience and handed over all my responsibilities as a parent to someone else, but . . . what kind of a man would I be? What example would I set for my children – and my country?'

'I hope you find the time,' said Eddie. 'It's definitely worth it. Even if,' he tapped Macy's toy, 'you end up buying a ton of rubbish you don't need.'

'Oh, so can I finally throw out your Fidel Castro cigar box?' Nina asked hopefully. 'Thank you so much for the tour, Your Majesty. I'm sure dinner will be just as good.'

'And I am sure your lecture on Atlantis will be most enlightening,' the Emir replied.

Ana led the family from the bridge. 'The royal dining room is on Deck 14, at the stern,' she said. 'But I can call for a golf cart if you don't want to walk the whole length of the ship.'

'Olivia, you want one?' Eddie asked.

'I'll be fine,' the old lady insisted. 'The day I can't walk a block and a half is the day I give up the ghost.'

Nina gave her grandmother a concerned look, but to her relief Olivia did indeed seem to be managing the trek perfectly well – if anything, better than she was herself, her feet starting to hurt in the high heels.

They took the lift down several decks. 'Ooh, look at this!' cried Macy, hurrying into the lobby. At its centre was a large circular display case, inside which was a slowly revolving representation of the *Atlantia* – but it was not a model. 'It's a hologram!'

'That's pretty impressive,' said Nina. She had seen holographic displays that could be viewed from any angle before, but this was a step up in image quality.

'I think there are four or five of them aboard,' said Ana. 'It shows you how to find anywhere on the ship.'

Eddie snorted. 'Probably cost half a million quid to do the same job as a bit of card with a map on it.'

Macy was already playing with a touchscreen. The computer-generated ship peeled open to reveal its interior. 'Mom, they've got a nail parlour . . . and a bowling alley . . . and a marina, look!' She pointed at the *Atlantia*'s stern, where a water-level dock extended from a giant hatch. 'You can even see the jetskis! Can we ride them?'

'I think you're too young,' said Nina. She didn't know if that were true, but fervently hoped it was.

'Show us where we're going,' suggested Eddie. Macy did so. The royal dining room was on a cross-deck high over the stern. 'It's bloody miles away! You *sure* you don't want a golf cart, Olivia? 'Cause I'm considering it myself.'

'If you do . . .' suggested Ana.

'We're okay, thanks,' Nina told her. 'Come on. The walk should help our appetites, if nothing else!'

'*I* want to ride a golf cart,' grumbled Macy.

They headed aft through the ship's long corridors, along the way traversing a lounge area with another giant ultra-high-definition screen. A tall Middle Eastern man in his early forties stood there, seemingly entranced by the reality of the three-dimensional display. The group passed him without so much as a second glance.

The hard-faced man waited for the VIP guests to retreat, then surreptitiously checked that nobody was nearby before moving to a planter. He slipped a cylindrical metal object from a pocket and carefully placed it beneath the leaves, then touched a finger to a small earpiece. 'This is al-Asim,' he whispered in Arabic. 'My bombs are in place. Everyone, report your status.'

He waited for the replies. All met his approval.

'Good. Return to your cabins and wait for the go signal. Our target is here.' He glanced after the departed group. 'Nina Wilde is aboard.'

3

Even by the *Atlantia*'s standards, the royal dining room was opulent, a chamber of marble and gold with a glass wall overlooking the liner's stern and the Mediterranean beyond. Ana introduced Nina to the other waiting guest. 'I'm sure you've heard of Gideon Lobato.'

'I have indeed,' said Nina. 'It's good to meet you, Mr Lobato.'

The gaunt man, his dark hair shaved down to a stubble, regarded her outstretched hand from behind his little round spectacles as if she had presented him with a rotting fish, hesitating before weakly shaking it. 'Dr Wilde,' he said. 'An honour.' Nina knew he was a naturalised American citizen, but he had a distinct accent: Turkish, she guessed. 'I am a great admirer of your work, specifically on the discovery of Atlantis. Fascinating.'

'Thank you,' she replied.

He withdrew his hand, then, without the slightest concern that she might be offended, took out an antiseptic wipe and cleaned it. 'Regrettably, I am not able to attend your lecture tonight. But I hope you will answer some of my questions during dinner.'

'I'd be delighted.' The white-clad billionaire's gaze alternated between avoiding hers and then locking on to her eyes with unnerving intensity. She got the impression he was well along the autism spectrum – which perhaps contributed to the unwavering focus that had made him a very rich man.

'And they must be your family?'

'They must,' said Eddie. He extended his hand, but Lobato's attention had already moved on as Alula and Snowcock entered.

34

'The Emir will join us soon,' Alula announced. She took a seat.

'If you please?' said the captain, gesturing for those still standing to join her. Ana quietly departed as Nina and her family took their places.

'Obnoxious *arriviste*,' muttered Olivia.

'Who?' Nina asked.

'Gideon. I've met him before, at events in New York and Boston, but he completely ignored me just now. He makes a big deal out of supporting the arts, but I doubt he could appreciate the difference between a Caravaggio and a child's crayon drawing. No offence to Macy, of course.'

Macy herself was talking to Lobato. 'I've seen you on television! Are you famous?'

'Yes,' he replied. 'I am a pioneer.'

'Oh, like an explorer? Like my mom?'

'In the sense that I am exploring the limits of possibility. I create products that humanity needs, even if they do not know it yet.' Coming from anyone else it would have seemed a shamelessly self-aggrandising sales pitch, but Nina had no doubt he fully believed it.

'Didn't you start out making video games?' asked Eddie.

The question was asked with a hint of sarcasm, which Lobato chose to ignore – or failed to detect. '*Realms of Warfyre* was my biggest success, yes. Did you play it?'

'No, I was in a real war once. Didn't see much point in mucking around with elves and goblins.'

'Ah, yes. You were in the SAS, I believe.'

Eddie snorted. 'Seems like everybody's been googling me today.'

'Knowledge and preparation are the key to success. But selling my company gave me enough money to pursue my true interests.'

'Are you very rich?' Macy asked.

Nina tutted. 'Macy, it's rude to ask people things like that.'

Lobato, however, treated the question literally. 'Yes, I am. The sale was for one point two billion dollars, and since then I have made a lot more.'

The young girl regarded him with sudden caution. 'Are you evil?'

For the first time, his mask of Vulcan implacability cracked. 'Why would you say that?' he said, surprised and slightly affronted.

'My mom and dad have met lots of billionaires. They said they always turn out to be evil!'

Nina and Eddie exchanged looks. ''Fraid so,' the Yorkshireman said. 'Kristian Frost, Richard Yuen, Rene Corvus, Pramesh Khoil, a whole bunch who called themselves "the Group" . . . and more; I've lost count.'

'I can assure you I am not evil,' Lobato said stiffly. 'My goal is to make the world a better place.'

'Which you are doing, my friend!' said the Emir cheerfully as he entered. Everyone stood. 'Please, please, sit.' He took his place at the head of the table. 'Gideon is my partner on a huge solar power project. It will supply all Dhajan's energy needs, and far more besides. We will soon sell electricity just as we sell oil.' He addressed Nina. 'As I told you, my country needs to diversify before our oil reserves finally run out.'

'Clean energy is the future,' said Lobato. 'It *has* to be; it is the only way we will survive as a species. I have started up new disruptive businesses in solar power, battery production, electric cars, tidal generators, even blue-sky ideas like orbital electro-dynamic tethers. People thought I was a fool, throwing my fortune away on dreams. But my dreams are now coming true – and I am richer than my critics. So we will see who is really the fool.'

'It is not you, Gideon,' the Emir assured him. 'Now, my chef has prepared a magnificent selection of dishes. It would be a shame to keep him waiting.'

The food lived up to its billing. 'Got to say, this is probably the best salmon I've ever had,' Eddie announced.

'Thank you,' said the Emir. 'What do you think of yours, Macy?'

The young redhead had gone for a vegetarian option. 'It's really yummy! I didn't think I'd like it, because it's got these weird bits on, but they're nice.'

'We're trying to expand her palate,' said Nina. 'One step at a time, but we're getting there.'

She was about to continue with her own delicious meal when Lobato leaned towards her. 'Dr Wilde, I was fascinated by one of your recent proposals about Atlantis. May I ask you more about it?'

'Sure,' she said, nodding.

'Your theory that the ancient Atlanteans either created or discovered a means to trap and store particles of antimatter; do you really believe they had such a capability?'

Nina groaned inwardly. There were many other aspects of her work she would rather have discussed; most of them, in fact. 'It's not so much a theory as a suggestion based on the available data,' she said. 'Do I actually believe it myself? I'd have to say . . . not really.'

'But it was your idea in the first place.'

'It was one avenue of possibility, sure – I've discovered several things that went beyond conventional science. Earth energy, for example. King Arthur's sword Excalibur could channel the planet's natural energy field to cut through almost anything, and I discovered several Atlantean artefacts that also used it to extraordinary effect. I've seen an ancient statue levitate across a room after being charged up by it.'

'But only in the hands of people with a particular genetic profile of Atlantean descent, correct?'

'Yes, that's right.'

'People such as yourself.'

She became uncomfortable. There was now no avoidance of direct eye contact; his unblinking gaze was fixed upon her. 'Yeah, but that's not exactly something I've shouted from the rooftops.' Eddie subtly shifted position at the change in the conversation's tone, ready to come to her defence – physically if necessary.

But Lobato shook his head dismissively. 'Earth energy is not an avenue of research I have pursued. The need for a human element makes it impractical as a power source. No, I am specifically interested in antimatter.'

'Antimatter?' asked Macy, mouth full.

Nina was about to explain when the Emir beat her to it. 'The opposite of normal matter,' he said. 'If matter and antimatter touch, they are both instantly annihilated in a total conversion of matter to energy. Einstein's formula $E=mc^2$ tells us how much energy, E, is explosively released, where m is the total mass of both matter and antimatter, multiplied by a constant, c, the speed of light, squared.'

'Thank you,' said Nina, surprised by the ruler's knowledge.

Fadil smiled. 'Gideon has shared his interests with me.'

'Personally,' said Eddie with a smirk of his own as he relaxed, 'I think of the world as made up of matter and doesn't matter.' Even Macy groaned.

'My interest in antimatter,' Lobato said with an impatient edge, 'is for its potential to provide the world with unlimited energy – and even propel us beyond it.'

'Been watching *Star Trek*, then?' Eddie remarked.

'Yes,' came the matter-of-fact reply. 'Since I first arrived in America in 1991. But I have always been interested in science, fact as well as fiction. So the theory about the Atlanteans being able to capture antimatter intrigued me.'

'Again, it's not really a theory,' Nina insisted. 'I certainly wouldn't author a scientific paper proposing it. Like I said, I don't really believe it myself – and certainly no other archaeologist does! It was more a thought experiment; practically sci-fi.'

'Science fiction often predicts the future,' said Lobato. 'Or even shapes it.' He took out a smartphone. 'Without *Star Trek*, and other supposed flights of fancy, would we have these as we now know them? They inspired the engineers down new pathways of possibility. And you have done the same yourself.'

'Hardly,' Nina countered. 'I just came up with a possible explanation – but the whole thing might be nothing more than Atlantean hyperbole. As an empire, they weren't given to modesty.'

'What exactly *was* discovered?' Olivia asked. 'I'm assuming it wasn't by you – you haven't been out in the field since that awful business in the Congo.'

'No, this was found by a joint team of Spanish archaeologists and the IHA – the International Heritage Agency, part of the United Nations,' Nina added, for the benefit of the Dhajanis. 'The ongoing excavations at Atlantis itself found evidence pointing to more Atlantean sites in south-western Spain, beneath the remains of Tartessian sites. The Tartessians,' she went on, preempting more questions, 'were a civilisation dating back at least as far as the seventh century BC. It looks increasingly likely that they built upon the remains of Atlantean settlements across the Iberian peninsula, or were even descendants of the Atlanteans themselves.'

'Intriguing,' said the Emir. 'How far did the empire of Atlantis reach?'

'Right around the world. They were at their strongest in the eastern Atlantic and the Mediterranean, of course, but I've been to two separate sites in the Himalayas, one in Nepal and the other in Tibet, and they also reached South America, into Africa, the Middle East . . . Their most famous explorer, Talonor, was fastidious about recording his journeys, and several volumes of his records have now been found and translated. I actually helped with the ones discovered in Spain – I wouldn't say I'm fluent in the Atlantean language, but I'm as good as anyone.'

'So how could a primitive society have used antimatter? I understand it is very hard to make, and even more expensive.'

'Atlantis was very ancient, but it wasn't primitive,' Nina insisted. 'The more we know about it, the more we realise how much we *don't* know. They had knowledge and techniques that were lost when the island sank, and that haven't been duplicated even now. They're almost a case of an alternate technological path, a road not taken. Our society is based on electricity and silicon; theirs on . . . who knows what? Earth energy, crystals, unknown meteoric materials – I know it sounds crazy,' she said, sensing scepticism round the table, 'but I've seen them myself. An Atlantean crystal was part of my own family's history.'

Lobato's expression revealed no scepticism; rather, intense interest. 'And you believe – you *posited*,' he corrected, 'that another of these crystals was the source of the Atlanteans' antimatter.'

'Maybe,' she said. 'An Atlantean text found beneath one of the Tartessian sites referred to weapons called "spearheads", which were supposedly hidden near the capitals of some of the rival empires of the era. If any of these rivals ever posed a direct threat to Atlantis, the Atlanteans would send out an emissary who would somehow prepare one of these spearheads, then issue an ultimatum – surrender to Atlantean rule or be destroyed. If the enemy didn't obey, or harmed the emissary, the spearhead would wipe them out.'

Eddie generally left his wife to get on with her research by herself; this was all new to him. 'Sounds like a doomsday weapon.'

'A doomsday weapon would only be an effective threat if the people being threatened knew of its existence, though,' said Olivia. 'You remember *Dr Strangelove*, surely.'

'Yeah, I married her,' Eddie joked.

'*You're* the strange one,' Nina retorted. 'But the Atlanteans *did* let their enemies know – at least, so they claim. They did . . . well, a demonstration, I guess, with the smallest of their four spearheads, for the ambassadors of some rival powers. It was kept in a vault on a small island somewhere in the Mediterranean. After the spearhead was taken out, it exploded – with what we'd consider nuclear force.'

'What happened to the island?' asked the Emir.

Nina regarded the blue Mediterranean beyond the windows. 'Gone. Completely obliterated. When they went back, after the tidal waves subsided, there was nothing left of it. The island was at least a mile across, so for it to be utterly destroyed would have taken a weapon of immense power, multiple megatons. That means a really big nuke – or antimatter.'

'But how? Antimatter explodes if it comes into contact with normal matter. How could it be stored?'

'Something I discovered in Nepal gave me the idea,' she explained. 'It was a crystal called the Crucible – the origin of the legend of King Midas. It could trap neutrons in such a way that they transmuted elements inside it into others. Mercury into gold, for one. I did some research, and found that theoretically – if something else with similar properties to the Crucible actually existed – naturally occurring antimatter could be trapped and stored safely, and over time build up into a very powerful weapon. For example, there are subatomic particles called positrons, one of the building blocks of antimatter, which are more common than you'd think.'

'How common?' Eddie asked.

'Remember those bananas we bought the other day?'

'Yeah?'

'They're spitting out positrons right now. Bananas have potassium in them, and a small amount of that is potassium-40 – which is radioactive and produces positrons.'

He was appalled. 'Wait, you mean we've got radioactive antimatter in our *kitchen*?'

She laughed. 'Only in tiny, tiny quantities. Like I said, positrons are *sub*atomic particles. But if you had a container similar to the Crucible that could trap and contain antimatter particles inside a magnetic field without them ever coming into contact with normal matter, then if you left it for long enough, the amount of accumulated antiparticles would go from the sub-micro into the macro. Just a gram of antimatter has more explosive potential than both atomic bombs used in the Second World War combined.'

Eddie shook his head. 'That part I can wrap my head around. The rest of it really does sound like *Star Trek* technobabble.'

'It is all perfectly sound theory,' said Lobato. 'I would be intrigued to hear more about the specifics, Dr Wilde. How would such a magnetic field be maintained?'

Nina laughed. 'Hell if I know! I'm an archaeologist. Weird science is just my hobby. The only reason I started doing this kind of research is because I've discovered plenty of things that *needed* weird science to explain them. Once it actually requires equations and formulae drawn on a whiteboard, I'll leave it to the real experts.'

The gaunt man nodded contemplatively, but others had questions of their own. 'How could the people of Atlantis have made such things?' asked Alula.

Nina shrugged. 'I don't know, but according to their records, they existed. Whether they're something formed by nature, something they adapted or something they actually made . . . again, I don't know. We'd have to find one to be sure.'

Lobato leaned towards her again, with renewed intensity. 'Do you believe they *can* be found?'

'If they still exist, then yes, I imagine so. The *marcadores de lanza* – the "spear markers" – discovered at the pre-Tartessian site near Seville supposedly point the way to the vaults where the spearheads are hidden. Nobody's figured out how yet, but given time, I'm sure somebody will.'

'And will that somebody be you? Are you going to search for them?'

'No.'

For all his implacability, an odd expression flickered across the billionaire's face at her blunt response. Nina got the feeling he had hoped for a different answer. 'Why not?'

'I . . .' She hesitated before replying. 'I've retired from fieldwork.'

'Why?'

Her response was reluctant. 'The last time I went into the field, in the Congo, it was . . . to follow another of my theories. And people lost their lives because of it.'

'But others have died on your expeditions, yet you continued,' said Lobato. 'Why was this time different?'

'If you don't mind,' Eddie said, his daughter's presence the only thing keeping him from expressing himself less politely, 'I think you should change the subject. Wouldn't want to spoil this very nice dinner.'

'Eddie, it's okay,' said Nina. 'Really.' She drew in a breath, then went on with fake cheer: 'My shrink keeps telling me that talking about it will help me get over it, right? Yes, in the past, people died on my expeditions, and no, that doesn't mean I downplayed those losses in any way. Some of them were . . . extremely painful. But this was different because it was all on camera. I went into the jungle with a documentary crew, who filmed the whole thing. And this time, I couldn't hide behind self-justification or rationalisation after the fact – everything was right there on screen, unvarnished, exactly as it happened. For the first time, I . . . I saw myself as others see me. And I didn't like it. I saw an obsessive egotist who put her own goals above everything else – and because of that, people got killed.'

'That's not what happened,' Eddie said sharply. 'That's not who you are.'

She gave him a sad look, but continued. 'And after *that*, when I got back to the States, I was sued by one of the surviving film crew. She claimed all the deaths were because of my negligence.'

'She sued the production company and the television network too,' Olivia reminded her. 'And she lost.'

'In the end. But it was still a year of hell on top of everything that happened – in the Congo, and in London too. Big Ben was destroyed and hundreds of people killed as a direct consequence of my deciding that I *had* to make one more big find, just to prove that I still could. Well, I don't need to prove anything else. I don't *want* to prove anything else. I won't risk any more lives just to satisfy my ego.'

The uncomfortable silence that followed was broken by Macy. 'Mommy, you're crying . . .'

'I'm okay,' Nina assured her daughter, wiping away tears. 'I'm fine, honey. Thank you.'

The other diners kept a respectful silence, but Lobato pressed on. 'Then there is no chance that you would search for these spearheads yourself?'

'Absolutely not. From now on, I'm happy to do all my exploration in libraries.'

'I understand. As you say, someone will find them eventually. Though it may take far longer than if you looked for them yourself.'

'That's not my problem. And considering everything that's happened because of me over the past fourteen years, it might be for the best if nobody ever *does* find them.'

She had not meant her last words to be the *literal* last word on the subject, but her vehemence made them exactly that. 'Well,' said the Emir, keen to move on, 'I believe the next course is ready.'

'You okay?' Eddie whispered to Nina as staff cleared the plates.

'Yeah,' she said flatly. 'Super-fine.'

The main course was followed by desserts that were every bit as exquisite. Lobato ate his quickly, then finished his glass of iced water. 'I must leave now,' he announced. 'I have to fly to Paris.'

'Business or pleasure?' asked Nina.

'For me, everything is business.'

'Doesn't sound much fun,' said Eddie.

'There is no time to waste to save the world, Mr Chase,' the skinny billionaire countered. 'Every day in which the problems of pollution are not solved is another day in which hundreds die needlessly, and many more suffer its effects. Before my parents came to America, we lived in Istanbul. Our house was beside a major road, and also close to the port. The pollution was . . .' For a moment he seemed to be genuinely struggling to breathe, the thought alone toxic. 'Particularly bad,' he concluded. 'I have asthma to this day, and I am convinced it was the main contributing factor in limiting my physical development. Fortunately, it did not affect my intellectual growth.'

'Modest, isn't he?' Eddie said, just loud enough for Nina to hear.

'Indeed it did not,' said Fadil. 'I believe you are going to speak at the renewable energy talks?'

'Yes,' Lobato replied. 'Then I will visit my battery development facility in Germany, before going on to attend the World

Economic Forum's regional meeting in Zurich, and after that I am giving a talk on climate change at the Scuola Grande in Venice.'

'San Rocco?' asked Olivia, suddenly perking up. 'Beautiful place, I know the Guardian Grando well.'

'Dr Pinto?'

'Yes, you must give him my regards.'

His small nod was utterly non-committal. 'Anyway, I must leave. It has been a great pleasure to meet you all.' The remark sounded almost mechanical, learned by rote.

'It's been . . . very interesting talking to you,' Nina replied. From his behaviour earlier she doubted that he would shake hands with his dinner companions before leaving, and she was right. The only person he treated to anything more than a perfunctory goodbye was the Emir, the two men holding a short conversation at the door before Lobato exited. Two large men in dark suits and mirrored sunglasses were waiting for him outside, falling into place with military precision to guard him.

'A very, very clever man,' said the Emir as he returned to the table. 'If anyone can keep the world from choking on its own smog, it is him! Now, would anyone like more to drink, or eat?'

'We're fine, thank you,' said Nina. 'It's been an amazing dinner. My compliments to the chef – and our host, of course.'

The Emir bowed his head. 'The honour is all mine, Dr Wilde. It has been a great pleasure to meet you – and I hope you are still willing to give me a private showing of the treasures in the Atlantis exhibition.'

'Of course. I'm looking forward to it.'

'Then shall we say,' he looked at his watch, 'in thirty minutes?'

'That'll be fine,' said Nina.

'Excellent. If we meet in the Sapphire Lounge on Deck 6, I will escort you there myself.'

Nina and her family said their goodbyes, then left the dining room. Ana was waiting for them. 'I hope you enjoyed your dinner. Are you going back to your cabins?'

'For now, yes,' said Nina. 'I'm meeting the Emir in a half-hour, but I'm sure everyone else has other things they'd rather do.'

'Wouldn't mind chilling out and digesting for a while,' said her husband as they started back through the ship.

'I want to go on the waterslides!' cried Macy.

'Or,' Eddie continued with a resigned sigh, 'I could go on the waterslides with Macy.'

'I'll come too,' said Olivia.

'You want to go swimming?' Nina asked, surprised.

Olivia gave her a haughty look. 'What, I'm banned from the water once I reach a certain age? I've been swimming Olympic lengths since I was eight.'

'Okay, you all go for a swim,' said the redhead, amused. 'I'll find you when I'm done.'

'I'll get towels for you,' Ana said. 'And anything else you need.'

Nina smiled at her. 'Ana, thank you, but really, you don't have to wait on us hand and foot. It's not our thing.'

'Speak for yourself!' said Eddie.

'We'll be fine,' she went on. 'You should take the evening off.'

'Are you sure?' asked the Brazilian. 'What if Mrs Garde—'

'I'm sure I can manage,' said Olivia. 'After all, I have a grandson-in-law to wait on me if I need anything.'

'Just 'cause I'm English doesn't mean I'm a butler!' Eddie retorted.

'Go on, Ana,' Nina insisted. 'Take a break.'

Ana nodded. 'Thank you. But I'm still on duty, so use your wristband if you need anything, okay?' She smiled, then headed away as the others continued to their cabins.

Once there, Eddie got changed into trunks, T-shirt and flip-flops, Macy putting on a swimming costume. Nina, meanwhile, considered donning something more casual, but decided to stay with her dress and heels. She *was* going to be in the company of a king, after all. 'Okay, I'll see you guys later,' she said as her husband and daughter headed for the door.

'Remember, he's got a country to run, so don't blather on about Atlantis for hours,' Eddie joked, before seeing what Macy was about to put into her bag. 'No, love. Leave that here.'

'But I need to practise,' she insisted, swinging the toy trikan on its cord. 'It's bigger than the one at home, it's harder to do tricks with.'

'Yeah, but if you do tricks in the pool, you'll have someone's eye out.'

'It's soft, look,' she said, bending one of the extended blades with her thumb. 'It won't hurt anyone.'

'Just leave it here, Macy,' Nina ordered, sharing a long-suffering look with Eddie. Their daughter pouted, but put the trikan down – after performing a quick flick-and-return of the yo-yo-like toy. 'Have fun!'

'You too,' he replied.

Once they had left, Nina freshened up before checking a map of the ship to locate the Sapphire Lounge. The Emir was not there when she arrived in the luxurious bar, so she ordered a glass of water and waited. He eventually appeared ten minutes later in the company of Alula, a male member of his entourage and a man Nina hadn't seen before, a tall, neatly bearded Caucasian with piercing grey eyes. 'Dr Wilde, my apologies,' the Emir said, bowing. 'I had to attend to business of state.'

'That's okay,' she said. Whatever his business had been, his sister's frown suggested her opinion had not matched his – but the monarch always got his way.

He turned to the bearded man. 'This is Monsieur Thomas Agreste, who is in charge of security for the Atlantis exhibition.'

'Good to meet you,' Nina said, shaking Agreste's hand.

'And you, Dr Wilde,' the Frenchman replied. The way he was subtly assessing not only her but everyone else in the bar suggested that his career before entering private security had been in law enforcement. She expected him to say more, but he was clearly not given to small talk.

'Shall we go to the exhibition hall?' asked the Emir.

'Please, lead the way,' said Nina.

He spoke to Alula in Arabic, dismissing her and the other Dhajani, then left the lounge with Nina and Agreste. 'We have three exhibition halls aboard,' he said. 'As well as Atlantis, there are also showings of Islamic art and the latest renewable energy technology. Our other ship, the *Pacifia*, will have a Picasso exhibition aboard its maiden voyage.' They descended a sweeping spiral staircase to Deck 5, then continued aft. 'Oh! I would like to make a brief detour. I am sure Gideon would appreciate you seeing this.'

He led the way into a large room containing numerous display stands and video screens, as well as impressive models of power plants, tidal generators, even a satellite suspended from the ceiling. A row of gleaming cars was also on display. 'Renewable energy, I'm guessing?' Nina said.

'Yes,' the Emir replied, guiding her to one of the models. 'This is the solar facility in Dhajan.' It was a section of rocky desert, bank upon bank of polished hexagonal panels resembling glass flowers surrounding a trio of towers. 'It is currently only a test facility, but it already produces and stores a great deal of power. Once it reaches its full size, my country will have total energy independence, without needing to burn a single drop of oil.' He turned to a row of electric vehicles. 'My hope is that every car in Dhajan will be electric in the next five years.'

'That's an admirable goal. I wish New York would do the same thing.'

One particular car was raised on a stand. 'Another project I am working on with Gideon,' said Fadil, striding towards the sleek futuristic vehicle. 'The Raiju. This is a mock-up, but we are testing the real thing in Dhajan right now.'

'It looks pretty fast.' The car was an aggressive wedge that seemed crouched to attack even while stationary, banks of blade-thin wings resembling razor heads running the width of its nose and tail.

'It is *very* fast!' he confirmed proudly. 'There have been electric supercars – this will be the first electric *hypercar*. It can accelerate faster than a Formula 1 car, has active aerodynamics and ground effect to keep it on the road . . . and it can even drive itself. Level five autonomous driving, it is called. It can do everything a human driver can, faster and more safely – it does not even need a person inside it.'

'Doesn't that kinda defeat the purpose of a car?' Nina said, peering through the gold-tinted windows. The interior had an unusual layout; the driver's seat was on the centreline, two others further back on each side. 'And there isn't much space for groceries.'

The Emir chuckled. 'There are two ways technology can advance, Gideon tells me. By starting at the bottom and working up, little by little – or by shooting for the moon. Little cars,' he indicated the smallest of the other vehicles, an uninspiring blobby pod, 'may be more practical, but this is more fun.'

'I suppose you'll be driving the finished version.'

'I already *have* driven it. And it is, well . . .' His features lit up with boyish glee. 'I have Ferraris, I have Lamborghinis. But this is something else.' He gazed lovingly at the low-slung mock-up, then turned back to Nina almost with embarrassment. 'But you have not come to see this! Let us go on to the Atlantis exhibition.'

'After you,' she said, amused.

They continued aft to a set of closed doors. 'The exhibition will be opened to the public after your lecture,' the Emir explained. 'Monsieur Agreste?'

The Frenchman went to the black glass panel beside the entrance and held up his ID card. The green symbol flashed in acceptance, and the doors unlocked with a mechanical clack. He opened them.

'After you,' the Emir said to Nina. She entered – and stopped at the sight greeting her.

She had known what to expect, as she had personally discovered no small number of the exhibits, but her host had spared no expense on their presentation. The hall was decorated in the style of an Atlantean temple, the walls almost hidden behind carved columns and bas-relief replicas of statues. But even they could not overshadow the main attractions. Dozens of items recovered from Atlantean sites all around the world, from small pieces of jewellery all the way up to a sarcophagus cast in the rare gold alloy known as orichalcum, glinted under spotlights. Glass cases housed the most valuable exhibits, but even these were positioned and lit to the best possible effect.

'This is amazing!' she said, delighted.

'Thank you,' the Emir replied. 'I wanted a most impressive display.'

'You succeeded. It's absolutely stunning.'

'Again, thank you. And I am honoured to have you tell me about these marvels.'

Nina smiled. 'The honour's mine.' She was reassured that the entire priceless collection was covered by multiple security cameras. 'So . . . where would you like to start?'

'At the beginning. What did you first discover, and how did you find it?'

She looked around, spotting with both pride and faint

embarrassment a large portrait of herself on a display stand of her own books and DVDs, before seeing pieces of an ancient orichalcum sextant in a case. 'A lot of my initial work was mathematical,' she began, leading him towards the navigational instrument. 'I used references to sizes and distances in Plato's *Dialogues* to calculate where Atlantis could have been situated in the Gulf of Cadiz . . .'

Elsewhere on the ship, a monitor showed Nina, the Emir and Agreste crossing to the sextant's case. It was a live feed from one of the hall's CCTV cameras, but the woman watching it was not on the bridge, nor in the *Atlantia*'s security centre.

She glanced at a second screen beside it. This showed a corridor outside the hall – not the one from which Nina and her companions had entered, but another further aft. A click of a mouse and the view changed to a different hallway. The door near the image's centre bore a prominent 'NO ENTRY' sign.

The woman's fingers danced over a keyboard. A message flashed up demanding a passcode. She entered six digits, then typed more commands – and the closed door slid open, revealing a white-painted crew access corridor beyond.

'Escape route is open,' she said into her headset. 'Dr Wilde and the Emir are both in the Atlantis exhibition with the Frenchman.'

'Get rid of him,' a man replied. 'We are ready to go when you give the word.'

'Stand by,' she said. 'I'll take care of Agreste; then you can deal with Dr Wilde.'

4

Nina continued her tour through the history of Atlantis, showing the Emir the various exhibits. 'This statue was recovered from the Temple of Poseidon at the heart of the Atlantean capital itself,' she said. 'It was brought up from eight hundred feet underwater.'

'Magnificent,' said Fadil, before going to another display case, leaning over the velvet rope cordon surrounding it to peer at a sword. 'And so is this!' The hilt was made of gold, orichalcum and silver, precious stones worked into it, but the blade itself was a bluish steel, free of corrosion even after thousands of years on the ocean floor. 'Is this really from Atlantis? It could have been made yesterday.'

'It really is,' Nina assured him. 'It's been cleaned and restored, of course. But the blade hadn't rusted at all. The Atlanteans were very advanced in metallurgy; some of their artefacts would be hard to duplicate, even now.'

'May I hold it?'

Nina hesitated, unsure of protocol. Normally she never let the public handle relics, but the Emir was hardly an ordinary visitor. 'I, ah . . . I suppose so?' she said, glancing at Agreste.

The Frenchman was less circumspect. 'Your Majesty, the cases must remain closed.'

The Emir raised an eyebrow. 'Even for me?'

'I am following your sister's instructions.'

'Ah, Alula,' the Dhajani sighed. 'Always trying to control her brother. I cannot convince you otherwise?'

Agreste shook his head. 'I am afraid not, Your Majesty.'

'As you see, Dr Wilde,' said the Emir, turning back to the case, 'it is a myth that Arab rulers have absolute power!'

Nina smiled, about to move on when Agreste's phone buzzed. 'Excuse me,' he said, taking the call. '*Oui?* No, I am with the Emir. I cannot—' He listened to the caller with growing annoyance. 'Very well.' He disconnected. 'Your Majesty, I apologise, but there is a matter I must attend to in person.'

'A security issue?' asked the Emir.

'It is nothing to worry about. I will return as soon as I can.' He went to the exit, using his card to open it. 'I will lock the doors after I leave.'

Fadil grinned. 'Do not worry, we will not steal anything!'

Agreste did not return the smile as he departed. The lock clacked behind him.

'We're locked in?' said Nina. 'Hope there isn't an emergency.'

'Do not worry. My personal code can access any system on the ship. Including,' the Emir added mischievously, 'these cases.'

'Even after what Mr Agreste just said?'

'He is only a functionary, and Alula is a minister in my government – but *I* am the Emir of Dhajan! This ship sails under a Dhajani flag, so while we are in international waters, it is Dhajani territory. My power may not be absolute, but,' his smirk widened, 'it is still considerable. Now, let us see . . .'

He moved one of the stanchions supporting the rope. Mounted upon the case's side was another touchscreen. He brought up the keypad, then slowly tapped in the same code he had used on the bridge. A lock clunked. 'There,' he said, swinging down the case's glazed front. 'That is security glass, it can stop a bullet. Nobody will steal anything from here.'

'As long as you remember to close the case,' said Nina, decidedly uncomfortable as he took the sword from its mount.

He held it up to the light in admiration. 'If there is trouble, the most valuable exhibits will retract into the ship's vault underneath us.'

She was not mollified. 'Wouldn't it be cheaper and easier just to hire a guard?'

'Computers never sleep, and cannot be bribed,' he replied, examining the blade's edge before carefully replacing the weapon.

'They can be hacked, though.'

'This ship does not run on Windows XP! One of Gideon's companies programmed the security systems. They are very secure.' He closed the case, the lock clicking.

'Unless someone's got your secret code.'

'I am the only person who knows it, I assure you. I have not even told Alula. Some secrets are for the monarch alone.'

Nina considered reciting it to let him know she had seen him type it in, but decided there was no way she could do it without sounding insulting – and besides, he was already crossing the room to another exhibit. She trotted after him.

The woman watched the monitor, tracking Nina and the Emir. 'Okay, they're approaching the marker,' she said. 'Security cameras along your route going down . . . now.' She hit a key. The second monitor showed a grid of CCTV feeds; red crosses appeared in the corners of several, though the pictures remained. 'Move!'

The doors of a row of four cabins near a secondary stairwell opened simultaneously. Two men emerged from each, all clad in black and carrying silenced handguns and Tasers. Each tugged a form-fitting balaclava mask over his face.

The last to cover up was at the head of the line: Hashim al-Asim, the man who had watched Nina and her family pass before planting a bomb. 'We are on our way,' he said into a throat mic. 'Be ready to detonate.' Gun at the ready, he led his men down the staircase.

On the bridge, an officer noticed that several security monitors were blank. 'Hey, some of the cameras are down.' He tapped commands into his console, frowning at the result. 'No faults registering.'

'It could just be a glitch,' said another man. 'Maiden-voyage gremlins.'

'Maybe.' But the problem was in a passenger area, which automatically made it a safety issue. The officer began a deeper diagnostic check, searching for the problem's cause.

Eddie burst out of the water in front of Macy. '*Raaaaar!*' he growled, splashing her. 'Shark attack!'

'Daddy,' she said, unimpressed. 'Sharks don't growl.'

'What if it's a *tiger* shark?' He grinned, then sloshed to the shallows. They were in one of the swimming pools on the long atrium deck, a family-oriented play area replete with waterspouts, artificial islands and a wave machine. The deep end was the landing area for several spiralling waterslides, people hurtling through the tubes with whoops and screams, which were echoed by those whizzing down the zip-line overhead. 'Olivia!' he called. 'You having fun?'

Olivia was doing a relaxed backstroke in a smaller, more sedate pool nearby. 'I'd prefer a longer lap, but yes. How's Macy?'

'Loving it,' he replied. His daughter had positioned herself over a waterspout, squealing as it gushed up beneath her. 'Hey, love – you want to race me down the slides?'

'It won't be fair,' Macy protested. 'You're heavier, you'll go faster than me.'

'Yeah, but I'm bigger, so I might get stuck! Shall we find out?'

She considered it, then beamed. 'Okay!'

'All right, let's go!' He dived back into the water beside her.

'Now these,' said Nina at the next display, 'are more recent discoveries.'

The case contained several items, but the Emir regarded one in particular. 'I recognise this! I bought it for Macy.'

The object in question was an Atlantean trikan. Its disc-shaped body was made of orichalcum, with a circle of dark polished stone inset at the centre, while the ornate blades around it were of a similar blue steel to the sword. 'This is one of the originals Macy's toy was based on,' Nina explained. 'Although I say "based on" in the loosest possible sense. The one in the movie can change direction in mid-air, snatch things out of people's hands, all kinds of crazy stuff. The real one isn't nearly as exciting. We know it was used as a weapon because we've found references in Atlantean texts, but as for how . . . well, no one's figured that out yet.'

'A cross between a boomerang and a yo-yo, you said.'

'That's in the movie. In real life, nobody's got it to work. It *does* have a wire like a yo-yo,' she indicated where it was attached to the protective metal handgrip, 'but there's too much friction for it to uncoil properly. The toy version works a lot better, ironically. The Atlanteans may have had some way of lubricating it that we haven't discovered – or it might not be used like a yo-yo at all.'

'I am sure you will find the truth.' Fadil moved on from the trikan to another golden disc. 'Perhaps you will find the truth about this too, despite what you said at dinner.'

Nina gave him a wry smile. 'So you know what it is.'

'One of the *marcadores de lanza*, yes. Does it really show the way to some great secret of Atlantis?'

'That's what its creators claimed, yes.' The spear marker was a flat circle slightly over eight inches in diameter and half an inch thick. One side was blank except for several square indentations, while the other bore the angular characters of Atlantean text. Even for someone who could translate the language, they were difficult to read; the lines wove snake-like around dozens of circular holes punched seemingly at random through the disc.

'Are the holes a map of some kind?'

'Possibly. I'm told that the other marker has pegs on its back that fit into the slots in this one, so they were clearly designed to work together. But nobody's come up with an explanation yet.'

'I see.' The Emir smiled conspiratorially, then moved the rope cordon aside. 'I am sure Mr Agreste will not mind if I take a closer look.'

'Y'know, he probably will,' Nina said, but he was already entering his code to unlock the case. 'I, ah, think it would be better if you wore gloves to handle it.'

He gave her a gently patronising look as he opened the front panel. 'I do not think a few fingerprints will hurt it. But if you would prefer to show me . . .'

She grimaced inwardly, but couldn't really refuse. At least this way she could minimise the amount of cleaning required. 'Okay,' she said. 'But if Mr Agreste comes back in, I'll tell him you ordered me to do it!'

He laughed. 'I will take the blame, do not worry.'

Nina smiled, then moved to the marker. She had seen it before, in Seville, having been invited the previous year to view the newly discovered trove of Atlantean artefacts, but it had still been undergoing restoration. Now, it gleamed beneath the display case's lights, the dirt of millennia removed. She picked it up carefully by its edge.

'Astonishing,' the Emir said as she turned it for him to see. 'Eleven thousand years old. An entire history we never knew about until you uncovered it.'

'The clues were there all along. Nobody believed them, that's all.'

'You did. And you were right.' He narrowed his eyes to pick out the inscribed characters. 'Could you hold it higher, please? It is very hard to see.' Nina raised her hands, backing up to catch the marker in a spotlight's beam. 'Ah, thank you.' He regarded the text, then continued: 'And there is still more to discover. Do you believe anyone *will* ever find these spearheads?'

'Like I said at dinner, if they really are some kind of weapon, it might be better if nobody does. But if anyone can, I'm sure it's the IHA.'

He nodded, then gestured for her to return the marker. 'If you are quick, Mr Agreste may not even realise what we have done.'

'What *you* have done,' Nina corrected with a smile, stepping back towards the open display—

'*Now!*' the watching woman snapped, stabbing at the keyboard.

The metal cylinder concealed in the planter detonated with a loud bang, thick grey smoke gushing out. More devices hidden around the *Atlantia* also exploded.

Alarms wailed, but it was not the grenades that had tripped them. These went off in every part of the ship simultaneously, the woman's intrusion into the liner's computers activating a global fire alert. The initial reaction of the eight and a half thousand people aboard was bewildered surprise . . . followed by growing panic as they realised the emergency warning was not a drill.

'What the hell?' gasped the bridge officer as his console lit up with multiple alerts. 'We've got fire alarms all over the ship!'

Another man frantically typed in commands. 'None of the temperature sensors are showing anything.'

THE SPEAR OF ATLANTIS

'I've got smoke alarms on Decks 5 through 10 . . . and now on Deck 4 . . . Deck 11 too. *Something's* wrong. Find the captain!'

Nina looked around in shock. 'What—'

More sirens shrilled, this time inside the hall – and the display cabinets began to lower with surprising swiftness into the floor.

The Emir had one hand on the open case. He lost his balance as it dropped away, clutching for support at the velvet rope – only for its stanchions to topple under his weight.

The open pane was sheared off and smashed as the cabinet reached floor level, then retreated through the deck into a steel chamber beneath. The Emir fell on top of it and was carried downwards, dragging the rope and several of its support poles with him before tumbling off and hitting the floor with a bang.

A large metal panel began to slide across the opening, about to seal the vault – but before it could fully close, it was halted by the trapped rope and a stanchion.

Still holding the marker, Nina hurried to the narrow gap. The Emir lay below, unmoving. 'Hey!' she cried. 'Your Majesty – Fadil! Can you hear me, are you okay?'

He did not respond.

Eddie and Macy were almost at the top of the waterslides when the alarm sounded. 'Daddy?' the young redhead said nervously. 'What's happening?'

'I dunno, but . . .' People were reacting with increasing concern as it became clear the warnings were not going to stop. 'We need to find your mum.' There was nothing to suggest the problem was anything to do with Nina . . . but he had the horrible feeling that given their past experiences, it was more likely than not.

The stairs behind them had already become a choke point as people retreated. 'Down the slides, quick,' he ordered. A woman blocked the top of the nearest tube, paralysed by indecision. He moved her aside firmly, then dropped on to the slide and hoisted Macy on his lap.

'Daddy,' she objected, pointing to a warning sign. 'It says only one person at a time!'

'Sometimes it's best not to do what you're told,' he replied, wrapping his arms protectively around her. 'Just don't tell your mum I said that!'

He pushed himself off, rushing water carrying them down the tube. Macy shrieked as they hurtled through it, picking up speed until they splashed down in the large pool. Eddie immediately swam clear, pulling Macy with him. 'You okay?' She spluttered, but nodded.

They reached the shallows, sluicing towards the poolside. Olivia was standing by the lounger where they had left their belongings, looking around in alarm. 'Olivia! We're over here!'

'Eddie!' she cried. 'Is Macy all right? What's going on?'

'I don't know, but I need to find Nina.'

'You think she has something to do with this? Why?'

'Because I married a bloody trouble magnet! Macy, you stay with Olivia. I'm going to—'

'Oh my God!' a woman wailed. 'The ship's on fire!'

Grey smoke gushed from a hatch halfway down the deck. The fear already susurrating through the passengers became full-blown panic. The crew tried to maintain order, but they were too few to handle the hundreds on the activity deck.

Eddie swore under his breath. The chaos would make it even harder to find Nina. But he had to try – and some instinct was also telling him something was *wrong*, beyond the obvious. The smoke . . .

No time to waste thinking about it. 'Stay with Olivia!' he told Macy again, before racing for the most direct way to the lower decks – the travelators descending into the mall. He was still dripping wet and clad only in trunks, but modesty was his last concern as he vaulted a barrier and weaved through the fleeing crowd.

Macy snatched up her bag and ran after him. 'Macy! No, come back!' Olivia cried in horror as her great-granddaughter disappeared into the throng, but it was too late to stop her.

The woman in the darkened room stared at her monitor, lips tight at the sight of panic spreading across the grid of CCTV feeds. She hesitated – then hit another key.

A plague of red crosses spread across the screen. The crew were now denied access to every camera aboard the *Atlantia*.

But they were locked out of more than merely the video systems.

Captain Snowcock hurried on to the bridge. 'What the hell's going on?'

The watch officer faced him with deep dismay. 'Fire alarms have been tripped all over the ship, and we can't shut them off.'

'*Is* there a fire?'

'We don't know, sir! Some smoke alarms have gone off too, but none of the automatic fire suppression systems have activated.'

The captain turned to the video wall. 'Where are the smoke alarms concen—' He broke off as all the CCTV feeds went blank. 'What's happened to the cameras?'

Another officer stabbed at his keyboard with increasing frustration. 'I can't access anything – I've been locked out!'

'Captain!' called another man. 'I was talking to the lifeboat deck, and the intercom just went dead!' He hit a button and spoke into a microphone, but to no avail. 'The PA system is down as well.'

'Someone's cut us off – we've been *hacked*!' Snowcock realised. 'All right. The safety of the passengers is our absolute top priority. Use walkie-talkies, use cell phones, run down and *shout* if you have to, but get everyone to assemble at their muster points.'

'We're going to launch the lifeboats?' asked the watch officer.

'I want to be ready if we need to,' the captain replied.

'Dammit!' said Nina. She had called to the Emir again, but he had not stirred. '*Now* what the hell do I do?'

Aside from the doors through which she had entered, there were two other exits from the exhibition hall: another set of double doors at the far end, and a single, noticeably more heavy-duty door in one corner. The vault entrance?

Try to open the vault, or get help? The latter, she decided, hurrying back to the entrance. Somebody from the Emir's entourage would surely be on their way – they might even be outside already, unable to unlock the doors.

The Emir's code came easily to mind: March 2015. The black glass panel lit up with a keypad as she raised her hand to it. She started to tap in the numbers.

The woman watched Nina over the CCTV feed. 'She's about to open the door. Get ready!' she snapped into her headset, simultaneously entering another command.

More alarms whooped, seven short, shrill notes followed by a prolonged wail. 'This is the captain,' came Snowcock's voice over the public address system. 'The ship is being evacuated for your safety. All passengers, proceed calmly to your assigned muster stations and follow the crew's instructions.'

Snowcock himself regarded the loudspeaker set into the bridge ceiling with shock. 'That was from the drill before we left Dhajan,' he said as the message continued. 'It's a recording! Can't someone shut it up?'

'No, sir,' replied an officer. 'We're still locked out.'

'It's telling the passengers to do what we wanted anyway,' the watch officer pointed out.

Snowcock fixed him with a withering stare. 'This is *my* ship, Mr Mallay. *I* give the orders, not someone using my voice!' He turned to the other bridge crew. 'Do we still have engine control?'

'Yes, sir,' the helm officer replied.

'Okay – all stop! Full reverse on the azipods, stop the ship! Get word down to the lifeboat deck and prepare the boats for launch!'

Pandemonium erupted around Eddie as he hurried through the mall. He imagined that the passengers had given the mandatory safety briefing the same attention as its counterpart before an airline flight – in other words, little to none – but now they had to find their way through the colossal ship to a point that could be several decks down and hundreds of metres along, through confined corridors filled with panicked crowds.

Screams ahead. Someone had fallen, people behind tripping over them in their blind rush. Where the hell were the crew? He hopped up on to a bench to check his surroundings. All the main exits were jammed with people – but then he saw a smaller side door open. A pair of crewmen hurried out.

Eddie glimpsed white-painted stairs beyond the doorway. The crew had a network of service corridors that let them carry out the nuts-and-bolts business of running the liner without inconveniencing the passengers. If he could get inside, he could bypass the crush in the public areas . . .

A fleeting gap opened in the crowd. He made a flying leap into it. The door started to swing shut. He shoved towards it. If it closed, he wouldn't be able to open it again—

He reached it just before it slammed. Throwing it wide, he rushed through and charged down the stairs.

★ ★ ★

Macy saw her father's leap just before she reached the bottom of the travelator. She climbed on to the bench to look for him over the crowd.

A familiar bald head disappeared through a doorway. 'Daddy!' she called, but he was already gone.

The door started to close again. Clutching her bag, she raced after him. 'Look out!' she shouted. 'I've lost my daddy, I need to catch him!'

The cries of a young girl were enough to halt some of the fleeing passengers, if only for a moment. But that was all Macy needed, gaps opening in front of her. 'Thank you, thanks!' she gasped, darting through the door just before it locked. She found herself at the top of a flight of stairs. 'Daddy!'

He was nowhere in sight. Worried, she scuttled down the stairwell.

'Where is His Majesty? Where is my brother?'

Snowcock turned as Alula and several members of the royal entourage swept on to the bridge. 'Your Royal Highness,' he said. 'If you would please let us—'

She glared at him, hands on hips. 'Nobody knows where he is, and now you are abandoning ship!'

'Someone has hacked into the ship's systems and triggered the fire alarms,' the captain told her. 'It appears to be a hoax, but the evacuation is precautionary until we're sure.'

'But I saw smoke.'

'I know; we're still investigating. And I assure you we're doing everything we can to regain control of the situation.'

Her dark eyes narrowed. 'Do it faster, *Captain*,' she said, the threat to his position clear. 'The Emir is missing. He must be found, now!'

★ ★ ★

Snowcock's announcement had made Nina pause. Now she jabbed in the last two digits of the code. Whatever was happening, she had to help the Emir.

The lock clicked. She reached for the handle—

An alert flashed up on the woman's screen: the exhibition hall's doors had unlocked. '*Now!*'

The door burst open, knocking Nina to the floor.

5

Dazed, Nina looked up – as men in black masks rushed into the room.

The leader thrust a silenced gun at her face. 'The marker! Where—' he began, before seeing the golden disc in her hand. 'Give it to me!'

Shocked, she held it up. He snatched it from her. 'I have it,' he said.

His controller acknowledged him. 'Opening the marina door now,' she replied, checking the grid of security cameras. 'Your escape route is clear – the passengers have run from the smoke.'

'How long before we can leave?'

'Two minutes to open the door and extend the dock. Go in . . . thirty seconds.'

The masked man acknowledged another radio message, then shouted a command to his companions – in Arabic, Nina realised. They moved towards the doors at the room's far end.

He kept his gun fixed upon her as he followed. 'Do not come after us,' he growled.

His companions reached the exit, then waited. He slipped the marker into a satchel. To her surprise, Nina saw that the others were leaving empty-handed. While the most valuable treasures of Atlantis had been lowered into the vault, even the smallest of those remaining were still worth thousands of dollars on the black market, but they had been completely ignored. The golden disc was their only objective.

A chill of realisation. There was only one reason why they could want it.

To find the Atlantean spearheads.

The service sections could be opened from inside without a keycard or code, which was a great relief to Eddie as he reached a door. He shoved it wide – then coughed.

The wide hallway he entered was full of smoke. But that alone wasn't what brought his instinctual feeling of *wrongness* rushing back. Rather, it was the smell. It was one he knew well from his time in the military, a sharp, sulphurous odour.

A smoke grenade.

'*Someone's* remembered *Speed 2*,' he muttered as he ran aft. The film's villain had created the illusion of a fire with smokers to prompt a cruise ship's evacuation, and somebody was doing the same here.

The hallway opened out into a lounge area at a cross-passage. One of the holographic ship's maps stood at its centre. He stopped, tapping at a touchscreen. He knew roughly where Nina had gone with the Emir, but he needed to find the exact route.

Exhibition halls . . . there. The rotating hologram of the *Atlantia* opened up to highlight his path. Further astern, one deck down. He rounded the display and hurried on.

The woman's gaze snapped to unexpected movement on one of the CCTV feeds.

A bald man wearing nothing but swimming trunks was leaving a lounge on Deck 6. That anyone was in the smoke-filled section at all was concern enough, but she recognised the face.

'Eddie Chase is coming your way!' she warned al-Asim. 'He must be trying to reach Dr Wilde.'

'Then stop him!' came the snarled reply.

She frowned, and quickly entered more commands.

Eddie raced down the new passage, the smoke becoming more dense ahead. Another bomb nearby, he guessed – whoever was behind the chaos wanted to drive people out of this part of the ship—

Amber warning lights flashed and a fire door began to slide across his path. He instantly knew it wasn't a coincidence. Someone was actively trying to keep him from Nina.

He increased his pace, easily clearing the rumbling barrier—

'*Daddy!*'

He whirled in alarm. Macy was running after him – and the door was closing between them. 'No, get back!' he shouted.

His daughter didn't listen, diving through the shrinking opening. She hit the thick carpet with a shriek as the door thudded shut behind her.

Eddie scooped her up. 'Oh my God! Are you okay?'

'Yeah, yeah,' she gasped. 'I almost got squished!'

'You almost . . .' Parental anger cut through his relief. 'Macy, that was stupid! You could have been killed!'

Her eyes went wide in dismay. 'But – but Eden jumped through a door like that in the movie.'

'This isn't a movie! This is real life, and you can get hurt!' He saw tears welling. 'But you're okay,' he quickly reassured her. 'I told you to stay with Olivia. Why did you follow me?'

'B-because you said Mom was in trouble! I wanted to help her.'

He couldn't fault her for that; it was exactly what he had done. He let out a humourless laugh. 'And I'm sure she'll appreciate it – after she's had a rant at me for letting *you* get into trouble!' He hugged her, then put her down. The door was now closed; the only way was onwards. 'Okay, stay with me.

And if I tell you to do something, you have to *do* it, no arguments. Yes?'

She nodded. 'Yes.'

'Good. Come on, then.' He took her hand. 'Let's go and find your mum.'

'Mom,' she said quietly as they started down the passage. His laugh this time was genuine.

'The route to the marina is clear,' said the woman in al-Asim's earpiece.

'What about Chase?' he asked.

'He won't reach you in time.'

'Good.' As the others ran out, he looked back at Chase's wife. She hadn't moved, but he knew she would spring up the moment he left the hall, either to follow the raiders or help the Emir. Both choices had been prepared for. He shot her a final menacing glower, then hurried after his men.

Nina waited until the sound of running feet faded, then jumped up. The intruders had the marker, and they also obviously had a plan to get it off the ship. If she could disrupt it . . .

But the Emir was still trapped in the vault. She looked through the gap. The Arab royal hadn't moved. 'Can you hear me?' she called.

This time, he stirred. 'What . . . what happened?' he mumbled.

'Some guys with guns just took the marker! This whole thing – it's a heist!'

'Then stop . . . you have to stop them . . .' He tried to lift his head, but slumped back down, falling still again.

'Shit,' Nina whispered. What should she do?

It took her less than a second to decide. Stop the bad guys, as he'd asked. If she encountered any of the crew, she could tell them the Emir needed help, and once she found how the thieves intended to escape the ship, either someone on the *Atlantia* could stop them, or the authorities in Spain or Morocco could be alerted.

A last look at the Emir, then she kicked off her high heels and ran after the raiders.

'Should be just down here,' Eddie told Macy as they pounded along a wide corridor. The smoke in the air had thinned almost to nothing.

'Here, Daddy!' she cried as they reached an open set of double doors. Gold gleamed in the large room beyond. 'These are from Atlantis,' Macy confirmed as they entered. 'Where's Mom?'

'I dunno.' But something had definitely happened; there were conspicuously large gaps behind rope cordons, as if whatever was on display had been removed. Hunks of broken glass littered the floor in one area, the base of a stanchion poking out from a narrow slot in the floor. 'Nina? Hello, anyone here?'

He went to investigate the hole – only to flinch as a panel retracted. The stanchion fell through with a clang. Other panels moved aside, glass display cases rising smoothly into the hall.

The cabinet before them was damaged, one of its sides missing. That explained the fragments on the floor – and Eddie immediately realised that something was missing from the display. Atlantean relics were laid out on dark blue velvet, but there was an obvious gap in the line-up.

'It's a trikan!' Macy said, worry replaced by excitement on seeing the ancient weapon. 'A real one, look!'

'I'm more bothered about what *isn't* there,' Eddie replied. He was about to take a closer look when a door across the room opened. 'Wait there,' he told her as he ran towards it. 'Nina! Is that you?'

But it was not his wife who emerged. 'Mr Chase?' said the Emir, surprised. 'What are— Where is Dr Wilde?'

'I dunno, I was hoping you could tell me! What happened?'

'I don't know. She was showing me the spear marker, then . . . then an alarm went off. I turned around and . . .' His eyes widened. 'She hit me!'

'You what?' Eddie said in disbelief.

'I fell into the vault, and – the marker!' he cried, seeing the damaged cabinet. 'She must have taken it!'

'Don't be bloody stupid,' the Yorkshireman snapped, not caring that he was addressing a king. 'Why would she do that?'

'She was talking about it at dinner – perhaps she has decided to find the spearheads for herself?'

Eddie shook his head. 'Nina didn't hit you, but whoever did, they've cost you a couple of million brain cells.' He turned at a noise from behind. Macy had gone to the case, one hand outstretched. 'Macy, watch your feet on that broken glass!' he cautioned.

A bearded man rushed into the room. 'Your Majesty!' he shouted. 'What has happened?'

'Your guess is as good as mine,' Eddie said. 'Who're you?'

'Agreste – I am in charge of security here.'

'Top work, mate,' was the sarcastic reply.

The Frenchman ignored him. 'Are you hurt, Your Majesty?'

The Emir rubbed his head. 'I am not sure. I was unconscious – I woke up in the vault.'

'Where is Dr—' Agreste stopped mid sentence as he saw the open case. 'The *marcador*! Where is it?'

'I think she took it,' the Dhajani ruler told him.

'She *didn't* fu— sodding take it!' Eddie barked, managing not to swear too badly in front of his daughter. 'Look, that smoke, it's from smoke grenades, not an actual fire. Someone's set this up! They've used it as a diversion so they can steal this marker thing, and Nina's probably trying to stop them getting it off the ship.' He looked towards the other double doors. 'We didn't see her

when we came in, so she must have followed 'em out that way.'
He rounded on Agreste. 'You're supposedly in charge of security, so either pull your thumb out of your *trou de cul* and get people looking for 'em, or I'll do it myself!'

Agreste pointedly turned away from him to address the Emir. 'I will get a doctor. And I will also order a search.'

'Not good enough,' said the Yorkshireman. 'Macy, stay here!' He took off at a run.

Macy hesitated, then followed him, slipping the object she had taken from the cabinet into her bag.

The trikan.

Nina hurried down to Deck 4. She was now deep in the guts of the huge ship, the corridors still accessible to the passengers but noticeably more functional in appearance. A residual haze of smoke hung in the air.

She had descended to follow a shout in Arabic, but there was no sign of anyone. Where had the raiders gone? They couldn't be using a lifeboat to get off the ship, as those were one deck above. Were there other boats on the lower decks?

A flash of memory, Macy cooing over the holographic map of the *Atlantia*. The marina! It was at the stern, and obviously at water level. That *had* to be where they were going. She ran with renewed determination.

Beyond an intersection, carpet gave way to painted metal, dark wooden ceiling panels disappearing to expose gleaming steel ductwork above a long passageway. The door to a crew-only section had been left open to aid the raiders' escape. She ran through it.

A shout from ahead, louder than the last. She was catching up.

Eddie pounded sternwards, following the smoke. The grenades had forced passengers and crew away from specific parts of the ship, creating an escape route. Follow it, and he would find Nina.

He reached a flight of stairs. Up, down or keep going? More smoke below: down. He descended and looked around.

A long corridor led aft – and he saw a figure running down it. 'Nina!' he shouted, haring after her.

Even over the alarms, Nina heard her name being called. She glanced back and saw Eddie, wearing only trunks, running after her. 'Eddie!' she yelled, slowing but not stopping. 'They took the marker, they're getting away! You've got to—'

She broke off in shock as someone else appeared behind him: their daughter. *Now* she stopped. 'Macy! *Macy!* Get back, go back!'

Eddie saw Nina stop and shout something, but between the clamour of the evacuation alarm and his own hearing loss, the result of close exposure to far too many gunshots and explosions, he couldn't make it out. 'I'm coming, hold on!' he yelled back.

The woman reacted with concern when she saw Nina stop on one of the CCTV feeds, her husband running towards her on another. The plan was at risk; the redhead needed to be alone . . .

She hurriedly typed new commands – and the metal door at the entrance to the service area began to close.

'Shit!' Eddie gasped as a barrier slid between him and Nina. He knew that he wouldn't reach it in time to get through, but he didn't stop running. 'I'll find another way down to you!'

The gap narrowed, cutting his wife off from view. He reached the intersection, spotting a sign pointing to a flight of emergency stairs, and ran for them as the opening shrank to its last few inches.

★ ★ ★

Macy had also seen the closing hatch – and remembered a similar moment in the most recent Mach and Crest movie. A stone block was sliding across a doorway, and Eden Crest had used her newly discovered powers to throw a trikan and block it. *If she can do it . . .* the seven-year-old thought.

She snatched out the trikan by its handgrip, swinging her arm to fling the ancient weapon. It whirled away on its thin wire, the blades a spinning blur . . .

Heading for a wall. The real thing didn't behave like its toy counterpart, and she had misjudged the throw. The door was almost shut, cutting off her mother behind it.

No!

She *willed* the weapon to go straight, to block the hatch . . .

And it swerved.

The trikan narrowly missed the wall, banking in mid-air to fly across the intersection towards the closing door—

Too late. The gap vanished, the trikan bouncing off the hatch with a clang.

Macy stared in astonishment. It had turned when she told it to, she *knew* it had—

Eddie heard metal hitting metal behind him and spun to see the trikan fall to the floor. '*Macy!* What the *hell* are you doing? I told you to stay where you were!'

Macy burst into tears. 'I'm sorry, I'm sorry! I just wanted to help Mommy.'

'Did you *steal* that? Jesus, Macy, it's not a toy. It's probably worth a million dollars!'

'I'm sorry!' she wailed again.

'Eddie! Macy!' Nina's muffled voice came from behind the hatch.

'Nina!' Eddie shouted. 'Are you okay?'

'Yeah,' Nina replied. 'Is Macy all right?'

'She's fine,' Eddie said, 'but we need to teach her about respecting other people's property!'

His wife had no idea what he meant, but there wasn't time to discuss it. 'I can't get out – this door's locked.'

'I know. Someone's messing us about.'

'They're heading for the marina. Listen, you warn the crew. I'm going after them!'

'The crew've got their hands full,' Eddie replied. 'I'll try to find another way to the marina. Don't do anything daft, just wait for me to – Nina?' No answer. 'Oh for . . . flip's sake! What is it with my family never listening to a bloody word I say?' He let out an exasperated breath, then turned back to the still-crying Macy. 'It's okay, love, it's okay. I'm not mad at you,' he assured her. 'I'm mad at whoever's done all this. And when I find 'em, I'm going to show 'em just how mad I am.' He started for the emergency stairs, then realised Macy was still holding the trikan's handgrip. 'Leave that here, love.'

'But it worked, Daddy,' she said quietly.

'What do you mean?'

'I made it fly where I wanted, like in the movie! I was trying to make it stop the door closing, and it nearly did.'

'It's just a fancy Frisbee. Like I said, this is real life. Come on, let it go.' She reluctantly dropped the grip, but looked back at the ancient weapon as Eddie led the way to the stairs.

The marina at the *Atlantia*'s stern was not a fixed structure, rather a pair of floating jetties that extended once a huge hatch had lowered. Numerous small craft, mostly speedboats and jetskis, were mounted on racks in a hangar, a turntable at the top of a launch rail allowing them to slide into the water between the dock's two arms.

The jetties were already in position when the raiders arrived, the automated process set in motion by their controller. With the liner stationary, it had been easy to haul two speedboats into the sea. The black-clad men took their places in the lead craft, and waited.

Impatience quickly grew. 'What's keeping him?' demanded one man, tugging off his hot and itchy mask to reveal Arabic features with a small burn scar on his left cheek. 'If we wait much longer, they'll catch us!'

'There aren't any crew near you,' came the woman's reply in his earpiece. 'You're safe. Hashim is following the plan.'

Knowing that things were going as they should did not ease his frustration. 'Start the engine,' he ordered, clambering back on to the jetty as another man pushed the starter.

Someone clanked down the stairs. The scarred man snapped up his gun, but it was only al-Asim. 'She's coming!' the team leader shouted, pulling off his own mask.

'What took her so long?'

'I don't know, but it doesn't matter. Get into the boat, Musad!' Al-Asim backed away, raising his gun, as he heard someone descending.

Eddie rushed out on to the stern. He had come up to Deck 8 after seeing a ship's plan on a wall; the only other way to the marina had been cut off by the hatch separating him from his wife.

The deck was a vast amphitheatre of pools, sunloungers and outdoor bars and cafés, the terminus of the zip-line next to a concert stage. It was also deserted, food and drinks left unfinished and personal items abandoned as passengers headed for the lifeboats. The scene felt almost apocalyptic. That suited his mood. *Somebody* would think it was the end of the world when he caught them . . .

'Okay, *now* wait here!' he told Macy. This time, she followed his instructions. He ran towards the stairs leading down to the marina – then on instinct continued to the rear railing. The Strait of Gibraltar opened out before him, but he had no time to admire the view. Instead he looked down. Twin jetties extended behind the liner's broad stern, a pair of boats waiting at them.

The larger of the two had several black-clad figures inside it, and as he watched, another man emerged from inside the ship, slowly backing towards his companions.

Then he stopped, right arm coming up.

Even from on high, Eddie could tell he was holding a gun.

Only one person could be his target.

Nina slowed at the bottom of the stairs, peering cautiously into the marina—

The lead raider, a tall, hard-featured Arab, was aiming a gun at her. She jerked back into the stairwell, expecting a bullet to sear past, but no shots came.

'Dr Wilde!' he shouted instead. 'You are very brave – and very stupid! Do not try to follow us!'

'Oh, shit,' she whispered. All he had to do to kill her was advance; even if she ran back up the stairs, she would never reach safety in time . . .

Tense seconds passed, then someone called out in Arabic. Nina crouched and briefly peeked out. Again, no rounds came at her, but now it was because the man had retreated, backing towards his boat.

The satchel containing the marker was still slung from his shoulder. If there was even a chance her theory about the spearheads was correct, she couldn't let him escape with it.

But how? He and his comrades all had guns, and were about to escape in a speedboat—

Something hit the water between the jetties, an explosive burst of water sending the man staggering.

'*Really* don't follow me!' Eddie yelled to Macy as he climbed over the stern railing – and jumped off.

He plunged towards the water like a bomb. The deck was some eighty feet above the ocean, giving him enough time to point his toes downwards and raise his hands above his head before he struck the surface. Even prepared, the impact was still punishing.

But he survived. He arched his back and threw his arms and legs wide to slow himself, then kicked back towards the churning splash above.

Nina didn't know what had happened, but she *did* know she only had one chance to take advantage of it.

The leader, briefly blinded, shook water from his eyes – and she charged, shoulder-barging him. Arms flailing, he skidded on the wet decking.

The satchel slipped from his shoulder. Nina grabbed it. Throwing it into the sea would not make her popular in the archaeological community, but she could live with that if it prevented the spearheads from falling into the wrong hands—

The man seized the satchel's strap and shoved her away. Nina caught herself at the jetty's edge, only to see his companions' guns swing towards her . . .

Nobody fired.

The leader rounded on her. His own gun came up – then he too changed his mind and swung a punch at her head. She intercepted the blow with an arm, but it still hit hard enough to knock her to the deck.

The man stepped up to her, gun ready—

A hand burst out of the water and grabbed his ankle.

He looked down in shock as Eddie pulled at his leg – then lashed out with his other foot. His boot caught the Englishman's head, sending him back into the water.

'Eddie!' Nina cried, but the man had recovered. His gun came back around . . .

Then he turned and ran for the waiting boat. He leapt in, the driver gunning the engine and sending the craft surging from the dock in a plume of spray. It powered away towards the Spanish coast.

Nina stared helplessly after it, then rushed to help her husband. 'Eddie, here!' she called.

Spluttering, he grabbed her hand. 'Jesus! It's a lot fucking warmer in the pool,' he gasped as she helped him on to the dock.

A life vest hit the water behind him, dropped from above. They both looked up to see Macy peering over the stern railing. 'Mom! Dad!' she shouted, scared. 'Are you okay?'

'We're fine!' Eddie managed to reply, waving. 'Thanks, love!'

He flopped on to the decking. 'Jeez,' said Nina, suddenly breathless after the adrenalin surge of the chase and fight. She looked northwards. Some of the *Atlantia*'s large orange lifeboats were moving clear of the halted liner, the speedboat lost to sight in the confusion. 'Goddammit. They got away.'

'What happened?' asked the Yorkshireman. 'Who were those arseholes?'

'I don't know. But they took the spear marker! We've got to contact the Spanish authorities—'

'Dr Wilde!' Agreste entered the marina, accompanied by a ship's officer and several crewmen.

'You're too late,' Nina told him. 'They got away.'

'Lot of bloody use you were,' Eddie added.

Agreste did not respond to the barb. 'The Emir wants to see you on the bridge,' he informed the couple. 'Right away.'

6

The journey to the bridge was almost unnerving, areas that had been thronged with people now deserted. There was nothing to fault about the *Atlantia*'s evacuation procedures; all five and a half thousand passengers and most of the crew were aboard the lifeboats just fifteen minutes after the alarm sounded.

'The *false* alarm,' Captain Snowcock told Nina and Eddie, the Yorkshireman having been provided with a dressing gown. 'Someone used a recording of me. The ship's systems were hacked.'

Also present besides the crew and Agreste were the Emir, Alula and several members of the royal entourage – and Nina couldn't help but notice that all eyes were on her. 'What – you think *I* had something to do with it?'

'You were in a locked room with the Emir,' said Agreste. 'When I arrived, the room was open, the Atlantean artefact was gone – and His Majesty had been attacked.'

'He wasn't attacked,' Nina insisted. 'When the alarm went off, the display cases retracted into the vault, and he fell in.'

'Is that what happened, Your Majesty?' asked Alula.

'I'm not sure,' the Emir replied. 'I remember the alarm going off – and then I woke up in the vault. Dr Wilde must have hit me; she was the only other person there.'

'That's not true!' protested the redhead. 'I mean, yeah, it *is* true I was the only other person in the room, but I didn't hit him.' She turned to Snowcock. 'There were cameras in the exhibition hall – they'll show you what happened.'

The captain indicated the video wall. All its monitors were dark. 'The hackers shut down the CCTV systems.'

Eddie shook his head. 'They weren't *all* shut down. Somebody was watching us – they kept closing doors to keep me from Nina. Maybe they cut off the bridge feeds, but they were still working. There might be recordings.'

'Check it,' Snowcock ordered an officer.

Alula's expression hardened as she spoke to Nina again. 'Assault on the Emir is a crime of the highest magnitude under Dhajani law.'

'I didn't assault him,' Nina said, frustrated. 'I was—'

'Mommy!' Two crewmen entered with Macy, the young girl wrapped in a towel. 'Daddy, are you okay?'

'Yeah, I am, thanks,' her father told her. 'What about you?' He gave her escorts a threatening glare. 'Nobody's hurt you, have they?'

She hugged her parents. 'No, they've been really nice.'

'Good job.'

'The *marcador de lanza* is missing,' said Agreste impatiently, 'and so is the Atlantean weapon, the trikan. What happened to them?'

'I can tell you where the trikan is,' said Eddie. 'It's in a corridor at the arse-end of Deck 4.'

'And why is it there?'

Macy spoke up timidly under the Frenchman's stern gaze. 'It . . . it was me. I'm sorry, I shouldn't have taken it.'

'You did *what*?' Nina said, aghast and embarrassed. 'You *stole* something from the exhibition?'

'I was going to give it back! I thought I could use it to help you, like in the movie. And it worked, it worked!' she added, suddenly thrilled.

'What worked?'

'The trikan, I made it steer in the air! I was trying to stop the door closing, and it went where I told it to!'

Nina had no time for fantasy. 'I very much doubt that, Macy.' She turned back to Agreste and the Emir. 'I am *so* sorry that—'

'It *did*, Mommy!'

'Macy! That's enough. I'm sorry my daughter took something,' she continued.

Macy started to cry. 'If it is found where Mr Chase said, then we shall say no more about it,' Fadil told her kindly. 'But what about the spear marker?'

'The men who stole it escaped in a boat from the marina,' Nina told him. 'They were headed for Spain.'

The Emir glanced at the starboard windows. The mountainous Spanish coast was a ragged line against the horizon, lit by the setting sun. Other ships were visible before it; some commercial vessels giving the stationary cruise liner a wide berth, others from the Spanish coastguard. 'Did anyone see this boat?'

'No,' said Snowcock. 'But everyone's been focused on the evacuation.'

'Maybe you should *re*focus,' Eddie snapped. He pointed at his temple, where the lead raider's boot had left a vivid mark. 'I didn't imagine getting punted in the head.'

'Sir,' said the officer searching for security footage. 'I haven't been able to access any CCTV recordings – I'm still locked out. But I *have* got the door recordings.'

'What are they?' Alula demanded.

'All the door touchpads have a camera,' said Snowcock. 'Every time someone uses a card or a passcode to open one, they're recorded. We can review them to make sure nobody's gaining unauthorised access.'

'And you can watch them?'

'Yes, Your Royal Highness.'

'Then do so! Find the recordings from the exhibition hall.'

The officer searched for the relevant file. 'It won't show

everything that happened in the room,' Snowcock cautioned. 'The recordings are only to check who's unlocked the door; they're not very long.'

'Then let us hope that is enough to clear you, Dr Wilde,' said the Emir.

'Here,' said the officer. He clicked the mouse.

Everyone crowded around the console. The video image was distorted, taken with a fish-eye lens, but the Atlantis exhibition was immediately recognisable.

Nina saw herself, one hand outstretched to touch the screen. The recording had begun as soon as the keypad appeared. Her past self tapped in the first digits, then paused, looking to one side as the evacuation alert sounded. Finally she resumed, entering the last numbers before reaching for the door handle—

The redhead on the screen suddenly disappeared behind the door as it burst open and black-clad figures rushed through. Then the recording ended. 'That's all there is, sir,' said the officer.

'It was long enough,' Alula told him, fixing Nina with an icy glare. 'She let them in!'

'I was trying to get help!' Nina replied. 'The Emir had fallen into the vault – I couldn't get him out, so I went to open the door and find someone.'

'The door was locked,' said Agreste. 'You used a code to open it – whose?'

'The Emir's . . .' she said, trailing off as she realised she was digging herself deeper into a hole.

Alula's response was almost explosive. *'What?'*

'How did you get my code?' the Emir demanded.

'Think it's about time you lawyered up, love,' said Eddie.

'Answer His Majesty!' shouted Alula. 'You are not in America – you do not get to stay silent!'

'I saw him type it in on the bridge, okay?' Nina shot back. 'It was a date, it was easy to remember.'

The Arab woman gave her brother a furious look. 'I should *never* have allowed Lobato to let you have a master code,' she said, before whirling back to Nina. 'And you opened the door for the thieves!'

'They knocked her flying!' Eddie countered. 'She didn't know they were there.'

'How would they have known to be there at that precise moment if she had not *told* them to be there? She is a part of this – she is probably *behind* this!'

'Enough.' The Emir spoke quietly, but there was anger behind the single word. 'Alula, you may be my minister of security, and my sister, but you do not, *ever*, tell me what I can or cannot do.'

She hurriedly bowed her head. 'I – Your Majesty, I am sorry. I did not mean—'

'But you *are* in charge of my security,' he went on, 'and you failed me. Perhaps I made a mistake by giving you such an important position; I should have given it to a *man*,' an unmistakable emphasis on the word, 'better qualified. If you cannot protect me, how can you hope to protect our country?'

Alula's face flushed in shame – and rage – but she had no reply. Nina had something to say, though, feeling oddly protective towards the other woman. 'Maybe you shouldn't have typed your damn code in where anyone could see it!' she told Fadil. 'You've never used an ATM? Actually, no, I guess you probably haven't. I suppose when your own face is on the banknotes, you don't *need* to carry cash!'

The Emir drew in a sharp breath at being challenged, but it was Alula who had the strongest reaction; any sympathy Nina had hoped to garner from her display of feminine solidarity failed to materialise. 'Do not *dare* speak to His Majesty like that!' she shouted. 'I want this woman arrested! Now!'

Some of the entourage's larger members moved towards

Nina. 'Don't even bloody think—' Eddie began, raising his fists to defend her.

'Eddie, don't!' Nina said, hurriedly pushing his hands back down. 'Don't do anything, especially not in front of Macy. They'll have to let me go, because I haven't done anything. You need to look after Macy while this is sorted out.'

The Yorkshireman nodded grudgingly.

'What's going to happen to you, Mommy?' Macy asked tearfully. 'Is this because I took the trikan?'

Nina hugged her. 'No, it's not your fault. You stay with Daddy, and everything'll be fine. Okay?'

Macy nodded, but with little confidence. 'Okay.'

'Good. I love you.' Nina kissed her. 'I'll see you again soon, all right?'

Alula issued an order. The men advanced again. Eddie tensed, giving them a venomous glare, but did nothing. With a last look back at her husband and daughter, Nina allowed herself to be taken from the bridge.

The last thing she expected to find aboard a luxury liner was a prison, but the *Atlantia* did indeed have one. Several small white-painted rooms in the bowels of Deck 2 acted as cells; their designers, Nina mused, had probably expected them to be used as drunk tanks or places to let overheated casino losers cool off, rather than to hold someone accused of conspiring to steal a priceless artefact and assaulting the ruler of a nation.

'This is insane,' she said aloud, lying back on the bunk. How was she going to prove her innocence? It should have been easy enough – since she *was* innocent – but Alula had been all too quick to leap to conclusions, and the others had followed suit.

The cell door opened. She sat up, hoping to see Eddie, but it was Agreste. 'Have you found the raiders?' she asked.

The bearded Frenchman shook his head. 'Not yet. But I will.' He spoke briefly to the Taser-armed crewman standing guard outside, then closed the cell door. The lock clacked. 'You are in a great deal of trouble, Dr Wilde. If you turn in your accomplices and tell me where to find the marker, I am sure the Emir will be lenient.'

She threw up her hands in exasperation. 'I can't turn in my "accomplices", because I don't have any! I didn't have anything to do with this.'

'That is not what the evidence suggests.'

'What evidence? You've got one video of me unlocking a door, and that's it. And it's pretty clear I got knocked on my ass when they kicked it open.'

He shook his head. 'That is open to interpretation.'

'Only if you've already made up your mind that I was helping the bad guys. Which I wasn't – I tried to stop them! And so did Eddie; he jumped off the back of the damn ship to keep them from shooting me. He could have been killed! He'd hardly take that risk if he was part of all this.'

'If I believed he was involved, he would be in the next cell.'

'What, so you think I secretly came up with a plan to steal an Atlantean artefact, then brought my husband, my daughter and my grandmother along as cover?'

'Whatever plan there is, I will uncover it, do not worry. I used to be an investigator for Interpol, and before then an officer in the Sûreté, and I was a very good one. But my job now is to ensure the security of the items in the exhibition; because I have not been completely successful,' a wry smile, 'my priority is now to return the spear marker to its rightful owners in Seville. You can help me do that if you cooperate.'

Nina pointed at her mouth. 'Hi. Read my lips. *I don't know where it is*, because *I didn't have anything to do with the robbery*. Okay?'

'I see.' Agreste stood straighter. 'Then I must inform you of the alternative.'

'Which is?'

'You will stand trial on charges of espionage and—'

'*Espionage?*' she yelped. 'Where the hell did *that* come from?'

'You used the Emir's passcode to open the door. Only the Emir himself should know it, so it is technically a state secret. As minister for state security, Princess Alula has the power to bring charges against you, and that is one of several she chose.'

'Oh, I see,' Nina replied with bitter sarcasm. 'He screws up, blames her, and she takes it out on me? Go on, then: what are her other bullshit charges?'

Agreste intoned them as if reading from a list. 'Assault on His Majesty; robbery; piracy; and conspiracy to commit all of the previous. Her Royal Highness is demanding the maximum punishment for each charge. I should also inform you that the maximum penalty for espionage under Dhajani law is death.'

'That makes the rest kinda redundant!'

'The penalties may, of course, be reduced in exchange for your confession and cooperation.'

Nina stood, gesticulating in frustrated anger. 'This is as much cooperation as I can *give* you, because I *didn't do anything*! I'm innocent!'

'That is for the court to decide.'

'Okay, so when do I get to call my lawyer?'

'When we reach Dhajan.'

She stared in disbelief. 'You're taking me to *Dhajan?*'

'This ship flies a Dhajani flag; the robbery took place in international waters, so it is under Dhajani jurisdiction. As I understand from the captain, once all the lifeboats are recovered, the *Atlantia* will head to Gibralter. The damage the hackers caused to the fire control and security systems means it is no longer safe to carry passengers, so they will be offloaded there. You will stay aboard until the ship reaches Dhajan—'

'Dhajan's in the goddamn Persian Gulf!' she protested. 'We're at the far end of the Mediterranean – it'll take days to get there.'

'Eight days, I believe.'

'Eight— Okay, this is ridiculous. If you're going to deny me a lawyer, then I demand to speak to the US embassy.'

'You will be able to speak to an official at the American embassy in Dhajan once we arrive.'

'You know damn well I didn't mean the one in Dhajan,' Nina snapped. 'I meant in Spain. Or Gibraltar – that's British territory, and I'm married to a British citizen. There must be a consulate there.'

'I will pass on your request to Her Royal Highness,' Agreste replied. 'But before I go, I will give you one last chance to tell me where to find the spear marker.'

'I. Don't. *Know*,' she said, infuriated. 'Why won't you believe me?'

'It is not my job to believe.' He rapped on the door. The crewman outside unlocked it. Agreste departed.

Nina dropped heavily back on to the bunk, mind reeling. A few hours earlier, she had been a king's guest of honour; now she was trapped in a nightmare worthy of Kafka.

'There she is,' Eddie said to Macy. They had returned to their cabin to get dressed, and after learning that Olivia was aboard the first lifeboat to return were now watching it being winched back up. The bulbous orange craft could carry almost four hundred people, but Olivia's age and lack of proper clothing meant she was amongst the first to be helped back aboard the *Atlantia*. 'Olivia! Over here!'

'Eddie! Macy!' she cried, hurrying to them. 'Are you both all right?'

'Yeah, we're fine. What about you?'

She was wrapped in a blanket. 'Cold. And very uncomfortable. The seats in that lifeboat were not exactly ergonomic.' She glanced around. 'Where's Nina?'

'Let's get inside first,' Eddie said, ushering her to a door. 'You know how I said she was a trouble magnet?'

'Yes? Oh *no*,' Olivia added in alarm. 'What's happened? Where is she?'

'In a cell, and they won't let us see her.' He put a supportive hand on Macy as she clung to him, trying not to cry. 'Someone robbed the Atlantis exhibition – they set off the alarms and forced an evacuation to cover what they were doing.'

'So why is Nina in a cell? Do they think she had something to do with it?'

'Yeah, and they won't listen to anyone who says different. Look, can you do me a favour?'

'Of course.'

'I need you to look after Macy while I make some phone calls. We've got friends in the US government and at the UN who can help, but some of them might need convincing, and I could get . . .' he gave her a faint smile, 'a bit heated. I'd rather Macy didn't hear me in full flow, if you know what I mean.'

'I do indeed,' Olivia replied as they reached a bank of elevators. 'Don't worry, I'll take care of her.'

'Great. Okay, we'll get up to our rooms, then I'll start ringing around.'

'Will Mommy be okay?' Macy asked.

'Don't worry,' Eddie told her. 'She won't be in that cell for long.'

The clack of the lock brought Nina out of her frustrated funk. She assumed it would be Agreste returning, another attempt to get her to confess. So it came as a surprise when Ana Rijo entered, carrying a bag.

'Ana?' she said, sitting up. 'What're you doing here?'

Ana waited for the man outside to close the door before speaking. 'Dr Wilde. I'm glad you're okay.'

'I'm glad too, but the accommodation's a definite downgrade.' She regarded the bag. 'Did Eddie ask you to bring me something?'

'No, I got these for you myself.' She seemed nervous, giving the door a worried glance. 'You have to get out of here.'

'No arguments there.'

'I mean, right now. You've been set up – you are the . . . the patsy?'

Nina stood. 'What do you mean?'

The Brazilian put down the bag and began taking out items: the high-heeled shoes Nina had kicked off in the exhibition hall and a pair of flats, then her passport and credit cards. 'I have heard people talking. You are being taken to Dhajan, to be put on trial – but you will be found guilty, no matter what. The royal family think you are one of the thieves, perhaps even their leader. They have made up their minds already. And in Dhajan, if the Emir says you are guilty, then . . .' A helpless shrug.

Nina felt a growing dread. She had already considered the possibility, but having it laid out so bluntly suddenly hammered the reality home; while the small Gulf state was a US ally, it was also a nation with a history of absolute monarchy that she doubted the Emir's programme of modernisation had much changed. 'So . . . what, you're busting me out of here? Why?'

Ana produced Nina's phone. 'Because I do not believe you are guilty. You are too kind. And I have seen what happens when the state decides someone is guilty before their trial has even started. Here.'

The last item she took out was a roll of banknotes in an elastic band. 'Those aren't mine,' Nina said.

'I know. They are mine. You will need them in Spain. Once you get there, you will be in a country that will not extradite you without evidence, and you will be able to make a legal defence.'

'I doubt breaking out of prison to get there will help my case.'

'You want to stay in here?' said Ana, with a little exasperation. 'If they find out I am helping you, they will put me in prison too. The man outside, I gave him money to let me in, but he will not protect me. Now I have to come with you.'

'You're putting yourself in danger to help me?' Nina said in disbelief. 'You barely know me!'

'Dr Wilde,' Ana said, imploringly, 'I've read about everything you have done. You have literally saved the world! Everyone owes you a great debt, even if they don't know it. And I believe in paying my debts. Now, please, we have to be quick.' She handed Nina her belongings. 'They are winching the lifeboats back aboard. The whole ship is in chaos, nobody knows what is going on. If we are fast, we can get to a motorboat and launch it before anyone stops us. We will be in Spain in less than twenty minutes.'

Nina donned her flat shoes. Her dress lacking pockets, she ended up putting her other possessions back in the bag. 'That's if you can get me out of the cell. There's a guy with a Taser out there, remember.'

She brought up her phone to call Eddie, but Ana stopped her. 'Please, there is no time now. You can call from the boat; the ship's cell towers have good range.' A more commanding tone entered her voice. 'Wait until I say.' She knocked on the door.

The guard opened it, ushering her out quickly. 'Okay, now go, go,' he muttered, turning to shut the door—

Ana snatched his Taser from his belt. Before he even registered that it was gone, she had already snapped it up and fired. Twin barbs stabbed into his back, fifty thousand volts of electricity dropping him to the floor.

Nina jumped back in surprise. 'Holy shit!'

The other woman kept her finger on the trigger for several seconds, the man convulsing before abruptly falling still.

'O-*kaaaay*,' the redhead said, hesitantly stepping over the fallen guard. 'I'd hate to see what you do to someone who leaves a bad tip at the end of the cruise.'

'I don't like this job anyway.' Ana dropped the weapon and peered cautiously through the exit. 'Okay, it's clear. Let's go.'

7

Nina followed the Brazilian out of the brig. 'Where are we going? The marina?'

'No, they're using it to help bring people back aboard,' Ana replied. 'It will be too busy. We can take one of the crew boats from the lifeboat deck.'

'You said they're lifting the lifeboats back up. Don't you think they might notice?'

'I'm a member of the crew – we are all trained to help during an evacuation. Nobody will think I should not be there. By the time anyone realises what we are doing, it will be too late to stop us.' They ascended a steep flight of metal stairs. 'When we get to the boat, you climb straight in. I'll start the crane to lower it, then jump in too. If anything goes wrong, there is an emergency release that will drop the boat into the water.'

'Isn't the lifeboat deck about five storeys up?'

'Yes. So hopefully nothing *will* go wrong!' They ascended another leg of the stairs. Nina tensed at the sight of a couple of crewmen, but Ana's uniform reassured them that both women were authorised to be there. 'Okay, one more floor, then—'

A harsh, shrilling alarm sounded. 'That *so* does not sound good,' Nina said.

'The security alert,' Ana replied, frowning. 'The guard must have woken up. Quick, quick!' They clattered upwards. Behind them, a crewman's walkie-talkie squawked, Snowcock's voice crackling from it. 'Shit! They know you've escaped.'

'Oh, great! How much further?'

'This way.' The Brazilian increased her pace, leading Nina into one of the public areas. A long passage ran the ship's length, clusters of people entering it from side hallways: passengers reboarding the liner from the lifeboats. 'Down here.'

Ana headed to an exterior door. An empty davit was visible through the glass. They emerged on the lifeboat deck, a chill wind hitting Nina. 'Where's the boat?' she asked, seeing that they were roughly halfway along the *Atlantia*'s length. The lifeboats already recovered were mostly towards the bow, though one was being raised further aft. Below, more of the orange craft bobbed in the water.

'There.' Ana pointed. Almost hidden amongst the cranes a hundred feet away was a smaller davit, this one bearing a rigid inflatable boat. It was unattended. 'Come on!'

They ran along the deck. Nina looked back, but there were no signs of pursuit – yet.

Ana reached the boat. 'Okay, I have to bring it out over the water,' she told Nina, going to a control panel. 'Get in as soon as you can.' She started the crane.

Nina ducked under the boat to wait at the deck's edge as it was swung outwards. The sea roiled vertiginously below, the lifeboats rendered toy-like by distance. She checked the deck again. More crew were emerging towards the bow, but they all seemed involved in the recovery effort, not looking for her.

'Get in!' Ana called.

Nina vaulted into the descending RIB. It rocked under her weight. She steadied herself and clambered to the front seat. The vessel's outboard motor was steered by a wheel; checking the dashboard, she saw the release handle her rescuer had mentioned beside a starter button. 'Are you coming?' she asked as the boat drew level with the deck.

'I have to start the winch.' Ana operated more controls. An

electric whine, and the RIB lurched as the cables suspending it wound out from their reels. 'Okay, I'm—'

Both women turned at a shout. Agreste was running along the deck towards them. The Frenchman's arm whipped up—

Fear hit Nina as she saw his gun. 'Ana! *Jump!*'

Too late.

Agreste fired. Ana fell against the controls and slumped to the floor, a spot of red on the chest of her white uniform jacket.

'*No!*' Nina cried. She looked back at Agreste. He lowered his gun, then marched along the deck towards the descending RIB's davit.

Sounds of alarm came as passengers reacted to the gunshot. Agreste maintained his pace, moving closer to the railing to keep sight of Nina as she was carried downwards, already clearing the deck below.

He reached the davit, staring down at her, then pulled back. The RIB continued its descent. Another deck passed—

The boat jerked to a stop, pitching Nina into the inflatable's footwell. Then it started to rise again as the winch reversed, hauling her relentlessly back towards the Frenchman.

He leaned out again, gun raised—

Nina pulled the cable release.

Both metal lines sprang free – and the boat plunged towards the sea. She screamed—

Her cry was abruptly cut off as the RIB hit the water. Spray rained over her. She sat upright, gasping, then looked up.

Agreste was still visible above. He targeted her again. Nina dived at the dashboard and pushed the starter button. The engine roared. She jammed the throttle to full power, and the boat's nose pitched upwards as it surged away. Another gunshot came from above, making her duck instinctively, but she wasn't hit. She straightened out, raising her head—

A lifeboat filled her view.

She spun the wheel, the RIB sweeping past the other boat with barely a foot to spare. It rocked as her wake hit it, passengers crying out in alarm.

More evacuation craft were dotted before her like orange icebergs, other boats that had come to assist mingling amongst them. One was a Spanish coastguard vessel. Nina hauled at the wheel to angle away from it as she swerved through the flotilla. Being arrested by the Spanish authorities was a better prospect than being gunned down by Agreste, but far preferable to either was not being caught at all.

Distant lights sparkled on the mainland. The nearest port was Tarifa, but the coastguard had almost certainly come from there, and she imagined they had other vessels available. Tarifa was the closest point in mainland Europe to Africa, and faced a constant stream of migrants crossing the strait, often risking their lives to do so and requiring rescue. She cleared the field of bobbing boats and aimed the RIB at a stretch of coastline west of the port. Intermittent lights told her she wouldn't be stranded in the middle of nowhere by making landfall there, but at the same time it appeared isolated enough that the police wouldn't arrest her the moment she stepped ashore.

She glanced back at the *Atlantia*. The liner was receding, the people on the lifeboat deck already reduced to mere dots against its enormity—

Eddie! She had to tell him what had happened while she was still in cellular range. Holding the wheel with one hand, she fumbled in the bag for her phone.

In his cabin, Eddie had called Oswald Seretse, a senior United Nations official whose responsibilities included oversight of the IHA. By the Yorkshireman's reckoning, Seretse owed him multiple favours for all the times he and Nina had prevented disaster, not least saving the lives of everyone at the UN itself.

The Gambian diplomat, however, while sympathetic, made it clear that any help he could provide would be limited. 'Unfortunately, Eddie,' he explained, 'the crimes of which Nina is accused did indeed occur on a Dhajani-flagged vessel. Now, while it could certainly be argued that any ship passing through the Strait of Gibraltar is actually within the twelve-mile territorial limit of either Spain or Morocco, in practice the right of free transit passage could equally be argued to apply under Part III of the UN Convention on—'

'I don't care about the legalese, Ozzy,' Eddie snapped. 'I just need to know if there's anything you can do.'

'I'm afraid that is likely to be in the hands of the lawyers. But I will of course do everything I can.'

'That'd be great. If we—' He broke off as his phone vibrated. 'Hold on, got another call coming in . . . It's Nina!' he exclaimed, checking the screen. 'I've got to take it, I'll call you back.'

He hurriedly accepted the new call. 'It's me, love. Are you okay?' There was a lot of background noise, as if an engine was running – and hadn't she left her phone in the cabin? 'Where are you?'

'I'm on a boat!' she replied.

'You're what? Why are you—'

'I don't have time to explain. That French guy, Agreste, killed Ana! She let me out of the cell because I was going to be railroaded by the Dhajanis, but he caught up and shot her! He took a shot at me too, but I'm okay.'

'Ana's *dead*? Jesus! And why are they trying to frame you?'

'I don't know. But Agreste told me they weren't going to let me off at Gibraltar – they want to take me back to Dhajan to put me on trial. I'm the only suspect they've got, so they've already decided I'm guilty.'

Her voice began to distort as she moved away from the liner. 'So what are you doing now?' Eddie quickly asked.

'I'm going to Spain, to Seville. This is all about the Atlantean spearheads, somehow – whoever took the marker from the ship will need the other one to find out where they are. I've got to make sure the bad guys don't get their hands on it.'

'So just tell the museum or whoever to stick it in a safe! Nina, if you go on the run, it'll make you look more guilty. I should bloody know, I once had to do it myself.'

'And you cleared your name by doing it. Which is what I've got—' Her words broke up into an unintelligible electronic stammer, then a series of rapid bleeps told Eddie that he had lost the connection.

The adjoining cabin's connecting door opened, Olivia peering through. 'What's happened? We could hear you next door – you sounded quite agitated.'

'That's putting it mildly.' Eddie opened the balcony door in the hope of spotting Nina, but it was now too dark to pick out much other than the flashing lights of the lifeboats. 'Nina's just broken out of jail, and now she's heading for Spain in a boat she nicked!' He chose not to mention Ana's death, seeing that Macy had just joined her great-grandmother.

'Is Mom all right?' Macy asked.

'She's fine,' Eddie assured her. 'But I need to have words with the Emir.'

'Not in your usual threatening way, I hope,' said Olivia. When he didn't immediately reply, she added: 'I mean it! We don't need you ending up in a cell as well.'

The Yorkshireman headed for the door. 'Depends if he's willing to listen. Look after Macy – I'll be right back.'

He made his way to the bridge, on the assumption that the Emir would be there as he waited for more news about the situation. The hallways were now packed with passengers returning to their cabins. It took him several minutes to squeeze through the crowds to the Deck 16 landing.

The bridge door was closed. He considered knocking, but before he could try, a young officer hurried to the entrance, waving his ID card at the reader before rushing inside. 'Gift horses,' Eddie muttered, darting in after him.

The bridge was considerably busier than before, the air a cacophony as officers communicated with crew members all over the ship via walkie-talkie. They were too occupied to notice the intruder, but Eddie was sure he would not stay invisible for long. He spotted the Emir and Alula with a couple of their entourage, engaged in deep discussion with Captain Snowcock.

And Agreste. Eddie felt a surge of anger at the sight of the Frenchman, but restrained himself from striding over and punching his lights out. Instead, he unobtrusively made his way towards the group.

Their conversation gradually became audible. '. . . ensure hotels are arranged for everyone – and transport to Spain too,' Fadil was saying. 'I do not imagine Gibraltar will have several thousand rooms free at short notice. Also give a full refund to every passenger. And arrange complimentary first-class flights to wherever they wish to travel – by Dhajan Airways if possible, but using the most expedient airline if not.'

Alula was equally unhappy, but for different reasons. 'That will cost millions of dollars, tens of millions!'

'This is the maiden voyage of our country's first cruise liner,' the Emir countered. 'And it is a public relations disaster! If we are to avoid becoming an international joke, and to be sure our *second* cruise liner does not leave port empty next week after every passenger cancels their booking, we must do what-ever is necessary to protect our reputation. Money is easily recovered; goodwill is not.' He looked back at his aide. 'First class. See to it. And,' he added to Snowcock, 'we must get the *Atlantia* back home as quickly as possible. I do not want to delay the repairs.'

'It'll take eight days to reach Dhajan, maybe even nine,' the captain noted. 'But if you overrode the speed limiter, we could do it in seven.'

'I will do that. If you—'

'Hey!' an officer shouted. 'You! You're not supposed to be on the bridge!'

Everyone turned to see Eddie in front of the dead video wall. 'Ay up,' he said with a disarming grin. 'Just thought I'd drop by.'

'Get him out of here!' Snowcock snapped. Several men bustled towards the intruder.

'No, wait,' said the Emir. They stopped. 'I would like some answers from Mr Chase.'

'That's funny,' Eddie replied, '"cause I'd like some answers from *you*. And him an' all,' he went on, jabbing a finger at Agreste. 'This twat tried to kill my wife – and he *did* kill Ana Rijo!'

The Frenchman gave him a look of haughty affront. 'I do not know what you are talking about.'

'No? They were getting into a boat, and you shot Ana! Then you took another—'

Alula interrupted him. 'How did you know your wife stole a boat?'

'She just rang me and told me,' Eddie replied.

'And where is she now?'

He answered with a protective lie. 'Halfway to Morocco. I mean, if you're being shipped off to a kangaroo court and get the chance to escape, you'd be daft not to disappear, wouldn't you?'

Alula scowled. 'Your wife has been charged with espionage, piracy and several other crimes – and a Red Notice has been issued for her arrest by Interpol on behalf of the Dhajani government. She will not get far, and when she is caught, she *will* be brought to Dhajan for trial.'

'And you've already got the guilty verdict sorted, right?' Eddie said with rising anger, stabbing his finger at Agreste again. 'What about a murder charge for him? Or does he already have a royal "get out of jail free" card?'

'He does not,' said the Emir. 'I do not know what lies you have heard about our country, Mr Chase, but I can assure you our trials are fair. Dr Wilde will be judged on the evidence. As for your accusations: where is *your* evidence? Where is Ana's body?'

'Probably chucked over the side with weights tied to her feet!' Eddie held up his wristband. 'Easy way to check if she's still here – I'll just call her. Let's see if she turns up.'

'Do not waste our time,' snarled Alula. 'Your wife has escaped, and you may have helped her. I should have *you* arrested for conspiracy!'

'Conspiracy, my arse!' he shouted back. 'Nina's been set up, and you've fallen right for it!'

'That is *enough*!' barked the Emir. 'Both of you, be silent.' Before the seething Yorkshireman could speak again, he continued: 'Mr Chase, I do not believe you were directly involved in the robbery. It has been confirmed that you were in the swimming pool with your daughter. But your wife *did* let the thieves into the exhibition hall using my personal code. She is the prime suspect in the crime – and now she has escaped from lawful custody, assaulted a crewman and stolen a boat. These are not the actions of an innocent woman.'

'They are if she thinks she's going to be blamed for something she didn't do,' said Eddie.

'That does not alter the fact that she is now a fugitive. And,' Fadil went on pointedly, 'if you were to aid her in any way, you would be committing a crime under Dhajani law. So, I shall ask you: where is she?'

The Englishman gave an exaggerated shrug. 'I don't know. Hopefully a long way from here.'

'He is deliberately obstructing us,' said Alula, scowling. 'Captain, I want him arrest—'

The Emir cut her off. 'No, no. He is just angry.' He looked Eddie in the eye. 'I would strongly suggest, Mr Chase, that you return to your cabin and calm yourself. And if your wife should call you again . . . you must inform us at once. Do you understand?'

Eddie's gaze was no less level. 'I'll do the right thing,' he said coldly. 'It's what I always do.'

'Good. Then if someone would escort our guest back to his suite?'

The crewmen surrounded him. With a last glare at the Dhajani royals, Eddie left the bridge.

8

Nina clung to the wheel as the boat was lashed by breaking waves. She was almost at the shore, but the rough water made the end of her voyage as scary as the start.

The craft rode over a retreating wave, pitching her against the wheel, then its keel thumped against the beach. She gunned the throttle. The RIB slewed around and slithered to a stop.

She knew it would not remain still for long. She grabbed the bag and jumped off the bow. Another wave sluiced past as she landed, the froth reaching her calves. She splashed onwards to dry sand. The boat was already being dragged back out to sea.

She surveyed her windswept surroundings. No flashing lights of approaching police cars, so that was a good start. Tarifa's lights were visible on a headland about three miles away. Turning, she saw the *Atlantia*, the brightly lit liner still standing out clearly even at a distance. It had come about, ready to head back into the Mediterranean. Completing her sweep, she spotted a hotel nestled amongst trees a few hundred yards to the west.

A hotel meant tourists – and where there were tourists, there was usually cellular service. She took out her phone and was relieved to find she had a signal. She looked towards the *Atlantia* as she called Eddie.

'Nina, where are you?' he asked urgently on answering. 'Are you okay?'

'I'm fine, just a bit wet,' she replied. 'I'm on a beach in Spain.'

'I wouldn't hang around. They've put a Red Notice on you. The cops'll have your picture – if they see you, they'll arrest you.'

She hurriedly started inland. 'As if I didn't have enough to worry about! Somebody's gone to a lot of trouble to make me the patsy. I think they're scared I might stop them.'

'Stop them doing what?'

'Finding the spearheads.'

'You weren't even sure if they were real,' he objected.

'*Somebody* obviously is. And they're sure enough of it to kill Ana to prevent me from interfering. Do you know if they arrested Agreste?'

'Not only did they *not* arrest him, the Emir and his people don't even believe Ana's dead. Or maybe they know she is, but they're part of it.'

She reached the top of the beach. 'You think the Dhajanis are behind this?'

'Maybe. Or Lobato – he seemed a bit *too* keen to find out about the spearheads, didn't he?'

'The thought had occurred. But I don't know for sure. The main thing now is making sure whoever it is *doesn't* find the spearheads. If they are what I think, they're much too dangerous to fall into the wrong hands. And the best way to stop that happening is to make sure they can't get hold of the second marker, the one in Seville. The one they stole is useless without it.'

'But why do you have to go there in person? Just ring 'em up.'

'There won't be anyone at the museum at this time of night, and I don't have anybody's personal phone numbers. Besides, if I'm on the international most-wanted list, the last thing I need on me is a literal tracking device! I'll have to get rid of my phone.'

'Are you kidding?' Eddie said in disbelief.

'I know – this is a new phone!'

'That's not what I meant. The cops won't know where you are, but I won't either. And you might need me. You *will* need me.'

'Macy needs you more,' she told him firmly. 'Is she there?'

'Yeah. But it might not be a good idea telling her you're doing a Lord Lucan. She's upset enough already.'

'I'll assume he's the British equivalent of D. B. Cooper. But I *have* to talk to her, Eddie. I don't know when I might get another chance.'

'Okay, okay,' he said with reluctance. 'Macy! It's your mum!'

Nina heard her daughter snatch the phone from him. 'Mommy! Are you okay?'

'Yes, I'm fine,' she replied. 'Are *you* all right?'

'I'm okay. Where are you? Daddy said you weren't on the boat any more. Are you still in trouble?'

'The Emir thinks I did something bad. That's why I had to get off the ship – they wouldn't let me go.'

'Does that mean you're a fugitive?'

Nina laughed; Macy's precociousness manifested at the most unexpected times. 'It means I'm going to prove I didn't do anything wrong,' she assured her. 'Then I'll come back to you and Daddy. Okay?'

'When?'

'As soon as I can.' She emerged from trees to find herself on open ground near a road. Some distance away, a car was speeding towards her. It wasn't the police, but they had probably been warned about her by now, and if they spotted the drifting boat, they would quickly find where she had come ashore.

And the cops were not the only people after her. 'Listen,' she said, 'I love you very, very much – and I *will* see you again soon. I promise.'

'I love you too, Mommy,' said Macy, struggling to hold back tears.

Nina felt much the same way herself. 'Can you put your dad back on, please?'

Eddie reclaimed the phone. 'What's wrong?'

'Nothing – beyond, y'know, the obvious. Look, I've got to go. I'll find a way to call you from Seville.'

'Nina, there's got to be another way. I already talked to Seretse, and there are other people I can try who could help us to fix this. Maybe Alderley—'

'There isn't time, Eddie,' she insisted. 'You said it yourself: the longer I wait, the closer the cops will get – and I doubt Agreste's sitting around eating croissants either. He killed Ana, so he'll want me dead too to cover it up.'

'I should've decked that arsehole on the bridge,' he growled.

'And then you'd be in a cell yourself – which is the last thing Macy needs. I've *got* to go,' she repeated. 'Tell her I love her – and I love you. I love you so much.'

'Nina! You—'

'Bye, Eddie.'

It took all of her willpower to disconnect. 'And this was a really good phone,' she muttered, trying to distract herself from far greater emotions.

She powered it down, then reluctantly tossed it away before tearing off her wristband – it was unlikely it could track her outside the ship, but she didn't want to take the risk – and turning towards the lights of Tarifa. As she set off, she could feel the cold on her bare arms and legs, and the squelching of her wet shoes. 'Viva frickin' España,' she sighed.

Eddie returned to his cabin's balcony, glaring towards the Moroccan coastline as he made another phone call. This was to someone as connected in the world of global diplomacy as Seretse – though in a very different sphere.

'How is it,' said Peter Alderley, the head of the British intelligence agency MI6, 'that whenever our paths cross, it's because you or Nina have caused another international incident?'

While Eddie and Alderley were hardly friends – the first time they met, when the Yorkshireman was in the SAS and the intelligence officer a field agent, the former had ended up punching the latter so hard that the bump of his resulting broken nose was still visible even now – they had over the years developed a grudging mutual respect. However, tonight Eddie had no time for their usual sarcastic banter. 'Neither of us *caused* it, but Nina's been framed for it,' he said impatiently. 'And now she's on the run in Spain, with whoever set her up wanting her dead. So I need to know if you or MI6 can do anything to help her.'

'I'm afraid that isn't really the Secret Intelligence Service's bailiwick. Nina's an American citizen, not British.'

'You wouldn't just be helping her,' Eddie snapped. 'You'd be helping *me*. Remember, the guy who helped stop Britain being taken over in a coup? Who got you your bloody job?'

Alderley made a noise of grim amusement. 'I wondered how long it would be before that came up.'

'I'm not joking, Alderley. Nina's in trouble, and I'm stuck on this bloody boat. So I've been seeing if anyone can put diplomatic pressure on Dhajan, but I thought you might be able to do something a bit more direct.'

'I should probably be flattered you think I have so much reach, but the sad truth is that I don't have field officers with time on their hands crawling all over southern Spain. This isn't *The Assassination Run*.'

'For fuck's sake!' Eddie banged a fist on the balcony railing in frustration. 'So you won't do *anything*?'

'I don't know what I *can* do! I like Nina, and I want to help, but I really can't think how.'

'Then think harder. She's going to the archaeology museum in Seville – if you get someone to watch it, you could—'

A noise caught his attention. With the balcony extending beyond the ship's flank, he was able to see its source: the lifeboat deck. A boat was being swung out on its davit – not one of the lifeboats, but a much smaller RIB. He stopped speaking as he realised who was standing beside the crane.

Agreste. The Frenchman was talking to someone obscured by the moving davit.

'Chase?' Alderley's voice. 'You still there?'

'Yeah, I'm here,' Eddie said distractedly. 'I've just seen the arsehole who set Nina up. Name's Agreste, he's French – supposed to be in charge of security, but he killed the woman who was helping her.'

'Agreste? I'll see if we have anything on him. Do you know his first name?'

'No, we didn't exactly exchange business cards.' He kept watching as the boat was carried clear of the deck, ready to be boarded.

But it wasn't Agreste who climbed into the waiting craft. Eddie felt a shock of recognition when he saw the Frenchman's companion.

It was Ana Rijo.

'Jesus!' he gasped. 'She's not dead!'

'Who?' asked Alderley.

'The woman Nina said got shot. She's still alive!' As he watched, Ana turned back to Agreste and shook his hand. 'She's bloody working with Agreste!'

Agreste returned to the control panel. 'I'll call you back,' Eddie said, rushing into the cabin. 'If you can help Nina—'

'I'll see what I can do,' Alderley assured him.

Eddie rang off. 'What's happened?' Olivia asked as he hurried past.

'I don't know, but I'm going to find out. Stay here,' he added as Macy stood. 'I'll be back as soon as I can.'

He ran from the cabin to the nearest flight of stairs. If he reached the lifeboat deck before Ana and Agreste departed, he could force them to give him some answers.

But he was too late. Agreste was gone, the empty davit reeling in its cables. He ran to the railing and looked down. A wake led his gaze out across the dark water to where the RIB was powering into the distance, Ana alone at its wheel.

'*Shit!*' he shouted helplessly after it, before retrieving his phone. If Nina still had hers, he could warn her she had been set up.

But the call went straight to voicemail. Her phone was probably in the sea or a ditch.

He glared after the boat. It was heading for Tangier—

Wait – he had friends in Morocco. Not in government, but in some ways more useful. He brought up his contacts list and made another call.

It was quickly answered. '*Salaam alaikum,*' a man replied, music playing in the background.

'Karim!' said Eddie. 'It's Eddie Chase.'

Karim Taysir switched from Arabic to English without pause. 'Eddie!' he said with great enthusiasm. 'My friend, how are you? It's been a long time.'

'I know – and this isn't a social call. I need your help.'

The Moroccan's genial tone became all business. 'What is wrong?'

'Dunno if you've heard, but there's a cruise ship off the coast, the *Atlantia*. It's had some trouble.'

'It has been on the news, yes. They said the lifeboats were launched.'

'They've brought 'em back on board,' Eddie replied, 'but another boat just left, a RIB, and it's heading for Tangier. The person in it's a Brazilian woman calling herself Ana Rijo. I need you to find her. She's framed my wife for stealing an Atlantean artefact, so I want to talk to her. She's going to tell me what's going on.'

Karim made a small *mm-hmm* noise. 'You can be very, very persuasive. As the Algerian discovered.'

'Think you can help?'

'Of course!' he boomed. 'This is Tangier, Eddie, it is my city – there is no one I do not know.'

'Thanks, Karim,' Eddie told him. 'I'll call you back soon.'

He disconnected and stepped back, thinking. If anyone could track Ana down in Tangier, it really would be Karim; he had only been slightly exaggerating when he claimed to know everyone in the city. Eddie himself had a wide network of contacts, but even he had been amazed at how many people on the streets of the Moroccan capital hurried to greet his friend, and while at the port, nothing more than Karim's wave had seen the Englishman escorted past a lengthy queue at customs, through a restricted area and on to a ferry for Europe with a passport check as fast as a nod.

But he wasn't going to leave everything to the Moroccan – he needed to find out more for himself. He re-entered the ship and pushed the button on his wristband.

It took several minutes, the crew still dealing with the aftermath of the evacuation, but eventually a white-jacketed steward hurried to him. 'Can I help you, Mr Chase?'

'I hope so,' he replied, adopting a concerned voice. 'Our steward, Ana – nobody's seen her since the alarms went off. We're worried about her, we think she might be hurt.'

The young man's badge gave his name as Jasni; his accent was Malaysian. 'I haven't heard anything like that,' he replied.

'Can you find out? We want to be sure she's all right.'

Jasni nodded. 'If you would wait in your cabin, I will come and tell you.'

Eddie leaned towards the slighter man, giving him a too-broad smile. 'I'd *really appreciate it* if I could come with you while you check . . .' He was still wearing his suit, his wallet in a pocket; he slipped his hand unsubtly towards its rectangular bulge.

The steward understood his meaning and smiled back. While the *Atlantia* was supposedly the world's most opulent cruise ship, Eddie was sure that the wealth did not trickle down very far. 'Of course, Mr Chase.'

Jasni led him down through the decks to a crew-only doorway. He obstructed the touchpad's camera with his body before using his card to unlock it. 'Quick, quick,' he told Eddie, who ducked through behind him.

He led the Englishman to a small office and went to a computer on the desk. 'Okay. I will find her bunk.' He started typing, soon making a quizzical sound.

'What is it?' Eddie asked.

'We all have to share rooms,' Jasni replied. 'But she has a cabin to herself!' He sounded jealous.

'Where is it?'

'Deck 3, Cabin C43.'

'Can you take me there?'

The response this time was more reluctant. 'All the cabins there belong to officers. I could lose my job.'

'Just tell 'em I'm drunk, I got lost, and you're taking me back to my room.' He took out his wallet. 'Two hundred dollars for five minutes' work. Sound fair?'

Jasni hesitated, then gave a wide smile. Eddie handed him the money. 'Mr Chase!' he exclaimed as he tucked the bills away. 'You are very, very drunk, you must have taken a wrong turn. Let me help you to your suite.'

'Cheersh,' the Yorkshireman replied, grinning.

The steward took him through the *Atlantia*'s innards to the officers' quarters. They encountered several members of the ship's complement en route, but the crewmen saw that Eddie was with one of their fellows and passed without comment. 'Here,' the Malaysian finally said. 'This is her cabin.'

The nondescript door had a keycard lock. 'Can you open this?'

Jasni shook his head. 'No, I do not have the right key. I am sor—'

The Englishman kicked it open. The steward yipped. 'That's okay,' Eddie told him, pushing into the cabin. 'I brought my own.'

'No, *no!*' Jasni cried. 'What are you doing?'

'Finding out why the steward who framed my wife gets her own private room.' The cabin contained a small bed, and a large desk. The reason for its size was obvious: it had to accommodate two big monitor screens, a computer and its keyboard, as well as various other pieces of electronic paraphernalia. Both screens were active, one a system display similar to those on the bridge, the other filled with a grid of live images. 'These are from the security cameras,' Eddie said. 'She really was watching us . . .'

'But the CCTV went out during the emergency,' said Jasni. 'We had to check all the corridors for lost passengers.'

'She blocked the bridge from seeing them.' The Englishman peered behind the monitors.

'What are you doing?'

'Making sure there isn't a bomb. *Speed 2,*' he added at his companion's blank look. 'You know, the film?'

'No.'

'Tchah! Nobody appreciates good bad movies any more.' Satisfied that the computer was not booby-trapped, he put his hand on the mouse. 'Let's see if she's got anything useful on here. A folder called "My Evil Plan" would be nice . . .'

Instead, a warning window popped up demanding a password. 'Arse,' Eddie muttered.

'Perhaps you should wait until the captain gets here?' suggested Jasni.

'My wife's in trouble, I don't have time. Okay, how about . . . "password"?'

He typed it in. The window flashed red, then returned to the password request. 'Bollocks! All right, what about "admin"?' Again, no luck. 'Clag nuts! "12345"? I've got the same password on my luggage,' he added, to the steward's bewilderment. 'Haven't seen *Spaceballs* either?'

This time, the failed entry produced a different result. Both screens went dark. 'Buggeration and fuckery!' Eddie exclaimed. 'It's locked me out.' He considered the situation. 'Okay, you wait here and guard this lot. I'll tell the captain what I've found.'

Leaving the worried steward in the cabin, he made his way to the bridge. The door was locked again – and he suspected that after his last intrusion, those inside would be more watchful. He banged hard on the metal barrier. 'Oi! It's Eddie Chase, open up!'

The door opened, a burly officer regarding him coldly. 'Yes?'

'Get the captain. I found out who sabotaged the ship!'

The man called across the bridge. Snowcock arrived swiftly. 'Mr Chase, if you're wasting my time—'

'Ana Rijo's not dead,' Eddie cut in. 'She just left in a RIB, heading for Morocco. She faked getting shot; she's working with Agreste. And she's got a computer in her cabin that's hacked in to all your CCTV and emergency systems.'

That caught his attention. 'What? Ana was a steward – she doesn't have her own cabin.'

'Think you need to check your records. Deck 3, Cabin C43. She could still see all the camera feeds even if you couldn't.'

'Get down there and see if he's telling the truth,' Snowcock told the other man. 'If he is, we might be able to get all our systems back online.'

Eddie decided not to tell him he had locked the system; hopefully somebody on the ship was good enough with computers to break in. 'The whole thing was done to set Nina up,' he continued. 'Ana made it look like she was involved in the robbery, and you all believed it. I need to get the Emir to call off the cops. Is he in there?'

'No, he's gone back to his suite – but Princess Alula is with me.'

'Okay, let me talk to her. Is Agreste there too?'

'Yes.'

Eddie clenched his fists. 'I might have words with him an' all.'

With clear reluctance, Snowcock retreated into the bridge, soon returning with Alula and Agreste. 'Your Royal Highness,' he said, 'Mr Chase wants to speak to you.'

She regarded Eddie with disdain. 'What do you want?'

'I want you to cancel the Red Notice on Nina. She's been set up. Ana Rijo isn't dead, she—'

'You told me she *was* dead,' Alula interrupted. 'Now you say she is not? Which is it?'

'She faked it to scare Nina into running – and *he's* working with her,' said Eddie, jabbing a finger at Agreste. 'I saw them both on the lifeboat deck fifteen minutes ago.'

Agreste shook his head. 'I was in the exhibition hall.'

'Must've been your twin brother, then. I *thought* it was dodgy how you turned up in the hall right after I got there. Were you watching the security cameras with Ana?'

'That is a ridiculous accusation,' Agreste sniffed. 'I came to make sure the Emir was not hurt.'

'But why would you even think the Emir *was* hurt, unless you'd been watching?' A new thought came to him – one he knew would not be taken well. 'And the Emir . . . he reckons he got knocked out and fell into the vault, right? But when I got there, he strolled *out* of the vault, fresh as a daisy – and he was surprised to see me there, like he was expecting someone else.'

Alula's expression darkened. 'You are accusing *His Majesty* of involvement in this robbery?'

'I'm just saying it's awfully bloody convenient,' Eddie pressed on. 'I mean, he invited Nina here in the first place, he asked her for a private tour of the Atlantis exhibition . . . and his story changed between him coming out of the vault and what he said on the bridge later. *Was* he in on it? Did he do all this to get Nina out of the way so he could find this spearhead thing without her interfering?'

Alula's nostrils flared in outrage. 'I will not stand here and listen to you accuse the Emir – my brother! – of being a criminal! Captain! I want this man arrested.'

Snowcock hesitated. 'On what charge, Your Royal Highness?'

'He is obviously in league with Dr Wilde, to embarrass His Majesty and discredit Dhajan!' When the captain did not instantly respond, she took an angry step towards him. 'Well? What are you waiting for?'

Snowcock called back into the bridge. 'Security! I need people out here!'

'Are you fucking joking?' Eddie said, aghast – but it was immediately clear that he wasn't. The captain stepped aside as officers and crew responded. 'Oh shit!'

Eddie turned and ran. Agreste moved to intercept him, but the Yorkshireman's special forces training had already kicked in. He twisted away from Agreste's outstretched hands, one arm swatting them aside as his other fist swept at the Frenchman's jaw. His target tipped his head away fast enough to save himself from a tooth-snapping impact, but was still knocked backwards.

Eddie sprinted for the stairs. Behind him, the men piling from the bridge pursued as Snowcock shouted into a walkie-talkie for backup.

The chase was on.

9

Eddie reached the stairs. Up or down? The crackle of Snowcock's voice from another radio below gave him his answer. He raced up to the top deck overlooking the vast central atrium.

More crewmen charged towards him from astern. He went to the railing. There were swimming pools below, but it was a twelve-storey drop—

The zip-line!

If he could ride it down, it would take him almost to the marina – his best hope of getting off the ship.

He ran to it, ducking under a chain to reach the boarding platform. Rather than individual harnesses for each thrill-seeker, this was more like a theme-park ride, a large cradle with a dozen seats suspended from the cable.

He went to the control panel. The cradle was held in place by a mechanical claw. He had to release it, but the panel was switched off – and needed a physical key rather than an electronic one. He doubted any of the men closing on him would be willing to provide it.

Instead he pulled the chain free and swung it over the cable, grabbed both ends – and threw himself into empty space.

The chain snapped tight under his weight, sending him swinging like a demented pendulum as it screeched down the zip-line. He tightened his grip, but could feel the metal slithering through his fingers, millimetre by millimetre . . .

And he saw movement at his destination. More crew were

running to catch him when he landed.

But he was still too high to risk dropping to the deck. A hundred metres to go, less, the men ahead scrambling on to the landing platform.

He crossed above the bowl-like stern deck, sunshades and loungers beneath him.

And swimming pools—

He let go.

The drop was over thirty feet. Just enough time for a surge of fear that the circular blue pool below wasn't deep enough to break his fall—

He pulled his legs up as he hit the water. The impact hurt, but less so than breaking an ankle on the bottom – which he would have done if he had landed vertically. His backside jarred heavily against the tiles. An involuntary expulsion of air with the pain, but he recovered and swam to the side.

Gasping, he looked around. The crewmen were already jumping from the platform. He dragged himself out. The marina access was not far away. Water streaming from his clothes, he hurried to it. Nobody below. He charged down the stairs and rushed out into the marina. The giant hatch was still open, but the jetties had been retracted.

Two crew members, a man and a woman, were pulling ropes on to the decking. They looked at him in surprise, just as the walkie-talkie on the woman's belt squawked a warning. 'He's gone down to the marina! Stop him!'

The man sprang up and rushed at the Yorkshireman. 'Oh fuck off,' Eddie growled impatiently, unleashing a stomach punch that folded the crew member to the floor. 'Now, I need a boat . . .'

The turntable at the head of the launch rails was aligned with a white-and-gold Kawasaki jetski. He pulled out the chock holding it in place, but now faced a new obstacle. The woman had darted to a control panel. A whine of powerful motors – and the stern door began to close, tilting upwards.

Eddie scrambled on to the Kawasaki. It slid over the turntable under his weight. The safety key was in its slot, a plastic lanyard dangling from it. He pushed the starter. The engine growled, a horrible dry rasp coming from the jetski's impeller duct – it was not supposed to be run out of the water.

He ignored the restriction, revving it to full power as the craft rattled down the rails. The awful noise became a splutter as the Kawasaki sucked water through its intake – then it dropped off the ramp's end, surging forward in a spray of froth.

The white wall of the door rose before him, a waterfall gushing over its upper edge as it breached the surface.

Eddie braced himself, holding the Kawasaki at full throttle—

The jetski slammed against metal, riding up the huge panel's inner face with a screech. It slowed as the slope steepened. Eddie desperately threw his weight forward as it stopped at the top . . . then tipped over and plunged into the sea.

Cold ocean water swirled around the Yorkshireman for the second time in a few hours. The craft rolled upright. Coughing, he wiped stinging brine from his eyes.

He was clear, but he still had a long way to go. And a lot to do.

He brought the Kawasaki around. The lights of Tangier swung into view as he moved away from the *Atlantia*. He fumbled for his phone, thankful that he had years ago realised the benefits of waterproof covers.

Two calls to make. The first was to Olivia. 'It's me!' he shouted when she answered. 'I'm not on the ship any more. There's been a . . . complication.'

'A *complication*?' Olivia hooted. 'What do you mean?'

'I found out that Ana set up Nina, and I think the Emir was in on it. But his sister didn't believe me, and they were going to arrest me so I had to nick a jetski to get away.'

Her response was one of weary resignation. 'So Nina's on the run, *you're* on the run – should I expect the Gestapo to kick down my door too?'

'You'll be fine, just don't tell 'em anything.'

'How can I? I have no idea what's going on.'

He managed a faint smile. 'Is Macy there? Put me on speaker.'

Olivia did so. 'Daddy?' Macy said, worried. 'Are you okay?'

'I'm fine, love. I've just got to take a little trip. Your great-grandma'll look after you.'

'No, Daddy!' she cried. 'You can't go as well!'

'I'm sorry, but I'll be back as soon as I can, I promise.'

'That's what you said when you went out – and now you're running away on a boat, like Mom.'

'I know, and I'm sorry. But your mum needs my help, and this is the only way I can do it. Olivia, you there?'

'Of course,' the elderly lady replied.

'They're going to turf everyone off the ship at Gibraltar, so you stay with Macy. They'll put you up in a hotel. I'll find you once I'm done in Morocco.'

'Eddie, what are—'

'I'm sorry, but I won't be in phone range for much longer, and I need to make another call. Macy, I love you. Never forget that, okay?'

'I love you, Daddy,' she said quietly.

Eddie reluctantly ended the call, then made a second. 'Karim, it's Eddie Chase again. Change of plans – I'm on my way to Tangier right now. I'll land on that beach near where me and Hugo met you that time. Might need you to use your charm on the customs people if they wonder what the hell I'm doing crossing the Med on a jetski.'

'You are on a jetski? Why are— Ehh, with you I should know

not to ask,' Karim said. 'Do not worry, my friend. I will meet you. Everything will be lovely jubbly.'

'Great. See you soon.' Eddie hung up, smiling at the use of the British slang, then pocketed the phone before slipping the safety key's lanyard around his wrist and turning his full attention to piloting the jetski through the choppy waves.

Tangier was roughly ten miles away. It would take him less than half an hour to reach it – if he could avoid being caught by the Moroccan navy, who could well have been warned about his escape. But something as small as a jetski in the swells of the Strait of Gibraltar would be tricky to track on radar, and the darkness would make him difficult to spot visually.

Besides, he had confidence in Karim. If anyone could talk him out of trouble, it would be his Moroccan friend.

He checked for any ships that might cross his path, then raced through the night towards the African coast.

Nina trudged into Tarifa, her shoes still damp. The journey had been far from a pleasant stroll; there were large stretches of road with no sidewalk or street lights, giving her a few worryingly close calls with passing traffic. She was also cold, the Atlantic wind harsh-edged.

But she had not let discomfort dominate her mind. There was too much to think about. She was still certain her best course of action was to reach Seville and warn the head of the city's archaeological museum about the threat to the second *marcador de lanza*. Once the relic was secured – and *only* then – she would consider going to the authorities to clear her name. The best place to do that would be the US consulate in Seville.

She had to *get* to Seville first, though. It was, if her memory of Spanish geography was accurate, about a hundred and twenty miles to the north. She checked her watch. Well after nine o'clock. If there was a rental car agency in Tarifa, it would probably be closed for the night – and even if it wasn't, the police could well have warned the staff to watch out for her. Hiring a taxi ran a similar risk, even if she could persuade anyone to take her on such a long trip.

Which left hitch-hiking, or the bus. The former was not an inviting prospect, so the bus it was.

Even in April, before the tourist season entered full swing, the long main street leading to the heart of the town was quite busy. She had little trouble finding someone who spoke enough English to direct her to the bus station. To her annoyance, she had walked right past it, forcing her to retrace her route to an anonymous grey building beside a gas station. The sign actually informing passers-by of its function was a masterpiece in modesty.

A timetable told her the first bus to Seville left at 8.30 the next morning. Eleven hours away – and she couldn't risk checking into a hotel, there being a high chance that the police would canvass every place in town for her.

She would have to either stay awake all night, or rough it. Neither prospect appealed. She found the money Ana had given her. Exactly two hundred euros, in crisp tens. That would surely be enough for the bus fare to Seville, and would also pay for a meal. If nothing else, she could stay in a restaurant until closing time, just to keep out of the wind.

She started back towards the town centre, girding herself for a long night.

Even at this late hour, there were still a few people on Tangier's Plage Malabata and the expansive white plaza inshore – and all were surprised when a jetski roared through the breaking waves and skidded to a halt on the sands. 'Evening,' said Eddie to the two young men having a smoke near his landing point. 'You want a jetski?'

They exchanged looks, then approached. 'Is for sale?' one asked in hesitant English.

'No, it's free,' he replied as he dismounted. They were understandably dubious about the sincerity – and legality – of his offer. 'Up to you.' He started up the beach, leaving the bewildered pair to debate their options.

He had just reached the plaza when a slow-moving old Citroën CX on the road beyond sounded its horn. 'Eddie!' shouted its occupant through the open window. 'I am here!'

Eddie hurried to him. 'Ay up, fancy meeting you here,' he said. 'Thanks for coming, Karim.'

'No problem, my friend. Get in. But quickly. You have attracted attention.'

Eddie slid into the car and looked back at the beached jetski. Beyond it, a spotlight flicked to life on the water, a piercing white beam locking on to the abandoned craft. The two young men hurriedly ran off. 'The harbour patrol,' said the heavyset Moroccan as he made a rapid U-turn – without checking his mirrors for anyone overtaking. His passenger winced, but said nothing. He had been to the country several times, and knew that drivers acting as if they were protected from harm by a force field, or Allah, was all part of the experience. 'But you landed before they caught you, that is what matters.'

'Close, though. Did you have any luck finding Ana?'

'Not yet,' said Karim. 'But I have spoken to the right people. If she is in Tangier, we will find her.'

'Let's hope she's here, then.' Eddie sat back, looking out to sea as the old car cruised past another long beach. In the far distance, he saw tiny shimmering lights: Tarifa. Somewhere across the water, on another continent, was Nina. Frustration rose once more at the knowledge that there was still nothing he could do to help her. All he *could* do was hope she was okay.

★ ★ ★

On the opposite coast, al-Asim was driving with his men away from Tarifa in a large SUV when his phone rang. 'Yes?' he said. 'Is something wrong?'

He listened to the rapid explanation. 'Understood,' he said at last, unsettled. 'We'll handle it.'

'What is it?' asked the man with the scarred cheek as al-Asim disconnected.

'A problem. We intercepted the Englishman's phone calls. He found out about the Brazilian woman, and now he's on his way to Morocco to find her.'

'How? It's a big city, and he doesn't know where she is.'

'It seems he has friends there. We can't let him get to her. She's just a mercenary, she doesn't have any loyalty to us.'

'So what do we do?' asked another of the raiders.

Al-Asim slowed the SUV. 'We're going back to Tarifa. Musad,' he told the scarred man, 'take the next ferry to Tangier. We should have more information on where Chase is and who his friends are by the time you arrive. Recruit whatever local help you need, and find them.' He swung the vehicle around to head back to the port. 'We've got to make sure Chase and the woman don't talk to anyone else. Ever.'

10

Nina awoke with a start, shivering. Confusion as she looked around, unsure where she was, then memory returned.

Tarifa's historic centre was beautiful, a maze of traditional buildings still partially surrounded by medieval walls, but she was in no mood to appreciate it. She had found a small restaurant that remained open until midnight, stretching out her modest meal as long as possible, but when she emerged, the temperature had dropped considerably. With only her thin dress to protect her, she had spent a miserable night wandering about in the forlorn hope of finding shelter, before exhaustion finally claimed her and she sat down on a bench beside the cathedral. Her intended five-minute rest stop had stretched into – *Jesus!* she thought, looking at her watch – over two hours.

It was still dark, though, nearing five o'clock in the morning. She rubbed her arms to warm them, then stood. A van emerged from a narrow side street. She watched it pass, then, on a whim, followed. She had plenty of time to kill before the bus departed.

A chill wind whipped in from the sea as she emerged at the harbour. It was fenced off, but a docked ferry rose high above the barrier. The sight of the ship made her wonder where the *Atlantia* was now.

That in turn made her think of her family. She wanted nothing more than to reassure Macy and Eddie that she was all right, but even if she used a payphone, it could open them up to charges of withholding information. The Dhajanis seemed determined to pin the theft of the marker on her, and might well snatch up her husband and daughter in their dragnet given the slightest excuse.

She was on her own. The last time she had felt so isolated, she had been kidnapped, held on an island by an apocalyptic religious cult. But even there, she had been able to rail against her captors. Here, she had only her own thoughts for company.

With nothing else to do, she started for the bus station, taking a circuitous route to minimise her chances of being seen by the police. By the time she reached the long road leading to the terminal, the eastern sky was starting to brighten. Just after seven.

A small shop was already open. She bought some food and a bottle of water, then went down a side street and sat on a wall to eat and drink. She estimated it would take her no more than fifteen minutes to walk to the bus terminal, but she wanted a safety margin to buy her ticket. She finished her unimpressive breakfast, then set off.

The walk was straightforward, and she heard no sirens, saw no flashing blue lights. Maybe she had overestimated the police response. But she was still on alert the whole way to the terminal.

When she finally reached it, to her relief, the ticket counter was open. Even with her limited Spanish, it was simple enough to buy a one-way ticket to Seville. She sat on a bench and waited. Ten minutes to departure, and the bus arrived. She started towards it—

A police car pulled up beside the terminal.

Nina froze, staring helplessly at it, then forced herself to keep walking. The two cops in the car didn't seem in any rush to get out, but if she behaved in an overtly suspicious manner, she would draw their attention. A couple of people had reached the bus before her, waiting for the driver to open the door. She glanced at the car. The policemen were still inside, one regarding the bus from behind sunglasses. Was he watching her? She couldn't tell . . .

He opened the door. Nina felt a rush of fear, looking for escape routes—

The cop got out and walked to the shop in the terminal.

She tried not to make her relief too obvious. The cop might not be fulfilling the American cliché of buying doughnuts, but he was definitely stocking up with snacks. Amusement overcoming apprehension, however briefly, she waited to board the bus.

The door hissed open. She filed in and showed her ticket to the driver. He looked up, expression flickering as he saw her face. Another surge of near-panic – had her picture been given to the bus company? – but then she realised it was simple lechery, a dumpy middle-aged man checking out a younger woman. She gave him a thin smile, then found a seat near the rear.

A few minutes later, the bus pulled out of the terminal. If it stayed on schedule, it would arrive in Seville at 11.30. Nina remained tense until the bus cleared Tarifa and started along the highway, then finally allowed herself to lean back in her seat.

Again she thought of her family. 'Hope you're keeping Macy's mind off all of this, Eddie,' she whispered.

In Tangier, Eddie was trying his best to do just that – but with father and daughter on different continents, he was having little success.

'I *know* you want me to come back,' he said to the distraught seven-year-old over the phone, 'but I can't, not just yet.'

'This *is* because I took the trikan, isn't it?' wailed Macy.

'No it isn't,' he insisted. 'You didn't have anything to do with it. It's not your fault. Okay?'

'But if I hadn't taken it, they—'

'Macy, Macy. Listen to me, love. It wasn't your fault. And the reason I left last night was because I had to find the person whose fault it *was*. When I do, I'm going to . . .' He opted not to tell her what he had in mind if Ana proved uncooperative. '. . . make them tell the Emir that Mummy didn't do anything wrong.'

'And then Mommy'll come back?' Macy asked.

'Yeah, she will. And so will I.'

'When?'

'As soon as I can. Okay?'

'Okay, Daddy.' She did not sound happy, but at least now she wasn't on the verge of tears.

'Good lass. Can I talk to Olivia?'

She handed the phone to her great-grandmother. 'Hello, Eddie,' Olivia said. 'Have you found Ana yet?'

'No, but one of my mates is on the case. If anyone can track her down, he can. Did you get off the ship?'

'Yes, we're in Spain. Algeciras, I think it's called.'

'I know it. Across the bay from Gibraltar. You in a hotel?'

'We are, yes. I imagine it was quite a feat to find everyone accommodation at short notice – I'm sure five and a half thousand people turning up in the middle of the night isn't an everyday occurrence, but somehow they managed it.'

'Everything's easy with money,' Eddie noted with dark humour. 'Chuck enough cash around and people'll find rooms in a hurry.'

'Quite. Do you still want us to wait here for you?'

'Yeah, for now. If I can get Ana to confess, that lets Nina off the hook. I'll let you know as soon as I can, then I'll get a ferry back to Spain.'

'It'll be good to see you.'

'Glad you're finally warming up to me after four years.'

'I was thinking more for Macy's sake,' Olivia said, but with humour.

Ending the call, Eddie left the room where he had slept. Karim and his wife Maysa had four children, and the posters of international footballers on the walls suggested that one of their sons had been evicted to make room for the visitor. Loud, tinny music reached him as he descended the stairs. He followed the noise to the kitchen. 'Hi, Maysa.'

'Good morning, Eddie!' Maysa replied brightly. She and Karim had been married for as long as he had known them, and while the latter had become considerably broader over the years, his always energetic wife's only sign of advancing age was strands of greying hair. 'Karim went out early, he said to talk to someone for you. He sounded confident.'

He nodded. 'That's great.'

'Would you like breakfast? There is coffee, mint tea, *khobz*,' she indicated a couple of round loaves of bread, 'pancakes, eggs . . .'

'Eggs sound good, thanks.'

'I will make you—' She broke off at a noise from outside and went to the open window, shouting up in irritated Arabic. After a moment, a pair of feet dropped into view and felt their way to the sill. A curly-haired boy in his early teens clambered through the opening and grinned at Eddie. 'Children!' said Maysa, shaking her head. 'One of them found a way on to the roof, and now I can't keep them off it. They jump over an eight-metre fall on to the next building. *Ya lawhy!*'

'Boys will be boys,' said the Yorkshireman, winking at Maysa's son as he ran past.

'Ha! The girls are even worse! How old is your little girl, seven? You will find that out for yourself soon enough.'

He laughed, then checked his phone while his hostess prepared breakfast. The faint hope that Nina might have emailed him was soon extinguished; there were no messages. But before he could put the phone away, it rang: Karim. 'Yeah?'

'My friend,' said Karim theatrically as Maysa turned down the blaring radio, 'the woman you are looking for? I have found her.'

'You have?' replied Eddie. 'Bloody hell, I knew you were good, but I didn't know you were *that* good.'

'How could you still not know after all this time?' Karim chuckled. 'One of my friends at Tangier-Ville port checked her through. He was suspicious – lone women do not often arrive in speedboats in the night – but her papers were in order, so he had to let her in. I called more friends in the taxi companies to find out who picked her up, and where they took her. Then I called the manager of her hotel – another friend of mine, of course—'

'Of course,' the Englishman echoed, amused.

'—and he told me she has arranged a taxi to the airport this evening.'

'So she'll still be around during the day?'

'She has to come back to the hotel to get the taxi, yes.'

Eddie was already formulating a plan. 'Good. Then let's get over there, because I want to have words with her right now.'

'Are you *sure* that is what you want to do?' The *sure* was drawn out to an almost comical length.

'Why wouldn't it be?'

'Because I know what happens when you "have words" with people. Like the Algerian, remember? And it would reflect very badly on me if one of my friends killed someone.'

'I'm not going to *kill* her,' Eddie said impatiently. Maysa's eyes widened. 'But Ana knows what's going on, and she's going to tell me, one way or another.'

'Then can I suggest something less . . . direct?'

'Like what?'

'You said this woman is Brazilian, yes? Then she probably does not have a connection to anyone in Dhajan – it is more likely she has simply been hired to do a job, and now it is over, she has come to Morocco to take her payment before going home.'

'It's possible, yeah,' the Yorkshireman grudgingly agreed.

'Lovely jubbly. So she is a freelancer – and with freelancers, there is always the possibility of negotiation. I can contact her through my friend at the hotel, tell her I would like to meet her about a job, a job with good pay. He will confirm to her that I am well known in Tangier. If I ask her to meet at a place where we have, as the Americans put it, the home-field advantage, we can put pressure on her to tell the truth – hopefully without violence.'

'Sounds like you've got somewhere in mind.'

'My restaurant. You remember it?'

'Up near the Kasbah? Course I do. Best kebabs I've ever had.'

'Thank you! But if I invite her there for lunch, she will still have time to catch her plane later, and hopefully be intrigued enough to come.'

'And if she isn't?'

'We still know where she will be later today.'

Eddie was dubious, but made a sound of agreement. 'So she turns up at the restaurant. Then what? I can't exactly interrogate her in front of the lunchtime crowd.'

'Everyone on the floor where you meet her will be a friend of mine. I know many people who will drop what they are doing for a free meal.'

'Very generous of you.'

'Very generous of *you*, Eddie. I take cash or credit cards!' Karim laughed. 'But the witnesses will be on your side if something should happen – which I would prefer it does not.'

'We'll see how it goes,' Eddie told him. 'You really reckon you can get her to come?'

'I shall call her now, and will tell you what she says. In the meantime, there is something I would like you to do.'

'What?'

'Go to the Medina and buy some new clothes. I do not want to be rude, especially to a guest in my house, but . . . Eddie, you smell bad. You smell of the sea. And the sea between Morocco and Spain is not very clean.'

'No offence taken, mate!' said Eddie in mock affrontery. 'But yeah, that's probably a smart idea.'

'I will text you the best places to go. If you tell them I sent you, they will give you a very good price.'

'Thanks. Okay, you'd better call Ana. Talk to you soon.'

He hung up. Maysa put the plate of eggs in front of him, then turned the radio back to its original volume. 'I told you he was confident,' she said, smiling.

'You did. Thanks.' He started eating, then paused. 'Maysa? Do I stink?'

Her expression, trapped between politeness and honesty, told him everything. 'I would not say so,' she managed.

'I would,' he said, grinning. 'I'll take Karim's advice and buy some new clothes. Right after I've had breakfast.'

Twenty minutes later, Eddie left the house and headed for the steep, maze-like streets of the Medina, Tangier's old market district.

Someone watched him go.

Musad, al-Asim's scar-cheeked lieutenant, lurked at a corner. He waited for the Englishman to approach an intersection, then started after him, making a phone call. 'Chase has left the house,' he reported. 'I'm following.'

'We intercepted another of Chase's phone calls,' al-Asim told him. 'His friend claims to have found the Brazilian – he's going to ask her to meet him at a restaurant he owns. Chase will be waiting there.'

'Are you going to warn her?'

The reply had a cold edge. 'She's a loose end, and so is Chase. If they're in the same place at the same time, you can deal with them both.'

'Understood,' said Musad. He ended the call and followed Eddie through the tangled streets.

★ ★ ★

Karim was as good as his word. The shops he had recommended to Eddie were all tucked away in obscure corners of the Medina, hard for the typical day-tripping tourist to find without help, and on dropping his friend's name he had been treated both to first-class service and a hefty haggle-free discount on the prices of his new clothes.

He emerged from the last shop, now clad in his standard uniform of jeans, a dark T-shirt and a black leather jacket. There was a mirror at the entrance; he regarded himself in it. 'Not bad for an old git,' he said. He had reluctantly accepted being middle-aged after passing forty-five two years previously, but had no intention of letting himself go to seed.

He retraced his route back uphill through the confined but brightly painted streets. His phone rang. 'Yeah?'

'It's Karim.' The Moroccan sounded even more enthusiastic than usual. 'She said yes! She has agreed to meet at my restaurant, at one o'clock.'

Eddie glanced at his watch; just under two hours away. 'She did? Bloody hell, you really *are* persuasive.'

'Did you doubt me? Once she is at her table, you can step out and . . . surprise her.'

'And you're going to get some mates to sit around us?'

'I will make some calls as soon as I get home. I am on my way there now, then I will go to the restaurant. I will meet you there in . . . an hour, we shall say. At noon.'

'Great. See you soon.'

'Lovely jubbly.'

Eddie smiled. It would take him twenty minutes to make his way through the maze to Karim's restaurant. Forty minutes to kill in the Medina – not exactly a hardship. He continued leisurely up the hill.

★ ★ ★

Behind him, unnoticed, Musad maintained his discreet pursuit. He followed the bald man for a few minutes, then his own phone rang. 'Musad,' said al-Asim. 'I have another update. The woman *is* going to the restaurant, and Chase is setting a trap. You must be there too.'

'I'm following him now,' he replied. 'Our local contacts can get as much backup as I need.'

'Get plenty. Chase is former SAS, so he's dangerous, but the Brazilian isn't helpless either. And you'll need to make Chase's friend cooperate.'

'I thought we would. I've already taken care of that.'

'Good. Get as many people as you can. I don't want those two to leave the restaurant alive.'

'Don't worry,' said Musad with conviction. 'They won't.'

11

Seville, Spain

Two hours of sleep had not been enough. Despite her best efforts, Nina dozed off not long after leaving Tarifa, waking to find the bus already entering Seville.

The additional slumber had not overcome her tiredness, but she couldn't let that stop her. She still had to devise a plan of action. The head of the archaeological museum was a man called Emilio Merlo, whom she had met before. It had not led to a firm friendship; she found the Spaniard arrogant yet oddly defensive about his achievements, as if offended that she was considerably better known than him. There was, she suspected, no small amount of sexism behind his attitude.

But he was the person who could best ensure the second marker's safety. Once she convinced him to increase security, then she could consider how to save herself.

It was a hot day, and also busy – she saw banners proclaiming Holy Week, the *Semana Santa de Sevilla*. The city's heart would be packed with people watching the day's various processions. Luckily, the museum was on the centre's fringe at the southern end of the large Parque de María Luisa, so she doubted the event would inconvenience her directly once she was on foot.

She still had to endure delays on the roads, though. Seville was a large city, with all the traffic problems that entailed, and the street closures for the processions aggravated them still further. The bus finally stopped almost an hour late. With relief, Nina disembarked, trying to remember Seville's layout. She was at the Plaza de Armas terminus, on the eastern side of the river bisecting the city. If she walked south along the riverbank, that would eventually take her to the Parque de María Luisa, and hopefully avoid most of the Holy Week crowds.

She considered calling Merlo to let him know to expect her, but decided against it for two reasons. The first was simple enough: she didn't know his number. There was also a second, more ominous reason not to forewarn him. Merlo would have been told by now about the theft of a valuable item from his museum's collection – and who had been blamed. If he knew she was coming, he would call the cops. But if she turned up out of the blue, she might be able to talk her way out of trouble.

She hefted her bag and struck out into the blazing sunlight.

The sun was even stronger in Tangier.

Ana Rijo squinted into its glare as she got out of a bright blue Dacia taxi. The straining cab had brought her up the hill overlooking the port to the southern wall of the Kasbah, the old fortress that once contained the palace of Morocco's last sultan. Her destination stood between steep, narrow streets, a stepped three-storey block of white plaster and elaborately patterned tiles. Like many of Morocco's buildings, most of the windows were covered by ornate bars, even on the higher floors. A sign above the door announced it as the Restaurant Vue Magnifique.

She went inside. A young waiter immediately approached her. 'I'm afraid we are full, madam,' he said in worried apology.

Ana frowned. 'Mr Taysir asked me to meet him here.'

'Oh, you are here to see Karim! Okay, I get him. Come, this way.'

She followed him into the ground floor of the restaurant.

It was indeed full, men eating at every table. Some looked up as she passed, the glints in their eyes suggesting their thoughts towards her were far from honourable. She ignored them, unfazed.

The waiter reached a set of swinging doors to the kitchen and asked someone inside a question. 'Karim will meet you soon,' he said on the reply. 'Please, come.'

He led her up a flight of stairs. Most of the next floor was a large and busy dining area, an open door leading to a balcony overlooking the city and the sea beyond. The waiter showed her to an empty table near a corner. 'Please, sit,' he said, pulling out a chair.

She took her seat. 'Where is Mr Taysir?'

'He will be here soon,' the waiter assured her, scurrying off.

Ana watched him depart with growing wariness. He seemed nervous, but she doubted he was a threat. The same could not be said of the other diners. All appeared to be locals rather than tourists, some giving her the same lascivious glances as those downstairs. This time, she treated each in turn to a stare of cold disdain. They looked away.

She belatedly registered that just as downstairs, they were all men. Another frown. Morocco wasn't a country that demanded separation of the sexes—

Hard metal pushed into her back. 'Ay up. Nice of you to drop by.'

Eddie had been waiting in a storage cupboard, silently emerging behind the Brazilian. 'Take out your gun, slowly,' he ordered.

'I don't have a gun,' said Ana.

'Well I *do*. And I'll use it if you don't give me yours.'

'You won't kill me in front of all these people.'

'You'd be surprised what I'd do when someone threatens my family.'

Hesitation . . . then Ana reluctantly reached inside her jacket. Eddie pushed harder against her spine. She flinched, and carefully withdrew a pistol, passing it back to him.

Eddie took the weapon. A stubby Taurus Millennium Pro, fully loaded with a round in the chamber. The safety had been on; he flicked it off. 'Thanks for that,' he said with sudden cheer, rounding the table. 'Worst this'd do to you is make you sneeze.' He held up his other hand to reveal he had been holding nothing more deadly than a pepper mill.

Ana's eyes widened in anger. 'That's all you had?'

'All I needed.' He put it down between a flickering oil lamp and a bowl of flowers, then sat opposite, the gun covering her beneath the heavy-topped table. 'I figured you were probably briefed on me – and that you knew I was in the SAS, so I tend not to fuck about.'

'I know you've killed a lot of people,' she said icily. 'I didn't want to be one of them. What do you want?'

His expression hardened. 'Nina, obviously. Without every cop in Spain chasing after her. You set her up – you can get her back.'

'I don't know where she is.'

'Your boss does, though. So who hired you?'

Ana leaned back, folding her arms. 'I'm not going to say.'

'Words come out, or bullet goes in.'

'I can't talk if I'm dead.'

'You'll only be dead when I let you die,' Eddie growled. But he could tell from Ana's unyielding stare that she was going to call his bluff. 'Look,' he said, trying a different tack, 'your boss must have known I was in Tangier, but he didn't bother warning you, did he? That means he doesn't give a shit what happens to you now you've done your job. I'm assuming that since you're not leaving Tangier until tonight, you haven't got your money yet. You tell me what I need to know, then you can collect it and fuck off home, while I deal with whoever's paying you.'

Her look of determination began to waver, but she still refused to give in. 'I know you're in the same business as me. We work for hire, we are both professionals.'

'*Worked* for hire,' Eddie corrected forcefully. 'Gave that up a long time ago.'

'But you are still in the security business. Yes, I did read your file. You still sometimes work as a consultant. And would you give up the trust of one of *your* clients so easily?'

'We're not talking about me. This is about saving Nina. You remember, the nice woman with the cute little girl who's really, really worried about her mum? Why did you frame her for stealing that thing?'

Again she seemed to be weakening, but before he could push her any further, Karim bustled up the stairs and hurried to their table. 'Ah, Eddie, Eddie, my most marvellous friend!' he said exuberantly – a bit *too* exuberantly, the Yorkshireman thought. 'Wonderful to see you again, lovely jubbly.'

'You're in a good mood, Karim,' Eddie replied.

'Of course I am! It is your birthday, after all. I will make you something special to celebrate.' Above his rictus grin, his eyes became almost pleading.

'It's not my birth . . .' Eddie trailed off. Karim knew full well it was months away.

He slowly turned to regard the other diners. He hadn't paid them much attention earlier, assuming his friend had done as promised and drummed up some reliable people to fill the restaurant. But now he realised that the men – and they were *all* men – were uniformly young, shabby and rough-edged . . . and ignoring their meals, instead paying far too much attention to the people at the corner table.

'What's going on, Karim?' he muttered.

'I am sorry,' the Moroccan replied in an anguished whisper. 'But they have my family! They said they would kill them if I did not do what they said. I know some of these men – they are bad people, bad.'

'You need to change your door policy,' Eddie said as he stood.

The men also rose, moving to block the way to the exits. The Englishman advanced a few steps and brought up the gun, which prompted a few nervous retreats. 'All right. Everyone fuck off out of my way, or—'

A hard metallic *click* from one side. He froze, knowing what it was – a pistol's hammer being thumbed back. An Arabic man with a scarred cheek was aiming an automatic unwaveringly at him. 'Put the gun down,' he ordered.

Ana stared at him, surprised. 'Musad? Why are you here?' He ignored her.

Eddie sized up the situation. There was no way he could bring his own weapon around fast enough to take out the scarred man before being shot, and even if he fired into the crowd while trying to break and run, sheer weight of numbers would quickly overpower him. He needed more room to manoeuvre . . . but there wasn't any.

No choice. He slowly placed the gun between the plates on a table beside him. 'Friends of yours?' he asked Ana sarcastically.

But her worried expression told him she too had been caught by surprise. 'No,' she replied, standing – and drawing herself into a ready stance for some form of martial arts. She was as prepared to fight as he was.

But it seemed unlikely they would get the chance. Musad gestured for Eddie to step back to his table, then pocketed the Taurus. 'You, go,' he told Karim. 'Remember, call the police and your wife and children die.'

Karim hesitated. 'It's okay,' Eddie told him. The Moroccan

gave him a look of despairing apology, then hurried towards the stairs. The crowd parted to let him through before closing again.

'Now you come with us,' Musad told Eddie and Ana.

'You're not going to just kill us here?' the Yorkshireman replied.

'If you prefer.'

'Actually, no.' Eddie searched for any way to tip the situation in his favour. There were items he could use, but going for them would get him killed as long as the gun was aimed at him.

A glance at Ana told him she shared his thoughts. They would have to become allies to survive, however unwillingly . . .

'Move,' ordered Musad. His men started to form a cordon around the prisoners. Eddie knew that once he was surrounded, escape would be impossible.

Ana realised it too. Another look passed between them: *ready*.

Eddie stepped forward. The gun tracked him—

Ana flipped the flower bowl at the Arab's face.

He flinched back, free hand snapping up to intercept it. The gun jerked away from Eddie, just for a moment—

It was all the Yorkshireman needed.

He threw something else from the table at the scarred man: the oil lamp. It hit his chest, flammable liquid splashing over him and igniting as it hit the flaming wick.

Musad reeled back with a yell as flames lashed at his face. His men gawped at him in stunned surprise . . .

And Eddie and Ana burst into motion.

12

Eddie grabbed the nearest table and hurled it at two men in front of him, knocking them down. At the same moment, Ana somersaulted over a chair, landing inverted on one hand and spinning her entire body to deliver a savage kick to another Moroccan's face before completing the roll and landing on both feet.

Eddie had just enough time to recognise the move as *capoeira* – a Brazilian form of martial arts – before a goon lunged at him—

He grabbed a kebab skewer and stabbed it up under the man's chin. The sharp metal spike punched through skin and flesh and tongue to pierce his upper palate, meat juice and fresh blood squirting over his neck. The thug screamed as best he could with his mouth pinned shut before a punch from the Yorkshireman knocked him to the tiled floor.

More men charged to take his place. Eddie dropped and rolled under a table, sweeping his legs across to scythe one man's feet out from beneath him. He hit the floor hard. The Englishman sprang back up, seizing a chair and whirling to crack it against another goon's head.

Ana was no less brutal, though more refined in her attacks. She swept one arm over a man's outstretched hands to deliver a fearsome chop to his larynx. His eyes bugged wide as he choked. She ducked and twisted beneath him before springing up to hoist him off his feet and propel him into the man behind him.

Another thug rushed at Eddie. The Yorkshireman punched

him in the face, flattening his nose with a wet crunch. He looked for another target as the man collapsed – only to take a blow to his own jaw that sent him crashing against a table. Plates smashed on the floor in an explosion of rice and sauce.

His attacker ran at him—

Eddie threw another plate at his feet. It shattered, splattering wet food over the tiles – and the running man slipped, face-planting on the floor. A kick to his skull ensured he would stay down.

Another look around, and the Englishman saw that Musad, the scar-faced leader, had batted out the flames.

The gun whipped towards him—

Eddie made a diving roll across a table, grabbing its edge and pulling it over after him. Musad squeezed the trigger, only for one of his own men to take the bullet in his hip as Ana kicked him across the line of fire.

The Dhajani was undeterred by the wounded man's shriek, sending a hail of rounds after the Yorkshireman. They smacked into the table's underside, but the thick wood stopped them from fully penetrating. Eddie hunched down, then grabbed a chair and lobbed it over the table. A satisfying thud of impact was followed by a pained grunt as the scarred man fell – and the clatter of metal as his gun spun away across the floor.

He was down, but not out. It would only take him seconds to recover the weapon . . .

Ana cried out as two men tackled her simultaneously, piling on top of her. 'Chase!' she gasped as one of her attackers pounded an elbow into her back.

Eddie jumped up. He glanced at Musad, who was scrambling after his gun, then charged to help Ana. A jaw-breaking punch to a man who tried to intercept him, then he snatched up a large knife from a table and jabbed it into the stomach of another before ducking under a sweeping haymaker to dive at Ana's captors – and stabbing the blade downwards through one man's hand.

It hit so hard that the tile beneath the Moroccan's splayed palm cracked, the point driving into the planks below and pinning him like a butterfly. The man screamed and tried to pull away, but his hand was trapped. Eddie twisted to smack Ana's other captor in the mouth with his boot heel. Broken teeth spun across the dining room.

Ana was free. Eddie smashed the haymaking thug's kneecap with a second heel strike, then dragged her up. 'We've got to get outside!' he shouted.

She was winded, but still nodded. Then they darted in opposite directions as more men charged at them.

The Brazilian jinked to avoid her new attacker's sweeping fist, responding by slamming the heel of her hand up against his nose. There was a hideous *splat* of collapsing cartilage. The man staggered back, blinded by his own sprayed blood.

Eddie, meanwhile, faced not only a much larger opponent, but one who was armed. A six-inch switchblade slashed at his throat. 'Whoa, fuck!' he gasped as he jerked away, the knife's tip slicing through his leather jacket's collar. 'That's brand new, you twat!'

The man took another swing. The Yorkshireman dodged again, but he was being backed into a corner.

Metal glinted on a table. A tray—

He snatched it up and raised it like a shield as the Moroccan lunged. Metal struck metal with a *clang*.

Eddie drew back, fending off more attacks, *clang*, *clang* – but was almost out of space to retreat—

The knife thrust again, but this time he didn't deflect it, instead leaping back squarely against the wall. The big man hadn't expected the move, his strike falling short and leaving him unbalanced . . .

Eddie's boot buried its steel toecap in his groin.

The big man dropped with a squeal. Eddie jumped over him to re-enter the fray.

Ana didn't need his help this time, the Brazilian woman delivering a spinning capoeira kick to a thug's stomach. He flew back against a pillar with such force that tiles shattered. 'Get to the stairs!' she called to Eddie.

They had thinned the crowd enough that the way to the exit was almost clear. She chopped another man's neck and sent him tumbling over a chair, then ran to the staircase. Eddie snatched up two plates, smashing one into the face of someone trying to block him and hurling the other across the room to explode against the back of Musad's head just before he reached his gun, before following her.

Alarm flashed across Ana's face. More men were thundering up the stairs.

She jumped and delivered a two-footed Shatner kick to the leading goon's chest. He back-flipped into the two men behind him, the trio bowling painfully down the steps. But within seconds, another wave trampled over the fallen.

Eddie lifted another table, swinging to crack a man's sternum with its corner before running to the stairs. 'Back!' he shouted to Ana. She rolled clear. He jumped down the top few steps with the table held ahead of him like a snowplough, wood banging loudly against the skulls of the men heading the charge.

The table was large enough to block the staircase. Eddie wedged it in place, then hurried to rejoin Ana.

She was trading blows with someone, but still shouted a warning to the Englishman—

Too late.

Another Moroccan rushed him and slammed him into a pillar. He dropped to the floor, dizzied. The man drew a knife – a nasty serrated blade, a reddish-brown residue against the hilt suggesting it had been used in many other fights.

Ana crouched to avoid a punch, rolling back and using her legs to sweep her attacker's feet out from under him. He thumped to the floor beside her. She twisted and pounded his face into the tiles with her elbow, then leapt to her feet—

A chair smashed against her back. The man wielding it threw aside the broken remnants and charged at the reeling woman like a bull, body-slamming her against a wall.

The knifeman advanced on Eddie as he rose. The man's mouth curled into a sadistic smile – then he thrust the knife—

Eddie twisted away. The blade caught his left biceps, ripping his sleeve and slicing a searing line into his skin but he was still able to bend his arm to trap his attacker's outstretched wrist in the crook of his elbow.

His right hand whipped up. The Moroccan's own elbow popped from its joint with an appalling crunch as Eddie's blow from beneath bent it the wrong way. He screamed.

Eddie didn't relent. He whirled the howling man around and drove him backwards into a window. Glass smashed, the frame breaking from its hinges, and the man hit the metal bars outside with such force that the whole grille was almost wrenched from the wall. The broken-armed thug crumpled to the floor, the knife clattering from his hand.

Eddie snatched it up and hurled it at Ana's attacker.

The blade thunked into the man's back just before he could kick her in the face. He screeched, desperately clawing over his shoulder to pull it out.

Ana leapt up and delivered a kick. He crashed into a chair, demolishing it. To his great fortune, he landed face-down, the knife still protruding from his back.

There was now only one Moroccan left standing. 'Seriously?' Eddie gasped as the man rushed at him, still fancying his chances despite his comrades' fates. The Yorkshireman jinked to take the impact, grabbing his attacker's arm to throw him over his shoulder – just as Musad recovered his gun.

Eddie instantly switched tactics to use the man as a human shield. A gunshot echoed through the room, the Moroccan convulsing as the bullet ripped a chunk of flesh from his buttock. The scar-faced man snarled and pulled the trigger again—

Snick. The magazine was empty.

'Let's go, *go!*' Eddie shouted, dropping the wailing man and running for the stairs.

The table blocking the lower flight jolted as men below pounded against it. 'We can't go down there!' Ana protested.

'Not down – up!' he shouted as he passed her.

'What's up there?'

'*Not* more bad guys!'

Musad fumbled for a replacement mag, then remembered he had a second weapon – Ana's Millennium Pro. 'Come on!' Eddie urged.

Ana hesitated, but then saw Musad draw her automatic. She ran after the Yorkshireman. Behind her, the obstructing table was finally barged aside.

Eddie hared up the stairs. He knew from a past visit to Karim's restaurant that a neighbouring building looked close enough to reach from the top floor's balcony—

A large vase smashed over his head.

He fell. He had been wrong: there *were* more bad guys upstairs, a handful of men ready for just such an escape attempt . . .

Ana vaulted him, outstretched fingers rigid as iron bars as she stabbed them into the eyes of Eddie's attacker. The man shrieked and tried to jump back, but she had already gripped his arm to propel him into another Moroccan coming at her with a knife. The blade sank into his side. The second goon realised what he had done and yanked it out, blood spurting.

The Brazilian was already attacking again, kicking the

wounded man in the stomach. He slammed against the knife-man, getting a matching stab wound to his other side as both of them fell down the stairs into the men coming up from below, starting a chain reaction of falling thugs.

Eddie raised himself from the floor. Ana was regaining her balance after her flying kick – oblivious of another man behind her. *'Look out!'*

She turned – but too late.

The Moroccan swung a cosh, a heavy lump of leather-wrapped metal. The home-made weapon was crude – but effective. It struck Ana's head with a flat thud, instantly felling her.

The man looked for her companion—

Eddie found him first.

The goons upstairs had taken full advantage of the restaurant's menu, slices of lamb sizzling on a hot iron skillet. The Yorkshireman grabbed its wooden handle and swung it at the man's face. The dull impact of thick metal on bone was backed by a hiss as the skillet's grooves seared into the Moroccan's flesh. He screamed, flailing back with raw red lines branded into one cheek.

Eddie finished him off with a punch, then threw the skillet down the stairs into the mass of thugs. A loud *clonk* of impact was followed by an agonised howl.

A door led to the small balcony. Eddie picked Ana up and kicked it open, emerging into sunlight. The Medina spread out below, a hotchpotch of multicoloured buildings jammed together at random. He looked over the edge. The closest rooftop was across an alley downhill from the restaurant, a good fifteen feet lower. He might make it if he was on his own. But he had to get Ana to safety – she was his only link to Nina. He doubted he could make the jump without injury while carrying her, and there was nothing to cushion her landing if he threw her across.

He needed another way down. The balcony of the floor below was off to one side, a canopy providing shade . . .

Someone shouted behind him. His pursuers had finally made it to the top of the stairs. Out of time—

'Sorry,' he told Ana – as he tossed her over the edge.

She landed on the canopy. The canvas caught her, only to rip loose, pitching the limp woman on to a table below.

Eddie jumped down, then scrambled to check on her. She was still unconscious, a new cut on her arm, but as far as he could tell had suffered no serious harm.

He hauled her over his shoulder. He was now on the wrong side of the building to reach the nearby rooftop, and the drop to the steeply sloping street was still too far to risk. He glanced back into the restaurant. Most of the thugs had charged upstairs. Could he get down to the ground floor?

No – another couple of men were rushing upstairs. If they blocked him, even for a few seconds, the others would return and swarm him. He could still reach the windows, but they were barred.

Although one was damaged.

Still lugging Ana, he charged back inside and ran for the broken window. The men reached the top of the stairs and charged at him, but he was already past them. He made a flying leap through the opening, twisting in mid-air to hit the bars with his back – and ripping the ironwork from the outer wall.

Three of the corners tore loose, one at the bottom just barely holding. But the metal buckled under the weight, the whole grille swinging downwards.

Eddie grabbed a bar with his free hand as he and Ana went with it—

It jerked to a stop. He lost his grip, falling . . .

And landing on a pile of garbage bags in the alley behind the restaurant.

Rubbish exploded around them. Eddie gasped, rolling his strained shoulder, then stood and hauled Ana back up.

Noises above. He was already running, risking a glance back. Musad leaned out of the window, spotting the fugitives.

He whipped up the Taurus—

Eddie weaved, bullets smacking against the walls behind him. He darted around the alley's end – just as another round exploded against the corner, brick fragments stinging his head.

A woman screamed, alarmed voices rising as people reacted to the gunshots. The gendarmerie would soon be called, if they hadn't been already. He couldn't let them catch him; even if they believed he was rescuing the unconscious Ana from their attackers, once she woke she could simply tell them he had been trying to harm her, then walk away while he dealt with the fallout.

And there were other people he still had to evade. Another voice called out: Musad, rallying what was left of his forces.

Eddie hurried downhill. His knowledge of the Medina's twists and turns was sketchy, having always relied on Karim to guide him. All he could do was get clear of the restaurant. Ana still over his shoulder, he headed down the narrow street as quickly as he could. Passers-by gawped at him and his cargo as he passed.

Extensions protruding from the upper floors of buildings on each side almost met overhead, forming a tunnel. He ducked into the half-light beneath, seeing an intersection ahead. Left or right? Left looked a more direct route down the hill. He took it, rounding the corner.

More shouts from behind. Musad's men had seen him. Ana was slowing him, badly. They would be on him in twenty seconds, less. He had to delay them . . .

The new street was stepped roughly every fifteen feet, enterprising locals setting up small stalls selling food and bric-a-brac on the relatively level sections. One even had a flock of chickens strutting around it, pecking at spilled grains – the birds were not caged, but Eddie imagined they were available to purchase in the same way as anything else. Opposite, a sullen man with a cigarette drooping from his mouth had stacks of knock-off toys balanced precariously on a folding table.

Eddie ran between them – then swiped the piled boxes with Ana's feet—

Musad's men charged around the corner after him – as an avalanche of Super Bat and Changing Robot and Marvellous Lady Bird figures cascaded into the flock.

The chickens flapped madly into the air to flee the trademark-violating bombardment. The running men hurriedly halted, hands shielding their faces as wings and claws lashed at them.

That had bought Eddie a few seconds. He ducked into a side alley. The walls were close enough to touch without even fully lifting his arms. He passed an even narrower passage, continuing for several metres before turning into a second and pounding down steep steps. Right at the bottom, under an archway, around another corner—

'*Bollocks!*'

Dead end.

He carried on nevertheless, hoping there was a wall or fence he could climb. But the tiny square was completely surrounded by run-down houses.

No way out. He turned to face his pursuers.

Four men. Five, Musad appearing behind them. The Dhajani still had the gun—

The others ran at Eddie, blocking their leader's line of fire. Small mercies, but he still had four guys to fight, and an unconscious woman over his shoulder.

But if his training had taught him one thing, it was how to turn a liability into an advantage.

The first thug came at him – only to take one of Ana's feet to his jaw as the Yorkshireman spun, centrifugal force whipping her legs upwards. He lurched back, colliding with the man following him. Both went down in a pile.

The next man hurriedly sidestepped to avoid them before readying an attack of his own—

Ana hit him in the face – not with her fist, but her entire body as the Yorkshireman flung her at him. He fell, the Brazilian landing on top of him.

Eddie stared at the last Moroccan in challenge: *think you can do better?* The man hesitated . . .

Whatever action he had been about to take was instantly forgotten as a police siren blared somewhere not far downhill. The man decided that staying out of prison overcame loyalty to his current employer. He turned and ran past Musad, the others scrambling up and following.

Musad shouted Arabic insults after them, then faced Eddie and raised the gun. 'This time, I have plenty of—'

Eddie broke and ran before he finished speaking. It took the scar-faced man a moment to react, speech hogging his brain's mental bandwidth, but then the Taurus snapped around and fired.

The Englishman hurled himself into the deepest of the square's doorways, slamming hard against thick wood as the bullet shattered on stone just behind him.

He rattled the door handle, but it was locked. Musad advanced past the fallen Ana to sight his target. Eddie shoulder-barged the barrier, trying to break it open. No luck.

Musad smiled cruelly and took final aim—

The door opened.

The startled Yorkshireman fell backwards as the round that would have hit his head cracked above him and struck the rear wall. The stooped old man who had opened the door flinched back in shock.

Musad brought the gun down – as Eddie flung a heavy cast-iron doorstop at him. It struck his chest, sending him staggering back in pain.

Eddie jumped up. The elderly man had a cane. 'Sorry,' said the Yorkshireman as he snatched it away and snapped it over his thigh. He rushed back outside, the broken stick raised like a lance.

Clutching his ribs, Musad straightened – to see his opponent charging at him—

The cane's ragged point stabbed into his neck.

The gun fell from Musad's fingers. The Yorkshireman ran to snatch it up, and turned – to find that his opponent was running, hand pressed hard to his bloodied throat. He briefly considered pursuing him to get answers, but the siren was getting closer. Shoving the gun into his jacket, he collected Ana once more.

'Do you know Karim Taysir?' he asked the bewildered old man. The name produced a nod; Eddie wondered why he found that remotely surprising. 'He'll get you a new cane!'

Ana dangling over his shoulder, he hurried back into the maze of the Medina.

13

Seville

The walk along the riverside under the midday sun had been hot. Nina was hugely relieved to reach the Parque de María Luisa, where she could find shade beneath the trees lining its broad avenues. As a redhead, she normally took precautions against sunburn, but on this occasion she was woefully under-equipped, without even sleeves to protect her arms.

The half-mile-long park was busy, tourists taking a break from the crush on the parade routes to gaze at the imposing architecture of the Plaza de España. Nina let a family on bicycles ride past as she headed through the gardens. The Museo Arqueológico was at the southern end, a handsome symmetrical art deco building that she knew from prior visits was home to many fascinating historical treasures.

The one she was interested in was not on general view, though. She hoped it was already under higher security; if not, she would have to convince the museum's head to up his game.

She climbed the steps to the main entrance, pausing at a vending machine to regard her reflection in its glass front. She did not, she had to admit, cut an especially impressive figure. While her shoes had dried out, they had been left stained and salt-crusted by their immersion in seawater, and after a night sleeping rough and a long bus ride, her hair was a mess. Her appearance was normally low on her list of priorities, but Emilio

Merlo was a man who paid great attention to what she considered superficialities – and he was the one who would decide what to do with the second spear marker.

Her high heels were still in the bag. She changed into them, using the elastic band that had held Ana's money as an impromptu scrunchie to tie her hair into a ponytail. She immediately felt more purposeful; it was how she always wore her hair in the field. Another look at her reflection. She still felt like a mess, but at least now she was a *businesslike* mess.

She went along a terrace into the museum proper, stilettos clacking on the polished floor. The sound drew the attention of two uniformed security guards, both men unsubtly checking her out as she approached. Neither rushed to apprehend her, so obviously the cops hadn't circulated her picture – though why would they? Nobody knew she was in Seville . . . she hoped. Still, the museum staff may well have been warned about events aboard the *Atlantia*.

Best to find out straight away. '*Buenas tardes*,' she began, hoping her Spanish wasn't too awful. '*Mi nombre es Nina Wilde. Estoy aquí para ver al Dr Merlo?*'

Her name produced a response from both men – fortunately one of recognition rather than alarm. She was, after all, the world's most famous non-fictional archaeologist. 'Dr Wilde, hello,' said one of them. 'I tell Dr Merlo you are here.'

'I don't have an appointment,' Nina added. 'But please tell him it's urgent.'

The guard made a call. Several tense minutes later, the museum's director arrived. Emilio Merlo was a broad-shouldered, barrel-chested but also rather short man in his mid fifties; Nina imagined he spent a lot of time in the gym to compensate for his below-average stature. His hair was also raised in a pompadour to give him that little bit of extra height, and she suspected he had wedges in his shoes.

His attitude towards her was also overcompensatory. In their previous meetings, he had made it very clear that whatever her achievements, inside the museum he was the big man – professionally, if not physically. This time would be no different. 'Dr Wilde,' he said. 'I did not know you were coming. You are lucky I am able to see you, I am very busy.'

'Hello to you too, Emilio,' Nina replied, forcing a smile and extending her hand. He shook it a little too firmly. 'It's very important – it's about the *marcador de lanza* that was aboard the *Atlantia*.'

He gave her a look that was suspicious but not openly hostile. 'Yes, I know. Terrible, shocking! And I was also told you were involved.'

She was briefly fearful, before realising that if he had called the cops, they would have arrived already. 'Well, obviously I *wasn't*, or I'd be sitting in a cell somewhere rather than here, wouldn't I?' she countered. He seemed to accept her logic. 'What else were you told?'

'A professional raid, they said. And they took only the *marcador*. Very strange. Although I should be relieved that they did not steal any more of our treasures.'

'I think I know why they were only interested in the marker. You remember my theory about—'

Merlo raised his hands dismissively. 'Please!' he scoffed. 'Not your antimatter idea? It is pure science fiction, total nonsense!'

'I didn't really believe it myself,' she said. 'It was just one possible explanation to fit what the Atlanteans said about the spearheads, in line with what I discovered about the Midas Cave in Nepal. But I think whoever stole the marker *does* believe it. They want to find the spearheads . . . and to do that, they need the markers. Both of them. They've got one already, which is why I'm here – to make sure they don't get the other.'

'They will not,' the Spaniard said firmly. 'I have already brought in more security.' He nodded towards the two guards. 'And there is another man at the door to the laboratory.'

'The guys who stole the other marker had guns,' Nina pointed out. The museum guards were armed with nothing more dangerous than truncheons.

'We are in a city, not out at sea. If there is any trouble, the police will be here in two minutes. You are worrying about nothing.'

'I'd like to see for myself,' she said. Sensing he was about to resist the proposal, she went on: 'Just for my own peace of mind. I'm sure you've taken every possible precaution, Emilio. If I'm happy, then I can stop bothering you.'

Merlo seemed considerably more enthused about that. 'Very well.'

He led her back past the main entrance and along another open-sided terrace to a hall containing an elevator. 'We have made much progress with the new Tartessian relics,' he said proudly, as the lift descended. 'Many interesting discoveries, all found here in Spain.'

'I'd love to see them,' Nina said truthfully as they emerged in the basement. Part of the lower level was dedicated to the Iberian peninsula's prehistory, but the majority was closed to the public, home to labs where the museum's archaeologists could examine and restore their discoveries. 'But I still want to check out the marker first.'

Merlo brought her to a door where, as promised, a security guard was stationed. Nina was less than impressed; the overweight man sitting on a chair did not suggest Fort Knoxian impenetrability. But at least it was *something*. Her host opened the door, beckoning for her to follow him.

She had visited the museum's labs before, so knew the layout. Partitions separated several work areas, though all were deserted. She wondered why, then remembered it was Holy Week – a public holiday. Merlo himself was probably there only to deal with the fallout from the marker's theft. He led her to the far end. 'Here, Dr Wilde,' he said. 'I will prove the *marcador* is safe.'

He unlocked one of numerous metal drawers. The object within was wrapped in soft dark cloth. Unlike the marker from the *Atlantia*, which was a flat disc, this bore a protrusion that made the shrouded shape almost conical.

The Spaniard reverently peeled away the cloth. Gold glinted beneath, a distinctive reddish tint to the precious metal. 'Here it is.'

Nina gazed at the historic treasure. She had only ever seen it in photographs before – it had been uncovered at the Tartessian site after her last visit. In pictures it had been unprepossessing, its golden gleam muted by dirt and most of the inscriptions obscured beneath hard-packed earth.

Now, though, it was restored to full magnificence. Like its stolen counterpart, it was riddled with small circular holes, Atlantean text snaking around them. She recognised the more common words immediately, and was sure she could translate most if not all of the rest, given time. But now her attention moved to the top of the golden arm extending from one edge to above the centre. A hoop about an inch across was fixed to its top, sitting parallel to the disc's plane. Its purpose was unknown, though theories included a mount for a lens or eyepiece that when looked through would give meaning to the pattern of holes.

She was familiar enough with the first marker to notice that its pattern was different from the one before her. When fitted back to back with the other disc, some of the holes would be blocked. However it pointed the way to the spearheads, only a subset of the pattern was important, not the whole thing.

'As you can see, it has not been stolen,' Merlo said smugly. 'And the security here at the museum will keep it safe.'

'A handful of unarmed doughy guys and some locked doors won't keep these men out,' Nina insisted. 'You need proper security, professionals – *armed* professionals. And this needs to be kept in a vault, not a glorified filing cabinet.'

Merlo's lips tightened at the criticism. 'The night guards have guns.'

'Then let's hope the place isn't robbed in the daytime.'

'Do you think we are all peasants here in Spain, Dr Wilde?' he snapped, starting to re-wrap the marker. 'The *marcador* is completely secure! And,' he went on, a mocking tone entering his voice, 'even if the *marcadores* really do point the way to the Atlantean spearheads, nobody knows how to use them. Not even *you* have solved their secret.' The last was said with considerable sarcasm.

'You can't take that risk!' Nina protested, growing angry at his refusal to take her seriously. 'If they have both pieces, all they need is someone who can translate Atlantean text. Once they know what it says, they *will* eventually find the spearheads – and they'll have a weapon that makes a nuke look like a firecracker!'

Merlo tucked the last corner of the marker's wrapping back into place. 'If that is what the spearheads are. Which I do not believe. Antimatter bombs, pah – this is not a Dan Brown book! You have spent too much time making television shows – you have lost touch with *real* archaeology.'

'So you're not going to do anything to protect it?' Nina demanded.

'I have done more than enough.' He stepped back, preparing to return the treasure to the drawer.

A mad idea flashed through Nina's mind. If Merlo wouldn't do what was necessary to keep the Atlantean relic safe, someone else would have to do it for him . . .

Almost before finishing the thought, she snatched the marker from him.

The Spaniard gawped at her in disbelief. She imagined her own expression was much the same. 'What are—' he began, before realisation struck. 'No!'

But Nina had already kicked off her high heels and bolted for the door.

14

Nina raced through the lab, clutching the marker. Merlo yelled in Spanish behind her.

The door ahead opened. The portly security guard jumped back in surprise as she ducked around him and ran for the exit. He hurriedly shouted into a walkie-talkie before starting after her.

She reached the elevator, but couldn't risk taking it. Instead she ran up a narrow staircase behind it, emerging on the museum's main floor. Going right would take her back to the entrance and the park—

She reached the terrace – and saw a guard pounding towards her. Bare feet skidding on the smooth marble, she hurriedly reversed and ran into the museum proper.

Carrying both her bag and the marker was awkward. She almost dumped the former, but remembered that literally everything she currently possessed was in it – including money, passport and shoes. Instead she stuffed the Atlantean treasure inside and held the bag shut as she ran.

Startled visitors jumped out of her way. The guard was gaining. Through more doorways, into a hallway with rows of Roman busts on plinths at the far end.

He was right behind her. A hand clutched at her ponytail—

Nina swung the bag at him. The heavy marker clonked against his head. She jinked aside, squeaking to a halt as he stumbled past.

The guard crashed against the front row of plinths. The

carved heads wobbled, an early-first-century bust of a woman toppling over. Nina shrieked and lunged to catch it before it burst apart on the floor, then laid it gently down.

The guard looked in confusion between her and the rescued bust, then pushed himself upright as Nina ran again.

Beyond the next room was the museum's central hall, a large oval chamber with a glazed ceiling. Its centrepiece was a perfectly restored Roman fresco on the floor, a rope cordon keeping tourists' feet off the ancient tiles.

The fastest route to the exit was straight across the fresco. She offered a silent apology to the archaeologists who had carried out the restoration, then hurdled the rope, racing through more rooms in a blur of pottery and Roman coins. Ahead was the room where she had first met Merlo. She was almost out!

She ran on to the terrace leading to the main entrance—

Merlo himself rounded the corner ahead, face filled with fury. 'Stop!' he yelled, holding out his arms to make a tackle.

Without stopping to think, she jumped on to the terrace's balustrade – and leapt off it.

She sailed over a wheelchair access to land on the plaza beyond. Pain flared in one ankle as her heel hit the stone slabs hard. Wincing, she looked back – to see Merlo and the others making a slower but safer descent to the zigzag ramp.

That gave her a head start, but not much. She ran into the broad space of the Plaza de América between the archaeological edifice and the Museum of Arts.

Where to go – and how? She couldn't run for ever; some of the guards were faster than her. She needed something quicker than her two feet . . .

A teenage boy slouched with a mountain bike, boredom clear on his face as he waited for his parents to take a selfie. 'Sorry, kid,' Nina said, yanking the bike from him. 'I need your wheels!'

She made a hasty rolling start. The bag's weight in one hand unbalanced her, the bike wobbling and almost pitching her off before she straightened out. The boy ran after her, screaming Spanish abuse as his startled parents looked around.

The guards were still chasing her. Nina pumped the pedals harder. She pulled clear of the bike's yelling owner, clicking up through the gears to gain speed. Her pursuers fell away behind.

She swung on to one of the boulevards, hooking the bag over the handlebars. Ahead was a crescent; she shot into it, making a wide turn to bring herself on to a tree-lined avenue. It was a busy route, horse-drawn carriages and bicycle rickshaws overtaking the ambling tourists.

But there was a motor vehicle on it too – a police car, lights and siren sending people scattering. Merlo hadn't been kidding about the cops' rapid response time.

Footpaths led into the trees on both sides. Nina swung down one to her right, bushes swatting at her as she whisked along the track. As long as she continued roughly north, she would head back towards Seville's centre, where she would have a chance of escaping the cops in the Holy Week crowds.

If she could get out of the park . . .

She burst out from bushes, making a quick swerve around a line of people at an ice cream stall to bring the bike back on to asphalt. She was almost at the Plaza de España. An exit from the park beyond it would bring her out near the University of Seville, where she had once given a lecture.

She reached another wide avenue and turned towards the Plaza. Behind, the police car peeled through an intersection after her. She clutched the bag more tightly and snicked up through the gears.

More cops ahead joined the hunt, officers patrolling the Plaza de España running in her direction. None was crazy enough to take a shot, the sheer number of tourists acting as a deterrent.

But the crowds made matters harder for Nina too, forcing her to weave through them.

She swung on to an avenue leading north-west out of the Plaza. Its end was fenced off, horse-drawn carriages lined up on the far side. She jumped the bike on to the pavement with a jarring thud and whizzed through the pedestrian entrance. Her ride immediately became several times more dangerous; she was now on a public road, badly parked cars on both sides and more drivers filing between them. She went with the flow of traffic, following a car circulating around the one-way loop to the park's gates before cutting alongside a line of vehicles at a stop light.

Ahead was a large traffic circle. The university was directly opposite. The road was clear, so she zoomed past the waiting cars – and instantly regretted her decision.

Traffic lights on another road turned green, and Spanish drivers did not take their time pulling away. Dozens of cars suddenly rushed at her. Horns blared, the oncoming vehicles weaving to avoid her. Metal and plastic crunched just behind. She glanced back. The two collided vehicles were blocking anyone else from coming up on that side. She turned and yanked up the handlebars to wheelie on to the grassy central circle.

That gave her a brief respite as she pedalled across it, but despite the fender-bender, drivers were still orbiting the round-about, squeezing past the two stationary cars and even putting their wheels on the sidewalk. 'And I thought they were impatient in New York!' Nina gasped as she continued at full pelt towards the exit ahead. A man who had narrowly missed her the first time seemed determined to finish the job, blasting angrily on his horn. She was able to spare just enough concentration to flip him the bird before sweeping on to the wide sidewalk outside the university.

She was safe—

Or not. Vehicles rounding another traffic circle further down the road parted to let a police car through. 'Oh, crap!'

More cops were approaching from behind. She swung the bike through a gate into the university's grounds. The oncoming police car screeched to a stop outside, stymied by a barrier.

Nina cut across a lawn and rounded the corner of the main building. A gate led back out on to the streets. No cars beyond; it was a pedestrianised zone. Dodging startled students, she sped through the opening.

Twin tramlines ran along the street's centreline, but while normal traffic was prohibited, the road was not inaccessible. Another police car was coming down it from the traffic circle, siren squalling. She followed the tramlines into a spacious square, where the Holy Week crowd became a crush. Music filled the air, a brass band blaring out a tune.

The parade itself gave her a moment of shock – at least until her knowledge of history overcame instinctual revulsion. Those marching were Nazarenos, members of a Catholic order following tradition by wearing long robes and tall pointed hoods that covered their faces. The same design had been adopted by the loathsome bigots of the Ku Klux Klan, only their concealment was out of cowardice rather than an exhibition of shame before God.

The music was surprisingly jaunty, the onlookers treating the parade more as spectacle than a sombre exhibition of penance. Amongst the hooded Nazarenos were *pasos*, elaborate floats bearing religious imagery, which at first glance appeared to be motorised but were actually carried on the shoulders of dozens of men hidden beneath their decorative skirts. They were being borne on to the street leading to the Cathedral of Seville.

Nina rode towards the parade until the thickening crowd forced her to stop. Gripping the bag, she jumped off the bike and ran. The wailing police car had already come to a halt.

The cops hadn't given up, though. She glanced back to see

two baseball-hatted men in sunglasses running after her. She was easy to spot; the vast majority of the visitors were Spanish, almost uniformly dark-haired, while her red tresses stood out like a beacon.

She ducked lower, shoving through the throng before emerging on the parade route itself. Robed figures surrounded her, eyes widening in surprise behind the holes in the pointed *capirote* hoods as she scurried past. '*Oye! Oye!*' someone shouted, a foot catching her painfully on her calf. Penitence clearly did not rule out anger, especially on a day that people had likely been anticipating for months. She gasped, but pressed on, more cries in her wake.

Keeping her head down, she pushed through the Nazarenos to scuttle alongside a lumbering float. A larger-than-life statue of Jesus on the cross regarded her disapprovingly from atop the *paso*. She spotted a small gap in the front row of onlookers and ducked into it.

A glance back as the crowd closed behind her. The closest cop was being hampered by his own religious upbringing – he was reluctant to disrespect the devout by barging through the Nazarenos. She took advantage of his hesitation and hurried onwards, forcing her way through the crush.

The parade turned into a plaza in front of the cathedral. Nina instead kept going down its side, the crowds gradually easing. A narrow street on her left; a quick check for police, then she took it. There were far fewer people here. A long line of parked mopeds led her to another junction. No cops there either. She rounded the corner and hurried along the new alley, then stopped, suddenly breathless.

The bag was heavy in her hand. She rummaged for her sea-damaged shoes and put them on her dirty, aching feet, then glanced back at her cargo.

The second spear marker was hers. The irony that she was

now actually guilty of what she had been accused of aboard the *Atlantia* did not escape her. A small disbelieving laugh. What the hell had she been thinking? For all Merlo's arrogance, he did have a point: there was no proof that the spearheads really were some kind of ancient superweapon, merely her supposition. She might have just committed grand larceny and set every cop in Spain after her for nothing.

But another part of her insisted she had made the right decision; the *only* decision. The raiders had specifically taken the first marker, and nothing else. They wanted it for a reason. And she was the only person with any explanation, however out-there, of what the spearheads might be . . .

It was something she could consider more once she was safe. She closed the bag, then headed off into the city.

15

Tangier, Morocco

'You know,' Eddie said to Karim as the Moroccan opened the Citroën's rear door, 'I never thought running around a major city with an unconscious woman over my shoulder would draw so much attention.'

Karim's usual ebullience was conspicuously absent. 'Get her inside,' he said. 'Quickly!'

The Englishman knew why he was so fraught. After getting clear of the restaurant, he had phoned his friend to learn that Maysa and the children were still being held hostage. Karim hadn't dared call the police out of fear for their lives. 'Thanks for coming, by the way,' he said as they put the limp Ana on the back seat. 'After I fucked up your restaurant, I wasn't sure you'd even pick up the phone for me.'

Karim shook his head. 'I should have warned you sooner. But I was afraid. They have my family, Eddie!'

'Not for long,' Eddie promised him. He made sure Ana was secure, then closed the door. 'Let's go.'

Karim's home was not far. He pulled up a few hundred feet away. 'I do not want to get closer, in case they are watching for me. What are we going to do?'

'*You* are going to stay here and look after Ana,' Eddie said firmly. '*I'll* sort this out.' He regarded the building, looking for points of entrance. Like most houses in the city, the windows on the ground floor – and even some higher – were barred, to deter opportunistic burglars. But those around the inner courtyard, he remembered, were not. 'Maysa told me your kids keep jumping across to the roof of another house. Which one?'

His companion gave him an uncomprehending look. 'Why do you—'

'Because if they can do it, so can I. Where's this other house?'

'Behind mine,' Karim said, pointing. 'The one with the red walls.'

Karim's home stood on a hillside; the other house was lower down the slope. 'I see it.'

'They jump across from a ledge. I keep telling them not to, but . . . in a way I am impressed.' His expression slowly changed from reluctant parental pride to despair. He murmured an Arabic prayer, then: 'Oh Eddie! What if they are hurt, what if they are – if they are dead? I do not know what—'

'You cooperated, they don't have any reason to hurt them.' Eddie could actually think of one very good reason why the bad guys *would* harm their hostages – to ensure their silence – but knew better than to tell his friend. 'Okay, wait here.'

He got out and crossed the street. He was sure one of the kidnappers would be on guard at the front door, so instead went down a narrow alley, then cut across the hillside until he was behind Karim's home.

There was the ledge, a protruding cornice three storeys up. He turned to examine the red house. An old cast-metal drainpipe wound down from the roof. That all the upper-floor windows near it were barred suggested it was climbable.

He made sure nobody was watching, then started his ascent. Plaster flaked beneath his feet as he hauled himself upwards, but the pipe held. He soon reached the top and stood on the sloping roof. The gap to the ledge was less than ten feet, so the jump would pose little difficulty. It was the landing that concerned him. The cornice was perhaps eight inches deep, the wall behind it lacking any handholds . . .

He took a step back, then jumped across the alley.

His raised hands took the impact against the wall. Even so, the touchdown was precarious. The twenty-five-foot drop rolled beneath him before he caught his balance. Once steady, he sidestepped along the ledge to a corner.

He gripped the flaking edge to ease himself around, then continued on to a point where he could pull himself up to the roof. Proof that Karim's kids had been here came in the form of chalk graffiti on the tiles. A small smile, then he carefully made his way across.

The courtyard opened out below, the radio blaring from the kitchen's open window. How had Maysa's son reached it? He must have climbed on to the sill of a closed window below, then lowered himself to swing in.

Hoping the hostage-takers weren't in the top-floor room, Eddie descended and perched on the sill. Karim and Maysa's bedroom: empty. But he couldn't take the chance of making noise by forcing the window open.

Instead he lowered himself down, hanging from the sill before dropping to the courtyard. It was a risk – he might be heard or seen if there was a bad guy in the kitchen – but it was also his best chance to get into the house undetected. He pressed his back against the wall and listened intently.

The radio was annoyingly loud, but not enough to blot out any sudden noises or shouts of alarm. He heard neither. A peek through the kitchen window. No one there.

Drawing Ana's gun, he slipped inside, senses on full alert. A faint sound somewhere deeper in the house. A sob. One of the children.

Suppressing anger, he crouched and looked through the doorway at the large dining room. The sound had come from a door ajar at the far end. The family were being held in the lounge. But by how many men?

He crept through the dining room to another door. This led into the main hall. He peered around the frame.

A scruffy Moroccan stood by the front door, staring out at the street through a small window. That meant at least two bad guys, one on watch and the other guarding their prisoners. Two he could handle; three would complicate things . . .

Hoping fate would keep his life simple for once, he went to check the lounge. The sobs grew louder. He dropped low again and slowly leaned around the door.

Maysa and her children were huddled on a long sofa against the far wall. None saw him, all their attention on their captor. Only one, thankfully, a rangy, scraggle-bearded man perched on a chair. He had a gun in his hand, but it was not aimed directly at them, rather a constant reminder of his power.

Eddie retreated and returned to the hall door. The lookout still had his back to him. Hoping the radio would mask the sound of his movements, he pocketed the gun and slowly advanced.

The guard shifted to look further down the street. Eddie moved up wraith-like behind him, both hands rising—

One clamped tightly over the unsuspecting man's mouth and nose, blocking all sounds as the other delivered a brutal knuckle-punch to his larynx. He hauled the guard backwards, punching his throat again before trapping his bruised neck in a chokehold. The man struggled for several seconds before going limp.

Eddie lowered him to the floor, listening. No shouts, no running footsteps. He released the unconscious man and searched him, taking a grubby snub-nosed revolver.

While simply stepping around the door and firing would now be the simplest way of handling the situation, the Yorkshireman didn't especially want to blow the remaining kidnapper's brains out in front of four children. Instead, he went back into the dining room and positioned himself beside the lounge door. Judging by their lack of coordination, the gang who had tried to kill him at the restaurant weren't a close-knit group, many possibly never having met before. So there was a good chance the two men here were also strangers . . .

He dredged some half-forgotten Arabic from his memory and called out in a loud whisper: '*Mahla! Huna!*' *Hey! Over here!*

The reply was beyond his ability to translate, but the tone was clear – impatient concern. '*Huna!*' Eddie repeated, hoping his low voice would disguise that he was not the other kidnapper – or even a native speaker. The chair creaked as the Moroccan stood, then approached the door. The last thing he did before reaching it was turn his head to check on his prisoners.

When he looked back, Eddie was right in front of him.

The Englishman's fist slammed into his face, snapping his nose and bursting both lips with a spray of blood. The Moroccan staggered backwards, blindly raising his gun – only for Eddie's revolver to crack against his skull. He fell. Maysa shrieked. 'With you in a second,' Eddie assured her, dragging the downed man out of the family's sight before pistol-whipping him into uncon-sciousness. He stepped over the slumped kidnapper, concealing the gun before returning to the living room. 'Are you all okay?'

'Eddie!' Maysa cried. 'Where is Karim, is he—'

'He's fine, he's outside. Did they hurt you?'

She hugged her children, tears streaming down her face. 'No, no. We are okay. Who are they, what do they want?'

'They want me, I'm afraid,' Eddie told her grimly. 'But you won't have any more trouble with them. I'll get Karim.'

He dumped the bloodied man beside his companion, then opened the front door and signalled. Karim was there in seconds. 'Where are they, are they all right?' he cried as he jumped out of the car.

'They're okay, don't worry.'

'Thank you!' Karim saw the unconscious kidnappers. He spat at them before hurrying into the house. 'Bring the woman inside, quickly.'

Eddie lifted Ana from the rear seat. Her eyes were still closed, body limp. That she had been out cold for so long was not a good sign; there were no outward signs of major trauma, but she had taken a hard blow to the head. He couldn't take her to a hospital, though. He still needed to find Nina.

The Yorkshireman carried her into the house. 'I'll put her in my room,' he called to Karim, who was having a tearful reunion with his family. 'Then we'll get rid of these two arseholes.'

'I recognise one of them,' the Moroccan told him. 'And I knew some of the others at the restaurant. They have made a very big mistake. I will tell my friends in the police who they are, and they *will* find them.'

'Tell 'em to start by looking in the nearest hospital. There'll be a big queue,' Eddie told him as he took Ana upstairs.

He laid her on the bed. She didn't stir, the only movement her breathing. He sat beside her. 'When you wake up,' he said darkly, 'you are going to tell me who you're working for. And then *I'm* going to find them.'

16

Seville

Nina stared at the face in the bathroom mirror, almost refusing to recognise it as herself. Her long red hair was gone, cut short into a ragged crop and dyed black. Below it, her face seemed nearly as unfamiliar: not because she had done anything to conceal her features, but out of fatigue and fear. Dark circles ringed her eyes, her lips pale. Normally people said she did not look her forty-two years, but right now she felt she was showing every one of them, and more.

It was the first time her hair had been so short. Even though she didn't consider herself to be particularly concerned with her appearance, the change was still a shock. She gave her shorn locks in the waste bin a regretful look, then went back into the bedroom.

She had used a chunk of her remaining cash to pay for a room in a *pensione*, a small hostel across the river from the bus terminal that offered a bed, a roof above it and little else. The owner was used to backpackers and other transients drifting through; he had not asked to see Nina's passport, or even any questions more probing than how long she would be staying.

The marker sat on the bed, surrounded by her few other belongings. The hours spent making her way through Seville had been fraught, every sighting of a police uniform treated as an immediate threat forcing a change of direction. She had ended up in a clothes shop, replacing her crumpled and dirty dress with a cheap outfit meant for someone much younger and less modest, and a floppy sun hat. Whether the disguise had worked, or whether she had simply been successful at avoiding the cops, she didn't know, but she had made it here.

Safe . . . she hoped.

She draped a towel over the pillow to protect it from dye, then flopped on to the bed. Her weight on the soft mattress caused the marker to nudge against her. She raised it and slowly turned it over in her hands. Despite her tiredness, she still couldn't help but be intrigued by the ancient relic. What secrets was it hiding? How did it work? The pattern of holes in the disc was the key, but what did it *mean*?

A flash of light through them from the single ceiling bulb triggered a thought. She turned the marker to examine the hoop on the end of the arm, then looked through it. A holder for an eyepiece, as had been suggested? Possibly. When combined with its sibling, many, if not most, of the little holes would be blocked; if it were then placed in the right position on some as-yet-undiscovered chart or text, any letters or symbols that showed through could be clues to the locations of the spearheads.

But why would an eyepiece be needed to read them? Unless it was a magnifying lens, or some kind of coloured filter, or a gem cut in a particular way to combine different kaleidoscopic fragments into a legible whole . . .

She shook her head. That was pure supposition. And unlike her theory about the spearheads, which had been based on the texts of the Atlanteans themselves, there was nothing to support it.

A closer look at the disc's inscriptions. She knew some words, but they didn't lead to any insights. She instinctively reached for her phone, on which were several gigabytes of research material on Atlantis and other historical topics, before remembering she had discarded it. 'Goddamn it,' she grumbled. Stuck in a poky room with no company, no Wi-Fi, not even her phone to pass the time . . .

That meant the marker itself was her only distraction. As much as she hated being separated from her husband and daughter, it was some time since she had been alone with an archaeological puzzle. If she had to endure solitude, she could at least make the best of the situation.

She looked back at the light bulb through the holes. It was only visible through a few at a time. They were angled so as to radiate outwards from a point at the hoop's centre, and she recalled that those on the stolen marker were similarly canted. The only way to see everything the two relics were designed to reveal was indeed by looking through the metal ring.

But something about the light still prodded her subconscious. The holes were small and would be relatively deep once both discs were put together. Not only would it be like trying to read a book through a drinking straw, but looking through the hoop would blot out most of the illumination needed to see the letters in the first place. The reader would need another light source between their eye and the marker. How would *that* work?

It wouldn't, she realised. She was going down the wrong track. But if the light source was placed *in* the hoop, and was strong enough . . .

She sat up, suddenly excited as a new theory formed, and turned the marker back over so the arm was on the upper side. The disc's shadow was solid, bar a few faint patches of light near its centre. This far from the bulb, only those holes running near-vertically through the artefact were at the right angle to let any illumination through. But if she brought it closer . . .

She hopped up and stretched to hold the top of the marker's arm against the bulb. The shadow expanded over the bed – and more points of light appeared within it, a fuzzy galaxy forming on the sheets.

'That's it,' she whispered. 'That's it!' The hoop wasn't for an eyepiece: it was a *torch holder*. Fit both markers together, shine a strong light through them, and it would create a pattern revealing . . . what?

That was as far as her discovery could go. Without the other marker, there was no way to create the correct pattern, so it would be impossible to deduce its meaning. On the plus side, the raiders couldn't find it either without the relic she was holding. Both sides had reached stalemate—

No! Nina realised she *could* create the right pattern, something the men who had stolen the first marker could never do. And the answer literally had her name on it.

But she couldn't follow up the revelation. It was already late in the day, and the chances of finding what she needed before Seville's shops closed were slim. She would have to wait until tomorrow.

But that gave her time to plan what she needed to do. Despite being hunted by every cop in Seville, despite being cut off from Eddie and Macy, she felt oddly enthused. She might have been forced back into her old world of archaeological discovery, but now that her freedom – and if she was right about the spearheads, the fate of the world – depended on it, she was damn well going to solve the puzzle.

She sat cross-legged, examining the marker again as her mind whirled into overdrive.

A hundred and fifty miles to the south, Ana's mind slowly clawed its way out of a deep, glutinous bog. She had been in a fight, trying to flee from . . . who? She wasn't sure. Half-recalled faces whirled before her, one in particular coming into focus . . .

Right in front of her. 'Ay up,' said Eddie coldly. 'Wakey-wakey.'

'What . . .' moaned the Brazilian, trying to sit up, only to flop painfully back on to the bed. 'Ow.'

'Here.' Eddie held out a cup of water and a couple of pills.

'They're just paracetamol, but they're the best thing to have after getting knocked out.'

She took them gratefully. 'Where am I?'

'My friend's house. The one whose restaurant we just wrecked.'

Her eyes widened in alarm. 'He set us up!'

Eddie shook his head. 'They were holding his family hostage. I rescued 'em.'

'Are they okay?'

He noted her concern; if her motivations were purely mercenary, she wouldn't have asked the question. 'Yeah. What about you?'

'I . . .' She tried to sit up again, this time managing to prop herself on her elbows. 'What happened? I was with you, we went up the stairs . . .'

'Someone clonked you on the head. You've got a bump the size of a tennis ball, but I don't think you've got a skull fracture or concussion.' He leaned closer to check her eyes, waving a finger from side to side. Her gaze instinctively followed it. 'You're focusing and your speech isn't slurred, so that's a good sign. Do you feel dizzy? Sick?'

'No. My head hurts, but . . .' She gingerly touched the bump, wincing. 'I'll live.'

'Good.' He leaned back, folding his arms. 'So now you can answer my questions – you know, the ones you wouldn't answer before someone tried to kill us. You knew the bloke in charge of that gang of fuckwits?'

'Yes, Musad. I met him once, briefly. He was with some people working for my employer.'

'And who *is* your employer? *Was* your employer, I mean. If *my* boss tries to kill me, I usually take it as a sign that the contract's been terminated.' A grim smile. 'Amazing how often that's happened to me.'

'You should take more care when you accept a job,' Ana said. 'But perhaps so should I.' She took a deep breath before overcoming her professional resistance. 'I was working for Gideon Lobato.'

'Lobato?' Eddie echoed. 'Jesus, Macy was right. Another fucking evil billionaire!'

She regarded him curiously. 'Another?'

'Yeah, there was a run of 'em. This is the first one for a while, though. So what does he want – and why did he frame Nina?'

'I don't know.'

'Really.' Though delivered flatly, the word contained no shortage of threat.

'He didn't tell me, and I didn't ask!' Ana protested.

'But you dealt with him directly?'

'Yes, on the ship before you arrived.'

'So what exactly did he want you to do?'

Another moment of reluctance before replying. 'My job was to make sure your wife left the ship and went on the run. So I told her the Dhajanis were going to put her on trial for the robbery, and then I worked with the Frenchman to scare her into taking a boat to Spain.'

'By faking your death.'

She nodded. 'Blanks and a blood pack.'

'So why set her up? You must know *something*.'

'I don't, really,' Ana insisted. 'I was paid well not to ask – at least, I thought I was going to be. Until Lobato decided to kill me rather than give me my money,' she added bitterly. 'I just had to get her into the boat. Once she left, my job was done.'

Eddie frowned. 'Well, it worked. And now I can't get hold of her to tell her who's behind all this. Fucking great.'

'If it's worth anything, I liked Nina. I'm sorry I've put you and your daughter through this.'

'No, it's not worth anything,' he snapped.

'I *am* sorry, even if you don't believe me,' she said.

He gave a dismissive shrug. 'Well, it doesn't matter anyway. I've got what I wanted from you, Lobato's name, so now you can fuck off home and not worry about it any more.'

Ana lowered her head. 'I can't go home,' she said quietly.

'Why not?'

'If I go back to Brazil I . . . I will be dead within twenty-four hours. I am a wanted woman.'

'Criminal?'

She looked up again, fixing him with a look of defiant pride. 'No. Cop.'

He was surprised. 'You've had a bit of a career change.'

'Not through choice. I was an officer in BOPE – Batalhão de Operações Policiais Especiais, the elite police unit in Rio. I worked undercover against the drug lords. I helped take down one of the big men, but my cover was blown, and the others put a price on my head. Literally. One million American dollars, for whoever brings my head to them in a bag. And many people want that money. If I return to Brazil, I will be killed.'

'And you're not worried I might claim it, especially after what you've done to Nina?'

'I read your file. I think you are a man of honour.'

'There's a lot that's not in my file,' he said, in a tone dark enough that for a moment she looked fearful. 'But no, I'm not going to. Got bigger things to worry about. Like how the fuck to get Nina back.'

A thoughtful moment, then: 'I will help you. If I can.'

'And why would you do that?'

'Lobato betrayed me. He tried to have me killed – and you too. That makes him an enemy to both of us.'

'My enemy's enemy is my friend, right?'

'If you like. But I have been betrayed before.' An edge of pain entered her voice. 'The man who sold me out was another cop, someone I trusted. Before I left Brazil, I made him regret it.'

'You killed him?'

'No. He has a wife and children, I could not have hurt them that way. But he is not a cop any more. You cannot walk the streets when . . . you cannot walk the streets.'

Eddie decided not to enquire further. 'So you want to help me?' he asked instead. 'How?'

'I . . . I don't know,' she sighed. 'I need to think.'

'Think fast, 'cause the longer Nina's out there, the more trouble she'll be in. The woman's a catastrophe magnet.'

Ana sat upright. 'Okay. The best way to help her is to prove she had nothing to do with stealing the marker.'

'Easy. Just tell everyone you were hired to set her up.'

A mocking look. 'And then I would be arrested in her place. But if we could make *Lobato* confess . . .'

'The Dhajanis'd call off the hunt *and* you'd get your own back on him,' Eddie concluded. 'Okay, that's a good start.'

'But we would have to reach him. And he could be anywhere in the world.'

'I don't know where he is now,' Eddie said, an idea taking shape. 'But I know where he's *going* to be. He's giving a talk in Venice in a few days.'

'We might be able to catch him there, yes. But I do not know the city.'

'Olivia does. She even knows the guy in charge of the place where he's doing the talk. If he can get us inside . . .'

'Where is Olivia? And Macy, is she with her?'

'They're both in Spain. I spoke to them while you were unconscious. If we get over there, Olivia can tell us more about Venice.' He looked at his watch. 'Bit late now, though. We're better going first thing in the morning.' He gave Ana a suspicious look. 'That's if you're still *here* in the morning.'

'Where would I go?' she objected. 'I was living in Mexico, but my payment for this job was supposed to get me out of there. And I can't go back to Brazil, so I am . . .' She threw up her hands. 'Screwed.'

Eddie still had his doubts, but he nodded. 'Okay. We'll get over to Spain tomorrow, then sort out a flight to Italy. And then we'll find Lobato. You can do whatever you want to him – but only *after* Nina's off the hook. Deal?' He held out his hand.

She regarded it with uncertainty, then shook it. 'Deal.'

'All right. Hope you like Cornettos, 'cause we're going to Venice.'

17

Seville

Wearing her floppy hat over her newly cropped hair, Nina hesitantly emerged from the hostel.

There was no SWAT team waiting for her, which was a good start. She didn't know if her previous day's escapades had made the news, but if they had, the hostel's owner didn't seem to have heard.

She wasn't prepared to assume he would remain in the dark. She had brought all her belongings with her rather than leave them in the room. It was a risk carrying a priceless Atlantean artefact, but not as much as returning to the hostel to discover the cops had staked the place out.

She headed for the city centre. Not having a phone made navigation harder, but she had at least found a tourist brochure with a street plan at reception. She still didn't know exactly where to go, and it took the better part of an hour before she found what she was looking for: a large bookstore. There was a Spanish edition of the book she wanted, which would have suited her purposes just fine, but as luck would have it, there was also a selection of recent English titles – and the one in question was on display amongst them.

Treasures of Atlantis, by Nina Wilde.

She felt vaguely embarrassed about buying a copy of her own book, but of more concern was that someone might recognise her even with her changed appearance. Not only was she a public figure, but her photo was right next to the barcode.

Her concerns came to nothing, though. The young woman on the till barely gave her more than a glance. The book was rung through, along with a pocket English–Spanish dictionary. Nina had already used the latter, haltingly asking: '*Me puede decir dónde encontrar una tienda de artesanía?*'

The woman regarded her as if she had just landed from Mars, but gave her directions she eventually managed to understand. The art and crafts store was on the other side of Seville's centre; a walk away, but she had plenty of time. '*Graçias,*' she told the assistant, setting out for her next destination.

Eddie and Ana had reached a destination of their own: Algeciras in Spain.

The Yorkshireman had been mildly surprised that the Brazilian had been as good as her word and not slipped out of the house in the night. Payback was clearly a strong motivator for her. After thanking Karim and Maysa – and giving the Moroccan some money to compensate for the trashing of his restaurant – they had taken an early ferry to Tarifa, then a cab for the fourteen-mile journey to the port town.

They met Macy and Olivia in their hotel. Macy was delighted to see her father again, Olivia relieved, though her reaction to Ana was less approving. 'What is *she* doing here?' the elderly woman demanded. 'You told me she framed Nina!'

'She did,' Eddie replied as he hugged Macy. 'But Gideon Lobato paid her to do it.'

'Gideon? That appalling little man, I *knew* there was something shifty about him! Why?'

'We don't know. But we're going to make him tell us.'

Olivia gave Ana another cold look. 'We? Why would she want to help you?'

He put Macy down. 'Because rather than pay her, he sent a load of goons to whack her. She's kind of peeved.'

'Quite understandably,' Olivia replied, raising her eyebrows. 'So how are you going to make Gideon talk? Actually, I don't want to know. Rather, how are you going to find him?'

'We'll catch him at that talk in Venice.'

'Ah, at the Scuola. Of course. I can try to get Gregorio to help.'

'That's what I was hoping. If you could give him a call—'

'A call?' said Olivia. 'A personal visit would be more effective. Gregorio and I are old friends, but I won't be able to twist him around my little finger – certainly not over the telephone.'

Eddie shook his head. 'No, I need you to take Macy back to New York.'

'We can't go home without Mommy!' Macy protested.

'I want to get you somewhere safe.'

'No, no!' she cried. 'We can't go without her! You've got to find her!'

'That's what I'm going to do, love. I'll go to Italy, talk to Lobato and find out where your mum is. Then everyone'll know she's not in trouble.'

'Ah . . . about that,' said Olivia, almost with resignation, as she held up a newspaper.

Eddie couldn't translate the Spanish headline, but the two pictures of his wife, one a publicity headshot and the other security footage of her running through what looked like a museum, told the story all too clearly. 'Oh bloody hell. *Now* what's she done?'

'It would appear,' Olivia told him, 'she stole an exhibit from the archaeological museum in Seville.'

He took the paper for a closer look. Nina was holding a disc-shaped object: the second spear marker. 'You're *kidding* me. She was supposed to tell them to put it in a safe!'

'I suppose it's one way to make sure the thieves couldn't get their hands on it.'

'Great. So the Dhajanis are after her, and now the *Spanish* are after her!'

'What's going to happen to Mommy?' Macy asked, trying not to cry.

'She'll be fine,' her father insisted, hoping he was being truthful. 'Like I said, I'll make Gideon Lobato admit he's the real bad guy. And I'm sure she'll have a really, *really* good explanation for why she robbed the museum.'

'If you're going to Venice,' said Olivia firmly, 'you'll need me to come with you. No, don't argue,' she went on as he started to object. 'I know the city well; it's one of my favourite places on earth. And I'm sure I'll be able to convince Gregorio to admit us to Gideon's talk. It's the only way you'll be able to get close to him.' She squeezed Macy's hand. 'And if I'm coming to Venice, Macy will have to as well. You can hardly send her home alone.'

Eddie knew she was right; it was his only opportunity to reach Lobato. And Olivia's knowledge of the city and friendship with the head of the Scuola might be invaluable. 'Okay, we'd better get organised. Lobato's giving his talk the day after tomorrow, so we'll need somewhere to stay, and we've got to sort out flights . . .'

'Oh, ours are already arranged,' Olivia said, with a little smugness. 'The cruise company is paying for us to fly to wherever we want to go next. First class, at that. We just have to let them know the destination. I'm afraid you and Ana will have to travel in coach, though.'

'All right, you can stop enjoying yourself now,' Eddie told her. He regarded the newspaper's front page again. 'Just hope we get to Lobato before Nina steals the Spanish crown jewels!'

Further thefts were not on Nina's mind. Instead, she was examining a picture of something that had already been stolen: the first spear marker.

She was at one of Seville's newer, and stranger, attractions. Its official name was the Metropol Parasol, but locals knew it descriptively as Las Setas – 'The Mushrooms'. It was a huge, curvaceous wooden lattice straddling La Encarnación square, acting as both a viewing platform across the city for those venturing to its highest levels, and a sunshade for those below.

Nina remained on the ground, hiding in plain sight amongst the crowds sitting on steps beneath the great structure. She had bolstered her disguise with a pair of oversized sunglasses, peering over them for an unfiltered look at the photograph of the marker in her book. It had a full page to itself in the large hardback, the text on its surface clearly legible.

Best of all, it was presented at its actual size.

She glanced at her bag, fighting the urge to place the second marker on the book for comparison. But at a glance, the dimensions seemed identical.

As well as the stolen – *borrowed*, she reminded herself – artefact, the bag also contained the fruits of her trip to the craft shop. Scissors, a scalpel, foam core board, pencils, glue, a ruler, an assortment of thin dowels, and a small but powerful LED torch. She hoped that when combined, they would reveal the secret of the markers.

But first she had to find somewhere to work. Returning to the hostel was now too risky. Her theft – *removal for safe keeping!* – of the marker dominated the headlines on newspaper stands throughout the city. At least with her hair now drastically changed, the staff at her next hostel might not recognise her.

She squeezed the book into her bag, then stood. A visit to a shop selling Apple products a couple of blocks from the Parasol had given her internet access, letting her write a list of nearby hostels. She set off to check them out.

The first hostel was full, as was the second – but Nina found herself being third time lucky. Luxurious it was not, but it gave her a bed, a small table on which to work, and most importantly, privacy.

She wasted no time. First she traced the marker's outline on to the foam board and cut it out, then mutilated her book by removing the picture of the first marker. After glueing it to the circle of board, she placed it beside the second relic. Their dimensions were as close a match as she could achieve. Grateful for her recent practice in arts and crafts with Macy, she cut out spaces into which the small pegs jutting from the Atlantean artefact could fit, then placed her home-made marker back-to-back with the orichalcum disc. They slotted together perfectly.

Now came the hard part.

She needed to put a hole through her craftwork in every place where there was one on the photograph – *and* make sure the angle of each converged at the same point. It would be a tedious and fiddly job, and she had to be accurate. With no way to know which holes were important, she had to duplicate them all.

A small sigh, then she began. One of the dowels matched the holes' size, so she used the scissors to pierce the photograph and slit the card beneath before aligning the wooden rod and pushing it through. The task was harder than it looked, the polystyrene compressing rather than splitting. She couldn't risk damaging the replica, so used a pencil's point to drill through the foam before trying again. This time, it was much easier. She felt for the faint bump where the pencil's tip had pushed against the other side of the card, then cut it open and pushed the dowel through.

She held the hole up to her eye. It was ragged, but checking it against the real marker, it seemed to be at the right angle to converge with the hoop. 'One down,' she said, her sigh much bigger this time. 'Only . . . eighty to go.'

18

Venice, Italy

The island city of Venice was one of the world's most popular tourist destinations, millions drawn every year to its beauty and history. But while Eddie was fully engaged in taking in his surroundings as he, Ana, Olivia and Macy approached the Scuola Grande di San Rocco, he was anything but sightseeing. Instead he was looking for positions of advantage, cover, blind spots, escape routes . . . anything he could use in his mission.

He noticed that Ana was doing the same as the group came around the imposing Basilica dei Frari. She may have been a cop rather than a member of Brazil's armed forces, but elite units like BOPE were effectively paramilitary – and their battleground was close-quarters urban combat in Rio de Janeiro's *favela* slums. Her training was finding a new use half a world away.

'I know Nina is more interested in considerably older history,' said Olivia, admiring the buildings around the small square they had just entered, 'but she would love to see this. There's the Scuola and the church of San Rocco, the basilica, the Leonardo museum . . .'

'We can crack the da Vinci code once she's safe,' said Eddie. 'This the place?'

The elderly lady was irked by his brusqueness, but chose not to respond in kind. 'Yes, here,' she said, pointing.

The Englishman took in the structure. The Scuola Grande

was a large, elaborately detailed piece of Renaissance architecture in white stone and pale yellow marble. The main block was technically only two storeys high, but each floor was on such a monumental scale that it appeared to have been built for giants. 'The bloke in charge *is* expecting us, right?'

'*Yes*, Eddie,' she said impatiently. 'I called him while you were buying your map. Which you won't need – I told you, I know my way around Venice.'

'We'll need more than the best routes to the art galleries,' he said as they entered the towering doorway. 'But we'll see if your mate can help us first.'

'Speaking of whom . . .' said Olivia as a grey-haired man in his late sixties approached, hands out wide.

'Olivia!' he proclaimed, kissing her on both cheeks. '*Mia bella signora, come stai?*'

'I'm very well, thank you, Gregorio,' she replied. 'And you?'

He patted his stomach through his well-tailored suit. 'Very good! I have lost fifteen kilograms. I became vegetarian, you know. It is not fashionable in Italy, but after my heart attack, I decided to leave the fashion to my wife.'

'And how *is* Mia?'

'She is good, thank you. Never puts on a gram, whatever she eats. And she likes meat too much to become vegetarian. I have tried to convince her, but she is my wife – she does not listen to me.'

'Oh, trust me, Gregorio,' said Olivia, smiling. 'A wife *always* listens to her husband – so she can remind him of something embarrassing he said when it best suits her.'

He laughed. 'Very true. You have brought friends?'

'Family, actually. My great-granddaughter, Macy, and her father, Eddie Chase. And his colleague, Ana. Everyone, this is Dr Gregorio Pinto, the Guardian Grando of San Rocco.'

'*Ah, bella, bella!*' said Pinto, crouching to greet Macy. 'A *great-*

granddaughter? I did not even know you had a granddaughter!'

'We were estranged – it's a long story. But we found each other while I still had time.'

The Italian nodded. 'If you do not have your family, then what *do* you have?' He straightened, kissing Ana's hand and shaking Eddie's. 'So, to what do I owe the pleasure?'

'We're staying in Venice for a few days, and I wanted to see you, of course,' Olivia told him. 'But I do have an ulterior motive, naturally.'

'Naturally,' Pinto echoed with a smile. 'I have known Olivia for forty years,' he said to Eddie. 'She is a most remarkable woman. But there is always a quid pro quo.' Eddie's only reply was a knowing smile of his own. Pinto turned back to Olivia. 'What can I do for you?'

'I believe Gideon Lobato is giving a talk here the day after tomorrow?'

The Italian nodded. 'About climate change – a subject close to the hearts of everyone in Venice.'

'I've met him several times; we had dinner a couple of days ago, in fact. A fascinating man. I'd love to continue our conversation, and I know your speakers always meet the guests afterwards.'

'Usually, yes. But Mr Lobato is a special case.' Pinto gave her a conspiratorial smile. 'He does not like . . . people.'

'Oh, I know. He's very reserved. But I would still like to see him again. If you could arrange it, of course.'

'All the seats are taken, but . . . well, I am sure I can do something for you. Quid pro quo.'

'A donation to the Scuola?'

'But of course. Tintorettos do not restore themselves.'

'We know each other so well, don't we?' They both laughed. 'Would a thousand dollars be sufficient?'

'More than enough. Come, we can talk in my office.'

Pinto led the way through the museum, taking them up a flight of stairs and through high-ceilinged halls lined with paintings. A uniformed security guard stood beside a door, both watching the exhibits and ensuring that members of the public did not enter the Scuola's private areas. He stood aside deferentially as Pinto and his guests went through.

A short hall beyond led to a staircase to floors above and below; the museum had a wing at the rear that stood taller than its grand facade. Eddie looked down the stairwell. At the bottom was an old wooden door with a heavy bolt. 'Is that a cellar?' he asked. 'Wouldn't have thought anywhere in Venice would be below ground level.'

'It is a cellar, yes,' Pinto replied. 'But we do not use it any more; it is flooded. The canals were lower when the Scuola was built. Another result of climate change – Mr Lobato is right that we need to act before it is too late.'

'Hope you've got good damp-proofing.' Eddie mentally filed away the information as they headed to the top floor.

Pinto brought them down a hallway to another door, unlocking it and ushering everyone inside. His office was at the Scuola's rear, overlooking a little piazza at the intersection of two canals. The red rooftops of Venice spread out beyond the tall windows, the lowering sun casting a gorgeous orange glow over the city. 'That is beautiful,' said Ana, entranced.

'I am very lucky to work here, yes,' said Pinto. 'Please, sit.' He helped Olivia into a comfortable armchair before sitting behind a heavy old desk of dark oak, tapping at the incongruously modern computer upon it. Eddie, Macy and Ana found places on a big chaise longue. 'Now, let me look at the guest list. Somebody may have cancelled, but if they have not, I will just put four extra chairs in the hall.'

'That's okay, you'll only need two,' said Eddie. 'I won't be able to make it. Nor will Ana.' The Brazilian gave him a questioning look, but said nothing, realising he was already devising a plan.

Macy was puzzled. 'Why aren't you coming, Daddy?'

'Me and Ana are going to help your mum, remember?' He put emphasis on the last word, hoping his daughter would take the hint.

'Okay . . .' said the little girl, still confused, but to Eddie's relief she didn't question him further.

Pinto was too involved with the computer to pick up on the unspoken. 'Ah! You are in luck, Olivia. Someone cannot attend, so there will be seats. I will add you and Macy to the guest list. Now,' he indicated the piazza below, 'Mr Lobato will be arriving by boat; will you be coming by water taxi, or on foot? We need to know so we can receive you.'

Macy excitedly answered for her great-grandmother. 'Water taxi! Can we, can we?'

Olivia caught Eddie's subtle shake of the head. 'No, Macy. It'll take longer than walking.' Macy huffed.

Pinto chuckled. 'You are stronger than me. I have four children, nine grandchildren and now two *great*-grandchildren, and still I have not learned how to say no to them.' He typed, then leaned back. 'There, everything is done.'

'Thank you so much, Gregorio.'

'It is my pleasure. Now, will you be able to stay for a little while? It has been a long time since we last had a chat.'

'You stay and catch up with your friend, Olivia,' said Eddie. 'Me and Ana need to sort something out. We'll meet you back at the hotel.'

'I'd love to stay, of course,' Olivia said to Pinto, covering her mild irritation at being told what to do. 'As long as you have some of that marvellous Liberica coffee you had when I was here last.'

'I rarely drink anything else,' the Italian replied. 'Well, except wine!'

She turned to Macy. 'Would you like to stay with me while your father and his friend do what they need to do?'

This time, the little girl didn't take the hint. 'No thank you, Grams. I want to go with Daddy.'

'That's okay,' Eddie said. 'She can come with us.' He stood, Ana and Macy doing the same. 'Have fun, Olivia.'

'I will show you downstairs,' said Pinto.

'I remember the way,' the Englishman quickly replied. 'Don't get Olivia too drunk!'

The Italian laughed, though Olivia was less amused. Eddie thanked him, then opened the door, glancing at its latch plate before exiting.

'You have thought of something?' said Ana as they descended the stairs.

'Maybe. But I'll need to check outside first.' They reached the floor on which they had entered the stairwell, but Eddie – after checking for security cameras – waved for Macy and Ana to stay put before hurrying to the foot of the steps.

The cellar door was old, thick wood, a faint scent of dampness coming from beyond. Drains in the floor suggested that the water in the canal outside had been known to make an entrance. He cautiously pulled the chest-height bolt. It was stiff, from both lack of use and the door's weight holding it in place, forcing him to apply more effort to pop it free. He winced as a loud *clack* echoed up the stairwell, then quickly opened the door.

The cellar beyond was dark, but he could see water gently shimmering within. He used his phone to take a flash photo, then switched on its torch. The ceiling was low, heavy beams stretching between carved stone pillars. He tilted the light down. Steps disappeared into the green water. Algae, broken wood and floating rubbish had collected in the corners. That meant there was a gap somewhere large enough for the trash to have come in . . .

On the sunken chamber's far side, just below the surface, was a faint rectangle of greenish light – an opening to the canal. He estimated its size, then quickly closed the door and rasped the bolt back into place. 'Okay, done,' he said, returning to Ana and Macy. 'Let's go, quick.'

'What did you find?' Ana asked.

'A way in – maybe. I'll need to check outside.' He opened the door into the gallery, the guard giving them a sidelong look as they exited.

'What are you doing, Daddy?' Macy asked. 'You're acting all weird.'

'I'm trying to help your mum,' he told her. 'The man I need to talk to, Mr Lobato? He'll be here in a couple of nights, and it's the only chance I'll have to talk to him. But he won't want to tell me anything, so I'll have to *make* him.'

She became unusually still. 'Is it going to be like when you rescued me from that man in England?'

'I really hope not.' The man responsible for the destruction of Big Ben had tried to take revenge on Eddie and Nina for exposing the attempted coup by kidnapping their daughter. Eddie had hoped Macy's subconscious had suppressed the memories of the traumatic event, but clearly she recalled it all too well. 'But I'll do whatever I have to do to help your mum.'

Macy looked up at him, wide-eyed but determined. To Eddie, she had never looked more like Nina. 'So will I. I want her back.'

'Me too, love. Me too.' He stopped in the middle of the gallery to hug her, not caring what the patrons thought. 'And maybe you *can* help.'

'How?'

'I'm not sure yet, but . . .' He kissed her, then straightened up. 'Let's have a look outside.'

The trio left the Scuola, Eddie leading them around its side to the canal. A small bridge just east of the museum crossed the narrow waterway, while a walkway led under high marble arches to the piazza he had seen from Pinto's office. He followed the latter route to the canal intersection, looking up at the Scuola's rear wing. Pinto's windows were a good fifty feet above.

He turned to survey the canals. Like most of Venice's waterways, they were directly abutted by buildings. Several apartment windows, he noticed, bore signs saying *Affittasi* – 'For Rent'. He had seen multilingual posters throughout the city railing against the plague of foreign speculators snapping up properties to turn into lucrative tourist lets, pricing Venetians out of their own city. While he sympathised with the locals, an unoccupied flat could be very useful.

But first he needed to find the opening he had seen in the cellar. 'Wait here,' he said, then went down a flight of stone steps to the water.

'What are you doing?' Ana asked as he leaned out to look along the canal's edge.

'There was a hole in the cellar wall. I'm trying to find it.' There: a lintel just visible beneath the surface. He went to a spot above it, rolling up his left sleeve before reaching into the water.

He found the opening's edge. Ignoring the curious looks of passers-by, he stretched further to feel inside. If there was a cast-iron grille blocking it, he could forget his idea before it had even fully formed . . .

His fingertips brushed wire. Chain-link, encrusted with muck. He pushed at it. The barrier flexed, but didn't give way.

'Daddy?' Macy asked. 'What have you found?'

'What I was looking for – I hope,' he said, swishing his hand to wash off the filth before withdrawing. He shook water from his arm, but left his sleeve rolled up. 'And the next thing I need to look for is somewhere with very hot water and loads of soap.'

'Why?' said Ana.

'Because Venice might *look* beautiful, but it doesn't *smell* beautiful, especially that close to the water. This canal's basically a big sewer!'

Macy wrinkled her nose and retreated from him. 'Daddy, I love you, but . . . when we walk back to the hotel? I don't want to hold your hand.'

19

Seville

Nina's estimate that there were another eighty holes in her replica of the spear marker was incorrect. It was only seventy-seven more, but the saving did not lessen her curses against the artefact's creators.

But now it was done. The question was: would it work?

She picked up the authentic marker and placed her newly made duplicate of its sibling against its back, the pegs in the former slotting into the holes in the latter, then held them both up to the light.

As she had expected, many of the openings in the golden surface were now blocked by the other disc behind it. Her painstaking, tedious work hadn't been for nothing; the angles of the holes pushed through the foam board did indeed align with those in the metal.

Now it was time to test her theory.

She picked up the flashlight and switched it on, then turned off the room's lights. Raising the two discs, she placed the brilliant little torch's head inside the metal hoop and aimed her apparatus at the wall.

A stellar display swept into view before her. Roughly a third of the holes had aligned to let light through – and she immediately saw that the points were decidedly organised. No random spatterings of stars arranged by human imagination into constellations here; there was a clear pattern, not quite repeating but certainly forming very similar blocks.

Not a star map, then, like the one she had used to locate the lost Pyramid of Osiris in Egypt. The heavens were not so regimented. So what did it mean?

Even as she asked herself the question, she realised the pattern was familiar. She had seen it, or something very similar, before. But where?

Holding the discs and flashlight together, she lay back on the bed and brought the display up to the ceiling. The Dendera Zodiac in the Louvre pointing the way to the pyramid had also been overhead – somehow there was a connection. Constellations on the ceiling, *patterns* on the ceiling . . .

She sprang back upright. 'Duh! Of *course!*'

Her first thought was to grab her phone, but that was no longer an option. She would have to find an internet café to confirm her revelation.

It was too late to search for one now, though. And she was tired, energy reserves depleted. She needed to sleep.

In the morning, she would check out her theory. One that she was already convinced was right.

Eddie heard a gentle tap at his hotel room's door. Expecting Olivia, he was slightly surprised to find Ana outside. 'Yeah?'

'Is it okay to talk?' asked the Brazilian.

'If you keep it down. Macy's just gone to sleep. Come in.' She entered, stopping in the short hallway as he closed the door. 'What did you want to talk about?'

'At the gallery, you seemed to have a plan. What is it?'

'I haven't fully worked it out yet, but I know it's not something I can do on my own – or even with the two of us together. So I've called some mates. Waiting to hear back how many of 'em might be able to help out.'

'You have friends who would drop everything to fly around the world to help you?'

'I'd do the same for them – I've *done* it for them. You back up your friends, they'll have your back when you need it.'

She sighed despondently. 'You have better friends than me.'

'You haven't got anyone you can rely on?'

'No. Since I left Brazil, I have been on my own. I have made contacts, acquaintances . . . but not friends.' She gave him a questioning look. 'Do you think I am attractive?'

'Not my place to say,' Eddie replied, uncomfortable – especially as she was almost face-to-face with him in the narrow hall. 'I'm married.'

A small laugh. 'Do not worry, you are not my type.'

'Why, what's wrong with me?' he said with mock offence.

'I like men who are my age. And have hair.'

'Tchah!'

She smiled, briefly amused before becoming serious once more. 'Many men do find me attractive. And they all think that because I am alone, and cannot return home, they can . . . take advantage. A favour for a favour – I am sure you can guess the kind they have in mind.'

'I can imagine, yeah.'

'I have been a freelancer for two years now, and I am good at what I do. But Lobato was the only man apart from you who was not . . . interested in me. Even though I am a professional, everyone thinks I am just – I do not know!' Anger entered her voice. 'A dumb girl, a whore. A plaything who is only there to please them.'

'After seeing you fight in the restaurant, I know you can hold your own,' the Englishman assured her.

Despondency returned. 'But you still had to save me.'

'Nobody can do everything on their own. Not even me – I would've been dead if not for you. And if the only people you're

meeting are arseholes, you need to meet some different people.'
He paused, then: 'Tell you what. When we're done, if you want
to stay in this line of work, I'll put you in touch with some
friends who can find you jobs. Ones where you won't be framing
innocent women.'

She nodded, taking his point. 'Thank you. But why would
you do that for me?'

'Because I'm *not* an arsehole. Well, I have my moments, but
generally I'm pretty clean.'

That elicited a genuine laugh, which she stifled so as not to
wake Macy. 'You know, you are not what I expected from your
file.'

'No? What did you expect?'

'Someone more . . .' She tried to think of the best English
word. 'More *grim*. You have been through so much, but you are
still . . . silly.'

'Being silly's how I stay sane,' said the Yorkshireman, smiling.
'I leave the grim Growly McTangodown stuff to Chris Ryan and
Andy McNab.'

She seemed about to say more, but his phone buzzed. He
checked the screen, then answered. 'Matt? Yeah, go ahead,
Macy's asleep.' He listened, then gave Ana a thumbs-up. 'You're
in? Fantastic. Reckon you'll be able to get here tomorrow? Yeah,
I know – good job you're in the States rather than Australia.
Have you got a gadget like the one I asked about? If there's one
thing Venice is famous for, it's water!' He shared a laugh with
the man on the other end of the line. 'Okay, call me when you
get here. Thanks, mate.'

'The first member of your team?' Ana asked as he disconnected.

'Second including you,' he replied. 'Although third including
Olivia . . . and fourth with Macy.'

She looked towards the little girl's bed. 'You are going to

bring your daughter into this?' There was both disbelief and disapproval in her words.

'I'm not going to put her in any kind of danger,' Eddie insisted. 'But she's got one advantage over everyone else I know.'

'What?'

'She's a seven-year-old girl.' He grinned, letting her try to puzzle out his meaning. 'Anyway, it's late, and we'll be doing a lot of walking tomorrow. So I'll see you in the morning.'

'All right. I will see you then.' She exited.

Eddie looked back at his phone. He had called almost thirty people all around the globe, but how many more would be able to respond was another matter. All he could do was wait and see.

And hope they could come up with a plan to snatch Gideon Lobato out from under the noses of his bodyguards.

20

Seville

The next morning was an exercise in frustration for Nina. Despite being a major city, Seville still worked on Spanish time: nowhere offering internet access opened until at least ten. 'Finally!' she grumbled as a café belatedly unlocked its doors. 'You would have opened at six in New York!'

But her annoyance quickly faded once she began her search. The subject was another Spanish city: Granada, about a hundred and fifty miles to the east. Like Seville, it was home to ancient archaeological sites, some dating back over seven thousand years, but she was looking for something considerably more recent.

It was still not a modern site, though. The Alhambra was a thirteenth-century Moorish palace complex, built on a hilltop over the ruins of much older forts from Roman times, and even earlier. It was one of Spain's greatest historical treasures – and if Nina was right, it held a secret nobody had ever even suspected.

A few quick refinements of her search terms brought up a collection of photographs. She was interested in one particular part of the palace – the Salón de los Embajadores, the Hall of the Ambassadors. Despite its name, it was not an embassy. Rather, it was a throne room, a place to impress diplomats and potentates visiting the Sultan of Granada with its magnificence.

Only one part of the room currently concerned her, however. The photos before her were all of its ceiling. It was a wonder in both size and beauty, the entire inner surface of the dome capping the hall decorated with elaborate clusters of stars. It was not an astronomical map; the constellations were too regular, forming repeating patterns across the wooden sky. The academic consensus was that it represented the Seven Heavens of Islam, a small hole in the centre revealing further stars beyond that were assumed to be Paradise. Certainly that was what all the guidebooks maintained.

But there could be more to it than that.

The repetition of the patterns was what had led Nina to connect the Hall of the Ambassadors and the stars revealed by the combined parts of the spear marker. Her frustration returned; she had no way to directly compare the two with her limited resources.

She was certain her theory was correct, though. The Alhambra might be a product of the Middle Ages, but the similarities between the throne room's ceiling and what she had seen in her hotel room couldn't be a coincidence. Somehow the two were linked – and that link might tell her the locations of the mysterious spearheads.

So how could she *test* her theory?

The answer was so stunningly obvious that she almost blurted it out, before remembering she was in a public place. Instead she carried out another search.

The new subject: *bus times from Seville to Granada.*

Eddie's day had also started early. His mission was reconnaissance, walking with Ana and Macy through Venice's narrow, twisting streets with Olivia as his guide. They had started from the Scuola Grande di San Rocco, making their way eastwards in a ragged zigzag. Eddie was paying particular attention to the canals, as the only way to travel with any speed through the labyrinthine city was by water, but he was also checking the bridges and piazzas. It wouldn't be enough merely to get clear of the Scuola; they needed somewhere to *go* . . .

They entered St Mark's Square. The long, arched marble arcades of the Procuratie flanking the expanse led their eyes to the Campanile di San Marco directly ahead, the red-brick bell tower the tallest structure in Venice. Beyond it stood the opulent domes and spires of St Mark's Cathedral. The great space was already filled with sightseers, selfie sticks waving in the air like flags. 'Isn't this magnificent?' proclaimed Olivia.

Eddie spotted something in the square's north-eastern corner. 'Ay up,' he said, pointing out a circle of blue glass set into a tall building. 'I know what that is – the Clock Tower of St Mark's. It's an astronomical clock.'

Olivia was impressed. 'It is indeed. Well done, Eddie. I think Nina must finally be rubbing off on you.'

A cheeky grin crept on to his face. 'James Bond threw a villain through it in the film *Moonraker*.'

Now she was less so. 'What?'

'That's what Dan Brown said about it in *Inferno*. Very educational.'

She shook her head. 'Macy, I hope you develop a better taste in literature than your father.'

'Nowt wrong with a book with a boat chase on the cover,' Eddie chuckled. 'How do we get to the water from here?'

'Right, past the Campanile,' Olivia told him. 'Although I'm not sure it'll be what you're looking for. That said, I'm not sure what you *are* looking for.'

'I need somewhere I can get out of a boat, quickly,' he explained. 'But it also needs to be somewhere anyone following me *can't* do it so fast, to give me time to get clear. Not sure how I'm going to manage it, but I'll know the right place when I see it.'

They rounded the Campanile into the piazza's southern leg, where the literally palatial Palazzo Ducale, the home of the

Doges, the former rulers of Venice, adjoined the cathedral. Beyond it was the great tidal lagoon from which the archipelago rose. The three female members of the group slowed to take in the wonder of their surroundings, but Eddie was concerned only with the water's edge. 'Well, that's not what I was after,' he complained as they approached it.

Olivia regarded the jetties and bobbing boats. 'What were you expecting? A convenient ramp?'

'Actually, yeah. Roger Moore drove right up one in his hover-gondola. Somewhere around here.' He looked along the quayside, but saw only narrow steps set into the stone.

'I hate to shatter your illusions, Eddie, but the James Bond movies are not documentaries.'

'You mean there *aren't* really hover-gondolas? Tchah! I've been lied to.'

'Movies aren't real, Daddy,' said Macy with a smile. 'You said that to me on the ship.'

'Always good to have my words chucked back at me by a seven-year-old,' Eddie said, laughing. 'Still got to find somewhere, though.' He opened his map. 'Are there any dead-end canals coming off the main one?'

He had asked the question almost rhetorically, but Olivia gave him an answer. 'Off the Grand Canal? Yes, quite a few; there's one not far from here, near the Venetian Institute.'

'Won't going down a dead end mean you are trapped?' said Ana.

'Depends how it ends,' the Yorkshireman replied. He found a truncated blue line on the map to the left of their position. 'Is that it?'

Olivia nodded. 'Yes. It's a little convoluted to reach from here, but I know the way.'

'We'll have a look. Are you okay, by the way? To walk, I mean.'

The old woman was using her cane, but the suggestion that she was not up to the challenge prompted a stern look at her grandson-in-law. 'Of course I am.'

'Just checking. So where do we go?'

'This way.' She started west along the waterfront.

Nina had also gone west, returning to the Plaza de Armas bus terminal. Buses to Granada were both cheap and relatively frequent. She bought a ticket, then found a seat to wait.

The spear marker was in her bag, along with her other belongings. She had protected the cardboard replica of the other disc, further desecrating her book – an act that caused a surprising amount of mental anguish – by tearing off its hardback covers and using them to sandwich her creation. She checked her watch. Twenty minutes before departure.

She passed the time by people-watching. Nobody paid her any attention. She still didn't feel safe, but once she left Seville, things should get easier. No one knew she was going to Granada, and if the local cops didn't find her in the next fifteen minutes, the chances of her getting caught would drop dramatically.

Ten minutes to go; five. Her bus pulled up. A quick check for police or security guards, then she joined the boarding passengers. An overweight, sour-faced woman shoved past her. Nina shot her a dirty look, checking that nothing in her bag had been damaged. She let the others on first, then found a seat behind the pushy woman.

More minutes passed, then the engine started. Nina waited impatiently for the bus to move off. A glance towards the main entrance for patrolling cops—

Her blood froze.

Agreste.

She saw the Frenchman through gaps in the milling crowd.

He was stationary, looking at something in his hand. Nina ducked lower before he could spot her.

How the hell had he found her? The only person she had told about coming to Seville was Eddie, and even if someone had eavesdropped on their phone call, the odds of Agreste turning up at the bus station at the exact time she was leaving the city were astronomical.

He had known exactly where she was. But *how*?

The bus started to pull out, but Nina's panic didn't subside. If Ana's killer had tracked her this far, he could follow her to Granada too . . .

The rational part of her mind rose through her fear. Agreste *had* tracked her, literally. The former detective was holding a smartphone, gaze fixed on its screen as he panned it from side to side. Suddenly his gaze snapped towards the departing bus.

Nina felt another shot of terror – had he spotted her? – but he was unable to see its passengers through the grubby windows. He glanced back at the phone as if to confirm something before watching it drive to the terminal's exit.

He knew she was aboard.

She looked down at her bag with fearful suspicion. Something inside had given away her location.

She carefully took out her belongings. It couldn't be anything she had picked up since leaving the *Atlantia*, so she put aside the ruined book, then used her hat to conceal the marker from her fellow passengers. What was left?

She still had some of Ana's euros. She held each note up to the window. Watermarks showed through, but none revealed anything that might be a tracking device.

It occurred that she didn't even know what a modern tracking device looked like. Probably not a black box with a flashing red light, she decided. For anything to have gone unnoticed, it would have to be small . . .

Small and *flat*. She eyed her passport. It was the one essential thing she needed to keep with her at all times. She carefully opened it. Her faintly embarrassing dead-eyed photo greeted her, reminding her how much she missed her long red hair. She thumbed through the little book for anything that didn't belong—

It was so inconspicuous she almost missed it.

Tucked between two of the pages was a square of transparent plastic, little larger than a postage stamp. Only when she tilted the passport to catch the light did she see a thin octagonal pattern of silvery metal.

She took hold of the plastic. It had been fixed in place with a spot of glue. With great care, she worked it loose and held it up to the window. Details became visible: a little chip and a minuscule battery, the GPS antenna spiralling around them.

Nina was almost impressed. The gadget was tiny, unobtrusive . . . yet it had brought Agreste right to her. And he now knew where she was going.

She had one advantage: he didn't know she had found the tracker. How could she make best use of that fact?

She had three hours to come up with an answer.

Eddie surveyed the small piazza of Campo Santo Stefano. He was less than half a mile from St Mark's, but the atmosphere was completely different. It had a more laid-back, youthful feel, and was considerably less busy.

That suited his purposes. He suspected he would make a spectacular entrance, and the fewer people there were in the piazza, the less likely anyone was to get hurt.

He went to the southern end and regarded a short, narrow stretch of canal. It ran alongside the Palazzo Cavalli-Franchetti, home of the Venetian Institute, for about a hundred metres. The little branch stopped at a wall below him, a couple of small boats moored to one side.

Something else caught his eye. Several large planks were stacked against the side wall, held fast by a grimy length of rope. From the accumulated sludge, it seemed they had been there for a while.

He made another mental note, then looked back at his companions. 'This might work. We'll see if there's anywhere else that's as good, but—'

He was cut off by his daughter. 'Daddy, my feet hurt,' Macy protested. 'I don't want to walk any more.'

'We *could* use a break,' Olivia added, leaning on her cane. 'Drink, food – you know, the essentials for ordinary people rather than SAS supermen.'

Eddie looked to Ana. 'You an' all?'

'I *am* quite thirsty,' she admitted.

'Bunch of wimps,' he said, grinning. 'All right, we'll find a café.'

They did not have to go far; the piazza was home to several. While they were refreshing themselves, Eddie had a phone call – one he had been particularly hoping for. 'Jared, hi.'

'I'm in,' came the simple reply.

'No small talk?'

Mocking amusement entered the other man's voice. 'You're old, so I thought you wouldn't want me to waste any of your precious remaining time.'

'Funny fu . . . dge-eater,' Eddie said, aware that Macy and Olivia were right beside him. 'When can you get here?'

'I'll be in Venice by eight o'clock tonight.'

'No trouble getting out of work?'

'I told my superiors I wanted to help you and Nina, and they said: what do you need? You did the Mossad a huge favour when you uncovered that little nest of Nazis, and we don't forget things like that. We help our friends – and I mean that personally as well as professionally.'

'I don't need to call in the whole Mossad on this, but thanks. See you soon.'

'You too, old man.'

Ana had heard Eddie's half of the conversation. 'Did you say the Mossad?'

'You know someone in the Israeli secret service?' asked Olivia.

'Friends in low places,' the Yorkshireman said. 'But yeah. He's someone I'd really hoped could help out. I think I've got enough people now to do what we need to do.' He looked back at the canal. 'Just as soon as I work out what that *is* . . .'

21

Granada, Spain

Under normal circumstances, Nina would have found the bus ride to Granada rather dull; the landscape, while pretty enough, was mostly flat farmland, and it wasn't until the ranges of the Sierra Nevada began to rise to the east that the scenery became worthy of any attention.

However, she spent the entire trip on a knife-edge of tension. She knew Agreste was trailing her. He wouldn't even need the tracker; he could just follow the bus. Somehow, she had to lose him.

Her window of opportunity would be limited. And she didn't know Granada at all – she would have to wing it with every step.

She made the most of the last few minutes of the journey to get a sense of her surroundings. Granada was an ancient city, but the bus terminal was in a relatively new part of town. Broad streets laid out in a grid, anonymous apartment blocks, a tram system, the ubiquitous McDonald's restaurants and Aldi supermarkets: it could have been anywhere in the world.

It was the older and probably more characterful section she was interested in, though first she had to get there – without Ana's killer catching her. But a plan was forming as the bus approached the terminal. After discovering the tracker, she had thoroughly searched all her other belongings to make sure Agreste hadn't planted a backup. He hadn't. So the first step was to get rid of the little device, in such a way that he didn't immediately realise . . .

The bus drove past a long modern building that she saw was her destination, then turned down a side street. There was a parking lot outside the terminal. If Agreste was following closely, he would probably stop there to watch for her as she emerged from the main entrance – the *only* entrance, as far as she could tell. She would have to find another escape route.

Another turn, and the bus went through a gate into the terminal proper. Nina held her bag with her left hand and the tracker in the other. She shuffled to the side of her seat, ready to move.

The bus pulled into a bay. The impatient woman in front of Nina was on her feet before the doors opened. Nina was right behind her. The two women bumped together. The Spaniard gave her an affronted scowl, then marched down the aisle. Nina followed, right hand now empty.

The Spanish woman had obviously made the journey before, and turned straight towards the exit. Nina quickly went the other way, ducking between parked buses. Agreste might be out of his car – she had to move fast.

She emerged from beneath the sunshade covering the bays. The entrance through which her bus had come was to the left, about ninety yards away; the exit was at the terminal's opposite end, slightly closer. Gripping the bag, she ran for it.

A man shouted in Spanish, waving for her to return to the passenger area, but she ignored him. A bus started to reverse out ahead of her. She swerved around it, sprinting for the exit—

Made it. A glance back. The shouting man was behind the moving bus, not following her.

Nor was anyone else. This was her chance.

She went left, hurrying across a street and through a small tree-lined plaza before taking a side road between some apartment blocks. The more buildings she could put between herself and the bus terminal, the less chance Agreste had of picking up her trail. Around a corner, down to a large traffic circle, then she turned again, running south-east. Doubling back was far from an original tactic, but she hoped it would confuse her pursuer long enough for her to lose him.

Another look back. No sign of Agreste. She continued past more apartment blocks to cross a street that led back to the bus station. The Frenchman was still not in sight. She reached the other side, then ran into a housing development, disparately designed properties piled together. She reached an empty plot, checking that nobody was watching before scaling a wall.

Beyond was a vacant lot, poles and orange tape marking where construction of another house would soon start, but for now there was nothing ahead but trees. Nina kept moving, before long reaching an RV park. She followed a road past the camper vans back to the main street. The bus terminal was a block away, to her left. She went right, heading for a shopping mall.

Agreste was still not in sight. She slowed to regain her breath.

She needed to get clear, in case the Frenchman started searching the surrounding streets once he realised the tracker was no longer on his target, but she needed food and water – and the mall would probably sell something else she needed. A last check, then she made her way to the shopping complex.

A couple of hours later, she had reached the heart of Granada. This was more what she had expected: narrow streets, old buildings, grand civic structures and churches.

The grandest of all was also the hardest to reach. The Alhambra had been built on a hilltop, but what the photographs hadn't shown was just how steep that hill was in reality. Legs aching, she finally reached the ticket office at the eastern end of the old fortress.

The Hall of the Ambassadors was in the section known as the Nazrid Palaces. With a certain inevitability, this was both the most popular and the most expensive part to visit. The only way to enter was as part of a guided tour with an assigned time slot. Resigning herself to acting like a tourist rather than an archaeologist, she bought a ticket, then made her way to her group's meeting point.

A guide eventually assembled everyone and led them through a gate. Nina hung back at the rear, using her hat and sunglasses to cover her features, and forcing herself not to correct the hapless man on historical minutiae as the tour progressed.

The Alhambra was an odd mix of eras and religions. Its history was predominantly Islamic, Spain ruled for centuries by the Moors before the Christian Reconquistas gradually drove them out to leave the Nasrid Emirate of Granada as the sole remaining island of Muslim rule on the Iberian peninsula. Once the last sultan finally surrendered in 1492 – a turning point in Western history, Nina mused, the same year that Christopher Columbus first reached the Americas – the Spanish royals wasted no time in stamping their own identity upon the fortress, destroying many priceless carvings and artworks in the process.

While the Reconquistas had worked hard to remove the touch of Islam from the Alhambra, some parts had been too remarkable even for them to desecrate. The sultan's palace had largely been left intact, albeit more for its monetary than cultural value. As a result, the deeper the tour group went into the complex of buildings, the more overtly Islamic the decorations became. Mosaics of stars adorned the walls, tiles bore elaborate Arabic inscriptions praising God or reciting poetry, and the ceilings were panelled in wood, exquisite carvings cut into the centuries-old timber.

The group made its way through a marble-paved courtyard to the great red block of the Torre de Comares. The guide halted outside and began a reverent spiel, but by now Nina was too impatient to listen. She slipped through the broad arched doorway and finally entered the Hall of the Ambassadors.

It was a large square room, occupying almost all of the tower's base. In its heyday, it would have been an explosion of colour and finery, the sultan showing off his wealth in a most extravagant manner. The silk curtains were long gone, the paint faded from the walls, but the stucco carvings were still there, still magnificent.

She raised her gaze higher. A row of windows ran around the upper walls, countless tiny squares of glass worked into elaborate filigree latticeworks. Beyond them, over fifty feet above her head, was what she had come to see.

Even half shrouded in shadow, the ceiling of the Hall of the Ambassadors was a marvel. Constellations of hundreds of precisely carved suns made of golden wood were set into the darker cedar of the firmament: the Seven Heavens of Islamic lore.

Nina was only interested in something very much of the physical world. But the rest of the tour group were now filing into the chamber. How could she test her theory without attracting attention?

She would have to wait until they left. Their guide had already shown himself lax at keeping track of his charges, needing to be told more than once that people had fallen behind the main group rather than counting for himself. If she hung back, she might have just enough time to get the room to herself before the next group arrived – or anyone in her own noticed she was missing. She took out a digital camera she had risked using her credit card to buy at the mall, and took pictures of the ceiling.

The tour guide pottered about, taking questions and delivering facts and figures about the hall. Finally he called for everyone to leave. Nina waited for her companions to filter out, standing just inside the door as if taking a final picture. The last tourists, an elderly Asian couple, passed—

She rushed into action, hurrying to the little square of tiles marking the room's exact centre, taking out the Atlantean artefact and placing it on the floor. Next, she removed the cardboard disc from her book's covers, then found the flashlight. Hopefully that would be all she needed.

If it wasn't, she was screwed.

She stood the real marker on its extended arm and fitted her home-made counterpart to its upper surface, then put the flashlight into the metal hoop. A moment of concern; its length forced the lens to stand a couple of inches proud of the floor. If the light source was meant to be flush with the hoop, the difference could throw off the result.

No choice now. Another tour group was entering the courtyard.

She switched on the flashlight and looked up.

What she saw almost made her gasp. She had been right. The pattern produced by combining the two markers was indeed connected to the image of the heavens, the repeating clusters of soft light closely matching the stars set into the ceiling. How, she didn't know, but before she could figure it out, she had to find out exactly *which* points were important.

She had not yet aligned the marker to any particular direction, so while the pattern she had created was similar to the carved stars, the lights did not correspond to any of them. She rotated the relic. The points rolled around the Seventh Heaven. Some passed over the wooden suns, but no deeper meaning leapt out at her . . .

Wait—

The discs fitted together in one specific way, and knowing the Atlanteans, it was unlikely to have been chosen at random. She looked at the orichalcum disc's arm. Maybe it wasn't just a spacer – it might also be a *pointer*. But to what?

The next tour group was getting closer. She was running out of time. Where to aim the marker?

The sultan's throne had long since disappeared, along with the rest of the chamber's furnishings, but she knew where it had been: directly opposite the main entrance, so he could watch his visitors approach. She turned the marker to align the arm with the space where he had once sat, then looked up again.

Disappointment filled her. Very few of the spots of light touched the ceiling's stars. She had been wrong.

Or had she?

Some *would* align – if they all moved slightly inwards towards the centre. The flashlight's lens was in the wrong position, higher than it should be. She couldn't push the torch down into the stone floor to meet the hoop . . . but she could raise the hoop to meet it.

The next tour leader was approaching the entrance. *Work fast, Wilde—*

She lifted the marker slightly, then raised her eyes once more – and this time she did let out a gasp.

The points of light were now sharper, the beams radiating from the flashlight passing cleanly through the angled holes. They didn't quite align with the stars, but were close enough for Nina to see that, had the flashlight been flush with the floor, they would indeed have matched perfectly.

No time to muse on their meaning. All she could do was grab the camera and take a couple of pictures, then shove the marker back into her bag just before the tourists arrived.

The guide gave her a suspicious look: visitors were not supposed to wander the Nazrid Palaces unattended. 'Sorry, sorry,' Nina said with a breathlessness that was not entirely feigned. 'Just taking a last photo!' She closed the bag and scurried for the exit.

Back in the courtyard, she saw that her own tour guide had

belatedly realised his party was one short and come back to find her. 'I'm here, I'm here!' she called out. 'Had to change my camera battery.' He rolled his eyes and gestured for her to keep up.

The tour continued, but Nina was no longer paying attention. Her mind was now fully occupied. Only some of the lights she had cast aligned with the carved stars above, which meant the pattern they formed had to be significant. When the group stopped in the next room, she took out her camera to check the pictures on its little screen.

Their quality was poor, but clear enough for her to make out. Twelve of the stars corresponded to the points projected through the marker. And as she stared at the image, a feeling of familiarity came to her. She had seen the constellation-like pattern before. But where?

Something connected to Atlantis, it had to be. She continued on, the Alhambra's wonders going unnoticed as she turned her mind to the problem.

Granada, like Seville, had its share of cheap hostels for the casual or fiscally strapped traveller. After descending back into the old city, Nina found one in a block of run-down buildings. Again, the man at the desk did not request identification, or anything other than cash up front, though he did ask, 'American?' She confirmed her nationality with a nod, only thinking afterwards that she should have claimed to be Canadian. Another degree of disguise, however small, could only have helped her.

She went to her room, which was directly above reception. Soundproofing had not been a priority for the hostel's builders, as she soon discovered she could hear every footfall, slammed door and conversational exchange of people coming and going. She sighed, but knew that once she became fully involved with solving the mystery, she wouldn't even notice the noise.

She sat on the bed and examined the picture on her camera again. She was more certain than ever that she had seen the constellation before, and that it was linked to Atlantis. How, though? Where had she seen the star map?

No . . . not a star map. An *actual* map. And there was a room in the submerged ruins of Atlantis dedicated to maps . . .

She snatched up her book – only to remember that she had gutted it in Seville, keeping only the covers. 'Oh goddammit!' she moaned. There had been a picture of exactly the room in question, but now she would have to buy another copy. It was already evening, too late to search for a bookstore in a city she didn't know.

That didn't mean she couldn't start working, though. She still had her memories of what she had seen in the Hall of the Ambassadors, as well as her knowledge of the Atlantean empire's history, and she was already developing an explanation for how a piece of fourteenth-century Islamic art might possibly be the key to a puzzle created millennia earlier.

The main door banged below her again, but she barely registered it, her mind already travelling through time and space.

22

Venice

Eddie faced the six other people in his hotel room. 'Hope you all enjoyed breakfast, 'cause it's time to get to work,' he said dramatically. 'Now, everyone knows me, but not all of you know each other. You can socialise over cocktails later, but for now I'll do a quick rundown.' Starting from his left, he indicated each person in turn. 'Matt Trulli. Underwater expert and submarine engineer. And I'm guessing the big box he brought has got one of his toys in it.'

'You guessed right, mate,' the chunky Australian replied. 'Had a few I could have chosen, but I figured *Ringo* was the best option.'

'Congrats on getting married, by the way.'

Matt smiled and showed off his ring finger. 'Thanks.'

'A shame your wife couldn't come,' said Olivia.

'Husband,' he corrected.

Her eyes widened. 'Oh! Ah . . . sorry. Not because you're, you know,' she added hastily.

Eddie smirked at Olivia's discomfort before he moved on to a tall, lean man in his early thirties with tightly curled black hair. 'Jared Zane. Works for . . . let's say the Israeli government. He's brought some useful bits and bobs as well. Knows his stuff – even if he is barely out of nappies.'

'At least I still have hair, *alter kocker*,' said Jared. The Yiddish insult was an affectionate way of saying 'old fart'.

The hulking, bearded Russian beside the Israeli was the only person besides Macy who had not understood Eddie's description of Jared as a veiled way of saying he was in the Mossad, a perplexed frown further crinkling his heavily scarred forehead. 'Oleg Maximov,' the Yorkshireman continued. 'Former Spetznaz commando, went freelance, started off on the wrong side from me and Nina. Luckily for him, he switched.'

'Lucky for *you*,' Maximov said, with a humorous jab of his thick forefinger at his host.

'Next, Ana Rijo. Used to be a cop until someone put a price on her head. Got me and Nina into this mess, now trying to make things right by getting us out.' Ana looked abashed, but still managed a faint smile. 'And then there's my family – Olivia Garde, who's Nina's grandma, and my little girl, Macy. Who really, *really* wants her mum back safe and sound, so if you can help with that, you'll be making her very happy. All right?'

'Ahem,' came a voice over Eddie's phone, which was on a table in speaker mode.

'And last, and very much least,' Eddie said with faux-weariness, 'Peter Alderley. He's the head of MI6, but don't get too impressed. He's still a bell-end.'

A sigh from London. 'I don't *have* to be here, Chase. I do have other matters requiring my attention – the defence of the realm and all that.'

'What's a bell-end?' Macy asked.

'Er, just, ah, the noisy part of a bell,' said Eddie hurriedly, as laughter came down the line.

The others exchanged quick greetings. 'So what's the objective?' asked Jared. 'Beyond "help Nina".'

'There's a bloke called Gideon Lobato,' Eddie began. 'You've probably heard of him – tech billionaire who's into solar power, electric cars, stopping climate change, all that kind of stuff. Sounds like a good guy, but nope. He's framed Nina for stealing an Atlantean artefact and put her on the run in Spain. *Why* he did it, I don't know yet . . . but I'm going to.'

'I should point out,' said Alderley, 'that Nina actually *did* steal a different Atlantean artefact. She's wanted by the Spanish police.'

'They haven't caught her yet, have they?'

'No.'

'Then we've still got a chance of fixing this before they do. So, back to Lobato. He's a hard man to find with the whole jet-setting billionaire thing, but tonight he's giving a lecture at the Scuola Grande here in Venice. He'll have bodyguards; we need to get him away from them so I can have a quiet chat. Once I knew who could help, I worked out a plan that'll let each of you do what you do best. But obviously, now I need to tell you what it is.'

'You make plans?' Alderley joked. 'I always thought it was more desperate improvisation with a hefty dose of luck!'

'Bit of both,' admitted Eddie. 'But if anyone's got any suggestions, I'm all ears. Okay, let's get started.'

Two hours later, his rough-and-ready plan had been considerably improved by his friends' advice. Whether it would work was a question that could only be answered in the field. But Eddie was confident – as much as he could be.

'So you can get that to us in time, Alderley?' he asked.

'It's . . . shall we say, pushing the boundaries of legality with regards to SIS operations in an allied nation,' said the spy chief, who had dropped in and out of the discussion to deal with other matters in London. 'But the nation owes you a considerable debt, so I'll see to it on my personal authority.'

'Great.' Eddie looked back at those in the room. 'Everyone knows what they're doing?'

Maximov nodded. 'Move planks, deliver boat, then pick up bag.'

'Open the grille, show you the way in, then stand by with the fireworks,' said Matt.

'Good so far,' Eddie said. 'Jared?'

'Follow you inside, then get Lobato's attention,' the Israeli replied. 'Once we've got him, I'll meet you at the Institute. I'll need to find the quickest route, though. You're not giving me much time to get there.'

'Once we're finished here, we'll check it out in person. Ana?'

She nodded to the Mossad agent. 'Keep Lobato talking after Jared finds him. Then slow down anyone following you.'

'Good. Alderley?'

'I'll have a courier from our Rome station deliver the juice to you,' Alderley assured him. 'They should have some in their medicine cabinet. Then once you're inside, I'll keep tabs on everyone in the building.'

'You can really do what you said earlier?' asked Olivia with a mix of scepticism and dismay.

'We can.'

'And I thought people were simply being paranoid about the intelligence services!'

'The only way to stay off our radar is to live in a deep cave and never communicate with anybody else, ever,' Alderley told her with a chuckle. Her concerns were not assuaged.

Eddie spoke to her next. 'And you remember what you're doing, Olivia?'

'Of course I do. I'm old, not senile. I'll do my dying swan act – not literally, I hope! – for Gregorio's benefit, then keep his back to Macy.' She gave him a warning look. 'Eddie, are you absolutely sure about involving her? You're putting an awful lot of responsibility on a seven-year-old – and it could be dangerous. If anything happens to her . . .'

'I can do it, Grams,' Macy insisted. 'I *want* to do it. If it helps get Mommy back, I'll do anything.'

'That's my girl,' said Eddie, before crouching before his

daughter. 'Are *you* absolutely sure, though? Because if you're worried at all, we'll think of some other way.'

'I can *do* it,' she repeated, with the total confidence of youth. 'I have to drop my toy down the stairs' – she held up the plastic trikan the Emir had bought her, with which she had been practising while the adults talked – 'and put the paper in the door. I tried it on the bathroom, look.'

Matt, closest to the bathroom, checked. 'She's right, Eddie. It's jammed in tight. Nobody'd better settle down on the dunny, 'cause that door'll pop open if a mouse breathes on it.'

'How long did it take you to do it?' Eddie asked his daughter.

'Five seconds? Maybe ten.'

'You'll have to be quicker, love,' he said, not wanting it to sound like a criticism.

She scurried to the bathroom door. 'I'll do it in *three* seconds. Watch me!'

Matt laughed. 'She doesn't take no for an answer, does she? Gee, I wonder where that comes from?'

'If it's good, from me. Anything else, blame Nina,' Eddie replied with a grin, which quickly disappeared at the thought of his missing wife. 'Okay, so I'll go in, grab Lobato, then escape with him.'

'It all sounds so easy when you put it like that,' Alderley said sarcastically.

'If I thought about it too hard, I'd probably bottle out of doing it at all.'

'Well, nobody's ever accused you of thinking too hard, Eddie,' said Jared, smirking.

Eddie made sure Macy wasn't watching before shooting the younger man an obscene gesture. 'What is this, a tag team? If we're all done, then—'

'Finished!' cried Macy. 'And I did it in less than five seconds, I timed myself!'

Her father checked her handiwork. 'That's in nice and tight,' he said approvingly. 'Macy?'

'Yes, Daddy?'

'Well done.' She beamed with pride. 'All right,' he told his team, 'let's get started.'

Nina had also spent the morning working. She had found a bookstore and bought another copy of her latest book, this time in Spanish, as well as an atlas.

The book did indeed contain the picture she was after. It had been taken in a chamber concealed inside the great Temple of Poseidon, at the heart of the Atlantean capital. Submerged for eleven thousand years, the temple had suffered considerable damage during Nina's first exploration of the lost city – not her fault, she always had to point out to counter the entirely unfair public perception that she was an archaeological wrecking ball. It had suffered a further collapse on a later survey – *again, not my fault!* – meaning that the hidden room now only existed in photographs.

One of which would help her solve the riddle of the spear markers.

She had spent the previous evening musing on how the celestial map in the Hall of the Ambassadors could possibly be linked to the far older Atlantean relics. Her answer was straightforward enough to satisfy Occam's razor: *the simplest explanation is generally the correct one.* In this case, knowing that the people of Atlantis had settled near Seville – the discovery of the markers beneath the Tartessian site proved that – made it reasonable to believe the expansionist empire had explored, even settled, the rest of the Iberian peninsula.

The Atlanteans had been here. The lights cast by the markers aligned to the Moorish star map. Therefore, the Moors had copied something made by the Atlanteans.

226

She knew there would be plenty of scholars, not just in the Muslim world, who would be offended by the suggestion. The carved ceiling was considered one of the world's greatest Islamic artworks. But she knew that even if the wooden firmament was modelled on an older version, the style of the Atlantean original would have been very different. The later interpretation had its own sense of beauty.

So the ancient Atlanteans had created a map, which a later civilisation replicated in its own fashion, probably without even being aware of its true meaning. But now Nina was on the verge of uncovering it. The reason the pattern of lights and stars seemed familiar was simple: she had seen it before.

She laid the book open at the relevant picture. The sunken chamber, amongst other treasures, had contained a map: the world as seen by the Atlanteans as they explored and conquered new territories. The ancient civilisation had established outposts across more than half the planet, from the depths of the Amazon rainforest to the Himalayas. The outlines of the continents were distorted, but recognisable – and upon them were marked places of great importance. Atlantis itself was the largest, but there were others in Europe, Africa and across into Asia. Nine in all, linked by lines to form a constellation.

It was distinctive enough for Nina to have remembered it – but the pattern the markers created had *twelve* points, not nine. Three extra stars.

Three spearheads.

The Atlantean texts recovered near Seville claimed that in addition to the one used to test their power, there had been a trio of spearheads left poised to destroy their enemies. And the marker was the key to finding them.

She compared the picture on her camera to the map in her book, picking out the interlopers. One in the eastern Mediterranean, south of Greece. Another somewhere in Turkey. And

THE SPEAR OF ATLANTIS

the last far to the east, in the islands of Indonesia. The Atlantean chart was too inaccurate to pin their locations down precisely, but she was sure that by using the maps in her atlas, she would be able to match them to modern-day locations.

Time to get to work.

'Time to get to work,' said Eddie, checking his watch.

He and his team were in an empty apartment not far from the Scuola Grande, Jared picking its lock with surprising ease. This particular flat had been chosen for a reason: it had a rear door opening directly on to the canal leading south from the museum. A plank running across an arched recess acted as a private mooring. The arch's inset meant anyone in it would be out of sight from the piazza behind the Scuola.

Olivia, wearing a formal dark blue dress, was having second thoughts. 'Are you sure this will work?' she asked him. 'If everything doesn't go perfectly, you'll be arrested. Or worse.'

'It doesn't have to go perfectly,' he assured her. 'Just good enough.'

'And you're happy for things only to be "good enough" when they concern your daughter?' She looked at Macy, who was showing off a yo-yo trick with her trikan to the impressed Maximov.

'Normally, no – if things aren't better-than-perfect for her, me and Nina kick up a stink. But this time we've got to make do.'

'And if something goes wrong, she could be in a lot of trouble.'

'She's seven, she can't be charged with anything. The age of criminal responsibility in Italy is fourteen.'

'I'm sure Macy will find comfort in that as she's led away by the *carabinieri*.'

'That's not going to happen,' he said firmly. 'Just stick to the plan, and you'll both walk right out of there.'

Olivia pursed her lips. 'I wish I had your confidence.'

There was not an ounce of doubt in his reply. 'I won't let anything happen to my family. You should know that by now.'

Before she could say anything more, Eddie's phone rang. He answered. 'Chase, it's me,' said Alderley. 'Your package will arrive in a couple of minutes.'

'Great, thanks. We're nearly ready here. You okay to be on the line when we need you?'

'I've cleared a space in my schedule. Which was surprisingly hard, actually. You'd think that as the boss I could decide when to do things, but there's always someone who just can't wait. In this case,' he added, 'it's a bald yob from Yorkshire.'

'It's actually a redhead from New York,' Eddie said pointedly. 'Okay, I'll call once we're set.' He hung up, addressing his team. 'That was Alderley – his courier's about to arrive, so we'll have everything we need. Matt, you all set?'

Matt was kneeling by the open back door. Before him was a small remotely operated vehicle – a vivid yellow underwater drone, the name *Ringo* written in elaborate flower-power script on its bow. The boxy little submarine was equipped with a robotic arm folded over its back. He was attaching a tool to it: a circular saw blade. 'Just got to plug in the fibre-optic line, then put it in the water.'

Ana eyed the ROV. 'What if someone sees it? It's a very bright colour.'

The Australian gestured towards the turgid canal. 'You seen the state of that? And she won't be near the surface – the arm can reach up to do the job.'

'How long will it take?' Eddie asked.

'Hard to say, mate. The wires shouldn't take long to cut, but I need to make sure you don't get sliced up by the stubs when you go through. You expose an open wound to that water, you might as well drink a bucket of typhoid.'

'Then take your time,' said Jared, donning a wetsuit.

'Not too much, though,' said Eddie as he headed for the front door. 'I'm off to meet Alderley's man.'

He left the flat and crossed a little courtyard, then waited at the end of an alley adjoining a narrow north–south street. Tourists wandered past.

It was not long before he heard his name. 'Chase,' muttered an unassuming dark-haired man, barely looking at him as he approached. He was holding a small package. Eddie held out a hand, the box being transferred to him as the man walked past.

'Not waiting for your tip?' the Yorkshireman said, knowing he would not get a response.

He returned to the apartment. 'Got it,' he announced.

Matt was lowering the ROV into the canal. 'That's the knockout juice?'

'That's right.' Eddie opened the package. Inside was a small black box, which in turn revealed a metal cylinder slightly larger than a lipstick tube. A button protruded from one end; there was a tiny hole in the centre of the other. 'One-shot injector. Stick it against Lobato, push the button, a needle pops out, and *squoosh*. He's out for the count.'

'How long?' asked Maximov.

'It's set to his body weight, and he should be out for thirty minutes. Takes about five seconds to work.'

Ana peered at the injector. 'What drug is it?'

'Dunno,' Eddie told her. 'Alderley said it was classified.'

'Probably a mix of remifentanil and a propofol derivative,' Jared remarked. Everyone looked at him. 'It's not the first time I've done something like this.'

Maximov eyed him, comprehension slowly dawning. 'You . . . do you work for the *Mossad*?'

'I can't confirm or deny that,' the Israeli replied cheerily.

The Russian looked perplexed. 'Does that mean yes?'

Macy put a hand on the big man's knee. 'I think it does,' she whispered.

Eddie chuckled. 'So long as it works, it can be Horlicks and turkey gravy for all I care.' He put the box down amongst a collection of other objects beside a large transparent zip-lock bag. 'Matt?'

'I'm ready,' Matt replied. He opened a laptop, into which was plugged a PlayStation control pad. 'Works as well as a normal remote control, and it's a lot cheaper,' he explained, seeing his companions' curious – or dubious – looks. 'Hey, if the US Navy can use Xbox pads in its submarines . . .' He brought up a view of the canal outside from the drone's camera. 'Right then. Here we go.'

He pushed one of the thumbsticks. The ROV moved away from the door, the image on the screen showing it slipping out from the archway. Gentle pressure on the other stick, and the sub descended beneath the surface. The buildings along the canal's sides were obscured by a dirty green haze.

'How will you see where you're going?' Olivia asked.

'I've tagged the route using GPS and an inertial positioner,' Matt replied. 'And *Ringo*'s got a low-power sonar system, like an ultrasound. Not very long range, but it doesn't need to be.'

Eddie watched over his shoulder. Even in the murk, he occasionally saw darker shapes rising up from below – junk on the canal's bottom. Another hazard to face on his own journey. The distance to the opening into the Scuola's cellar was roughly fifty metres, about a hundred and sixty feet – the length of an Olympic-sized swimming pool. Normally an easy swim, but pools weren't filled with hazardously filthy water and littered with potentially dangerous debris . . . and in a pool, he would also be able to surface for air.

'Going round the corner,' Matt reported, nudging a stick to the right. 'Heading for the cellar.'

'How deep are you?' Eddie asked.

'About half a metre. Is that it?'

The dark shadow of the opening appeared. 'Yeah.' From the small submarine's perspective it seemed cavernous, but Eddie knew from his exploratory groping that it was barely big enough for a person to fit through. 'Can't see much.'

'I'll turn on the sonar.' A click on the trackpad, and a monochromatic outline of the stonework was overlaid on the grimy green. The sonar return was fuzzy, but still showed individual wires of the chain-link blocking the gap. 'Don't think it'll give the cutter any trouble.'

Matt guided the sub to the opening, issuing a command for it to hold position, then switched the controller to operate its robot arm. Working both sticks at once as well as the triggers, he carefully brought the blade into contact with the first piece of wire. 'All right . . .'

The saw whirled, tiny bubbles spewing from it as it sliced into the metal. 'Someone might see that,' warned Ana.

'They'll just think the bubbles're from a pipe or something,' said Eddie.

'You hope.'

'Yeah, I hope. Been doing a lot of that lately.'

'One down,' Matt announced. The saw withdrew, the chain-link neatly severed. 'On to the next.'

'Nice work,' said the Englishman. 'How long to do the whole lot?'

'At this rate? Fifteen minutes, maybe.'

'Great. The rest of us'd better get ready. I'll squeeze into my rubber suit – no jokes in front of Macy, please.'

Muted laughter from Jared and Matt. Macy looked up at her father in confusion as Olivia sighed. 'Has Nina ever mentioned the topic of age-appropriate humour to you?' she said.

'Yeah, but it sounded boring and grown-up, so I didn't listen.'

He picked up his wetsuit, then indicated the items beside the zip-lock bag. 'Jared, if you can pack that lot, we'll be ready to go as soon as Matt brings the sub back.' Another time check. 'Olivia, Macy, you'd better get to the museum. I'll text you when we're in position.'

Olivia joined her great-granddaughter. 'Come on, Macy. And don't forget your toy.'

'I've got it,' Macy replied, holding up the trikan.

'You remember what to do?' Eddie asked.

'*Yes*, Daddy,' she replied, with a little impatience.

'Just wanted to be sure, love. But if anything goes wrong, just leave it, okay? I'd rather stop and give up than have anything happen to you.'

'But that would mean you'd be giving up on Mommy,' said Macy firmly. 'So I *will* do it right.'

Eddie gave her a hug and a kiss. 'You know you're the best kid in the world, right? I love you.'

'I love you too, Daddy. Now let's go help Mommy.' She took Olivia's hand and led her to the front door.

Matt smiled at Eddie. 'You've got a right little firecracker there.'

'Tell me about it,' he replied proudly. 'She's going to put some poor lad through absolute hell when she's older. Or lass; I'm not going to stop her doing what she wants.'

'Could you even if you tried?' asked Jared, amused.

'I doubt it.' He hefted the wetsuit again. 'Okay, I'll get changed. And then . . . I'm going to get into deep shit. Probably literally.'

23

By the time Eddie and Jared had prepared themselves, Matt had finished cutting away the grille. After piloting the little submarine through the opening to check that the chamber beyond was actually accessible, he returned the robot to the apartment's rear door. 'Okay, I'll hook up the bag,' he said, collecting the now sealed zip-lock with the mission's equipment and two bundles of clothes inside. 'You guys ready?'

'Almost,' said Eddie. He and Jared were in wetsuits and swimming fins, sealing their extremities with neoprene gloves and socks so they would be protected from the canal's polluted water. There was one part of their bodies they couldn't cover with conventional diving gear, though. Full-face hoods that left no skin exposed simply didn't exist – beyond very specialised latex clothing suppliers, at least, and Venice did not exactly have fetishwear emporia on every street corner.

But swimming in the canals, even briefly, posed a great risk of infection to eyes, noses and mouths, even ears. Their heads would have to be completely enclosed, and the only way to do that was literally by taping a plastic bag over them. Making matters worse, once in the water they would have no air to breathe beyond however much was sealed in; the cellar's opening was too small to fit through while wearing a scuba tank.

Jared drew in his lips as Maximov opened a transparent bag. 'I'm having really bad memories of my training to resist interrogation,' he said unhappily. 'Waterboarding in the morning, suffocation in the afternoon. That was not my favourite lesson.'

Eddie took rapid deep breaths. The more oxygen and less CO_2 in his system, the longer he would be able to resist the urge to breathe. 'Sub ready, Matt?'

The Australian was attaching the large bag to the little craft's stern. 'Nearly done . . . there.' He watched the zip-lock sink beneath the rancid water. The ROV tipped backwards with the weight. 'Huh. Hope *Ringo*'s strong enough to pull all that.'

'You think of that *now*?' said Eddie. 'Okay, Jared. Ready?'

'No, but it's too late to back out,' the younger man replied. 'The trouble I get myself into for you, *alter kocker!*'

'If you didn't love trouble, you wouldn't do what you do.' Eddie turned to Ana and Maximov, both now holding bags open in their hands. 'Let's get started. And don't try this at home, kids.'

'Good luck,' Ana said, with trepidation. She pulled the bag over Eddie's head, and he held it against his shoulders while she quickly wrapped duct tape around his neck, squeezing it tight against the neoprene wetsuit. Maximov did the same to Jared. The Mossad agent gave Eddie a nervous look through the plastic.

Eddie exhaled slightly. The bag inflated, but the seal at his neck held. Jared's also stayed firm. The Englishman gave a thumbs-up, and both men entered the water. Matt had already returned to his laptop, sending the ROV back beneath the surface. Eddie followed it under.

The water pressure pushed the bag against his face. The sensation was horribly like being smothered, but he would have to endure it. If there had been more air inside, the extra buoyancy would have pulled his head upwards, making it almost impossible to swim.

He started up the canal, four feet beneath the surface. The ROV was an indistinct grey shape ahead, colour leached away by the dirty water. But Matt had added something to make it easier to find: a small LED strobe light on its underside, blinking every few seconds. Eddie glanced back. Jared was not far behind him.

Fifty metres had never seemed so far. He had swum without an air supply in colder, darker, deeper waters, but the bag seemed to be actively sucking the energy from him, a plastic facehugger sliding revoltingly across his skin. He looked for the ghostly submarine to make sure he was not falling behind. The distance was hard to judge in the gloom, until the strobe pulsed a few metres ahead.

The flash also picked out lengths of mangled metal jutting from the canal floor, an old bed frame or broken scaffolding. Matt had already seen it, the ROV adjusting course. Eddie also angled clear of the obstacle. He could tell from the light above that he was coming to the intersection where the canal joined another at the Scuola Grande. Halfway there. He looked back at Jared again.

The younger man was continuing on their original course. He hadn't yet seen the submerged junk. Eddie twisted to warn him – but too late.

The Israeli finally saw the scrap, but even as he swerved, his own momentum carried him into it. The impact dislodged one of the lengths of metal. It toppled, hitting Jared's shoulder and knocking him into the slimy sediment below.

Eddie hurriedly swam back, groping with gloved hands. The rusted pole was pinning the other man down. He grabbed the heavy spar and braced his feet against the canal bed to lift it. Jared pushed backwards, the bag over his head brushing the corroded metal. The Yorkshireman used a splayed hand to protect the plastic, then, as soon as his friend was clear, pulled him up.

The bag wasn't punctured. Relieved, Eddie looked for the ROV—

It was gone.

The drone had continued without them. With no guidance, he would have to guess at the direction to the cellar's entrance, costing valuable time, or surface to check – which would expose them to onlookers, including security at the Scuola Grande.

He had to keep going. He swam on, trusting Jared to follow even with the shock of his close call.

He reached the intersection and turned right. He still couldn't see the sub, or even its strobe. Matt had probably guided it to the opening already, not realising the swimmers had stopped . . .

He suddenly became aware of a noise over the rustle of the bag – the growl of an outboard motor.

He looked around to see a boat coming straight at him, a propeller slicing through the water beneath it—

Eddie kicked downwards, flattening himself into the muck and trash on the canal bed as the craft swept right overhead. The prop's churning wake lashed at him, threatening to rip the bag.

Then the boat passed.

Forcing himself not to take a relieved breath, he looked back to find Jared. The Israeli had also gone to the bottom.

Eddie set off again. If Matt had stopped the ROV at the opening to wait for them, he should spot its light. But if he had already taken its cargo inside . . .

And there was now another danger, growing with every passing moment. The two close encounters had between them taken only forty seconds, but that was over half a minute extra that he would need to hold his breath – and his body was already demanding more air.

He kept going, each stroke more tiring than the last. How much further? It couldn't be more than sixty feet, but it felt like sixty miles . . .

A flash of light, off to his right. The sub.

He turned towards it, suddenly reinvigorated. Another flash, closer. Thirty feet, twenty, and then he saw the boxy ROV, right in front of a dark rectangle in the wall.

Ten feet. Five – and he reached the sub, which obligingly

moved aside. Matt must have realised the swimmers hadn't kept up and turned to look for them. No time for gratitude, though. A sickly fire was rising in his chest, his lungs desperate to expel foul air. He pulled himself through the gap into the darkness beyond—

Something stabbed at his stomach.

A stub of severed chain-link stood a couple of millimetres proud of the grille's frame, but that was enough to gouge into his wetsuit like a claw. He felt the neoprene stretch, then tear. If it cut his skin as well, there was no telling what might infect the wound . . .

He drew his stomach muscles as tight as he could, forcing himself upwards. The wetsuit kept stretching . . . then snapped free.

Eddie dragged himself into the cellar. The moment his feet were clear of the opening, he surfaced and clawed at the suffocating bag. His gloved fingers slipped over the plastic, unable to find grip. He clenched both fists, scrunching it up, and pulled with all his remaining strength.

The bag tore open.

He almost choked in his rush to exhale, then drew in a deep, whooping breath. Something bumped against his legs: Jared. He moved to let the Israeli surface beside him. The younger man breached the surface, ripping away his own bag and gasping for air.

Eddie trod water until he was able to speak. 'You okay?' he wheezed.

'Yeah,' was the breathless reply. 'Let's not do that again.'

'Might be easier than getting into the building,' the York-shireman cautioned. The chamber was dark, but enough sickly light came through the submerged opening for him to pick out the steps. He swam to them, trudging gratefully to solid ground.

Jared followed. Behind him, Matt's ROV surfaced. The

Mossad agent detached the zip-lock, and the little sub bobbed in acknowledgement before heading back towards the canal.

'Everything still dry?' Eddie asked.

Jared pulled off his gloves, then unsealed the bag. 'Looks like it.'

'Thank God. Might make people a bit suspicious if we walk around stinking like we just came out of a sewer. Which we kind of did.'

'How do we get out?'

Eddie rummaged in the bag, producing a torch, which he switched on, and his phone. He pointed the former towards the top of the steps. 'There's the door – but it's bolted from the other side.'

'Which is where Olivia and Macy come in?'

'Yep. Better tell 'em we're here.' He sent a brief text message to Olivia, then took out the rolled-up clothing. 'So now we get changed – then hope a seven-year-old and a ninety-three-year-old can pull off the next part of the plan . . .'

The atmosphere inside the Scuola Grande di San Rocco was very different from Olivia and Macy's previous visit. During the daytime it was a haunt for lovers of Renaissance art, but they were vastly outnumbered by tourists, treating it as simply another tick on the checklist of Venetian attractions.

Now, though, the museum was hosting one of its regular private functions, and its visitors were more than mere sightseers. The lectures it hosted by globally renowned figures drew an elite audience from all over the world. As a result, security had been bolstered, the pair having to pass through a cordon and a metal detector before being allowed entry.

Once in, the air was more upscale cocktail party than art gallery. The guests – Macy was the youngest by about three decades, and even at ninety-three Olivia was not the oldest –

were more concerned with networking than appreciation of Tintoretto. Macy regarded everyone nervously, holding her great-grandmother with one hand while the other clutched the trikan. 'Where are we going, Grams?'

'Let's find Gregorio,' Olivia replied. 'This way.'

They went up to the next floor. Macy glanced towards the door they had passed through to reach Pinto's office. As before, it had a security guard stationed at it, but he seemed much more alert than his predecessor. 'What if he doesn't let us through?'

'He will, don't worry.' But the elderly woman was hiding her own concerns. She had been in the field with Eddie before, but that had been a matter of escape and survival. Walking into potential danger was another thing entirely.

A quiet buzz from her handbag. She took out her phone to see a text from Eddie. Just one word: *Go*.

'Is that from Daddy?' Macy asked.

'Yes, it is. They must be in the cellar, so now we've got to get them out. Do you remember what to do?'

Macy nodded, holding up her toy trikan unhappily. 'It's going to break, isn't it?'

'I'm sure your father will buy you a new one. Oh, there's Gregorio.' She spotted Pinto amongst a cluster of people in front of one of the paintings.

'The bad man's with him,' said Macy, worried. The little crowd had formed around the evening's guest of honour, Gideon Lobato. Three large suited men stood at a respectful distance: the billionaire's bodyguards. The white-clad man did not seem remotely comfortable in the close proximity of so many others, his expression suggesting he wanted to spray them all with an antibacterial – or pesticide.

'You have to pretend that we don't know he's bad,' Olivia told her as they headed across the room. 'We don't want to scare him away.' The thought had occurred that her mere presence might make Lobato suspicious, but the plan depended on her speaking to Pinto, and she guessed he would stay clamped to his VIP guest like a limpet.

That proved to be the case. When the Italian saw her, he waved for her to join them rather than come to greet her. 'Ah, Olivia! *Ciao, bella!* And Macy, too. *Ciao, piccola.*'

'Lovely to see you again, Gregorio,' said Olivia, kissing his cheeks. 'And Gideon, hello.'

'Mrs Garde,' said Lobato. He was clearly unsettled by her arrival. 'I did not expect to see you.'

'I told you, Gregorio is a good friend. And your mentioning that you were coming here inspired me to see him. Not that I need any excuse to visit Venice.'

Lobato eyed Macy. 'And you brought Dr Wilde's daughter with you?'

Olivia's tone became sombre. 'I thought it best to take her mind off everything that's happened.'

'I see. And . . . her father?'

'In Spain, dealing with the police. He's trying to bring my granddaughter home safely.'

'I would imagine that might not be for some time. Several years, perhaps. I do not know the Spanish sentence for robbery.'

'I'm sure that whatever Nina did, it was for the best of reasons,' Olivia replied, prickling. 'She *has* saved the world several times; she knows what she's doing. I expect she's preventing some megalomaniac from obtaining a dangerous archaeological relic.' Her eyes were fixed on his.

He didn't even blink. 'A megalomaniac? Highly unlikely.'

Pinto gave Olivia a concerned look. 'Your granddaughter is in trouble?'

'Yes,' she replied. 'She's Nina Wilde, the archaeologist.'

His eyes widened. '*She* is your granddaughter? I saw in the news that she stole something from a museum in Spain!'

'As I said to Gideon, I'm certain she'll be vindicated. But it has been . . . very distressing.' Her voice quavered, and she wobbled a little, supporting herself on her cane. 'For Macy, of course, but also for me. Knowing your granddaughter is on the run, being hunted by the police for something she didn't do, is terribly stressful. Terribly . . .'

She staggered, then crumpled to the floor.

'Grams!' Macy cried, horrified. Gasps came from those around her.

Lobato stared at the fallen woman in confusion. Pinto, however, was quicker to respond. 'Olivia!' he said, crouching. 'Are you all right?' He signalled to the security guard, who hurried over. '*Veloce! Chiama un'ambulanza!*'

'No, no,' Olivia insisted, straining to sit up. 'I'm all right, Gregorio. Just . . . a moment of dizziness. I'll be fine. Perhaps . . . perhaps if I could lie down for a few minutes?'

'I will take you to my office,' said Pinto. He spoke to the guard in Italian.

'Thank you,' she said. The two men carefully brought her to her feet.

'Are you okay, Grams?' Macy asked, stricken.

Olivia leaned closer. 'I'm fine, my dear,' she said – then, when she was sure nobody else could see, winked at her. 'Now, let's go to Gregorio's office. And don't forget your toy.'

Comprehension blossomed on the young girl's face, followed by a smile that she fought to conceal. 'I won't.'

'Good.' Olivia took Pinto's hand, holding her cane with the other. 'Thank you, Gregorio. Follow us upstairs, Macy.'

Pinto offered apologies to his guests, then he and the guard walked Olivia and Macy to the stairwell door. Lobato watched them go, struggling not to recoil as the other guests closed in around him.

The guard opened the door to let Olivia and Pinto through.

Macy trailed behind, fidgeting with the trikan. She looked down the stairs, seeing the cellar door below. A moment of hesitation, fuelled by fear of being caught . . .

Then she reached over the banister and dropped the toy.

It hit the tiles two storeys below with a loud crack of plastic. 'My trikan!' she cried as both Italians turned. 'I dropped it, I dropped it!' Remembering what she had to do, she ran down the stairs after it.

'No, wait!' called Pinto, reluctant to have an unaccompanied child haring around the building. He turned to the guard to tell him to go after her—

'Oh!' gasped Olivia, wobbling. Her escorts hurriedly steadied her. 'I'm sorry, I felt dizzy again.'

'Are you sure you are all right?' Pinto asked. 'I can still call an ambulance.'

'No, don't be absurd. I just need a few minutes off my feet. And,' a small smile, 'a drop of Casavecchia would help enormously.'

His own smile was wider. 'Ah, as always, an ulterior motive.'

By now, Macy had reached the bottom of the stairs. She looked up. Both men were still concerned with her great-grandmother, but she only had a few seconds to complete her task. She reached up to the bolt and pulled—

It didn't move.

The door's weight was pressing the bolt against its rusty staple. She tried again, harder, but barely shifted it, and the attempt produced a metallic squeak. Another fearful glance up. Pinto's shoulder was visible above the railing. If he turned his head, he would see what she was doing.

'Macy!' Eddie's low voice rumbled from behind the door. 'Are you okay?'

'I can't open it!' she replied in a desperate whisper. 'It's stuck!'

'Hold on.'

She didn't know what he was going to do, so she glanced up again. Olivia was talking to Pinto, but it was no longer enough to distract him. He started to turn . . .

The door drew more tightly against its jamb as Eddie pulled at it. 'Try now!'

Macy tugged the bolt again – and this time it popped free.

'Macy, are you all right?' Pinto called. He leaned over the banister –

She just barely managed to whip her hands down. 'I – I,' she stammered, before coming up with a response. 'It's broken! It broke!' Pieces of the toy trikan were scattered around her.

'We'll get you another one,' said Olivia. 'Have you finished down there?'

It took Macy a moment to understand the question's dual meaning. 'Yes, yes,' she said, collecting the plastic fragments.

'Leave them, do not worry,' Pinto told her. 'I will send someone to clean them up.'

'No, no, it's okay, I've got them,' she gabbled. If anyone came down the stairs and saw the unlocked bolt, they would either close it again, or open the door and find her father. 'I've got them all.'

'Good lass,' came a whisper from the door. 'Now get back to Olivia, quick!'

She followed her father's instruction and ran upstairs. Pinto regarded the broken pieces sympathetically. 'I am sorry. I hope it was not expensive.'

'Her father thinks anything above a dollar fifty is expensive,' Olivia told him.

'Ah, yes. The English, they are . . . *frugal*, yes?'

'And Yorkshiremen particularly so.' They shared a smile, then Olivia remembered she still had a job to do. 'Oh, but I do need to lie down.'

'Of course. *Avanti*,' he told the guard, who gently supported her arm as they climbed the stairs, Macy behind them. On reaching the top floor, the little girl shot a last worried look at the cellar before following them to the Guardian Grando's office.

Pinto unlocked it, then opened the door, guiding Olivia to the chaise longue before going to a cabinet. 'Please, rest. I will get you a drink. *Va bene, puoi tornare indietro,*' he told the guard, who nodded and started back to his station downstairs—

The moment both men's backs were turned, Macy darted after the departing guard, whipping a foot into the gap just before the door slammed shut. She clenched her jaw to hold in a squeal of pain.

Quick, quick! Olivia mouthed. Macy hurriedly produced a wad of folded paper wrapped in black masking tape and stuffed it into the box of the frame's strike plate. Behind her, Pinto took a wine bottle from the cabinet. She gave the makeshift bung a last push, then retreated.

The door closed, catch clicking . . . but it was the lock she had jammed. There was no way to know if she had been successful, though – not until Pinto locked it again.

The Italian turned. Macy gave him an innocent smile, trying to hide the fact that she felt sick with fear. He smiled back, then collected two glasses. 'Here. I am sure this will make you feel much better.'

'Are you unwell too, Gregorio?' Olivia asked, smiling.

'I call it prevention. Much better than cure.' He poured wine into the glasses and gave one to her. '*Buona salute e benessere!*'

'Good health,' Olivia echoed, giving her great-granddaughter a look of praise over the glass.

24

In the cellar, Eddie and Jared had changed into the clothes from the zip-lock bag. The Israeli now wore a dark suit, the Englishman a spy-style black turtleneck. Both outfits were crumpled, but the hope in Jared's case was that the colour would camouflage the creases.

Eddie, meanwhile, hoped nobody would even *see* him to note the state of his clothing. He opened the cellar door a fraction, listening as someone descended the stairs. They went through the door above, the murmur of conversation from the galleries briefly reaching the Yorkshireman.

'That must've been whoever went upstairs with Macy and Olivia,' he said. 'Probably one of the guards.' He opened the door wider and peered out. The stairwell was empty. 'Okay, let's get ready.'

The two men took out the rest of their gear. Jared collected only a phone. The Englishman, on the other hand, ended up with a small bag holding the gas injector and a couple of other items, plus a large folded canvas sack containing a long skein of rope. He also pocketed his phone and donned a paired Bluetooth earpiece. 'Think we're all set,' he said. 'Come on, Macy. Do your dad proud . . .'

'How do you feel now?' asked Pinto, finishing his wine.

'Much better, thank you, Gregorio,' Olivia replied, sipping from her own glass. 'I just needed to sit down. That's the problem with growing old; what you used to be able to do with no trouble starts to exhaust you.'

Macy sat beside her, swinging her feet with increasing boredom. 'Can we go now?'

'I think that was a subtle hint that my great-granddaughter may have had enough,' said Olivia. She used her cane to stand.

'Are you sure you will be all right?' Pinto asked.

'Yes, thank you. And we should get back downstairs anyway. It would be a shame if I missed Gideon's lecture – and a terrible faux pas if you did!'

'We still have time,' he assured her. 'Come, I will escort you.'

Macy followed them to the door. Pinto let them through, then closed it and put his key in the lock. A grunt as he had to apply more force than expected, but finally it turned. 'Now, let us see what Gideon has to say.' He took Olivia's hand and led her to the stairs.

Macy looked anxiously back at the door. The lock had clicked, but she didn't know if the wad of paper and tape had kept it from closing properly.

And her father would only find out when he tried to open it.

'Sounds like Macy and Olivia,' said Eddie, hearing footsteps in the stairwell. 'They must be going to Lobato's talk.'

'Do you think Macy managed to jam the door?' Jared asked.

'If she didn't, I'll have to come up with a plan B.'

'You know the B doesn't stand for "break things", yes?' Both men grinned. 'So how long do we stay down here?'

'Until Olivia tells us Lobato's finished.' He checked his watch. 'He's supposed to start at seven o'clock, and it's ten to now. So we've got a bit of a wait.' He sat down on the cold floor. 'Got any games on your phone?'

★ ★ ★

Almost unwillingly, Olivia found Lobato's talk an interesting one. While the tech billionaire seemed nearly robotically devoid of personality in conversation, he became noticeably more animated once he took to the podium on a subject about which he was clearly passionate. She couldn't fail to notice, however, that many of his proposed solutions to the looming problems of climate change happened to be illustrated with examples developed by his own companies. The event was as much sales pitch as soapbox.

The combination of Lobato's often technical discussion and her personal antipathy to the man who had put her mother on the run meant Macy was far less involved, however. 'Is he done?' she muttered when after forty minutes he stepped down and the Scuola's upper-floor Chapter Hall filled with applause.

'I think so,' Olivia replied, taking out her phone. 'You know, you should have paid more attention. I'll be long gone, but your generation will be the one that has to save the world.'

'Yeah, Grams,' was the reply, in the dismissive tone of a much older girl.

Olivia sighed. 'You sound just like your grandmother. And your mother.' She sent a text with just one word: *Now*.

Eddie's phone vibrated. He quickly checked the screen; it was the message he had been expecting. 'Okay, Lobato's just finished,' he told Jared as he made a call.

'Alderley,' came the reply.

'It's me,' said the Yorkshireman. 'You ready?'

'All set,' Alderley told him. 'Starting the phone ping . . . now.'

The British intelligence services had ploughed a colossal amount of money into electronic surveillance technology, to the point that their spy agency, Government Communications Headquarters – GCHQ – was second only to America's National Security Agency in its ability to penetrate other nations' communication systems. In this case, the order Alderley had just given to MI6's sister agency was aimed at Venice's phone network. The cellular masts near the Scuola Grande now became tracking devices, every phone in range silently reporting its location and allowing GCHQ to triangulate their positions.

'Okay,' said Alderley, 'there are, let's see . . . one hundred and eighty-seven phones inside the museum, including yours. They're almost all in the Chapter Hall. Lobato's is there, and so is Olivia's.'

'How many in the rest of the building?'

'Ah . . . seventeen in total, with four in the wing above you. That's phones, of course – which might not be the same as people. Two of them look to be in one room, so I'd say they're staff, and the others security.'

'Are they patrolling?'

'Have to wait for the next ping to see. Hold on . . .' A pause, then: 'Only one is moving. Let's see where he's going . . .' Another pause. 'Okay, he's on one of the higher floors, moving west – away from you. He's not in a hurry.'

'How long between pings?' The GCHQ updates were not in real time, and the longer the gap, the more chance there was of an unwelcome surprise encounter once Eddie and Jared left the cellar.

'Ten seconds or thereabouts. It's a trade-off between speed and positional accuracy, I'm afraid. And the faster the updates, the more chance there is of someone in Italy noticing we're hijacking their bandwidth. I can tell GCHQ to speed up the pings, but I'd rather not draw attention – especially as this isn't exactly an approved operation.'

'Keep it as it is,' said the Englishman, hoping he wasn't making a mistake. 'Is Lobato moving yet?'

'He's still in the hall, but nearer the exit . . . Ha, looks like Dr Pinto's buttonholed him. There's a wall of phones in his way.'

'He won't hang around for long. All those non-billionaires breathing on him? He'll be desperate to disinfect himself.' Eddie opened the door and checked the stairwell. 'Clear here. Let's go.' He collected his belongings, then he and Jared made their way up.

The younger man stopped at the hallway 'How long should I wait?'

'Alderley, has anyone come back into the gallery?' Eddie asked.

'They're just starting to,' was the reply.

'Give it a minute, then go through,' the Yorkshireman told his companion.

'I should warn you,' Alderley added, 'the guard is right outside the door.'

Eddie relayed the information to Jared, who frowned. 'So how do I get past him?' he asked. 'He'll know none of the guests were in this part of the building.'

'I think we can arrange a distraction,' said Alderley.

Eddie had his own ideas. 'Just walk past like you own the place,' he told Jared, 'and if he says anything, tell him you were looking for the loo. In Hebrew. It'll confuse the hell out of him, and by the time he gets his head back into gear, you'll be gone.'

The other Englishman was less than impressed. '*Or* we could arrange a distraction! Just tell me when.'

'Go in a minute,' Eddie instructed the Israeli again. 'I'll see you soon. I hope.'

'Good luck, *alter kocker*,' Jared told him.

'You too, kid,' Eddie replied with a smile as he resumed his ascent.

Olivia and Macy slowly made their way downstairs from the Chapter Hall, letting others past as the guests dispersed through the Scuola. 'Mr Lobato still hasn't come out,' whispered Macy.

Her great-grandmother smiled. 'I imagine Gregorio is trying to push all the Scuola's benefactors in front of him before he leaves.' They reached the intermediate level. 'We won't miss him, though. He has to come this way.'

'I can't see Daddy's friend. Where is he? He's supposed to be here.'

'He will be, don't worry,' Olivia assured her. She looked back up the stairs as the level of ambient conversation became more excitable. Lobato was on his way. 'Although he needs to hurry . . .'

Eddie reached the uppermost floor. 'I'm at the top,' he whispered to Alderley. 'Is anyone up here?'

'I don't think so,' the older man answered.

'You don't *think*? I thought you could pinpoint their phones to a couple of feet.'

'In longitude and latitude, yes. *Altitude* is another matter. The system's less accurate on the Z axis.'

'*How* less accurate?'

'About fifteen feet precision.'

Eddie fought to keep his voice down in his exasperation. 'So that guard might be on *this* floor?'

'He's stopped moving, but when he sets off again we'll be able to get a better idea.'

'You take your time,' said the Yorkshireman sarcastically. 'Not like I'm in a hurry or anything . . .'

Jared reached the exit. He tugged his jacket straight, lifted his head high, then opened the door and strode out into the gallery.

He rapidly assessed his surroundings. Few people in the room would pose a threat, the vast majority beyond both middle age and peak fitness, but the guard to his right, who had just registered that the man passing him was not a member of the museum's staff, could be a problem. '*Mi scusi, signore,*' the man said, starting after him—

Jared waved a dismissive hand as he walked into the throng of visitors. 'I was looking for the toilet,' he said airily – in Hebrew. Faced with an unfamiliar language and somebody acting as if he had every right to be there, the guard hesitated. By the time he overcame his uncertainty, the Israeli had disappeared from view amongst the chatting guests.

Jared continued through the Scuola, occasionally glancing back until he was sure the guard was not following. A small smile at the fact that Eddie's suggestion had actually worked, but within moments he was again all business.

He saw Olivia and Macy, giving them a brief nod before looking up the stairs. Lobato was on the way down, surrounded by a gaggle of guests. The one beside him, based on Olivia's description, was Pinto. He steeled himself and marched towards the descending group.

'Tracking Jared's phone – he's moving towards Lobato,' Alderley reported.

Eddie opened the door and slipped through, heading for Pinto's office—

'Chase! *Hide!*'

The urgency in Alderley's voice warned him that the danger was immediate: no time even to ask questions. He looked around frantically. No doors nearby. His only choices were to run back to the stairs, or dart into an alcove containing a water cooler. He opted for the latter, squeezing into the narrow gap beside the incongruous dispenser.

'The guard's coming!' the MI6 man continued. 'He *was* on your floor.'

'Thanks for fucking telling me *now*!' Eddie hissed. He fell silent, listening.

Old floorboards creaked faintly under the approaching man's weight. The guard was in no hurry. Eddie hadn't been seen – but if he didn't get to Pinto's office soon, the plan would fall apart.

And he might still be found. Unless the man was missing an eye on the Englishman's side, there was no way he could fail to notice the intruder.

The footfalls drew closer. Eddie tensed. Taking the guard down would be straightforward, but assaulting a civilian hadn't been part of the plan.

He might have to do it, though. The man was now just feet away. Eddie clenched his fists—

A phone chimed. The guard stopped, taking it out to read a text – then gasped and ran past the alcove without so much as a sidelong glance before rushing down the stairs.

Eddie cautiously peeked out. 'Dunno what just happened,' he whispered, 'but it was bloody lucky that it did.'

'Luck had nothing to do with it,' Alderley said smugly. 'I told you we could arrange a distraction. We drilled into his phone and accessed his text messages. Turns out he's having an affair. So we spoofed a text from his wife saying she knows about the other woman and is leaving and taking the kids *right now.*'

'I'm impressed. Didn't realise you were so devious.'

Alderley chuckled. 'I know you have a rather low opinion of me, but I am the head of SIS, remember? I *have* done this kind of thing before.'

'Wouldn't want to be that bloke when he gets home.' Eddie stepped into the hallway. 'So there's *definitely* no one else on this floor, right?'

'No, we're certain,' Alderley replied. 'You're all clear.'

'Good.' The Yorkshireman continued to Pinto's office. 'Let's see how Macy did . . .'

'You're putting a lot of faith in a seven-year-old, you know.'

'Yeah, I am.'

He slowly turned the handle, pushing at the door. A scrape of metal from the bolt as it caught . . . then popped open. 'That's my girl,' he muttered with pride as he tugged out the mashed wad of paper. 'All right. I'll get into position. Just hope Jared can get Lobato in here.'

'We'll find out soon enough,' Alderley reported. 'Looks like they're about to meet.'

Jared approached Lobato and his hangers-on. With the tech billionaire's bodyguards preventing anyone else from getting too close, Pinto was acting as an impromptu moderator, passing on questions from other guests.

Lobato gave somebody a terse reply. More questions immediately bombarded him. Pinto looked between the other visitors to choose one—

'Hey, Lobato!' Jared shouted, voice echoing from the high ceiling. Pinto's gaze snapped towards him, drawn by the disrespectful nature of the cry. Confusion crossed his face; he didn't recognise the young man.

'Lobato!' Jared called again, holding up his phone. 'Ana Rijo wants to talk to you!' Lobato froze at the name.

'I – I don't know who that man is,' said Pinto. 'He is not a guest. I will have him removed.'

'No, wait,' said Lobato hurriedly. 'Let me speak to him.' He glanced at the curious faces surrounding him. 'Is there somewhere we can talk in private?'

Pinto nodded. 'In my office. Ladies and gentlemen, if you will excuse us? I am sure Mr Lobato will return soon.'

'This will not take long,' Lobato said, regarding Jared coldly.

Pinto led the way to the stairs. Lobato gestured for his bodyguards to follow, and whispered something that drew grimfaced nods in response. The Mossad agent assessed the pair. They were large, almost certainly ex-military, probably even special forces; Lobato could afford the best. He could probably take on one of them alone, but not both. He would need help.

He hoped Eddie was in a position to provide it.

Outside the Scuola Grande, a red speedboat puttered along the canal. Oleg Maximov was at the helm, the hulking Russian glancing back to make sure the cargo in the rear seats was still there before bringing his craft to the little piazza. Several of the boats that had transported VIP guests to the museum were tied up; he stopped beyond them and tossed a looped mooring rope loosely over a stone stanchion.

Nobody seemed concerned about his parking there. He clambered out, leaving the boat behind as he lumbered west down an alley.

Pinto led the little group to his office. 'Please, come in,' he said. 'Shall I stay, or—'

'I would prefer privacy,' Lobato told him.

The Italian nodded. 'Of course. I will wait for you downstairs.' He left, closing the door behind him.

Lobato regarded Jared icily. 'What do you want?'

Jared moved to the windows, his face turned a golden-red by the sunset. He peered down at the piazza before facing Lobato. Pinto's desk was between them, the bodyguards flanking it on each side to block the way to their boss. 'Ana Rijo's not happy about what happened in Morocco.'

Lobato frowned. 'She got what was agreed to. There is nothing more to say.'

'Oh, she's got *plenty* more to say.' Jared started a video call, then turned the screen towards the billionaire. 'You shouldn't have double-crossed her. Now she wants more money – a *lot* more money – or we'll go to the cops and the media and tell them how you set up Nina Wilde aboard the *Atlantia*.'

Lobato's features tightened. 'What double-cross?' he demanded as Ana appeared on the screen. 'Ms Rijo. What is this about? We had an agreement – why are you violating it?'

'You know why,' Ana snapped. 'You tried to have me killed!'

He blinked. 'What are you talking about?'

'Don't pretend you don't know! You sent men to kill me in Morocco, and Eddie Chase too.'

The thin man was now fixated on the image on the phone, as were his bodyguards. Behind them, a figure slid silently from beneath the chaise longue.

'I did not,' Lobato told Ana, indignation breaking through his usual affectless front. 'Why would I? You did your job, exactly as planned.'

'Then where is my money?' she cried.

'If you did not follow the instructions to collect it, that is not my problem.' A frown. 'You met Chase? What did you tell him?'

'I told him everything! My loyalty to you ended when you tried to kill us.'

Lobato stepped towards the phone as if to get closer to Ana. 'And where is Chase now?'

'Ay up,' said the man in question from behind him.

Lobato and his bodyguards whirled, shocked – only for one of them to be literally shocked as Eddie fired a Taser point-blank into his chest, dropping him to the floor. Before the other man could react, Jared vaulted over the desk and tackled him, slamming him against the wall and seizing him in a chokehold. The guard tried to throw the Israeli off his back, but the Mossad agent's merciless grip quickly cut off the blood supply to his brain. A last strangled gasp, then he collapsed.

Lobato remained frozen in disbelief during the brief explosion of violence. Eddie dropped the Taser and stepped in front of him. 'Remember me?' he growled. 'You framed my wife. You're going to tell me why.'

'I can explain,' said Lobato, now fearful. 'What you think is happening is not—'

'I didn't mean this second, arsehole.' Before the skinny man could react, Eddie stabbed the little injector into his arm. Lobato stared at it – then wobbled, eyes rolling, and flopped to the floor as if his bones had liquefied.

Jared stepped over him. 'These two won't be out for long.'

'Open the window,' Eddie told him. Jared did so as the Yorkshireman retrieved his gear. 'You fix up the rope, I'll bag Marty Hopkirk here.' He tossed the rope to the Israeli, then far from gently bundled the limp white-clad figure into the canvas sack.

Jared looped one end of the rope around the legs of the heavy wooden desk, then pulled it with him to the window as Eddie tugged a cord to close the bag. 'You sure this is the best way?'

'We won't have time for owt else.' The Englishman dragged the sack to the window, then picked up the coil of remaining rope. 'Go, quick.'

'See you at the bottom.' Jared waited for Eddie to brace himself before gripping the line firmly and climbing out of the window.

Eddie grunted as he took the other man's weight, then let the rope out, foot by foot. Jared descended towards the piazza. It only took seconds for him to reach the level of the floor below; three more to go until he was on the ground.

One of the bodyguards moaned. The Yorkshireman's eyes snapped to him. If he recovered while Jared was still too high up to survive a fall . . .

He let out an extra foot of rope each time, the line burning his hands as he took Jared's weight. The Israeli was more than halfway down. Another fifteen feet and he would be able to drop safely to the ground. 'Jared!' he called. 'They're waking up!'

The shout drew attention, people on the canalside looking up in surprise at the descending man. 'I'm going to jump!' Jared replied.

'You'll break your legs, you bloody idiot! Hold on!'

Eddie let out more rope as quickly as he dared, then lurched back as the weight on the line suddenly vanished. He looked down at the piazza. Jared scrambled back upright in front of the startled onlookers. 'I'm okay!' the younger man called. 'Send him down!'

The Yorkshireman hooked a quick-release clasp attached to the rope's other end through metal eyelets in the sack, then hauled it up. Despite his rail-thin build, Lobato was heavier than he'd expected. 'Must be that giant fucking brain,' he grumbled as he manoeuvred his cargo to the window.

One of the bodyguards groaned, levering himself on to his side. The other man stirred with a moan of his own.

The moment they saw Eddie, anger and adrenalin would blow away the lingering fog of their unconsciousness. He had to speed up the escape—

'Jared!' he shouted. 'Get ready to catch him!'

'What do you mean, catch?' Jared replied, before realising he meant it literally. 'No, wait!'

But Eddie had already tossed the billionaire through the window.

25

Lobato plunged towards the piazza five floors below.

Eddie hurriedly grabbed the rope – not the coiled length attached to the sack, but the one Jared had used to reach the ground. He clamped both hands around it and jammed a foot against the heavy wooden desk to brace himself—

The rope yanked tight.

His palms seared as the top layer of skin was rasped off, but he kept hold and bent his raised leg to absorb the shock as he caught the falling man. Straining to support Lobato's weight, he looked out of the window.

The sack was swinging ten feet above the ground. Jared stared up at him, aghast. 'I wasn't ready to catch him!'

'I wasn't ready to *drop* him!' Eddie shot back. One of the bodyguards sat up and saw him. 'Wait until I get down there!'

'How are you going to get— Oh *shit*!'

The Israeli got his answer as Eddie jumped from the window.

He dropped, the rope immediately pulling taut, and gasped in pain as he slammed against the Scuola's wall. But his fall had been slowed, Lobato acting as a counterweight. The sack bumped back up the side of the building as Eddie descended.

Not quickly enough. Lobato weighed less than he did, but the difference was not huge. Realising he couldn't rely on gravity alone, Eddie leaned backwards until he was practically horizontal, soles scraping against the wall as he walked himself down it.

He passed the ascending sack—

One of the bodyguards peered out from above, bewildered by the scene – until he realised who was in the canvas bag. He ducked back, shouting to his comrade.

'*Now* get ready to catch him!' Eddie yelled as he reached a tall arched window on the first floor. Jared darted into position below as the Yorkshireman returned to the vertical . . . then let go of the rope.

He fell – and caught the window ledge. The onlookers gasped.

The rope shot back up to the window. A yelp of sheer panic came from above as the bodyguard realised his boss was plummeting towards the pavement. Jared's own reaction was barely less frantic.

Eddie had already let go of the marble sill, dropping to the ground. Even rolling on touchdown, the landing was still painful, but he ignored it and threw himself in front of Jared as the bag hurtled towards them.

The Israeli caught it, but not even a Mossad agent at the peak of physical fitness could take the weight of a man falling from nearly four floors up. He collapsed – on to Eddie, the Englishman's breath pounded from him as his friend and the unconscious Lobato bounced off his back.

'*Chara!*' Jared yelled. 'Eddie! Are you okay?'

'Fine,' Eddie croaked. His ribs hurt, but there was none of the piercing pain of a broken bone. 'All those years . . . of Macy using me as . . . a trampoline paid off.'

Both men looked up as the rope jerked. They had not taken the full force of Lobato's touchdown by themselves; the bodyguards had grabbed the line just before it disappeared, slowing the billionaire's fall. 'Time to go,' said Eddie, staggering upright. He released the clasp, the rope springing upwards, then started to drag the sack across the piazza towards the red boat Maximov had moored. Jared hurried to help him.

One of the bodyguards shouted down at them angrily before

retreating into the office. 'They'll be here in a minute,' Jared warned.

'They'll have to join the queue,' said Eddie. A museum guard at the VIP arrival area was already gabbling into a phone. 'Come on, quick!'

They shoved the sack into the boat's rear. Eddie jumped into the front as Jared unhitched the mooring rope. 'Go!' shouted the Israeli. He turned and sprinted east, back past the Scuola Grande. 'See you in five minutes!'

'Four would be better!' Eddie retorted, starting the engine. He jammed the throttle to full power and peeled away from the piazza, heading west.

The canal he entered was the Rio de le Muneghete, one of the many narrow channels cutting through the old city. Its speed limit was just five kilometres per hour. This being Italy, that restriction was ignored by practically everybody – but even the locals yelled as he powered past them, kicking up a frothing wake that smacked against the walls and sent other traffic rocking uncontrollably. He glanced back to see large men running out of the Scuola, then the museum was blocked from view by the canal's curve.

He looked ahead again. The plan would require precise timing. He kept his hand on the throttle as he headed for his first rendezvous.

'He went that way!' yelled one of Lobato's bodyguards as he reached the quay. The speeding boat's churned trail was impossible to miss. 'Get after him!'

The men with Lobato in Pinto's office had been joined by another pair. The first two each commandeered a moored craft, the new arrivals vaulting into a third behind them. Any objections the museum staff had to the triple piracy were silenced as the last boat's passenger drew a gun. Onlookers retreated fearfully as the three vessels swept away.

The leader followed his quarry's wake into the Rio de le Muneghete, weaving between the rolling locals. The walls quickly closed in, brickwork cliffs on both sides as the canal curved northwards. He didn't know how far ahead Mr Lobato's kidnapper was, but he should come into sight as the waterway straightened—

A low bridge ahead – and just beyond it was the red boat!

It surged away in a spitting spray of froth, but the three pursuing boats had closed the gap enormously. The bodyguard clenched the steering wheel in angry triumph. It wouldn't be long before they caught up, and then the bastard who had kidnapped Mr Lobato would get what was coming to him.

Eddie glanced back as he accelerated to see the first of the three boats roar under the bridge, its driver ducking beneath the low archway. The Yorkshireman had lost valuable seconds, and didn't know if he could make them up again.

He powered past more moored boats, sending them thudding against the walls. Under another small crossing, then the way ahead was clear for about a hundred metres until a sharp bend in the canal. Just before it was a further arched bridge.

The distance was eaten up with alarming rapidity. Eddie aimed for the gap between the stationary boats on each side of the canal, bracing himself for the turn – and flicking his gaze towards the figure standing at the waterline.

Ana.

He roared past her – ducking and turning hard as he swept beneath the bridge, just as she kicked out at the prow of one of the stationary boats.

It swung into the path of the oncoming vessels. The leading bodyguard saw it in time to throw his craft around it, glancing off another moored boat before recovering and powering under the bridge.

The man behind him was not so lucky.

He tried to swerve, but was going too fast. His boat hit the obstruction and was flung into the base of the bridge, wood and fibreglass smashing into splinters.

The third boat snaked through the wreckage before following the other vessels around the corner. Ana paused long enough to see that the crashed bodyguard was still alive before hurrying up the steps and disappearing down a nearby street.

Eddie heard the collision, but realised that the trap had not caught all the pursuing boats. He cursed and pressed on. The new leg of the canal was longer, an almost straight two-hundred-metre stretch before the next turn—

A *crack* from astern, and a bullet slammed into the back of his boat.

He dropped as low as he could as another round tore past barely a foot overhead, putting his boat into a serpentine weave. The next shot went wide. A glance back. The man in the lead boat was firing one-handed, steering with the other. Ahead, the canal began to curve to the left. Eddie followed it around, his pursuer forced to take the wheel with both hands as a sharper bend approached.

Eddie made a hard turn through the corner, flinging a wave against the wall of another of Venice's grand buildings. The bodyguard swung after him—

A bright yellow ROV burst out of the water into his path.

Matt Trulli had positioned *Ringo* under the surface, waiting for Eddie to pass – and now the little submersible unleashed its new cargo. A simple compressed-air cannon, a short length of plastic tubing connected to a small gas cylinder, fired its contents into the air ahead of the onrushing boat—

Where the stun grenade exploded.

The Israeli weapon was designed to be used indoors. Outside, the effect of its dazzling flash and ear-splitting bang was reduced, but the detonation still overpowered the bodyguard's senses.

Only for a moment . . . but that was enough.

He recovered – and saw the building looming before him. He screamed, spinning the wheel—

Too late. The boat skittered sidelong into the wall with a stucco-shattering impact. The man was thrown into the water as his battered craft rebounded.

The third boat slowed. Its pilot angled towards the frantically splashing bodyguard, but his companion shouted angrily, pointing after the disappearing Englishman. With a half-hearted apology to the floundering man, the driver powered away in pursuit.

Another one down, though it still wasn't enough to ensure Eddie's escape. But at least he had opened up some distance—

He reached a crossroads – and saw a motor launch in police livery rumbling towards him from the right. He immediately turned to surge past before it could block him. It was the route he had actually meant to take, but the appearance of the police complicated things enormously.

The launch swung sharply about to follow him, but before it could finish its turn, the bodyguards' boat burst out of the side canal and rushed past it, the wake almost sending the cops into a wall. Furious at the affront, they charged after the fleeing boats, a wailing siren echoing off the surrounding buildings.

The new canal was wider, but also more busy, plodding cargo barges joining the smaller boats and tourist gondolas. Eddie ducked through a narrowing gap between two of the lumbering vessels, then brought his boat under a pair of bridges. He was now approaching the intersection with the Rio de San Polo, a main artery leading to the Grand Canal. His pursuers would expect him to head down it to reach the broad waterway.

Instead, he turned hard to the right, swinging into the Rio de San Stin.

It was far narrower. Not only were boats moored on each

side, but traffic was traversing the canal in both directions. He weaved through the logjam. The bodyguards rounded the corner to follow him, the police launch behind them. It was much faster than its prey.

Ahead was a bridge, a ninety-degree turn beyond. Eddie could see people on the crossing, the siren's wail catching their attention.

He knew two of them. As he drew closer, Olivia and Macy stepped apart, stretching something out between them.

He rounded another boat, its occupants yelling abuse at him, then raced under the bridge and hurled his craft into the hard left turn. Lobato's bodyguards and the police passed on either side of the boat he had just overtaken. His two pursuers were almost level, the bodyguards narrowly in the lead. They reached the bridge—

The net that Macy and Olivia had been holding splashed into the water just ahead of them.

The bodyguard driving realised the danger and threw his vessel hard over to avoid it, spinning around – but the cops, focused on their quarry, didn't see the net until it was too late.

Their boat rode over it, ploughing the floating nylon lines under its keel—

The roar of its engine became a shrill of disintegrating metal as the net entangled – and instantly jammed – the propeller. The cops were thrown to the deck, then the police boat continued onwards in abrupt silence, thunking against a flight of stone steps.

The Yorkshireman was already speeding down the Rio dei Frari, but was now out of tricks. The net had been his team's last booby trap. To escape, he would now have to rely on his own skill – and as much luck as he could muster.

He thundered under two more bridges, then made another sharp turn into a new waterway. This was the narrowest yet, barely wide enough to take two boats abreast. Nobody was traversing it, fortunately, but another right-angled turn was coming up fast. Behind, the roar of another outboard told him Lobato's men had entered the canal.

He made the turn – as a gunshot echoed between the buildings, shards of red brickwork exploding mere feet behind.

A low metal bridge loomed right in front of him, forcing him to duck or lose his head. 'Shit!' he gasped as he cleared it, hoping his hunters didn't have quick reflexes.

The hope was dashed as both men stooped low to whip beneath the bridge. The passenger was the first to rise, raising his gun again – only to duck once more as he saw an even lower bridge in their path.

Eddie had to drop practically beneath the gunwales to avoid decapitation. Bushy ivy dangling from the old stonework lashed him, leaves flying like green shrapnel, then he was through. Tourists gawped at his narrow escape, their amazement repeated seconds later as the bodyguards followed him under.

The canal curved to the right, widening enough to let three boats pass abreast – much to Eddie's relief, as he swerved past a dawdling motorboat. Even with the extra space, his craft still scraped a wall. He grimaced, then roared under another bridge. There was a junction beyond, an arm of the canal leading left, but he kept going straight, seeing more open water ahead.

He had reached the Grand Canal.

One of Venice's busiest waterways, and certainly its most famous, the Grand Canal divided the old city in two, languidly snaking from north-west to south-east. Eddie had emerged about three-quarters of the way down its length, but even though this section was not nearly as great a draw for tourists as the likes of the Rialto Bridge, visible about half a kilometre to his left, it was still packed with traffic. Motorboats, cargo barges and traditional gondolas mingled with large *vaporetti* water buses and luxurious pleasure cruisers.

The passengers aboard the cruiser Eddie had to swerve to

dodge found their enjoyment abruptly curtailed, dirty spray drenching them as he accelerated into the canal. He swung in front of a long barge, then powered across the bows of a *vaporetto* going the other way.

His pursuers took a wider route to follow him. That reopened the gap a little, but the space between the two boats was still too slim for the Yorkshireman's liking.

The sweeping wooden arch of the Ponte dell'Accademia traversed the curving canal ahead, specks of sunlight glinting off the hundreds of padlocks attached by lovers to the bridge's railings despite the Venetian authorities' regular rounds with bolt-cutters. His destination was just beyond it – and so was Jared.

He hoped . . .

Jared pounded across the Ponte dell'Accademia, weaving between the tourists. He had taken a more direct route than Eddie, the Englishman deliberately following a circuitous path to give the younger man as much time as possible to reach their rendezvous.

He glanced at his watch. Five minutes had already passed. He was late – and the sight of the red boat cutting perilously close to the piers along the north side warned him that he was almost out of time.

Resurgent adrenalin pushing him on, he reached the shore. His destination was on the far side of the Palazzo Cavalli-Franchetti, forcing him to go all the way around its walled grounds. Would he get there before Eddie?

He would have to.

Eddie's boat swept beneath the bridge. More piers stabbed out into the Grand Canal, candy-striped poles marking the palazzo's private mooring – but he could see his final turn beyond them, a narrow channel between the art gallery and its equally grand neighbour.

He made a sweeping turn into the shadowy tributary. Lobato's bodyguards followed, another gunshot accompanied by a burst of shattered plaster from the brickwork just behind him.

They were still willing to kill him to save their boss. And now he had entered a dead end.

The little canal terminated at a wall at the southern end of the Campo Santo Stefano: a wall towards which he was racing at full speed.

'Hope you're here, Jared!' he said, aiming for its base.

Two sturdy planks angled out of the water to the piazza's edge six feet above, forming a ramp. Eddie had no time to make a precise approach. He drove straight at the beams and braced himself—

The boat hit the planks, the impact flinging him backwards as his craft skidded up the makeshift ramp and smashed through the railing at its top. People screamed and ran as the vessel spun across the piazza, keel rasping over the stone paving.

Eddie clung to his seat as the boat ground to a halt. The sack in the rear thumped into the footwell. Dizzied, he looked back at the narrow canal. Lobato's bodyguards would try to follow him up the ramp . . .

And would fail.

Jared had reached the canal's end mere seconds earlier. He grabbed a rope tied to one of the planks, and pulled it off the piazza's edge into the water.

The bodyguards saw it splash down just before they reached it. The driver jammed the throttle into reverse and hauled on the wheel – but in the confined channel, he had nowhere to go.

The boat hit the remaining plank, nearly flipping over before slamming side-on into the wall. The driver was hurled against the gunwales, his companion flying out to hit the stonework with a heavy thud before sliding almost cartoonishly back into the hull.

Jared hurried to Eddie's beached boat. 'You okay?' he gasped, breathless from his mad dash.

Eddie clambered out. 'You cut it a bit bloody close!'

The younger man managed a grin. 'You're okay.'

'What about them?'

'Still alive, if that's what you mean. Come on.'

Phones had turned towards them. Jared raised a hand to block his features from the startled tourists' lenses and started northwards at a run. Eddie gave the canvas sack a brief look, then followed.

One of the bodyguards climbed up a ladder to the piazza. But there were too many civilians between him and his fleeing targets to risk a shot. Instead, he limped to the abandoned boat. The sack was still inside, its contents unmoving. 'Mr Lobato!' the man shouted fearfully. 'Mr Lobato, are you okay?'

He grabbed the cord holding the bag closed and tugged it open—

The second bodyguard staggered to his shocked comrade. 'What's wrong?' he said. 'Is he . . . is he dead?'

'No . . . I mean, I don't think so,' said the first. 'I don't know. I don't know!'

He pulled the sack from the boat. Its contents clattered on to the pavement.

Pieces of a mannequin. Its blank head bore a child's crude crayon drawing of a face. An adult had added a speech balloon: *Suckers!*

Both men gawped at it. 'Wait,' said the second. 'So if we were chasing this . . . where's Mr Lobato?'

26

Eddie and Jared returned to the apartment. 'Daddy!' Macy cried as they entered. 'Are you all right?'

Her father embraced her. 'I'm fine, love,' he said, giving her a kiss. 'Did you get out of the museum without any trouble?'

'After Gideon went with Jared, we made our excuses and left,' Olivia told him. 'I assumed from the chaos a few minutes later that you'd managed to get out of there as well.'

'Yeah, the quick way down. What about Lobato? Is Oleg back yet?'

Ana gestured towards another room. 'In there.'

Eddie and Jared entered to find Maximov and Matt standing watch over the unconscious billionaire, who had been laid out on a bed. 'Ah, Chase!' said the scar-faced Russian, greeting him with an overpowering bear hug. 'You are okay!'

'Yeah,' Eddie replied. 'You have any trouble getting him here?'

Maximov shook his head. 'After I pull him up from boat, I just put sack over my shoulder and walk.' Eddie's stop beneath the first bridge had been just long enough for the huge former Spetznaz soldier to lower a rope, the Englishman to hook it to the sack, and the bag to be hauled up as if it contained nothing heavier than pillows. 'No one even look at me.'

'More likely they were too *scared* to look,' said Matt, smiling. 'I mean, an ugly two-metre-tall guy built like a brick shithouse? He could've been carrying the crown jewels and people would've still looked the other way.'

Maximov glared at him. 'Who is ugly?'

'Ah – not you, mate!' the Australian hurriedly backtracked.

Eddie laughed. 'We got him, that's the main thing. Nice work with the flash-bang, by the way.'

'Nobody got hurt, did they?' Matt asked.

'Nothing fatal,' Eddie assured him, before turning his attention to the man on the bed. 'Can't promise the same for this twat, though.'

He looked at his watch. Almost thirty minutes had passed since his escape from the Scuola Grande. If Alderley was correct, Lobato would soon regain consciousness. 'All right,' he said, returning to the main room, 'everyone except Ana, it's time to go. I don't want Lobato seeing you.'

'Are you sure?' asked Jared. 'I can help you interrogate him.'

'Thanks, but I can manage. Macy, go back to the hotel with Olivia and wait for me, okay?'

Macy shook her head. 'I want to stay with you, Daddy.'

Olivia gently took her hand. 'No, no. Your father needs to . . . talk to Mr Lobato.'

The little girl looked Eddie directly in the eyes. 'Are you going to kill him, Daddy?'

He didn't break her gaze. 'No.'

'But he's a bad man, and he tried to hurt you and Mommy.'

'Just because someone's bad doesn't mean you have to kill 'em.' That brought an assortment of disbelieving looks and mocking coughs from his friends. Eddie glowered at them. 'Trying to set a good example for my daughter, thank you very much! But no,' he went on to Macy, 'me and Ana need to talk to him on our own. Nobody else needs to get involved.'

'Bit late for that,' Matt noted sardonically.

'I'll let you all know what's happened once we're done,' the Yorkshireman assured the others. 'But right now, you need to go – he'll wake up any minute.'

Reluctantly they started to leave. Jared paused at the door. 'If you have any trouble with him . . .'

'We won't. Trust me. All right, come on, shift!'

Everyone except Ana left the apartment, Eddie giving Macy a loving farewell before returning to Lobato's room. The skinny man was beginning to stir. 'Looks like Alderley was bang on with his timing.'

'So what do we do?' Ana asked.

'Wake him up.' Eddie hauled Lobato up by his collar – then slapped him hard across both cheeks. 'Oi! Dickhead! Nap time's over.'

Lobato gasped in pained surprise. He looked blearily around as the room came into focus, only to freeze in terror, suddenly fully awake, as he recognised the man looming over him. 'No! Don't— Where am I? How did you get me away from my bodyguards?'

'Knowledge and preparation are the key to success, some idiot once told me.'

Lobato tried to adopt a defiant air, but his fear was impossible to mask. 'You've kidnapped me! You'll spend the rest of your life in prison for—'

Eddie slapped him again, harder. 'Talk without me telling you to, and you'll start losing teeth. Now, Ana said she'd read my file, and I assume you did too. So you know what I've done to people who've tried to hurt my family. Yeah?'

The billionaire's eyes flicked towards Eddie's clenched fist. 'Y-yes,' he whispered.

'Good. So you give me answers, and maybe, just maybe, you'll get out of this room without me breaking every bone in your body.'

'Th-there are two hundred and six bones in the human body,' Lobato stammered. 'I doubt you could—'

Eddie punched him in the mouth. 'Did I ask for a fucking anatomy lesson?'

'I'm sorry!' Lobato feebly spat blood down his chin. 'But the likelihood of your breaking every single bone is so small, I had to point it out! I couldn't help it, it . . . it's a compulsion.'

His captors exchanged looks. 'Great, he's not just a sperg, he's a pedantic one,' the Yorkshireman rumbled. 'All right, Mr Logic, let me make this clear.' He leaned closer. 'I. Can. *Kill*. You.' As Lobato quailed, he went on: 'Nobody knows you're here, and nobody'll be able to find you before I'm done. So just answer the questions without quoting Wikipedia, and you might stay alive for longer than the next five minutes. First one's easy. Where's Nina?'

The wide-eyed Lobato licked his bloodied lips. 'She . . . she is in Granada, in Spain.'

Eddie frowned. 'Granada? What's she doing there? She was in Seville.'

'The artefact she stole from the museum in Seville must have led her there. Agreste is following her.'

'Why did you frame her?'

The billionaire hesitated, before the Yorkshireman's rapidly darkening expression convinced him to reveal the closely held secret. 'So she would find the Atlantean spearheads, of course.'

'Of course,' came the sarcastic echo. 'Still waiting for the *why* part, though.'

Lobato's fear was not enough to fully hide his condescension. 'If they still exist, and Dr Wilde's theory about their nature – that they are some kind of trap and containment for particles of antimatter – is correct, they represent a source of potentially limitless power. My intention is to find and secure them.'

'*If* they still exist,' Eddie said pointedly. 'Which they might not after over eleven thousand years.'

'Dr Wilde found Atlantis after the same amount of time.'

He gave the white-clad man a humourless smile. 'Yeah, I do remember.'

'Why did you need Nina to find these things?' Ana asked. 'You are rich. You could have paid anyone to find them for you.'

Lobato shook his head. 'Dr Wilde is the world's foremost expert on Atlantis. She is therefore the person with the greatest chance of decoding the markers. But she had made enough of her theory public for others to follow through on her research, given time. So when she rejected my attempt to convince her to work with me willingly, I was left with no choice but to implement my plan.'

'And set her up,' Eddie growled. 'You made it look like she'd helped steal the marker, got Ana to break her out of jail – and then she and Agreste faked a shootout to scare her into going on the run!'

'I'm sorry,' Ana said quietly.

Lobato, on the other hand, offered no apologies. 'It had to be done. Fear is a great motivator – as is,' he went on, 'the desire to prove oneself intellectually superior.'

'I'm sure you'd know all about that,' Eddie said sarcastically.

'Yes.' The response was matter-of-fact. 'I created a scenario giving Dr Wilde no choice but to find the spearheads, both to prove her innocence and to prevent the "bad guys" – who were of course following my instructions – from obtaining them by locating them first, all while making her believe the actions she took were of her own volition. In reality, she was being directed at every turn.'

'Bollocks,' said the Yorkshireman. 'You can't have planned for everything she might have done.'

Lobato became almost smug. 'But I did. I used to design games, and the art of successful game design is forcing the player to follow the paths you have prepared, while making them believe they have total freedom of action.'

Eddie shook his head. 'Life isn't a game.'

'The basis of all human civilisation is the creation of systems,'

Lobato countered. 'Systems of government, of economics, of morality. And all systems can be controlled and manipulated if you are aware of their mechanics. A game is merely an abstraction of reality – or conversely, reality is a more complex iteration of a game. The same logic can be applied to both, if you have sufficient intellectual prowess.'

'Which you do, right?'

'Yes.' Again, there was no immodesty in the billionaire's reply; he was simply stating what he considered an inarguable fact. 'Aboard the *Atlantia*, I offered Dr Wilde multiple choices of action, and prepared responses for each. For example, when the raiders left the ship with the marker, a second boat was waiting which she could have used to pursue them. They would have led her to Spain, and from there to Seville and the second marker. She instead opted to stay aboard – so the scenario then became about framing her, giving her motivation to clear her name. When Ana freed her, Agreste then took on the role of a dangerous pursuer, to force her onwards – again, to Seville. There were many other potential branches, but every possibility had been planned for.'

Eddie stared at him . . . then without warning punched him again. 'Didn't plan for *that*, did you, Nostradamus?' he growled as Ana flinched and Lobato squealed in pain. 'So you know exactly where Nina is right now? Then you're going to call Agreste and get him to tell her she's been set up. You're also going to tell the Emir to call off Interpol and straighten things out with the Spanish cops.'

'Interpol never were involved,' Lobato whined. 'That was a fiction, to increase the fear effect and add motivation.'

Eddie was sorely tempted to increase Lobato's own fear effect, but realised the revelation's implication. 'The Dhajanis lied to us? So they're involved too?'

The skinny man nodded. 'I was already in partnership with

the Emir on the solar energy plant and other projects. Once Dr Wilde made her theory public, we realised that if the spearheads were what she believed, they represented a source of antimatter in almost infinitely greater quantities than could ever be produced in a particle collider. That would provide a new source of energy for the world – and it would be one we controlled. We could ensure it would be used for the good of humanity, not as a weapon. That was why I could not allow Dr Wilde to work with the IHA,' he added. 'They cannot be trusted to keep the spearheads from those who would use them for the same purposes as the Atlanteans – destruction.'

'I'd trust the IHA to look after 'em more than you,' said Eddie. 'Especially as you tried to have me and Ana killed in Morocco.'

'I did not,' Lobato objected.

'Thirty-odd guys in hospital say otherwise.'

'I did my job exactly as you asked,' Ana told Lobato angrily. 'But you betrayed me!'

'I did not!' the billionaire repeated, more agitated. 'Why would I? You completed the task I asked of you exactly as required. '

'So if you didn't want us dead, who did?' Eddie demanded – but even as he spoke, he realised Lobato had already given him the answer. 'Who else apart from you knew about the plan? Knew *everything* about it?' He was not so much asking the other man as telling him.

Understanding dawned on Lobato's face. 'Sheikh Fadil,' he said. 'The only other person who knows everything is the Emir!'

27

Granada

The sun had fallen behind the mountains, the sky turning a lurid red. But Nina only belatedly registered the night's arrival, so engrossed in her work that it wasn't until she had trouble reading her notes that she registered her little room was in darkness.

She switched on a bedside lamp. The marker's two halves sat by her feet, her book and the atlas open before her and pages of her hastily scribbled deductions spread out around them. She had been busy for several hours, barely noticing the passage of time.

But her hard work had paid off – almost.

Comparing the stars highlighted on the Alhambra's ceiling to those on the map in the Temple of Poseidon had given her the approximate locations of the vaults containing the spearheads. The Atlantean text on the marker had, once translated as best she could, let her narrow down their positions. There was nothing so clear as a place name, though; being an archaeologist sometimes required the talents of a detective, and this was one of those times.

'The place where to our enemy we are unseen, yet we observe their every act, their city laid out before us' had been the first riddle she solved. A veiled reference to hilltops, she deduced, suggesting the Damoclean weapons had been hidden higher than their targets, to prevent the blast from being blocked by terrain.

The vaults were within line of sight of their targets, but not so close that the Atlanteans would be caught while planting the spearheads.

The line 'as many stadia distant as the Gardens of Pelnius and the Temple of Cleito' seemed to confirm that. She knew from the underwater excavations in Atlantis that the Gardens of Pelnius, an Atlantean king, were roughly six miles from the Temple of Cleito, Poseidon's wife, which in Atlantean terms was seventy-nine stadia, the ancient civilisation's unit of distance. So the vaults were that far from the cities they threatened, near or at the highest point. But in which direction?

The answer seemed to come from another inscription: one translating as 'from the domain of Boreal'. Boreal was a god shared by the Atlantean and ancient Greek pantheons, the personification of winter and the north wind. His domain was, naturally, to the north. The Atlanteans had cloaked the vaults' locations beneath riddles that would be obvious to them but obscure to anyone else . . . except for obsessive archaeologists millennia later.

So now she knew not only the regions where the vaults had been hidden, but how to pinpoint their exact positions. She made some final notes, then picked up the atlas to regard the spots she had marked on a map of the world.

There were three, corresponding to the highlighted stars in the Hall of the Ambassadors that did not appear on the map from the Temple of Poseidon. And at two of them, she already knew, there would be nothing to find.

The first was in the southern Aegean Sea, at the Mediterranean's eastern end. She did not need precise coordinates to figure out exactly where. Its position, north of Crete and roughly equidistant between Greece and Turkey, meant it could only be one place: the island of Thera, now Santorini. An important hub of the seagoing Minoan empire, and with sketchy archaeological evidence suggesting it was home to another civilisation long before that, it had been obliterated by a massive volcanic eruption three and a half thousand years ago.

Had the spearhead itself been responsible? It was possible. Nobody in the present day had been insane enough to use a nuclear bomb to set off a volcano, but she knew from a previous adventure just how large a hole a powerful nuke could rip into the earth. The biggest bomb of all time, the Soviet 'Tsar Bomba', had been fifty megatons of fusion fury unleashed, and despite detonating more than two miles above the ground it had still blasted a crater almost half a mile wide. The explosion of just three pounds of antimatter would be even more destructive.

And the Atlanteans had used it as the ultimate leverage against their rivals. Obey, submit, surrender – or be utterly annihilated.

It seemed unlikely they had actually carried out such a threat; Atlantis had sunk over seven thousand years before Thera's eruption. But perhaps their doomsday weapon had remained *in situ*, forgotten . . . until something set it off. And the result had been one of the largest volcanic eruptions in human history.

She looked across the map to the second cross at the site of *another* of the largest eruptions ever recorded.

Krakatoa.

The Indonesian islands had seen much volcanic activity, but the eruption of 27 August 1883 put them on the map, while ironically all but wiping several of them from it. Had Krakatoa too hidden a spearhead?

There had not yet been any direct evidence of the Atlanteans reaching Indonesia, but Nina had followed their trail across Asia as far as Nepal and Tibet, and was convinced she had only scratched the surface. If they had travelled beyond the Pacific's western shores, the great island chain sweeping from Thailand practically to Australia would have been the first thing they found. She knew that an even more ancient civilisation, known only as the Veteres, had made the same journey; it was not a stretch that explorers from Atlantis could have followed suit.

And the Atlanteans were conquerors, regarding any land they crossed as part of their dominion. If they encountered a civilisation in the archipelago powerful enough to be considered a threat – a possibility, since evidence of human population there dated back over forty thousand years – they might have deemed it dangerous enough to deploy their ultimate deterrent.

Which, like its counterpart on Thera, had been lost to time . . . until the nineteenth century.

'Or not,' she said, with a small shrug. She was realistic enough to know all of this was nothing more than theory, even pure speculation. But she had discovered Atlantis, and more besides, from the same starting point. What if there was truth to this too?

If so, there was also great danger.

Her gaze went to the last cross. It was in eastern Turkey, not far north of the Syrian border. The site of an ancient civilisation – and this one was well-documented fact.

Gobekli Tepe was one of the world's oldest known cities, at least a contemporary of Atlantis and possibly dating back even further. Lost and buried for millennia, it was only rediscovered in the 1960s, and its full extent and importance not realised for another three decades. Excavation of the neolithic complex was still ongoing, but nobody in the archaeological community believed all its secrets would be uncovered for a very long time.

A civilisation, advanced for its era, existing at the height of Atlantis's power, on the route from Europe into central Asia. A gatekeeper – a potential rival. That was something the Atlanteans would not allow to stand without challenge.

Had they planted the third spearhead nearby?

She flicked through the atlas to a map of Turkey. The level of detail was relatively low, but it was enough to show that while Gobekli Tepe was situated on a plateau, higher mountains rose all around it. If the pattern was repeated for all three vaults, the spearhead would have been hidden on the highest hill roughly six miles to the north. It would be straightforward enough to find the most likely candidate once she had access to proper maps and an internet connection.

Getting a little ahead of ourselves, aren't we? she thought wryly. There was the minor matter of being hunted by the police to deal with . . .

Before she could mull any more on that problem, a commotion from the reception area below caught her attention. She had been so engrossed in her work that the hostel's comings and goings hadn't even registered, but the voices coming up through the floorboards were particularly loud – urgent, even. She listened, realising they were speaking in English. One voice was the hostel's manager, the other someone asking for a room—

Sudden fear struck her. The man wasn't asking for *a* room. He was asking for *her* room! 'The American woman, with long red hair! Where is she?'

The manager's reply was indistinct, but clearly a confused denial of any knowledge. It took Nina a moment to remember she no longer *had* long red hair. The other voice grew louder. 'I know she is here! An American woman, alone! What room?'

Nina jumped from the bed. Her pursuers had found her!

She had to get out of here. But even as she donned her shoes, she heard footsteps running up the stairs. More than one person. The main staircase was the nearest way out of the building, and now it was blocked.

The window.

She threw it open. Street lights had come on outside, revealing a man at the hostel's entrance. He looked up at the noise, and saw her.

The leader of the raiders. The same hard-faced man she had faced aboard the *Atlantia*.

A glance back at the bed – at the markers, her notes. *Shit!* She had to take them; combined, they led straight to the last spearhead's location—

No time. The pounding feet were almost up the stairs.

She jumped on to the windowsill and leaned out, stretching to grab the bottom of the small balcony of the room above. Her fingers scraped through bird droppings and cigarette ash before hooking over the crumbling brick around its edge. Feet scrabbling against the twisted skeins of electrical cables running up the building's side, she hauled herself upwards just as the door of her room was smashed open.

Someone shouted in Arabic. She glanced down. The raiders' leader had disappeared, probably into the building, but he had been replaced by a much closer threat. A young Middle Eastern man leaned from her window. He grabbed her foot, but she jerked it clear before he could get a firm hold.

The man started out after her. Nina dragged herself over the rust-bubbled railing on to the balcony. It was little more than a foot wide, narrow French doors opening inwards. She shoulder-barged them. They burst open, sending her reeling through on to the bed. The two men sharing it sat up in shock, one of them yelping something in German. 'Sorry!' said Nina, rolling off and scrambling to the exit. 'Go about your business!'

She threw the door open, emerging in a hallway identical to the one below. The main stairs were to her right, but she could already hear someone hurrying up them. Another startled German cry warned that the man following her had reached the balcony.

Nina ran left, hoping the hostel had a fire escape. The hall turned, taking her deeper into the old building. Someone shouted orders: the leader, sending his men after her. At least three pursuers, and if it was the entire crew of raiders from the *Atlantia*, over twice that many. She had to get out of the building, fast.

A door was marked *Salida*: exit. She crashed through to find herself in a gloomy stairwell at the rear of the hostel. Down—

Light flooded in below as someone kicked open a door. *Up!*

She hared upstairs. Two more storeys, then she reached the final landing. A door led into the hostel's top floor, but there was another exit. Nina rushed through to find herself on a small roof terrace, cheap metal tables bearing ashtrays and cigarette burns. The deep red sky cast an unsettling half-light over the old cityscape before her.

No way down. She looked around. The hostel was midway along a street, the adjoining buildings a mismatched jumble of styles and heights. A two-storey drop to her right, but the rooftop to the left was within reach.

She used a table as a step to climb on to it. Tiles clattered beneath her feet, one shifting under her weight and almost making her stumble. She recovered and continued up to the ridge, grabbing a chimney stack for support as she got her bearings.

No apparent way down to ground level. She set off again, arms outstretched for balance as she hurried along the rooftop. A loud bang behind: her pursuers had reached the terrace. Someone shouted. They had seen her.

She jumped to a lower roof, skidding as she dislodged moss and dirt from the old tiles. There was another terrace at the rooftop's rear, a lower level beyond. She angled towards it.

Two men were already running after her, menacing silhouettes against the bloody sky. A third man scrambled up from the hostel's terrace behind them. The leading man was gaining quickly, crossing the sloping surface as sure-footed as a cat.

Nina reached the terrace, dropping down – and recoiled as a small but vicious dog snapped at her, defending its home against the unexpected intrusion. 'Whoa, whoa, it's okay!' she cried, skittering around the furious animal as it lunged repeatedly at her ankles. 'Good boy, girl, whatever!'

There was a squeaky rubber chicken on the floor. She grabbed it, the dog targeting its plaything instead. She was about to toss it at the apartment door to get the animal out of her way, then had a better idea.

The first man vaulted down into the terrace as she ran for its far end – and threw the toy at him. The dog charged after it, barking angrily. The raider reacted to the seemingly frenzied beast with fear. He kicked at the animal, which only doubled its fury. It latched on to his lower leg, sinking its teeth into his flesh. The man shrieked.

Nina jumped on to another roof, one of a line of three or four buildings of roughly the same height. Still no direct way to the ground, but there was a promising gap beyond them. She ran again.

Behind her, the second raider reached the terrace. He did not share his comrade's fear of dogs, swatting the animal with the rubber chicken before lobbing it. The dog released its prey and scrambled after the toy. The man pulled his companion back upright, then turned to pursue Nina once more.

The third man overtook them both. He had bypassed the terrace by traversing the apartment's rooftop, making a flying leap down to Nina's level. Tiles smashed with the impact of his landing, but he stayed on his feet and raced on as broken pieces skittered down the sloping roof in his wake.

Nina looked back. The man was closing fast. She hopped up on to a slightly higher building, hurriedly rounding an illuminated skylight and ducking behind a chimney. The Arab followed—

And took a television antenna to the face.

Nina had pulled the aerial's pole with her as she passed, releasing it to spring back at him. The man screamed and reeled backwards on to the skylight. The glass shattered beneath him, pitching him into the room below to smash down on a startled family's dining table.

But now the other two men had jumped from the terrace. Nina kept going, hopping on to the next roof and reaching the gap she had spotted.

It was completely vertical: an alleyway, the ground three storeys below. No way down. Nor could she jump across, the gap a good fifteen feet and the roof higher on the far side. Even with a run-up, she would fall short. She looked around in desperation. The two men were getting closer.

There was a top-floor balcony at the front of the other building, a furled patio parasol at its corner. The terrace was small, but it was her only option. She hopped back then ran, leaping across the alley—

She barely cleared the railing on the far side, one foot clipping its top as she made a punishing landing. The parasol toppled to land beside her.

The two raiders halted at the roof's edge. The man who had been bitten retreated to make the leap, but winced at the sting of his wounds. A brief exchange, then the second man took his place.

He broke into a run, jumping after their target – to find himself hurtling helplessly towards a waiting spear. Nina had flipped the parasol around, pointing its top over the balcony wall. Even though the shaft was capped by a plastic ball, the blow to his chest was still agonising – and there was more pain to come.

The collision robbed him of the momentum he needed to reach the balcony. Instead, he slammed against the railing and rebounded off it, falling—

Nina cringed, expecting to hear a bone-breaking thud. Instead there was a metallic tearing sound, like a giant guitar string snapping – *then* came the flat thump of a body hitting the ground. She wasn't sure whether to feel relief or dismay when it was followed by a groan; the raider had survived his plunge.

She pushed herself up and peered over the balcony. The man

was sprawled in the alley below. Strands of wire coiled around him – telephone lines. He had fallen on to a clutch of cables, breaking his fall.

Two pursuers down, but the third was still on the rooftop opposite, staring in dismay at his fallen colleague before looking back at Nina with rising anger. And behind him, she spotted another silhouette hurrying along the rooftops.

A light came on in the apartment. Glancing through the window, she saw a middle-aged couple, their expressions first startled, then furious as they saw the trespasser on their balcony. The woman yelled something; Nina picked out the word *policía* clearly enough.

She rushed to the balcony's other end, jumping diagonally from its railing to the slightly lower roof of the next building. The fading light caused her to underestimate the distance, giving her a heart-punching jolt of terror as her feet barely cleared the rotten guttering.

She hurried along the roof's crown. Still no way down, none of the buildings in the row less than three storeys tall, and she would soon reach another alley. This one looked wider than the first. She glanced towards the back of the row. Maybe there was a lower extension at the rear—

A tile broke loose under her foot. She staggered as it slipped away from her, landing hard on her side. More tiles were jarred free, skittering down the sloping roof . . .

And she went with them.

'Shit!' Nina gasped, clutching at the rooftop – but she was already moving too fast, her fingernails scraping over the old tilework. She slid towards the edge, the street opening out below . . .

She twisted, jamming her heels down to catch the gutter. They slammed against the mouldy, leaf-clogged wood – and a yard-long section of guttering broke away, tumbling down to smash into splinters on the sidewalk. She followed it over the edge—

A desperate roll, scrabbling for any last iota of grip – and finding it.

Nina caught the surviving gutter's ragged end with one hand. She dangled above the street, shoulder joint straining. The wooden channel creaked, the rusty peg holding it in place inching from the eaves.

Her other hand found a crack in the wall's scabbed plasterwork. She dug her fingertips into it . . . feeling it crumble.

Another ominous groan from the gutter. She looked up, terrified. The old wood was giving way. She tried to find purchase with her feet, but the movement caused the peg to edge out still further.

One toe caught a protrusion on the wall, but slipped off before she could steady herself. The gutter moaned again, sagging.

She was going to fall—

Dirt dropped on to her face. She shook it off, then looked up again.

The third raider was standing over her.

Nina felt a new surge of fear. He was going to kick her off—

The man stood unmoving for a moment . . . then bent down, stretching out a hand.

A rush of conflicting emotions hit her. Her attempt to escape had failed and the raiders were about to capture her, but at least she would still be alive. She tried to reach up—

A shout from below.

The man froze. Another yell – a command, in Arabic. Nina risked a glance down. It was the raiders' leader. A second man with him was holding something.

She realised with horror that it was all her notes, and the atlas. They had everything they needed to locate the last spearhead.

She had literally drawn them a treasure map marked with an 'X'.

Which meant they no longer needed her.

The man on the roof withdrew his hand and straightened, watching his leader and the other man run off . . . then he looked back at Nina.

His foot edged towards her hand.

'No, please,' Nina gasped as his sole pressed against her knuckles. 'Don't do it!'

He gave her an almost apologetic look, then lifted his boot slightly, about to stamp down—

A clatter from behind him as the last pursuer caught up. The man standing over her turned – and to Nina's shock, crumpled as something struck his head.

His attacker caught him before he toppled over the edge and pulled him back, then peered down at her.

Agreste.

Nina's fear returned at the sight of the Frenchman. He had killed Ana, and now he was going to finish her off too—

His first words were the last thing she expected. 'Let me help you.' Like the raider before him, he reached down to take her hand. Her first instinct was to refuse, before the rational part of her mind took back control; friend or foe, he was the only person who could save her. Nevertheless, she still readied herself as he hauled her back up. If she had to push him off, she would . . .

'Please do not do anything foolish, Dr Wilde,' he said, as if reading her mind. 'Nothing is what it seems.'

'Oh, so that guy *wasn't* just about to kick me off the roof?' she snapped, glancing at the unconscious Arab.

'I am afraid he was. Why, I do not know. It was not part of the plan, and as my instructions are to protect you, I had to become involved directly.'

'Protect me!' The moment she was securely on the roof, she

jerked free and retreated. 'You tried to *kill* me! And you killed Ana!'

He shook his head. 'Ana is still alive. We were working together.'

'*What?*'

Agreste regarded the street below as a police siren began to wail. 'I will explain. But this is not the best place, no? There is, I think, a way down on the other side.' He dragged the raider a few yards back up the roof before continuing towards the ridge.

'Why should I trust you?'

'I saved your life. Is that not enough?'

'I've had bad guys save my life before. It's usually because they want me for something.'

He halted, his wry smile just visible in the encroaching darkness. 'My employer did want you for something, yes. But I am not a bad guy, and,' he went on, glancing after the departed raiders, 'I am afraid someone else has taken it.' He continued to the top of the roof, beckoning for her to follow. 'When we get down, I will tell you what is going on – at least, as much as I know.'

Reluctantly, Nina went with him.

28

Several people had called the police, including the hostel's manager. Nina waited on a nearby street while Agreste went to investigate the *pension*. She almost took the opportunity to run, but she had nowhere to go – and even if she did, without passport or money she would not get far.

He returned after several minutes. 'What's happening?' she asked.

'I spoke to the police,' he replied. 'They are looking for you.'

'Well, yeah. They have been ever since I arrived in the country.'

'That is not what I meant. The manager did not know who you really are, so nor do the local police. All they know is that a group of Arab men broke in looking for you, so they are treating you as a possible victim until they know otherwise.'

'They'll realise who I am when they find my passport, though.'

'That will not happen.' He reached into a pocket and produced that very item.

She took it. 'How the hell did you get hold of *this*? My room must be full of cops!'

'I still have my old identity cards from Interpol and the Sûreté. I assured the young officer guarding your room that it would be returned. When it is not, I doubt he will admit to letting a stranger take it.'

'What about the marker? And my notes?'

'The marker is still there, but I am afraid your notes are gone.

Just before I reached you on the roof, I heard al-Asim tell his man they had all your work, and a map.'

'You know him?' she said, suspicion rising again.

A nod. 'Hashim al-Asim. He is Dhajani, one of the country's senior intelligence operatives.'

'So you were working with him.'

'Not directly. He and his team were also part of the plan, but we were acting independently. Once they took the marker from the ship, that was supposed to be the end of their involvement. Either they have exceeded their orders . . . or they have been given new ones.'

'*What* orders?' she demanded. 'What plan?'

'I can only tell you my part of it,' Agreste said. 'I was employed to provide security for the exhibition aboard the *Atlantia*, yes – but I also arranged that you were alone in the room when the raiders broke in.'

'You set me up?'

'I am afraid so. My apologies.' There was not much contrition in his words, but nor were they completely devoid of sincerity. 'After you were arrested, Ana and I worked together to free you, and then frighten you into going on the run to prove your innocence. She was not hurt.'

Nina struggled to take in the revelation. 'And all this was so . . . so I'd try to stop the bad guys from finding the spearhead by beating them to the marker in Seville?'

'The expectation was that you would examine it and obtain the information you needed. That you would actually steal it came as a surprise.' A small smile. 'I then had to keep the police away from you – a task you made much harder when you discovered the tracking device in your passport.'

'So how did you find me here?'

'I told you, I used to be a detective. I knew you would not stay somewhere requiring you to present identification, which left cheap hotels and hostels. So I visited each in turn until someone told me they had seen you. It was clever of you to change your hair, by the way,' he added. 'Long red hair is a very distinctive feature, and most people would remember that over anything else. However, you are an attractive American woman, travelling alone. In such places, that is also memorable.'

'So how did the Dhajanis find me? They didn't seem like detectives.'

'My attention was on following you,' Agreste told her apologetically. 'I had not even considered that anyone was following *me*. Come, we should leave.' They started down the street. 'I would not want to go to the trouble of finding you again only to have the local police arrest you. You are, after all, a wanted woman.'

'If this whole thing was a set-up, does that mean you're not going to hand me over to the Dhajanis?'

'You were never wanted by the Dhajanis,' he said. 'That too was a ruse.'

'So Interpol didn't have a Red Notice on me?'

'No. Although now, who knows?'

Nina ignored his amusement. 'Eddie told me they did – so the Dhajanis lied to him too?'

'Yes. The Emir backed the plan. But it was devised by—'

'Gideon Lobato,' she cut in.

'Yes. He employed me. How did you know?'

'There weren't many other people trying to convince me to search for the Atlantean spearheads. That son of a bitch!' she snapped. 'He's going to have his ass kicked so hard you'll be able to see the bootprint through his stomach. If I don't do it, I'm sure— Eddie!' she cried. 'I need to tell Eddie and Macy I'm okay!'

Agreste took out a phone. 'Of course. Use this.'

She snatched it from him then gave him a sheepish look.

'This will sound ridiculous, but . . . I can't remember his number.'

'The curse of modern technology,' he replied. 'But I have it, and also your grandmother's. A contingency in case I needed to contact them.'

She didn't want to dwell upon what contingency might have required him to call her relatives. Instead, she waited impatiently for him to find the number, before taking the phone again. 'It's ringing,' she said eagerly, only for anticipation to become annoyance as the tone continued. 'Okay, why isn't he answering? Seriously, I'm on the run – why isn't he hanging on the frickin'—'

'Hello?' The familiar voice was tinged with wariness at receiving a call from an unknown number.

'Eddie, it's me, it's me!' she cried.

'Nina!' He was as relieved and excited as her. 'Jesus Christ, love, are you all right?'

'I'm fine, I'm fine! I'm in Granada, in Spain.'

Oddly, he didn't seem surprised. 'And you're okay? What's happening with the police?' he added, concern in his voice. 'You haven't been arrested, have you?'

'No, but I'm with Agreste. He just saved me from the assholes who raided the ship. Listen, this whole thing has been a set-up! I worked out where the spearheads were, where the last surviving one probably still is, but the guys chasing me got all my notes – they'll be able to find it themselves if we don't stop them. They're working for—'

'The Emir of Dhajan and Gideon Lobato.'

She was stunned that he already knew – and oddly deflated. 'Uh, yeah. How did you find out?' Agreste gave her a questioning look. She put the phone on speaker.

'Lobato's right here. He's just told me everything.'

'O-kaaay . . .' How on earth had he pinned down the billionaire? 'So where are you?'

'In Venice. Ana's with me – she decided to help after the Emir sent a bunch of goons to kill us both. Turns out he double-crossed Lobato as well, so we're all on the same team now, more or less. Olivia and Macy are here too.'

'So Ana really is alive,' she said, giving Agreste a brief glance. 'Is Macy okay?'

'Yeah, she's fine,' Eddie assured her. 'Misses her mum, though.'

'Well, hopefully we can take care of that soon. How did you track down Lobato?'

'He said he was coming to Venice, remember? So I rounded up some of my mates and we persuaded him to have a chat.'

'This is one of those times when it's probably best I don't enquire any further, isn't it?' Her eyes widened at an unwelcome thought. 'Oh my God – you didn't involve Macy in this, did you?'

Her husband hesitated before answering. 'Ah . . . a *little* bit.'

'*What?*'

'Don't worry, she was never in any danger. Plus she's too young to go to prison in Italy, I checked.'

'Oh, well, that makes everything all right. Jesus, Eddie!'

'You can have a go at me in person when we're back together. But the most important thing is that we *get* back together.'

'That'll be easier said than done. I'm still wanted by the cops here in Spain.'

'I may be able to assist,' said Agreste. 'I have contacts in the Spanish government. As the marker is intact and undamaged, I can ensure it is returned to the museum safely, and will do what I can to have the charges against you dropped.'

'Good luck with that,' Nina said. 'Emilio Merlo would probably love to see me locked up even if I *hadn't* stolen the marker!'

A new voice over the phone: Lobato. 'I am sure I can persuade him.'

'Why would *you* want to help her?' Eddie demanded. 'You dropped her into this bloody mess in the first place!'

'Dr Wilde is not the only person who has been deceived by the Emir,' the billionaire replied. 'I feel I have a responsibility to correct the situation.'

'I'd say that you damn well do, yeah,' Nina snapped.

'I will do everything I can. You said you found the locations of the spearheads, and that you believe one is still intact?'

'Yes, but I'm sure as hell not going to tell you over the phone. I want you to get me out of this situation that you created first. And even then I might not tell you. I'm not convinced *anybody* should have it.'

'If you do not,' he countered, 'the Emir's men will surely use your notes to find it.'

He was right, she was forced to admit. 'I'll decide what to do once I meet up with you and Eddie. Just get me off the hook with the Spanish cops, okay?'

'I will arrange a flight for you as soon as I have dealt with the authorities,' said Lobato.

'Great,' said Nina. 'I'll see you and Macy as soon as I can, Eddie.'

'Can't wait,' her husband replied.

'Nor can I. Venice, huh? I've always wanted to go there.'

29

Venice

Macy gasped as her mother entered the hotel room. 'Mom! Your hair!'

Nina had forgotten about her changed appearance. 'What do you think?' she said, opening her arms for an embrace. 'Do you like it?'

Macy came to hug her, a little hesitantly. 'It's . . . different,' she said, touching her mother's crudely cropped hair as if expecting it to be as bristly as a broom.

'It's definitely that,' Eddie agreed. 'Gives you a bit of a Tank Girl look.'

'Gee, thanks,' Nina replied. 'That wasn't exactly on my mind when I did it.'

'I kind of like it. Dark hair suits you.'

'Thanks, but it's not staying like this. I'm a redhead and proud of it! And I miss my ponytail.'

'Oh, gosh,' exclaimed Olivia as she entered from an adjoining room. 'Not your usual style.'

'Well, now that I'm off Spain's most-wanted list, I can get back to normal. In however long it takes to grow my hair back.' She kissed Macy, then did the same to her husband and grandmother. 'So. Apparently while I was on the run, you were causing chaos in Venice!' She glared at Eddie. 'I cannot *believe* you dragged Macy and Olivia into whatever the hell you were doing.'

'It was easy,' Macy assured her. 'All I had to do was open a door for Daddy. Oh, and I had to jam the lock in a different door as well.'

Nina was not impressed. 'What, you're teaching our little girl to be a cat burglar now?'

'It all worked out, that's the main thing,' said Eddie. 'Nobody got killed, there wasn't *that* much property damage, and Lobato's on our side now. He's in the penthouse.' He glanced at the five-star Venetian suite's ceiling.

'I'm still not sure if I'm on *his* side,' Nina retorted. 'Yes, he helped get the Spanish to drop all the charges, but it was his fault the cops were after me in the first place!'

'He didn't expect you to nick the marker from the museum . . . but no,' Eddie said, quickly changing tack under her glare, 'I don't trust him either. He wants to talk to you, though; we'll see what he has to say.'

'He can damn well wait, can't he? I only just arrived. I want to be with my family . . . and I could really, *really* use a wash.'

He grinned. 'I didn't want to say anything, but . . .'

Nina returned the grin, more thinly. 'Thanks. You got me some new clothes, right?'

'Yeah. And a phone too.'

Macy pointed at some shopping bags. 'I picked the clothes for you.'

'Lobato'll get a surprise when you turn up looking like a Disney princess,' Eddie joked – at least Nina *assumed* he was joking. Elaborate, flouncy dresses were not Macy's thing, their daughter already preferring more adventurous characters; considering who her parents were, she supposed that was inevitable.

'I'm sure you've got me something I'll like,' she told Macy, who smiled. 'In the meantime, I'll be in the bath.'

★ ★ ★

After everything Nina had endured, being able to submerge herself in a huge tub of hot water and let her thoughts drift was exactly what she needed.

Once immersed, though, she found to her annoyance that her mind refused to relax. She had been manipulated, used – *played*. She should have seen it sooner . . .

But self-recriminations would achieve nothing. There were more important issues – not least the last spearhead. Everything suggested it was hidden somewhere near Gobekli Tepe in eastern Turkey. Now that they had her notes, al-Asim and the rest of the Emir's agents would almost certainly be able to track it down.

Turkey . . . Lobato, she now knew, had been born in the country, even though he was a naturalised American citizen. Considering the ease with which he had acted on her behalf with the Spanish, maybe he also had high-level connections in his homeland. But did she really want the Turkish government, which over recent years had descended ever deeper into repressive autocracy, to get their hands on something potentially so devastating?

There were other options, but the more she thought about them, the less certain she became. The spearhead couldn't be allowed to fall into the wrong hands . . . but whose were the *right* hands?

A knock on the door. 'Nina?' called Eddie. 'Lobato just rang. I told him you'd see him when you were ready.'

'I'll come now,' she replied, rising reluctantly from the water. 'Let me get dressed.'

The new clothes were, to her relief, mostly things she would have picked for herself: earth-toned safari trousers and an over-sized shirt intended to be worn almost like a jacket; although Eddie hadn't been entirely joking about her daughter's choices; the T-shirt meant to go underneath it bore the image of some big-eyed CGI super-heroine of whom Macy was a fan. Oh well, she could always button the larger garment over it.

'What, you didn't keep your short skirt?' was Eddie's first comment when she emerged. 'Shame.'

'I'll wear it if you wear a mankini,' she replied. 'No, wait – you're actually considering it, aren't you?'

'Lime green suits me,' he said, smirking. 'But you look like you're back to your usual self. Except for the hair.'

She scrunched it in her hands. 'I don't want to keep it like this, but I'll tell you something – it's a lot quicker to dry.'

Eddie rubbed his own bald head. 'Tell me about it.'

Nina smiled. 'Where's Macy?'

'With Olivia. They went for a walk.'

'Good. I think their involvement should stop here, don't you?'

'Be good if ours did too, but I doubt that's going to happen.'

She sighed. 'So do I. Okay, let's see what Lobato has to say.'

They took the elevator to the top floor. The penthouse door was opened by a surly bodyguard, who regarded Eddie with hostility. 'Something I should know?' Nina asked.

'Had a bit of a run-in with him yesterday. I'm not on his Christmas card list, put it that way,' Eddie told her.

They entered the penthouse's lounge, the tall windows giving a magnificent view across the waters of the Venetian lagoon to the beautiful renaissance basilica of San Giorgio Maggiore. Lobato stood before the windows, as always clad entirely in white. 'Dr Wilde,' he said. 'I am glad to see you.'

'You'll excuse me if I'm not all sunshine and smiles at seeing *you*,' she responded.

He nodded. 'I suppose you are quite angry about what I put you through.'

'Oh, no. I mean, I have to steal ancient artefacts and go on the run across Europe on a regular basis.'

A moment of puzzlement, then: 'Ah. You are being sarcastic.'

'No shit, Mr Data. So what do you want to talk about?'

He waved towards a large sofa. 'Please, sit down.' Nina and Eddie did so, Lobato perching on the edge of an armchair facing them. She noticed he had a swollen lip; her husband's handiwork, she guessed. 'The spearheads. We have a problem.'

'Well, yeah,' she said. 'Thanks to you, something that should have stayed buried is probably going to fall into the hands of people who almost certainly aren't planning to bring peace and love to the world.'

Lobato raised an eyebrow. 'Having studied your previous adventures, I could say that is practically your modus operandi.'

'And I thought you didn't understand sarcasm,' said Eddie with a crooked smile as his wife glared at the slender man.

'I was not being sarcastic.'

'Well, whatever you were being,' Nina said impatiently, 'it's your fault. The question is: what are you going to do about it?'

'What are *we* going to do about it,' he corrected. 'You possess information I do not: the location of the spearheads. I can do nothing until you share it with me.'

'I'm not sharing a damn thing until I'm one hundred per cent sure I can trust you.'

'Total trust is only possible in the world of cryptographical mathematics. With humans, I have found that an acceptable level is the best that can be achieved. But I assure you,' Lobato went on, 'I have no intent to deceive or betray you. Our interests are aligned: we both want to locate the spearheads and prevent them from being obtained by persons who might use them for nefarious purposes. Do we not?'

Eddie snorted mockingly. 'Christ, you really do sound like Mr Data. Glad I didn't punch you any harder; I might've cut my hand on a circuit board.'

'He does have a point, though,' said Nina. 'If the spearhead were used as a bomb, it'd make a nuke look like a firecracker.'

'And those arseholes chasing you in Spain can find it?'

'Afraid so. They got all my notes. It won't take them long to piece everything together and find the last spearhead.'

'So there's only one left? What happened to the others?'

Nina regarded Lobato again before answering. The billionaire did indeed seem sincere, but his entire plan up to this point had been about deceiving her. On the other hand, in conversation he came across as almost painfully direct and unfiltered. If he wasn't expecting to have to lie – or had no reason to – she might get the truth. 'Can I ask you a question?' she said.

'Of course,' Lobato replied.

'You said you didn't want the spearhead to be used for nefarious purposes. What are *your* purposes for it? You tell me, and if it all sounds genuine, I'll tell you what I learned.'

'Very well.' He leaned towards his guests, eager to impress. 'At dinner on the *Atlantia*, I told you about the solar energy project I began in partnership with the Emir. We constructed a power plant and electrical storage facility, which is already functioning and exceeding expectations. However, its isolated location also made it ideal for research into the use of antimatter as a non-polluting, highly efficient power source. When I first learned of your theory about the spearheads, Dr Wilde, I constructed a small facility that would be able to extract antiparticles from them and use them in a device known as an annihilation laser. That would in turn permit the total conversion of matter into energy in a controlled manner – the ultimate source of power.'

'Wait, you've actually *built* something?' Nina exclaimed. 'Already? I only made my idea public eight months ago!'

'The scientific principles concerning the utilisation of antimatter have been known for decades. It was merely a matter of application. From your theories about the spearheads, I was able to deduce their probable nature, and design a means of utilising them accordingly.'

'Huh. Well I guess you really are a genius, seeing as not even *I* know exactly what the spearheads are – and I've translated everything the Atlanteans had to say about them!'

'Which brings us to your side of our deal, Dr Wilde. What else have you discovered about them – and their location?'

'Okay,' she said, with reluctance. 'The two halves of the marker combine to form a kind of map. I won't waste time describing the specifics, but it's why I went to Granada, to see the Hall of the Ambassadors in the Alhambra; it contains an Islamic replica of an Atlantean map. I compared the results with another map in Atlantis itself, which gave me three new locations – one for each of the spearheads.'

'You said there was only one spearhead remaining. How do you know the other two no longer exist?'

'If I say the name "Krakatoa", would that be a hint?'

'As in *Krakatoa, East of Java*?' said Eddie. 'Even though it's west of Java and whoever made the film didn't bother looking at a map?'

'The same.'

'The volcano?' asked Lobato. 'You are saying the Atlanteans placed one of the spearheads in Indonesia?'

'It's a long way from Atlantis, I know, but their most famous explorer, Talonor, got as far as Tibet, and others followed in his footsteps – we're still making new discoveries even now. Another of the spearheads was a lot closer to home, though.'

'Where?'

'The island of Thera, in the Aegean. It's now known as Santorini.'

Lobato nodded again. 'I know Santorini. You are saying the volcano there was also destroyed by one of the spearheads?'

'It fits with what I discovered on the markers, yes.'

'Ancient history is not my speciality, but I thought the eruption was much later than the period of Atlantis?'

'And Krakatoa didn't explode until the nineteenth century,' Eddie added. 'The film got *that* much right, at least.'

'Atlantis was long gone,' Nina explained, 'but the spearheads stayed in place, forgotten . . . until something caused them to explode, and made the volcanoes where they were hidden erupt absolutely catastrophically. What's terrifying is that the last one is still out there – and we don't know what might set it off.'

'But you know where it is,' said Lobato.

'Yeah. It's in Turkey.'

The billionaire's face revealed genuine emotion: shock, and alarm. 'Turkey? Where?'

'Near Gobekli Tepe, the Neolithic ruins. My guess is that the Atlanteans considered the civilisation that existed there a threat, and planted a spearhead to force their submission. Do what we tell you, or we blow you to hell.'

'And you know exactly where it is located?'

'Yes . . . but I'll keep that to myself for now. At least until I know how we're going to proceed – and what we're going to do with the spearhead if we find it.'

'If it's a bomb that could go off any time,' said Eddie, 'we've got to warn people.'

'We will, if it's an imminent threat. But it's been sitting there without any trouble for eleven thousand years, so we need to examine it first. And no offence to your birthplace,' she added to Lobato, 'but I'm not keen on handing over something so dangerous to a government that's one step away from becoming a full-on dictatorship.'

Lobato was still disturbed by her relevation. 'I became an American citizen so I could leave Turkey,' he said, 'but that does not mean I do not care about what happens there. I still have many connections, family. However, I agree about the current government. I feel the same about keeping the spearhead away from *any* nation that might use it for destructive purposes, and that includes America. I had thought Dhajan could be trusted as a guardian, but I was mistaken.'

'So where exactly *would* you take it?' Eddie asked. 'If you don't trust the States to look after it, Russia or China won't be any better. Or Britain, for that matter. It might be a different government now, but after what happened in the Congo two years back, I wouldn't trust the old-boy network any more than I could juggle a tank.' He turned to Nina. 'What about the IHA or the United Nations? They could hold on to it until everyone decides what to do.'

The billionaire was about to object, but Nina beat him to it. 'Hold on to it *where*?' she said. 'They're based in New York – a mile and a half from our home! Do you really want them to keep a potentially unstable antimatter bomb in their basement?'

'Put it that way, no,' her husband replied.

'There's another problem with getting the IHA involved. Lester Blumberg – the head of the IHA,' she added for Lobato's benefit, 'has already said publicly that he thinks my theories about the spearhead are wackydoodle sci-fi horseshit. Not his exact words, but he'd be very, very hard to convince. And he's also extremely by-the-book and bureaucratic. Even if I did bring him aboard, it could take days or even weeks to get an IHA team into the field, as he would want to clear everything with the Turks.'

'As soon as they knew about the spearhead, they would claim jurisdiction over it,' Lobato pointed out. 'That is an undesirable outcome.'

Nina nodded. 'Plus,' she went on, 'we might not even have days to find it. The Emir's people have all my notes – they'll figure out where it is soon enough. And Agreste told me they're members of Dhajan's intelligence agency. They won't waste time dealing with Ankara; they'll just go incognito straight to the spot and start digging for the vault.'

'Your notes are that accurate?'

'I know the direction, distance and even altitude from Gobekli Tepe. I haven't had a chance to do a proper topographical search yet, but the number of possible sites I find when I do will probably be pretty small. For all we know, the Emir's men have done the same search already.'

'They might be on the way there,' Eddie said, with growing concern.

'We have to find it first,' Lobato insisted. 'Dr Wilde, you must tell me where it is. The spearhead cannot be allowed to fall into the hands of the Turkish government *or* the Dhajanis.'

'I agree,' said Nina. 'But there's no way I'm going to tell you where to find the vault and let you send a team of hired goons to dig it up. It's a new relic of Atlantis, a major archaeological discovery – and that's *my* speciality.'

Dismayed realisation dawned on Eddie's face. 'Oh for fuck's sake,' he snapped. 'So much for "I'm done with fieldwork, it's too dangerous" – now you want to race the people who just tried to kill you to a fucking doomsday device that could blow up if someone breathes on it!'

'I know, I know, I *know*,' she said over his objections. 'But what else can we do? If the Emir's people find the vault and take the spearhead, then Dhajan suddenly becomes the owner of the most powerful bomb in the world. And I really can't see much good coming from that. What if the Dhajanis decide to take out one of their regional rivals?'

'They'd get bombed to shit themselves, though,' Eddie replied. 'Soon as anyone realised what they'd done—'

'That's just it. Nobody *would* know what they'd done! It would be like when Brice blew up Big Ben. We were the only people who knew about the Shamir and what it could do – if I hadn't gotten that video of him to the US embassy, he would have carried out the perfect false-flag attack. This is the same thing. The best weapon is one nobody knows you have. If Tel Aviv or Tehran or Bahrain disappeared in a flash without any warning, who would blame Dhajan?'

The reminder of the terrible events in London two years previously, the rogue MI6 agent having stolen the Biblical artefact that destroyed the city of Jericho, put a grim cast over Eddie's face. 'You're saying we're the only people who can stop them.'

'I'm saying we're the only people who can stop them *in time* . . . without handing the spearhead over to someone just as bad, or possibly even worse.'

'And if you're wrong about it being there?'

'If I'm wrong, and we can't find it, they won't either. They're working from my notes! But either way, there's still an incredibly powerful weapon buried somewhere, waiting to go off. And we don't even know what the trigger is, nor will we unless we find it.'

'Fuck's sake,' Eddie muttered again, shaking his head. 'But what do we do with the thing when we find it? We can hardly stick it in your research station for safe keeping,' he looked at Lobato, 'since that's in fucking Dhajan!'

'I guess that's a bridge we'll have to cross when we come to it,' said Nina. 'But the most important thing is that we *do* find it.' She continued more softly: 'Eddie, I *need* you. I can't do this without you. I don't think I've ever felt more alone in my life than after I went on the run in Spain without you. I can't leave you again.'

'You managed okay on your own,' he said, but his anger was fading. 'All right,' he reluctantly agreed. 'So we need to get to Turkey, quick and on the quiet. We'll need backup, too. I'll see if any of my mates here in Venice can come with us.'

'I will be able to get us into Turkey,' said Lobato. 'I have influence, contacts – and a private jet.'

'That last one's a big advantage,' said Nina. She turned back to Eddie. 'Olivia will have to take Macy home, though.'

'Definitely,' her husband agreed. 'I want her safe. And I'll get someone in New York to keep an eye on her as well. Just in case.'

Nina knew he was not impugning Olivia's ability to look after her great-granddaughter, but rather taking extra precautions to ensure the safety of both of them; Macy had been targeted before. 'Good idea.'

Lobato stood. 'I will make the arrangements.'

'We'll need off-road vehicles, and some equipment. I'll make you a list.'

'I will also bring bodyguards.' He started to speak to his men.

Eddie rose to interrupt him. 'You don't need your bodyguards,' he said, advancing. 'You'll have me.'

Lobato eyed him nervously. 'I would feel safer with my own people.' One of his men started across the room, ready to intervene.

The Yorkshireman stopped just short of the skinny man. 'Oh, I'll keep a close eye on you, don't worry.' He grinned wolfishly, exposing the gap between his front teeth.

'You want to help find the spearhead?' said Nina, backing up her husband. 'You'll do it our way. We can always take a commercial flight.'

Lobato hesitated, then waved for his bodyguard to withdraw. 'Very well. But my security team will at least accompany me to Turkey. I will feel safer knowing they are close by, even with Mr Chase's most generous offer of protection.'

Eddie grinned. 'Now *that* sounded like proper sarcasm.' He stepped back. 'All right. I'll talk to my mates, see who can come with us.'

'We've got to talk to Macy first,' Nina reminded him. 'I'm sure that'll be fun . . .'

★ ★ ★

'But *why* can't I come with you?' demanded Macy, upset.

'I'm sorry, honey,' her mother told her softly, 'but it's too dangerous.'

'But I helped Daddy get you back! That was dangerous too!'

Nina gave Eddie an aggrieved glance – *I still can't* believe *you involved her!* – before looking back at Macy. 'That was different. Nobody would have hurt you then, even if you'd been caught. But the men who stole the marker are looking for the same thing as us. I hope we don't run into them, but if we do, it won't be safe for you to be there.'

'It won't be safe for you or Daddy either,' the little girl pointed out. 'But you're still going!'

Nina couldn't fault her logic. 'When did they start running a debate club in second grade?' she asked rhetorically, before looking to her husband and grandmother for support. 'You'll be flying home with Olivia – you can stay with her until we get back. And we'll get back as soon as we can.'

'You said that before,' Macy said sulkily. 'When you went to Africa.'

'You were *five*! How would you even remem—' Nina caught herself. 'That was different, honey. I was . . . I was being selfish then. This time, though, we have to move fast, because we're the only people who can stop the bad guys.'

'But why does it always have to be *you* who stops the bad guys?'

'That's a good question,' said Eddie. 'Been asking it myself since about 2008.'

Nina smiled. 'I don't know,' she said. 'I guess that sometimes you find yourself in a situation where what you do next is really important. You have to make sure you do the right thing. If the bad guys get the spearhead before we do, they can use it to hurt a lot of people. We can't let that happen. Can we?'

There was no reply for a few seconds, Macy looking down at the floor, before a quiet 'no' finally emerged.

Eddie hugged her. 'I know you don't want us to go without you, but we'll come home soon.'

She looked up at him, eyes wide. 'Do you promise, Daddy?'

'I promise, love.'

'So do I,' said Nina. 'And we always keep our promises, don't we?'

Macy half smiled. 'Daddy promised he'd get me a new trikan after the other one got broken.'

Eddie sighed. 'Looks like I'd better nip out to a toy shop before we go.'

Nina kissed Macy, then straightened. 'And I need to look at a map. If we're going to Turkey, it'd help if I knew exactly *where . . .*'

30

Turkey

The late-morning sun glared over the desolation of southern Turkey, a harsh wind sending dust across the paths of the two BMW X5s. Nina and Eddie were with Lobato in the lead SUV, Ana and Maximov in the second. The huge Russian was the only one of Eddie's friends who had been willing and able to join them. Jared had reluctantly returned to his duties in Israel, while Matt had pointed out that while he would have been happy to help, there was little use for a submarine engineer in the desert.

Macy had, to her parents' relief, flown back to the States with Olivia. Nina still felt unhappy about splitting the family up so soon after reuniting, but there was no way she was going to put her daughter in danger in the field.

In the field. Despite everything, after the nightmare of the Congo and all that had ensued, she was once again leading an archaeological expedition. She had convinced herself that that part of her life was over, that she had retired from actively seeking out the lost relics of the past . . . but here she was again.

And deep down, she was glad. She wasn't sure whether she should be ashamed of the feeling. The realisation that people kept dying because of her obsessions had been hammered home in the worst way possible two years earlier, but this time, she told herself, was different. She had not begun the quest voluntarily;

she had been tricked into it by the man in the rear seat. That Lobato had himself been played in turn hadn't lessened her anger at him.

But he was now cooperating, and appeared sincere in his desire to make things right. For all his manipulation and deception – based on past experience, Nina doubted that *any* billionaire had become so rich without screwing others over – he did genuinely seem motivated by the prospect of bringing about a new era of clean energy, albeit in a technocratic and almost robotically dispassionate way.

Right now, he was looking at a map on his phone. 'How much further, Dr Wilde?' he asked. 'Surely it is now time to tell me where the vault is hidden.'

She exchanged a look with Eddie, then held up the paper map she had been studying. 'According to the markers, all the vaults were buried in the same general position relative to their targets. My guess is the Atlanteans did it so that even if the exact locations were lost, anyone who could use the markers correctly would be able to find them.'

'And where are they?'

'North of the cities, on the highest hill, at a distance of seventy-nine Atlantean stadia – about six miles.'

'There are several hilltops in that area,' Lobato noted. 'Which is the correct one?'

'That's what we have to find out,' Nina replied. 'The directions are still vague. Is the site precisely due north, or just generally in that direction? Where's the distance measured from: the city's exact centre, its edge, some landmark within it? Is the vault buried at the very top of the hill, or partway down it? The Atlanteans would have known, but we don't – so we'll have to find out the hard way.'

'Which is why you need an archaeologist,' Eddie chipped in. 'Rather than sending a bunch of goons with shovels.'

'Yeah. I'm hoping my experience – and intuition – will help us narrow down the options.'

'In my *own* experience,' said Lobato, 'intuition is merely another name for guesswork.'

'You'd be surprised how often it pays off in archaeology,' Nina retorted. 'But then it's one of the humanities, isn't it? The logic's always more fuzzy than the yes/no binaries of a game.'

'Maybe that's how the Emir tricked you,' said Eddie. 'He took advantage of human nature – even though you probably don't like admitting you're human.'

The white-clad man eyed him, then looked back at Nina. 'So what does your *experience* tell you about the location of the vault?'

'I've narrowed it down to two possibilities based on the topography and satellite views,' she said. 'When I actually see them in person, I'm hoping my knowledge of the Atlanteans will tell me which is the right one. What would they have done? Where would the best place be to plant this weapon? If I can find the right answer, we'll be able to reach it before the Emir's people.' She checked her map again. 'We'll need to turn off for the first hill soon, Eddie. Next exit to the left.'

Eddie kept driving until the turn came into view. 'We're going off-road,' he warned. 'It'll get bumpy.'

Nina, well used to traversing bad terrain, braced herself as he brought the BMW on to the rutted track. Lobato, on the other hand, was evidently accustomed to a smooth ride, clutching at the door handle as a lurch sent him skidding across the leather seat. Husband and wife grinned at each other. Ana guided the second SUV after them.

The track climbed higher. Nina surveyed her surroundings. Although they were technically passing through farmland, the sandy-brown soil sprouted nothing but stones. She looked back at her map. This hill was, she already suspected, the less likely prospect, but it was the one closer to the airport – and there was always a chance her intuition was wrong.

'Going to run out of road in a minute,' Eddie remarked. The track petered out below the summit, where a gnarled rocky ridge rendered it useless for even the most hardscrabble farming techniques.

'Just get as close as you can,' she told him. 'I want to see the view from the top.'

More bumps and jolts followed, the last few testing the strength of the seat belts, before Eddie finally stopped. 'Everyone okay?' he asked.

'Just glad I wasn't doing my make-up,' Nina joked. Behind her, Lobato unclawed his fingertips from the upholstery.

She climbed out. The wind hit her immediately. With almost no vegetation in its path as it swept down from the mountains, it was dry and gritty, unpleasant. This was not somewhere she would choose to live.

But several millennia ago, people had. The buried ruins at Gobekli Tepe – their real name still unknown, no traces as yet having been found of their inhabitants' written language – stretched far beyond those so far fully excavated. It was a place where under normal circumstances she would have been positively itching to conduct a dig of her own.

But that would have to wait. It was a relic of Atlantis she was searching for, a time bomb from the past. Was the vault somewhere beneath her feet? She clambered to the hilltop and gazed at the view beyond.

Eddie arrived behind her. 'So, is this the place?'

'I don't know,' she said, though she was already coming to the conclusion that it wasn't. She took out her phone and brought up its compass to check a bearing, then stared intently in that direction.

Only bleak, crumpled hills met her gaze, inactive volcanoes

rising in the distance beyond them. They were roughly six miles from Gobekli Tepe but the site was hidden from view beyond a rise.

Lobato scrabbled to the top of the hill, brushing dust off his hands with distaste. 'Well? What have you found?'

'I've found,' she replied, 'that we came up here for nothing.'

'How can you tell?' he demanded in disbelief. 'We have only just arrived! You have not even started to search.'

'I can tell, because I'm thinking like an Atlantean – and like one who's planting a doomsday device. Gobekli Tepe is over there,' she pointed, 'but it's out of sight behind that hill. So for one thing, your scouts can't keep an eye on your target to make sure they're not sending an army in your direction. For another, it means the city would be shielded from the explosion.'

'If it's as powerful as a nuke, it'd still cause plenty of damage,' said Eddie.

'Maybe, but the Atlanteans wouldn't want to just *damage* their enemy. They'd want to *obliterate* them, utterly – to serve as an example of their power. They'd need to be sure the blast would hit its target directly, so the vault would be in line of sight.'

'So on to the next hill?'

'Yeah. It's . . . over there,' she said, pointing towards a summit about a mile and a half away.

Lobato looked. 'There is a building on it.'

'I saw it on the satellite photos. It's a little farmhouse – with half the roof missing. I don't think we'll be bothering anyone.' She started back to the car.

Ana and Maximov had just emerged from the second BMW. 'We are not stopping?' complained the Russian. 'We had bumpy ride for nothing?'

'Thought you'd enjoy being bashed about,' said Eddie as he followed Nina. While in the military, Maximov suffered a head wound that had not only required a steel plate to rebuild the front of his skull but had also scrambled some of the nerve impulses to his brain; he now experienced pain as pleasure.

The huge man put a hand to his stomach. 'That, no problem. But seasick? No, no!'

'There were only two possible locations,' Nina explained. 'I don't think it's here, so it has to be on the other hill.'

'And if it isn't?' asked Ana.

'Then the Emir's people won't find it either. They're working from the same data as me.' She climbed back into the SUV. 'Well, come on, then. Let's go!'

Ana came closer to Eddie. 'Nina was . . . *different* on the ship,' she said quietly. 'Is she always this impatient?'

'When she's after something archaeological, yeah,' he told her.

'Huh. She is a lot more rude.'

He smiled. 'You get used to it. Well, *I* just ignore it. Have to, really, otherwise—'

'What are you two talking about?' demanded the subject of their discussion.

'Nothing, dear,' Eddie replied, sing-song. He got back into the X5, still smiling smugly as Nina gave him a sidelong glare. He turned the car around, leading the other SUV back down the hill.

The distance between the two hills was not great as the crow flew, but the journey along winding dirt tracks took over an hour. Finally the travellers neared their destination – where Eddie noticed something unexpected. 'This road's been flattened out,' he said as he guided the BMW upwards. 'Someone's put new gravel on it.'

It was indeed smoother than the rutted, stony path they had traversed earlier. 'There are tyre tracks along the sides,' said Nina. 'Maybe someone's brought a tractor up here.'

'The land hasn't been ploughed, though,' Eddie said. The hilltop came into sight. 'And *that'd* be why.'

Lobato looked ahead. 'It would appear the satellite images were out of date.'

'No kidding,' said Nina, startled.

She had expected to see a little cottage ahead, but instead was greeted by a sprawling house. It was brand new, plastic sheeting covering a still-incomplete corner of the roof. A small yellow excavator stood near a water bowser on a rise, part of which had been dug away to make room for a swimming pool. The pool was not yet finished, a pallet of lurid blue tiles waiting beside it.

The house itself was a gaudy architectural catastrophe, a wedding cake of unnecessary columns, tiered gable ends and windows of different sizes and styles. It seemed as if someone had taken the worst excesses of wealthy American suburban housing, and rather than mocking them had instead decided to celebrate them by cramming as many examples together as possible.

'Have to admit,' Nina went on, 'I didn't expect to see a McMansion on top of a hill in Turkey.'

'It'd be more of a Mansionoglu,' said Eddie. She gave him a confused look, only to notice that Lobato appeared almost amused. 'Yeah, I know a little bit of Turkish.'

'I love that even after fourteen years, you still manage to surprise me,' she said. 'But now I'm not sure what to do. We've turned up at someone's house!'

'You could just knock on the door, tell 'em who you are and ask to poke around the place,' Eddie suggested, bringing the X5 to a stop.

Nina considered that. 'You know, I could.' She got out of the car.

'And I thought it was just *you* who didn't get jokes,' he told Lobato with a sigh as he followed.

Ana emerged from the other SUV. 'Is this the right place?' she asked, confused.

'We'll soon find out,' Nina replied. The house had several entrances; she headed for the largest and most elaborate. As Eddie caught up, she pushed the doorbell.

A man and woman in their thirties, both wearing casual-but-pricey clothing and ostentatious gold watches, opened the door and regarded them suspiciously. The man spoke in Turkish. 'I'm sorry,' said Nina, 'but do you speak English?'

'English? Yes, I do,' he replied, chest swelling at the chance to show off his linguistic skills. 'What do you want?'

'This will sound odd, but . . . I'm Nina Wilde,' she said. The couple regarded her blankly. 'Dr Nina Wilde, the archaeologist.' Still no recognition. 'I discovered Atlantis? Found the Ark of the Covenant?' Nothing. 'Saved the world at least three times, Hollywood made some movies about me? Oh, come on!'

The man sniffed, shaking his head. 'No, I do not know you.'

Eddie chuckled. 'You always tell me you don't care about being famous. Now you know what it's like!'

The others had by now joined them – and the woman gasped and tugged at her husband's sleeve. 'Gideon Lobato! It's Gideon Lobato!'

The man's response was no less awestruck. He spoke in Turkish to Lobato, who replied with a small nod and what Nina realised was a request for him to speak in English. 'Yes, yes,' said the man, grinning uncontrollably. 'Whatever you want. You are our . . . the word, the word . . .' He snapped his fingers in frustration, saying something to the woman.

'Idol,' she told him, before addressing Lobato. 'You are our idol, a hero. You began with nothing here in Turkey, and now you are one of the richest men in the world. You are a big inspiration!'

'We are rich too,' said the man with a complete absence of modesty. 'Not as rich as you, but one day we get there. What can we do for you?'

Lobato gestured towards Nina. 'Dr Wilde can explain better than I.'

'Why, thank you,' she said, trying to hide her annoyance. Eddie was right; she *had* become used to people knowing who she was, and finding out that not everybody did was a small slap to her ego. 'As I said, I'm an archaeologist, and there may be a major archaeological site buried on this hill. I would like your permission to look for it.'

Even before she finished, it became clear that the couple knew something, and also that they were concerned about telling her. 'An archaeological site,' the man echoed. 'Are you, ah . . . are you from the government?'

'Not the Turkish government, no,' Nina replied. They both visibly relaxed. 'But I worked,' she de-emphasised the past tense as much as she could get away with without outright lying, 'for the International Heritage Agency at the United Nations in New York – and Turkey is one of the IHA's contributors.' A pleasant but pointed smile. 'Why, does that make a difference?'

The house's owners were now decidedly nervous. 'It is very important,' said Lobato. 'Please, if you know anything, you must tell us. It is a matter of safety.'

'Safety!' cried the woman. A rapid-fire exchange with her husband, then she looked back at Nina. 'Are we in danger?'

'That's what we need to find out,' the American replied.

'You . . . you should come in,' said the man, with a blend of worry and resignation.

'Thank you,' said Nina. 'By the way, you are . . . ?'

'Elmas,' the woman replied. 'Elmas Onan. And my husband, Berk.' Eddie suppressed a snort of amusement.

'Eddie,' Nina cautioned quietly. 'I'm Nina Wilde, and this is my husband, Eddie Chase. Mr Lobato you're already familiar with, and these are Ana Rijo and Oleg Maximov.'

Any hope of Berk's that he might be able to reassert his

dominance once he was inside his own house faded as the giant Russian ducked through the doorway and stared down at him, arms folded. 'Hello, yes. Welcome,' he managed.

The interior was as ostentatious as the outside, positively Trumpian in its unrestrained use of gilt. 'This is a . . . very big house,' was the best compliment Nina could manage. 'I wasn't expecting it to be here, though. There was only a small building on the satellite photos.'

'My grandfather's old farmhouse,' said Elmas. 'He had not lived there for a long time, but it still belonged to him, and he left it to me in his will last year.'

'The house was worth nothing,' Berk continued, 'but the view? Very valuable! Come, see.' He led them into a large lounge, from where more doors led to other parts of the expansive house. One wall was dotted with framed photographs of the couple in the company of people whom Nina assumed were well-regarded Turks, though the only one she recognised was the country's president. Berk's smile in the picture had the intensity of a cult member.

He made sure all his guests saw the wall of fame by leading them right past it, before bringing them to panoramic picture windows. 'Look! It is worth living all the way up here for that view. Do you agree?'

'I do, yes,' said Nina. 'It's very impressive.' But she was less interested in the vista as a whole than in what she could pick out upon another rise. 'That's Gobekli Tepe, isn't it?'

'The old ruins, yes,' said Berk, unenthused. 'But if you look over there, we can see all the way to Sanliurfa!'

'That is where we work,' added Elmas. 'Our friends in the city have big houses, but ours is bigger – and we can look down on them from here.'

Nina wasn't sure if the Turkish woman meant it literally or in a snobbish way, but her attitude suggested a bit of both. She went closer to the window. Sanliurfa was indeed visible in the distance to the south-west, a grey sprawl across the dusty brown terrain.

This had to be the place. It would have provided the Atlanteans with direct line of sight to their target at Gobekli Tepe – but now, if the spearhead were to explode, it would also flatten a city of half a million people. 'I think this is it,' she said to Eddie and Lobato.

'Then we have to find the vault,' Lobato said. 'And quickly, before the Emir's men get here.'

'Has anyone else come to see you in the last few days?' Eddie asked the Onans.

Elmas shook her head. 'No. Only the men building the pool, and we know them.'

'We got here first, at least,' he said to Nina. 'Question is, can we find the thing before they turn up?'

'Before who turns up?' asked Berk.

Nina adopted what she hoped was a reassuring tone. 'Okay. Like I said, I'm an archaeologist, and my speciality is Atlantis. You *had* heard it's been discovered, right?'

'Of course,' said Berk, affronted.

'Just checking. Now, there was a recent discovery – a kind of map. Long story, but it brought me to this hilltop. I think the Atlanteans buried a vault here, and it contains something that might be extremely dangerous.'

The couple's eyes went wide. 'Perhaps you should sit down?' Ana suggested.

'Yes, perhaps,' said Berk, leading his wife to a large sofa. They dropped on to it, holding hands. 'What do you mean, dangerous?'

'I don't want to be too alarmist,' said Nina, 'but it's basically a bomb.'

'A *bomb*?' Elmas shrieked. 'There is a *bomb* here?'

'As far as we know, right now it's safe,' Nina went on. 'But there are other people looking for it – people who want to use it as a weapon. We have to find it before them. Now, when I first mentioned an archaeological site, I got the impression you knew something about it?'

There was a brief whispered exchange in Turkish. Berk exuded reluctance, while Elmas was entirely the opposite, swatting her husband's chest in annoyance. 'Yes, yes,' she said to Nina. 'We found—'

'Elmas!' protested Berk.

'If it is dangerous, we have to tell them!' she snapped. 'I am not having a bomb under my house!' She turned back to Nina. 'When we were building, we found some big stones under the ground. One had writing on.' Her gaze shifted away evasively. 'We . . . did not tell anyone because we thought it was something to do with the ruins at Gobekli Tepe. If the government learned about it, they would have taken away our land and given it to the archaeologists.'

Nina was not impressed. 'So you bulldozed a priceless archaeological site because you didn't want to give up your view?'

'We did not bulldoze it!' Berk objected. 'We kept the pieces.'

She stood. 'Show me.'

The Onans exchanged worried looks, then Berk reluctantly rose too. 'Come with me.'

He led Nina and the others deeper into the house. 'The guy really is a berk,' Eddie whispered.

'Okay,' Nina said, 'what's so funny about his name?'

'Berk? It's Cockney rhyming slang. Like "butcher's hook" means "look", and Londoners say "I'll have a butcher's". Well, berk's short for "Berkshire hunt". It means someone's a right c—'

'Yeah, I get it,' Nina hurriedly interrupted. 'Poor guy – and he doesn't even know his name's an insult in another language.'

Her husband grinned. 'He'll find out pretty quickly if he ever visits England.'

Berk opened a set of double doors. Beyond was another lounge, this one with a high ceiling and an upper-floor balcony overlooking the cavernous space. A large fireplace dominated one wall, leather sofas arranged in a semicircle before it.

'This is it,' said the Turk, going to the fireplace. 'This is what we found.'

At first Nina didn't see what he meant – then she gasped in horror as she realised that the mantel, a large stone slab protruding from the wall, bore inscriptions in a language she knew all too well. 'That – that's Atlantean text!' she cried.

'We did not know what it was,' Elmas said, unconvincingly.

'You knew enough not to tell anybody in case it got confiscated! My God! You've destroyed an Atlantean site for this monstrosity of a house – and you've turned the one thing that survived into a goddam *conversation piece*!'

Elmas pursed her lips, insulted. 'My house is *not* a monstrosity!'

Lobato held up a placating hand. 'Was this all that you found?'

'This was the biggest,' Berk told him. 'There were others, but they were broken. They did not have writing on them, though,' he added hastily.

'What does this say, love?' Eddie asked, indicating the ancient writing.

Still angry at the couple, Nina read the text. Some of the characters were chipped and cracked, but she was able to garner its meaning. 'It's definitely connected to the vault,' she announced. 'It says it marks the entrance – although it was buried, so . . .' She looked back at Berk and Elmas. 'How deep down did you find it?'

Berk thought for a moment. 'A metre and a half, maybe. It was covered in dirt.'

'Eleven thousand years on a windy hillside'll do that. It was probably just beneath the surface originally. So the vault would be behind it . . . *Where* did you find it? Exactly?'

'I will show you,' said Berk.

Everyone followed him back through the house, entering the main hall. 'Excuse, please,' said Maximov. 'Where is toilet?'

Berk stopped and gestured uncertainly up the sweeping staircase, unwilling to give him the freedom of the house but also not daring to deny it. 'Upstairs and down the hall. On the right.' Maximov clomped upwards. Elmas watched the Russian go with extreme disapproval.

Her husband took their guests through a door and down a wide hallway. 'This place is huge,' Ana said quietly. 'My whole house in Brazil had only three rooms!'

A large dining room, dominated by a long table of heavy dark wood, had French windows leading to a patio. Beyond was the unfinished swimming pool, the hilltop rising beyond it. Berk opened the doors. 'We found the big stone here,' he said, pointing into the pool. 'About halfway along.'

Nina dropped into it. 'Show me where – and tell me which direction it was lying.'

'There,' Berk called. She stopped about ten feet from the far end. He clambered down to join her. 'It was like this.' He held out his arms to show the stone's orientation.

It had been roughly perpendicular to the pool's length. Nina looked up towards the summit. The very top was some hundred feet away, about thirty feet higher. Subtract a metre and a half, five feet, to give her the topography in the Atlantean era . . . 'There's room for something to have been buried under the hilltop,' she told the others. 'If the stone marked its entrance, the way in would have been . . . here.'

She walked to the pool's end. A raw concrete wall cut into the dusty soil, the unfinished tiling reaching a third of the way up. 'When you dug the pool out, was there any sign of a tunnel?'

'Not a tunnel,' Berk answered, 'but the builders did not take as long to dig as I expected. As if it was easy.'

'The tunnel might have collapsed,' said Nina. She climbed out and went to the edge of the excavated area, prodding at the dusty soil. It was loosely packed, slipping free with little effort. 'It could be right under here! We need to check.'

'How will you do that?' demanded Elmas. 'It is behind the pool.'

'Then we need to *move* the pool.' Nina pointed at the little excavator. 'You've got a digger, right there.'

'What?' gasped Berk. 'You cannot dig it up! It is almost finished!'

'Well, it'll give you a chance to rethink your tile choices,' said Eddie. 'That blue's a bit eye-poking.'

'The way I see it, you've got two options,' Nina said firmly. 'Either we dig up the pool and see what's under there . . . or I get the Turkish government involved and tell them you've kept quiet about finding an Atlantean archaeological site. And I can assure you, the Ministry of Culture *will* know who I am. You think a handshake with the president will be enough to keep them from taking your land?'

Berk looked stricken, while Elmas's expression was one of barely contained fury. 'You are trying to *blackmail* us?' she hissed.

'I'm trying to *save* you,' Nina shot back. 'Your house is on top of something that could explode without warning – and it won't only kill you. It'll take out Sanliurfa too. And I told you, we're not the only people trying to find it. The others won't ask politely to dig up your property. They'll do it at gunpoint – assuming they don't shoot you the moment you open the door.'

'She is telling the truth,' said Lobato. 'It is very important that we find it before anyone else.'

The couple held another emotional exchange. Finally Elmas

spoke to Nina. 'Okay . . . you can dig up the pool. But if there is nothing there, you will pay for the repairs!'

'If there's nothing there, I'll be happy to,' Nina replied.

Berk glanced towards the garage. 'We should stay in town while they are working.'

'I am not leaving my home,' his wife insisted.

'But if—'

'I am *not* leaving my home!' She glared back at Maximov as he emerged from the French windows. 'Do you want them treating it like their own?'

'We will stay,' Berk quickly agreed.

Nina shrugged. 'Up to you. Just give us the keys to the digger and we'll get started.'

Maximov reached them. 'Sorry, took wrong turn,' he said. 'Had to come down different stairs back there, house is like maze. You should give guests map!' He belatedly registered the frosty atmosphere. 'What did I miss?'

31

Both Eddie and Maximov had experience operating tracked vehicles and earth-movers from their military careers. However, the Englishman carried out the bulk of the work for one simple reason – the Russian was too big to fit in the little excavator's cab. He instead ended up acting as practically a second earth-mover himself, dragging chunks of broken concrete clear as Eddie used the machine's hydraulic arm and bucket to smash the pool's end wall apart. Each impact made Berk grimace and Elmas clench her jaw ever tighter, until finally the couple retreated into the house to save her teeth from shattering under the pressure.

Nina divided her time between observing the dig and watching the track to the house. There had as yet been no sign of anyone approaching the Onans' property; as much as she hoped that would remain the case, she was growing increasingly concerned about unwelcome visitors. Her notes had contained enough information for others to follow the same path.

'It is possible,' remarked Lobato, to whom she had voiced her worries, 'that al-Asim and his men have simply been unable to comprehend your work. Being members of an intelligence agency does not by definition make them intelligent. I found them quite thuggish.'

'Maybe, but I bet you thought the same about Eddie, didn't you?' she said. 'I'd rather not take that chance.'

Both turned back to the pool at the loud bang of collapsing concrete. 'We've got something!' Eddie yelled over the excavator's roar as he reversed.

Maximov hauled another piece of smashed wall aside as Nina hurried to see what they had found. Where the poolside had been demolished, she saw dark earth containing hunks of stone-work, voids beneath some of them. Holes in the soil. There *had* once been a tunnel there, but it had collapsed. Earthquakes were the most likely cause – this was a volcanic region.

She reached into the largest hole for the better part of a foot before her fingertips touched rubble. The stone felt smooth, carved. 'It's definitely man-made,' she said, withdrawing. 'I think this was once the way to the vault.'

Eddie left the excavator to see. 'The ground's pretty soft,' he said. 'Shouldn't take too long to dig it out.'

'If there is anything still left to find,' Ana said, handing the grateful Maximov a bottle of water.

'There *has* to be,' Nina insisted. 'The inscriptions on the slab in the house said the vault was here.' She checked the time. 'Okay, it's after three o'clock. We should have a quick break to eat, then get back to work and do as much as we can before it gets dark.' She regarded the hollows in the soil. 'Then we'll see what's hiding down here.'

The Onans were far from enthused about feeding their guests. However, while Elmas was a study in resentment, she never-theless felt compelled to act as a good hostess and provide a meal of grilled aubergines and couscous salad, if only to retain Lobato's favour.

Eddie wolfed down his late lunch and returned to the pool, Nina going with him. 'Lobato said you were worried about the Emir's guys turning up,' he said.

'You aren't?' she replied.

'Yeah, but they had a head start, and they're still not here. Maybe they haven't worked out where to look yet. Maybe they won't ever.'

'That's very optimistic of you. Especially based on past experience.'

'Thought I'd try being positive for a change.' They shared a smile. 'I'm also hoping no arseholes turn up looking for trouble, 'cause we haven't got any guns.'

She raised an eyebrow. 'That's not like you.'

'I didn't want Jared or Max to bring any to Venice, because I didn't want 'em around Macy. I could have asked Alderley to send something to Sanliurfa, but after what you said about not trusting governments with the spearhead, I didn't want to tell him what we were doing.'

'Probably for the best, yeah. I trust Peter, but considering what some people in MI6 were willing to do to their own country to get hold of the Shamir, letting them know we've found an antimatter bomb might not be the best move.'

'That's if we *have* found it.' He climbed into the excavator and restarted the engine. 'Only one way to find out!'

Nina stepped back as he drove the machine over the broken rubble and scooped out more volcanic earth. Lobato, Ana and Maximov joined them, the Russian hopping down to help clear more debris.

With the concrete now broken open, the excavation proceeded relatively quickly. Nina occasionally cringed as the bucket's steel teeth ground against buried stonework, but this was an occasion when speed trumped archaeological reverence.

Nevertheless, the work still went on for another couple of hours, the sun lowering, until there was a sudden breakthrough – literally. 'Ay up,' Eddie announced, quickly withdrawing the scoop. 'Think we've found it!'

Nina rushed to look. A crooked hole had opened up. She peered inside. 'It's definitely a tunnel,' she said, seeing the dim outlines of ceiling cross-beams receding into the blackness. 'Eddie, Oleg, widen it. I'll get my gear.'

She went to the SUVs, collecting a backpack. It contained equipment from the list she had given Lobato, but right now, there was only one thing she needed: a flashlight. She hurried back to the pool. Eddie and Maximov had by now widened the hole enough for her to fit through, so she shone the powerful torch inside.

The beam revealed a narrow tunnel, trapezoidal in cross-section, with slanted stone pillars supporting the ceiling slabs. The walls were lined with wooden slats, but many were broken, earth spilling through the gaps. The passage extended around thirty feet to a rectangular opening, beyond which was a larger space that contained . . .

She couldn't tell *what* it contained at first glance. Something metal, the glint reflecting back at her, but she had no idea what it might be. It seemed spherical, but if that were the case, it was *big*. At least twenty feet in diameter, maybe more. The reddish-gold tint suggested it was made from orichalcum. Definitely Atlantean. Could it be the vault?

Eddie returned from backing the excavator out of the pool and peered over her shoulder. 'Wow. Took long enough, but I knew that sooner or later we'd find a UFO!'

'It's *not* a UFO,' she insisted – but on this occasion, there was at least a glimmer of uncertainty. The mysterious object certainly *looked* the part, the gleaming metal seemingly cast as a single seamless piece. She had seen Atlantean statues of similar size, but they had been made near their final locations. How this huge object had been brought across rough terrain over a hundred miles from the nearest coast – in a region under the control of an adversary – without being discovered was a mystery.

There were far more urgent questions, though. First and foremost: was the spearhead here?

She swept the beam over the ceiling before turning it to the floor. 'The roof looks intact,' she said. 'I can't see any cracks or fallen soil from above.'

'Is that the vault?' asked Lobato, gazing down the tunnel.

'If it's not, we've found one hell of a Kinder Egg,' the Yorkshireman replied.

Nina was more serious. 'It must be. It's been buried here for eleven thousand years . . . and it's still intact. So the spearhead must be inside.'

Lobato moved as if to push past her, but Eddie held out an arm. 'Hang on there, Sheldon. Let's let someone who knows what she's doing go first, eh?'

'Nothing I like more than being the first person to walk up to a bomb,' his wife quipped as she stepped through the opening. The tunnel smelled stale and damp, but did not appear to have suffered any recent flooding that might have left it unstable.

A bigger concern was booby traps. She had encountered too many in the past; the Atlanteans liked to protect their treasures with lethal force. But the light revealed no tripwires or lurking mechanisms – just stone and dirt.

And the vault itself. She moved closer, stopping when Eddie came through the hole. 'Here,' she said, taking another flashlight from the pack and switching it on. 'Let's make sure we can all see what we're doing.'

She passed the torch to Eddie, who moved up alongside her. Behind him, Lobato entered. 'Wait, wait,' Nina told him, but the billionaire was already inside, brushing distastefully at earth smeared on his white sleeve. 'Okay, Gideon,' she said with a sigh. 'This is *my* game, so here are my rules. One: do what I tell you. Two: don't touch anything. Three: if you're *that* dirt-phobic, maybe don't come into an underground tunnel?'

Lobato was not amused. 'I will defer to your experience,' he said, fingers still fidgeting.

'Good. So wait there until I've checked things out, okay?'

'Don't suppose I can stay back here too?' Eddie asked hopefully.

'Yeah, right. Get your butt over here, mister.'

He chuckled and followed her down the passage.

The rectangular opening was bounded by hefty stone pillars. Nina saw familiar angular characters upon them. 'Atlantean text . . .'

'What does it say?'

She paused to translate, then let out a half-laugh. 'Basically, "this is the spearhead's vault". It's just a sign to tell the emissary from Atlantis that they're in the right place.'

'Yeah, 'cause I'm sure every hilltop in southern Turkey's got a random tunnel dug into it.'

She smiled, then entered the chamber proper. The object at its heart was indeed spherical, or nearly so; it was slightly flattened, roughly twenty-five feet across. The stone-walled room matched its shape, large enough to allow people to walk around its centrepiece.

The light from outside dimmed as Ana and Maximov looked through the hole. 'Is it safe?' the Russian asked.

'Seems to be,' Nina called back, 'but let's not take any chances. Eddie? You go around it clockwise – carefully. I'll go the other way.'

'Okay.' Eddie cautiously went left as she headed right around the golden artefact. He offered a running commentary. 'Floor's clear, walls and ceiling are intact, not seeing anything on the UFO . . .'

'It's not a UFO!' Her own exploration also revealed nothing – until she reached the far side. 'Wait, there's something here.'

She brought her flashlight closer. A thin line was cut into the smooth metal surface, forming a rectangular shape.

A door.

'It's a way in,' she gasped. 'It *is* the vault, and we just found its entrance!'

Eddie reached her and raised his own light. 'So how do we open it?'

'I'll take a wild guess and say *that* has something to do with it.' She illuminated an indentation at the door's exact centre, in the shape of a splayed hand.

'Palm-print reader?' said Eddie. 'Bit high-tech, surely. Unless—'

'*Not* aliens.' She examined it more closely. Inset at the open palm's centre was a circle of polished stone . . .

'We've seen something like this before,' she said, suddenly on alert. Her warning tone prompted Eddie to rapidly check his surroundings for threats. 'In Ethiopia, the Temple of the Gods. The Atlanteans put a handprint just like this at the entrance.'

'Yeah – and it was a trap, remember?' He looked up at the ceiling. On their previous encounter with such a device, it had turned out to be a decoy, the real entrance hidden nearby. Anyone who put their hand into the indentation hoping to open the door would be crushed. 'Not seeing any giant hammers here, though.'

'There wouldn't be room to fit one, not this close to the hilltop. But that doesn't mean there aren't any other death-traps.' She turned, examining the walls and ceiling. In their starkness they were typically Atlantean, but there didn't seem to be any way an unwelcome surprise could pop out, stab up or swing down. 'Can't see anything,' she said. 'This place was well hidden – they might have thought security through obscurity was enough.'

'What have you found?' Berk called from the tunnel.

'What are *you* doing here?' Nina demanded.

'This is our property!' said Elmas, affronted.

'It's a UFO,' Eddie replied. 'The place is full of dead space aliens! Wait, wait – one of 'em's moving! There's something coming out of its chest – no, *no!* Aaah! *Eeaarghhhhh!*'

Nina folded her arms impatiently as he flailed about, pretending to strangle himself. 'Are you *quite* finished?'

'*Gaahhhh* . . . yeah, I'm done.' His grin widened as her eyes narrowed.

'So it *is* UFO?' Maximov asked uncertainly.

'It's not a frickin' . . . Ugh, whatever.' Nina shook her head. 'We've found the vault, but its entrance might be booby-trapped. Nobody else come down here until I'm sure it's safe, okay?'

She moved her light around the door's edge. The narrow gap was a constant width, precisely crafted. The rest of the vault's surface was smooth and unmarked except for the dust of ages.

'All right,' she said, regarding the handprint. 'This is the only feature I can find. So either it's a way to open it, or it'll kill me.' She looked more closely at the inset disc. A purple stone, thin veins of some dark metal running through it. Something else she had encountered before, and it had never led to anything good. 'Great. I thought the whole earth energy crap was behind me, but apparently not . . .'

'It's earth energy?' Eddie asked.

'It's the same stuff the Sky Stone was made of. And we know how well *that* went for the Atlanteans.' The Sky Stone was a large meteorite, exact composition still unknown, that somehow channelled and focused the earth's natural energy flows in a way that certain people could control. The rulers of Atlantis had sought to use it as a weapon – but the attempt went catastrophically wrong, bringing about the destruction of the Atlantean civilisation itself. 'That might explain how they were able to transport something this big, though. Maybe they used the earth-energy effect to levitate it.' She registered her husband's disbelief. 'Hey, come on. We both saw a chunk of rock the size of a house floating in mid-air! Don't tell me you've forgotten.'

'I've seen so much weird shit since I met you that I've lost track,' he said. 'But I'm not bothered right now about how they got this thing down here. I'm more worried about it blowing up any fucking second!'

Nina raised a hand to touch the vault's curving flank beside the door. 'Maybe if—'

She gasped in surprise, jerking back.

'Jesus!' said Eddie. 'What're you bloody doing? Don't touch it, you might set it off!'

'I didn't touch the handprint,' she said. 'If anything's going to happen, it'll be when someone touches the stone.'

'So what's wrong?'

'Feel for yourself.'

He put a dubious fingertip against the metal. 'It's buzzing!'

'Here as well,' she said, testing another spot. 'The whole vault's . . . humming. Earth energy, it has to be.'

Eddie backed away. 'What, so the spearhead's charging up and getting ready to explode?'

'The earth energy might be *keeping* it from exploding.' At his confused look, she elaborated: 'The test the Atlanteans carried out, when they blew up an entire island – they said they kept the spearhead inside the vault until they were ready. Once they took it out, the last men who got away said it started to flash and shake, more and more violently. If the spearhead contains anti-matter particles, then however they were trapped, it would need a lot of power to contain them without their coming into contact with normal matter and exploding. Earth energy might be that source of power. And the vault could be how they channel it.'

'I thought you needed a person to channel it,' said Eddie, dubious. 'It's how it worked before. Excalibur, that death-ray DARPA built from it, the Sky Stone – they all needed you touching 'em to work.'

'Me, or anyone else descended from the right line of Atlanteans. Even back then, only a few people could focus the energy.'

'I doubt there's still anyone alive inside there to do that. They'd be bloody hungry after eleven thousand years.'

They both turned at a sound from the entrance. 'Hey!' Nina

snapped, looking around the vault to find Lobato staring at it in wonderment. 'I told you not to come down here.'

'We cannot waste time, Dr Wilde,' he reminded her. 'We must secure the spearhead.' He tried to peer past her. 'Have you opened it?'

'No, not yet, because I don't want to blow everyone for ten miles to atoms!'

'Is the bomb really that big?' asked Berk from behind him.

Nina huffed in exasperation. 'Oh, sure, why doesn't *everyone* come in? Jesus! I'm remembering why I retired – so I didn't have to babysit any boat-footed gawkers!'

Eddie laughed. 'There's the woman I married.'

'This was here all the time?' asked Elmas. 'Is it made of gold?' She sounded thrilled at the prospect.

'It's a gold alloy called orichalcum, and yes, it's been here for thousands of years. Now if everyone would let me work . . .' But when the new arrivals showed no sign of taking the hint, she reluctantly accepted she was stuck with an audience. 'All right, just stay back, and don't touch anything.'

Lobato nevertheless advanced until Nina's annoyed glare reached an intensity even he could not fail to interpret. Berk and Elmas went the other way to watch from behind Eddie. 'What have you found?' asked Ana from the tunnel entrance. 'Can we see?'

'Sure, why not?' was Nina's sarcastic reply.

Eddie's was more measured. 'Someone needs to stay on guard, in case we get visitors.'

'I stay outside,' Maximov replied. 'Roof is too low for me anyway!'

The Brazilian made her way into the chamber, standing beside Lobato. 'Everyone got a good view?' said Nina, before focusing. 'Right,' she said, staring intently at the handprint. 'This is either a lock or a trap. Which is more likely?'

'I would say the probability—' Lobato began.

She cut him off. 'Shush! Rhetorical question. It's more likely to be . . . a lock.'

The billionaire was irked at being silenced. 'I hope your reasoning is based on experience rather than *intuition.*'

'The vault was well hidden,' she explained, 'and it can only be opened by someone of the right Atlantean bloodline. Only about one per cent of people today are of Atlantean descent, and even in Atlantis itself, very few could focus earth energy. So the number of people who could have opened the vault would be very small. Anyone else would have to force the door open. *That's* where the trap is.'

'Try to break it open, and *boom?*' Eddie suggested.

'Exactly. The only people who would try to force their way in would be its targets. That would make them a danger to Atlantis – they couldn't be allowed to gain control of a spearhead. So breaking open the vault would get them blown up as surely as if the Atlanteans had set it off themselves.'

'You are sure about that?' Ana asked.

'As sure as I can be. But there's only one way to know for certain, and that's to open it.' She sensed distinct uncertainty from her audience.

'Anyone who isn't convinced had better get out of the blast radius,' said Eddie, pointing down the tunnel. 'About thirty miles that way.'

The Onans looked to be considering it, but Lobato was more confident. 'You are sure you are correct, Dr Wilde?'

'I am,' she replied.

'Then I will trust your judgement.'

Nina gave him a nod of thanks. 'Okay. Let's do this.' She cautiously raised her hand towards the indentation and pressed her palm against the stone disc.

A moment passed . . . then relieved exhalations came from

around the chamber as everyone's atoms remained intact.

Nina's response was different. The moment she touched the lock, she felt a bizarre sensation, as if some tremendous power was flowing through her. With it came almost an *image* in her mind, a flash of knowledge: that she had indeed found the object for which she had been searching. 'It's here!' she gasped, stepping back. 'The spearhead – it's here!'

'You okay?' Eddie asked, concerned. 'You looked like you just got zapped! Is it electrified?'

'No, it's . . . it's hard to describe,' she told him, recovering. 'But I *know* the spearhead is inside – it's almost as if I saw it. I've felt something like it before, with the three statues that led to the Sky Stone. I was . . . *connected* to it.'

'In what way?' asked Lobato.

'I . . . I don't know. Like I said, it's hard to describe. As if I had an extra sense, but only for a split second.'

'But nothing happened,' Ana pointed out. 'The door is still closed.'

'Something *did* happen,' Nina insisted. 'In the vault, at least. Maybe I need to—'

Before she could finish, a flat metallic *thump* caught everyone's attention. 'What was that?' said Berk, alarmed.

'It came from inside,' said Eddie. 'Maybe we should get out—'

'No, no!' Nina insisted. 'It's opening!'

As she spoke, another sound came from the metal sphere: a low creaking noise, as if a giant spring were being released from centuries of compression. The thin line marking the door's edge gradually widened, the barrier reluctantly moving outwards before starting to hinge open. Eddie sidestepped to stay with Nina as it swung out into the chamber. The vault was thick, more than a foot of metal emerging before the first glimpse of the interior was revealed.

To everyone's shock, it was not dark. A strange shimmering light came from within. 'What is *that*?' asked Lobato.

'What we came to find,' said Nina, waiting for the door to open wider before leaning through.

What she found was remarkable even by the standards of Atlantis. Inside was a circular space, the metal walls inset with columns of some kind of crystal. The spaces between them were scribed with Atlantean text. But translating it was far from her first thought, her attention instantly dominated by what sat at the room's centre. A pillar of dark stone rose from the floor, its top cupped to hold the object the vault had been built to contain.

To hold it. But not touch it.

She knew she was looking at the spearhead, the image that had flashed into her mind returning like a lost memory. It was an elongated and slightly flattened diamond shape, just under a foot in length, formed from translucent crystal. The light came from within it, blue-white motes sparkling and flickering as they lazily swirled like a miniature galaxy.

But that was not the most astonishing thing about it.

The spearhead was *levitating*, suspended a few inches above the pillar's top. 'Look at that,' she whispered. 'It's incredible!'

Lobato's view was obstructed by Eddie. 'What is it?' the billionaire asked impatiently.

'Just your everyday glowing diamond the size of a rugby ball floating in mid-air,' the Yorkshireman replied. 'No big deal.'

'A diamond?' exclaimed Elmas, all worry in her voice instantly evaporating.

'This isn't a damn Tiffany's,' said Nina. 'Everyone get back. I need to read this text.'

With Eddie acting as bouncer, she warily stepped into the vault. The door opened fully, stopping with a thud that made the golden sphere shudder. She flinched, but the spearhead, silently hovering above the purple stone altar, was unaffected.

A moment of wonder as she peered into the crystal's shimmering depths, then she forced her attention to the Atlantean inscriptions, starting with the most prominent. 'Okay,' she said after reading the first blocks of text, 'this confirms what I thought about the spearhead's purpose. It's definitely a weapon – a doomsday device that Atlantis could use to blackmail or destroy the civilisation that existed here.' She cocked her head as she continued her translation. 'The Atlanteans obviously thought they were a major threat, but they also didn't have a very high opinion of them. They're referred to as "barbarians" and . . . "the skull desecrators". Actually, that would tie in with some of the archaeological findings from Gobekli Tepe—'

'Nina,' Eddie cut in. 'Glowy bomb thing. Top priority.'

'*Ugh*, okay.' She looked back at the ancient writing. 'More about their enemies, which is fascinating but I'll skip it for now . . . Ah! These,' she indicated a new section, 'are instructions for the "Emissary of Perses".'

'Perses?' said Berk. 'He was a Greek god.'

'One of the Titans rather than an Olympian deity, actually, but yes.'

'But this is from Atlantis, not Greece.'

'The Atlanteans and Greeks shared a pantheon,' she explained. 'The roots of ancient Greek mythology date back much further than was once thought, but it wasn't until Atlantis was discovered that—'

'Bomb thing,' Eddie said impatiently.

'Argh! Okay, okay. Perses was essentially the god of destruction – whenever he got personally involved in a conflict, there wouldn't be much left standing. If the spearhead really is an antimatter bomb, that fits. So after the emissary opens the vault, she – interesting, it specifies the emissary will be a woman – she then confronts the leaders of Gobekli Tepe, and issues an ultimatum . . .' She frowned, falling silent as she read on. 'Oh, crap.'

Eddie stiffened. 'Yep, when I'm standing ten feet from a bomb, *that's* what I want to hear.'

'What does it say?' asked Lobato.

Nina hurriedly reread the inscriptions, hoping she had translated wrongly. But if anything, her second attempt only made the words more chillingly clear. 'It says . . . when the emissary opens the vault, the spearhead is . . . "freed" is the word they use, but it can also be translated as "unleashed". Once that happens, their enemies have less than a day to surrender – or be destroyed.' She looked at the others in appalled fear. 'I've just started the countdown on the world's biggest bomb!'

32

E ddie stared at his wife. 'You've done *what*?'

'It's a kind of fail-safe – well, a fail-*deadly*!' Nina frantically scanned the rest of the inscriptions. 'The vault didn't need any deathtraps, because it *is* the deathtrap. The emissary opens it, activating the spearhead, and *then* goes to the target's rulers with the ultimatum from Atlantis. That way, if they imprison or kill the emissary, the bomb goes off. The only way to stop it from exploding is . . .'

'I hope there is a description of the procedure,' said Lobato drily.

'Yeah, me too! Okay, something about . . . the emissary asks for . . . nope, useless. Ah . . . this might be it! The spearhead goes through three phases . . .' She read the ancient words as rapidly as she could. 'All right. In the first phase, which is what it's in now, the flashes inside it get brighter over time – although apparently there's a very bright flash a few minutes after it's taken off the altar. Which, incidentally, is something else that starts the countdown.'

'So we don't move it,' suggested Ana.

'Wasn't planning to anyway,' Nina assured her. 'This phase lasts . . . half a day. Then in the second phase the flashes get brighter and more . . . violent, I think that means, and the light changes colour. Once it gets into the third stage, it starts to shake from inside. That's the point of no return.'

'I believe I know what it is describing,' said Lobato. 'The spearhead must indeed contain particles of antimatter, which are contained by some sort of magnetic field, preventing them from coming into contact with normal matter. Once this field starts to weaken, the antiparticles begin to escape, whereupon they collide with matter and explode. At a certain point, the spearhead is so damaged it can no longer contain the remaining antiparticles. The field collapses, they are all released at once – and the result is an antimatter detonation of enormous force.'

'So how do we stop it?' demanded Eddie.

'I'm workin' on it!' Nina replied. 'There must be a way, otherwise why have the ultimatum?' Her gaze flicked over various sections of the Atlantean text in the hope of picking out some key word that could help her, and to her relief, eventually she found one. 'Ah! Here – I hope.'

'Don't suppose there's an abort button, is there?' said Eddie.

'Not exactly, but there *is* a way to bring the spearhead back to normal, if you do it in time. Let's see . . .' She crouched to read the inscription. 'Great, *now* I find a bunch of words I don't recognise. Okay, context, context . . .'

Maximov's voice echoed down the tunnel. 'Eddie!'

'Hold on, Max!' the Yorkshireman shouted back. 'Got a situation here!'

'What kind of situation?'

'The "we're gonna get blown up" kind! Give us a minute.' He turned back to Nina. 'If we *have* a minute . . .'

'I think I've figured it out,' she replied, though she was far from confident. 'This text describes some kind of ritual, so a lot of the words are specific to it – they're probably religious terms. But it's all to do with this altar.' She indicated the stone column. 'Opening the door – correctly, rather than forcing it open – somehow affects the flow of earth energy into the spearhead, and causes whatever field contains the antimatter to gradually decay. I'm guessing that if the door *is* forced open, the field collapses immediately and everything explodes. But as long as the spearhead hasn't entered the final stage, putting it on the altar and performing the ritual stabilises it.'

'Ritual?' said Lobato dubiously. 'You are not suggesting the Atlanteans used magic, surely?'

'Not in the Harry Potter sense, no. But there's some hands-on physical process involved, the emissary touching the altar to affect the flow of earth energy. Ancient cultures almost always attach ceremony to certain acts over time – you see it in healing rituals throughout the world – and eventually the mumbo-jumbo comes to be seen as the driving force of what- ever's being done, rather than just baggage attached by the gatekeepers. But enough anthropology, more archaeology, huh?' She read on.

Maximov shouted again. 'Eddie! We have problem!'

'No shit!' Eddie replied, but the urgency in the Russian's voice gave him concern. 'I'll see what's wrong,' he said, heading for the tunnel.

Nina looked back at the inscriptions. 'If I'm reading this right, the emissary is supposed to stabilise the spearhead by *willing* it to stabilise. As in, they hold the altar, then really, really *want* it not to explode.'

'Like saying a prayer?' said Ana.

'Prayers do not work,' Lobato scoffed. 'They are another example of religious mumbo-jumbo.' The Brazilian scowled at him.

Nina was also sceptical, but she could not afford to be so dismissive. 'Well, the Atlanteans certainly seemed to think they worked – to the point of relying on them to keep their asses from being blown into the stratosphere. And this might sound weird, but I've definitely had . . . I won't say "visions", because that sounds ridiculous, but *flashes* where I've felt a connection to things channelling earth energy, even at a distance. It happened before I found the Sky Stone in Ethiopia, and it happened again here when I opened the door. I *felt* that the spearhead was in here before I saw it.'

'Now you are saying that you have *psychic powers*?' Lobato's usually flat voice took on a tone of mocking disbelief.

'No, I'm not,' she snapped. 'But I *am* saying that some people can sense – and even affect – the earth's natural energy fields when they use the right kind of conductor. This,' she indicated the altar, 'is one of those conductors. If the inscriptions are right, then an effort of willpower while touching it is enough to return the spearhead to its normal state.' Sensing ever-greater incredulity, she went on: 'Think of it as using electrodes to read people's brainwaves in order to control machinery – that's something we can already do. This is the same kind of thing. And the Atlanteans were using it – had *weaponised* it – eleven thousand years ago.'

'I remain to be convinced,' said Lobato.

'If she is wrong,' Ana pointed out, 'the spearhead will explode in less than twenty-four hours.'

'I hope she is not wrong,' said Berk anxiously, before addressing Nina. 'You are not wrong, are you?'

'Not usually,' she replied, but something else in the inscriptions had snatched her attention. 'Okay, this is weird . . .'

'What is it?' Lobato asked.

'The text explaining how the emissary is supposed to stop the spearhead from exploding . . .' She read it again, thinking she must have translated it wrongly but at the same time certain she hadn't. 'It says the ritual was given to them by "those who came before". But who came before Atlantis?'

Before she could puzzle over the question any further, Eddie rushed back into the chamber. 'Everybody out – we've got a big fucking problem!'

'What is wrong?' asked Elmas.

'There's a helicopter coming in, and I doubt it's your friends dropping by for cocktails. Nina, you've got to get that thing out of there!'

'I can't!' Nina protested. 'It'll explode unless I can stabilise it.'

'Can you do that in less than – Max! How far away are they?'

Maximov shouted from the tunnel entrance. 'They are jumping out at house!'

'Less than twenty seconds?' Eddie continued.

'No, of course I can't!' she said.

'Then grab it, 'cause we've got to go! If we get to the cars, we can make a run for it—'

Maximov's sudden cry of alarm was followed by the rattle of automatic weapons fire, accompanied by the *plunk-plunk-plunk* of bullets penetrating sheet metal. 'What was that?' yelped Berk.

'That was the cars,' said Eddie grimly. 'Okay, we'll *literally* have to make a run for it. Nina, grab that thing! Everyone else, go!'

The Onans hurried for the exit, Ana following. Lobato started after her, but halted when he realised Nina was not moving. 'If it leaves the vault, there's no way to stop it exploding,' she insisted as Eddie reached the golden door.

'All right, so let them take it!' Seeing her surprise, he explained: 'They take it to Dhajan, it blows up in their faces. Problem solved!'

'And what if they take it to a city full of innocent people?'

His face fell. 'Problem *not* solved.'

'They will probably take it to the solar facility,' said Lobato. 'It is isolated, in the mountains.'

'Problem *re*-solved. Nina, come on!'

'But they may be able to use my containment facility to extract the antimatter.'

'Oh, for fuck's sake! Okay, we grab it, get away, take off in your jet and chuck the fucking thing out over the sea. But we've got to go! *Now!*'

Nina reached reluctantly for the spearhead, but before she could take it, another burst of gunfire came from outside, followed by a woman's scream. 'Elmas!' she cried, fearing the worst—

The scream continued, getting closer. Elmas and her husband were running back down the tunnel. 'We're cut off!' Ana shouted as she returned with them. More weapons fire followed, closer – then Maximov, squeezing through the opening, let out a loud gasp. '*Oleg!*' the Brazilian exclaimed.

'I am okay,' he grunted. 'Hit in arm, not too bad.'

'You are . . . smiling,' said Elmas, shocked.

'Yeah, he's weird like that,' Eddie said as the hunched Russian reached the chamber. Maximov was holding his lower biceps, blood dripping from his fingers, but he did indeed have a look of pleasure. 'How many of them are there?'

'Seven, maybe eight,' Maximov replied as Ana examined the wound. 'All have guns.'

'What do we do?' Berk asked fearfully.

'Not much without guns of our own,' Eddie said. 'Can we call the cops?'

'We left our phones in the house,' said Elmas unhappily.

The Yorkshireman pulled out his own phone. 'Shit! No network. Anyone else?'

The others reported the same lack of reception. 'The phone signal is bad up here,' Berk admitted.

'Plus, y'know, we're underground,' Nina added.

'Get back, away from the tunnel.' Eddie peered towards the ragged slash of light. Voices were audible outside, but he couldn't tell what they were saying. They were getting closer, though. 'They're coming,' he warned.

Maximov clenched his fists. 'We make them regret it, no?'

'No.'

'No?' The Russian regarded him in surprise.

Ana was also taken aback. 'You are going to surrender?'

'I don't like it, but we don't have much choice,' Eddie replied. 'If they shoot their way in, we'll all get killed.'

'They might kill us all anyway,' said Nina as she exited the vault.

'We've got the only person who can translate Atlantean and the guy who designed the antimatter thing they'll need to use,' he said. 'We might be able to make a bargain.'

'But they'll have the spearhead.'

'They'll have it no matter what – there's nowt we can do to stop them.'

She looked back at the hefty door. 'I could try to seal the vault.'

'And then they'll either use the rest of us as hostages to force you to open it again, or just blow it open – and set off the fucking bomb.'

'Dr Wilde!' a man shouted from the swimming pool. 'We know you are in there. Surrender!'

'Any chance of an "and you will not be harmed" at the end of that?' Eddie called back. A mocking laugh came from outside. 'Arse. So much for being positive!'

Nina joined her husband. 'If you guarantee our safety, I'll tell you how to make the spearhead safe. Gideon Lobato is here as well – he can help you use the facility in Dhajan to stabilise it.'

'Lobato is no longer needed,' came the reply. The billionaire twitched in dismay.

A man slipped through the opening, gun at the ready as he advanced. Another of the Emir's agents followed him in. 'Everyone get back by the vault door,' Eddie said grimly. 'They might not shoot if they think it could damage the spearhead.'

Everyone retreated to the opening in the orichalcum sphere. Nina climbed inside, regarding the spearhead's shimmering light. 'I should at least try to stabilise it while I've got the chance.'

'You won't have time,' Eddie warned. The first man was almost at the chamber, the beam of a small but powerful flashlight stabbing through the entrance.

'I have to *try*.' She examined the inscriptions. 'I don't think I have to touch the altar in any particular way. It's what I'm thinking – what I'm *willing* – that matters . . .'

'Then will faster!'

The intruder's torch beam locked on to the golden sphere – before a shouted command from al-Asim overcame his greedy amazement and he swept his gun to each side. 'We're not armed!' Eddie told him, raising his hands and edging into the man's line of sight. The Dhajani stared coldly at him but did not fire.

The second man arrived, more advancing behind him. 'Nina,' the Yorkshireman muttered, 'if you're going to do something, do it *now*.'

Inside the vault, Nina gave the inscriptions one last desperate look before facing the altar. She had not translated enough of the text to learn exactly what she needed to do; too much was masked by metaphor, referring to events she had yet to discover. Another way to ensure that only an Atlantean could control the spearhead, perhaps, but it meant that she could either do nothing . . .

Or try – and hope.

She crouched, closed her eyes . . . and gripped the altar.

The coldness of the stone was overpowered by an almost electric sensation, the mysterious energy field of the earth itself suddenly flowing through her. She had felt it before, but not with this intensity; she had to force herself not to pull away. It was not painful, more . . . *unnerving*, a sense that she was in contact with something both forbidden and dangerous.

But there was something else there. The spearhead.

Even without seeing or touching it, she could *feel* it – *know* it. How, she had no idea, but somehow she perceived the ceaseless whirlpool of power running through it, forces she didn't yet understand containing antimatter particles inside the crystalline shape. She also instinctively knew that it had indeed started to become unstable, a small but rising dissonance faintly scraping the fringes of her new sense.

But she could repair it, she was sure. It was almost as if she could touch the vortex in her mind, shape it . . .

Willpower. That was what the Atlanteans meant. The rare few who could make contact with the planet's unseen energies were able not only to sense them. They could affect them, maybe even control—

'Dr Wilde! Move away from the spearhead! *Now!*'

The harsh command snapped her back to reality. She opened her eyes, momentarily dazzled by the spearhead's light before turning to see a man at the doorway of the vault.

Hashim al-Asim.

The Dhajani agent was pointing a gun at her. Behind him was Eddie, hands raised – and staring at her with an expression of more than simple concern. 'What's wrong?' she asked. 'Apart from, y'know, the obvious.'

'What's wrong?' Eddie echoed. 'You were in a bloody trance!'

She blinked. 'For how long?'

'Thirty seconds, more? I was talking to you and you didn't even hear me.'

'But I only just . . .' She looked back at the altar and the strange artefact suspended above it. 'It . . . it didn't seem that long.'

'Well it was, trust me. Did . . . anything happen when you touched it?'

'I wasn't able to change anything,' she replied, recognising that his vagueness was deliberate; he didn't want to give away anything about the spearhead to their captors. She stood, withdrawing from the stone column.

As she moved, al-Asim turned his attention to the spearhead itself. His eyes widened. 'It is floating in the air! What is this? Magic?'

'Science,' Nina retorted. 'Weird science, but still science. It's a kind of magnetic levitation produced by the earth's natural energy fields. Don't ask me to explain it, because I honestly don't think I can.'

'Lobato's your man for that,' said Eddie. 'Be a really good idea to keep him alive. And Nina too, because she can read the inscriptions in there. In fact, keep us *all* alive. Consider it your good deed for the day. Just take the spearhead, and go. You're best off getting as far away from here as possible.'

Al-Asim ushered Nina from the vault, then gave her husband a suspicious look. 'You are very keen for us to take it, Mr Chase.'

'I don't want anyone to get killed.'

The Dhajani's expression did not change as he stepped inside. He slowly circled the altar, waving a hand beneath the hovering crystal as if to assure himself it was not a trick, then addressed the man guarding Eddie. 'I am going to take the spearhead,' he announced. 'If anything happens . . . kill them. Kill them all.'

He shouldered his weapon, then held both hands around the spearhead. He flexed his fingers, giving Nina a challenging look – and took hold of the crystal.

She twitched, half expecting something drastic to happen, but after a moment, al-Asim spoke. 'It is . . . warm,' he said, sounding almost disappointed. He stepped back. Whatever suspended the spearhead above the altar's top also held it there, the Dhajani having to apply definite force, but then it came free.

The motes of sparkling light inside it subtly changed, their swirling motion becoming more of a random fuzz, but their intensity remained the same. Al-Asim regarded the glow, then cradled the spearhead in one arm and returned to the vault's door. 'I have it,' he announced triumphantly, issuing another

350

command in Arabic before gesturing with his gun for Nina and Eddie to move. 'Outside.'

His men started to march the others at gunpoint towards the tunnel. 'So you've got the spearhead,' Nina said angrily. 'Now what? I'm guessing you don't want it for peaceful purposes.'

'That is no longer your concern,' al-Asim replied dismissively.

'But you *must* take it to our facility in Dhajan,' Lobato implored as everyone filed into the passage. 'It is the only way to contain the antimatter safely. The spearhead is a weapon, a bomb; if it is not kept stable—'

'I know it is a bomb – that is why we want it! We are taking it to the facility, yes, but you are not coming with it.'

Elmas clutched her husband's hand. 'They are going to kill us!' she cried. Maximov tensed, glowering at the nearest raider, but the man had stayed just beyond the huge Russian's reach.

'You and your fucking game plan,' Eddie growled at Lobato. 'Didn't see *this* fucking outcome, did you?'

'I . . . did not, no,' the billionaire replied stiffly, trying to contain his fear.

'Keep moving,' ordered al-Asim. His men guided the prisoners towards the opening. 'Into the pool. I will make it quick and painless, I promise.' Elmas moaned in fear, almost stumbling, but one of the raiders shoved her onwards. 'I have—'

The spearhead's light suddenly flared. Al-Asim stopped. 'I felt something!' he cried, as his men brought their prisoners to a halt. 'It – it shook! What is happening?'

'I don't know,' Nina replied, seeing that Eddie was ready to react to whatever might happen. 'Maybe that was the flash mentioned in the inscriptions.'

'The *flash*, with a *bang*,' Eddie added, glancing at Maximov and Ana. The Brazilian immediately knew what he meant, but it took the huge man a couple of seconds longer to pick up on the message, his mouth opening in a silent 'Ah!' of understanding.

'Is it going to explode?' al-Asim asked Nina, alarmed.

'I think taking it out of the vault was a very bad idea,' she said. The seething glow rose in intensity then held, as if straining against the walls of its crystalline prison. 'Look at it!' She pointed.

As the Dhajanis' gazes instinctively followed her finger, Eddie and Nina closed their eyes—

A dazzling flash of unearthly light filled the tunnel.

33

Even with her eyes shut, Nina felt as if she was staring straight into a paparazzo's flash gun. But for those looking directly at it, the effects were literally stunning, their senses overwhelmed by a silent explosion of light.

'Jesus!' said Eddie. 'No bang, but one hell of a flash!' Ana and Maximov had shielded their eyes, but Lobato and the Onans had not understood his veiled warning, and were now staggering as helplessly as their captors.

The nearest Dhajani to Eddie blindly waved his Glock 18 machine pistol at comrades and captives alike. That danger quickly ended as the Yorkshireman snatched away the gun, then delivered a punch that left him even more insensate. 'Everyone get out!' he shouted. 'Ana, Max, bring 'em!'

Maximov and Ana grabbed Elmas and Berk, Eddie seizing Lobato's arm and hauling him towards the tunnel's mouth. Nina, though, had gone the other way – plucking the spearhead from al-Asim's hands. It was heavier than she expected, weighing at least ten pounds.

'No, get his *gun* – oh, for fuck's sake!' Eddie cried as she ran after him. 'You can't shoot anyone with a fucking crystal!'

'They can't blow anything up with it either!' she fired back as they reached the tunnel's end. Ana went through with Elmas, Maximov shoving Berk after them before causing a jam as he squeezed his hulking frame into the narrow gap. 'We've got to get this thing as far away from anyone as we can. Dropping it into the sea from ten thousand feet sounds like a good plan!'

The Russian finally popped free, Eddie propelling Lobato after him. The sun had set while they were inside the chamber, the sky a dusky purple. The helicopter in which the raiders had arrived was orbiting the hilltop, several hundred metres distant.

'Oh, great!' said Nina, noticing their bullet-riddled 4x4s. Smoke wafted from one BMW's hood, the other's front tyre shredded. She ran towards the house after Maximov, who was carrying the Onans under his arms. 'These guys must have a car, right?'

Eddie followed, bringing Lobato with him. 'There was a big garage at the other end of the house.' The group entered the building. Nina paused to slam the door shut. 'Yeah, that'll keep them out,' he said sarcastically, rapping the gun barrel against the glass.

She glowered. 'Just find the car, smartass.'

He glanced back at the pool. Nobody had emerged from the tunnel, but it wouldn't be long before the raiders recovered – and realised they had lost their prisoners *and* their prize. 'No, I'll need to hold 'em off until we're ready to go. You take Lobato.' He pushed the billionaire towards her, then surveyed his surroundings. He needed a higher position to fully cover the tunnel entrance and pool, the parked earth-mover partially blocking his line of fire. But there was a turret-like chamber directly above the dining room. Its large windows would give him an excellent vantage point, if he could reach it in time. 'Berk, Elmas! The round room, right upstairs – how do I get to it?'

The couple had recovered enough to protest the indignity of being carted around like wet rugs, struggling until Maximov put them down. 'The . . . the hot tub,' said Berk. 'There are stairs, through there.' He indicated the hallway just outside the dining room.

Eddie rapidly ejected the gun's magazine, finding it fully loaded, then reinserted it. He ran for the exit. 'I hope you've got a car in your garage, 'cause we'll need it,' he told the Turks.

'Of course we have a car!' Elmas snapped after him. 'We have two, an Audi and a Mercedes.'

'Why am I not surprised? Start 'em up – and don't leave without me!' He rushed up the stairs.

'Where's the garage?' Nina demanded.

Berk steadied himself. 'This way.' He started back down the long hall, the others following.

Eddie reached the top of the stairs, throwing open a nearby door at one end of a long landing to enter a circular room housing a large hot tub. The windows ran down to knee height, presenting anyone relaxing in the raised bath with a panoramic vista.

He was more interested in the view over the pool. From here, he had clear line of sight – and fire – on the tunnel entrance. The raiders had not yet emerged, but he glimpsed lights moving inside the ragged opening.

He swung a window outwards and crouched at its foot, sighting the gun at the hole. The lights went out, almost as one. They were about to move—

Someone leaned into view, weapon readied. Eddie sent a single shot at him. The bullet smacked into the soil just above the man's head. The Englishman instantly refined his aim, but the raider had ducked back.

They were pinned for now, but that wouldn't last. From what he knew of Dhajan's intelligence agency, its operatives were well trained – in part, ironically enough, by Britain, which considered the little emirate a useful ally in the Gulf. If the situation were reversed, he would have his men take up positions flanking the tunnel mouth, ready to blast suppressing fire at the turret while someone sprinted for the shelter of the excavator. He had no doubt that al-Asim was doing exactly that.

He readied himself for the inevitable assault.

★ ★ ★

Berk led the way to a door. 'The cars are in here.' He rushed into the garage – and stopped, horrified. '*Hassiktir!*'

'Whatever you just said, I agree with it,' Nina replied. The Onans' two large and expensive German sedans were both damaged, a line of holes in the garage doors where the raiders had swept gunfire across them. Dirty water from the Audi's ruptured radiator trickled across the floor, and the Merc, facing the other way, was dribbling gasoline. 'Okay, we need a new plan!'

'The phones!' Ana exclaimed, turning to the Onans. 'We are out of the tunnel – you can call the police.'

'But they will take a long time to get here,' said Berk. 'We will all be dead by then!'

His wife was less defeatist. 'I will not let anyone kill me in my own home,' she growled, pushing past Maximov. 'My phone is in the lounge. Come, quickly!'

Nina followed, still holding the shimmering spearhead. 'Oleg, Ana, go help Eddie.' They acknowledged the order and ran back the way they had come. 'We need to get somewhere safe while you make the call. Which room has the most shelter?'

'The pantry,' said Elmas. 'It is the only room with no windows.'

'Okay, let's go.' They hurried away.

Eddie kept his eyes on the tunnel entrance, awaiting the attack—

Guns whipped around the hole's sides, unleashing a hail of automatic fire at him. He shot back, but was forced to drop as rounds smashed against the house's exterior. The open window exploded, shards raining over him. 'Jesus Christ!'

But he knew that the Glocks, even with their extended magazines, could only sustain full-auto fire for two seconds before exhausting their ammunition. And the opening was so narrow nobody would be able to fit through until the shooting stopped. He just had to wait . . .

The staccato stereo clatter abruptly became mono, then cut out. They were reloading—

A man rushed through the opening and sprinted along the pool towards the excavator. The Yorkshireman tracked him, only to see a second raider hare off at a different angle. He stayed with his first target – then realised the man was unarmed, the original owner of his gun. Shit! He'd been decoyed! He hurriedly locked on to the second runner, who *did* have a gun, only for another double blaze of fire to erupt from the tunnel.

More windows burst apart, wood and plaster shattering as rounds penetrated the outer wall. Eddie dropped again, but knew he was not safe. His opponents now knew exactly where he was and were concentrating their fire on his position, smashing apart his cover chunk by chunk – faster than he expected. 'Fucking cheapskates!' he gasped, the insult aimed at his hosts. 'They built this place out of cardboard and Weetabix!'

He scrabbled sideways – as a fist-sized hole blew open where his head had just been. He crawled to the next window and swung up to fire again.

The second man was still his target. He dived as Eddie's shots cracked tiles in his wake, rolling to flatten himself against the pool's end wall. The Yorkshireman risked one more shot before retreating again, but it impacted harmlessly on the coping's edge. The raider was now in full cover.

Eddie swore, but there was nothing he could do as another fusillade ripped into the house. He heard al-Asim shout something, then a third gun, and a fourth, joined the barking chorus. The rest of the raiders were spilling out of the tunnel.

Berk and Elmas clutched each other fearfully as they huddled with Lobato in the pantry adjoining the kitchen. But Nina's concern as she heard bullets thud into the house was for Eddie. 'Are they coming?' she demanded. Elmas had been calling the police when the assault started.

'Yes, yes,' the other woman replied. 'But it will be at least fifteen minutes before they can get to us!'

'Then let's hope Eddie can hold them off for that long!' But Nina knew that was unlikely – and the window of survival abruptly shrank further as she heard a new noise. An engine had just started up outside.

And it was not one of the cars.

Eddie heard it too. Why were the Dhajanis starting the digger? He checked the magazine. About half its rounds left. Each one would have to count.

Bent low, he scuttled to a broken side window and peeked over the sill. Below, the excavator's lights were on. The unarmed man was in its cab, working the controls to raise the front scoop. The Yorkshireman rose higher, aiming down at him – only for a man running through the pool to fire wildly at his position.

The shots landed close enough to make Eddie flinch back. He recovered and pulled the trigger, but the scoop was now high enough to act as a shield, the rounds ricocheting off the thick steel.

More shots stormed up at him – and this time it wasn't wild-fire. At least two gunmen had reached flanking positions, opening fire simultaneously. Bullets tore through the walls, the few remaining windows disintegrating. Eddie dropped to the floor, but the assault continued, swathes of lead hosing into the room.

The streams of fire dropped lower, exploding plaster and skirting and floor tiles. The raiders knew he had fallen flat and had him pinned, closing in—

He hurled himself into the hot tub just before the deadly barrage reached him.

The tub juddered and rang like a great flat bell as gunfire struck it, but while it cracked and splintered, it didn't shatter. It was ceramic rather than fibreglass, apparently the one part of the house where the Onans hadn't skimped on materials.

The gunfire stopped. Eddie shook off broken wood and tile, then raised his head. The room had been reduced to Swiss cheese, gaping holes in the curved outer wall and one of the supporting pillars between the windows blown almost completely apart . . .

A loud bang, but not from a gun. The surviving plasterwork sloughed away from the damaged pillar, the concrete beneath cracking—

The support collapsed, bringing most of the ceiling with it. Wood and concrete and slate cascaded into the room, flattening everything below.

'Hold fire!' al-Asim shouted, watching almost with glee as a section of the house imploded in a roiling dust cloud. Even if Chase had fled in time, he would be badly shaken by his narrow escape, and almost out of ammo.

And if he *hadn't* got out of the room, well . . .

'What now?' asked one of his men. 'Move into the house and find the others?'

Al-Asim's gaze moved to the idling excavator. 'No,' he decided. 'We drive them out to us!'

The ceiling's fall shook the entire building, loose items falling from the pantry shelves. 'What was that?' gasped Berk.

'My house!' Elmas wailed. 'They are smashing my house!'

'I don't care about your damn house,' said Nina. 'I care about my husband! *Eddie!*'

Ana heard Nina's cry from downstairs as she ran for the hot tub room. 'I'll find him!' she shouted.

She reached the door, but it didn't open. She barged it with her shoulder. It shifted slightly, enough for her to see that a fallen ceiling beam had blocked it. More debris was piled on the floor. 'Eddie! Can you hear me? Eddie!'

No answer. 'Oleg!' she shouted. 'I need help! Eddie's hurt!'

Maximov had gone to the upper floor's rear to act as lookout. His reply was muffled and distant. 'I come to you! Where is—'

The house shook again, more violently, as the excavator ploughed through the outer wall.

The jolt shook Eddie back to full awareness. He opened his eyes, but saw only darkness. What had happened? He had dropped flat in the hot tub as the ceiling came down . . .

He was still in it, broken wood and plaster around him. He tried to sit up, but something blocked him.

He groped a hand over it. A large panel, covered in cracked plaster – part of the ceiling. He pushed at it, but it barely moved.

The tub shuddered again, loud crashes reverberating from below. Jesus! The raiders had driven the digger into the house, and from the sound of it, they weren't stopping. He had to get out.

He used his phone's screen as a light, seeing the dust-covered Glock. If his count had been accurate, it had just enough bullets left to take out all the attackers . . .

If he ever got the chance to use it.

He shifted, trying to lift the panel on his back. It flexed, but didn't move. There was too much weight on top.

'Shit,' he growled. He was trapped!

Cracks lanced through the wall beside Ana as the excavator tore through the floor below her.

She jumped clear with a shriek as a section of the landing smashed down into the dining room. Water sprayed her from ruptured pipes. She gasped, turning to shield her eyes, and saw the whole passageway twisting, warping like a moment from a nightmare as structural supports were knocked out.

She couldn't help Eddie; she would be lucky to save herself. She ran for the stairs—

The floor fell away beneath her. She dived, landing hard in the stairwell. Wood creaked, splintered . . .

And snapped.

The whole staircase collapsed, pitching her into the void below.

Maximov hurried angrily through the upper floor. He had again taken a wrong turn, somehow going in a circle. Retracing his steps, he reached what he hoped was the right door and charged through it. 'Ana! I am—'

It was not the hallway he expected, but a room sparsely populated by fitness equipment. He stopped, looking with rising frustration for another exit but finding none. 'What is *wrong* with this fucking house?' he growled, turning back to the door—

A tremor almost pitched him to the floor. Plaster sheared from the ceiling as a fearsome crack of overstressed wood came from above. He looked up – then flung himself back in fright as a hefty wooden beam crashed down in front of the door.

A shelf broke loose, spilling its contents over the pantry's occupants. Lobato yelped as a jar struck him.

'We've got to get out of here,' Nina said. 'The whole damn house is about to fall down!'

'If we go out, they will kill us,' Berk protested.

'Two tons of roof'll kill you as dead as a bullet.' She peered into the kitchen. The excavator's rumble and crash was getting louder, but she couldn't see any of the raiders. She gripped the spearhead, readying herself for action. 'Nobody here. Okay, I'll—'

An earsplitting crunch of rending drywall and cinderblock – and the excavator's scoop burst through the kitchen wall like a steel fist. The rest of the machine followed a moment later, pulverising the countertop and crushing the oven beneath its tracks. Gas hissed from ruptured pipes.

'Holy *shit*!' Nina cried as the vehicle ground towards their hiding place. 'Get out, go! *Now!*'

She and Lobato rushed into the kitchen, Berk pulling the horrified Elmas with him. The earth-mover snarled almost triumphantly as its headlight beams found them. The driver yanked at the control levers, bringing it around to chase its prey as they ran through the nearest door.

Nina found herself in a room she hadn't seen before, containing a long table with ornate chairs around it. 'How many damn dining rooms do you need? Come on, quick!'

She ran for the exit, the others following—

The excavator ploughed through the wall behind them. Flying masonry hit Lobato's leg. He cried out and fell into the machine's path.

Elmas screamed – but her husband lunged back and dragged the billionaire clear just before the tracks crushed him. Lobato's fallen glasses were not so lucky. They disappeared under one of the steel belts with a faint tinkle of crushed glass.

Berk pulled the slender man upright, then grabbed his wife and ran with them after Nina. 'Thank you!' Lobato gasped.

Berk's expression was one of startled shock – not so much at Lobato's near-death as at the fact that he had put himself in danger to rescue him. 'No – no problem!' he stammered.

Nina reached the door, opening it to find the main hall beyond. She looked back as the excavator smashed the dining table to splinters. 'Split up!' she shouted. 'It's me they're after – and the spearhead!'

She waited for Lobato and the Onans to catch up, then rushed out into the hall. The twin staircases curved upwards, but even though she was desperate to find and help Eddie, ascending would limit her options for escape. Instead, she sprinted to a door at the hall's rear, while her hosts headed across it into the other wing of the house. Lobato hesitated, blinking at his blurred surroundings, then doubled back into the hallway leading to the pool.

A shout came from behind Nina as she reached the new exit. The excavator's driver was calling out to his comrades.

They were coming for her.

She flung the door open and ran through, just as a man rushed out of the dining room. He saw her and raised his gun—

Nina slammed the door and dived sidelong as bullets blew holes through the wood. One of the spearhead's pointed ends jabbed painfully into her chest, the other jarring against the floor. She gasped, but jumped back up, more worried about damage to the artefact than herself. If it broke and the antimatter was released . . .

It seemed intact. Relieved, she looked around. Elmas and Berk obviously fancied themselves as musicians; the room was dominated by a white grand piano, a cello on a stand nearby. Nina was only interested in the exit in the far wall, however. She ran for it.

The bullet-riddled door burst open behind her. The gunman rushed in and fired.

She shrieked and threw herself under the piano, skidding along the marble floor on her front with the spearhead in her outstretched hands. Rounds slammed into the instrument above her, playing a cacophonous tune as they shattered keys and severed strings.

The raider aimed lower, chipping the floor and shredding the piano's rear leg—

Nina kicked it as she scrambled past. The damaged support

gave way, the piano's end hitting the floor with a monstrous chord that almost deafened her. But the noise staggered the gunman too, the gunfire stopping just long enough for her to reach the exit. He fired again, a wild spray of shots picking out a new melody on the wrecked instrument before hitting the door, but she was already gone.

The man's magazine was empty. He angrily ejected it, slotting in a replacement as he pursued her.

34

L obato hobbled down the hallway towards the exit to the pool. It ran behind the kitchen, which the Emir's men had already searched – or rather, destroyed, but the result was the same – so in his mind they were unlikely to return. If they were all in the house, he might be able to escape downhill—

The excavator smashed through the wall behind him. He shrieked and started to run, only for his injured leg to buckle. He fell.

The menacing machine pivoted like a tank to face him. Diesel fumes spewed from its exhaust, filling the passage with a foul fog.

The billionaire struggled upright and desperately limped along the hall. The excavator snarled after him. The passage was just wide enough to accommodate it, though the tracks' edges carved into the walls whenever the driver failed to keep it in a straight line.

Lobato reached the kitchen door, only to reel back as the stench of gas hit him. He hurriedly continued along the hallway. To his alarm he saw as it came into focus that the far end was strewn with debris where a section of ceiling had collapsed. But he had no choice except to negotiate it – the stairs Eddie had gone up had been destroyed as well. He began to pick his way over the obstacle, glancing back—

Rubble shifted underfoot. He fell again.

The excavator rolled remorselessly towards him—

Ana leapt out from the stairwell and hurled a chunk of broken concrete at the cab.

The driver flinched as it crazed the windscreen, one hand jerking on the control lever. The excavator turned sharply, its right track tearing into the drywall before hitting something more solid behind it and slamming to a stop.

'Get out of here!' Ana shouted, pushing Lobato into the dining room. Parts of its ceiling had caved in, beams and wreckage from the devastated hot-tub room above strewn about.

The billionaire staggered away as she retreated. The earthmover lurched into motion again, reversing out of the wall before straightening. It smashed through the doors, charging like a bull.

Ana took on the role of matador, hurling bricks at the cab to keep the furious driver focused on her as she angled away from Lobato. The excavator followed her, grinding over wood and brick. She kept up her retreat – until she backed into a heavy joist that had punched almost vertically down through the ceiling.

Sensing victory, the driver brought the machine surging forward to crush her—

Ana dived aside. The scoop smashed into the beam, the excavator driving it backwards and ripping the hole in the ceiling even wider.

Realising that he had been tricked, the driver braked—

Too late.

The hot tub plunged down from the floor above, landing squarely on top of the machine and crushing its cab.

More debris fell with it, scattering across the dining room – and amongst the flying detritus came a bald-headed man in a leather jacket. 'Bugger-fucking-*ation*!' yelled Eddie as he bounced over the dining table, demolishing several chairs.

Lobato had reached a gunfire-shattered window to find relative safety outside. He squinted fearfully back into the dining room. 'Ana! Are you all right?'

The Brazilian shook off wood and cement. 'I'm okay,' she panted. 'I heard Eddie! Where—'

'Here,' Eddie groaned. He regarded the damaged digger and its hot-tub hat. 'I took out a bad guy while I was in the bath? That's a first.'

He went to the excavator. 'What are you doing?' Ana asked. 'The others will be coming!'

'I need to find my gun.' He climbed up to look inside the tub, but found it piled with chunks of the bathroom's marble floor. 'Arse!' He started to toss them aside, then heard a moan from the flattened cab. Looking in, he was surprised to see the driver had survived. The machine's roll cage was buckled, but had done its job: the man was slumped in the footwell with the mangled roof inches above his head. 'You are one lucky bastard,' Eddie told him – then he punched him in the face. 'Not *that* lucky, mind.'

'Someone is coming!' Lobato cried, looking outside.

'Ana, take him that way,' Eddie ordered, pointing down the hall. 'I'll be right behind you.' He groped in the tub again.

Dark grey metal was revealed beneath a jagged slice of marble. He tugged the gun out – and cursed. It was damaged, the slide bent where falling masonry had pounded it like a hammer. It almost certainly wouldn't cycle correctly; the single bullet in the chamber was all he could be sure of firing.

But even one bullet was better than none. He jumped down after Ana and Lobato. 'Where's Nina?' he shouted.

Nina ran through the lounge containing the Atlantean marker stone. The pursuing raider fired a couple of wild shots as she darted through a door into a short hallway. Stairs led upwards, but she went instead to an exterior door. If she could get clear of the house and stay ahead of al-Asim's men until help arrived . . .

She pulled the handle. It didn't move.

Locked!

'Shit!' She turned and raced up the stairs as her pursuer barged into the hallway.

She reached the top and sprinted desperately through the upper floor. 'Eddie!' she cried. 'Eddie, help!'

No reply from her husband – but there was one from someone else. 'Nina?' came Maximov's muffled shout.

'Oleg!' She ducked through a side door to keep the gunman from shooting her in the back, finding herself on the balcony overlooking the lounge. A section of plaster had broken away from the wall, cracks running from it. 'Someone's right behind me! Where are you?'

'Stuck in room! I hear you through wall, but—'

Whatever he said next, Nina didn't catch – she was too busy trying to catch *herself* as the balcony swayed under her weight. The excavator's rampage had weakened the cheaply constructed house well beyond the rooms it had destroyed. She grabbed the handrail, almost dropping the spearhead.

The man chasing her burst through the door, only to be caught by the unexpected lurch. But he quickly steadied himself, bringing up his gun—

He held fire as the door at the other end of the balcony was kicked open by a second armed Dhajani. If either shot at Nina, they could hit the other.

But that was little help to her. She was trapped between them, the only way out a fifteen-foot fall to hard marble.

'Nina!' Maximov shouted again, his voice coming from the other side of the cracked wall.

'Oleg, they've got me!' she wailed as both men advanced—

A growl became a roar, getting louder – and the huge Russian exploded through the wall.

The two gunmen froze in shock. 'Down!' yelled Maximov. Nina dropped as he whipped out both arms and spun, one of his hock-sized fists hitting the nearest Dhajani's head hard enough to send teeth flying from the balcony. Their owner followed them as the fearsome blow cartwheeled him over the railing.

Nina threw herself aside as the Russian whirled out of his spin to charge the second raider. The other man recovered from his shock, and pulled his Glock's trigger just as Maximov grabbed him.

Its muzzle was pressed against the big man's left arm. The bullet ripped through it, blood splattering the wall. Maximov howled. The raider pulled back to aim a lethal shot at his chest, thinking the pain had rendered his opponent helpless . . .

But it wasn't pain the former Spetznaz trooper was feeling. The startled Dhajani realised this as he saw the other man *grin*—

Maximov bent back, winding up – and delivered a brutal headbutt to the other man, the steel plate in his skull magnifying the attack to sledgehammer force. The blow was so hard that the already weakened floor gave way beneath the Dhajani's feet. He fell through the balcony, bouncing off the marble to end up beside his equally stunned companion.

Maximov turned to Nina, blood smeared across his forehead and an extremely unsettling smile on his face. 'You okay?' he asked.

'Uh, yeah,' she replied.

'We find Eddie, *da?*'

'*Da,*' she said, hopping over the hole in the floor to the door at the balcony's far end. 'Was he still in the—'

A sudden jolt threw her against the railing. She yelped, catching herself – as the middle of the balcony broke away and fell. Maximov went with it.

The Russian slammed into the rubble below with a snap of bone that made Nina cringe. She looked down. He was sprawled over the balcony's remains, one foot twisted at a sickening angle. 'Oh my God! Oleg!'

He squinted up at her. 'I am okay,' he said, voice slurred. 'I am . . . *very* okay.' He peered at his broken ankle and smiled in grotesque ecstasy. 'Very, very, *very* . . . okay . . .'

His eyes rolled back, then he slumped.

Nina was about to drop down to help him when one of the Dhajanis groped groggily for his gun. She hurriedly retreated through the door. There was nothing she could do for the Russian now – her first priority was keeping the spearhead from their attackers.

She rushed through the upper floor. She almost called out Eddie's name, but silenced herself. Al-Asim's men would close in if she gave her position away. Instead she ran on, hoping her husband was still in the turret – and still alive.

Eddie followed Ana and Lobato down the excavator-ravaged hallway. A noise caught his attention: someone was running along the floor above. He was about to call Nina's name when his nostrils warned him of something more urgent. 'Shit! There's a gas leak.'

'The kitchen,' said Lobato, indicating an open door ahead. 'The pipes were broken.'

'Like we don't have enough trouble already.' Eddie looked back towards the wrecked stairwell. 'Nina! Is that—'

'Look out!' cried Ana.

A raider appeared at the passage's far end. He raised his gun and fired—

Ana threw herself in front of Lobato. The bullet that would have hit him in the chest instead struck her shoulder.

Eddie whipped around to shoot back, but another armed man had already joined the first. He only had one bullet: whichever raider he shot, the other would kill him. Instead he tackled both Lobato and the wailing Ana through the kitchen door. Automatic fire tore down the hallway behind them.

The kitchen had been devastated by the earth-mover, debris turning the room into a treacherous obstacle course, but that was not Eddie's biggest concern. The room stank of escaping gas.

Metal pipes jutted from the wrecked wall, propane hissing from their torn ends.

Lobato gagged. 'We can't stay in here!' he said, coughing.

Eddie agreed, but for different reasons. The trail of destruction had opened up a direct path to the main hall, and the two gunmen were already following it towards them. Both hesitated at the stench of gas, then lifted their fingers off their triggers before running for their prey. 'In here, quick!'

He pushed Lobato and Ana past the shrilling pipes into the next wrecked room. The excavator had made its entrance here, the exterior wall caved in. 'Go that way!' he ordered, pointing at the opening as he dropped behind an overturned table. 'And keep your heads down!'

Despite her pain, Ana turned to look back at him as Lobato helped her through the hole. 'What are you going to— *No!*'

But Eddie had already taken aim. He pulled the trigger – and sent his last bullet at the ruptured pipes.

The red-hot metal whipped through the gushing gas, setting it alight – and the kitchen erupted in fire, the two gunmen screaming and hurling themselves backwards as a swelling wall of flame rushed at them.

The blast tore the leaking pipes apart, more gas bursting out and igniting. The shock wave was transmitted back through the metal in a chain reaction, shattering joints and cracking welds. The conflagration swept through the house's foundations to its source—

The Onans' isolated mansion was not connected to the country's gas network, instead using large cylinders of liquefied gas. They were kept in a metal shed tucked against the house's side – which blew apart as the valves ruptured, ripping the tanks open and detonating all the remaining propane in a huge blast. Every window on that side of the building shattered as a churning fireball erupted into the twilight sky.

The whole house shook. Lobato pulled the wounded Ana clear as dislodged tiles cascaded over the eaves. Eddie took several painful strikes as he raced after them. He swore, then looked back.

The kitchen was in flames, but the inferno had spread far beyond it, the explosion having practically split the building in two. Tongues of fire rose from the roof, smoke swirling from windows. He couldn't see the gunmen, but if they were still alive, they would be decidedly singed.

He hurried to Lobato. The billionaire had found cover behind a patio wall and was crouched over Ana, who lay on her side, face twisted in pain. 'What do I do?' he asked, sounding lost.

Eddie quickly examined Ana's wound. 'Got an entry and an exit – looks like the bullet deflected off a bone. Not much we can do right now except stop her bleeding out. Put your hands over the holes and keep pressure on them.'

Lobato stared at Ana's shoulder in horror. 'But – there is lots of blood!'

'Yeah, that usually happens when someone gets shot! Come on, do it.'

The skinny man raised his hands, but couldn't bring himself to touch the wound. 'Okay, Gideon, listen,' said Eddie, trying to contain his impatience. 'I've got to find Nina before these arseholes do – which means you're the only person who can help Ana. You can do it,' he added, seeing the other man's uncertainty. 'You're one of the richest men in the world, for fuck's sake. If you can build a business, you can do first aid. You want to save the planet? Start with saving one person.'

'I . . . can do it. I *can* do it.' Lobato steeled himself, overcoming his revulsion and hesitantly placing his palms on Ana's shoulder. She gasped, making him recoil.

'Stay there,' Eddie growled, pushing his hands back into place. 'Yeah, it'll hurt her, but it'll keep her alive. I'll be back.'

He checked his surroundings for enemies. Nobody in sight.

He vaulted over the wall. If the person he had heard upstairs was Nina, she would be at the pool end of the house. He ran towards it.

Nina had been stymied in her attempt to reach Eddie by the hole outside the hot-tub room. She stood at the edge of the gap, unsure what to do – until a massive explosion shook the house. She whirled—

And saw flames charging down the hallway.

With a wail of '*Shiiiiit!*' she spun back around and leapt desperately into the hole.

Nina hit a broken beam side-on, her thigh and hip taking the impact. She cartwheeled over its top, the debris-strewn floor spinning at her. She instinctively threw out both arms to protect her head . . .

Letting go of the spearhead.

She gasped as she realised her mistake. The spearhead tumbled past her and hit the rubble. The swirling flecks of light within it flared . . . then stabilised.

The relic bounded onwards, clattering to a stop just inside the wrecked dining room. Nina let out a long, relieved breath. The spearhead was tougher than it looked; if the blow had weakened it in any way, the antimatter would have been released and she, the house, the hill and everything else for miles around would have been annihilated.

Groaning at new bruises, she crawled to the glowing object—

Boots crunched down in front of her.

She looked up to see al-Asim. His gun was aimed at her head. 'Dr Wilde,' he said, mouth curling in triumph. 'You have caused us a great deal of trouble.'

35

'You'll get a lot more trouble if you take that thing,' Nina snapped. 'Unless I put it back in the vault, it'll explode – and you won't even know when!'

'But *you* know, don't you?' Al-Asim picked up the spearhead, then gestured for her to stand. She reluctantly obeyed. Behind him, she saw that the excavator had been partially crushed beneath, of all things, a hot tub. Its cab was empty, though; the driver must have survived. Flames from the fireball danced around the hole in the ceiling above it. 'You are an expert on Atlantis. It is how you found the vault, after all – and I think the inscriptions inside have told you all about it.'

'They didn't tell me anything,' she lied. 'We'd only just opened up the vault when you arrived. I didn't have time to translate anything.'

'We shall see. Move.'

She started for the French windows. 'Where are we going?'

'You are coming with us, to Dhajan.' He smiled, far from reassuringly. 'You are an expert on Atlantis. I am an expert on interroga—'

He was slammed to the floor as Eddie leapt through a broken window and tackled him.

The spearhead skittered across the room. 'Nina, get out of here!' the Yorkshireman shouted as he grappled with the Arab.

'I've got to get the spearhead!' she cried, starting towards it—

Al-Asim squirmed beneath his opponent to point the Glock at

374

her. He pulled the trigger – just as Eddie yanked his arm upwards. Nina jumped back in fright as bullets struck the ceiling. Burning wood fell from above. 'Get out!' her husband shouted again. This time she ran for the nearest window.

The two men struggled. Al-Asim was younger and taller, but Eddie had the edge in raw strength. He made the absolute most of his slight advantage, shoving his forearm against al-Asim's throat while trying to tear the gun from the agent's grip with his other hand.

The choking Dhajani clawed at Eddie's eyes. The Englishman twisted to block the other man's arm with his shoulder. Al-Asim's fingertips caught his chin – and Eddie snapped at them like an angry terrier, catching his little finger in his teeth and biting it, hard.

Bone crunched. Al-Asim screamed, wrenching his hand back. Eddie felt something tear as it jerked free. He spat. Blood and an entire fingernail hit the raider's eyes.

His adversary flinched. Eddie grabbed for the gun again, this time finding a hold on the grip—

Al-Asim kicked out, not at Eddie, but the surrounding debris. His foot hit a hefty section of broken beam. The sudden jolt as he found leverage unsteadied the Yorkshireman. His arm slipped from al-Asim's neck, and before he could pull it back, the other man struck at his face again, delivering a brutal punch that knocked Eddie sideways.

Al-Asim forced his adversary away – but in doing so, gave Eddie an opportunity of his own. He rolled, tearing the gun from the Dhajani's hand as he scrambled back against the earth-mover and whipped the Glock around—

Something hard and *sharp* smashed against his hand.

The impact knocked the gun away. Eddie cried out, blood running from a deep cut in the ball of his thumb—

The object rushed at him again, heading straight for his face.

He threw himself sideways. The weapon flashed above his cheek as he fell, metal blades glinting, then arced around to snap back at al-Asim. The Arab whipped up his wrist to intercept it. It was on a wire, reeling back into his watch—

It *was* his watch, Eddie saw as it clacked magnetically into place on its band, the razor-like blades retracting. Al-Asim jumped up, pulling the bizarre device free again and holding it by the wire as he whirled it like a bolas – or rather a perdida, the single-weighted variation of the throwing weapon. The blades popped back out with a *snick*.

Eddie's hand closed around wood: part of a broken chair. He snatched it up as the perdida swung at his head. It smacked against the chair leg, spitting splinters into his face, but the blades buried themselves in the wood. 'Gotcha!' he crowed, dropping his makeshift shield as he went for the gun.

Another *snick*, al-Asim touching a button on the watch band – and the blades retracted again, the perdida falling free. He jerked his arm back, the wire winding in with a faint whine like a fishing reel, only to shrill out again as he snapped the weapon back at his target.

It struck Eddie's head with a crack just as his hand found the Glock, the gun falling to the floor. The blow was like being struck by a cricket ball – the weapon was small but heavy. He fell against the excavator. Only al-Asim's lack of time to unfurl the blades had saved him from being stabbed in the skull.

Al-Asim recalled the perdida and spun it from his hand once more. He extended the blades, winding up to deliver a deadly strike—

A loud *bang* from above – and a burning beam smashed down between the two men.

Rubble followed it. The ceiling was about to collapse. Eddie retreated, expecting another attack. To his surprise, he saw that the Dhajani had withdrawn – but he had snatched up the spearhead as he went. Al-Asim shot Eddie a victorious look, then ran through the doors to the swimming pool, shouting commands into a walkie-talkie.

The blazing debris prevented Eddie from following directly, and more was coming down around him. The hot tub shattered as a falling marble slab struck it edge-on like an axe. He leapt aside as broken pieces crashed to the floor, then hurriedly scrambled over the rubble until he was clear of the flames. He vaulted through a broken window into the open.

'Eddie!' Nina cried, hurrying to him. 'They've got the spearhead!'

'I know!' he shouted. The helicopter had touched down on the drive, rotors whirling just below take-off speed as al-Asim climbed aboard with his prize. More Dhajani agents emerged from the burning house. 'Keep down!'

He and Nina both ducked, but the raiders were no longer concerned with them, instead piling into the chopper. Some of the men were injured, their comrades helping them, but all had survived the conflagration.

Whether the same was true of his friends, Eddie didn't know. He looked back at the house, spying Ana and Lobato behind the patio wall, but there was no sign of Maximov or the Onans. 'Where's Max – and those two yuppie arseholes?'

'Oleg saved me,' Nina told him, 'but his ankle's broken. He was in the big lounge with the Atlantean marker stone; I don't know where Berk and Elmas are.'

The helicopter's engines roared, the aircraft taking off and immediately wheeling towards Sanliurfa. In the distance beyond it, Eddie saw flashing lights. 'Cops are coming.'

'Great,' Nina replied, 'but we don't need the police – we need the fire department!' She reacted in alarm as she saw how far the fire had spread. 'Oh my God, Eddie! Oleg's still in there!' Flames were coming out of the ground-floor windows beyond the main entrance.

'No way a fire engine'll get here in time,' he said grimly. He started to run up the slope. 'We'll have to make our own.'

His wife followed him. 'What do you mean?'

'Here!' He reached the water bowser, a large tank on wheels that could be towed like a trailer. 'Help me move it!'

A length of lumber acted as a chock under the wheels. Eddie kicked it away. He banged a fist on the bottom of the tank, making a dull thud, then again higher up with the same result. 'It's got water inside. Just hope it's enough.' He went to the rear, where there was a large valve. 'I'll get this open, then we push!'

He hauled at the valve wheel. It creaked, reluctant to turn . . . then suddenly water sprayed out with enough force to make him stagger back, soaked. 'Okay, come on!'

Nina took up position on one side of the tank as he shoved at the other. The sheer weight of water had made the wheels settle into the ground. 'It's stuck!'

'Pull it back!' He hauled at the chassis, rocking the bowser, then pushed again. Nina added her own weight, and at last the wheels jolted free of the ruts.

The tanker rolled down the slope, slowly at first but with increasing speed. 'Uh, I don't think we'll be able to stop it,' Nina said.

'I don't *want* it to stop,' Eddie replied, still pushing. 'We need to get it into that lounge, and there's a wall in the way!'

'Yeah, but Oleg's on the other side!'

'He won't be any worse off unless this thing actually squishes him.' A section of roof collapsed, a volcanic gush of sizzling embers spewing from the hole. Eddie applied more force, adjusting the bowser's course. 'Come on! Keep pushing!'

Nina did so. The water tanker rolled across the driveway,

passing the bullet-riddled BMWs and careering towards the wall. The flames rose ever higher through the broken windows, the heat now reaching them. 'Eddie!'

He grimaced. 'Keep going, keep going – okay, *let go!*'

Nina scrambled back, Eddie giving the valve a final twist before stumbling to a halt. The bowser rumbled on, water spouting from its rear – and smashed through the wall.

Fire erupted through the hole, only for the blaze to shrink back from the tanker as gallons of water sluiced over it. Loud crashes came from inside the house as it ploughed on, demolishing furniture before burying itself in an interior wall. Arms raised to shield his face, Eddie ran inside.

His aim had been accurate; he saw Maximov lying in the wreckage, ankle snapped. The escaping water had driven the spreading fire away from him, but flames were swelling outside the arc of spray.

'Nina!' he yelled, running to the downed Russian. 'Help me!' His wet clothes would not protect him for long.

Nina came to the opening, regarding the flames fearfully, but took a deep breath and ran to her husband. Maximov was unconscious but alive; the two men he had sent over the balcony had decided survival was more important than revenge.

Eddie strained to lift the huge man. 'We'll have to drag him.'

'What about his foot?'

'Just hope it doesn't come off!'

Together they hauled at the Russian. Maximov weighed well in excess of two hundred and ninety pounds, and it was all dense muscle. For a moment it seemed his wounded foot was going to stay put as the rest of him moved, but then it came free from the rubble with a nauseating little crackle of bone. Nina almost retched.

They pulled him towards the opening. The bowser was running low, the spray's pressure dropping fast. Terrifying creaks and groans came from the burning ceiling. 'It's coming down!' she cried.

'Nearly there!' Eddie grunted as he brought the huge man through the broken wall.

A crack like a thunderbolt exploded above them – and the roof gave way, the central beam plunging down into the lounge. Joists and tiles fell with it, masonry exploding like grenades against the floor.

Nina and Eddie had just got Maximov outside, but the impact still knocked them both down. Eddie yelled as he took a painful blow to his legs, then felt burning. He kicked away a chunk of burning timber and hurriedly patted out the flames scorching his already dry jeans. 'Nina!'

His wife had been hit by a chunk of tile, her short hair glistening with blood from a nasty gash in her scalp. She put a hand to the wound. 'Aah! Jesus!'

'We're not safe,' he warned, struggling upright. More crashes came from the burning house as its internal walls gave way. 'Grab Max!' Maximov's clothes, and even his beard, were smouldering where flaming motes had landed on him. Eddie swatted them off, then with Nina's help hauled the big man clear of the building.

Nina put him down with relief. 'Holy crap,' she said, looking back. Fires now burned throughout the house's length, the remaining windows shattering in the heat. A flat *whumph* came from the garage as the leaking petrol tank ignited – followed by a blast that ripped the doors from their frames as both cars blew up. 'Oh my God! Elmas and Berk, what if they're still inside?'

'They're not,' Eddie said with exhausted relief. The Onans had staggered zombie-like over an earth bank, staring in horror at the remains of their home.

'Eddie!' Ana cried. They both turned to see Lobato supporting her as they limped closer.

'I told you to stay with her!' the Englishman shouted at the billionaire. 'She's got a fucking bullet wound, why did—'

'I told him to,' Ana gasped. 'I had to . . . see you were . . . all right.' She saw Maximov. 'Oh! Is he . . .'

'He's alive,' Nina told her. 'His leg's broken, but I think he'll be okay.' She glanced back at the Russian. 'Although *that's* not disturbing or anything.' Even unconscious, his face bore a demented smile. 'He must really have gotten hurt.'

Lobato squinted at him. 'But he is smiling.'

'Long story,' said Eddie brusquely, pushing him aside to check Ana's wound. 'Here, sit down.'

He helped her to the ground, leaving Lobato to stand in awkward bewilderment. Nina noticed that he kept glancing at his bloodied hands as if desperate to remove and discard them. She went to him. 'Are you okay?'

'I . . . No,' he mumbled, before giving her a curious look. 'After everything that has happened, you are still concerned for me? Or are you merely being polite?'

'I'm being a human,' she replied. 'You know, caring about other people? You should give it a try.'

He clenched his lips. 'I suppose I deserved that.'

Elmas and Berk arrived. 'Our house!' the Turkish woman cried, tears rolling down her face. 'What have you done to our house?'

'I am . . . very sorry,' Lobato told them, taking Nina's point to heart. 'But I will see to it personally that everything is rebuilt exactly as it was.'

The Onans stared at him for a moment . . . then Elmas rushed to embrace him, while Berk grabbed his hand and shook it with tearful enthusiasm. '*Sen bizim kahramanimiz!* Oh, thank you, thank you!' Lobato bit his lip, clearly uncomfortable with the unwanted physical contact but forcing himself to endure it.

'It won't be *exactly* as it was,' Nina pointed out. 'For a start, there's a major archaeological site right there.' She indicated the swimming pool. 'And you won't get to keep your centrepiece, either.' She looked back at the remains of the lounge. The Atlantean marker stone set into the chimney breast was, ironically, the only thing that had survived intact.

'The spearhead!' Lobato said, finally squirming loose from the Onans. 'The Emir's men have it!'

'We know where they're taking it,' Nina told him. 'Your facility in Dhajan.'

'They won't keep it there long,' said Eddie. 'Not if they can't stop it from blowing up.'

Lobato faced Nina. 'Will they be able to stabilise it there?'

'You're asking *me*?' she protested. 'I don't know! The inscriptions said it would explode in less than a day unless it was returned, which suggests there's an earth-energy confluence point here. The vault must channel it somehow and keep the spearhead stable. Unless there's another confluence point at your solar power station, which would be a pretty damn big coincidence, they won't be able to stop whatever contains the antimatter from decaying.'

'So it *will* explode,' said Lobato. 'Then either they will damage their own country . . .'

'Or they've got somewhere else in mind to let it go off,' said Eddie. He finished his examination of Ana's wound. 'I can't do anything else with it here. You'll live, but you need to get to a hospital.'

Although she was breathing heavily, Ana managed a feeble smile. 'I hope . . . I have paid my debt for . . . what I did to you both.'

'I'll be the judge of that,' Eddie said, feigning coldness before cracking a grin to tell her he was joking. 'We need to get Max to hospital as well. I doubt he'll be running any marathons for a while.'

'He'll be lucky to *walk* for a while,' said Nina, regarding Maximov's broken ankle with a shudder. 'Okay, so: al-Asim is taking the spearhead to Dhajan. What can we do about it?'

'Can the UN get involved?' asked Eddie.

She shook her head. 'Dhajan's a sovereign country. Normally you'd get the diplomats to talk to its ruler . . . but in this case, the ruler's behind the whole thing! And if any of the other countries they'll pass over en route to Dhajan stop their plane, the spearhead will explode while it's on the ground. Unless it's brought back here – which opens up a whole new can of worms, because I *definitely* don't want to give the Turkish government a free antimatter bomb.'

'Then we have to get to my facility in Dhajan,' Lobato said. 'We know the spearhead will be there, at least for a time. And it is the only other place where it may be possible to stabilise it.'

'Maybe,' said Nina, 'but there's a slight problem. We can't just hop in your private jet and fly to Dhajan! The Emir's people would arrest us the second we landed.'

'There might be another way in, though,' Eddie said thoughtfully. He looked towards Sanliurfa. The police cars were now only minutes away. 'Soon as we get the chance, I'll make a phone call . . .'

36

Saudi Arabia

'There he is,' said Eddie, looking out from Lobato's taxiing jet to see a middle-aged Arab man waiting beside a Toyota Land Cruiser.

Nina didn't recognise him. 'Who is he?'

'Abdul Rahji. Saudi secret service; met him in Mecca.'

Lobato, wearing new glasses, blinked curiously at him. 'You are not a Muslim. Why did the Saudis let you into Mecca?'

'When you're the only person who can find a doomsday cultist before he gases fifty thousand people, they bend the rules.' The plane stopped beside the SUV. Lobato's cabin crew opened the door, then the three passengers stepped out.

Rahji came to meet them. 'Mr Chase! Welcome back to Saudi Arabia.'

Eddie shook his hand. 'How are you? Last time I saw you, you'd taken a bullet.'

'I am fine. I have a scar my grandchildren find fascinating, and sometimes it aches when it is cold. Fortunately, I live in Saudi Arabia. Cold is not often a problem. Except,' he added pointedly, 'when someone calls me to the desert early in the morning!' The jet had landed at al-Ahsa airport in the country's north-east, from where a broad, nearly featureless sandy plain stretched to the Persian Gulf.

'Sorry. I wouldn't have done it if this wasn't urgent, though.

384

And you're the best person I know in Saudi to help out.'

'You saved Mecca. In a just world, every Saudi – every Muslim – would consider you a hero and give you whatever help you need.' A small shrug. 'But this world has never been just, so . . .'

'I'll settle for whatever you can manage, thanks.' Eddie made introductions. 'My wife, Nina Wilde, and Gideon Lobato. This is Abdul Rahji.'

'Mr Lobato, welcome,' Rahji said, shaking the billionaire's hand. 'I have heard of you, of course. Your solar energy project means you are not the most popular person amongst my country's rulers,' he added with a sly smile, 'but I am still honoured to meet you.' He turned to Nina, placing his hand on his heart and giving her a small bow. 'And Dr Wilde. I have also heard of you! Like your husband, you have saved the world.'

'Well, I hope we can do it again,' she said.

'The situation is that serious?'

'Let's just say that if we don't get into Dhajan soon, without them knowing, today'll be memorable in a really bad way,' said Eddie.

'Is my country in danger?'

'Probably not directly,' said Nina. 'But there could be collateral damage – and worst-case scenario? A lot of people die, and the whole Gulf gets thrown into chaos.'

Rahji's eyes narrowed. 'But you will not tell me why?'

'It's nothing personal,' Eddie told him. 'But there's nothing anyone in Saudi can do to stop it. Nina and Gideon might be able to, though.'

'*Might* be able to? That is not the same as *will* be able to.'

'It's the best we've got,' said the Yorkshireman apologetically. 'So can you help us?'

'I will,' Rahji replied, though he was less than approving. 'Come with me – I will drive you across the border. Dr Wilde, I am afraid you will have to cover your hair. The rules for foreign women are more relaxed than for Saudis, but if the situation is as critical as you say, we do not want to draw attention.'

Nina was about to object, but saw his point. If the notorious Saudi religious police stopped them, the security agent should be able to pull rank, but they would lose valuable time. 'Okay,' she huffed. 'It's not as if I've got much hair left anyway, but I'll cover it up.'

'Thank you.' The Saudi opened the rear door. Nina got in, followed by Eddie, while Lobato took the front passenger seat. She found a dark blue scarf waiting for her. Giving Eddie an eye roll, she donned it as Rahji set off into the climbing sun.

The road to Dhajan was also the road to Qatar, the tiny emirate tucked between its two larger neighbours at the southern end of the Gulf of Salwah. The highway Rahji followed took his passengers through mile upon mile of emptiness, the great barren plain home to nothing but rock and sand.

By the time they approached the border, the temperature outside was already over twenty-five degrees Celsius, the number on the dash rising almost by the minute. Rahji put on sunglasses. 'You picked a good place to build a solar plant,' Eddie said to Lobato. 'No shortage of sun.'

'There are regions of the Sahara that would have been superior in terms of sunlight hours,' Lobato replied. 'But the logistical difficulties of construction in remote desert would have made it uneconomic. And there were also political considerations; the nations of north Africa are not stable.'

'I'm sure the Emir of Dhajan putting up most of the money didn't hurt,' said Nina. 'And he let you play with . . . other toys.' She caught herself before mentioning antimatter, not wanting to let Rahji know what they were facing.

Lobato not only failed to catch her hidden meaning, but took her words literally. 'My electric cars are not "toys", Dr Wilde,' he sniffed. 'They are the future; the only one possible if we are to avoid environmental apocalypse.'

'So long as we don't get any other kind first,' Eddie rumbled.

'Cars that do not use oil,' said Rahji, shaking his head in amusement. 'That is why you are not popular with my country's rulers. You will put them out of business!'

'There are many other uses for oil,' Lobato replied. 'The need for plastics will only become greater over time. But I have also invested heavily in companies working to make them fully biodegradable—'

'We are almost at the border,' the Saudi cut in as they crested a low rise. There was not much to see ahead; the highway continued in a great sweep along the coastline towards the unimaginatively named Dhajan City several miles distant. A small cluster of low buildings, a customs post, marked the boundary itself.

'I thought it was an open border,' said Nina, eyeing the waiting vehicles.

'For Saudis and Dhajanis, yes, but passports are still checked – which is why your husband called me,' Rahji added. 'I can get you across without any official record, so the Dhajani authorities will not know you are in the country. Once we are clear of the border, I will leave you. If that is what you wish.' He looked back at Eddie. 'Are you *sure* you do not want to tell me more? The Saudi government may be able to intervene.'

'Intervening might make things worse,' said Nina. 'If we can neutralise the threat, we will. If we can't . . . we'll do all we can to minimise it.'

The Saudi gave his passengers a harder look. 'If something happens that affects my country, and it could have been stopped had you warned us, you will be to blame.'

'We'll do everything possible to make sure that doesn't happen,' Nina assured him. 'You said when we first met that I'd saved the world; I hope you can trust me enough to do it again.'

Rahji did not seem convinced, but the Toyota reached the checkpoint before he could reply. Rather than joining the queue, he pulled over to one side. That immediately caught the border guards' attention, two men starting towards them. 'I will take care of this,' he said, getting out.

He met the guards, presenting his identification. A rapid exchange, then all three went into a building. '*Should* we tell him?' said Nina. 'If the spearhead blows up, the blast could hit Saudi Arabia as well.'

'There's nowt they can do to stop it,' Eddie pointed out. 'Besides, Saudi "intervention" usually involves bombing the shit out of everything, like in Yemen. And even if we stop the thing from blowing up, I don't want the Saudis to get hold of the spearhead. We stopped them from buying nukes from North Korea a few years back, so I *definitely* don't want them adding an antimatter bomb to their arsenal.'

'Yeah,' she agreed unhappily. 'It's kind of a bad situation all round, isn't it? Unless we come up with a way of permanently stabilising the spearhead and making it useless as a weapon, *or* it blows up somewhere it can't hurt anyone.'

'The solar facility may be the best option in the latter case,' said Lobato.

'How far is it from Dhajan City?' Eddie asked.

'Twenty-three kilometres.'

'Is that out of the blast range?'

'I do not know,' the billionaire admitted. 'We do not know how much antimatter the spearhead contains. One-point-two kilograms of antimatter would exceed the destructive force of the most powerful nuclear device ever detonated.'

'Be good if it was only one-point-two *milligrams*, but I'm not counting on it,' Eddie said. He saw movement outside. 'Ay up. Rahji's coming back.'

The Saudi was returning to the SUV. As well as the two border guards, a uniformed officer had also exited the hut and was walking to another building beyond the barriers. Rahji climbed back in. 'Everything is taken care of,' he announced. 'We have certain arrangements with the Dhajani border guards. We will be allowed through without showing our passports.'

A short wait, then the officer reappeared and waved to Rahji. 'Okay,' he said, starting the car, 'we can go.'

Nina nervously regarded the men on the other side of the checkpoint. 'They're definitely not going to stop us?'

'No. Just look straight ahead, and there will be no problem.'

She took his advice, but could not help giving the Dhajanis a worried sidelong glance as the Land Cruiser crawled through the checkpoint. If the Emir and his agents even *suspected* they might try to enter the country, the border guards would surely have been given their photographs and descriptions.

A long, tense moment . . . then the vehicle cleared the check-point. Eddie looked back. The guards hadn't moved. 'Think we made it.'

'I told you there would be no problem,' said the Saudi, accelerating down the highway. 'Now, I will wait for you so I can take you back across the border, but you will be on your own in Dhajan.'

They crested a rise. Dhajan City shimmered in the heat haze ahead. The vast white slabs of what Nina realised were the *Atlantia* and its sister ship the *Pacifia* stood out clearly in the harbour, but she was more interested in the landscape outside the capital. 'The solar plant's in those mountains?' she asked Lobato.

'Yes,' he replied. 'We will turn off this road to reach it soon.'

'They are hardly mountains,' Rahji chuckled. 'We have taller *dunes* in Saudi!'

'There is no internationally agreed definition of what constitutes a mountain,' said Lobato. 'The Dhajanis named them as such, so . . .' He registered that his companions were giving him mocking looks. 'But that is not important, apparently.'

'You're getting the hang of this whole not-acting-like-a-robot thing,' Nina said, amused.

After another mile, Rahji pulled off on to a side road. Another SUV waited beyond the intersection. 'This is where I leave you,' he said, stopping beside the other vehicle. 'Eddie, there are guns in the trunk compartment if you need them.'

'I hope we don't,' said Nina.

'So do I. But it is good to be prepared, don't you think?'

Eddie nodded. 'It is. Thanks.'

'Good luck. *Allah yusallmak!*' He got out. Eddie took his place in the driver's seat as the Saudi climbed into the other SUV.

'All right,' said the Yorkshireman, 'let's go. This way, right?' The line of black tarmac stretched through the desert towards the rising rocky hills.

Lobato nodded. 'It is impossible to get lost; it is the only road.'

'I like it when I don't have to worry about directions.' They set off down the new road, leaving Rahji's vehicle behind.

The route was totally straight for the first few miles, but began to curve as it rose into the foothills. Nina looked ahead. As Rahji had noted, the mountains were hardly on the same scale as the Himalayas, but the bare, sun-scoured rock meant they deserved the name for their appearance, if not their altitude.

There was something up there other than barren stone, though. As Eddie brought the SUV around another ascending bend, Nina caught a flash of reflected sunlight from between the peaks. 'Is that the solar plant?' she asked Lobato.

'Yes,' he replied. 'One of the solar furnaces. The facility has three, as well as a large photovoltaic—'

'Your solar energy plant,' Nina interrupted as a thought came to her. 'Your antimatter facility's at the same site – why did you pick that location?'

'It was the only suitable location in Dhajan. It is a small country, and the Emir was not willing to sacrifice any land with farming potential, which ruled out the coastal areas. The solar array also required an area of relatively flat, unshadowed land. The only place meeting all the requirements was in the south-eastern mountains.'

'So you chose the location out of necessity, right? And I'm guessing you put your antimatter lab there because the solar plant gave you effectively unlimited power.'

'Only in the daytime, though,' Eddie joked.

Lobato shook his head. 'At all times. That is the purpose of the power storage units – the world's largest lithium-ion battery banks. They can store almost five hundred megawatts, enough to power the whole of Dhajan through the night.'

'I don't care about some oversized laptop battery,' Nina said impatiently. 'The point is, without the vault *and* a source of earth energy, I don't see how you could stabilise the spearhead, no matter what gadgets you've built there.'

'The theories behind the containment systems are all scientifically sound,' the billionaire insisted.

'Did any of them take earth energy into account?'

That question brought an uncharacteristic uncertainty to his face. 'They . . . did not. But I am sure—'

'Levitating crystals? Weird purple stones that only people with Atlantean DNA can affect?'

'Again, no. I am beginning to see what you mean.'

'Good. Because I just realised something. I said in Turkey that it would be a damn big coincidence if there was an earth energy confluence point at your solar plant. But it's *also* a damn big coincidence that there must be confluence points where the Atlanteans hid their vaults in Turkey, Krakatoa and Santorini. They put them in the same relative positions to their targets, so either they were spectacularly lucky that they happened to be places where they could channel earth energy to stabilise the spearhead, or . . .'

'Or?' Eddie prompted after a moment.

'Or,' Nina continued, still deep in thought, 'they had some way to use it even without being at a confluence. Those other crystals in the vault's walls – I've never seen anything like that before at any Atlantean site. They're something new.'

'Crystals? Sounds a bit hippy-dippy to me.'

'Er, you did *see* the big-ass floating one full of sparkling antimatter, right? And the Midas Crucibles before that. And when we were underground in northern Canada, the cave with the pool of eitr was also full of crystals. There's obviously a lot more to them than cleansing your chakras. It seems the Atlanteans knew that – and took advantage of it.'

Lobato was also sceptical. 'I cannot deny the spearhead has characteristics yet to be explained,' he said. 'But attributing an entire alternate path of science and technology to the Atlanteans? That pushes the bounds of plausibility.'

'Most people thought that about my theory on the spearheads,' Nina retorted sharply. 'But you believed it enough to get us all into this mess.' She took out her phone and flicked through pictures she had taken of the inscriptions inside the vault before leaving Turkey. 'The Atlantean texts said something about "those who came before" – as if the Atlanteans used earlier knowledge to create the spearheads and the vault. That's something else I've never seen before, a reference to a civilisation preceding them. One they held in great reverence, which is unusual. The rulers of Atlantis believed they were the world's apex culture – they didn't like to admit anyone else might have done something first, or better.'

'So they were like Americans,' Eddie said with a grin.

'Ha ha. But the only earlier civilisation more advanced than Atlantis was the Veteres, and they were wiped out over a hundred thousand years before. I can't see how they would be the same people.'

'The Veteres?' said Lobato. 'I have never heard of them.'

'You wouldn't have,' Eddie told him. 'Some very powerful people went to a lot of trouble to make sure every trace of 'em was wiped out.' He glanced back at Nina. 'I still reckon they were aliens.'

'They *weren't* aliens,' Nina said, sighing. 'And keep your eyes on the road!'

They were now high enough for deep canyons to have opened up, the route winding along the edge of one. Eddie brought the car around a tight bend. 'All under control, love.'

'When the laws are changed to allow my cars to operate in fully autonomous mode, you will not need to worry even on roads like this,' said Lobato. 'They can drive better than any human.'

'Plenty of people'll argue with you about that,' replied Eddie. 'Like every single Italian.'

'The proof will speak for itself.'

'I'm not planning on getting into some robot car,' said Nina. 'Right now, I'm more worried about your antimatter lab. We're assuming al-Asim took the spearhead there like he said, but we don't *know* if he did. Or even if he was telling the truth.'

'He intended to kill us,' Lobato observed. 'He had no reason to lie.'

Nina smiled. 'Let's hope the Blofeld fallacy holds true, then.'

He seemed puzzled. 'I am not familiar with that.'

She put on a deep, oddly accented voice. 'Since I'm going to *keel* you anyway, I may as well tell you all the details of my *eeevil* plan. Muwah-hah-hah!'

Eddie gave her a look. 'Was that meant to be Blofeld? Sounded more like Skeletor.'

'Well, I can't do accents,' she huffed. 'And nor can you, before you say anything!' He laughed and drove on.

The road twisted through the mountains for a few miles before finally straightening out and dropping into a vast, bowl-like plateau. 'Bloody hell!' complained Eddie, squinting as light flooded into the cabin – from below rather than the sky. 'You could've warned me I'd need shades.'

'Still, look on the bright side . . .' said Nina.

'Oi! I'll do the crap jokes, thanks.'

Lobato had also narrowed his eyes, but his expression was still proud. 'Welcome to my solar power facility.'

The landscape before them had been transformed from empty rocky desert to a high-tech wonderland. At its centre were three tall, widely spaced towers surrounded by sweeping arcs of large mirrors, all angled to direct reflected sunlight at the white pillars topping each structure; the spill from those in line with the sun was what was dazzling the onlookers. Around them in turn were endless banks of solar panels.

'The towers,' Lobato continued, 'house concentrated solar thermal generators. Sunlight from the ten thousand four hundred and sixty-two heliostats—'

'The whats?' Eddie asked.

'—the *mirrors* is focused on them, heating a steam turbine to produce electricity. The system uses molten salt as a storage medium rather than water, so it can retain heat and produce power even after the sun has set. Look,' he added, 'you can see the heliostats moving. They reorient themselves for maximum efficiency as the sun changes position.'

The mirrors were indeed shifting, a subtle Mexican wave passing through them as the heliostats panned and tilted to refocus the beam. 'So they can generate electricity all day?' Nina asked.

'Precisely. And unlike some similar plants, it does not need to burn fossil fuels to preheat the generators before sunrise. The stored energy in the battery banks does that.' He indicated the huge fields of solar panels beyond the mirrors. 'There are also over five million photovoltaic solar arrays. Between them, the plant can generate an average of two thousand and fifty-six megawatts of power. That is more than the solar energy output of the entire United States, from a single facility.'

'I think we need to get our butts in gear and fix that,' said Nina.

'I have tried,' Lobato told her, with a faint sigh. 'Unfortunately, the fossil fuel industry is entrenched in Washington, and opposes anything that threatens its profits. But this facility will show that it will inevitably become as extinct as the dinosaurs from which its fuels are derived.'

'Good intentions. You might need to make your slogan snappier, though.'

'I leave the humour to my advertising agency,' he said. Nina wasn't sure if that in itself was a joke. 'The white blocks,' he indicated long, squat structures dispersed around the facility, 'are the power storage units.'

'The batteries?'

'Yes. As you rather disparagingly said, they indeed use the same technology as laptop batteries. They are on a much larger scale, however.'

'I'd noticed. This whole place must be over two miles across.' She diverted her squinting gaze to the facility's perimeter, seeing what at first glance she thought was an access road running around it, before noticing its seemingly gratuitous twists and turns. Several hangars sat beside it to the south. 'You've got a racetrack here as well?'

'A test track for my electric cars,' Lobato told her. 'They have an unlimited supply of power, and its isolation deters most corporate spies. The Emir also enjoys driving fast cars, and this allows him to do so away from public roads . . .' He trailed off at the reminder of his partner's betrayal.

'What's the security like?' Eddie asked.

'There is a small contingent of guards, but the majority of the security is electronic. Dhajan has a very low crime rate.'

'Except at the very top, I guess,' snarled Nina.

'Most of the security measures exist to keep people out for their own safety. The beams from the heliostats produce a temperature of well over one thousand degrees Celsius. Anyone entering the beam would be instantly incinerated.'

Eddie pretended to write a note. 'Adding that to my list of safety tips, thanks.'

'What about the antimatter facility?' Nina asked.

Lobato pointed. North of the three solar generators was a cluster of buildings, an observation tower standing above the largest. 'It is adjacent to the plant's operations centre.'

'So . . . we're just going to drive in there?'

'Yes.'

She raised an eyebrow. 'Okay, you can stop with the attempts at humour now.'

'I am being serious,' he said. 'It is extremely unlikely that the Emir knows we are in the country. Therefore he will have had no need to revoke my access.'

'You hope,' scoffed Eddie. 'And what about us?'

'This is my facility as much as the Emir's. If I tell the gate guard you are my VIP guests, he will accept that. As long as you do not appear to be making me act under duress.'

'I'll put on my nicest smile, then.' The Yorkshireman drew his lips back wolfishly.

'Please don't,' said Nina. 'You'll get us both shot.'

'Tchah!'

They descended into the shallow bowl. A striped barrier blocked the entrance in the outer fence, a white building with mirrored windows beside it. As the SUV approached, two men emerged.

'They've got guns,' Eddie noted as he slowed.

Lobato was unconcerned. 'I will speak to them.' He lowered his window.

The Toyota stopped between the two Dhajanis. Even behind sunglasses, the guard on Eddie's side was clearly suspicious, but his partner snapped to attention on seeing the man in the passenger seat. 'Mr Lobato, sir! Good morning. We were not expecting you.'

'I am here to show my guests the Raiju,' Lobato replied.

The guard nodded. 'Yes, sir. May I take their names?'

Lobato froze, apparently not having expected the question, but Eddie leaned across the console to speak for him. 'I'm Tarquin Bostick, and this is Mabel Otterthorpe. Amazing place you've got here. Must get warm in that hut, though.'

'It does, sir,' said the guard, tapping the pseudonyms into a tablet computer. 'But we have air conditioning.'

'Good to know that Mr Lobato cares about his people.' Eddie smiled and sat back. He rested his foot on the accelerator, then subtly moved his hand to the drive selector, ready to go forward – or back – at high speed.

But the guard merely checked the tablet's screen before giving the visitors a respectful bow of the head. 'Enjoy your visit, Mr Bostick, Mrs Otterthorpe.'

'I'm sure we will,' said Nina.

The man returned to the hut. After a few seconds, the barrier rose. Eddie drove through, keeping his eyes on the second guard in the mirror. No sign of alarm, or hostility. The car had barely gone a hundred feet before the Dhajani strode back to the welcoming air-conditioned cool of the gatehouse. 'Looks like we're clear.'

'As I predicted,' said Lobato, a little smugly.

'All right, smart-arse. But we've still got to get the spearhead, if it's even here. What about security at the antimatter facility?'

'There may be more guards,' the thin man admitted. 'But we have the advantage of surprise.'

'We'll see,' Eddie said dubiously.

They drove down the access road, passing beneath the test track at an intersection before entering the field of solar panels. The photovoltaic arrays, each bank the size of an articulated lorry, were fixed in position, the majority facing due south to capture the most sunlight, with the remainder angled to catch the rising and setting sun. Once they reached the heliostats, though, it felt more like entering a forest. The mirrors were mounted on hefty steel masts, a universal joint allowing them to rotate and tilt to track the sun. This close, dust in the air caught the beams reflecting up at the towers, turning the deep blue sky a sickly yellow.

Lobato directed them left at a junction. 'There is the operations centre.'

Eddie saw the buildings through the steel thickets. A few cars were parked beneath sunshades. 'Doesn't look too busy.'

'The plant is mostly automated. Apart from the guards, there are probably no more than ten people here.'

'How many in the antimatter facility?' asked Nina.

'Four technicians at most. There may also be some security personnel.'

'Hopefully not too many.' Eddie brought the car to the complex and parked under a shade. The antimatter facility was a smaller block behind the main centre. He noticed a large helipad nearby, but it was empty. 'Okay, the quicker we do this, the better. I'll get the guns.' He looked at the billionaire. 'Do you know how to use one?'

'In theory,' Lobato replied.

Nina eyed him. 'And in practice?'

'You ever actually *held* one?' Eddie demanded.

'No . . . but the operating principles are very simple. I am sure that—'

'So just you and me, love.' He got out and went to the tailgate.

She followed, frowning as the heat hit her. 'Nothing I love more than waving guns around.'

'Better than walking in there and waving bananas around.' He opened a floor compartment, finding the promised weapons: a pair of compact Beretta Nano handguns. 'Ha! Rahji didn't think Lobato could handle a gun either. Here.' He checked both were loaded, then handed one to Nina. 'Keep it out of sight until we're inside.'

She tucked the automatic as best she could into a pocket, hiding the protruding grip with her right hand. Eddie shoved his own weapon inside his leather jacket. 'It's a hundred degrees out here,' Nina said as they started towards the building, Lobato joining them. 'Don't you *ever* get hot in those damn jackets of yours?'

'Nope,' he replied.

'Why not?'

'Because they make me cool.' She groaned.

Lobato gave him a puzzled look. 'But you are sweating. You cannot be . . . Oh, I see. "Cool" in the sense of—'

'Of something you'll never know,' Eddie interrupted. They reached the entrance. 'Okay. Play everything cool – in a non-temperature sense – until we find the spearhead. Then we grab it and get the fuck out of here. You go first and do the talking,' he told the other man.

Lobato took the lead. The reception area felt almost arctic compared to the desert heat. A guard sat behind a desk, reading his phone; he stood in surprise on seeing the man in white. 'Mr Lobato! I did not know you were coming. I will—'

'That is all right,' Lobato replied. 'Is Dr Oto here?'

'Yes, sir.' The man nodded towards a metal door. 'In the test chamber.'

'Thank you.' Lobato led Eddie and Nina to it, placing his

hand on a palm-print reader. It lit up to scan his hand, then flashed green. The door slid open. 'Follow me,' he told them.

They went through, leaving the guard behind. Beyond was an airlock chamber. Lobato scanned his hand again to enter the large room beyond.

The gleaming machinery within was oddly familiar. 'It's a particle accelerator,' Nina whispered, taking in the wiring-entwined metal cylinder occupying most of the room. The ceiling above it was almost lost to sight behind a mass of stainless-steel pipes: a coolant system. 'Like the ones we saw in Greece and North Korea.'

'It is not an accelerator,' Lobato corrected. 'It is a storage system for antiparticles – a Penning trap. They are confined in a vacuum by magnetic fields so they do not collide with matter.'

He brought them to the machine's far end. Three men in lab coats were there, as surprised to see him as the guard outside had been. 'Mr Lobato?' said a balding Asian. 'My apologies, we were not expecting you.'

'That is all right, Dr Oto,' the billionaire replied. 'I wanted to see the spearhead as soon as possible, so I flew in this morning.'

The explanation seemed to satisfy them. 'Of course,' said Oto. 'It arrived in the middle of the night. We immediately placed it in the vacuum chamber. But I regret to say we have not yet managed to extract any antiparticles. It is . . . something we do not understand.' He sounded embarrassed by the admission.

Lobato peered through a small window in a thick metal sphere attached to the Penning trap. Light shimmered within: the spearhead.

Nina looked around him. 'It's changed,' she said, trying to contain her alarm. 'The light's different.' There was now a blue tint to the glow, and the flickering inside the crystal was more intense, almost violent, as if the infinitesimal points of light were battering against an invisible barrier. 'It's reached stage two.'

Oto regarded her uncertainly. 'Stage two?' he said. 'Are you familiar with its nature?'

'Yeah. It goes boom,' said Eddie.

One of the other scientists looked between Lobato's companions and his boss. 'Sir, may I ask,' he began, his accent Russian, 'who these people are? I know they are your guests, but you have many times told us of the need for secrecy.'

'They are indeed my guests,' Lobato said firmly. 'That is all you need to know.'

'Of course.' The Russian backed down, but his gaze kept going to Nina's right hand.

Eddie had a good idea what had drawn his attention; she had unconsciously closed her hand around the gun's grip in a way that was hard to mistake. 'Let's have a look at it,' he said, moving between Nina and the technicians. 'A proper look.'

Lobato stepped back to address his staff. 'Repressurise the chamber and open it, please.'

He may have been their employer, but the command still sent concerned looks between the three men. 'With all respect, Mr Lobato,' said Oto, 'are you sure? Our orders were—'

'I am giving you new orders,' he replied. 'Open the chamber.'

More hesitation. Eddie sighed – then drew his gun. 'All right, bollocks to this. Get that box open. Now!' He thrust the Beretta at the three startled scientists as Nina pulled out her own weapon.

'Mr Lobato!' Oto cried, looking to the skinny man for support, and finding none.

'Come on,' Eddie said impatiently. 'Open it up.'

Oto hesitated, then went to a control panel. 'It will take a few minutes to repressurise,' he said nervously. 'We do not want to risk a sudden pressure change damaging the spearhead.'

'He's not stalling for time, is he?' Nina asked Lobato.

'No, the system was designed to work that way,' the billionaire replied. 'But it should take no more than three minutes.'

401

'Great, I'll boil an egg,' said Eddie. He watched the other two technicians as Oto worked the controls. 'Keep an eye on the door,' he told Nina, 'in case that guard comes in.' She shifted position.

A rumbling thrum came from the chamber as valves opened, followed by the hiss of air through pipes. A digital counter slowly ticked upwards. The Russian kept glancing towards Nina, as if contemplating lunging at her, but his eyes hurriedly went to the floor when he realised Eddie was glaring at him.

A minute passed, two, the hiss becoming louder as enough air entered the vacuum chamber to transmit sound. 'Open it as soon as the pressure has equalised,' Lobato said.

'If I may ask, sir,' said Oto, 'why are you doing this? We have only just begun our work – there has not even been time to calculate how much antimatter is trapped inside the spearhead.'

'Too much,' said Nina. 'And the Emir isn't planning to use it to keep Dhajan's air con running. It's a bomb.'

All three scientists expressed shocked disbelief. 'I – I refuse to accept that,' said Oto. 'The Emir has always assured us this technology will be used for peaceful purposes.'

'Well, gee, I guess he lied.'

The Japanese scientist was about to respond when a shrill bleep came from the panel. 'The chamber is fully pressurised,' he announced.

'Open it,' Lobato told him. Oto operated controls. The hiss of air faded, but the rumble continued, now seeming to come through the floor. Nina had no time to consider the oddity, as motors purred and the chamber's heavy door opened. The polished stainless-steel tray bearing the spearhead slid out.

She quickly moved to examine the crystal. 'It looks intact,' she said with relief. 'I was worried it was damaged when it fell.'

'It was dropped?' said Oto in concern.

'Yeah. It didn't exactly arrive here legitimately – the Emir's people tried to kill us for it. *All* of us.' She indicated Lobato.

'The Emir tried to *kill* you?' gasped the Russian.

'There's been a whole lot of double-crossing going on,' Nina told him. 'But right now, that doesn't matter. What *does* matter is that this thing is going to explode – before sunset, and probably a lot sooner.'

Oto's eyes widened. 'How do you know?'

'I read the manual. The moment it was removed from the vault where it had been kept, whatever field keeps the antimatter contained began to deteriorate. At stage one, you can just put it back and it'll be as if nothing's happened. Stage two – this,' she said, pointing at the seething cloud of lights inside the spearhead, 'means the particles are starting to escape and hit the inside of the crystal. Each one of those flashes is a little antimatter explosion.'

The three men were horrified. 'We detected gamma radiation,' said the Russian, 'but at a low level only. We thought it was the item's natural state.'

'Well, think again. The whole thing's being eaten away from the inside, atom by atom. Up to a certain point, the field can still be restored by putting it back in the vault. After that, though, it enters stage three, where it's so damaged that nothing can stop it from collapsing. When it does, the antimatter escapes—'

'And like I said,' Eddie concluded for her, 'boom.'

'That would be . . .' Oto struggled to find a suitable word, 'catastrophic.'

Nina nodded. 'So we need to get this thing as far from Dhajan as we can before it blows up. As far from *anything*, actually.'

Her revelation was greeted with stunned silence. She belatedly registered that the rumbling had stopped, but by then Oto had overcome his shock to speak to Lobato. 'Is this true? Has the Emir lied to us?'

'I am afraid so,' the billionaire told him solemnly. 'So now the spearhead must be removed, and quickly. If it explodes, the blast could destroy Dhajan City, even from this distance. Over half a million people would die. I cannot allow that to happen, and I hope that you could not too.'

'Of course not!' the Russian cried.

'Then let's get it out of here,' said Nina. She checked Eddie was still covering the technicians, just in case any placed loyalty to the Emir over Lobato, then pocketed her weapon and picked up the spearhead.

'What's wrong?' Eddie asked, seeing her shudder.

'I just remembered,' she replied, unsettled. 'These guys said it's pumping out gamma radiation!'

'The emissions have not yet reached a harmful level,' Oto noted.

'Easy for you to say; you don't have to take the damn thing with you!' She held the shimmering crystal at arm's length, then turned to Lobato. 'Okay, so we get in the car, cross back into Saudi, get to your jet, and either head to Turkey to put this back into the vault, or throw it out in the most isolated place we can find. Good plan?'

'It could be finessed,' Lobato replied, 'but it is all we have, so yes.'

'Let's get the fuck out of here, then,' said Eddie. He started towards the exit only to hear a bleep from the other side. 'Shit! Someone's coming!'

The airlock's inner door slid open, to reveal the Emir of Dhajan.

37

The Emir stared in surprise at the group. 'Gideon?' he said. 'I wasn't expecting you so soon.'

Eddie snapped his gun up at the startled Arab, but others emerged behind him. The Emir's sister, Alula; two uniformed members of the royal guard; the security guard from the lobby . . . and Hashim al-Asim.

'Guns down or I shoot the Emir!' the Englishman barked, but the ruler's protectors had already snatched out their own weapons. He couldn't cover them all—

The besuited monarch shouted a command. His men froze. 'Stop, stop!' he repeated in English. 'What is going on here?' He regarded Nina in puzzlement before recognising the now black-haired woman in a headscarf. 'Dr Wilde!'

'Hello, hi,' Nina replied, trying to control her fear. The Emir might have stopped his guards shooting them, but their guns were still drawn and ready – and now al-Asim had produced one too, positioning himself before Alula. 'I guess you weren't expecting to see me again, huh?'

'I said drop your weapons!' growled Eddie, tightening his finger on the trigger.

'You cannot escape,' sneered al-Asim. 'Put down your gun.' He gave an order, and one of the other men switched targets, locking on to Nina. 'Do it now, or your wife dies.'

The Emir was shocked. 'Nobody is going to die!' He put his hands on his hips, issuing more commands. His men looked to al-Asim for confirmation. He nodded, with clear reluctance, then

405

all four holstered their weapons. 'Now, Mr Chase, I have given you a show of good faith. Would you be so kind as to lower *your* gun?'

The Yorkshireman was not so ready to surrender his advantage. 'Should've thought of that before you sent this arsehole to try to kill us.' He glanced at al-Asim.

The Emir frowned. 'I do not know what you are talking about. Gideon, what is going on?'

'There is no point continuing this deception, Fadil,' said Lobato. 'You betrayed me to use the spearhead as a weapon. I cannot allow that.'

'A weapon!' The Emir's eyes went to the glowing crystal. 'Why would you think that?'

'It's funny,' said Nina, nodding towards al-Asim, 'but when someone literally says "we're going to use this as a bomb" and then tries to kill me while they steal it, I'm inclined to take their word for it. And he works for you.'

'He does, yes, but – but I did not order him to kill you. I did not order him to kill anyone! Gideon and I deceived you, yes, but it was necessary to find the spearhead. For that, I apologise. I will make sure all is put right with the authorities, and that you are compensated for the inconvenience.'

'Mighty generous of you,' she said sarcastically.

'Inconvenience, my arse,' snapped Eddie. 'He was going to fucking execute us! Give me one good reason why I shouldn't do the same to you.'

His gun had not wavered from its target: the Emir's heart. Al-Asim's hand shifted millimetre by millimetre back towards his holster – but the monarch picked up on it, issuing another order. Visibly angry, al-Asim lowered his arm.

'Because, Mr Chase,' said the Emir, 'I honestly do not know anything about what you are saying. I worked with Gideon to use the spearhead for the good of humanity. Why would I build all this,' he held out a hand to encompass the laboratory, 'to safely extract antimatter as a source of power if I merely wanted to blow something up?'

Nina had an answer. 'It seems to me that having a way to take antimatter out of the spearhead and store it is a good way to make a *lot* of bombs. You blow up the spearhead and you're killing the goose that laid the mutually annihilatory egg, but take out what's already inside it and you've got not only the most powerful explosive in existence, but potentially a way to create more of it. *If* you can figure out how to extract the antimatter. Which you haven't.'

'I do *not* want to make bombs,' the Emir said firmly. 'And the spearhead has only just arrived. There will be plenty of time to study it and find a way to transfer the antimatter.'

'If by "plenty of time" you mean "by this afternoon, if you're lucky",' Eddie told him.

Again the monarch was puzzled. 'Gideon, what do they mean?'

'They are telling the truth,' Lobato replied. 'The spearhead became unstable the moment it was removed from the vault. Whatever force contains the antimatter is gradually deteriorating. The Atlanteans believed it would collapse and explode in under twenty-four hours. Fourteen hours have already passed.'

Fadil looked to the scientists in alarm. 'Is this true?'

'We do not know, Your Majesty,' said Oto. 'But if it is, we have no way to stop it.'

'If it is returned to the vault,' said the Emir, pursing his lips thoughtfully, 'would that stabilise it?'

'It should,' said Nina, 'if we can get it there in time. But it's already reached the second stage of destabilisation. Once it reaches the third stage, nothing can stop it – and it'll blow up within an hour or two.'

His eyes widened in alarm. 'And when will it reach the third stage?'

'I don't know. But in the next few hours. I don't know if we'll have time to get it back to the vault.'

'But we must try!' Concern vanished, replaced by commanding determination. 'My helicopter is outside. We will fly the spearhead to the airport, and I will have a jet take it to . . . Where is the vault?'

'Outside Sanliurfa, in Turkey,' Lobato told him.

'You shouldn't have any trouble getting hold of a chopper at the other end,' said Eddie witheringly. 'Just use the same one al-Arsehole and his mates rented.' He nodded towards al-Asim.

The Emir rounded on his agent. 'Hashim, what is going on? Did you really try to kill Gideon and Dr Wilde?'

'And me an' all,' Eddie added in mock offence.

Al-Asim practically forced out a reply. 'I . . . Yes, I did.'

Again, the Emir was shocked. '*What?*' he cried, marching to the other man. Eddie tracked him with his gun, still determined to deter his guards from redrawing their weapons. 'Why? Explain!'

'I was doing what was necessary to obtain the spearhead for Dhajan,' al-Asim replied stiffly.

'Not by killing! That was not part of the plan!'

Alula suddenly broke her silence, stepping out from behind al-Asim to face her brother. 'Actually,' she said, her voice filled with contempt, 'it was. Not your plan: mine.'

The Emir stared at her. 'What do you mean?'

She did not answer, instead issuing a sharp order in Arabic. All three guards instantly whipped out their weapons.

'Guns *down!*' the Yorkshireman roared. 'Or the Emir dies!'

The guards ignored the threat. Two aimed at Eddie and Nina, the third covering the others in the room. Eddie knew his bluff had been called; his target was as surprised at the reversal of fortune as he was, and if he pulled the trigger, he and Nina would die a fraction of a second after the Emir himself.

'Go on,' said Alula. 'Shoot him. Let us see what you are made of. Could you kill an innocent man?'

The Emir was speechless. 'So he really *wasn't* behind this?' asked Nina.

'Oh, he and Gideon did plan their little game for you together,' the princess replied mockingly. 'But they didn't go far enough. The ultimate power on earth, and they wanted to use it to make *electricity*?'

Despite the situation, the Emir was affronted rather than frightened. 'I told you before, Alula. We have no more oil! If we do not find a new source of income, our country is doomed.'

'And *you* will have doomed it!' she shouted back, startling him with her genuine anger. 'When our enemies realise the spearhead's power, they will attack and take it for themselves. The Saudis, the Iranians – even the Americans. How naïve *are* you, brother? They will not let us control it. So we must use it first, to strike them down before they destroy us!'

Fadil turned to his guards. 'This has gone far enough,' he said coldly. 'Arrest Her Royal Highness immediately. She has clearly gone mad.'

Nobody moved. Now it was the Emir's turn to show a rising anger, but this time tinged with fear. 'I said arrest her!'

Alula folded her arms. 'They are loyal to *me*,' she said smugly. 'As is everyone in the Ministry of State Security. I have been working towards this day – I did not expect it to come so soon, but then Dr Wilde's theory caught your attention, and now? Here we are.' She regarded Eddie and Nina coldly. 'Drop your guns. Now.'

With no choice, Nina discarded her Beretta. Eddie held position for longer, but then angrily tossed his weapon away. Al-Asim gave an order, a guard collecting them.

'This is *treason*!' the Emir cried. 'Why? Why have you turned on me – why have you turned on my country?'

Alula's face expressed sheer, almost despairing disbelief at his ignorance, before the fury returned. 'Your country?' she screamed. 'It is *my* country! You stole it from me the moment you were born! I was the oldest, the throne should have been mine – but men always come before women, even if they are younger!'

'We were born three minutes apart,' said the Emir, flabbergasted.

'Three minutes that should have made all the difference, but they did not, because our father could not countenance a woman ruling Dhajan. And nor could you! All the laws you changed in the name of *liberalisation*,' the word was almost spat out in disgust, 'turning our country into a whorehouse for Saudis and infidels, even selling out our claim to the Gulf of Salwah in return for the so-called protection of the American navy . . . but the one thing you did not change, the one thing you would never *dare* change, is the rule that let you steal the throne from me!'

'Even if I wanted to give you the throne, I could not! The moment Father died, I became the Emir – it is not a mere appointed position, a *job*, from which I can resign. I will hold the title until my heir succeeds me. If I have a daughter before a son, I will be happy to name her as my successor, but I cannot give up my rule to you.'

'But you do not have an heir,' said Alula. 'And you never will.'

He blinked in confusion. 'What—'

She pulled out a gun and shot him.

'Holy *shit!*' Nina cried as the Emir fell to the floor. Blood slowly swelled around the scorched rent in his jacket's chest.

Lobato wailed in horror. 'Fadil! My God!' He stared at the fallen man. 'Is – is he *dead*?'

'He just got shot in the heart at point-blank range,' said Nina, appalled. 'That's not something people generally recover from!'

410

'Under Dhajani rules of succession,' said Alula, returning her slim weapon to a concealed holster, 'if the Emir dies without an heir, the throne passes to his closest relative.' A cold smile of triumph. 'I am now Emira of Dhajan!'

Al-Asim knelt at her feet. He bowed his head, speaking in reverent Arabic, then stood. 'Your Majesty. You have my eternal loyalty.'

'Thank you, Hashim,' she replied. The guards offered their respects in turn, though at least one kept their prisoners covered at all times. Alula removed her headscarf and dropped it, shaking out her long dark hair. 'Free at last. In all ways.'

'Congratulations on your inauguration, *Your Majesty*,' Nina said sarcastically. 'So what's going to be your first act as Emira?'

Alula approached her, gazing at the spearhead in the American's hands. 'I will use this as my brother never dared even dream,' she said. 'To wipe out Dhajan's enemies in the Gulf. Bahrain and Qatar will be obliterated, as will the American navy at their Bahraini base, and Saudi Arabia will suffer a blow that will take them decades from which to recover.'

'I thought you were *partnered* with the Yanks?' said Eddie.

'A deal made by my brother,' she told him, sneering. 'A deal that turned us into the whining sycophantic *dog* of other countries. But we will no longer be anyone's pet!'

'But even an antimatter bomb wouldn't take out Bahrain, Qatar *and* Saudi,' said Nina. 'They're too big.'

Alula rounded on her. 'Do you think I am an *idiot*, Dr Wilde? Of course I know I cannot destroy them all with a single bomb.'

'Then what?'

'The *Pacifia* has just set sail from Dhajan City,' al-Asim told her.

'The other liner like the *Atlantia*?' Eddie asked.

'A grotesque and decadent waste of money, another of my brother's attempts to make us more . . . *Western*. But its maiden voyage will also be its last!' Alula's mouth curled into a nasty smile. 'It will deliver the spearhead to our enemies by sailing straight into the American naval base in Bahrain. They will not dare sink a ship with ten thousand civilians aboard, but by the time they realise the danger, it will be too late. Bahrain will be destroyed, the American Gulf fleet wiped out, and Qatar and Saudi will be flattened by the tidal wave.'

Lobato broke the speechless silence. 'A tidal wave powerful enough to flood Qatar and the Saudi coast would also sweep southwards to hit Dhajan as well,' he pointed out. 'Dhajan City would suffer massive damage and loss of life.'

'Dhajan City?' she scoffed. 'A cesspit of sin hidden behind glass and steel. I know why foreigners come to my country – and it makes me sick. I have seen the depravity beneath the surface.' An almost messianic fervour entered her voice. 'It is time to drag it into the light and exterminate it! Only when the parasites are dead can a body be healthy. It must be cleansed and purified, so we can rebuild and start afresh. A new rule: *my* rule!'

'You're insane!' said Nina, appalled.

Alula stormed closer. 'No – I am *angry*!' she snarled. 'I have been angry my whole life. The royal palace is a *prison* for a woman. I could do nothing without the permission of a man – first my father, then my brother, and all their lackeys and servants who still think they are better than me. Only one ever treated me with respect.' Her gaze flicked towards al-Asim. 'I studied hard, worked hard, learned to do anything a man can do, while my brother acted like a playboy in the casinos and brothels of Monaco and Macau – but I still had to *crawl* to him to be allowed to serve in his government.'

'But he let you,' Nina said. 'And you must have done a good job, because you're still there.'

'A *good job*?' she spat. 'I protected my country from spies, sabotage, criminals, terrorists – but the credit for all successes went to my brother, and the blame for every failure, however small, was put upon me!'

'Believe me, I *know* what you're talking about. Every woman does! We've all had to put up with crap from patronising or stupid or just plain misogynist men, even when we're better than them. But there's no need to kill millions of innocent people – men *and* women – to get revenge on one person.'

Alula narrowed her eyes. 'This is not about revenge on my brother. This is about destroying the corruption at the heart of my country. And the spearhead,' she looked down at the object in Nina's hands, 'will be the blade that cuts it out. Give it to me.'

With no choice, Nina surrendered the crystal. Alula clutched it to her chest. 'It is mine,' she crowed. 'Hashim, tell the pilot to start the helicopter. We will fly straight to the *Pacifia.*'

Al-Asim's eyes were fixed on the prisoners. 'And them?'

'Kill them, of cour—'

A hand closed around Alula's ankle.

She gasped, stumbling back as the Emir pulled at her leg.

Everyone reacted with shock at Fadil's unexpected resurrection. The guards all turned towards him—

Eddie lunged for al-Asim's gun. The other man reacted just in time to pull the weapon away – but not clear. The Englishman managed to tear out the extended magazine.

Al-Asim spun to bring the still-chambered Glock around at him. But Eddie had already twisted to body-slam his opponent before smashing the magazine's corner hard against his temple. The Arab staggered – and Eddie grabbed the gun before kicking him in the stomach and sending him to the floor.

The other men whirled back to face the new threat, guns rising—

Eddie aimed his own unwaveringly at Alula's head.

'*La tutliq alnaar!*' she cried. 'Stop!'

The three guards fixed their guns on the Yorkshireman . . . but did not shoot.

A stand-off: that could not last.

Alula overcame her fear. She yanked her leg from her brother's feeble grip and faced Eddie. 'If you kill me, my guards will kill you.'

'Maybe,' Eddie replied stonily, 'but you'll still be dead.'

'You won't get your revenge,' Nina added.

Alula raised her chin defiantly. 'Hashim will carry out the plan even if I am gone.'

'Maybe I should kill him an' all,' said Eddie.

She almost smiled. 'You only have one bullet.'

'Whatever you do,' growled the bloodied al-Asim, 'you will die. And Her Majesty will win.'

'Not if I shoot the spearhead.' Eddie glanced at the pulsating artefact. 'Nina, you think it'd blow up?'

'Who am I, the Mistress of Crystalline Knowledge?' his wife replied. 'I don't know!'

'The blast could still reach Dhajan City,' warned Lobato.

'And you would not kill innocent people, would you, Mr Chase?' said Alula with contempt. 'You cannot win.'

Al-Asim slowly began to stand. 'Get back down,' Eddie snapped.

The Dhajani ignored his warning. 'I will give you all a quick death if you surrender, Chase. Otherwise you will suffer.'

'All right,' said Eddie, lifting his gun away from Alula and towards the ceiling. 'Chill out.'

Triumph lit Alula's face. She started to issue a command.

Eddie fired – and the cooling system exploded.

38

Superchilled freon burst from the ruptured pipe, the spraying liquid instantly evaporating into a freezing, choking cloud.

It gushed over the three guards, sending them staggering as the vapour burned their skin and seared their throats. Al-Asim was caught on the jet's fringe. He jumped away, gasping, only for the Yorkshireman to deliver a kick to his groin that sent him flying back into the miasma.

Alula snatched out her gun, but Eddie swatted it across the room. '*Khinzir!*' she spat, clawing at his face with her nails.

He grabbed her wrist, easily overpowering her, and drew back his other arm as if to strike her. She cringed. 'I don't hit women,' he said. She shot him a scathing look, its meaning clear: *then you are too weak to beat me.*

'She does, though,' he went on, stepping aside as his wife rushed up with her own fist clenched.

Before Alula could react, Nina punched her in the face with enough pent-up fury to send her reeling backwards. 'Inaugurate *that!*' snarled the American.

Alula staggered – and tripped over her fallen brother's legs. Her elbow jarred painfully against the floor, sending the spearhead flying from her hand. It disappeared into the gushing chemical fog.

'Shit!' Nina yelped. 'We've got to get it!'

'We've got to get out of here,' Eddie countered. 'Help me with the Emir!'

'You want to take *him* rather than the spearhead?'

415

Alula crawled clear as he crouched to lift the wounded man. 'If he's alive, he can countermand Alula.'

'*If* he's alive.' The Emir's chest wound was still bleeding.

'He won't be for long if we don't help him. Gideon!'

Lobato came out of his stunned fugue and took hold of the Dhajani. Nina stared helplessly after the Atlantean crystal. It was lost in the rushing fog . . . but the jetting vapour's pressure was falling, most of the coolant escaped. 'I can get it!' she said, spotting a faint light within the haze.

'Don't!' Eddie shouted, but she was already running—

The vapour hit her – and she recoiled from the sub-zero assault on her exposed skin. Sheer shock made her cry out, only to choke as the freezing gas entered her mouth. Panic rising, she abandoned her search and staggered blindly back.

She forced her eyes open – to see Alula scrambling towards her fallen gun.

Coughing, Nina ran after Eddie. Behind her, the escaping jet was now just a desultory billow, the vapour dispersing to reveal the royal guards.

They still had their guns – and were recovering.

Eddie reached the airlock's open door, Lobato with him as they supported the wounded man. 'Come on!' he yelled to Nina.

Alula reached her gun as one of the royal guards opened his streaming eyes and saw the fleeing American. He brought up his weapon—

'Nina! *Dive!*'

Eddie's roar told Nina she was in immediate danger. Without hesitation she threw herself into the airlock, hitting the floor with a thump as the guard's bullets smashed tiles on the wall above her.

But now Alula had locked on to her target—

Lobato jabbed a button on the control panel – and the steel barrier slid closed, intercepting the princess's round with a shrilling clang before clunking shut.

Alula nevertheless kept firing, the impacts ringing stridently through the airlock. Eddie hauled the unconscious Emir to the exit. 'Get this fucking door open before they get *that* one open!'

'Just a moment,' said Lobato, oddly calm as he concentrated. His fingers danced across the control panel, a new window popping up. He tapped it, and a message flashed on the screen. 'There!'

'What did you do?' said Nina as she breathlessly stood.

'Locked the door,' he said, a little smugly, as a muffled pounding came from the other side. 'One of my companies designed the operating system for this facility, so I inserted a back door that would give me unrestricted access.'

'The same thing you did on the *Atlantia*, right? And you gave your code to the Emir?'

'No, that was a different code with the same function.' He quickly joined Eddie and opened the outer door before helping lift the Emir again.

'Can they override it?' Nina asked.

'There is an emergency manual release, so yes.'

'The technicians know about it?' said Eddie as they carried the Emir into the reception area.

'Of course.'

'Then we've got less than a minute. Get to the car, quick. Nina, you drive.'

Nina led the way to the Saudi SUV. She looked around for any more of Alula's forces – and saw something more menacing than any soldier. 'Shit!' Parked side-on to her on the helipad were two aircraft: the Emir's personal helicopter, a gleaming Sikorsky S-76 bearing the Dhajani flag and royal coat of arms . . . next to an Apache gunship in desert camouflage. She had once faced off against a similar chopper – an experience she and Eddie barely survived.

'Well, that's all we fucking need!' the Yorkshireman growled. The Apache was the latest AH-64E version, an airborne tank designed to kill targets on the ground with great efficiency. The pilot and gunner were visible in the cockpit, and he had no doubt they had been personally chosen by – and were loyal to – Alula.

The two helmeted men spotted the fleeing group, reacting in alarm at the sight of the Emir. 'Buggeration and fuckery!' said Eddie as the pilot hurriedly threw switches. 'They're powering up!'

Nina reached the Toyota and flung the rear door open before jumping into the driver's seat. 'How long before they can take off?' The war machine's rotors were stationary.

'They don't need to!' Eddie replied as he lowered the Emir into the back. 'The gun's electric – they can shoot us while they're on the ground. Gideon, get in!' Both men rounded the vehicle, Lobato taking the seat beside Nina as Eddie glanced at the gunship.

The chain gun beneath the Apache's cockpit swung down from its stowed position. It performed a brief sequence of tilts and pivots as it ran through a self-testing routine . . . then snapped around to lock on to the Land Cruiser, the gunner tracking them with his helmet-mounted sight.

Eddie threw himself on to the back seat. 'Go!'

Nina jammed her foot on the accelerator. The big vehicle surged forward, bounding over the kerb on to the sand beyond the parking lot.

The chain gun followed – then opened fire, unleashing a rapid-fire stream of high-explosive shells—

Nina screamed as the barrage whipped past just behind them. One of the technicians' cars took the brunt of the attack instead, metal shredding like paper in a shotgun blast and sending the mangled wreckage cartwheeling across the lot. Other shells smashed into the heliostats beyond, mirrors exploding. 'Oh my God! They missed!'

Eddie raised his head. The cannon had reached the limit of its firing arc. 'They can't turn the turret any further. Good job you went this way rather than staying on the road – we'd have been dead.'

'All I was thinking was that we'd go faster forward than in reverse,' she replied, clutching the wheel fearfully.

Lobato peered through the rear window. 'So are we safe?'

'Course we're not fucking safe,' Eddie replied, still watching the Apache. 'They'll be in the air soon, and then we're fucked – shit, get down!'

He ducked, Nina doing the same as gunfire clattered from the reception area. Al-Asim and the guards had opened fire from inside the lobby, destroying the windows in their haste to stop the escapees. Rounds struck the tailgate and shattered the rear windscreen. Lobato shrieked and dropped, covering his head with his hands.

Nina powered over a rocky rise. They briefly went airborne before slamming down on the other side, now shielded from their attackers. 'Jesus!' Eddie cried, struggling to hold the Emir on the seat. 'We're not trying to *shake* the bullet out of him!'

'Oh, I'm sorry, would you like me to engage hover mode?' she snapped back. Ahead lay the sweeping forest of heliostats, giant gleaming sunflowers directing their reflected rays at the power towers. 'Gideon! How do we get out of here?'

The billionaire nervously straightened, gripping the centre console as the SUV bounded across the plain. 'The road to the main gate is . . . that way,' he said, pointing.

Eddie looked back. The helicopters were partly visible beyond the rise; the Apache's rotors were still stationary. 'The chopper's not moving yet, so we might have a chance of reaching it.'

'I'll try not to throw the Emir around too much,' said Nina.

She followed a sweeping route through the heliostat masts as Eddie examined the Dhajani ruler.

Alula strode out of the reception area to see a cloud of dust rising in the solar forest. 'They got *away*?' she snarled.

'I'm sorry, Your Majesty,' said al-Asim, bowing his head. His men looked abashed.

She glared at them, then indicated the Apache. 'Send the gunship after them!'

'They'll need a couple of minutes to bring the rotors to take-off speed – but I'll order them to skip the safety checks,' he added hastily as her angry gaze returned to him. Taking out a walkie-talkie, he issued rapid commands to the aircrew.

Alula turned her attention to the guards. 'You three! Get after them!'

They exchanged nervous looks. 'Ah . . . how, Your Majesty?' one asked.

'Take a car, idiot!' She pointed at the remaining vehicles in the parking lot.

The technicians, who had earned their survival – for now – by showing their captors the airlock's manual override, emerged. The Russian gawped at the mangled wreckage. 'My car!'

Alula had no sympathy. 'Your keys,' she demanded, jabbing a finger at Oto. 'Now!' One of the guards snatched them from the quivering Japanese scientist's hand. A push of a button on the fob unlocked a Cadillac Escalade SUV beneath a sunshade. The three men ran to it.

As al-Asim finished his call, the Apache's twin engines started up, the rotors slowly beginning to turn. 'The gunship will be airborne in two minutes,' he reported. 'They won't escape.'

'I want to be absolutely sure of that,' Alula replied. 'My brother must *not* survive.' She turned towards the larger building adjoining the antimatter facility: the operations centre for the solar plant itself. An observation room, walled in mirrored glass, was located at the top of a five-storey tower, giving the technicians an unobstructed view across the huge field of mirrors. 'Up there. We are going to *burn* them.'

'Road's coming up,' Nina announced with relief. Traversing rough terrain at speed while trying not to crash into any solar panels or heliostat masts had been neither easy nor enjoyable. 'How's the Emir?'

Behind her, Eddie had managed to keep the injured man in place by fastening a seat belt around his waist. 'Not good, but he's not dead, either.'

'How?' she asked. 'He was shot in the heart, point blank!'

'Something in his chest pocket took the impact. Don't want to move it yet, though – it might be the only thing keeping him from bleeding to death.'

'There is a medical unit at the test track,' Lobato told him.

'We need to get *away* from here, not back through the middle of the fucking power station!' Eddie put his palm on Fadil's chest, trying to staunch the bleeding.

'Okay, here's the road – hold on!' Nina cried. She slowed to bring the Toyota through a small ditch, then swung it on to the route to the gate.

'They are following,' warned Lobato.

Nina checked the mirror, seeing another vehicle weaving through the masts. She accelerated. Back on smooth asphalt, the 4x4 surged away. 'We've got a clear run now.'

Alula, holding the spearhead, stared across the plain. From the observation tower, it seemed as if she was overlooking sea rather than desert, the heliostats reflecting blue sky. 'Can the mirrors be aimed manually?' she demanded.

The head technician had not been expecting gun battles or his country's ruler to be usurped on his watch, and was in considerable agitation. 'It, it would not be—' he stammered.

Al-Asim pointed a gun at his head. 'The correct answer is "Yes, Your Majesty".'

'Y-yes, Your Majesty!'

'Show me,' Alula ordered.

The man, suddenly sweating despite the air-conditioned cool, led her to a console. 'These dials move the focus of the reflected sunlight – we call it the prime beam,' he said, indicating a set of controls. 'If one tower is out of action, we can shift its beam to either of the others to increase the amount of light falling on it. We select the mirrors on this touchscreen.' He tapped a large glass panel.

'Can you control all the mirrors at once?'

He blinked. 'Yes, but – but it has never been done. We have not needed to—'

'Do it,' she snapped. 'Set all the mirrors to focus together. Then aim it at *that*.' She pointed.

The technician's mouth dropped open as he saw her target: a vehicle racing away on the access road. 'But there are people inside it!'

'Her Majesty is well aware of that,' said al-Asim. 'Do it!'

Mouth dry, the man entered commands, bringing all the thousands of heliostats under one set of controls. Alula felt almost wonderment as the mirrors began to realign. Great ripples swept across the 'sea' as each rotated and tilted to direct the sun's rays towards one particular spot.

The road, and the SUV racing along it.

39

'What the hell's happening?' said Nina. All around them, the great mirrored flowers were starting to move. To her growing alarm, she realised that those on her left were turning in the opposite direction to those on the right, swinging around to point at the road.

Lobato regarded the synchronised display. 'All the mirrors are realigning. But they are not aiming at any of the towers. They are—'

'They're aiming at *us!*' she cried. 'Alula's gonna fry us like an ant under a goddamn magnifying glass!'

Eddie looked back. Nina was right – the great mirror-lined bowl was becoming brighter by the moment as every single heliostat turned to reflect the sun at them. 'Shit! Is there anywhere we can hide from it?'

Lobato searched the hillside for cover, but saw nothing. 'No. We will just have to stay ahead of it.'

'You ever tried to outrun the sunrise?' the Yorkshireman said cuttingly. As if incineration was not enough of a danger, he also saw the pursuing Escalade vault on to the road – and the Apache rise above the vast shining bowl. 'Nina, new plan – get off the road again! If you stay under the mirrors, they won't be able to see us, and what they can't see, they can't melt.'

'And what about the helicopter?' Nina demanded.

'Let's worry about one horrible death at a time. Get under the mirrors!'

'*Really* not liking this plan,' she said, but she swerved the Toyota off the road.

Alula watched the SUV disappear beneath the shifting mirrors. 'Follow them!' she snapped. The combined beam from the heliostats started to form, the air shimmering as it was super-heated by ever more intense sunlight.

'I – I can't see them,' protested the technician.

'Are you blind? Follow their dust trail – Hashim, hold this.' She thrust the spearhead at al-Asim and shoved the technician aside to take the controls herself. The Apache had by now cleared the pad and was heading in pursuit. 'Tell the helicopter to hover above them. I will do this myself!'

She adjusted the dials. The heliostats all responded, sending the searing point of light sweeping after the Land Cruiser.

In normal operation, each of the three prime beams would be created by a third of the mirrors, the temperature at the focus point roughly one and a half thousand degrees Celsius. All the mirrors combined, however, produced something far more intense. Heliostats toppled in the monstrous new beam's wake, flower heads of glass and metal scythed off as a beam half as hot as the sun's surface sliced through them like a laser.

The technician stared in horror as his facility crumbled before his eyes. Alula ignored him, an almost maniacal smile forming as the dazzling beacon of destruction drew ever closer to her brother and his rescuers.

'What was that?' said Nina, hearing explosive crashes behind them. 'The chopper?'

Eddie turned – to see mast after mast shearing apart, the huge mirror arrays falling and smashing in a blizzard of mirrored fragments. 'No, but I almost wish it was!' Lower down the slope, the other SUV was angling towards them. A man leaned out of its window. *'Incoming!'*

Everyone ducked as the royal guardsman sprayed full-auto fire at them. The cargo area's side window blew apart, followed by *thunks* as bullets punched through the bodywork. Lobato cried out as a metal fragment tore into the back of one hand, another round narrowly missing the Emir's legs before striking the frame of Nina's seat. 'Jesus!' she yelped.

'Are you okay?' Eddie hurriedly asked.

'Yeah, I'm fine,' she assured him as she lifted her head, 'but we're running out of places to go!'

Ahead was a gap in the ranks of heliostats to accommodate a line of electrical pylons, but the space left to ensure that the power lines were not damaged by the mirrors' beam had been filled by photovoltaic arrays, banks of solar panels running directly across her path. 'You will have to go around!' said Lobato, clutching his wound.

'How? It goes half a mile in each direction!'

'What're they made of?' Eddie asked Lobato.

He looked back in confusion. 'I do not understand.'

'The panels, the frames! What're they made of?'

'The panels are polysilicon cells mounted on glass, and the frames are aluminium—'

'So they're lightweight? Nina, go *through* 'em! Fast as you can!'

'You think I wasn't already going that fast?' She lined up with a set of panels. 'Brace yourselves!'

Everyone tensed, Eddie holding the Emir—

The Toyota ploughed into the solar panels.

Dark glass exploded, flying shards raining over the hood. The SUV lurched, about to roll over as the angled panels acted like a ramp – then their frame collapsed under its two-ton weight and the vehicle slammed back down, dragging the wreckage for several yards before the mangled framework fell away.

But they were not clear yet. Another set of panels loomed—

Nina spun the wheel and hit it head-on. This time, the whole array disintegrated on impact, part of the aluminium framework cracking the windscreen. She gasped, but held course, powering the dented 4x4 back into the endless maze of mirrors.

Another burst of bullets followed them. The Escalade was still closing. But the sizzling solar beam had overtaken it, drawing ever nearer to its prey.

'The pylons!' cried the technician, unable to hold his silence any longer as the blazing point of light approached the power lines. He reached for the controls. 'Your Majesty, you must stop—'

Al-Asim threw him to the floor. 'Do not touch her!'

'But if you cut the power lines—'

'Shut up!' Alula yelled, fixated on her target. The Toyota had come back into sight, and she sent the beam after it as fast as the mirrors could realign. 'I've almost got them!'

The dazzling spot raced across the gap after the retreating Land Cruiser, vaporising the solar panels on the ground – and slicing through a pylon.

Skeletal aluminium flashed white-hot, melted – and fell.

Eddie stared through the rear window in horror as the beam rushed towards them, feeling its heat rising on his face—

It abruptly halted.

The bisected pylon crashed down in front of the pursuing Escalade, the severed power lines whipping furiously. The driver braked hard – but too late. The vehicle ploughed into the fallen structure, flipping end over end and smashing down on its roof.

But the inferno remained stationary, burning sand into glass in a searing cauldron. 'Christ!' Eddie said. 'Dunno why, but the beam just stopped moving.'

'Of course,' said Lobato, with relieved realisation. 'It cut the power lines, which caused a feedback surge in the power storage units. The safety systems activated automatically to prevent an overload, affecting the entire facility.'

'So are we safe?' Nina asked, swinging the vehicle back into the now-stationary heliostats as fires erupted behind them.

'No. It will only take a few seconds to reboot . . .'

'What's happened?' Alula demanded, rounding angrily on the technician. The finger of God chasing her brother had abruptly stopped, the controls no longer responding to her commands. The screen showing the heliostat status blanked out, then returned with a large warning banner obscuring most of the display.

'I tried to warn you,' he replied fearfully. 'When you cut – I mean, when the main power lines to Dhajan City *were* cut,' he corrected, trying not to imply that the country's clearly ruthless new ruler was in any way at fault, 'the system shut down to keep the power storage units from overloading. But look, look,' he went on as the warning disappeared, 'it's already reset!'

Alula took hold of the controls again. The heliostats responded, the point of intense light emerging from the flames and smoke. She searched for the fleeing SUV, but it was hidden by the mirrors. 'Tell the helicopter to find them,' she ordered al-Asim. 'I want to kill them myself!'

Eddie heard a new noise above the crashes and thumps of the Toyota's overworked suspension. 'Chopper's coming in!' He glimpsed the Apache's angular dragonfly silhouette between the moving mirrors, feeling a rush of fear. If he could see it, it could shoot *them*.

But the chain gun remained silent. Instead, the gunship drew closer, its rotor downwash kicking up a whirlwind of sand. Dust blew in through the smashed windows. 'What's it doing?' said Nina, coughing.

'Marking us,' her husband reported, 'so Alula can zap us!'

'Why would she do that?' asked Lobato. 'It would be much easier for the helicopter to shoot us.'

'Never underestimate the human element,' said Nina. 'She's pissed at us and wants to kill us personally!'

Eddie saw another line of pylons some way ahead. He tracked them back to their source: one of the power storage units. 'Gideon, you said the system shut down to protect the batteries, right?'

'Yes,' Lobato replied.

'So how long would it shut down for if the batteries got fucked up?'

'Until the batteries were . . . un-fucked up.' The obscenity sounded almost comically strange in his precise, accented voice, but nobody had time to laugh.

'Nina—' Eddie began.

'Already on it,' she replied. 'Hold on!' She made a hard turn to angle downhill towards the storage block.

The Apache followed, dropping lower. The beam sliced across the desert bowl after them. Nina weaved between the masts towards the power unit. What looked from a distance like a single white building was now revealed as a cluster of closely packed modules, fat skeins of cables connecting them. They would reach it in seconds.

But the ravenous beam was right behind them, the scorching heat rising again.

'Nina!' warned Eddie.

'I'm doing it!' she said, pushing the accelerator all the way down.

'I mean it!'

'*I'm doing it!*' The wheel kicked in her hands as the SUV

pounded over the rough ground; at this speed, she was more guiding than controlling it. There was a gap between the banks of modules, access for maintenance vehicles. She forced the car towards it—

The air around them glowed, the cabin temperature rocketing.

Heliostats exploded, metal flashing white-hot. The Toyota's rear paintwork burst into flames even before the blinding beam reached it, the remaining windows cracking. Eddie dropped over the Emir to shield him, but he knew it was too late—

The blinding light faded.

Nina braked hard, skidding the SUV into the concrete channel between the white blocks. 'We're in!' she gasped. They were shielded from the beam, and another safety shutdown had already triggered as the battery banks overheated, locking the mirrors in place. Safe!

Or not. 'No, no, get *out!*' cried Lobato, looking in alarm at the nearest module. Smoke belched from its ventilation louvres.

'What's happening?' Eddie demanded.

'They are lithium-ion batteries,' the billionaire replied as Nina hurriedly set off again. 'Just like laptop batteries, but hundreds of times larger. If they get too hot, they explode!'

'Great move bringing 'em to the fucking *desert*, then!' shouted Eddie.

The Land Cruiser's rear end was still on fire, trailing smoke and flame as it surged through the storage unit, but bigger blazes were sweeping through the modules. A sizzling hiss rose over the clamour of the hovering helicopter: a battery bank igniting under the pitiless beam—

It blew apart. Its neighbours following suit in a catastrophic chain reaction.

Alula's triumph at the sight of the distant SUV wreathed in flame vanished as the vehicle disappeared behind a white building

– and then the controls cut out again. 'What's wrong?' she barked.

'The beam set fire to one of the battery units!' said the technician. 'The whole system has shut down!'

A new warning flashed on the screen, and unlike its predecessor, this one did not disappear. The princess pounded her fists on the console in frustration. 'Hashim!' she snapped. 'Order the gunship to kill them!'

Al-Asim raised his walkie-talkie, but an explosion caught their attention. 'We may not need to,' he said.

'Oh *shit!*' Nina cried as another detonation shook the storage unit. A large piece of electrical equipment blocked what she had hoped was the route out of the battery block, forcing her to slow and make a sharp turn. Sizzling meteorites rained around the SUV, burning lumps of lithium from the ruptured batteries. 'The whole thing's gonna go up!'

There was a junction box in her path, but there was nowhere else to go. She floored the accelerator. The flaming Toyota lunged forward. 'Brace!' she shouted.

The big 4x4 smashed into the obstruction and ripped it out of the ground, one corner of the hood crumpling upwards. Eddie kept hold of the Emir, for the first time hearing a response from the wounded man as he gasped in pain. 'I've got you!' the Yorkshireman told him. 'It's going to be okay—'

A sizzling hiss from behind – and several modules blew apart as one. Debris showered the fleeing vehicle as it vaulted off the storage unit's concrete base.

Nina and Lobato both screamed – then their cries were cut off by the airbags firing as the SUV slammed down, the front suspension collapsing.

They couldn't stop, though. More battery blocks were exploding behind them. Nina kept the power on, the still-functioning rear wheels forcing the mangled vehicle through the sand—

A heliostat tower loomed ahead.

She turned the wheel. Nothing happened. The steering column had snapped. 'Hang on!' she cried as she braked. The burning Toyota ground to a standstill just a few feet short of the mast.

Eddie released the belt holding the Emir and opened the rear door. 'Out, out!' he shouted, hauling the semi-conscious man with him. 'This thing'll blow up any second!'

Nina needed no urging. She ran past the heliostat, looking for the gunship. The Apache had moved well clear after the first explosion, only now starting to circle back towards them. 'Gideon, get out of sight!' she yelled to the white-clad man as he staggered from the burning SUV. 'Eddie, come on!'

Eddie had no time for medical niceties. He raised the Emir in a fireman's lift and lumbered down the slope after his wife. Catching up with the limping Lobato, he pulled the other man with him under another heliostat. 'Get down! It's gonna expl—'

The flat *whump* of escaping fuel igniting warned that his prediction was accurate. He dropped into a barely controlled skid to land beside the base of the mast. Lobato tumbled down next to him as the SUV exploded in a raging fireball.

'Jesus!' said Nina. 'Is everyone okay?'

'I am no worse off than before,' said Lobato shakily.

'Help me with the Emir,' Eddie grunted, struggling to lift Fadil. Between them they laid the injured man on his back as gently as they could. He was half awake, face screwed up in pain. The Yorkshireman looked at his chest wound. 'Shit, it's still bleeding. If I don't do something soon, he'll die. How far to this place with the medical centre?'

Lobato pointed at the hangar-like buildings near the top of the bowl. 'Over there.'

'It must be half a mile away,' said Nina. 'We'll never get there – not with that chopper after us!' The Apache was now coming back towards them.

Eddie stared at the approaching aircraft, then up the slope at the erupting power storage unit. He jumped to his feet. 'You two carry the Emir,' he said. 'Stay behind the mirrors so they can't see you.' He helped them lift the wounded man, then stepped back, still watching the helicopter.

'Where are *you* going?' Nina asked.

'Away from you. They'll start shooting any second, and you don't want to be anywhere near where the shells land!'

'I remember,' Nina said grimly. She still had a shrapnel scar from her last face-off against an Apache. 'Gideon, come on!'

They hurried into the blind spot behind the heliostat, then Eddie broke into a run. He followed a weaving course, ducking in and out of sight amongst the huge reflectors. If he was lucky, the chopper's crew wouldn't realise that only one of the fleeing group was moving . . .

Some sixth sense screamed in warning. He dropped low – as the heliostat behind him was ripped apart by a storm of explosive 30 mm cannon shells, fragmented glass and aluminium adding to the lethal spray of high-velocity fragments.

The chain gun's chattering thud reached him, the shells outpacing their own sound. He kept running, swerving as more projectiles punched through the mirrored forest. Most hit the sandy ground, but a few struck the heliostat masts, scattering more deadly fragments.

Pain shot through his left arm. He yelled, but didn't stop moving. His leather jacket's sleeve was ripped as if someone had slashed a razor across it. Two spikes of sharp metal were embedded in his arm. If he hadn't changed direction, he would have taken many more in his back.

The gunfire stopped. He glanced back. Where was the

Apache? If it went after Nina and the others, they wouldn't stand a chance . . .

He spotted it a few hundred metres away, lower than he'd expected. The pilot had dropped to get a better view under the confusing canopy of mirrors.

A glint of reflected light from the sensor pod on the chopper's nose as it pivoted towards him. The cannon followed, fire flashing beneath the fuselage. Eddie changed direction, screwing up his eyes against the rising brightness. The air grew hotter, as if he was running towards an open furnace.

Another mirror disintegrated in a storm of pulverised glass. The gunship swept towards him. A fearsome barrage struck the heliostats, what little shelter they offered shredded by the storm of shells. He kept going, head down as the world exploded around him.

The Apache's engine noise became a deafening roar, the sandstorm kicked up by its rotor wash scouring his skin. It thundered at him—

And burst into flames.

Eddie threw himself flat as it hurtled past. He was a couple of hundred yards clear of the battery bank, but the heliostats were still locked on to it, focusing the sun's relentless power – and he had drawn the gunship straight through the beam. Like the car before it, its paintwork instantly ignited, turning the aircraft into a cruciform torch streaking through the sky.

The Apache lost height, the pilot blinded—

Its forward landing struts and cannon hit a heliostat, scything it from its mast and pitching the aircraft down still further. It ploughed into the gleaming forest, flung into a spin as it demolished the next mast like a wrecking ball. The whirling rotors hacked through the mirrors, glass and carbon fibre shattering.

The gunship hit the ground hard, carving a swathe through a

bank of solar panels before slamming to a halt against another mast. Both men inside were still alive – the cockpit was designed for maximum survivability even in a crash – but neither was in any condition to pose a threat.

'That's what I call catching some rays,' said Eddie, grimacing as he pulled off his shredded jacket to check his arm. Blood was leaking from the two shrapnel wounds, but he would survive.

He hurried back to Nina. 'Eddie!' she called as he approached. 'Oh my God! Are you okay?'

'I'll live,' he replied. 'How is he?'

'I'm not sure,' Nina told him as he checked the Dhajani. 'I think the bleeding's slowed, but that's not necessarily a good sign, is it?'

'Nope.' The Emir's face was paler, his breathing shallow. Eddie looked towards the hangars. 'We've got to get him up there. Gideon, are there guards at the test track?'

'None specifically assigned there,' Lobato replied. 'The guards for the facility as a whole carry out regular checks.'

'Let's hope they're all with Alula, then.' Eddie picked up the wounded man, Nina and Lobato assisting, and they struck out towards the test centre.

Alula glared across the solar plant, searching for movement amongst the mirrors, but saw only columns of smoke. 'I can't see them, Your Majesty,' said al-Asim, scanning the facility through binoculars. 'They must be dead.'

'I won't believe that – I *can't* believe that – until someone finds their bodies,' she said. 'Order the guards to search for them. And call in more forces from Dhajan City. They can't be allowed to escape, or to warn anyone what's happened. Cut the landlines and shut down the cellular network.'

Al-Asim handed the binoculars back to the technician, then picked up the spearhead. 'Just here at the facility, or . . .'

Alula knew the implications of the unspoken words. 'No,' she said firmly. 'It's time. Over the whole country.'

'It's sooner than planned,' he cautioned. 'Not everybody will be ready.'

'They'll have to improvise. Give the order – Dhajan is now under martial law. Then start my helicopter.' She regarded the cosmic forces seething inside the crystal with almost predatory anticipation. 'I have a ship to catch.'

40

The journey to the test centre under the unblinking sun left the fugitives sweating, parched and exhausted. They reached the entrance with relief, but Nina looked around at a distant noise. The other helicopter was taking off. 'Oh crap.'

But rather than come after them, it headed north. Eddie watched it go. 'Must be Alula going back to Dhajan City.'

'Or the *Pacifia*,' she said. 'She's still got the spearhead.'

Lobato went to the entrance and, grimacing in pain, pressed the palm of his injured hand against a touchscreen. The mirrored doors slid open. 'The medical unit is in here,' he said, limping through.

Eddie paused, seeing a vehicle following a road through the solar plant towards them. 'Shit. They'll be here in a couple of minutes.'

'Can you stabilise him before they get here?' asked Nina as they carried the Emir inside.

'I might be able to get the bullet out, but that's all.' His eyes adjusted to the soft light. While the building was a test facility, it was also a showcase for Lobato's technology, the spacious lobby home to display stands bearing large photographs and scale models of his electric vehicles. 'Christ, it looks like a car dealership. Think we could buy one while we're here?'

'It'd be a fast way out,' Nina replied.

She had meant it as a joke, but then she caught Eddie's eye. 'Oh no,' she said.

'Oh yes,' he countered with a grin. 'Gideon!'

Lobato looked back. 'Yes?'

'This place is where you test your cars, right?'

'Yes?'

The Yorkshireman's smile widened. 'So let's have a test drive.'

An SUV bearing the solar facility's logo pulled up outside the portico. Three guards emerged, drawing their guns. 'They definitely went inside,' said the leader into a radio, peering at the doors but seeing only himself and his companions reflected in the mirrored glass. 'I can't see through the windows, though.'

'Go in and kill them,' was al-Asim's blunt response. 'That's a direct order from Her Majesty. Everyone in that building is a threat to Dhajan and must be eliminated. *Everyone.* Do you understand?'

'Yes, sir,' said the guard, recognising which way the political wind had blown. He replaced the radio on his belt. 'Move in.'

The trio advanced cautiously, the leader sidling to the touch-screen. 'You two cover me. If you see anyone inside, shoot them.'

His companions took their positions. The guard reached up, then hesitated at a noise over the constant whip of wind across the desert. He looked around, but saw nothing. 'What's that?'

The other men tipped their heads. There *was* a new sound, a soft, purring whisper, but it was getting louder.

Getting closer, *fast*—

The mirrored windows burst apart as a sleek and futuristic car smashed through them.

Nina jinked the electric-blue supercar between the guards as they dived out of her way, then swung it towards the pit lane leading to the test track. The cockpit was beyond crowded. Lobato's pride and joy had only three seats, Nina's in the centre with the other two behind on each side. Lobato himself was on the left, the Emir tightly buckled into the right, with Eddie forced to squeeze into a small luggage space behind his wife.

The tinkle of glass faded, replaced as she accelerated by . . . almost nothing. The Raiju was eerily quiet, a muted whine from its electric motors the only sound – except for the distinctly 1970s tune her husband was humming. 'What's that?' she asked.

'*The Professionals* theme,' he replied. She could tell from his tone that he was smirking.

'I don't even want to know . . .'

Gunshots cracked behind them. Carbon fibre splintered as one of the swooping wings sculpted into the rear bodywork took a hit, but the car's mechanical components were undamaged. Nina glanced at where she expected to see a wing mirror, finding instead a small screen set into the window's bottom corner. The rapidly shrinking figures on it sent a few last rounds after them, then ran for their SUV. 'Hope this thing's as fast as it looks.'

'It is faster,' said Lobato, wrapping her headscarf around his wounded hand. She gave him a sardonic glance as she brought the car into the pit exit, then floored the accelerator.

The response felt more like a rocket than a road vehicle, G-forces kicking her into the seat. 'Oh my *God*!' she squealed. 'This ain't no Prius!'

'Nina, ease off!' Eddie barked as the semi-conscious Emir gasped in pain. 'You'll put the bullet out through his bloody back!'

'Sorry,' she said, glancing at the speedometer as she lifted her foot. They were already doing – she blanched – a hundred and seventy kilometres per hour, over a hundred mph. Despite that, the Raiju felt firmly planted on the road, boosting her confidence. 'I don't think we'll have trouble outrunning them. How fast can it go?'

'This car was recently upgraded, but has not yet been fully tested, so I do not know,' said Lobato.

'Okay, but pedantry aside, ballpark figure?'

'It will easily exceed two hundred miles per hour. Our simulations suggested the potential to reach two hundred and seventy. We intended to beat the world record for a road car.'

'Don't think we'll fit the bloke from Guinness in here with us,' said Eddie. He returned his attention to the Emir. 'Okay, let's see what we've got.'

He opened Fadil's jacket and peeled back the bloodied material, then carefully unfastened his shirt to expose his chest. The object in the monarch's pocket had both slowed and deflected the bullet, the entry wound angling into his flesh. Blood oozed out, but to Eddie's relief it was not gushing. He felt the skin around it. The Emir moaned, but the Yorkshireman's fingertips sensed a bump against his ribs that did not belong. 'I can feel the bullet,' he said. 'Gideon, I need forceps or tweezers.'

They had taken an emergency kit from the medical centre. While Lobato searched through it, Eddie took a moment to see what had saved the Emir's life. He removed the rectangular object from his jacket . . . and let out an unexpected laugh.

'What is it?' Nina asked.

'The thing that stopped the bullet?'

'Yeah?'

He held it over her shoulder. 'It's that book Macy made for him!'

The little volume was mangled and blood-soaked, a charred hole almost ripping it in half, but still recognisable. 'You're kidding! He still had it?'

To their surprise, Fadil spoke. 'I thought it was . . . sweet,' he whispered. 'So I left it in my pocket and . . . just happened to choose this suit today. Divine guidance, perhaps . . . or luck. It was indeed . . . useful.'

'Macy'll appreciate that,' said Nina. 'Although I might leave out the gory details when I tell her.'

Lobato found a packet containing a pair of stainless-steel

tweezers. Eddie opened it. 'I'll be as careful as I can, but this'll hurt,' he warned the Dhajani. 'You ready?'

The Emir grimaced. 'Do it.'

'Okay. Nina, hold us steady.'

'Not a problem.' The test track was possibly the smoothest road Nina had ever driven on, and the Raiju's active suspension and aerodynamic aids made it feel as though it was floating above the surface rather than on it. 'But we'll have to turn soon; I can see the main gate.'

'How far?'

'Couple of miles – so at this speed you've got maybe a minute.'

'Slow down, just until I've done this.'

She was shocked to find that without conscious effort she had taken the car to almost a hundred and fifty miles per hour. Bringing it back below the ton now felt as if they were moving at walking pace. 'Okay, I don't want to go any slower – those guys behind'll catch up.'

'This is fine. Right,' Eddie told the Emir, 'here goes.'

The Dhajani clenched his teeth as the Yorkshireman slid the tweezers into the bloody wound. Lobato looked on in white-faced fascination. Eddie kept gently pushing until he felt resistance. His patient let out a strained moan. 'That's the bullet,' he said. 'Let's get it out.'

He gripped the piece of metal, slowly squeezing until the tool had a firm hold, then started to pull. The Emir let out a choked cry. Eddie drew in a sharp breath, but continued.

'Eddie,' said Nina.

'Just a sec,' he told her, easing the tweezers upwards.

'Eddie!'

'*What?*'

'There are two jeeps coming to the gate!'

'Nothing *I* can do about it.'

'Oh, thanks!' Nina stared ahead. They were rapidly approaching the intersection of the test track and the access road. Uphill, two military vehicles were heading for the perimeter barrier – which was lowered, blocking the exit. 'How the hell are we going to get out? Don't suppose this thing has a universal garage door opener?'

'It was not on my list of priorities,' said Lobato.

'Eddie, I'll have to brake for the turn. Hold on—'

'That will not be necessary,' Lobato interrupted. 'The ground-effect system will maintain full grip even at this speed.'

They were still doing over ninety. 'You've gotta be kidding,' said Nina in disbelief.

'Trust me.'

The tweezers were inside the injured man's chest. 'If you're wrong, it's the Emir's life,' Eddie warned.

'He is my friend,' said the billionaire simply. 'I do not want him to die – so trust me.'

Nina swallowed. 'Okay . . .' she said, forcing herself not to brake as they swept into the intersection. Instead, she turned the wheel to bring the car down an off-ramp. To her amazement, it obeyed without the slightest fuss. She was expecting to have to grapple with the wheel, but the Raiju might as well have been on rails, the suspension adjusting automatically to minimise the lateral G-forces. 'Jeez! Is this for real?'

'It could go even faster in autonomous mode,' noted Lobato. 'The computer can drive better than any human.'

'We'll put it into KITT mode when we don't have anyone shooting at us,' said Eddie. He looked past Nina. 'Which is going to happen any second!'

The car swept out of the bend on to the access road. The two guards hurried from the gatehouse, the jeeps approaching the other side of the barrier – which was still down. 'Oh crap!' said Nina. 'What do we do?'

Eddie stared at the striped pole. 'It's about waist-high – Gideon, how tall's this car?'

He was not surprised to get more than an approximation. 'One thousand and fourteen millimetres.'

'So, a metre – Nina, go *under* it!'

'We'll never make it!' she protested.

'The front's sloped, it'll act like a wedge.'

'Okay, but everyone better keep their heads down!'

They hunched as low as they could as she aimed the car at the barrier, Eddie hurriedly withdrawing the tweezers. The guards waved for her to halt, then ran clear when they realised she was not going to stop—

The supercar's nose whipped under the barrier – then the polycarbonate windscreen struck the metal pole itself. The whole car shook, the window's top crazing with the impact, but the obstruction was flung upwards. Nina gasped in fright, but kept going, swerving around the jeeps as they tried to block her way and reaching the open road beyond.

She stamped on the accelerator. The car leapt forward, shoving her back into the seat. 'Easy, easy!' Eddie shouted. 'There's a man here with a hole in his fucking chest!'

She lifted her foot off, bringing the Raiju more gently up to a hundred along the road into the mountains. A hard-edged trill came from the dashboard, a speed limit sign flashing up on one of its displays; the car was warning her that she was breaking the local traffic laws now she was on a public road, but she didn't care. 'Okay, we're clear,' she said, checking the rear-view screens. 'So where are we going to go? Meet Rahji and get back into Saudi Arabia?'

'No, no. If . . . we can get to Dhajan City,' the Emir whispered, speech a strain, 'I know a . . . place that will be safe.'

'That's a big if,' said Eddie.

'You have got me . . . this far. I have faith. It is . . . *all* I have!'

442

Nina checked a large touchscreen to the right of the wheel. It showed a map, the highway a straight line heading north. She pushed a button to zoom out until the series of curves descending towards the coast came into view. 'We've got a couple of miles before things get twisty,' she said. 'If you're going to get that bullet out of him, now's the time.'

Eddie looked back at the Emir. 'You holding up?'

'No,' he replied. 'But the pain means . . . I am not dead!'

'It'll be over soon. Hopefully in the good way.' The Yorkshireman brought the tweezers back to the wound. 'I've got to find the bullet again,' he told the Dhajani, slipping the bloodied metal pincer back into the hole.

The Emir tensed, trying not to cry out. Eddie probed deeper. The tweezers found the bullet where he had been forced to leave it. The tips caught it, then slipped off. He tried again—

'Got it!' he exclaimed as they found a firm hold. 'Okay, let's get it out.'

He eased the piece of metal upwards, only for a rivulet of blood to sluice from the wound. The Emir spasmed. Eddie halted. He had to apply pressure to slow the bleeding while he worked, but in his awkward position he needed his other hand to support himself. 'Gideon! Put your hand above the hole and press on it.'

Lobato twisted and tried to reach past the Englishman with his uninjured hand, but there was not enough room. 'I can't.'

'Shit!' Eddie attempted to straighten, but the cabin roof was too low. 'Nina, he's bleeding, but I can't do anything about it like this. You'll have to stop so I can—'

'Wait, wait,' she said. 'Gideon, the auto-drive – it's really as good as you say?'

'It is,' Lobato replied.

'Okay, how do I turn it on?'

'Hey, car,' he said. An airy chime came from the dash in response. 'Auto mode.'

'Destination?' a female voice asked.

'Dhajan City.'

'Confirmed.' The displays in front of Nina changed colour, taking on a purple tone. Simultaneously, the mood lights around the cabin did the same.

The wheel twitched in her hands. 'Whoa!' she yipped.

'You can let go,' Lobato told her. 'The purple lights mean it is now in fully autonomous mode.'

'But it's slowing down.' The speedometer dropped to precisely one hundred and twenty kilometres per hour.

'It is programmed to obey national speed limits. If we need to go faster, you can deactivate it.'

'The Emir'll be deactivated in a minute,' Eddie warned impatiently. 'Nina, can you help me?'

'Hold on.' She unfastened her seat belt, then, fighting every instinct gained in years of driving, pulled herself around to face backwards, trusting the computer to do its job. To her relief, it continued along the road without so much as a twitch. 'Okay, where do you want me to press?'

'Just above the wound,' he told her. She held her hand against the Emir's chest. He flinched, drawing in a shuddering breath. Blood was still trickling from the bullet hole, but the pressure had slowed the flow. 'Thanks. Just keep it there for a minute . . .' Eddie teased the bullet upwards. 'Nearly got it, nearly . . .'

'Oh!' Lobato said in alarm. 'Look!'

'Little *busy*, Gideon,' Nina hissed.

'But there is another helicopter!'

She glanced ahead. The angular black dot of an aircraft was visible above the mountains, coming straight towards them. 'Crap! Eddie, I think it's another gunship.'

The Yorkshireman couldn't look away, a glint of metal visible within the gore. 'Get back on the wheel.'

'But he'll start bleeding again—'

'*We'll* be bleeding if they shoot at us! We need to go faster – and start dodging!'

Nina reluctantly withdrew. A gush of trapped blood immediately escaped from the wound. Eddie had no choice but to ignore it. He worked the tweezers upwards, the bullet taking on form inside the wet redness. 'Almost got it, almost . . .'

His wife took the wheel. The helicopter – another Apache – was dropping towards them. 'How do I take back control?' she asked Lobato.

'Just push the brake,' he said.

She tapped it gently. The purple lighting instantly reverted to its earlier colours. 'Manual control restored,' the car told her breezily. 'Please use caution.'

'Sorry, car, not happening,' she replied, accelerating again. Her gaze snapped between the approaching gunship and the road, watching for the first sign of cannon fire—

The chain gun flashed, smoke belching out behind it. Nina swung the car to the other side of the road as a line of tracer rounds streaked down at them. 'They're shooting, they're shooting!'

'Yeah, I gathered!' Eddie snapped, bracing himself. A series of crackling detonations came from outside as the incoming shells hit the road beside them. Shrapnel clattered against the car's flank, but it was already powering clear.

He looked back at the Emir's chest. The bullet was almost free. One last pull. He steadied himself, then eased the tweezers upwards—

'*Gotcha!*'

The Emir gasped as he tugged the bullet clear, and held it up to the light. Macy's book had robbed the round of much of its lethal force, the piece of lead mashed flat. 'The bullet's out,' he announced. 'I'll bandage him up – you get us out of here!'

Nina saw more fire erupt from the chain gun. 'Hang on!' She darted back across the road, shells bursting along the car's previous course, then accelerated hard. More searing rounds streaked directly overhead to explode behind them. The Apache continued its descent towards the road, as if trying to physically block their path. 'It's coming straight at us!'

'Just keep going,' said Eddie. He pressed his hand over the Emir's wound. 'Gideon, bandages! Now!'

She weaved from side to side, using the road's whole width to avoid the lancing cannon rounds. The gunship rushed at her, still dropping – then suddenly pulled up. Lobato shrieked as the car whipped beneath it, a rush of rotor-blasted sand and spent shell casings battering the windscreen. 'Holy *crap!*' Nina cried. 'That was too close!'

She checked the rear-view screens. The Apache was turning in place. She jammed her right foot down, hard. The Raiju's motors whined to full power, again throwing everyone backwards. This time, she didn't ease off. The speedo shot past one hundred, one-fifty, and kept rising. The helicopter fired again, but the cannon rounds hit nothing but the empty road behind them. It tipped nose-down and climbed in pursuit.

But the gap between the car and the chopper was still widening. 'How fast can an Apache go?' Nina asked.

Eddie put a gauze pad over the wound. 'I dunno – two hundred knots or so?'

It took her only a moment to convert the measurement. 'That's about two hundred and thirty miles per hour – we can outrun it!'

'We can't outrun its gun, though.'

'But if we get far enough ahead, it can't lock on to us. If it just keeps firing and trying to get lucky, it'll run out of ammo!' She

446

pushed her foot all the way down. The desert became a blur.

'How long before we get to the twisty bit, though?'

'A couple of—' She checked the map, and saw they were almost at the weaving section of road. '*Seconds!* Oh shit!'

The landscape opened out as the Raiju rocketed towards the end of the high plain. Nina slowed, hard, panels on the car's rear popping up to act as air brakes. One-fifty, one hundred, the first bend swinging away to the right. She had to fight with the wheel to maintain control. 'Shit, *shit!*' she gasped as the barrier came closer, the chevron signs flicking past like a stroboscope. 'Come on, come on . . .'

The car lurched as all four wheels finally regained grip. She gasped, sweeping through the bend – only to have to slow again as the road snaked back the other way around the canyon's edge. 'What happened? It felt like it was glued to the road before!'

Lobato's eyes were as wide as an owl's. 'I do not believe it is a fault with the car.'

'Oh, so I'm a bad driver?' she shot back. 'I'd like to see *you* do any better!'

'I doubt I could – but the computer can. Hey, car.' The chime sounded again. 'Assisted mode.'

The displays and lighting changed colour again, this time turning turquoise rather than purple. The wheel squirmed in Nina's hands once more. 'What's that?' she asked suspiciously.

'The car will steer itself, but you control the speed,' he replied.

'How fast can we go?'

'I do not know, but it will not let you crash.'

'Sure, and the *Titanic* was unsinkable,' she retorted. But she lifted her hands from the wheel, unable to escape a sense of unease as it turned without her assistance. The speedo read barely forty-five. She cautiously lowered her right foot. The needle rose, the car continuing to navigate the road with no difficulty. Sixty, now past the point where her own nerve would have failed, but it followed the lane perfectly. 'This is just . . . weird.'

Eddie had a more pressing concern. 'Where's the chopper?'

The answer came as the car swept around a tight bend – and the Apache came into sight off to their left, charging down the canyon after them. 'You had to ask!' Nina complained, accelerating again—

Nothing happened. The chiding alert sounded. The automatic systems not only warned the driver about speed limits; they enforced them. 'Oh come on!' she shouted. 'Go faster, you stupid—'

'Wait, wait!' said Lobato. He reached past Nina to a dashboard panel. As well as the inevitable touchscreen, this had a small cross-shaped joypad and some buttons. He hurriedly tapped at them. 'Up, up, down, down, left, right . . .'

The helicopter was rapidly approaching, but held fire. Nina wondered if it was low on ammo, or if the gunner simply wanted to get in close to prevent the supercar from taking evasive action. Not that it could. As long as the computer was in control, she was limited to going slower or faster, and right now couldn't even manage the latter. 'What're you doing?' she demanded.

'. . . and A!' Lobato concluded. 'Hey, car! Disable speed limiter!'

'Disabling the speed limiter may result in legal penalties,' the car replied. 'Lobato Inc. cannot be held liable—'

'Confirm, confirm!'

'Speed limiter disabled. Please drive responsibly.'

'God, it's as annoying as its creator!' Eddie sniped.

'Now what?' Nina asked.

Lobato sat back. 'Go!'

She shoved down the pedal just as the helicopter opened fire.

Cannon rounds exploded behind the Raiju as it surged forward, the needle leaping past the speed limit – and well beyond as it kept accelerating. Nina had to force her hands away from the wheel as they swept into a seemingly suicidal series of turns. But the car remained planted on the road, the computer's icy confidence unshakeable.

She looked for the helicopter. Its crew were equally surprised by the supercar's abilities, but they quickly recovered, the gunship drawing alongside. The gunner's head turned towards her, the turret beneath the cockpit matching the movement.

Locking on—

She stamped on the brake.

The deceleration was so violent, not even the car's driving aids could fully compensate. The Raiju fishtailed, burning black streaks of rubber on to the asphalt as the cannon fire ripped into the cliff along the roadside ahead of it. The gunner turned to track his target, but the Apache had already flown on, the gun hitting the limit of its firing arc.

With their seat belts unfastened, Nina and Lobato were pitched forward; only her braced legs kept her from ending up in the footwell, while the billionaire crashed into the dash. Eddie, wedged against the back of Nina's seat, came off better, but was still sent flailing. 'For fuck's sake!' he yelled over the Emir's scream. 'You *trying* to kill him?'

'Oh shut up!' Nina snapped, her patience at an end. The gunship was already looping around for another attack. She accelerated again. The sudden stop had not affected the car, which quickly regained its insane speed through the curves. 'Hang on – I'll have to weave in a few seconds!'

The Apache completed its sweeping turn. The cannon tilted down to find its target—

Nina gripped the steering wheel, then tapped the brake with her left foot, while keeping her right firmly planted on the accelerator. The turquoise lights went out. She clenched her jaw and jinked into the other lane as the gunship opened fire.

The impacts were much closer this time. The Raiju shook as blasts pummelled its side, metal fragments punching through the carbon-fibre bodywork and cracking the rear window. She applied another burst of speed – then braked hard, swerving back into her original lane. Another furious burst of cannon shells stitched holes into the road ahead, then the firing stopped as the Apache overshot them again.

Another bend swept the supercar into a fold in the canyon's side. Nina powered through it. They were already nearing the bottom of the winding road. The desert plain leading to the Dhajani coast came into view as she rounded the final curve. 'Hey, car, assisted mode,' she gasped. The displays regained their turquoise tinge.

Foot down again, the needle flicking upwards as the Raiju descended on to the long, straight highway. She searched for the Apache. It had fallen behind, making a second looping turn for another attack run only to realise too late that its prey had reached its natural habitat: the open road.

'Okay,' she said. 'Let's see what this baby can do.'

Even though they were again exceeding a hundred miles per hour, the acceleration was still forceful enough to give the car's occupants a jolt of adrenalin. At one hundred and fifty, the ride remained smooth; only when they passed the two hundred mark did it start to vibrate, the sheer volume of wind rushing over the bodywork causing turbulence even as the fins and flaps adjusted to smooth the airflow.

'How's the Emir?' she asked Eddie.

He had finished covering the wound. 'He'll be okay if we get him to a hospital fast enough.'

'I don't think speed'll be a problem.' They were at almost two hundred and fifty mph, covering a mile every fifteen seconds. Nina was glad the computer was handling the steering; even on a straight, empty road, she wasn't confident she could react quickly enough to avoid anything they encountered.

'Unless that chopper starts shooting again.'

She checked the rear view. The Apache was now just a sand-coloured spot against the rocky backdrop, the supercar easily outpacing it. 'They're not firing. Out of ammo, or . . .'

'Or there's something else ahead of us,' Eddie concluded grimly.

Lobato struggled back into his seat. 'We need to decide where we are going.'

'I will . . . tell the computer,' said the Emir weakly. 'Hey, car?' The chime sounded, and he spoke to it in Arabic. It confirmed his command in the same language, the map zooming out to show a route to an address in Dhajan City. 'An old friend. Someone I . . . I trust with my life.'

'Bet you thought that about Alula, though,' said Eddie.

'I did. I hope I have not . . . made two mistakes . . . in one day.'

'Oh, me and Nina usually manage eight or nine.'

'Before breakfast,' Nina added. The car briefly overrode her control of the accelerator, slowing to a mere two hundred to bring itself on to the coastal highway. 'Hey, there's Rahji—' The Saudi's parked SUV flashed from dot ahead to blur to dot behind. 'There *was* Rahji.'

'At this speed, we will reach the city in just over a minute,' said Lobato. The Raiju guided itself around a lone car traversing the route, then snapped back into its original lane.

The skyscrapers of Dhajan City rose over the dunes, the highway a shimmering black line sweeping towards them. Nina frowned as shapes emerged from the heat haze. 'There's something on the road. Something big.'

Lobato peered ahead. 'Trucks?'

Eddie looked past his wife. 'No – those are fucking *tanks*!'

'Oh crap,' she gasped. 'They really, *really* want to stop us! Is there another way to the city?'

'Not . . . from here,' the Emir told her. 'This is the only road.'

'So we've got to get past them.' The squat and angular war machines rapidly took on form, main guns pointing ahead as they rolled side by side along the highway. Nina accelerated once more.

'You sure about this?' asked the Yorkshireman. 'You're driving straight at a couple of Leclercs at two hundred miles an hour!'

'I'm going to drive straight *between* them – well, the car is. Gideon, can it do that?'

Lobato stared at the rapidly approaching tanks. 'It is not a situation that has been simulated . . .'

'Great! Let's hope we're moving faster than they can aim!'

They would find out all too soon. The supercar had eaten up the distance in seconds, racing towards the tanks like a wheeled missile. Nina glanced at the speedo. Two-sixty, and the computer was not trying to slow down. It had apparently calculated that it could fit through the gap, and she was now committed to trusting its judgement.

She looked back up – to see the turrets turning towards her.

'Incoming!' she gasped—

Both tanks opened fire, but with their secondary machine guns rather than the main cannons. Tracer rounds streaked at the car, the initial sprays going wide before the gunners homed in on their target. Nina had to force herself not to grab the wheel to swerve. Their lives depended on the computer.

The searing lines of bullets closed in – and hit.

Rounds ripped into the car's nose, shards of shattered carbon fibre flying up over the windscreen, which cracked as the bullets punched through the polycarbonate. The whole vehicle shuddered as the incoming fire hit the heavy battery packs. Nina ducked, Lobato shrieking—

The pounding suddenly ceased, even though the guns were

still firing. The Raiju was closing so quickly, the gunners couldn't redirect their weapons fast enough to track it.

The supercar rocketed towards the gap between the two tanks. But they were now turning towards each other, trying to block its path.

Nina cringed and closed her eyes—

A *whump* of displaced air jolted the car as it shot through the narrowing space with mere inches to spare. If it had had wing mirrors, they would have been sheared off. She opened her eyes again to see the tanks rapidly receding in the rear-view screens. 'Jesus!' she cried, scarcely believing she was still alive. 'We made it!'

'Still got to get to where we're going,' Eddie reminded her, raising his voice over the roar of wind through bullet holes. One of the dashboard screens was broken, the round that had smashed through it buried in the side padding of Lobato's seat. 'Everyone okay?'

'Yes,' said the shocked billionaire, 'but the car is damaged.' A surviving screen was flashing urgent warnings. 'The batteries are on fire!'

'The same kind of batteries as at the solar plant?' said Nina. 'The same kind of batteries that *exploded like a goddamn – bomb* when they got too hot?'

'Time to get out,' said Eddie. 'Where are we?'

They were approaching the fringes of Dhajan City. A couple of miles ahead was the country's main harbour, tower cranes and hulking container ships rising high above the water, but all were dwarfed by the *Atlantia*. The liner had returned to its home port for repairs, its long voyage completed just in time to witness the departure of its sister ship. Inland, the gleaming skyscrapers of the city's business district stabbed into the blue sky, but the map told them they would soon turn away towards the suburbs. 'We are going to . . . my friend Mamun bin Junayd,' the Emir said, struggling to be heard over the wind. 'He was my mentor in the . . . Dhajani army. A good man. A loyal man.'

'Let's hope he's loyal to you personally,' said Nina. She checked the map. About a mile and a half to go, the freeway exit not far ahead. 'Is it always this quiet?' Even as they entered the city's outskirts, there was a distinct lack of traffic.

'No,' said Lobato, concerned. 'This road is always busy.'

'That'd be why.' Eddie pointed to the bottom of the approaching slip road. There was a jumbled line of stationary vehicles at the intersection, where a military roadblock had been hastily erected. 'Alula's kicked off her coup!'

Smoke started to boil from the vents and bullet holes in the car's nose. An alarming sizzling sound rose; more batteries overheating as the flames from the damaged packs spread. 'This thing's about to kick off too,' said Nina as an acrid stench hit her nostrils. Another glance at the map: less than a mile to their destination. 'We've got to get out!'

'We will . . . never get past the soldiers,' groaned the Emir.

Eddie coughed as more smoke coiled past him – then jabbed a finger at the roadside. 'Stop here, stop!' he snapped.

Nina knew from his tone that he had a plan. She braked hard, halting the Raiju alongside a large billboard. The hoarding was directly in line with the roadblock, obscuring them from the waiting soldiers' view. She swung up the scissor door and clambered out, Lobato exiting too as Eddie unbuckled the Emir and lifted him from the car.

'This will not hide us for long,' said Lobato. 'The soldiers are waiting for us – they will come looking!'

'They're waiting for the *car*,' Eddie corrected. Still supporting the wounded man, he leaned back into the cabin. 'Hey, car! Auto mode.'

'Destination?' the computer asked.

'Er . . . the current one?'

'Confirmed. Please close all doors to proceed.'

He slammed the door, signalling Lobato to do the same. The billionaire looked confused, but did so. The moment both were shut, the smoking supercar set off – with nobody inside it. 'Quick, over here,' Eddie said. He and Nina carried the Emir towards the end of the billboard.

Lobato hurried after them. 'What are you doing?'

'Causing a distraction.' Eddie leaned around the hoarding to observe the slip road. The car was already heading down it, the soldiers at the junction raising their weapons. Civilians trapped by the roadblock scrambled from their cars as they opened fire.

The Raiju's windows blew apart, bodywork fragmenting as rifle bullets riddled it. But it kept coming, the computer still guiding it onwards until its sensors picked up the stalled traffic ahead. It came neatly to a stop at the rear of the muddled line even as the soldiers kept shooting.

The squad's commander let loose a final burst, then shouted a command to cease fire. He advanced warily, weapon trained on the pockmarked cabin. His men followed, all reacting in surprise as they saw there was nobody inside . . .

Flames gushed out from beneath the stationary vehicle – and its burning, bullet-torn batteries exploded.

The soldiers scrambled for cover as blazing lithium fragments rained around them. Panicked screams rang across the inter-section.

'Come on,' said Eddie, starting down a sandy embankment. Nina helped him with the Emir, Lobato limping along behind them. Low-rise housing blocks backed on to the highway; they scaled the wall of the dusty garden area behind one and headed for the road on its other side. 'Hope you remember how to get to your mate's house,' the Yorkshireman said to the Emir.

'I do,' came the strained reply. 'It is not far.'

'Listen!' said Lobato in alarm. Over the shouts and cries from the roadblock came the rattle of more gunfire. This was from further away, within the city itself.

'Sounds like people aren't happy about your sister taking over,' Eddie said. 'This keeps up, you'll have a civil war on your hands.'

The Emir moaned. 'Alula, what have you *done*? People will *die* because of you!'

'A *lot* of people, if the spearhead blows up in Bahrain,' Nina reminded him. 'We've got to stop her.'

'How?' asked Lobato.

She gave him a fraught look. 'I'll tell you as soon as I know myself.'

41

Alula gazed from the co-pilot's seat of the royal helicopter at the vessel below. The *Pacifia*, identical bar minor cosmetic features to its sister ship, sat stationary in the blue waters of the Gulf of Salwah. It had departed on its maiden voyage a few hours earlier, heading northwards on what was scheduled to be a four-day cruise around the more tourist-friendly quarters of the Persian Gulf.

It would not complete it.

The spearhead sat in a metal case on her lap. She opened it. The strange light spilled out, bright even in the midday sun. What was going on inside the crystal, she wasn't sure – but then *nobody* knew for sure, Wilde and Lobato and everyone else with a theory offering nothing more than that: a *theory*. What mattered was what would happen in practice. And based on Wilde's discoveries in Turkey, it would do exactly what its creators had claimed.

Obliterate her country's enemies.

The pilot responded to a radio message. 'We're cleared for landing, Your Majesty.'

'Good,' she replied. 'Have the captain meet me on the pad.'

She closed the lid, leaning back as the Sikorsky S-76 descended. The *Pacifia* had stopped to receive its unexpected visitor, but she wanted it under way again as soon as possible. It would take over three hours to reach Bahrain, and she needed the huge ship to be at its target when the spearhead exploded.

The helicopter dropped towards the *Pacifia*'s bow, bay doors swinging open and landing gear extending. Passengers lounging on the upper deck watched as if its arrival was another show laid on for their amusement. *Parasites*, she thought with contempt. These were the people Fadil had been so intent on courting? Prostituting their country for fat, debauched old Westerners?

She hid her disgust as the S-76 landed side-on to the super-structure, presenting her door to the waiting officers. The moment the wheels came to rest, crew members scurried to secure them with steel cables.

Al-Asim exited first, surveying the bow for potential threats before opening Alula's door as the rest of his team of seven men emerged. She passed him the case. He held it in one hand, extending his other to help her out. 'Your Majesty,' he said as she stepped down.

'Thank you, Hashim,' she said. Heads low beneath the still-whirling rotor blades, they strode across the helipad to the waiting contingent.

A grey-bearded man in a crisp white uniform stepped forward to greet her. 'Your Royal Highness,' he said, bowing. 'I'm Jesper Ingels, captain of the *Pacifia*. We are all honoured to have you aboard for our maiden voyage.' The Dane peered past her at the helicopter. 'I was under the impression the Emir himself would also be here?'

Alula fixed him with a cold look. 'There has been a change of government. *I* am now the Emira.'

He was shocked. 'I . . . I am not sure what to say.'

'You can start by pledging your loyalty to Her Majesty,' growled al-Asim.

'Of course, of course!' Ingels bowed again, more deeply. 'Your Royal Hi— Your *Majesty*, on behalf of the *Pacifia*'s officers and crew, I extend our deepest congratulations and respect.' He looked up at her. 'Does this mean the previous Emir is—'

'My brother is dead,' Alula said curtly. 'I have declared a state of emergency in Dhajan to ensure calm. As this is a Dhajani-flagged vessel, the same applies here.'

'But we are in international waters, so . . .' The captain saw her growing hostility and hastily changed tack. 'But as you say, this is a Dhajani vessel. What are your orders, Your Majesty?'

Alula marched towards the superstructure's entrance, al-Asim and his men forming a protective cordon around her. Ingels and his staff hurriedly followed. 'I want all communications cut off,' she told him. 'Cell phones, two-way radio, satellite television, internet – everything.'

'*Everything?*' echoed Ingels in alarm.

'Her Majesty does not want the passengers panicked by news of what has happened in Dhajan,' al-Asim told him.

'I see. But would it not be better—'

'You will also set course for Manama harbour in Bahrain,' Alula went on. 'Get under way immediately.'

Ingels became more concerned by the moment. 'But we aren't scheduled to stop there for three days. With everything that has happened in Dhajan, wouldn't you prefer to be there rather than in Bahrain?'

'Do not question Her Majesty!' snapped al-Asim. 'Cut off all external communications, and set course for Manama. Now!'

They entered the ship. 'What should I tell the passengers?' the captain asked.

'Tell them nothing,' Alula replied.

'Your Majesty,' he said, standing straighter, 'the safety of the passengers is my absolute priority as captain. If there is anything that—'

Alula stopped and faced him, her bodyguards shifting position to trap him in a menacing circle. The other officers retreated, worried and confused. Even though the Dane was a head taller, he shrank back as she leaned closer, almost snarling her words. 'The passengers will be safe. Your job is not. If you do not do as I say, I will replace you with someone who will – and have you arrested.'

'Arrested!' Ingels cried. 'On what charge?'

'We are in a state of emergency,' said al-Asim. 'Failure to obey Her Majesty's orders is a crime.'

The captain summoned all his remaining reserves of dignity. 'Very well. I will do as you say. But I must put the safety of the passengers above all other demands – even yours, Your Majesty.' He delivered the title with just a hint of challenge.

'Just do as you are told,' Alula ordered.

The guards pulled back. Ingels gestured to one of his men for a walkie-talkie, then used it to speak to a bridge officer. 'Get us under way. Set course for Bahrain – I'll confirm the heading when I get up there. And close down all external comms, including the cellular phone masts.' That last predictably provoked questions. 'Just follow my orders,' he said.

The officer acknowledged. 'Good,' said Alula. 'Now take us to the bridge.'

The elderly bearded man shook his head as he finished applying bandages to the Emir's chest. 'I always said you were careless, *al'amir alshabu*,' he sighed. 'So much time spent thinking about the future that you don't see what's happening right now.'

'Thank you for your support, Mamun,' the Emir said weakly, managing a half-smile.

The group had made their way to the modest but comfortable detached house of retired colonel Mamun bin Junayd, the ruler's former mentor. A high wall around it ensured their privacy. 'Will he be okay?' Nina asked.

Junayd stood back. Despite no longer being in the military, the Emir's old commanding officer had still been prepared for action, producing a well-stocked medical kit after overcoming his shock at finding Dhajan's wounded monarch at his door.

With Eddie's assistance, he had cleaned and disinfected the wound, then stitched it closed. 'He is stable,' he announced as he washed his hands. 'But he needs to go to a hospital.'

'Not an option right now,' said Eddie, joining him. 'If Alula's people find him, they'll kill him.'

The older man shook his head again. 'Alula. Hmph! I always thought she was an angry girl. But angry enough to try to murder you?' he remarked to his patient. 'I would not have believed that.'

'If men kept calling me "girl", I'd be angry too,' Nina said sarcastically.

Junayd dried his hands. 'And who are you again?'

She bristled, but the Emir spoke before she could give a cutting answer. 'She is Dr Nina Wilde, the famous archaeologist, and she saved my life. So please, treat her with the same respect you would give me.'

The colonel looked surprised, then bowed his head. 'Of course, Your Majesty.' He turned to Nina. 'I am sorry. I meant no disrespect. This has come as . . . a surprise.'

'To me too,' said the Emir. 'Help me up.'

'I do not think that would be wise.'

'If I had been wise, I would not be in this situation. Please.' Reluctantly Junayd and Eddie helped him sit upright. Even after taking painkillers, agony still shot across his face. 'You . . . were right. That was not wise.'

Lobato was relieved. 'But you are still alive. That is what is most important.'

'What's most important is stopping Alula before she kills a few million people,' said Nina. 'How are we going to do it? She's probably aboard the *Pacifia* already.'

'We need to warn the US Navy in Bahrain,' said Eddie. 'If they know there's a nuke-sized bomb heading their way, they'll do everything they can to stop it.'

'But how can we warn them? I doubt it'll be as simple as

phoning the naval base and saying, "Hey guys, you might want to stop that ship."'

'Can't hurt to try.' There was a landline phone in the room; he picked it up. 'Or maybe it can.' An Arabic voice was already coming from it. 'Dunno what they're saying, but I doubt it's good.'

Junayd took the phone. 'A recording,' he said grimly. 'The Emir is dead . . . murdered by foreign terrorists. State of emergency, martial law declared . . .'

'Foreign terrorists?' Lobato said, puzzled. 'What foreign terrorists?'

'They mean us,' Nina explained.

'Don't know if you noticed, but the Emir's not dead either,' Eddie added. 'It's this new-fangled thing called lying.'

'The cellular networks and internet will also have been shut down,' said the Emir. 'Unless we can get out of the country, we will not be able to contact anyone – and all routes will now be under Alula's control.' He turned at a noise from outside: a voice echoing from a loudhailer, issuing orders. 'They are telling everyone to stay in their homes and await instructions from the Emira.' He scowled at the thought of his usurper.

The voice grew louder, then gradually Dopplered away as the vehicle carrying the speaker continued past. 'But if you show yourself, that will prove she is not telling the truth,' Lobato suggested.

Eddie shook his head. 'Can't risk it. Even if the regular soldiers are still loyal, as soon as any officer who's on Alula's team gets involved, the Emir'll be whisked to somewhere "safe". And nowhere's safer than a grave.'

'Then we've got to go after the spearhead itself,' said Nina. 'It could enter the final stage any time, if it hasn't already. We've only got a few hours before it explodes.'

'How?' asked Junayd. 'If this bomb is on a ship, the only way to reach it is by helicopter. And every helicopter in the country will be under guard.'

'Plus Alula and al-Asim are bound to have backup with 'em, just in case the crew decide they don't want to go on a suicide cruise,' Eddie added. 'They'd shoot down a chopper before it could put anyone aboard. Same with a boat.' He paused, suddenly thoughtful.

'What is it?' Nina asked him.

'Unless it was a *big* boat . . .' He turned to the Emir. 'Dhajan's navy – have you got any ships that could stop something the size of the *Pacifia*?'

'I am afraid not,' was the reply. 'Dhajan is only a small country, and the American navy handles most of our defence in the Persian Gulf. We have patrol boats and a few corvettes, but that is all.'

'Our naval base will also be protected by Alula's forces,' said Junayd. 'Even if we had any larger ships, we would never reach them.'

'You've got *one* ship that's larger,' Nina said, remembering what she had seen while approaching the city. 'A *lot* larger – the *Atlantia*! It won't be as heavily guarded as the navy base.'

'You are suggesting we chase a cruise liner . . . in a cruise liner?' said the Emir in disbelief.

'They won't be able to stop it once it gets moving,' Eddie pointed out. 'And you wanted to try for a speed record – now's your chance. Stick your override code in, redline the engines, and we might catch the *Pacifia* before it reaches Bahrain.'

'And then what?' said Lobato. 'Even if we get on the other ship, and even if we take control of the spearhead, we will be trapped aboard with a bomb!'

'I don't know,' protested Nina. 'But at least we have a chance.' She turned to the Emir. 'If it's the only option we have, we've got to try it.'

'The ship's got satellite links and ship-to-shore radio, an' all,' said her husband. 'If we can get aboard, we can warn someone.'

Fadil looked pensive. 'It is not the option I would choose, but . . . you are right, Dr Wilde. Any smaller boat would be blown out of the water by our own ships, but the *Atlantia* . . . I am not even sure the Americans could sink a ship so large.'

'They might have to try,' Eddie warned. 'How do we get to the port? If Alula's forces are in control of the city, we're bound to run into them.'

Junayd stroked his chin. 'There may be a way. But you will have to give me a few minutes.'

'Why?' asked the Emir.

'Because, *al'amir alshabu*, I need to change into my old uniform,' the retired soldier said with a wry smile. 'It has been some time since I last wore it – it may not fit!'

It was a squeeze, Junayd having to suck in his stomach before he could fasten his uniform jacket, but he managed. 'I can hardly breathe,' he complained, regarding himself in a mirror and straightening his collar. 'I should have kept up my exercises. But it is so easy to fall out of good habits when you have nothing to work for.'

'I should never have let you retire,' said the Emir, putting a hand on his shoulder. 'If you had stayed at my side, perhaps none of this would have happened.'

'Who knows?' Junayd straightened. 'But we don't have time to waste on such thoughts. We must stop Alula.'

'We can start now,' said Eddie. 'Another jeep's coming.' An amplified voice was slowly growing louder.

Junayd donned a belt and holster, then retrieved a metal box from a drawer and took out an automatic. 'You're a bit short on ammo,' the Yorkshireman noted. The gun was missing its magazine.

'I never thought I would need any,' the old soldier replied, slipping the weapon into the holster.

'Hope they don't look too closely,' said Nina. The open space in the gun's grip was clearly visible.

The Emir smiled. 'They will have more to worry about, trust me.'

Lobato had gone upstairs to watch the street. 'I can see them coming!' he called.

Junayd donned a black beret, then marched to the front door. 'I will be back soon,' he told his guests, before speaking in Arabic to the Emir. The two men embraced, then the older stepped outside.

The moment he was gone, the Dhajani gasped in pain and staggered to a seat. 'Are you okay?' Nina asked.

'I will be fine,' he whispered, breathing heavily.

'Looks to me like you were trying to impress him with how tough you are.'

A strained chuckle. 'It would seem that, once again, I cannot fool you for long.'

'I'll look after him,' Eddie said. 'You see what's happening outside.'

Nina hurried upstairs. Lobato was hunched beside the bedroom window. 'What's going on?' she asked.

'There is a Humvee coming,' the billionaire replied. 'Junayd is walking towards it.'

Nina peeked out at the street. About a hundred yards away was a Dhajani military vehicle, a man's voice booming from a loudspeaker. Soldiers armed with rifles leaned from the windows, watching for anyone breaking the newly imposed curfew. They all turned to aim at Junayd, only to waver at the sight of his uniform.

The colonel signalled for the Humvee to approach, standing with his hands on his hips as he waited. It halted beside him.

A junior officer spoke insouciantly from the front passenger seat.

Junayd said nothing for a long moment, merely glaring at him until the young man become visibly nervous – then he erupted, bellowing into his face. The lieutenant scrambled out and stood to attention, his comrades hurriedly following suit. Junayd continued his tirade, circling the hapless officer like a shark before finally standing before him, shaking his head.

'Wow,' said Nina. 'Even I'm scared, and I know he's not in the army any more!'

Junayd was now issuing orders. The soldier got back into the 4x4 and gabbled into a radio handset, then spoke to the colonel again. Junayd nodded, then waved a dismissive hand before turning on his heel and starting towards the house without a backwards glance. The other soldiers quickly returned to the Humvee, which set off, moving considerably faster than before. The officer's voice echoed from the loudspeaker again, but his first few words were quavery enough that he had to clear his throat before resuming in a forced baritone.

Lobato and Nina hurried downstairs to meet Junayd. 'What on earth did you say to them?' she asked.

'The same I would have said if I was still serving,' he replied, amused. 'A state of emergency is no excuse for lax discipline! But,' he went on, 'I told them I had been called to duty, but my car had not arrived. So I ordered them to radio a friend of mine – someone I trust completely,' he added to the Emir, 'and tell him to pick me up. We will then have a military vehicle to take us to the port.'

'Very clever,' said the Emir admiringly. 'I am glad you are on our side!'

'Always and for ever, Your Majesty.' Junayd saluted him.

'So now we just wait for the car?' said Nina.

He nodded. 'He will be here soon.'

'I hope so,' Eddie said. 'Because the *Pacifia*'s getting further away every minute.'

Alula stood on the liner's bridge, staring imperiously through the broad windows. The *Pacifia* was sailing north through the Gulf of Salwah, Dhajan now far behind them. To the east were the desert shores of Qatar, Saudi Arabia an equally empty line of desert far to port. There was a mist on the horizon ahead, blurring sea and sky together, but she didn't need to see through it to know they were on course. The ship's computerised navigation displays were simple enough to read even for a non-sailor; their heading took them directly to Bahrain, the island state at the entrance to the Persian Gulf proper.

The screens also told her the estimated time of arrival: just before three o'clock, with the ship sailing at a solid but not excessive twenty-three knots. She knew it could go faster, but for now she was content to hold this speed. Remaining inconspicuous, insofar as a vessel the size of a supertanker could do so, would help her plan's chances of success.

Its most critical part remained unpredictable, though. She had regularly checked the spearhead. Its shimmering pulses of light seemed to be getting stronger, but as yet it did not appear to have reached the point of no return . . .

She caught the tail end of a whispered discussion between Ingels and one of his officers. 'What is going on?' she demanded, stalking to them. Her guards had stationed themselves around the bridge, unnerving the crew.

'The passengers are complaining about the loss of communications,' said the Dane. 'The internet in particular, but also the satellite television. They are—'

'Tell them there is a technical fault and the crew are working to repair it,' she cut in, annoyed. Whining about losing access to their pornography and pabulum! She could barely contain her disgust. The sooner they were all destroyed, the better.

But when would that happen? She gestured for al-Asim to place the case on a plotting table. He did so, then opened it, angling it so the crew couldn't see what was inside. 'It hasn't changed,' she whispered, frustrated. 'Did Wilde say anything else about how long it would take to explode after reaching the final stage?'

'No,' he replied, closing the case. 'Only that it would happen within two hours.'

She regarded the navigation display again. 'The ship will reach Bahrain before then. If it arrives too soon, the Americans might take action.' A moment of thought, then: 'Captain!'

Ingels hurried over. 'Yes, Your Majesty?'

'I want the ship to arrive in Bahrain at three thirty. Change our speed to do so.'

'Of course.' He issued the order.

Alula watched as an officer adjusted the thruster controls, reducing power to the three huge azipods propelling the ship. The speed readout eased back to eighteen knots, the estimated time of arrival creeping upwards.

Alula exchanged a satisfied glance with al-Asim. If the spearhead exploded earlier than expected, it would still have much the same effect: the tidal wave would flatten Bahrain and much of Qatar, as well as inflicting considerable damage on the Saudi coastline. But if it reached its target, the blast would obliterate the rival emirate *and* the American military base controlling the western Gulf. The balance of power in the entire region would shift, and Dhajan, under her rulership, would be perfectly placed to take advantage.

'The change has been made, Your Majesty,' said Ingels.

'Thank you, Captain,' Alula replied, with a small, cold smile. 'Thank you very much.'

42

'H e is here,' Junayd called from the upper floor.
Eddie helped the Emir to stand. 'You ready?'

The deposed ruler was still weak and pale, but with his wound closed and the painkillers taking full effect, he was steadier on his feet. 'Yes, I think so. Thank you.'

'Don't thank us yet,' said Nina. 'We haven't even made it out of the front door. We still have to get right across the city.'

Junayd, still in uniform, hurried downstairs. 'We will do it. I trust Rakin.' He and Eddie supported the Emir. 'Now, quickly.'

Nina opened the door and the group crossed to the gate. Junayd eased it open and peered through. A Land Cruiser in sandy camouflage colours waited on the street. 'It is clear. Go!'

They hurried to the 4x4, Eddie helping Junayd slide the Emir into the second row of seats. 'I'll sit back here with him,' he told the older man. 'You get in the front – we'll need you to do the talking.'

'I will have to start right away,' Junayd replied. The driver, a Dhajani army major, was staring at his royal passenger in utter shock. 'He thought the Emir was dead!' He climbed in and began a hasty explanation in Arabic.

Lobato and Nina took their places in the rearmost row of seats. 'At least nobody'll be able to see in,' she said. The windows were all tinted.

Lobato was less confident. 'They will not stop bullets.'

'Actually, they will,' said the Emir. 'All our military vehicles are armoured.' A faint smile. 'We buy them from a company in Bahrain, ironically.'

'Let's hope they're still in business by the end of the day,' Nina said. 'Still in existence, even.'

'I have told Rakin everything he needs to know,' Junayd announced. 'He will help us – he is loyal to the country, and to its true ruler.' The Emir expressed his thanks.

'What's the situation on the streets?' Eddie asked as the SUV set off.

'There are roadblocks at every major intersection. Even driving a military vehicle, Rakin was stopped twice. But he was able to talk his way through.'

'By "talk", you mean he shouted at them until they backed off, right?'

The colonel smiled. 'I taught him well, no?'

'Let's hope you're both loud enough to stop anyone from looking in the back,' said Nina nervously. A barricade was visible ahead.

The SUV approached the roadblock, slowing as a soldier waved it down. The other men on guard watched warily as it stopped. Their guns were held at the ready, but nobody had their finger on the trigger – yet.

The soldier walked towards Rakin's window, but Junayd wound down his own and barked an impatient demand. The man hesitated, then crossed in front of the Land Cruiser to speak to him, reacting with uncertainty when he saw a senior officer.

Junayd did not unleash the same verbal flaying as he had upon the Humvee crew, but he still made his displeasure at being delayed clear. The soldier apologetically explained that he was merely obeying orders, but under the colonel's increasingly hostile glare he eventually caved in, telling his comrades to move the barrier. Junayd raised his window as Rakin brought the Toyota through the blockade.

Even with the heavily tinted glass, Nina still hunched low until they were clear. 'One down,' she said. 'How many more before we get to the docks?'

'I do not know, but there *will* be more,' replied Junayd.

'I hope your voice holds out,' said the Emir, smiling.

Rakin drove on, taking the Land Cruiser on a circuitous route to avoid Dhajan City's gleaming centre, where the majority of the military forces were concentrated. Even so, he still had to make two more stops; the checkpoints were well positioned, making it impossible for anyone to traverse the city without encountering one. The first was circumvented by the same means as before: high military rank and a loud voice. The second, though, had a more senior, less easily browbeaten officer in charge. It took a few minutes of persuasion, Junayd getting out to speak to him face to face, before he allowed the SUV through, by which time the other soldiers had started to pay an uncomfortable amount of attention.

'Perhaps I should show myself,' said the Emir, as a particularly nosy sergeant retreated under Rakin's icy stare. 'If they know I am not dead, Alula's lies will be exposed. They may choose to follow me.'

'And they may not,' Eddie countered. 'It only takes one guy who's loyal to her to fuck things up and make you dead for real. And the rest of us with you.'

Junayd got back in, catching the tail end of the exchange. 'I'm afraid that is true, Your Majesty. You can only show yourself if we have no other choice. It is too great a risk.' The Emir unhappily accepted his friend's advice.

Rakin set off again, turning on to a wide highway along the edge of the business district. Dockyard cranes were visible at its end. 'How much further?' asked Nina.

'Only a kilometre,' said Junayd. 'I do not see any roadblocks ahead, but the entrance to the docks will certainly be under guard.'

She exchanged pensive looks with Eddie and Lobato. 'What if they won't let us in?' There was an uncomfortable silence. 'That wasn't a rhetorical question, guys.'

'Have to do what we always do,' Eddie suggested. 'Improvise and hope we don't end up too deep in the shit.'

She gave a humourless laugh. 'The sad thing is, that's probably the best idea any of us have.'

'Ay up,' said the Yorkshireman as the car rounded a corner. 'There's the ship.'

The *Atlantia* came into view, the enormous vessel looking for all the world as if one of the skyscrapers had toppled into the water. 'And there's the checkpoint,' Nina added. Large arched gates of white marble marked the entrance to the docks, which was blocked not only by barriers and soldiers, but also by several jeeps and, most alarmingly, a tank.

Armed men waved the SUV to a stop at the roadblock. 'Oh,' said Junayd, seeing an officer in mirrored sunglasses advancing.

'That did *not* sound like a good "oh",' said Nina.

'I know him. Colonel Isam.'

'Friend of yours?' Eddie asked.

'Unfortunately not. And he knows I am retired.'

'Can you bullshit him? Tell him Alula called you in specially?'

'We shall see.' Junayd got out and marched to meet the other colonel. Isam reacted first with surprise on seeing him, then frowned.

Even without understanding what was being said, Nina could tell the discussion between the two officers was not going their way. Isam was clearly calling Junayd out on his retirement. The older man tried to keep their conversation quiet, but his rival was having none of it, drawing increasing attention from his men. 'I don't think Junayd's convincing him.'

Eddie scanned the checkpoint for escape routes, but saw

472

none. Too many soldiers, too many guns, and this time they were in a vehicle the tank crew would have no trouble targeting. 'If the shit hits the fan, best option'll be to crash the barrier and try to get behind that,' he pointed at a small building, 'before they turn the car into Swiss cheese. After that . . . I dunno.'

'I think the fan's about to get splattered,' Nina warned.

Isam jabbed an angry finger at Junayd's chest, then called out to his men. A pair of large young soldiers advanced on the older man, whose shoulders dropped in defeat. He shot a heavy-hearted glance at the Land Cruiser, then led Isam and his companions to the 4x4. A few more words to the other officer, then he opened the rear door.

The glowering colonel leaned in – and gasped when he saw the Emir. He started to speak, only for his ruler to raise a finger to his lips: *be quiet*. Junayd began a low-key but intense Arabic exchange. The Emir joined in, Isam bowing his head deferentially.

Nina became more concerned about what was happening outside the car. The two soldiers accompanying Isam were both sidling closer, trying to peer inside. Others manning the roadblock were also moving closer. 'Crap,' she whispered. 'If anyone else sees the Emir . . .'

'Everyone else'll know in no time,' Eddie rumbled. 'Gossip travels faster than bullets.'

'Even for soldiers?'

'*Especially* for soldiers. You have no idea how fucking boring guard duty is!'

Isam withdrew. Junayd closed the door, but at least one of the waiting soldiers had glimpsed the man to whom their commanding officer had been talking, his mouth dropping open. Eddie tensed. 'Tell Rakin to get ready to go,' he said to the Emir. 'If we have to—'

The front passenger door opened. Everyone flinched, but it

was only Junayd. He quickly took his seat as Isam shouted a command. His men opened the barrier, waving the Land Cruiser through.

'What did you say to him?' Nina asked.

'I appealed to his loyalty as a patriot,' the Emir replied, 'and as a traditional Dhajani. No matter what his orders, what he thinks about my reforms, he agreed that if I am alive, Alula cannot be the country's true leader.'

'And you believed him?' said Eddie.

'Isam has many faults,' said Junayd wryly, 'but he is indeed a traditionalist. Even if His Majesty was dead, I do not think he would accept Alula as the new ruler.'

'Oh, so he's just a plain old-fashioned sexist,' Nina snipped.

'Perhaps, but it has worked in our favour.'

'For now,' said Eddie. 'One of the soldiers back there saw the Emir. That means the whole squad'll know he's still alive within five minutes. And it only takes one of 'em to tell Alula's people for the whole fucking army to come down on us.'

'Then we have to act quickly,' said the Emir. 'The *Atlantia* is that way.'

'Yeah, it's kinda hard to miss,' Nina pointed out. The tallest building in the dockyard was four storeys tall, but the liner stood five times higher, a white-and-gold metal wall slicing the facility in two.

Rakin brought the Toyota through the docks. The curfew had affected its workers, the only people they saw a few patrolling soldiers and some worried faces looking out from buildings. It did not take long to reach the *Atlantia*.

The huge vessel required its own purpose-built dock, a great finger of concrete half a mile long lancing out into the harbour. Massive doors at its seaward end showed it was a dry dock, able to be closed and drained so the liner could be maintained below the waterline, but they were currently open. Several gangways extended into hatches along the length of the ship's starboard side. Rakin pulled up beside the nearest, at the bow. A gantry bearing numerous thick power cables extended to the hull nearby.

Eddie got out, helping Junayd with the Emir. 'We likely to have any trouble once we get aboard?'

'We can trust the captain,' the Dhajani ruler replied. 'I was personally involved with his hiring; Alula had no part of it.'

'What about the crew?' Nina asked.

'Very few of them are Dhajani, so they would have no reason to support Alula over me.'

'Unless you paid 'em crap wages,' Eddie said with dark humour as they hurried up the ramp.

A Hispanic officer appeared at the entrance, raising a hand in challenge before recognising the Emir and reacting in surprise. 'We need to see Captain Snowcock,' Fadil told him. 'Where is he?'

'On the bridge, Your Majesty,' the officer said. 'But they said on the radio—'

'Everything they said is a lie. I am alive, I am still the Emir of Dhajan, and I need to speak to the captain, right now.'

'Of course, of course!' the man stammered. 'Follow me, please.'

The group entered the ship. With no passengers, the *Atlantia* had a very different atmosphere. 'Christ, it's like the hotel in *The Shining*,' said Eddie as they traversed the deserted corridors. 'How many people are aboard?'

'I'm not sure,' the officer replied. 'There's a skeleton crew of about sixty people. Some of them went ashore after we arrived this morning, but when the curfew started they weren't allowed back.'

'Are there enough people to run the ship?' Nina asked.

'I don't know, but we've only just docked for repairs – we

aren't setting sail again for a few weeks.' He sensed the new arrivals knew something he didn't. 'Are we?'

'You might want to put your sea legs back on,' said Eddie.

They reached the lifts, riding up to Deck 16 and emerging on the landing behind the bridge. The officer used his ID card to open the door, then ushered everyone inside. 'Captain!' he called out.

Snowcock was talking to another officer. He turned, gasping when he saw the Emir. 'Your Majesty!' he cried. 'Are you all right? We were told you'd been killed!'

'I am still alive, Captain,' the Emir told him, gesturing for Eddie and Junayd to let him stand unaided. They released their hold; he grimaced, but held firm. 'My sister has launched a *coup d'état*, and tried to murder me. She failed, thanks to my friends,' he indicated his companions, 'but there is a much greater danger. How soon can you get the ship under way?'

Snowcock stared at him. 'Under way, Your Majesty?'

'Yes. We have to catch the *Pacifia*. There is a bomb aboard, as powerful as a nuclear weapon. Alula intends to drive the ship into Bahrain harbour to destroy the American naval base and the entire city – and cause a tidal wave that will devastate Qatar, Saudi Arabia and even Dhajan itself. The *Atlantia* is our only hope of stopping her.'

The captain's eyes went wide. 'I . . . Okay, I guess we need to get under way!' He took in the status displays. 'We're currently on shore power so we don't have to run the gas turbines in dock, but the batteries are at . . . seventy-two per cent charge. We can run entirely on them until the turbines complete their start-up sequence. If we shut down all non-essential power to the passenger decks, that'll give us some extra juice.'

'Are there enough crew to run the ship?' Nina asked.

Snowcock questioned another officer. From his concerned expression, the answer was right on the borderline. 'As long as we don't have an emergency situation . . . yes.'

'Can't guarantee that,' said Eddie ominously. 'What about the turbines? How long will they take to start up?'

'Ten minutes.'

'You had better begin right away,' said the Emir. 'We need to leave dock. Now.'

'Yes, Your Majesty,' Snowcock replied, with deep trepidation. He raised his voice to a commanding bark. 'You heard the Emir! Begin expedited departure procedure. Clear all moorings and commence gas turbine start-up.' He continued issuing orders, the bridge officers hurrying to obey.

'How long before we start moving?' Nina asked.

'We can engage the electric drive systems in under a minute,' said Snowcock, 'but it'll take at least five minutes to retract all the gangways and disconnect from shore power.'

'Too long,' snapped Eddie. 'What happens if you just, you know, *go*?'

'We – we'll damage the ship!' the captain spluttered. 'If we don't retract the gangways, they'll be dragged along until they either fall into the water or hit something on the dockside – and that will probably rip a hole in the hull.'

'Big enough to sink us?'

'No, they're all a long way above the waterline—'

'There you go. Your Maj?'

'Do it,' said the Emir.

Snowcock took in his crew's stunned looks, then went to the pilot's station. 'I'll do this myself,' he announced. 'If there's going to be any damage, I'll take full responsibility.'

Nina moved to the observation pulpit at the centre of the panoramic front windows. 'You'd better do it fast!'

Eddie ran to join her. Below, he saw several military vehicles tearing through the dockyard towards the *Atlantia*. 'Alula's people are coming!' he shouted. A glance to port; there was a good twenty metres of open water between the liner and the dry dock's other side. 'Go sideways – we've got to pull clear of the gangways before they get aboard!'

'Moorings are clear!' an officer shouted.

Snowcock took a deep breath. 'Well . . . here we go,' he said, turning all three thruster controls through ninety degrees . . . and applying power.

The great ship tipped top-heavily towards the dockside as the azipods whirled to speed beneath it, then wallowed back upright. Nina took a firm hold of a handrail as Junayd and Rakin hurriedly supported the Emir.

The leading jeep skidded to a halt beside the Land Cruiser. 'Shit, they're here!' Eddie yelled. 'They'll be on the gangway any second – go, go!' He sprinted for the starboard wing bridge. 'Stand by to repel boarders!' Snowcock reluctantly applied more power.

The Yorkshireman ran into the wing bridge, vaulting down a small flight of steps to land in what was essentially the main bridge in microcosm, duplicating its primary controls. The reason it and its port-side twin existed was literally clear: the glass-walled room extended out more than twenty feet from the ship's side, providing an unrestricted view of the *Atlantia*'s flank. The floor had thick glass panels set into it so the crew could view what would otherwise be a huge blind spot directly below.

He fought momentary vertigo to look down through them. Soldiers scrambled from the first vehicle, trucks and Humvees disgorging their occupants behind it. The *Atlantia* was pulling away from the dockside, the gap between the white metal wall and the concrete quay opening up to reveal churning water below.

Not fast enough. The running soldiers began to race up the gangway. 'They're coming! *Faster!*' he shouted through the open door.

Another surge of power – and a great wall of spray erupted from beneath the ship, sweeping across the dock and knocking the newly arrived soldiers off their feet. The wave's force swept the gangways around, one of the smaller ones plunging into the frothing water.

The soldiers already on the larger ramp staggered as it lurched. A few men hastily ran back to shore, but others continued upwards. The ship pulled out still further – and the gangway's upper end fell away from the hatch. It plunged into the water, taking the screaming soldiers with it. 'Got 'em!' Eddie shouted.

The Dhajani troops resurfaced, only to be tossed helplessly against the wall by the relentless force of the ship's thrusters. Some of the soldiers on the quayside recovered and searched for life belts to throw to their comrades.

Others raised their weapons and took aim at the bridge.

Triumph suddenly turned to fear. Eddie turned and launched himself up the steps. Bullets cracked against the deck and windows behind him, glass exploding. He dived into the main bridge as more rounds clanged against the bulkhead. 'They're not happy,' he announced.

The gunfire stopped. 'Are all the gangplanks gone?' Nina asked.

'I don't know,' said Snowcock, focused on manoeuvring the ship. 'We managed to restore some of the hacked systems, but the CCTV is still down.'

'Whoops, sorry,' said Eddie, glancing at the darkened video wall at the bridge's rear. 'But nobody made it up the one at the front.'

A female officer called out from the port wing bridge, warning that the ship was getting close to the other side of the dry dock. The captain quickly reversed the direction of the azipod thrusters, then turned the controls to ease the *Atlantia* backwards out of its berth—

The ship jolted, sending everyone reeling. An alarm honked

over the sound of metal shrilling outside. 'What was that?' demanded the Emir.

'The power lines!' Snowcock cried. 'They're still connected!'

'I can see them,' said Nina. The cables running to the bow were now stretched taut, the gantry visibly twisting and straining as the enormous vessel pulled at it. 'They're gonna break – hold on!'

She gripped the handrail as the pylon buckled – then tore from its base and collapsed on to the quay with a colossal crash. Soldiers fled as sparking cables whipped at them. The *Atlantia* jolted again as it broke free, its stern swinging out diagonally into the dock. Snowcock tried to compensate—

'Captain!' the woman screamed. 'The crane! We're going to hit—'

The liner shook again as the jib of a tower crane on the dock's far side speared into the topmost deck. Broken glass rained into the water as it scythed through the still-reversing ship, tearing away radio masts and satellite dishes and sending debris cascading down the *Atlantia*'s sloping front. Everyone instinctively ducked as the battered crane smashed on to the foredeck, disintegrating in an explosion of flying struts and girders.

'Is everyone okay?' Snowcock called. Relieved responses came from around the bridge. 'Damage report, quickly! And tell me how much stern clearance we have – I need to straighten her out.'

The woman ran back into the wing bridge and shouted again. 'Sir! They're closing the dry-dock gates!'

'*What?*' said Snowcock. He called another officer to his position. 'Hold station,' he ordered, before running to the wing bridge to see for himself.

Eddie and Nina went with him. The two enormous gates at the dock's far end were slowly swinging inwards. 'How long before they close?' Nina asked.

'About ten minutes,' Snowcock replied. 'But we'll never make it through in time – the ship's so wide, they won't even need to get halfway to block us in.'

'So go faster,' said Eddie. 'Just whack it to full power and cane it through!'

'We can't see where we're going! All our cameras are down.'

The Yorkshireman gave him an incredulous look. 'You've got *eyes*, haven't you?'

Snowcock scowled. 'It took us nearly an hour to manoeuvre into the dock, and that was with my crew and port control guiding us in. You're asking me to bring a quarter-million-tonne ship through a closing gate backwards, at high speed, while steering it from almost half a kilometre away!'

'So I'll guide you in.' Eddie returned to the main bridge. 'I saw some walkie-talkies in here – they've got enough range to cover the whole ship, right?'

Snowcock and Nina followed him. 'Yes,' said the captain, 'but you're not a sailor. You don't know the terminology you'll need to direct us.'

Eddie found the rack of radios and took one. 'Don't worry, I'm pretty good at making myself understood.'

Nina laughed. 'You're from Yorkshire! I'm married to you, and half the time *I* have trouble understanding what you're saying.'

'Tchah! Okay, I'm on channel eight. I'll call you when I get to the arse end.' He ran for the exit.

'You mean the stern, and you'll never get there in time,' Snowcock protested.

'I know a short cut! Just get the fucking boat moving!'

'It's a *ship*!' the captain shouted after him, but Eddie had already gone.

He rushed back to the lifts, riding up to the top deck. It was littered with debris. He quickly picked his way through it to the edge of the balcony overlooking the huge atrium along the ship's centreline, then scaled the steps to the platform at the top of the zip-line on the starboard side.

He found a length of chain and flicked it over the cable. ''Cause this was so much fun the first time,' he muttered, taking a firm hold of each end. He backed up a few steps – then leapt off the platform.

43

Sparks flew from the chain as Eddie screeched down the cable. The waterslides and pools whipped past below him. But he kept his eyes fixed on the terminus below, riding all the way to it.

This time he was able to use the bungee lines attached to the cable to brake. Even so, he was flipped forward, losing his grip on the chain and hitting the padded wall with a thud. Swearing, he ran for the steps to the higher deck around the stern.

The massive dry-dock gates came into view, slowly but unstoppably grumbling shut. Beyond them was Dhajan's harbour, two long breakwaters enclosing it. Another obstacle to negotiate, but there was no point worrying about it until they cleared the first – if they could.

The *Atlantia* was still askew in its dock. He took out the walkie-talkie. 'Hello! Can you hear me?'

'I'm here,' said Snowcock. 'Can we fit through the gates?'

'Yeah, but you'll have to get moving!' The liner was drifting towards the opening at less than walking pace. 'Straighten out, bring the back end over to the left.'

A low thrum came through the deck as the azipods increased power. The ship began to pick up speed. 'Come on, faster!' Eddie ordered. 'Otherwise the fucking gates'll cut us in half! To the left!'

'*Which* left? The ship's left, your left – or do you mean to the port side?'

'My left . . . I mean, shit, hold on.' He got his bearings. 'Starboard, starboard!'

'And *that's* why we use nautical terminology,' the captain said scathingly as he adjusted course.

'Yeah, very funny.' The stern started to swing lazily back towards the dry dock's centre. 'That's it, keep going. And I shouldn't have to keep saying this, but *go fucking faster!*'

Another surge from the drive systems, though he could almost feel Snowcock's huffy resentment transmitted through them. The *Atlantia* was now moving at a strong jog, then a run.

But it was still on a collision course with the gate as it swung inwards. 'Back end hard to starboard – and push the front to port,' he ordered. 'Straighten out or we'll crash!'

The gates were less than a hundred metres away. They were rapidly running out of space.

Eddie grabbed the railing as the ship swayed. Snowcock had directed the fore and aft azipods in opposite directions, turning the liner around its centrepoint. The stern came about more quickly. 'Okay, that's it, that's good! Ease off, ease off . . .' The *Atlantia* wallowed again as the thruster pods counteracted their previous movement. He glanced back along the ship's length to judge its alignment, then: 'That's it, you're straight! Hold it there – and go, *go*! Full fucking power!'

Even with more than a quarter of a million tonnes of metal to move, the acceleration as the engines went to full throttle made him sway. The stern drew level with the dock's end, passing the massive machinery driving the gates—

And into the open water of the harbour.

Eddie exhaled, but there was still a long way to go – specifically, the four hundred metres of cruise ship behind him. 'The back end's out of the dock!' he reported. 'Keep going, faster!'

'We're at full speed!' Snowcock replied.

'So tell the Emir to override the speed limiter!'

A brief silence, which Eddie hoped meant that the captain was passing on the message, then Snowcock returned. 'How much clearance do we have?'

The Yorkshireman looked to each side. The gates were sweeping relentlessly inwards. 'About . . . twenty metres to port, a bit less on the right. Has he put his code in yet?'

The answer came in the form of another surge of power. The *Atlantia* increased speed again, but Eddie realised it wouldn't be enough. He ran to the port side, leaning out to look along the ship's length. The barrier was still closing, only around fifty feet of clearance – and the gap was shrinking with every second.

'You've got to go faster!' he yelled. 'We're not gonna make it!'

Nina heard her husband's frantic radio message. With the captain at the controls and the Emir having used his code to unleash the full power of the *Atlantia*'s engines, there was nothing she could do to influence events, but nor was she just going to stand there and wait for the crash.

Instead she ran to the port wing bridge. The female officer, whose name tag read *Dimakos*, had been calling out the remaining clearance, but now she was frozen, staring down the ship's side with growing horror. Nina joined her. 'Oh *crap*.'

The liner was halfway out of the dock, but the lock gate was drawing ever closer. Even with the *Atlantia* still accelerating, it would only be three-quarters of the way through when the gate caught it. The bow began to narrow not far beyond that point, but there were still several protruding sections – to say nothing of the lifeboats. At best, the ship would suffer major damage; at worst, it would be ripped open on both sides, or trapped and crushed.

She exchanged a worried look with the other woman, then they both gripped the handrail. The gate moved closer, closer, not even the redlining drive systems able to get them clear—

The barrier struck.

It caught one of the lifeboats, the orange vessel exploding into fibreglass shards. The boat ahead of it met a similar fate – then the great blade caught the *Atlantia*'s hull proper.

Even holding on, Nina was almost thrown to the deck. A hideous screech of tortured metal echoed through the vast vessel as steel panels crumpled like paper. The awful sound grew louder as the wave of destruction swept towards her, more lifeboats disintegrating—

The gate smashed into a glass-walled lounge projecting from a lower deck. The entire vessel jolted, hurling Nina and her companion against the wing bridge's rear wall – then the lounge was sheared away, leaving a ragged hole framed by twisted girders.

Nina scrambled to the glass panels to look down as the gate swept past a hundred feet beneath her. The bow was by now curving inwards, but the barrier was still closing, biting huge chunks out of the main deck's edge with a terrifying tattoo of pounding metal—

The noise stopped.

For a moment Nina feared she had been deafened, but then she heard flat splashes as wreckage dropped from the battered ship. She jumped up to look out of the front windows. Both gates fell away beyond the *Atlantia*'s bow as the liner pulled clear of the dry dock and began to turn for the harbour mouth.

She ran back into the main bridge to find the crew recovering from the rough ride, Snowcock clinging to the thruster controls as if lashed there like Odysseus. 'We're clear!' she cried. 'We made it—'

A deep echoing *whump* – and everyone was sent flying as something ploughed into the ship's side.

Eddie had grabbed a stanchion and clung on as the ship jolted. The hammering ceased, and he stood – only for another impact to knock him down again.

It wasn't the dock gate. This blow was near the stern. He looked over the railing.

The collision wasn't an accident.

A bright orange harbour tugboat had rammed the *Atlantia* about a hundred feet forward of him, hitting hard enough to buckle the hull plating. Black smoke belched from the funnel as its engine roared, pushing the far larger ship sideways.

Another tug was coming in beyond it, and a third rounded a quay further along the harbourfront. 'Tuggeration and fuckery!' Eddie said, then whipped up the radio. 'Snowcock! A tugboat's rammed us – it's trying to force us aground! Push it back!'

'What do you think I'm *trying* to do?' came the terse reply.

The liner rolled again as the azipods changed orientation to resist the attacker, but with little success. The huge ship's bow was slewing around, the furious tugboat acting as a pivot. It would hobble the *Atlantia* long enough for its companions to arrive and drive the liner into the shore. Eddie looked at the two approaching boats, then across the harbour for anything that could turn the battle in the ship's favour—

He raised the radio again. 'Don't go sideways – steer us *backwards* at . . .' He had no idea what bearing they were on. 'At seven o'clock! Go backwards as fast as you can on a course of seven o'clock!'

'Why?' demanded Snowcock.

'Because you'll push that fucking boat into something that'll scrape it off us!'

'*What* thing?'

'A crane boat thing, I don't know what it's called – I'm not a bloody sailor!' The craft he had spotted was a squat rectangular barge with a large red-and-white counterweighted crane arm rising from it, anchored a few hundred metres out into the harbour. 'Just do it!'

Snowcock didn't reply, but the ship's wallow told Eddie that the thrusters had changed direction again. The liner began to push backwards once more. Froth churning beneath its stern, the tug came about, its strengthened nose buried in the white hull – but against the full colossal horsepower of the *Atlantia* it was fighting a losing battle.

The ship picked up speed, carrying the unwelcome remora with it. 'How far are we from the crane?' Snowcock demanded. 'Are we on course?'

'Come left – port – a bit more,' said Eddie; the tug was still bullying them away from it. 'We're about two hundred metres away. Keep going – left hand down!'

The *Atlantia* swung towards its target. The Englishman looked back at the tugboat. Its occupants hadn't yet noticed the approaching danger, focused on preventing the cruise ship's escape. 'That's it,' he told the captain. 'Keep going, you'll smack 'em right off the side!'

A hundred metres, less, the ship forcing up a heavy swell from its stern as it powered onwards – but the tug's crew had finally realised what their opponent was trying to do. The boat's engines reversed, trying to pull away – but its bow was caught in the hole smashed in the *Atlantia*'s side. Another burst of foul black smoke as it attempted to tear loose, but too late—

The crane's jib rolled past Eddie – and the tugboat crashed sidelong into the barge.

The impact ripped it free of the liner, the barge's angular corner slamming into its hull like a mason's chisel and cracking it wide open. Both crewmen flung themselves overboard as their vessel capsized.

But they were not the only ones in danger. The barge was knocked into a spin by the collision – and the crane wheeled about even faster, the jib scything at the stern—

Eddie hurled himself down a flight of steps to the pool deck and dropped flat as the crane slashed around, demolishing everything in its path. 'Christing arse!' he yelled as debris rained about him.

The barge rebounded off the liner and reeled away. The crane arm swung out, the whole machine finally toppling into the water.

Eddie staggered back up the stairs. The railings were gone; he went as close as he dared to the edge of the wreckage-strewn deck and looked down.

The tugboat had rolled over, its cracked hull rising from the water like a turtle's shell as its crew floundered nearby. But the threat was not over, the two other tugs still homing in. He took out the radio to warn Snowcock – only to find its antenna had been snapped off by his hard landing. He tried to call the bridge, but got no reply. 'Shit!'

He started running. Over three hundred metres and eight decks to the bridge – and this time, there were no short cuts.

'One boat down!' Nina shouted. 'Still two more coming at us.'

'Where are they?' Snowcock called back.

Dimakos reported their positions, but Nina was more concerned about fending them off. One tug had almost overpowered the *Atlantia*; two would force it ashore.

She looked down through the glass floor panels. The liner was still angling diagonally backwards, and the ship's enormous flank was driving a hefty wave ahead of itself . . .

'Go straight at them!' she cried to the captain. 'Broadside on, at full speed – if they're smart, they'll get out of the way, and if they're dumb, we're kicking up such a big wave, they'll be swamped!'

'If they hit us, we'll take a lot of damage,' Snowcock objected.

'The ship's already trashed. And if we don't get out of here, Alula's people will kill us!'

Snowcock looked towards the Emir. 'Do whatever you must to get us out of the harbour,' Fadil told him.

'Yes, sir,' the captain replied. He brought the liner around side-on to the approaching tugs, presenting them with a colossal wall of metal. 'Full power.'

He pushed the throttles to their limit. The engines surged, rocking the ship. The wave of displaced water rose higher as the *Atlantia* picked up speed. The closer of the two tugs turned and tried to power clear. But it had been aiming to hit the liner amidships, and had two hundred metres to cover in either direction before it could escape—

It wasn't fast enough.

The pilot hurriedly tried to turn back into the swell to ride over it, but couldn't bring his craft around in time. The wave hit, slamming the tug almost on to its side before it rolled back – and swamping it. A burst of foul fumes erupted from the funnel as the lower deck was flooded, drowning the engine.

But the last tug was still coming, aiming for the *Atlantia*'s prow. Its bow was flung clear of the water as it crested the wave, then it slapped back down in a burst of spray and homed in on its target.

'Brace yourselves!' Nina yelled, grabbing a console—

The *Atlantia* shook as if it had struck a mine, the impact almost flinging Nina to the deck. A deep, echoing *boom* like the beating of a monstrous gong rolled through the ship's innards.

'Jesus!' she gasped. The tug had hit hard enough to tear a crooked rent in the larger vessel's prow. She couldn't tell if it extended below the waterline, the attacker's nose buried in the white steel.

The tug's crew had already recovered from the collision. Its engine roared, and the *Atlantia* slewed around as the powerful craft drove hard against its bow. Snowcock rotated the azipods to compensate, but the tug's position at the front of the hull gave it an advantage, as if pushing down the end of a seesaw with nothing more than a fingertip. Even with all three huge thrusters at full power, the liner could no longer hold course.

A bridge officer shouted from the observation pulpit. 'They're trying to force us into the container docks!'

'You've got to shake them loose!' said Nina, trying to see if the *Atlantia* was taking on water through the rip—

Something caught her eye – *above* the tug rather than below. An anchor, thirty tons of white-painted metal inside a recess in the hull.

She drew back, frantically checking the console. She was certain she had seen an anchor control panel . . .

There! A plan-view outline of the ship marking the positions of its anchors: one on each side of the bow, and a single one at the stern. A button beside the port-side forward anchor was labelled *Release*.

She pushed it.

A buzzer sounded. Dimakos looked at her in alarm. 'Wait, what are you—'

The anchor dropped, heavy-duty chain snaking after it. It plunged towards the water – and smashed down on the tug's bow.

The foredeck caved in. The boat's stern flipped out of the water, exposing its whirling propellers, then it rolled back into the froth. The crew were catapulted from the open cabin door into the harbour.

'I got it, I got it!' Nina cried. 'We're clear – go!'

Dimakos could only stare in astonishment, while Snowcock asked, 'Got *what*?'

'The tugboat! I dropped an anchor on it!' It was now the captain's turn for stunned disbelief. 'Don't worry, the crew are okay.'

'I think, Captain,' said the Emir before Snowcock could explode at her disregard for maritime safety, 'we should take this opportunity to leave harbour. At the greatest possible speed.'

'Yes, Your Majesty,' Snowcock replied, regaining his composure. 'Mr Moretti, take the helm.' Another man took his place as he went to the pulpit. 'Hard aport, bring us to the harbour mouth.' He snapped out more commands to his crew as the great ship began to turn. The deck shook again as the crushed tugboat struck the bow. 'Throw life vests down to the men in the water – and raise the damn anchor!'

The *Atlantia* turned towards the gap in the breakwaters. Nina came back into the bridge, watching as the docks slid past to starboard. The liner might be huge, but its three azipods made it surprisingly manoeuvrable – and with the speed limiter overridden, it would reach the harbour exit in just a few minutes. They still had to catch the *Pacifia*, but at least nothing could stop them—

The thought was premature. Dhajan's naval base came into view across the bay – and charging across the waters from it was a corvette. The small warship was only a fraction of the *Atlantia*'s size, but it was still packed with firepower.

One of the weapons was turning towards them.

'They're gonna shoot!' she cried. 'Get back from the windows – everybody down!'

Snowcock saw it too. He turned and ran from the pulpit, grabbing the Emir and pulling him behind the consoles. The rest of the crew followed suit—

A barrage of 27 mm Gatling gun shells hosed across the liner's forward superstructure. Explosive projectiles ripped into the bridge with a deafening cacophony of shattering glass and tearing metal.

Nina hunched beneath a console and covered her ears as debris showered around her. The gun was so much lower than the bridge that its shots mostly struck the ceiling, but some were hitting the level below and ripping up through the floor. She felt the deck judder with increasing ferocity as cannon rounds punched through it, getting closer and closer—

The onslaught ceased.

She peered out fearfully. 'Is anyone hurt?' she called, ears ringing.

'I am all right,' said the Emir from beneath another console nearer the bridge's rear. Then, in alarm: 'Captain! You're hit!'

Snowcock grunted as he rose, revealing a slash of red across his thigh. 'I'm okay, I can stand.' He looked anxiously for the rest of the crew. Some had shrapnel injuries, but there had been just enough warning for everyone to get clear of the room's now-devastated front. 'Evacuate the wounded before they start shooting again,' he ordered as he limped forward, squinting into the wind blowing through the shattered windows. 'The main pilot station's been destroyed. Moretti and Calvos, with me into the starboard wing bridge. We've got to get the ship back under control.'

The corvette was still closing. 'Why've they stopped firing?' Nina wondered aloud.

In the next moment, she saw why. They were preparing a more devastating attack. The turret housing the ship's main gun was turning, bringing its cannon to bear.

'*Get out!*' she screamed, hauling Snowcock with her towards the starboard wing bridge. 'Everyone get out! They're going to blow up the bridge!'

Most of the crew raced for the exit at the rear, two men bodily lifting the Emir as others carried their wounded colleagues. Another man helped Nina with the captain as they barged through the door and clattered down the steps into the wing bridge. The room had taken no damage from the Gatling gun, its fire concentrated on the ship's centreline.

Nina looked back at the corvette. The main gun tilted upwards – then stopped.

She dived against the bulkhead beside the stairs, dragging

Snowcock and the other man with her and pressing her hands to her ears—

A chilling moment, as if time had frozen – then the windows above her blew out as a 76 mm shell exploded in the main bridge.

Even shielded from the blast, it still felt as if a giant had kicked her in the back, sending her skidding over the floor. The two men were booted across it with her, the younger officer striking his head against the console's base.

Nina shook off pulverised glass and looked up. If the first attack had left her ears ringing, they now felt as if her head had been inside a bell when someone struck it with a steel sledgehammer. Snowcock crouched to check on his companion, but she knew there was a more urgent issue. 'That ship's gonna blow us out of the water – you've got to stop it!'

'How?' said Snowcock. 'They have weapons, we don't!'

'You've got one – the *Atlantia* itself! It must weigh a thousand times more than that thing. You could roll right over it and not even feel a bump!'

'I can't—'

They both flinched as a second cannon round blasted the port wing bridge into flaming scrap metal. 'Yeah, you *can*,' she insisted.

'I can,' the captain agreed.

Nina helped him stand and take the duplicate controls. He turned the azipods to direct the liner – straight at the corvette.

Full power. The distance between the two ships shrank rapidly, their closing speed well over fifty knots and increasing as the *Atlantia* accelerated. The gun traversed, sweeping from one side of the cruise liner to the other, but now it couldn't elevate quickly enough to track the remaining wing bridge as the towering vessel rushed towards it.

It fired again. Nina's heart froze—

Then restarted as the shell screamed past beneath her, arcing harmlessly out to sea.

'Brace for impact!' shouted Snowcock as the other ship's captain ordered a frantic evasive turn away from the juggernaut—

The collision was glancing, the *Atlantia*'s prow clipping the corvette's stern – but with a quarter of a million tonnes behind it, the liner carved straight through the far lighter warship's hull, ripping away a chunk of its aft section and one of its two propellers. The Dhajani ship reeled as water rushed into the engine room. Sirens and alarms wailed as the crippled vessel's captain immediately realised his command was doomed and ordered an evacuation.

Snowcock was already altering course, bringing his own ship back towards the harbour entrance. 'Look after Calvos,' he ordered. Nina crouched to help the fallen officer. The cut on his head was quite deep, blood running down his face, but he was still breathing.

'Nina!'

She looked up as she heard her husband's voice from the remains of the main bridge. 'Eddie! I'm down here!'

He ran to her. 'Christ, I thought you'd been blown up!'

'So did I, for a moment – it was *way* too close a call. Are you okay?'

'Yeah, nothing too fatal.' He saw the blood on Snowcock's leg. 'What about you, Captain?'

'I'll survive,' the white-haired man replied. 'Get Mr Calvos somewhere safe.' He nodded towards the injured man. 'Is the Emir all right?'

'He's okay – well, as okay as someone who got shot in the chest can be.' With Nina's assistance, Eddie lifted the younger officer and started up the steps.

She looked back at Snowcock. 'As soon as we're in open water, get up to full speed and head north. We've *got* to catch the *Pacifia*.'

'Aye aye, *Captain*,' he replied, more than a little sarcastically.

The couple brought the officer out of the wrecked bridge and through the lobby to a muster station, where the rest of the bridge crew had gathered. 'Got a man with a head wound here!' Eddie announced.

Blankets had been laid out as makeshift beds. 'Are you all right?' asked the Emir as they put the officer down. 'And where is Captain Snowcock?'

'Driving the ship,' Eddie told him. 'We'll live. As long as we stop the spearhead from blowing up, that is.'

'What if we are too late?'

'Even if there's no way to stop the explosion, we've still got to try,' Nina insisted. 'We have to catch up.'

'And then what?' said Eddie. 'They're not going to stop so we can hop aboard.'

'Then,' she said with grim determination, 'we *make* them stop.'

44

Nina looked out from the wing bridge, wind from the broken side windows ruffling her hair. With no passengers, a skeleton crew and a minimal fuel load, the *Atlantia* was powering through the waves even faster than during the Emir's demonstration on her first visit. Somewhere ahead was the *Pacifia*, but mist obscured her view of the horizon.

There was no way to locate the huge liner by other means, either. The tower crane that had smashed into the *Atlantia*'s upper deck had demolished the ship's main radar. Making matters worse, the swathe of destruction had also taken out most of its radio antennae, as well as the satellite links for the internet and cellular phones. All long-range communications were down; the more limited ship-to-shore radio was still working, but reception was overpowered by a repeating message from Dhajan announcing alternately in Arabic and English that the country was in a state of emergency and to await further information.

Eddie tried the radio again, then put the handset down in frustration. 'How long before we get out of jamming range?'

'Marine radios use VHF,' Lobato observed, 'which is generally range-limited by line of sight. In theory, once we pass over the horizon from Dhajan, we will regain use of the transmission frequencies. Unfortunately—'

'How did I know there'd be an unfortunately?'

'—the *Atlantia* is a very tall ship, so we will have to travel a greater distance to clear the jamming. We will probably be approaching Bahrain before we are able to transmit a message without interference.'

'We should keep trying, though,' insisted Nina. 'We might get lucky and reach someone in Qatar who can pass on our message to the US Navy.'

The Emir was resting in a chair. 'We might,' he echoed morosely, 'but that depends upon the message being relayed quickly and accurately. And there are many people in Qatar, and beyond, who would be happy to see the American naval base blown up. You are our allies, but that does not mean you are popular.'

'It won't just be the navy base, though,' she pointed out. 'They'll be hit by the tidal wave themselves not long after.'

'If some random person radioed you and said there's a super-nuke sailing past on a cruise ship, would you believe 'em?' asked Eddie.

Nina saw his point, but before she could reply, Snowcock spoke. 'Your Majesty, I really think we should slow down.' He indicated a screen. 'We're holding at forty-four knots, but the drive systems weren't designed to run this fast for this long. The engines are starting to overheat. If there's a fire on the battery deck—'

'Yeah, we know what'll happen, Scotty,' she cut in. 'But we don't have a choice. If we don't catch the *Pacifia*—'

'I'm aware of the danger, Dr Wilde,' Snowcock said irritably.

'We have to keep going,' said the Emir. 'How long before we catch up?'

'Assuming the *Pacifia* holds a normal cruising speed, I'd say it'll be . . . about an hour and fifty minutes. We should see it long before then, as soon as that mist clears.'

'If the spearhead's entered its final stage, we might not *have* much longer than that,' said Nina. She regarded the screen. Some of the bars showing the engines' status had indeed moved upwards, going beyond a green line marking normal operating temperatures into a yellow zone. As she watched, one rose in height by another pixel, creeping ever closer to an ominous red line.

She looked back at the shrouded horizon. They would enter the mist in minutes, but there was no telling how long they would take to clear it. All she could do now was wait . . . and hope they had enough time to make a difference.

Alula paced impatiently across the *Pacifia*'s bridge. Her gaze kept returning to the display showing the liner's estimated time of arrival at its final destination. Bahrain was now less than two hours away, half the hundred-mile voyage completed, but the spearhead's state had not changed. If she ordered the liner to slow still further, the American navy might take an unwelcome interest . . .

'Your Majesty,' said al-Asim urgently. 'Something has happened. I can feel it.' He indicated the spearhead's case.

Alula cautiously touched the lid and felt a surge of excitement. The box was *trembling*. She opened it.

The spearhead was still aglow, but the light had changed. More vivid shades of blue and purple and even red were spreading through the pure white, which itself was visibly brighter. 'It's starting,' she said. 'Wilde was right – it's reached the final stage.'

'Which means . . . nothing can stop it.'

She gave him a quizzical look. 'Are you having second thoughts, Hashim?'

'Of course not, Your Majesty. But knowing there's now no turning back is . . . a great responsibility.'

'A responsibility I'm willing to take for the sake of my country,' Alula said firmly. She closed the lid. 'Our enemies must be destroyed, inside Dhajan and out. That time has come – and so has mine!'

★ ★ ★

'The fog's clearing,' said Snowcock.

The *Atlantia* had been ploughing through the bank of mist for over an hour, the horizon in all directions blanked out by a featureless grey. Now, though, the dividing line between sea and sky began to fade in. 'Any sign of the *Pacifia*?' asked Nina.

'Not yet, but once we get full visibility, we should be close enough to see it.'

Eddie took a pair of powerful binoculars from a clip and scanned the gulf. 'There's something, but . . . no, it's the wrong colour, it's black. Must be an oil tanker. I can see land, though.'

Snowcock glanced at a chart laid out on the console; with the radar and GPS down, he had to navigate the old-fashioned way. 'The southern tip of Bahrain should be to the north-west.'

'Yeah, that must be it,' Eddie replied. He slowly panned the binoculars eastwards from the thin line of sandy terrain. 'Got her!'

Nina looked. In the far distance was a pale rectangle – a megaliner seen from directly astern, rising over the horizon like a monolith. 'How far away?'

'Let me see,' said Snowcock. Eddie gave him the binoculars. 'From this height, the horizon's about fifteen miles away. I can see the stern deck, so they can't be more than a mile beyond that.'

The Emir stood, Rakin and a crewman helping him. 'How long will it take us to catch up?'

'We're closer to her than I expected, so she must only be making twenty knots, or less,' said the captain. 'We have at least a twenty-four knot advantage, so . . . about thirty-five minutes.'

Nina examined the chart. Their current position was between Bahrain proper and its smaller territory of the Hawar Islands just off the Qatari coast to the south-east; the American naval base was in a large bay at Bahrain's northern end. She checked the map's scale, estimating the distance to Alula's target as around thirty-five miles. 'We'll only be about five miles from the harbour when we reach the *Pacifia*,' she said in dismay. 'That's cutting it *way* too fine.'

'And we still have to get the spearhead clear,' said Eddie. He took back the binoculars. 'Christ, I can actually see people on the decks. They don't have a clue what's going on—' A thought struck him. 'Shit, if we can see them, they can see us!'

'Damn it, they can,' Nina said. 'Alula'll know we're coming!'

Captain Ingels put down a telephone handset and turned to Alula. 'Your Majesty? I've just been informed of something . . . odd.'

'What do you mean?' she demanded.

'I will show you.' He spoke to an officer, who tapped at a keyboard, then gestured towards the video wall at the bridge's rear. 'There.'

She drew in a sharp, angry breath as a view directly astern filled all the screens. A towering shape was clearing the mist smearing the horizon. 'The *Atlantia*!'

'What's it doing here?' said al-Asim, surprised.

'Following us,' Alula snarled. 'It's Fadil! And Wilde and Chase must be with him.'

'Why would they be there?'

'Because nobody else would be insane enough to steal a cruise liner!' She faced Ingels. 'Bring us to full speed. We can't let them catch us.'

The captain regarded her in confusion. 'Your Majesty?'

'Are you deaf? Full speed! Now!'

Ingels' lips tightened in anger, but he maintained a level voice. 'Increase to twenty-five knots,' he ordered the helm officer.

'No, faster!' Alula snapped.

'That – that is as fast as she can go, Your Majesty.'

'No, it isn't! The *Atlantia* reached almost forty knots.'

'You would have to override the speed limiter to do that—'

'Then override it!'

'I can't.'

'Out of my way, you idiot!' she shouted, storming past him. Al-Asim shoved him aside for good measure before joining her. The rest of his men took up menacing positions nearby, daring the bridge crew to challenge them.

The helm officer hurriedly gave up his seat for Alula, who brought up the passcode entry screen and typed in the code her brother had used aboard the other liner: 032015—

The screen flashed red, a warning message telling her it had been rejected.

'*What?*' She tapped it in again, more carefully, but with the same result. 'Why isn't it working? It should— Oh, that *bastard*.'

'What is it?' asked al-Asim.

'The code Fadil used on the *Atlantia* isn't working because it's not his *real* code! He kept it from me!' She pushed all the throttles as far forward as they would go. It made no difference, the speed display staying constant at twenty-five knots. Her face flushed with pure fury. '*No!*'

'We're gaining,' Snowcock reported. The *Pacifia* now stood tall on the horizon, fully visible. 'They've increased speed, but I'd say they've topped out at twenty-five knots.'

'The limiter,' said the Emir, managing a smile.

'Alula can't override it?' asked Nina.

'No,' said Lobato. 'The access code you used on the *Atlantia* was devised to be easy for you to remember – and was only ever meant to be used there. It was not programmed into the *Pacifia*.'

'So she didn't know your real code?' Eddie asked Fadil.

'Of course not. A ruler must have some secrets, even from his own family. Don't you have secrets from your wife?'

'Only my internet search history,' Eddie replied, waggling his eyebrows at Nina.

She sighed at her husband's attempt at humour. 'It's not nearly secret enough – I have to keep deleting it from the browser so Macy doesn't see it.' She turned to Snowcock. 'When will we catch up?'

'About twenty minutes,' said the captain. '*If* our engines hold. One of the battery banks has had a five-degree temperature spike in the last ten minutes. If it goes much higher, I'll have to slow down.'

'We can't stop now,' said the Emir, pre-empting Nina's own response by a split second. 'We have come this far, and we are so close to them.'

Eddie stared at the other ship. 'How far are we from Dhajan now?'

Snowcock glanced at the chart. 'About seventy miles.'

'Out of jamming range?' the Yorkshireman said pointedly.

The older man hurriedly picked up the radio handset. '*Pacifia*, *Pacifia*! This is Captain Arnold Snowcock aboard the *Atlantia*. Do you read me?'

'Sir!' called one of the *Pacifia*'s bridge crew. 'We're getting a radio message from the *Atlantia*.'

Ingels crossed to the man's station, but Alula and al-Asim pushed him aside. 'Let me hear!' she snapped.

The young man switched the radio to loudspeaker. The transmission was distorted, the Dhajani emergency message still interfering, but the American's voice was just about discernible. 'I repeat, this is Arnold Snowcock on the *Atlantia*. The Emir is alive. His sister tried to murder him in an attempted coup, but failed—'

Shock rippled around the bridge, but another voice had cut in: an American woman. 'Not important right now!'

'Wilde!' snarled Alula.

'*Pacifia*, if you can hear us,' Nina went on, 'Alula has a bomb that's as powerful as a nuke. She's going to use your ship for a suicide attack on the US base in Bahrain!'

All eyes turned to the usurper. 'Is this true?' Ingels asked.

Alula glared at the increasingly hostile officers – then shouted an order. Her men snatched out concealed Glock 18 machine pistols and pointed them at the bridge crew, who retreated in fear. 'Whether my brother is alive or not does not matter,' she announced imperiously. '*I* am the ruler of Dhajan, and this ship will go where I order it. Turn that off.' The officer reluctantly silenced Nina's ongoing message. 'Stay on course for Manama. How long before we reach the harbour?'

Ingels checked a screen. 'Just over forty minutes.'

Alula looked back at the video wall. The *Atlantia* was still powering after its sister ship, visibly gaining. 'Hashim, bring the spearhead,' she said. 'The rest of you, guard the bridge. No one enters, no one leaves. If anyone tries to slow the ship, change course or use the radio, shoot them.' Her men moved to cover the entire room.

Al-Asim picked up the case. 'Where are we going, Your Majesty?'

'The vault,' she replied. 'If we lock the spearhead inside, nobody can interfere with it. Captain, you will open it for me.'

Ingels nodded reluctantly. Al-Asim ordered his agents to watch the crew, then followed Alula and the captain from the bridge.

There had been no reply to Nina's message, nor had the *Pacifia* changed speed or course. The *Atlantia* charged after it, the gap steadily closing. Ten miles, five, less . . .

'Will the US base be able to hear us yet?' Nina asked, looking past the other liner at the Bahraini shoreline.

'I don't know,' the captain replied. 'We're still fifteen miles out. But they'll know something's wrong. *Pacifia* wasn't scheduled to stop in Bahrain for another three days.'

Eddie picked up the binoculars. The busy harbour mouth was becoming visible on the horizon, long breakwaters and piers stretching out into the shallows. Inland, a small forest of gleaming skyscrapers stood above the capital's sprawl. 'We've got to keep trying. They might be able to get a special forces team on to the ship by chopper—'

He broke off as a new voice came over the radio – an American man. The words were muffled, the transmitter in Bahrain using brute force to overpower the jamming, but clear enough to make out. 'Approaching Dhajani cruise liners, this is Naval Support Activity Bahrain. You are making an unscheduled and unauthorised approach to Bahraini waters and a United States naval facility. Stop your engines and await further orders. I repeat, *Atlantia*, *Pacifia*, you are making an unauthorised approach to a US naval base. Stop your engines immediately.'

'NSA Bahrain, this is *Atlantia*,' Snowcock replied. 'I have the Emir of Dhajan with me. Please stand by.' He gave the handset to Fadil. 'Your Majesty.'

The monarch composed himself, then spoke. 'This is the Emir of Dhajan. My country has suffered an attempted *coup d'état*, and the lead conspirators are aboard the *Pacifia*. As an ally of the United States, I am asking for your help to stop them.'

A pause, then the voice returned. '*Atlantia*, I repeat: stop your engines immediately and await further orders.'

'I am the Emir of Dhajan!' Fadil repeated, frustrated. 'Let me speak to your superior officer!'

'I don't think they believe you,' said Eddie.

'I'll get their attention,' said Nina, grabbing the handset. 'NSA Bahrain, the *Pacifia* has been hijacked with ten thousand innocent people aboard, and there's a bomb on it big enough to take out your base and a lot more besides. It's not going to stop – and since we're the only ship that can catch it before it reaches you, nor are we. Got that?'

The pause before the naval officer replied was longer this time, and when he did resume, his tone was harder. '*Atlantia*, *Pacifia*, if you do not stop immediately, we will sink you.'

Nina looked at Eddie, aghast. 'That went well,' he said.

'Why won't they listen to me?' the Emir asked.

'They won't believe you're the Emir without proof, which means stopping the ship and letting them board,' said Eddie. 'And their response to a bomb threat is pretty much going to be "blow the shit out of the *Pacifia*". Although will they be able to get anything out of dock in time?'

'The Fifth Fleet's stationed in Bahrain,' Snowcock told him. 'They could probably start up a cruiser or destroyer quickly enough to intercept.'

'We've got to stop the *Pacifia* before they do, then,' said Nina. They were closing rapidly on the other liner, passengers now visible to the naked eye on its rear decks. 'Although . . . how?'

'Ram it from behind and take out the engines,' Eddie suggested.

'That wouldn't work,' said Snowcock. 'The gas turbines aren't right at the stern like an old steamship. And even if we caused enough damage to shut them down, the azipods can still run off battery power. Ramming it would kill hundreds of people for nothing.'

Lobato gazed nervously at the ever-nearing glass spires of Manama. 'Even if we stop the ship, if the spearhead explodes, we are close enough to Bahrain that the blast would destroy it.'

'Then we've got to get the spearhead itself,' said Nina. Her gaze danced over the other liner, fixing on its stern. 'The marina! We could put the spearhead in a speedboat and send it out into the Gulf!' She indicated the empty horizon to the north-east, beyond which was nothing but open water for a hundred miles until the shores of Iran.

'All well and good,' said Eddie, 'but first we've got to *get* the spearhead – which Alula's not going to just hand over. And there's the slight problem that it's on *that* ship,' he indicated the *Pacifia*, 'and we're on *this* ship.'

'So we get *from* this ship to that ship. Somehow.' The silence that followed almost made her expect a cricket to chirp. 'I'm open to suggestions?'

'We're less laden than the *Pacifia*, so we're higher in the water,' Snowcock offered. 'If we came right alongside, someone could jump from our top deck down to theirs.'

Eddie regarded the approaching ship. At a casual glance, the liner's side appeared to be a flat wall, but on closer inspection, all manner of extensions jutted from it – balconies, viewing lounges, lifeboats, to say nothing of the twin of the room in which they were standing. 'Won't the wing bridge be sliced off if you get that close?'

'Not if I'm careful – and since I'll have to be in it, I'll be *very* careful! The best place to jump from would be the promenade.' The captain turned to point out a long, sweeping protrusion from the uppermost deck about halfway down the *Atlantia*'s length. 'There's an emergency evacuation gantry. You'll be able to jump straight on to the sun deck.'

'Get someone to show us there,' said Nina.

Eddie eyed her. 'You're coming, are you?'

'Don't even start, you know I am. Captain,' she went on to Snowcock, 'the more people we have with us, the better our chances. Will any of your crew be willing to volunteer?'

'I'll put out a call,' he replied.

'I will come too,' said Junayd as Snowcock began an announcement over the public address system.

'No!' protested Fadil. 'Mamun, you are retired!'

'I will never be too old to do my duty – or protect my Emir,' the old man replied. 'Stay well, *al'amir alshabu.*' The monarch was about to object further, but then gave a reluctant nod.

The *Pacifia* was now only a few ship lengths ahead, the nineteen-knot speed difference eating away at the gap by ten metres every second. 'We need to go,' said Eddie.

'Wait,' said the Emir as they turned to leave. 'My access code – the real one. It will let you into all of the *Pacifia*'s systems.'

'You wouldn't give it to your own sister, but you're giving it to us?' said Eddie.

'A secret is worthless if it is not used when it is most needed. The code is nine-three-seven-six-four-four.'

Nina repeated it. 'Thank you.' She and Eddie hurried into the wrecked main bridge, Junayd and Rakin following.

They quickly made their way to the top deck. Four officers, including Dimakos, and several crewmen were waiting. 'You need our help?' said one of the officers, a burly young Australian man whose name badge read *Rignall*.

'We need to get across to the *Pacifia*,' Eddie told the group, getting disbelieving looks in return. 'The captain said there's an emergency gantry on this deck?'

'Yeah, yeah. This way.' Everyone hurried aft.

The *Atlantia* pulled out to overtake its twin on its port side. It drew closer, the passengers on the exterior decks beginning to realise from the damage to its bridge and bow that this was no publicity stunt. People retreated indoors, the exodus speeding up as it became obvious that the other liner intended to get very close indeed.

Alula and al-Asim emerged from the *Pacifia*'s vault, waiting for Ingels to use his access code to close and lock the heavy steel door before climbing the stairs and entering the exhibition hall. Unlike the Atlantis exhibit aboard its sister ship, this was a display of Picasso's artworks. Alula gave the priceless display a dismissive sneer – Western degeneracy! – then headed into the passageway outside.

It was immediately clear that something had happened. Several passengers ran past them towards the front of the ship, worried voices echoing through the luxurious halls. 'What's going on?' al-Asim asked.

'The *Atlantia* must be catching up,' said Alula.

'But why are they so worried?' A frightening possibility occurred to the security officer. 'Are they going to *ram* us?'

'Fadil would never allow it,' she replied, but there was a definite sense of fear rising around them. 'We have to get to the bridge. Quickly!'

They hurried up the hallway – then halted in astonishment as they reached one of the 3-D video walls. 'My God!' cried Ingels. The screen showed the view outside the ship . . . which was mostly obscured by the shell-ravaged *Atlantia* drawing alongside.

Alula stared at the jaw-dropping image, then broke into a run. 'We've got to stop them! *Move!*' One hand on his hidden gun to force the captain onwards, Al-Asim sprinted after her.

45

Snowcock realised he was holding his breath as he guided his ship alongside the *Pacifia*. The leading liner's roiling wake meant he had to make constant tiny course adjustments to maintain the gap. One mistake, and the wing bridge would be mashed flat against the other ship's side . . .

'Your Majesty,' he said to the Emir, 'you should get to a safer place.'

'I must admit, the thought had occurred to me,' the Dhajani replied. 'Gideon?'

'Absolutely,' Lobato quickly agreed. He limped up the steps.

The crewmen helped the Emir after him. 'Captain,' Fadil said, pausing, 'thank you – and good luck. I will make sure you are honoured for your bravery.'

'I just hope I'm there to appreciate it,' Snowcock replied with a brief smile. The Emir returned it, then departed.

The captain returned his full attention to the task at hand. The *Pacifia*'s stern slid past, the holidaymakers who had been sunbathing and swimming now fleeing as the battered juggernaut relentlessly closed in.

Alula waited for Ingels to open the bridge door, then rushed in and hurried to the port wing. Al-Asim followed.

She looked back down the *Pacifia*'s length at its twin. What was her brother doing? Trying to stop the spearhead from reaching Bahrain by crashing the two ships into each other?

No, she decided. Doing that would kill hundreds of

passengers. Even with far more lives at stake, he was too weak to make such a decision. So did he mean to overtake her liner and block its path?

That would also result in deaths – she was more than willing to ram anything that tried to stop her, and he would know that. Which left . . .

'They're going to board us!' she realised. 'Send the men to the top deck – and kill anyone who tries to jump over!'

Al-Asim ran back into the main bridge, issuing orders. Six of his team rushed for the exit, one staying with him to guard the crew.

'Here's the gantry,' said Rignall. The promenade deck curved outwards amidships over the liner's side around a swimming pool and wet bar. At its outer edge, behind a gate in the tall glass windbreak panels enclosing the deck, was a white-painted piece of equipment resembling a crane's jib. 'It's for lowering people to the water if they can't reach the lifeboats,' the Australian went on as he unlocked the barrier, 'but I'm guessing we're not going all the way down?'

'I hope not,' said Nina. The *Pacifia*'s upper deck was about twelve feet below. Snowcock was holding steady on a parallel course that seemed terrifyingly close to the second liner.

Rignall worked a control panel. Warning lights flashed, the gantry starting to swing outwards. Eddie watched the approaching ship. 'We'll reach it in about thirty seconds,' he said. 'Everyone get ready.'

'We can jump down by the basketball court,' said the Australian, pointing to the rear of the *Pacifia*'s top deck, where a blue rectangle stood out against the pale teak. 'I'll go first.'

The gantry stopped, extending perpendicular to the deck's edge. Rignall locked it in place, then held the single handrail and carefully walked out along the metal grillework floor.

Eddie took up position on the gantry's base. The *Atlantia*'s side dropped vertiginously away below. The ship was riding more heavily as it crashed through the other liner's bow wave, rolling him out above the water before swinging sickeningly back.

The other vessel's upper deck was clearing in a hurry as the sunbathing passengers realised the very real danger of over half a million tons of metal colliding. But then he saw people running against the tide, black-clad figures racing towards the stern—

'Get back!' he shouted to Rignall. 'They're going to shoot!'

Full-auto gunfire erupted from the *Pacifia*'s deck. At this range, the Glock 18s of Alula's security detail were not especially accurate – but firing twenty rounds per second, they didn't need to be.

Bullets sprayed up at the gantry, shattering the glass panels. Nina and the two Dhajani soldiers dropped at the Englishman's warning, but others were not so quick. A bloody chunk of flesh exploded from an officer's arm, a crewman clutching at his neck as a round ripped through his trapezius muscle. Another man's face was slashed by flying glass.

Rignall, exposed on the gantry, had nowhere to hide. A bullet smashed his left shin as he ran back towards the deck, and he fell screaming over the gantry's side—

His momentum saved him from a long plunge into the seething sea. Ranks of cabin balconies lay below, and he landed hard on one three decks down, demolishing its table and chairs.

'Jesus!' Eddie gasped, braving the gunfire to look down. 'He fell back on the ship!' He couldn't see the other man directly, but a smear of bright blood on a white railing told him where he had ended up.

The firing stopped, the Dhajanis having exhausted their magazines – but they would quickly reload. 'Is he alive?' Nina asked.

'He got shot and fell thirty feet, so if he is, he'll be fucked up. We can't get across this way; they'll cut us to fucking pieces.'

'Rakin has a gun,' Junayd reminded him. 'He could give covering fire.'

'Not against six guys. We need to find another way over.'

'We've got to help Mr Rignall!' said one of the crewmen, pulling an injured comrade clear of the edge.

'We can do both,' Nina said. 'We go down, find Rignall, and then jump across.'

'Are you crazy?' said Dimakos.

'If we don't get on that ship, everyone on it will die – and maybe millions more!'

Eddie risked another look at the *Pacifia*, ducking back as more shots clanged off the ship's side below him. Alula's men were now congregated on the upper deck, waiting for them; any attempt to cross the gantry would be suicide.

He retreated to check on his companions. The injured officer had a walkie-talkie, as did one of the crewmen. The Yorkshireman took the officer's radio, then addressed the *Atlantia*'s personnel. 'Do what you can for them. We'll go down and find Rignall. Anyone who still wants to come with us, we're going across.'

One of the officers and two crewmen volunteered, the others staying to tend to the injured. Dimakos used the remaining radio to call for help as Eddie led the way back through the gate. 'He landed three decks below us, a couple of cabins back,' he said. 'Anyone got a key?'

'I have,' said one of the crewmen.

'Good.' He hurried to a flight of steps nearby, his companions right behind. 'Snowcock, are you there?' he said into the walkie-talkie as they descended.

'Yes,' the captain replied. 'Are you on the *Pacifia*?'

'No, we got shot at. Some of your people are wounded. They're getting help, but we need you to help us as well. We can't get across from the top deck, so we're going to jump over from one of the balconies below.'

'You'll never make it! It's too far.'

'I know, which is why you need to get closer.'

'It's too dangerous! If I get any nearer, the suction effect will pull the two ships together.'

'Yeah, it sucks, deal with it,' Eddie snapped as he reached Deck 17. A narrow corridor was lined with cabins. 'Okay,' he said, heading aft, 'he must be in one of these.'

The crewman with the key opened the first door and entered. 'He's not here.'

'Try the next one.' Another door was opened. This time, it was immediately clear that they had found Rignall's landing site; one of the glass balcony doors was smashed, a stiff wind blowing through it. 'In here!'

The Australian was sprawled over the wrecked furniture. Both his legs were broken, one bent sickeningly below the knee. More blood had pooled around his head. 'Oh, Jesus,' gasped the officer.

Eddie checked the room number. 'There's a badly wounded man in Cabin 17326,' he radioed. 'If there's a medic aboard, get them here now!' Rignall was still alive, a small bubble of blood swelling and shrinking in one nostril. 'Get a blanket and cover him,' the Yorkshireman ordered. 'Back into the other room – we're going across.'

The crew attended to their shipmate, the boarding party now down to himself, Nina, Junayd and Rakin. They returned to the first cabin, Eddie leading them to the balcony.

'Can we make it?' Nina asked.

'Nope.' The two liners were about twenty-five feet apart – too far to jump. He lifted the radio. 'Captain, you've *got* to get closer!'

★ ★ ★

On the wing bridge, Snowcock heard the message and grimaced. There was less than ten feet between the windows to his right and the *Pacifia*'s side. 'I'll come in as near as I can,' he replied. 'You just be ready to jump across.'

He delicately adjusted the thruster controls, reducing the *Atlantia*'s speed to match its sister's and bringing it closer as carefully as he could.

Alula felt relief and satisfaction when the boarding attempt was repelled, but the other liner was still dangerously close – and now it was slowing, matching speeds. Her enemies were up to something . . .

She realised what as the gap between the two huge vessels started to shrink. Her men were guarding the upper deck, but there were literally hundreds of balconies below from which people could jump from one ship to the other. No way to cover them all.

She was about to shout an order for Ingels to turn away, but a more aggressive idea came at the sight of a silhouetted figure in the other ship's surviving wing bridge. Don't defend: *attack!*

'Captain!' she yelled. 'Turn to port – crash into them!'

The Dane went white. 'What? But Your Majesty, we have almost ten thousand passengers aboard!'

Al-Asim marched towards the captain, raising his gun. The rest of the bridge crew shrank back. 'Turn the ship. Or you die.'

Ingels stared at the weapon, then, dry-mouthed, ushered the officer manning the helm station aside. 'I – I will do it,' he said. 'I can't ask anyone else.'

'I do not care who does it,' Alula told him. 'Only that it is done. Now!'

Ingels took fearful hold of the azipod controls and turned them, hard.

★ ★ ★

Snowcock watched the white wall of metal to starboard inch nearer – then suddenly it lunged at him.

He was thrown to the floor as the wing bridge pounded into the *Pacifia*'s side, windows shattering. The floor crumpled like a concertina, folding around him.

Eddie was about to climb on to the railing to make the jump – when the daylight from above was abruptly blotted out as the *Pacifia* rolled towards him like a falling skyscraper. 'Shit!' he yelled, throwing himself backwards. 'Down, get down!'

Nina and the others dived into the cabin—

The windows exploded as the two liners slammed into each other.

46

A lula clung to a railing, barely staying upright as the *Pacifia* lurched as if struck by an earthquake. The bridge crew were flung across the deck or slammed against consoles.

The chaos in the rest of the liner was far worse. The corridors were packed with holidaymakers fleeing the collision; hundreds were hurt as they were thrown against walls or sent tumbling down stairs.

But the armed men on the top deck suffered the most severe whiplash as the huge ship reeled beneath them. One broke a leg against the unyielding steel support of a sunshade canopy – and another was catapulted over the atrium railing, falling with a scream into a swimming pool twelve decks below. The others were barely better off, ending up bruised and dazed amongst a sea of broken glass.

Alarms screeched throughout the *Atlantia*. Snowcock dragged himself back to the console. He had survived only by chance, the mangled wing bridge jammed into the spacious balcony of one of the *Pacifia*'s larger cabins. A few feet higher or lower, and his eyrie would have been crushed like a beer can.

But he still wasn't safe. The display told him the collision had inflicted major damage upon his ship, fire suppression systems activating in several sections – including the battery banks.

His worst fear had come true. One battery fire could be contained, but with several along the ship's length and not enough crew to deal with them, the chances of a chain reaction became terrifyingly high. If the batteries went up, the rest of the *Atlantia* – including its fuel of liquefied natural gas – would rapidly follow.

He had to sound the evacuation order, but he also needed to give his visitors one last chance to carry out their mission. He recovered the radio. 'Chase! I can't hold her! You've got to get across, *now!*'

Nina heard the captain's voice squawk from the walkie-talkie. 'Eddie!' she cried. The view from the balcony was now almost a mirror image, one of the *Pacifia*'s cabins just a few feet beyond it.

'I heard, I heard,' her husband replied groggily. He went back to the balcony, clutching the railing as the deck shook. A sonorous moan of straining metal echoed through the ship, glass hailing from both vessels. They were entangled, protruding sections mashed together, but they would not hold for long.

Nina joined him. 'Shit,' she gasped. The gap between the two ships was about six feet, but the *Atlantia* was rising and falling in the swell. The slightest misjudgement would send her plummeting to her death in the colliding wakes below.

'We can do it.' He climbed on to the railing, holding position until the *Atlantia* rose higher . . . then leapt across.

He cleared the other railing by mere inches, hitting the wooden deck with a bang. 'I'm okay!' he shouted to Nina. 'You can do it!'

She clambered up. Rakin moved to support her from behind, but it was what lay ahead – or rather below – that worried her. The remains of lifeboats from both ships clattered between the hulls as debris fell past them into the churning water.

She readied herself . . . and leapt—

A new alarm shrilled in the battered wing bridge. Snowcock looked at the monitor, and saw every readout turn red. The fires were spreading, the overheated drive systems shutting down. He activated the PA system. 'Abandon ship!' he cried. 'This is the captain – abandon ship! Everyone get to the port-side lifeboats—'

Explosive cracks and screams shook the ship as the *Atlantia* ripped away from its sister. Snowcock knew the end had come for his vessel. He ran up the steps and dived through the doorway as the embedded wing bridge was torn away from the superstructure like a rotten tooth, tumbling down the *Atlantia*'s side to smash into the sea far below.

Nina had just jumped when the liner veered apart from the other ship. The balcony rolled away from her—

The archaeologist desperately threw out her arms. She hit the railing – at chest height.

Pain cracked across her ribs. Overcome, winded, she fell—

Eddie grabbed her wrist.

'I've got you,' he gasped, straining to lift her – only to freeze as he looked back at the *Atlantia*. 'No, don't!'

Too late. Rakin had hurled himself across the gap, both hands outstretched to catch the top railing – but the two ships were still separating. His fingers brushed a lower rail, slipped off . . . then his arc continued inexorably downwards.

The Dhajani hit a balcony two floors below with a crack of breaking bone. He screamed, someone sheltering inside the cabin crying out in fright. Junayd looked on in helpless horror as the gap between the twin liners widened.

Eddie couldn't spare the injured man a moment's thought. All he could do was cling to Nina as the *Pacifia* reeled back over, his wife swinging beneath him like a bell's clapper – though the flat thud as she hit the ship's side was anything but musical. He braced himself, waiting for the liner to right itself, then hauled her upwards. 'Grab the railing!'

Her free hand clamped around it. He strained to lift her

higher. She found a foothold and pushed, all but falling on to the balcony beside her husband.

'Oh Jesus!' she wheezed, clutching her bruised chest. 'I thought I was going to fall!'

'Rakin did,' he said. 'He landed lower down. Just hope someone can help him, 'cause we don't have time.'

'You're right,' she reluctantly agreed. 'We've got to find the spearhead and get it off the ship.'

'Yeah. So where is it?' They looked at each other, neither having an answer. 'Oh for fuck's sake!'

'It'll either be with Alula,' Nina reasoned, 'or she'll have put it somewhere nobody can interfere with it. So on the bridge, or . . . the vault!' she exclaimed. 'The only people who can open it are the senior officers, and they're probably all being held at gunpoint.'

'So how do *we* open it?' Eddie asked.

She smiled. 'The Emir gave me his code, remember? Come on!' Adrenalin partially overpowering the pain across her chest, she hurried out, the Yorkshireman following.

Alula watched the *Atlantia* drop behind as her own ship powered onwards. Smoke billowed from the other liner's lower decks, and with the port wing bridge torn off, the vessel was now crippled.

The threat to her plan was not over, though. She had seen tiny figures leap across the gap as the two ships pulled apart; at least three people had made it over, and even at a distance she was certain one of them was Nina Wilde. She unconsciously rubbed her nose at the thought of the American, the only person ever to lay a hand on her in anger, and the resulting spike of pain stoked her own anger still further.

She returned to the bridge. 'Wilde and some others got aboard,' she told al-Asim. 'Send the men after them.'

'It's a big ship,' he reminded her. 'How will they know where to look?'

Alula nodded towards the video wall. 'Use the cameras,' she ordered the bridge crew. 'Find them!'

Alarms echoed throughout the *Atlantia* as the enormous vessel lost speed. With no passengers aboard, the crew could bypass normal procedures and instead run straight for the port-side lifeboat deck.

Snowcock was determined to be the last man off. Three boats were already being lowered, another waiting for the last evacuees. 'Come on, hurry!' he yelled as a crewman led Junayd to the last lifeboat. 'Where are Dr Wilde and the others?'

'They made it to the other ship,' Junayd told him. 'Is the Emir safe?'

'He's in the lifeboat.' Snowcock stood back to let them board.

A dull thump echoed through the hull. 'That was a battery explosion!' warned Lobato. 'We have to go before a chain reaction starts.'

The captain hurried to the control panel. 'Everyone hold on!'

He activated the winch. The lifeboat juddered, then began to lower from its davits. Snowcock moved to jump through its hatch—

Another explosion – nearer, and more violent. The captain staggered, one foot slipping over the edge.

He fell—

One flailing hand caught the bottom of the hatch. He hung for a moment, before losing his grip – only for the crewman to grab him. Others inside scrambled to drag the dangling man into the descending craft.

'Captain!' the Emir cried. 'Are you all right?'

'I'm fine,' Snowcock gasped. He thanked his crew as he stood and closed the hatch. 'I'm very sorry about your ship, though,' he told Fadil apologetically. 'As maiden voyages go, it's up there with the *Titanic* . . .'

'There they are, *there*!' snapped Alula, pointing at a screen. The *Pacifia*'s corridors were crowded with panicking passengers, but she had just seen two unpleasantly familiar faces pushing against the flow. 'Where is that, and where are they going?'

An officer checked a computer screen. 'Deck 10, section Port D. They're heading aft.'

'So they're going back through the ship,' said al-Asim, watching as the couple reached a stairwell and descended, 'and down. What are they doing?'

'They're going to the vault,' Alula realised in alarm. 'Send the men after them!'

Al-Asim made a rapid radio call to his team. 'But the vault's closed. They can't reach the spearhead, can they?'

'They shouldn't have escaped from the solar plant, they shouldn't have reached the *Atlantia*, and they shouldn't have got aboard this ship,' she said angrily. 'Don't underestimate them – just kill them!'

Nina and Eddie reached Deck 5. Even this deep in the liner, panicked passengers were running in all directions. After the collision with the *Atlantia*, thousands of people had fled the port side, only to find nowhere to go. With the *Pacifia* running at full speed, it was impossible to lower the lifeboats without risking numerous deaths.

Eddie took the lead, one arm raised to fend off anyone charging blindly into him. 'Stay behind me!' he told Nina as he shoved away a jabbering Russian in a tracksuit. 'Which way?'

Apart from differences in decor, the *Pacifia*'s interior was identical to its sister's. 'Down here, then left,' she said, following him.

They rounded a corner, coming to a set of double doors. 'This it?'

'Yeah.' They were locked, but there was a dark glass panel beside them. She raised her hand, and it lit up. 'Okay, let's see if the code works . . .'

She brought up the keypad, then tapped in the Emir's secret access key. Green, and the lock clicked. 'That's a good start.'

'Let's hope Alula didn't stick a padlock on the vault door, or we're fucked,' Eddie said as they ran inside. The softly lit treasures of the Picasso exhibit greeted them, but neither could spare the cases a glance as they hurried to the vault entrance.

Nina quickly entered the code a second time. The door unlocked. They went through to find themselves in a small antechamber. Stairs led down to the vault's gleaming steel door. There was another access panel at the top of the flight. Unlike the one outside, this was not blank, instead displaying a message in multiple languages: *Security Systems Active.*

Eddie looked suspiciously down the stairs. He could see numerous cameras and sensors, faint red lines of laser light visible in the air. 'You think the code'll work on this?'

'Let's see. Y'know, I'm never going to buy one of Gideon's cars if they've all got back doors like this . . .'

To their relief, the code was again accepted – and a low rumble of powerful motors reached them. 'It's opening!' said Eddie as the huge door started to move. They waited . . . and waited. '*Reeeeally* slowly.'

'It's a big-ass door,' Nina noted.

He glanced back into the gallery. 'I don't like this. Opening the vault's probably tripped a warning on the bridge, and with all these cameras, it's not like they can't see us – shit, they might have seen us already!'

'You think they're on the way?'

'You wait here. I'll watch the door.' He started back across the exhibition hall, looking for anything he could use as an improvised weapon—

A shout from outside as someone was barged aside. Eddie's eyes snapped back to the entrance to see a black-clad man rush through it, whipping up his Glock.

The Yorkshireman dived behind a display cabinet as the automatic blazed, fire scything across the room after him. The toughened glass crazed with the first few impacts, then shattered as more rounds struck it, fragments showering over Picasso's bronze *Death's Head*.

An alarm shrilled – and all the cabinets suddenly began to drop into the floor.

Both Eddie and the Dhajani were taken by surprise, though the Yorkshireman's shock was tinged with fear as his cover disappeared. He burst out from behind the shrinking case and sprinted for a taller one a few metres away. His attacker swept the Glock after him—

Bullets seared past as Eddie hurled himself headlong behind the new cabinet – then the gunfire stopped. The Dhajani had burned through his ammunition. He immediately ejected the empty magazine, reaching into his clothing for a replacement.

Eddie looked for better cover. But he was too far from the vault entrance to reach it before the man reloaded, and the holes into which the cases were descending were closing one by one as metal hatches slid across them—

There was a moment between their clearing the floor and the openings being sealed – and a neighbouring case was just vanishing into the vault. He sprang at it as the gunman fired again. More rounds tearing at his heels, he rolled into the hole and fell a couple of feet to thud down on the cabinet's top. The hatch sliced into place above him.

He dropped to the vault floor. The rest of the cabinets were lowering around him. The chamber was lined with deposit boxes, places for paranoid passengers to leave their valuables during the voyage – but what instantly drew his eye was something conspicuously out of place. A large metal briefcase sat near the entrance. The spearhead; it had to be.

The heavy door was closing again, Nina's override itself overridden by the new alarms. He ran for it—

A thud behind. The Dhajani had ridden down on a different cabinet.

Eddie snatched up the case without breaking stride. The door was two feet of solid steel, slowly but relentlessly swinging shut. The gap was narrow, and shrinking fast.

He dived through the opening as the gunman raised his weapon—

The Yorkshireman's right knee hit the frame's edge – but he was clear, landing heavily at the foot of the stairs as a deafening fusillade of gunfire clanged against the barrier behind him. Then the noise was abruptly cut off as the door slammed.

Nina ran to him. 'Eddie!'

'I'm okay,' he assured her breathlessly, standing. 'And I got the spearhead. At least, I hope I did. Be annoying if it's just six hundred million dollars in negotiable bearer bonds.'

'I'll assume that's a movie reference and move on,' she said. 'We need to get out of here before more of Alula's people arrive. Can you run?'

He followed her up the stairs. 'I'll bloody have to, won't I? So what are we doing with this?'

Nina checked nobody else had reached the gallery before running for the exit. 'We need to get it as far from land as possible, so we'll take a speedboat from the marina.'

'You know somebody'll have to *drive* the boat, don't you?'

'Yeah, I do,' she said grimly. 'And the list of choices is exactly two names long.'

★ ★ ★

Alula watched the monitors, seething, as the American and her husband disappeared from frame. 'They have the spearhead! Find them, kill them! Get it back!'

The images changed, switching to cameras near the exhibition hall. Nina and Eddie flitted from screen to screen. Al-Asim relayed their position to their three remaining hunters.

Alula turned to him. 'I want to talk to my pilot.' He changed the walkie-talkie's channel, then handed it to her. 'Get the helicopter ready to take off,' she commanded. 'I will be leaving soon.' The pilot confirmed, then she returned the radio. 'I want you to make sure the ship stays on course for Bahrain. Nothing must stop it.'

It took a moment for her words to sink in, and when they did, shock dawned on al-Asim's face. 'You . . . you don't want me to come with you?'

'Hashim, you . . .' She looked down, voice softening. 'You are the only man I trust in this world. I trust *you* to see this through. It's the only way to save our country.' Her eyes came back up to meet his, almost pleading. 'Please. You must do this. For me.'

'Your Majesty . . . Alula,' he said quietly. One hand reached out and squeezed hers; she did not resist. 'If you want me to finish this for you, you know I will. I have always been there to do whatever you needed.'

'You have, I know. And I will always be grateful.'

'But there's no other way?'

'I wish there was,' she said, sadness clear. 'But I know you won't let anyone defeat us. Not my brother, not the Americans, not this ship's crew . . . and definitely not Nina Wilde.'

'I will not,' he said. 'You have my word. But there is something I must tell you before you go. I . . .' He took a deep breath. 'I lo—'

'I know, Hashim,' Alula whispered, closing her hand around his. 'I know.'

They stood still, looking into each other's eyes, then al-Asim straightened, drawing away. 'Nobody will stop you, Your Majesty. You will take the throne of Dhajan, and you will save our country. It has been . . .' He swallowed before continuing. 'It has been the greatest honour a man could have to serve you.'

'Thank you. For everything.'

As she turned to leave, al-Asim spoke again. 'Your Majesty, please let me take you to the helicopter. I have to be sure you leave the ship safely.'

'I need you here,' she told him, indicating the screens. 'You have to guide your men to the spearhead – and make sure the ship stays on course. I will be all right.' A hint of a smile. 'I am not a girl any more, Hashim.'

'I know, Your Majesty. Then . . . goodbye, and good luck. May God protect you.' He bowed his head.

'And you.' A brief but respectful nod of her own, then she left the bridge.

'Anyone following us?' Nina asked as she and Eddie reached a lounge area towards the *Pacifia*'s stern. One wall was taken up by a 3-D screen. The sandy coast of Bahrain rolled past upon it, the image almost hyperreal.

'Don't see anyone,' he said, looking back. 'Let's check we've actually *got* the spearhead.'

He laid the case upon a sofa and opened it. 'I'd say that's a yes,' Nina said, narrowing her eyes against the shimmering light within the Atlantean crystal. Its colour had changed, lurid purples and blues and reds erupting amidst the intense white glow. 'Damn, I think that's definitely stage three.'

'Better get it to a boat—' He broke off as the view changed to an angle astern. Even though the *Atlantia* had fallen some way behind, the crippled liner still dominated the image. Smoke poured from its hull, a few lifeboats making hasty retreats. As the couple watched, an explosion blasted out a section of the ship's side, debris spinning into the sea.

'Oh my God,' said Nina, appalled. 'I hope everyone got off in time.'

Eddie counted. 'I can see four lifeboats, and there might be more behind—'

He was silenced again, this time in stunned shock, as fireballs erupted along the ship's length. The entire enormous vessel *jumped*, over a quarter of a million tonnes of metal leaping higher in the water as shock waves slammed against the inside of its hull—

Then the *Atlantia* blew apart.

47

Even deep inside the *Pacifia*, the force of the *Atlantia*'s destruction reached Nina and Eddie, the whole ship quivering as if feeling its sister's death. They stared in silence at the liner's burning hulk, then the view changed again. The new camera was near the bridge, looking over the bow. 'Shit, we're getting closer to Bahrain,' said Eddie, seeing the artificial headland marking the harbour's southern entrance. He shut the case, about to set off again.

'Wait, wait!' Nina cried. She pointed. 'Look!'

A helicopter was on the landing pad. It was starting to power up, the rotor blades turning lazily. 'It's the Emir's,' said Eddie, recognising the royal coat of arms. 'Well, Alula's now.'

'Exactly! It's Alula's – which means she hasn't left yet! But she's about to.'

'That's assuming she even came aboard.'

'You think she'd trust anyone else to look after the spearhead? But she's bugging out now that it's in its final stage – so if we can get to the chopper before it takes off . . .'

He realised where she was leading. 'We'd get the spearhead clear a lot faster than any boat.' A look at the screen. 'It'll take a couple of minutes to get the rotors up to speed – and it's still got cables holding it down. We can make it!'

They ran back the way they had come. 'The pad's on Deck 8,' said Nina, 'so we need to go up three decks, then head forward.' They found an access stairwell and pounded up it.

★ ★ ★

'Where are they going?' al-Asim demanded. He had been directing his forces to intercept Wilde and Chase at the marina, which seemed their most likely destination, but they had now apparently changed their plan.

'They've gone up to . . . Deck 7,' Ingels told him, spotting the Arab's targets on another screen. 'Looks like they're heading for the bow.'

Al-Asim didn't catch the significance of his statement, instead growling commands into his radio. 'They're on Deck 7, going towards the front of the ship.' He watched the monitors for a moment. 'They're going into the shopping mall. Jakeem, you're closest – get them!'

Eddie and Nina ran through the mall's entrance. The shopping complex was all but identical to that on the *Atlantia*. Considering the chaos, it was unsurprisingly sparsely populated – though there were still a few people milling around, as if even imminent disaster could not tear them away from shopping.

'The chopper hasn't taken off,' said Nina, catching a view of the bow on a screen. 'We can still hijack it.'

'What's with this "we"?' Eddie asked. 'If we both die, Macy'll be an orphan! I'll do it.'

'Why are *you* so keen on the possible suicide mission?'

'I'm the only one who can fly the bloody helicopter!'

'You had *three lessons!*' she objected. 'Eight years ago. And on the last one, you crashed into Trump Tower!'

'All right, so I'm not exactly Stringfellow Hawke— Oh fuck!'

He grabbed Nina and dived with her into the toy shop as one of Alula's men ran towards them. The handful of people in the mall screamed as he opened up with his Glock, shattering the store's windows.

'Get behind that!' Eddie yelled, pointing at a heavy display case. Nina reached its cover as he scrambled behind a free-standing shelf unit. The gunman fired another burst. Stuffed toys exploded above the Yorkshireman, showering him with the fluffy innards of Mickey Mouse and the PAW Patrol. He dropped the case, then kept moving as the shelves splintered, more toys cascading over him. One landed hard on his head. 'You're taking the piss, right?' he said as he saw it was a Jason Mach action figure.

The gunfire stopped. Eddie glanced out to see the Dhajani slapping in a new magazine. He looked for anything he could use to his advantage. There was a large cabinet of expensive drones and remote-controlled vehicles nearby, the wooden base of which would give him concealment, maybe even some protection against bullets. If he reached it unseen, he might be able to catch their attacker off guard—

The crunch of boots on glass warned him that his plan had already failed. He had expected the man to come through the shop's door, giving him the couple of seconds needed to reach the cabinet, but instead he had taken a short cut through a smashed window.

Eddie hunched down as the footsteps drew closer, but he knew he would be seen any second—

'*Hey!*'

Nina's shout rang across the shop as she popped up, arm drawn back to throw something—

She hurled it as the Dhajani agent whipped around – and took a replica trikan to his face. The toy was only plastic, but it was still hefty enough to jar his senses, however momentarily.

The Englishman took that moment and ran with it, literally, ploughing into the shelf unit and lifting it as if making a tackle. He charged at the gunman. The Glock snapped back around, but Eddie was already on him.

Toys flew everywhere as they crashed together, the Dhajani stumbling backwards. Bullets blazed wildly from his gun – then he tripped over the window frame and fell on his back, Eddie and the shelves landing heavily on top of him.

The winded agent looked up – to see the Yorkshireman's fist rushing at his face. The impact was considerably harder than Nina's trikan. 'Night-night, fucko,' Eddie growled as the Dhajani slumped.

He collected the Glock, quickly checking the magazine as Nina retrieved the case. Less than half full, about a dozen rounds remaining. There wasn't time to pull the shelves clear and root through the Dhajani's clothing for extra mags; instead, he switched the fire selector to single-shot. If any more of Alula's goons arrived, he would just have to aim well.

'I'm okay,' he said, pre-empting Nina's inevitable question. 'We've got to keep going.'

They set off again. 'How many more of them do you think there are?' she asked.

'How many arseholes can you fit in a helicopter? At least the crew aren't trying to stop us as well.'

'I doubt they'd willingly let themselves get blown up— Oh crap!'

Another Dhajani agent appeared at the top of an escalator to the atrium. The pair hurriedly swerved into a perfume store, Eddie sending a couple of shots at him before he could fire. The man hared down the escalator after them.

He was not alone, another of al-Asim's team following. The first man reached the bottom and dropped behind one of the water features along the mall's centreline, opening fire on the store. More glass shattered, the windows joined by bottles of fragrances as bullets hit them.

Eddie and Nina ducked behind a display. 'Shit, we're pinned,' he said, then flinched as a perfume bottle blew apart, spraying him with Chanel.

Nina recoiled; the scent was pungent in such high concentration. 'God!' she gasped. 'It's like that time in Beverly Hills all over again.'

'At least we're not in a limo that's on fire,' Eddie said – then an idea came to him. 'That cloth there, give it to me!' She tugged a silk handkerchief from a nearby table and passed it to him. 'If you see 'em, take a shot.' He gave her the gun, then pulled a larger perfume bottle from the display.

'A shot of *vodka* would go down fine about now.' She unleashed two suppressing rounds at the first man as he peered over the water feature, forcing him down.

Eddie soaked the handkerchief Nina had given him in perfume, then stuffed it into the neck of the bottle. 'Okay, give me the gun. Hope this works . . .'

He took the Glock, positioning the gun's muzzle beneath the dripping fabric – then fired.

The bullet smacked against a wall, but he wasn't concerned about its target – rather its flash. It caught the alcohol-soaked handkerchief . . . and ignited it.

Nina hurriedly pulled back. Eddie winced as hairs singed on the back of his hand, then lobbed the bottle. It arced over the water feature to smash on the marble floor beyond.

Perfume splashed out – and caught fire. Liquid flame sluiced over the first gunman's legs. He screamed, leaping up in panic. An alarm sounded, valve heads in the ceiling gushing out a dense fog of tiny water droplets.

The Dhajani did not wait for the fire suppression system to take effect. Instead he threw himself into the water feature. A splash, followed by a rush of smoke, then he slumped into the shallow pool, moaning.

The second man fired another burst. Eddie pushed Nina back as bullets blew more bottles to pieces. Their attacker moved for a better angle – stopping beneath a large and gaudy golden chandelier.

Eddie snapped up his Glock, locking on to the base of its stem as the gunman rose to attack again—

The Yorkshireman fired first.

He pulled the trigger so rapidly, the shots sounded fully automatic. The rounds ripped into the gold-plated support rod. The chandelier broke from the ceiling – and fell.

The Dhajani looked up – and the heavy chandelier smashed down on his head, knocking him cold.

'Lights out,' Eddie said, standing. 'Let's go before any more arrive.'

He and Nina ran from the shop. The escalator's foot was now almost completely obscured by the mist from the HI-FOG fire suppression system, which had already choked out the flames from the pungent Molotov. They traversed the haze and charged up the moving stairway to the atrium.

Eddie had his gun ready as they reached the top, but saw only fearful passengers. 'Maybe that was the last of them,' Nina suggested hopefully.

'Someone must still be on the bridge, or the crew would've stopped the ship by now,' he replied as they ran forward. 'If Alula's leaving, that means they're going to sail right into the US base. The navy'll do whatever they need to stop it – which means trying to blow us out of the water.'

'But there are ten thousand people on the ship!'

'They'll still do it – especially as we've told 'em there's a bomb aboard.' They reached the atrium's forward end and entered the superstructure. The elevators to the bridge were not far away – giving him an idea. 'Hold on a sec.'

'What is it?'

'Change of plan. Here.' He gave her the gun. 'Take that, and the spearhead – get to the chopper and make sure it doesn't take off.'

'How?'

'Gun, the pilot, his head – put 'em all together and you'll come up with something!' He grinned as she gave him an irked frown. 'If I'm not at the pad in four minutes, force the pilot to take you out over the Gulf until you're far enough from land to drop the spearhead. If you fly north-east at full speed for ten minutes, that should do – it'll *have* to do. Then turn around and get as far away as you can.'

'What if Alula's in the chopper?'

'Shoot her before she shoots you! I'll get to the bridge and try to stop the ship.'

Nina looked at the gun. 'I don't like this plan.'

'Me neither, but it's the only one we've got.' He ran for the lifts. 'Four minutes. I'll see you down there!'

'Goddammit, Eddie!' she shouted after him, before reluctantly turning for the helipad.

On the bridge, al-Asim had been watching the monitors, dividing his attention between the hunt for Wilde and Chase and Alula's progress towards the helicopter – with, despite his best efforts, more spent on the latter. The Dhajani monarch finally reached the waiting aircraft, letting him concentrate on his enemies. To his alarm, he saw that they had managed to evade all his men and reach the forward section, just eight decks below.

Wilde was carrying the spearhead, but her husband was the most immediate threat, entering one of the elevators. 'Khadim! He's coming up here!' he shouted to the remaining man guarding the bridge crew. 'Go into the lobby and kill him!'

The agent ran to the exit. Al-Asim changed position to cover the officers. Beyond the bridge windows, Manama's harbour entrance grew ever larger. In just a few minutes, the *Pacifia* would make its final turn for the American base.

He glanced back at the screens. The pilot helped Alula into the idling helicopter before scurrying to release one of the cables securing the aircraft. Wilde was running down a hallway, Chase still ascending in the lift.

It stopped. The bald Englishman peered through the doors, then ran out. Al-Asim waited for the sound of gunfire outside the bridge . . .

None came.

The other monitors revealed the reason: Chase had emerged on the deck *above*. What was he doing?

Eddie was entering the landing on Deck 17. A relaxation spa was ahead; off to each side were cabins, the doors of some to port still open after their occupants had fled the collision with the *Atlantia*.

He hurried to one of the two curving staircases flanking the lifts, then crept down it. The deck beneath came into view. He leaned over until he could see the bridge entrance. Was there a guard?

Yes – a shadow against the white-painted bulkhead revealed the form of a man holding a gun.

He retreated. Unarmed, he wouldn't get more than a couple of steps into the lower landing before being gunned down. He needed a distraction. . . .

There was a touchscreen panel near the lifts. He glanced at the ceiling, seeing several of the same features that had been present in the mall, then ran to the screen. 'Now, what was that code again?' he muttered.

Khadim waited outside the bridge with impatience and rising concern, his gun sweeping between all the possible entrances to the landing. The Englishman had been on the way up; why hadn't he arrived?

He looked back at the elevators. The digital displays told him that one was now on the deck above. Still warily checking the other potential access points, he started towards the stairs, watching for movement above—

An alarm shrilled, amber emergency lights flashing. Khadim recoiled as the nozzles in the ceiling blasted out a thick, soaking mist. He quickly withdrew to the bridge door as the fog grew thicker, reducing the staircases and elevators to vague shapes in the haze. His finger tightened on the Glock's trigger . . .

Movement on the stairs to his right.

He whirled and fired, sending half his magazine into the shadowy form. It tumbled heavily down the steps. Exultant, he ran over to confirm his kill—

It wasn't the Englishman.

Lying on the ground was a bullet-shredded mattress. A decoy! So where was—

'Ay up,' said a voice behind him.

Eddie had taken the single-width mattress from a cabin, hurling it down the stairs into the fog he'd triggered with the Emir's code before haring down the other flight. He slammed a fist into the startled man's face as he turned, following it up with a brutal assault that left the Dhajani broken-nosed, bleeding and unconscious on the bedding. 'Least you've got something to lie on,' he said, taking the Glock.

Clothing drenched, he went to the bridge door, about to use the code – then stopped. The ship hadn't slowed or changed course, so there was still at least one of Alula's people inside. And with this the only way in, he would be an easy target.

Another plan formed. He liked it even less than the idea of simply walking through the door, but it was his only chance of entering the bridge without being cut down. 'Buggeration and fuckery,' he growled as he ran up the stairs.

48

Gun in one hand, the spearhead's case in the other, Nina cautiously peered from the doorway to the bow deck.

The helicopter was still idling on the pad. The pilot crouched beside the aircraft, releasing one of the taut steel cables holding it. Alula was in the co-pilot's seat, a shadow behind the tinted windows.

The man's back was to her. She quickly advanced on him. A moment of alarm as the helicopter tilted, the edge of the rotor disc dropping a few feet towards the deck; with the *Pacifia* still ploughing through the waves at twenty-five knots, the wind was strong enough to affect its aerodynamics.

She ducked lower, but the chopper tipped back upright. The pilot had paused, ready to jump clear; he now resumed his task, slackening the cable, then releasing the clasp. Even though it had been loosened, the metal line still twanged away across the pad.

He sidestepped to the next cable. Nina readied the gun, then hurried towards him.

Al-Asim raised his Glock, aiming at the bridge door as he watched the Englishman approach it on the monitors . . . but then the bald man rushed away, heading back up the stairs. Where was he going?

All thoughts of Chase's plan vanished as he saw a new danger on another screen. The helicopter was still on the pad, its pilot having just released the second of the cables holding it, but now a new figure had appeared.

Nina Wilde.

The American was moving quickly across the bow deck, the case containing the spearhead in one hand and a gun in the other. 'No!' Al-Asim instinctively cried out in warning, even though he knew the pilot couldn't hear him.

The pilot reached the penultimate cable and crouched to unfasten it—

'Don't move!' Nina shouted.

The pilot looked back at her, eyes widening – then clawed for his weapon.

She fired. The bullet ripped bloodily through his thigh. He screamed, falling on to his back.

Nina kicked his pistol away, then ran to the S-76's door, yanking it open and thrusting her gun inside before Alula could draw hers. 'Drop it!' she snarled.

Eddie reached the *Pacifia*'s uppermost deck. He headed forward into the glazed geodesic dome covering a bar and sun lounge. A stiff wind hit him; several panels had shattered when the ship collided with the *Atlantia*. Passengers were huddled around the room, crew members trying to maintain order and calm, but it evaporated when people saw his gun.

He had no time to waste explaining the situation. Instead he ran to the front of the deck, angling to a broken pane large enough to fit through. To his alarm, he saw a warship powering towards the harbour entrance; the US Navy had indeed got a destroyer under way. It would be in a position to fire torpedoes in two minutes, or less. He had to stop the *Pacifia* before then.

The superstructure sloped away towards the bow, the bridge marked by a line of greenish glass running its entire width four decks below. Nina was now on the pad beside the chopper, its pilot lying nearby as she aimed her gun into the aircraft.

There was nothing he could do to help her from so far away. But he trusted her to take control of the situation while he dealt with his own.

Alula gave Nina a poisonous glare, but eased out her pistol and tossed it over the back of her seat. 'You are like a cockroach, Dr Wilde – I stamp on you again and again, but you do not die.'

'Oh, please,' Nina scoffed, gesturing for her to climb out. 'Lady, you're not even in the top ten of people who've tried to kill me. And you're not going to kill anyone else, either.'

The Dhajani eyed the metal case. 'You are mistaken. The spearhead will explode very soon, perhaps in thirty minutes . . . perhaps in thirty seconds.'

'If it does, you'll be right here to see it. Now move!'

Alula reluctantly stepped down from the cockpit, her eyes not leaving Nina as she watched for any chance to fight back.

Eddie held the broken window's frame as he brought both legs through and perched on the lip of the deck. The bridge's protruding central pulpit was about thirty feet to his left. He spread his feet apart, aiming the gun down the metal slope between them, then flicked the Glock's fire selector to full auto. He would only have a split-second window of opportunity – in this case a *literal* window – and couldn't afford to miss, even if he had to use up all his ammo in the process.

He readied himself – then slipped over the edge.

The white-painted metal was like a colossal playground slide. He picked up speed quickly – *too* quickly. Even with both heels jammed against the smooth surface, he couldn't find enough grip to control his descent.

Portholes flashed past. He slapped his free hand down flat. Rivet heads slashed at his skin, but he slowed, slightly.

But not enough. And now he was swinging around, about to tumble out of control as he careered towards the bridge windows—

He desperately took aim – and held the trigger.

The Glock blazed, tearing through its remaining ammunition in less than a seond. The rounds clanged off steel – then the wild storm of fire reached the line of glass.

One of the floor-to-ceiling windows burst apart, its fragments raining into the bridge. A split second later he followed them, plunging through to land with a bone-jarring bang.

'So how are you going to take the spearhead out to sea, Dr Wilde?' sneered Alula. She glanced at the pilot. 'He is in no condition to fly the helicopter.'

'Eddie can fly it,' Nina said defiantly.

'But he is not here.'

'He will be. Now get away from—'

Gunfire erupted behind her.

Nina spun, fearing that one of Alula's men had come to her rescue, but saw nothing – until she looked up. Eddie was sliding down the front of the superstructure, firing wildly. She gasped, horrified—

Alula dived at her.

The gun went off as Nina hit the deck, its slide locking back. She lashed the empty pistol at her opponent. Metal struck bone, Alula crying out, but then the princess threw herself on to the other woman.

Nina's head cracked painfully against the deck. She tasted blood, but recovered quickly—

The case containing the spearhead was torn from her grasp.

Eddie sat up. He had been left winded and battered by the fall, but knew he had to move. The crew were frozen in astonishment at their stations, but there was one person not wearing a white uniform.

Al-Asim. Eddie snapped the gun up at him—

Its slide was locked back. Empty.

The Dhajani overcame his shock at the other man's dramatic entrance and spun to bring his own weapon to bear. Eddie rolled against a console as he fired. Its screens blew apart under a hail of bullets.

Al-Asim swore, then charged across the bridge. He leapt out into the front of the wide room, unleashing another searing burst of fire at the Englishman's hiding place—

He wasn't there.

The Arab glared at the smoking holes in the deck, then realised his target had squeezed through a footwell beneath the console. He darted around it to find Eddie getting to his feet, and pulled the trigger again.

Nothing happened. His own gun was empty.

He yanked out a replacement magazine – as Eddie leapt at him.

Alula jumped up with the case. She looked about her, then started around the helicopter's tail towards the prow.

Nina knew what she planned: to drop the spearhead into the sea. It would be impossible to recover, but in the shallow waters this close to Bahrain, the antimatter explosion would be almost as destructive as if the *Pacifia* had sailed right into the harbour.

Alula had given the helicopter's whirling tail rotor a wide berth. Nina forced herself up and cut under its rear boom to charge after her. The Dhajani tried to dodge, but too late. Nina tackled her, both women falling at the edge of the pad.

The case skidded towards the railings. Nina scrambled in pursuit, grabbing it just before it went over. She swung around, skidding it back towards the helicopter – then gasped as a kick caught her hard in the side.

Alula hesitated, torn between continuing the fight and recovering the spearhead. She chose the latter, running after the case. Nina rose clumsily to follow.

The S-76 shifted again as the *Pacifia* pitched over rough waves. The rotor dipped towards Alula, who retreated in fear – allowing Nina to catch up. She yanked the Dhajani back by her long hair and punched her in the face as she fell. Alula shrieked, only for her cry to be cut off by a harsh chop to her throat.

Nina delivered one more punch to keep her down, then shakily stood and headed for the chopper. A hole was visible in the bridge windows eight decks above. Eddie's insane stunt had gotten him inside the command centre, at least—

A loud metallic *thwack* rang across the pad – and something struck her back so hard it threw her across the helipad.

Eddie and al-Asim collided. The Dhajani was knocked back, dropping the new magazine. He smacked his weapon against Eddie's head, drawing blood and a yell of pain – but the furious Yorkshireman immediately drove him against another console so hard he flipped backwards over it. The officer manning the station scrambled clear as al-Asim crashed down on his chair, his gun flying across the room.

Eddie still had his Glock. He was about to dive at the Arab to pistol-whip him when he realised the full magazine was on the floor nearby. He rushed to it, ejecting the empty to make room for its replacement—

Al-Asim sprang up, pulling his watch from its band and flinging the concealed weapon at his opponent. A *snick* of metal as the perdida's blades extended – and the Yorkshireman cried out as it slammed against the side of his wrist, slashing open the skin. The blow knocked the magazine from his hand, sending it under a console.

He gripped his wounded arm, blood flowing between his

fingers. The cut was deep, but if it had hit him a moment earlier, it would have sliced through the arteries in his wrist.

Al-Asim saw his enemy's pain and launched the perdida again. Eddie jerked aside as it whistled past his head. He edged towards the magazine, but was forced to retreat as al-Asim pulled his weapon back into a spinning motion and whirled it at him again.

Eddie backed away. Any possible avenue for a counterattack was blocked by the perdida. He changed tack and hurled the empty gun at al-Asim's head.

The Arab instinctively jerked up his raised arm to shield his face. The Glock was deflected by the whirling wire, but the perdida's smooth orbit suddenly became a crazy wobble.

The Englishman saw his chance. If he stopped the weapon from spinning, it would become useless. He lunged—

The perdida whirled gyroscopically back into alignment as al-Asim straightened his arm. The weapon rushed at Eddie's head. He ducked, but not fast enough. It clipped him above his temple, slashing an agonising line across his forehead.

Nina tumbled to a stop near the helicopter, the pain across her back so intense she could barely think, never mind move. Her eyes struggled to focus, the bow finally congealing into a coherent image. Alula was on all fours on the opposite side of the helipad, something moving snake-like across the deck between them . . .

Another cable.

The lines securing the helicopter were attached to large eyelets set into the deck. Alula had released the clasp on one of them, sending the taut cable lashing across the helipad like a whip. It had torn Nina's clothes, wind-blown salt in the air searing the exposed wound across her back. The only thing preventing a scream was her lack of breath.

The *Pacifia* rolled again, and the helicopter slithered sidelong across the pad. There was now only one cable holding the

Sikorsky – and it was acting like a pendulum, the aircraft reeling as the ship moved beneath it.

Alula had started towards the spearhead case, only to beat a frantic retreat as the tail rotor scythed at her. The last cable strained as it took the aircraft's full three-tonne weight. Despite his wounded leg, the pilot managed to drag himself clear of the pad.

Nina had no choice but to get closer. Despite the pain, she crawled for the case. The helicopter reached the end of its arc, then juddered back; even though its wheel brakes were on, the combination of the rotor's gyro effect and the liner's constant sway was enough to overcome them, the aircraft skipping terrifyingly over the deck with little shrieks of tortured rubber.

Only a few feet between her and the spearhead – but the S-76 was coming at her. One wheel left the deck as it tipped, the rotor carving downwards.

She grasped the case, twisting painfully to fling it clear, and dropped flat as the blades scythed towards her—

The pain from his forehead was excruciating, but Eddie knew that was the least of his problems. He could already feel blood running down his face. He dashed it away, but it would keep flowing until the wound was covered. If it reached his eye, he would be temporarily blinded.

A new, malevolent confidence came to al-Asim's face. He advanced, spinning the perdida towards what would soon become the Englishman's blind side.

Eddie wiped at the blood again, but felt his eye sting as the first trickle reached it. Al-Asim whipped out his arm. The Yorkshireman jumped back, the bizarre weapon chopping a chunk from his lapel. He kept retreating, almost at the bridge's centre. The crew looked on helplessly, nobody willing to risk injury or death by intervening.

Another strike at Eddie's face. He jerked away, the blades whisking so close to his nose that he felt a rush of displaced air – and stumbled against the helm console.

Al-Asim rushed at him, whirling the small but deadly weapon straight at his head—

The Yorkshireman whipped up his left arm to intercept it: not the heavy disc of the perdida itself, but the wire. It looped around his forearm, picking up speed as it wound in – to carve through his sleeve and embed a blade into his flesh with a wet thud.

He let out a pained cry, but it was also fuelled by fury – and the knowledge that he had just disarmed his enemy.

The Dhajani tried to yank the perdida back. The wire tightened around Eddie's arm, but the weapon stayed put. He grabbed the steel line with his other hand, then pulled as hard as he could. Caught off guard, al-Asim staggered towards him—

Eddie released the wire and delivered a punishing uppercut to the other man's jaw. Blood spurted from al-Asim's mouth as he bit off the end of his tongue. He shrieked and tried to retreat, but the Englishman used the wire to hold him as he pounded his face again and again, breaking his nose and knocking out teeth.

Reeling, al-Asim clawed at his watch band and released the clasp. Eddie lurched back as the wire's tension was suddenly released. The Dhajani spat out more blood, then kicked him hard in the stomach, sending him sprawling over the helm console.

Eddie's empty gun had landed not far behind al-Asim. The Arab snatched it up, then scrambled for the magazine.

Agony coursed through the Yorkshireman's left arm where the perdida was still embedded. He could barely move his fingers, the blade having slashed muscle. He was about to pull it out when he saw al-Asim load the magazine. The Glock's slide clacked forward, chambering the first round.

The Dhajani spun towards him, raising the gun—

Eddie jammed the azipod controls around, hard.

The *Pacifia* rolled into a full-speed turn, the forward thruster pivoting to push the bow to port, and the rear azipods swinging the stern to starboard. The deck tipped, pitching Eddie against the console . . . and throwing al-Asim off balance.

The Dhajani stumbled backwards, arms flailing. A burst of bullets tore into the ceiling. The liner's turn tightened, the floor tilting ever more steeply. He grabbed a console to stop himself from falling, only to see Eddie charging down the slope at him, wounded arm raised – with the bladed perdida still jutting from it.

The Englishman swung – and slammed the watch hard into al-Asim's throat.

The Arab choked, eyes bulging. Eddie pulled his arm back. Blood spouted from the deep wound. Al-Asim let out a gargling shriek and dropped the gun, clapping a hand over the gushing rent. Eddie kicked the Glock away and shoved him to the floor. 'Watch yourself,' he growled, extracting the perdida from his own injury and unwinding the wire.

Nina screamed as the rotor blades sliced at her – then the helicopter reeled away as the ship rolled sideways.

The spearhead's case skittered down the slope, towards Alula. The Dhajani staggered for it.

The helicopter hit the railings. A smashed section broke away and fell into the *Pacifia*'s churning bow wave. The S-76 rebounded and squealed back towards the superstructure.

The ship wallowed back upright. Nina forced herself into an unsteady run down the deck as Alula closed on the case.

The princess caught it – then the archaeologist body-slammed her to the deck. Nina rolled off her, then scrabbled for the handle. Her fingers closed around it—

A heel slammed into her stomach. Winded, Nina fell

backwards. Alula stood and kicked out again, this time aiming for her face—

Nina swung the case to intercept the blow.

Alula yelled as she struck metal rather than flesh and bone. She recoiled – and Nina smashed her own heel against the princess's kneecap. Cartilage crunched. The Dhajani shrieked and toppled to the deck.

Nina struggled upright. Alula was already trying to rise, unwilling to give up the battle—

The case pounded down on her head like a sledgehammer. She flopped to the deck. 'Stay the fuck down, *Your Majesty*,' Nina panted.

Ingels rushed to the controls and pulled back all the throttles, then brought the azipods back into alignment. 'Get a medic up here!' he shouted. 'And radio the US base, quickly – tell them we've got control of the ship!' The destroyer was clear of the headland and turning towards them.

His crew rushed to obey, an officer grabbing a first-aid kit from a cabinet and hurrying to Eddie. 'My God!' he said, seeing the bloody cuts on the Englishman's head and arm. 'Here, let me help you.'

'No time,' Eddie replied. He glanced at the wounded, squirming Dhajani. 'Patch that arsehole up, and get the crew to find his men and chuck 'em in the brig.'

The officer examined al-Asim's injury. Ingels strode to the Yorkshireman. 'Who *are* you?'

'Name's Eddie Chase,' he replied, wiping more blood from his eye. 'I save the world occasionally – but right now, I need to save my wife.' He retrieved the gun, then went back to the broken window. Below, Nina was standing over the fallen Alula, holding the case. She had secured the spearhead, but they still had to get rid of it.

The cabinet from which the officer had taken the medical kit also contained other emergency equipment, including a coil of rope. 'I need to get to the helipad,' Eddie said. 'Someone secure that line for me – I don't think I'll be much good at tying knots right now.' He could barely move his blood-soaked left hand.

Ingels fixed the rope around a console with a mariner's practised ease. Eddie pocketed the gun, then looped the line around his right arm and took hold of it. 'What are you going to do?' the captain asked.

'The bomb's still down there. We've got to get it clear of land before it goes off!' Eddie climbed out of the window, taking his weight on his arm as the rope pulled taut, then started a barely controlled slide down the superstructure.

Nina limped away from Alula and looked around. The helicopter was now slithering tail-first towards the pad's rear. Its engine was still running, though, and she was sure the ship's abrupt turn was Eddie's doing. If he reached the helipad quickly enough, they still had a chance to get the spearhead a safe distance out to sea—

Movement above. Her husband was indeed on the way, taking a short cut. She limped to meet him – then moved faster, alarm rising. The helicopter was still heading for the super-structure . . . directly beneath him.

Eddie picked up speed down the metal slope. He gripped the rope more tightly, its coils dragging against his sleeve. With only one useable hand, he could barely restrain his descent.

He looked down. Nina was coming towards him – and so was the helicopter.

The buzzing tail rotor was directly in line with him. He was about to drop straight on to its blades!

Unless—

He rolled to the right – and released the rope.

He was still three decks up. Eddie slid ever faster towards the bow, completely out of control.

And the chopper remained on a collision course with the superstructure. He wasn't far enough clear – he would still be hit by razor-sharp shrapnel as its blades smashed against the steel—

The cable snapped tight. The helicopter jerked to a halt. Its tail swung around – towards the Yorkshireman. All he could do was yell, '*Fuuuuuck!*' as he slithered helplessly at the whirling saw—

The S-76 rebounded sharply on the overstretched line. Eddie slammed down on the deck as the aircraft skidded back across the pad. But any thoughts of celebration were overpowered by the resurgent pain in his left arm, which was now joined by a new spike of agony through one ankle.

He tried to move his leg. Faint relief: it wasn't broken. But he wouldn't be moving faster than a hobble for a while.

'Eddie!' Nina reached him, holding the case. 'Oh my God! Are you—'

'I'll be okay,' he gasped, trying to stand, only to slump back. 'Not right this second, admittedly . . .' His eyes went to the case. 'You got the spearhead?'

'Yeah, but can you fly the chopper?'

'I'll have to. Might need you to help, though. How long've we got?'

She opened the container. The lights inside the spearhead had taken on a new fury, the crystal quivering as subatomic explosions ate it away from within. 'It can't be long.'

'Help me up, and get me to the—' He broke off as he looked back at the helicopter.

Alula, blood running down her face, had managed to get back up – and had released the last cable before staggering to the Sikorsky. 'Shit!' Nina gasped. 'If she takes off, we're stuck with the spearhead!'

Eddie hurriedly reached for the Glock, but found his pocket empty. 'I had a gun – where's the fucking thing gone?'

Nina spotted it wedged against a light fixture a deck above, out of reach. She turned back, to see Alula climbing into the helicopter. 'Okay, either she can fly a chopper, or she's putting a lot of faith in beginner's luck!'

'Get me up so I can—' Eddie began – but she had already slammed the case shut and was running with it after the Dhajani. 'Nina, wait!'

She didn't stop. The chopper's engines roared as Alula increased power; she *did* know how to fly. But the door was still open. If Nina could reach it, she might be able to drag the other woman out—

The helicopter shifted, its landing struts extending as the pressure on them lessened. The nose tipped upwards, the Sikorsky rolling back on its rear wheels for a few metres as Alula balanced the controls, then it left the pad.

Nina was still short of the door. Instead she leapt at the starboard rear landing leg – and hooked an arm over the wheel.

The chopper tilted with the extra weight, sideslipping across the bow. Still clutching the case, Nina struggled to pull herself higher. Alula leaned out of the open door and saw her. Pure hatred flared on the princess's face. She shouted something, but it was lost in the wind. The Sikorsky climbed, ten feet up, twenty. Nina twisted, swinging her other arm at the landing strut—

Hydraulics skirled – and the leg began to retract into its well, the streamlined door slicing down at her like a guillotine.

And now the helicopter was sweeping her over the broken bow rails, and the sea far below—

She released her hold – and fell.

49

Eddie got to his feet – or more accurately *foot*, barely able to take any weight on his aching ankle – and hobbled in pursuit of his wife. But he was still fifty feet away when Nina let go, trying to drop back on to the deck instead of into the ocean—

She hit the bow's edge with a crack he heard even over the helicopter. Ignoring the S-76 as it tipped into forward flight, he hurried towards the slumped figure. But before he could reach her, she rolled limply over the side.

'*No!*' Eddie screamed – but she had already disappeared.

He reached the gap and looked down to see her hit the water eighty feet below. Even though the *Pacifia*'s thrusters had stopped, the ship was still moving, needing miles to drift to a halt. The bow wave swept over her splash.

Without a second thought, he dived after her, head down, arms outstretched—

And hit the water.

The impact as he hit the water was punishing, all the more so against his injuries. His left wrist and forearm burned, the salt water like molten metal against the bloody cuts, and the slash across his head stung as if doused in acid. But he forced himself to ignore the pain, bringing himself upright.

He breached the surface, drawing in a gasping breath – only for the bow wave to pound him back under.

Churning turbulence threw him helplessly over and over. Then the widening hull struck him with a bang that almost knocked him unconscious. He spun, bringing his arms up to cushion another collision with the towering metal wall, and kicked himself away.

The undertow was pulling him down. He swam harder. Waves shimmered above him, for a terrifying moment receding as he was dragged deeper, then he broke loose.

Coughing, tasting blood as well as brackish water, he surfaced. The *Pacifia* sliced past, impossibly huge. Its horn began to sound, three long blasts – the bridge crew had seen him and Nina fall and sounded the person-overboard alarm. But where *was* Nina? He turned in the water, desperately searching.

The alarm sounded again. Something smacked down into the sea behind him. He saw a bright orange life vest bobbing fifty feet away. If he swam for it, he would survive long enough for someone to reach him in a boat, but doing so might take him further away from Nina. A few seconds could mean the difference between life and death . . .

A dark shape bobbed briefly into view between the wave crests. Eddie fixed his eyes on its position and started to swim. It might just be a piece of floating flotsam – or it could be the woman he loved. But he didn't know which, the mystery object still out of sight—

There! The liner's expanding wake had pushed it further away. He swam harder to catch up.

Fear struck him. It *was* Nina – face down, unmoving.

He reached her and hurriedly rolled her over. 'Nina, can you hear me? Nina!'

No response. Her eyes were closed. She wasn't breathing.

He tipped backwards, holding her clear of the surface as he swam for the floating vest. The *Pacifia*'s horn sounded another triple blast, the noise now almost funereal. He caught sight of the helicopter, but Alula's escape was no longer of any concern to him. Only one thing mattered. 'I'm not giving up,' he raspily assured Nina, reaching for the life vest.

There wasn't time to don it properly. All he could do was shove his injured arm through the straps, then he manoeuvred Nina over it and tilted her head back to open her airways.

Recovery training had been drummed into him in the SAS, the procedure instantly leaping to mind even after two decades out of military service. He squeezed her nostrils closed, then turned her towards him, letting water drain from her mouth before locking lips and beginning resuscitation. Four strong breaths into her lungs, then he withdrew and checked for movement. She remained still, no sounds of respiration. A second round of mouth-to-mouth – again with no result.

Fighting back horror that he might have lost her, he tried once more, driving another four breaths deep into her, willing her to breathe—

Nina convulsed. Eddie pulled away, turning her on to her side. She coughed out brine, then vomited. 'I've got you, I've got you!' he said, letting her expel another mouthful before easing her upright so he could put the vest on her. 'I'm here . . .'

She was in no condition to reply. He secured the vest, then kept hold of her, treading water.

The *Pacifia* continued past like a gold-trimmed iceberg. A boat came around its stern from the marina, three crew aboard. One man held out a boathook. Eddie painfully closed his wounded hand around the pole and allowed himself to be pulled closer. 'Are you hurt?' another man asked.

'Take a guess,' was the bloodied Yorkshireman's sarcastic reply. 'We need to get her to your hospital, fast . . .' He trailed off. 'Oh, shit.'

'What is it?'

He hadn't seen the spearhead's case on the bow – which meant it must have fallen into the water with Nina. 'I don't think a hospital'll make much difference. For any of us!'

★ ★ ★

Alula checked the instruments. The helicopter was at ten thousand feet and climbing, heading out over open sea at one hundred and fifty-five knots. It was travelling at almost five kilometres every minute, and she had taken off more than five minutes ago.

While her brother and Lobato had investigated the potential of antimatter as an energy source, she had done her own research on its more destructive applications. If there was enough antimatter inside the spearhead to equal the fifty-megaton force of the Soviets' Tsar Bomba, to be clear of the blast she would need to be at least fifty-five kilometres from the *Pacifia*; another six minutes of flight. There was the risk that the Atlantean artefact could blow up at any moment, but every passing second brought her a little closer to safety.

The blue sea rolled past far below. For the first time since leaving the ship, Alula smiled, a hard smirk of triumph. She had overthrown Fadil, taken control of the country that should have been hers by birthright, and was on the verge of smashing its rivals. Victory was almost hers – and nobody could keep it from her.

Not even Nina Wilde.

'Come on, come on!' Eddie shouted as two crewmen carrying Nina on a stretcher hurried along behind him. He in turn was ignoring the pain in his leg as he followed another man to the *Pacifia*'s medical centre. 'Get her in here!'

They rushed into the ward. It was packed, tending to passengers injured in the collision with the *Atlantia*, but a space was found for the new arrival. Eddie waited beside her as a harried nurse began an examination. 'She went overboard and wasn't breathing,' he told the woman. 'I gave her mouth-to-mouth.'

She nodded, checking Nina's pulse before looking for other

injuries. Even barely conscious, the archaeologist still jerked in pain as the nurse touched her right shin. 'I think it's broken,' the woman said. 'Hold on, I need to cut off her trousers.' She bustled away to find scissors.

Eddie took a closer look at his wife's leg, seeing an ugly bulge beneath the wet fabric. He held her hand. 'Hey, it's okay, I'm here. You're on the ship, they'll take care of you,' he whispered, but his attempt to sound reassuring didn't even convince himself. 'Until the fucking spearhead blows up.'

To his surprise, Nina laughed. It was only quiet, but genuine, not a final expression of resigned despair. He squeezed her hand more tightly. 'Are you okay? What is it?'

'Oh, I'm definitely *not* okay,' she whispered. 'But I might be. We all might be.'

'How? The spearhead fell into the sea – it's right behind us!'

She managed a faint smile. 'It's not right behind *us* . . .'

From thirteen thousand feet up, the Persian Gulf spread out below Alula like a sapphire carpet. Bahrain and Qatar's northern headlands were now a long way behind, the shores of Iran a faint line on the distant horizon. Far away, she saw dark motes on the sea, oil tankers from Iraq and Kuwait, but there was nothing below her. She was alone, almost sixty kilometres from land – and from the spearhead. She was safe.

All she had to do now was keep flying, wait for the spearhead to explode, then, once the danger had passed, return to Dhajan to take control. Her people would need strong leadership in the disaster's aftermath, and through her, they would have it . . .

A noise rose over that of the engines. She had subconsciously registered it a few minutes earlier, but now it was loud enough to demand her attention. No warnings on the instrument panel; all the engine gauges displayed normal readings. But there was definitely something rattling in the fuselage behind her, with increasing force—

A rush of utter terror hit her.

The spearhead!

Wilde must have thrown the case into the wheel well just before it closed. The bomb was no longer aboard the *Pacifia* – it was behind her!

She stabbed at the switch to lower the landing gear and drop the spearhead into the sea—

Too late.

The magnetic field inside the Atlantean crystal finally weakened to the point of collapse – releasing all the remaining antimatter.

Freed of their constraints, the antiparticles slammed against the spearhead's pitted and corroded inner surface. Matter touched its inverse, causing mutual annihilation in an unimaginable burst of primal energy.

Alula and the helicopter were not merely vaporised. They ceased to exist, every molecule torn apart in a billionth of a second. The atmosphere itself became a searing sphere of plasma, for an instant a thousand times hotter than the heart of a star – then the explosion's force blasted it outwards at hypersonic speed, compressing the surrounding air almost to a solid before the shock wave burst free.

A new sun rose over the Persian Gulf.

Ingels and his bridge crew watched in horror as the initial dazzling flare faded to reveal a seething fireball. The warning from the *Atlantia* had been true: Alula had indeed been using their ship to carry a weapon of mass destruction.

The bomb might have gone off at a safe distance, but the ten thousand souls aboard the liner were still in danger. 'Bring us about!' he ordered. 'Turn the bow towards the blast! Sound the general alarm, and get all the passengers into cover!'

His officers scrambled to obey, the man at the helm station rotating the azipods to bring the great ship into line with the explosion. A white haze obscured the horizon beneath it – the oncoming shock wave.

There were no windows in the medical centre, but the general alarm – seven short bursts followed by one longer – told Eddie and Nina something had happened. It was not hard to guess what. 'Everyone hold on!' the Yorkshireman shouted. 'A bomb's just gone off – we're gonna have a rough ride!'

The nurse looked up from cutting away Nina's trouser leg. 'What kind of bomb?'

'Let's just call it a nuke to save time!' Shock and fear spread through the room as an urgent voice boomed over the PA system, ordering people to seek shelter away from any windows. 'If you can get down on the floor, get down – otherwise, hold on tight!' Everyone hurried to obey.

Nina readied herself for a terrifying – and potentially terminal – experience. 'Oh, I'm *so* not going to enjoy this, am I?'

For once, Eddie didn't have a tension-relieving wisecrack. Instead, he took hold of her. 'I've got you,' he whispered.

She managed a smile. 'You always have.'

They kissed, then held each other—

A growing rumble shook the ship, the wind outside rising as the shock wave closed in – then the *Pacifia* reeled violently as if struck by a giant hammer. A colossal boom echoed through the enormous vessel as the blast wave hit, windows shattering along its length. But even this noise was not enough to drown out the horrifying sound of thousands of people screaming as one.

Loose objects flew across the infirmary, several patients flung from their beds as the deck bucked beneath them. Eddie clung to

Nina, but even braced, he couldn't withstand the earthquake-force impact. 'Nina, hold on!' he cried as he fell.

She gripped the stretcher, but the cot itself slid sideways as the ship pitched. It tipped over, throwing her to the floor—

Her broken leg hit the deck. An explosion of pain – and everything went black.

The spearhead's detonation hit far more than just the liner.

There was no nuclear fallout. Like an atomic blast, the explosion released huge amounts of gamma radiation – but the sheer force of the explosion actually served to absorb it, the shock wave compressing the atmosphere around it as densely as the thickest lead shielding.

There was still considerable destruction, though. Even though much of the blast wave's energy dissipated over its thirty-mile journey, windows were smashed and buildings damaged throughout northern Qatar. The gleaming skyscrapers of Manama had their facades shattered, though luckily the explosion's distant flash had provided enough warning for those within to get clear of their glass frontages before they were shredded by flying shards.

Injuries were inevitable – widespread, often serious – but astoundingly, the only person killed as a direct result of the Atlantean artefact's annihilation was Alula herself.

Nina opened her eyes, squinting at the painful brightness. It took a moment for the brilliance to fade, revealing that she was no longer in the *Pacifia*'s infirmary. The last thing she remembered was Eddie holding her, then an explosion of pain, then nothing . . .

Eddie! Where was he? She tried to sit up—

And flopped back down as she discovered her broken leg was now immobilised in a cast.

'Whoa, easy!' said Eddie, jumping up from a chair beside her bed. A bandage covered the laceration across his head, other dressings on his left hand and arm. 'How're you feeling?'

'Like crap,' she replied. 'Where are we? How long was I unconscious?'

'Hospital in Dhajan,' he told her, perching on the bed. 'You've been out for about eight hours, although some of that was because the doctors gave you a sedative. And a shitload of painkillers.'

'Yeah, I thought "crap" seemed remarkably good, considering.' She looked down at her leg. 'How bad is it?'

'You won't be riding around Central Park with Macy for a while. You broke your shin when you fell off the chopper.'

Nina winced. 'Ow.'

'Yeah. But it could've been worse. Seeing as you drowned.'

'I *what*?' she yelped.

'You went over the edge of the deck into the sea. You weren't breathing – I had to give you mouth-to-mouth.'

'Saved by a kiss, huh?' They both smiled. 'So what happened? The ship got hammered, so the damage on the shore must have been bad.'

'The glaziers in Bahrain'll be quids-in. Lots of skyscrapers with broken windows. But the spearhead blew up far enough out that the actual blast didn't do too much damage on land. I was talking to the Emir earlier, who'd been talking to someone in the States – they reckon the explosion was about forty megatons.'

'Much less than it could have been.' She rested her head on the pillow. 'I suppose the antiparticles inside the spearhead would have decayed over time. And maybe it didn't capture many new ones inside the vault. Gold's nearly as effective a shield as lead, after all.'

'Well, whatever, we got lucky. There's been loads of property damage, but I haven't heard about anyone being killed. Well, except Alula, but fuck her. Lots of the *Pacifia*'s passengers were hurt, but apparently everyone got off the ship alive.'

'What about the *Atlantia*? You said you spoke to the Emir . . .'

'The US Navy recovered the lifeboats. Everyone's okay, including Lobato.'

Nina nodded. 'What about Macy? Have you called her?'

'Yeah, a couple of hours ago. She's flying over with Olivia tomorrow – the Emir's sending a private jet.'

'Good. I want to see her. I need to be back together with my family.'

'Had enough of going on adventures on your own, eh?'

'Had enough of adventures, period,' she scoffed. 'After the Congo, I just wanted to work on my books and my research. I'm thinking that twice as much now! Maybe it's time to get back into academia – professors usually have a quiet life.'

Eddie raised an eyebrow. 'So you never want to go out into the field again?'

'Well, never say never. But I really, really, *really* would like to be able to work without guns and explosions and massive destruction all around me. Just *once*.'

He laughed. 'Won't make for a very exciting film, but we'll see how it goes.'

Nina managed to raise herself on one elbow. She put her other arm around her husband's waist and hugged him to her. 'So long as we go there together.'

Epilogue

New York City

Two Months Later

'What do you mean, the vault is *gone?*' Nina demanded in disbelief.

She had called Oswald Seretse at the United Nations to check on the IHA's plans to secure the buried Atlantean chamber in Turkey. The last she had heard, a couple of weeks previously, the IHA had reached an agreement with the Turkish government – under considerable pressure from the US and other major powers – to excavate the vault and transport it elsewhere for examination by experts. While she still had no intention of returning full-time to the IHA, she had hoped to help discover more of the strange structure's secrets.

Seretse had dashed those hopes, though – and raised chilling questions. 'I mean that quite literally, Nina,' said the Gambian. It took a lot to worry him, but this was one of those rare occasions. 'An IHA team arrived on site two days ago to begin digging out the vault. They found that the hilltop had already been excavated and the vault itself removed. By helicopter, apparently, as there were no heavy vehicle tracks. Whoever was responsible worked quickly, as the site had been visited by the IHA the day before and everything was still intact. But the culprits remain persons unknown.'

'Persons unknown!' she echoed sarcastically. 'What, Berk and Elmas didn't see all this going on fifty feet from their house?'

'The Onans relocated last month. The Turkish government expropriated their property. They were far from happy with the amount paid, I understand, but had little choice but to accept it. Such is the nature of autocratic regimes.'

She shook her head. 'So the Turks have the vault?'

'They deny all knowledge of its removal.'

'Well, of course they would!'

'For what it is worth, I believe them. I have not been idle in this matter, Nina,' he went on, a little condescendingly. 'I spoke to my sources in the military and intelligence communities, and all heavy-lift helicopters belonging to the Turkish government were accounted for on the night in question. That does not rule out the use of privately owned aircraft, of course, but it is a start.'

'It's not an end, though,' she said. 'If it's not the Turks, who has the resources to dig out and steal something that must weigh twenty tons from right under their noses?'

'That is a very good question,' Seretse replied. 'I will keep you informed should I learn anything.'

'That'd be great, Oswald. Thank you.'

She hung up and sat back, thinking. The amount of work needed to excavate the Atlantean vault over a single night would have been phenomenal . . .

Eddie opened her study door. 'Something up, love? You were getting a bit loud.'

'Oh no, nothing's wrong,' she said sarcastically, running a hand through her hair – it had returned to its natural red colour and was growing back from its close crop. 'Only that Oswald just told me the vault's been stolen, and nobody has any idea who did it.'

'What did they steal from the vault? There wasn't much in it.'

'No, they didn't steal anything *from* the vault – they stole *the vault*, the whole thing.'

'You what? It must weigh twenty tons!'

'Yeah, tell me about it.' She stood, wincing a little. Her cast had been removed a week earlier, but she was still suffering some residual pain. 'So much for my plan to finish my paper about the spearheads with an analysis of the vault. I was kinda hoping to have a closer look at the Atlantean technology. If it even *counts* as technology, that is. I mean, it was crystals powered by earth energy! I don't think it could have been more stereotypically New Age if it had been tie-dyed.'

'Could it be dangerous?' Eddie asked. 'Last time someone tried to use something like that, they were planning to take over the world.'

'Yeah, I remember. And the time before that, they wanted to start a world war. I thought I'd seen the last of it, but I guess the Atlanteans had other ideas.'

'Bunch of arseholes for burying secret weapons all over the world, eh?'

'Damn right. Why couldn't I have gone into a safe and non-controversial line of archaeology like, I dunno, looking for the body of Christ?'

They both laughed, then went into the living room. Macy, playing with a toy trikan, looked up. 'Are you okay, Mommy?' she asked. 'You were shouting.'

'I wasn't shouting, honey,' Nina assured her. 'I just had some news I wasn't expecting. What are you up to?'

'Trying to do the trick I did on the ship.' The little girl flicked the elaborate yo-yo out on its line. It whizzed away almost horizontally, spinning at the end of the string before looping back and snapping into its holder.

Her mother was impressed. 'You're getting really good at that.

When I had a yo-yo as a kid, I could barely get it to come back to me.'

Macy frowned, not accepting the compliment. 'No, it's *wrong*. When I was on the ship, I made it go a different way just by *wanting* it to. Why can't I do that now?'

'It's just a toy, love,' Eddie reminded her. 'Maybe there's something different about the way the real one works.'

'I can't believe you even got the real trikan *to* work,' said Nina. 'Everyone who's examined it says there's too much friction in the mechanism to throw it, never mind have it come back.'

'It *did* work!' Macy insisted angrily. 'If you'd been there, you *would* believe me!' She scowled, then stalked out of the room.

'I didn't mean it like that!' Nina called after her, but her daughter was gone. A few seconds later, the apartment reverberated to the sound of her bedroom door slamming. 'Oh, she's a handful,' she sighed.

'You think she's bad now, wait till she's fifteen,' Eddie said, smirking.

'It's all right for you. She's a daddy's girl; she never gives you any trouble. Me? I'm just remembering how much trouble I caused *my* mom in my teens.'

The smirk grew wider. 'Karma's a bitch, innit?'

'I'll remember you said that the next time something bad happens to you. Oh well. Life goes on.' They sat together on the couch, Nina gingerly stretching out her sore leg. 'Hopefully nice and quietly.'

'Well, you won't get that with a seven-year-old, but at least nobody'll be shooting at us. Fingers crossed!' He slipped his arm around her; she snuggled against him, glad of the chance to relax. 'You fancy watching a film?'

'Got anything in mind?' she asked.

'How about *Speed 2*?'

* * *

565

The Yorkshireman's cackling 'Oof!' as his wife hit him was loud enough to reach Macy, but she ignored it, still fuming. Why wouldn't anyone believe her? The trikan *had* gone where she'd wanted it to – where she'd *told* it to. She *knew* it had!

She snapped the toy version out and back, out and back, sweeping it around in increasingly elaborate loops and twirls. She practised with it whenever she had a spare moment, trying to repeat what she had done aboard the liner – and to show her parents she hadn't been imagining things, or lying. But while her skills had improved hugely, so far she hadn't reached her ultimate goal.

She knew what had happened, though. She had done something amazing – but nobody believed her.

Some day, she was going to prove it. To everyone.

WHEN I WAKE UP

BORN IN Sweden, Jessica moved to London
to pursue a career in publishing. She has
also lived in the USA and Middle East,
where she worked in PR and taught
journalism to undergraduate students.
Writing is her true passion and in 2016,
Jessica won a Montegrappa First Fiction
Award at the Emirates Festival of Literature.
She balances her time between writing and
her young family.

WHEN
I WAKE
UP

JESSICA JARLVI

ⓐ

First published as an ebook in 2017 by Aria,
an imprint of Head of Zeus Ltd

First published in print in 2017 by Aria

9 7 5 3 1 2 4 6 8

A catalogue record for this book is available from
the British Library.

ISBN (HB): 9781786696090
ISBN (XTPB): 9781786696779
ISBN (E): 9781786695451

Typeset by Divaddict Publishing Solutions Ltd

Printed and bound in Great Britain by
CPI Group (UK) Ltd, Croydon CRO 4YY

Head of Zeus Ltd
First Floor East
5–8 Hardwick Street
London EC1R 4RG
WWW.HEADOFZEUS.COM

To Mark, Julia, Leo and Max

for your love and support, always

She staggers backwards, her back ramming into the car door. There is no sense of time. Instinctively, she puts her hand to her head. There's blood on her fingers. She stares at the dripping redness, amazed. Bewildered she looks around. Did anyone see?

She's about to speak when another blow strikes her head. Her back bangs into the door again and this time she falls over. She immediately tries to get back up but a boot explodes into her stomach and she screams, or at least she thinks she does; nothing comes out as she gasps.

She feels dizzy, her eyes won't focus; they're getting increasingly damp and sticky and she wipes them, only to see her hands covered in even more red. It looks like paint. Another boot and it sounds like something breaks. She hopes it's a tree branch and not her ribs but the agony is unbearable. Despite the pain, she clambers to her hands and knees. A blur of movement and her head smashes against cold metal.

Then everything turns eerily quiet.

PART ONE

I

Erik

March 2016

T EACHER OF THE YEAR BRUTALLY ATTACKED IN SCHOOL
PARKING LOT.
Life-threatening injuries... coma.
No eyewitnesses.
Erik tries to make sense of the words in the newspaper.
They read like badly written lyrics. He's holding Anna's
bruised hand; her fingernails are raw and scraped for evid-
ence. He feels sick, emptied of emotion; he stares at his wife,
he stares at the white walls.

Then a rainbow of colours. Her wedding ring catches the
sunlight, cascading beams of light across the dull room, and
he's reminded of the beginning, seven years earlier, when
he sold a collection of records to pay for the diamond. Her
calm, grounded and responsible nature made him feel loved.

He needs to hang onto that feeling. The beginning. Not
the end. Not even the in-between when life rushed past and
he sometimes struggled to remember why they were married.

"There was still cash in her purse," the police say. "Money isn't a likely motive."

"Of course not," Erik says. "We live a modest life."

He's not sure if this adds value even if it's true. They live in a small, white-brick house from the sixties and share a second-hand Volvo V70. They bought the station wagon when they left Stockholm for the southern countryside with its widespread, yellow colza fields. Anna had just accepted a job at a local school. He was between assignments and followed her lead. That's when her career started to dictate their lives. The students became her life and he was left to create his own.

The words 'rape kit' bounce harshly against the sterile walls. He switches off, stares at Anna instead, trying to read her: *why did this happen to us?*

Her body is heavy on the white bedding, the long dark hair arranged in a neat ponytail. He feels an urge to pull it out, to make it messy. They've made her look different.

If he squints, she could be someone else. Half her face is dark red, almost purple, her right eye swollen, reflecting the attacker's anger. His insides tighten.

"Her head injuries are consistent with the damage on the car door."

"So it could have been an accident?"

"Not likely. Her ribs are bruised, her right arm broken, the head... it hasn't just hit the car door once... sorry... we understand you need time."

"For what?" he says. To cope? To grieve? To hope? What is it that they want from him? He looks around the room, bewildered. There's no one there to respond to. Just Anna. They've left him alone.

The respirator next to her bed dominates, its overwhelming sound filling the room, reminding him that her chest is no longer rising on its own. Oxygen flows through a mask. As if she's in the sea, deep under water.

They did a test dive on their honeymoon in the Maldives; she wanted to become a certified diver but then the twins were born. He imagines the machine next to her bed as a gas cylinder and the tube a diving regulator. Her head could be filled with the colours of the ocean. In her dream-like state she might be happy.

Tears form in the corners of his eyes, one by one. Blurring.

The doctors haven't told him much. Or maybe he didn't listen properly. He finds the whole hospital machine intimidating: the overwhelming smell of disinfectant, the physicians in their unbuttoned, sloppy white coats, the nurses annoyingly officious. There is this unspoken requirement of him to behave a certain way but he has no idea how to conduct himself. This is not something you can prepare for.

He is immature. Anna has always said so and she's been right. When they first started dating, she found his juvenile nature endearing. "You can get away with anything," she would laugh. Although her patience seemed to diminish as time went on.

He blames her bloody job. Being a teacher is a calling for her. She is consumed by her students – people she isn't even related to!

Now he must nod and say 'yes, she's a great teacher' even though he secretly thinks she should have been a better mum. Then she would have been at home.

He keeps it to himself, must act maturely.

There's a monitor next to her bed that measures her heart

rate, her vitals; a reminder that she is alive... just. A flick of the switch and the machines go quiet; her chest won't rise again. It feels like a threat, like he's God.

A vibration in his pocket and he pulls out his phone.

WhatsApp now

Pernilla Arvidsson: How are you doing? Thinking of you... Sebastian and Lukas can stay late if needed. Hugs

His heart jolts. He's forgotten to pick up the children from day care. They don't know about the attack. Only that mummy is sick.

He writes a response.

Thanks. Thinking of you too.

He stares at the screen. Yesterday he would have clicked 'Send' without much thought. Now it feels inappropriate. He retypes it.

Thanks. See you.

*

"Erik?"

His mum is at the door. At the sight of her, the tears start to fall more heavily until he breaks down completely. The chair shakes under his unstable frame.

"Oh, Erik." She hugs him tightly.

Tears and snot run into a single stream but he doesn't care. "Any improvement?"

He shakes his head. Mum's eyes are teary when she hands him a bag but she doesn't cry. She always remains strong and calm.

"Clothes," she explains. "I'll get the boys."

He wishes she would scream instead of being so organised and practical. That at least someone would react. Everyone is too peaceful; they speak in monotonous, slow voices, as if he's retarded. The doctors, the nurse, the police. Has the world not stopped while his wife fights for her life? It feels like it should.

"I agreed with the teacher that we would keep their routine normal," Mum continues. "Is her name Pernilla?"

He nods and wipes his face with the back of his sleeve. Anna would have hated that. He smiles faintly. If she wakes up, he's going to be the husband she deserves.

2

Anna

September 2015

"Erik collecting the boys?" Kent asked, handing Anna a cup of coffee.

She looked up from the paperwork, happy for the interruption.

"Yes, I'm marking exam papers."

It was a cold and bleak afternoon; autumn was on the doorstep with woolly cardigans making an appearance in the teachers' lounge. She wrapped her fingers tightly around the hot cup.

"How's it going with the new student, Daniel?" Kent made himself comfortable on the corduroy couch next to her desk. "Is he still testing the limits?"

She shrugged. "Basically, yes. I've tried reaching out to the parents but there seem to be a number of problems at home."

"What about the school counsellor?"

"He won't talk to 'a shrink'. His words, not mine. I've explained that it's confidential but he doesn't buy it. He's very private, on edge, you know."

Living in a small town did make it harder for people to open up. Students and parents were often worried that everyone would know their business.

Kent sipped his coffee, nodding. "Should we involve social services?" he asked.

She smiled at him, relaxing her shoulders from the stressful day; she loved that he cared, not just about his own students but also about hers. Their friendship kept her coming back to this school every year.

"I'm not sure," she said.

"Anna, you can't save every child on your own."

"I know," she said defensively. "I'll think about it. I don't want to cause him more harm. He's obviously just trying to get attention."

"Causing fights will definitely achieve that."

"That's why I need to find a way to reach out to him."

She wanted to tell him about the letters Daniel had written to her but she couldn't. Kent would worry, and although it wasn't her job to protect him, she was determined to deal with this on her own.

She had received the first letter in August, when school started after the summer break. As was always the case with new pupils, she had secretly hoped for a studious and conscientious addition, although this had quickly turned out to be a fantasy.

I hate school and I know I'm going to hate you. People like you think you rule over me, but you don't. No one does. If you understand that, we have no problems. If you don't... you'll see what will happen.

At first she had felt threatened. Scared even. Then she had

taken a step back and viewed it from a different angle. After all, it was ridiculous to be intimidated by a seventeen-year-old. She was nearly twice his age. He was simply reaching out to her. That's what her years of experience told her, that it was a cry for help.

The next letter had been similar in nature but then they had become milder.

I hate you. You think I can't read. That's why you don't write back. You think I'm stupid?

He wanted her to reply. So far she hadn't. Was it ethically correct to correspond with a student in this way? Didn't it mean she was showing favouritism? She wanted to ask Kent's advice but she had a feeling he would object to any written communication with a student.

"His writing is good," she said. "Above average actually."

"Well, at least that's something." He looked tired. The stress of the new school system was getting to him. "Good thing I'm retiring soon," he would say. "Let me know if I can help in any way."

"I will," she said.

She had fancied Kent once. Even though he was much older and his khaki trousers and check shirts weren't obviously sexy, his clear blue eyes had made something stir in her. He was an attentive listener, unlike Erik, who had the attention span of a two-year-old.

"You're very ambitious and extremely caring," Kent said, tilting his head. "I admire that, but there's a life outside of this school as well. Don't let the students get to you."

They exchanged a knowing glance. He knew that her troubled students reminded her of her own upbringing.

"I know," she said.

"Anyway, I have to go," Kent said and got up. "Taking Märta to the cinema."

She watched him leave, feeling an unexpected surge of jealousy. It wasn't Märta, a fifty-three-year-old accountant who dressed like a seventy-year-old; it was the feeling of being cherished the way she was. Kent adored her.

Sighing, she leaned back in her chair. It was half-past five. Outside the window, birch trees were bending in the strong wind, the sky thick with clouds. Sebastian and Lukas would be inside, eating dinner. She picked up the phone to call them but decided against it. They would be busy telling Erik about their day. The thought made her smile. She needed to focus on the two wonderful boys they had given life to. Somewhere, there was a video of the twins as babies, highlighting the joyous moments as opposed to the sleepless nights and arguments about whose turn it was to load the washing machine. She should watch it to revel in the smiles and snuggles. Her boys made her happy, and Erik had too. To bring her back to the early days, she often reminisced about his proposal, which had been unexpected and therefore highly romantic: slumped on the couch in pyjamas one evening, he suddenly got down on one knee. No ring, but still.

After Kent's exit, other teachers started to leave and soon she was on her own. She welcomed the ensuing silence. Picking up the red pen, she inhaled the serene school air: paper, newly sharpened pencils, old books, cardboard boxes, gingerbread and coffee. She loved the late afternoon and evenings when everyone had left the building.

"Hi, Anna."

The raspy adolescent voice cut through the air. Surprised,

she looked up. The doors had automatically locked at five o'clock. But there he was, in his worn-out, small denim jacket, backpack thrown over the shoulder, shoelaces undone.

"Daniel?"

3

Erik

March 2016

Anna's parents haven't visited their daughter in the hospital yet but instead of feeling bitter, Erik is relieved. They would only make the situation worse. Like a drama train they would pull in and off-load their own issues. Erik needs to focus on his own family now, on his children.

"I think it's scandalous," Mum says, and it's the closest he has seen her to being upset. "She could die, for goodness sake!"

"It's a long drive for them," Erik says.

He's in the doorway, taking his jacket off. It's been a long night, sitting by Anna's side. This morning he was told to go home, to take a shower and sleep. The nurses promised to call if there were any developments.

"They could get a train," Mum says. "That would only take a few hours. It's not as if they live in a different country."

"They're just busy with their own lives."

He wants the conversation to be over.

"If I had a daughter like Anna…" Mum says and her eyes momentarily tear up.

He's not sure if he should put his arms around her. He hesitates. Mum likes Anna a bit too much sometimes. When he first brought Anna home, he was happy that his mother approved. But when he realised that she had taken the top spot on the likeability chart, with him dropping down to second place, then it became… well, not a competition, but definitely annoying.

"Anyway," Mum says. She wipes her eyes and is back to her normal self and there is no need for a hug. "The boys don't have any clean underwear. Doesn't anyone do laundry in this house?"

*

Erik walks up the stairs to take a shower. Mum has promised to visit Anna this morning so that he can rest. The sun outside is radiating an annoying sense of warmth and happiness, not reflecting his mood. He feels cold and out of place, like this is no longer his house, the bed no longer his, the shower foreign. He glances at Anna's shampoo and scented soaps. Should he throw them out or leave them where they are?

Before Mum leaves, she pops her head into the bathroom.

"Please hang the washing in the drying cabinet when you wake up," she says. "I will pick the boys up from day care this afternoon so that you can go back to the hospital."

"Thanks," he says.

"Oh, and Erik?"

"Yes?"

The hot water burns into his back.

What is it now? Just leave me alone.
"Everything is going to be okay."
"Sure."
Whatever you say. Just go.

*

With the washing machine whirring in the background, Erik pulls out Anna's laptop from her school bag and places it on the kitchen table next to a strong cup of coffee. He pulls the blinds down to block out the neighbours and anyone else walking past. Even though it's still cold outside, the town seems to come alive when the sun is out. It's all very formal and polite. People walk and talk and nod with a high-pitched "*hej*" when they pass each other. Anna loves how friendly this place is but Erik thinks it's fake. He prefers bigger cities where you mind your own business. At least their house is on the main street of Mörna which means they're not tucked away in a cosy neighbourhood with weekend barbecues and coffee mornings. They only have two immediate neighbours: a ninety-year-old woman they hardly ever see and a family with grown children who they're only required to wave to every now and then. The mother has made an appearance since the news about Anna broke. With sad eyes she offered to help Erik with the children or food shopping – "anything at all" – but he has politely declined. He can cope. He *will* cope, and for now, Mum is here.

He should be sleeping as per the nurses' orders, but he can't. No one knows that he has Anna's laptop and it makes him feel guilty. That night when she had to "dash down to school", she left it in her workbag at home and when his band-mate Rob hurriedly drove him to the hospital, Erik grabbed the bag on his way out. It was parked by the door, as if she had forgotten it.

"She might need her bag," he told Rob.

"What the hell is wrong with you?" Rob said. "You don't even know what state she's in, mate."

"Yeah, but it can't be that bad. Otherwise, they would have said, right?"

How wrong he was.

"I wasn't thinking," he said. "I'm... I mean... she's going to be okay though, isn't she?"

He started crying then, the full waterworks. Obviously she couldn't use her laptop. He ended up leaving it in Rob's car and by the time Rob gave the bag back to him, the police had already searched the house. He should have handed it over but something held him back. It's not that he doesn't trust the police; he just doesn't think they will prioritise it. Too often, he reads about the lack of resources in the newspaper, people having to look for their stolen goods themselves. Only last week, two teenagers had to turn investigators and search for their stolen mopeds. That's just wrong. Erik can't leave this in someone else's hands.

*

He flops onto a white, Danish designer chair, the motion sparking a recent memory of Anna's persuasive decision-making. She insisted they buy these chairs.

"They're expensive *and* uncomfortable," he said at the time. "That's a bad combination."

She bought them second-hand. Avoiding conflict but still getting her way.

He grabs a pillow and places it behind his back to make himself more comfortable while also delaying the inevitable: logging on to her computer. It doesn't feel right. Yet it's necessary. The police will need his help.

"Anything you can think of, let us know," they said.

He wants to be obliging and more importantly, he wants to be involved.

Pressing the start button on Anna's laptop, he realises that he has never used it before. The children haven't even been allowed to play games on it. "My work laptop", she called it, even though she had bought it with her own money.

A blue screen stares at him, requesting a password. He tries various combinations. The usual ones. Birth dates, mother's maiden name, name of the pet she had when she grew up.

Please try again.

He tries again and again but has no luck. He snaps it shut. It was a bad idea anyway.

That's when it hits him. The whole situation. It's completely surreal! His wife is in a coma and he has no idea when – or even *if* – she will ever wake up. It's indescribably painful, this limbo... His knuckles whiten as they press hard around the edges of the laptop. There's a cramp inside his chest. He slams the computer down and punches the table, releasing the pressure. What the hell is he going to do?

He breathes deeply, composes himself the way Mum would do. Takes a sip of coffee "to calm his nerves".

"Bloody hell!" He burns himself on the Filippa K mug that's been designed without a handle. Stupid invention.

One of Anna's classes gave her a whole set for Christmas. Looking around, he realises that Anna is everywhere.

Even the furniture is a reminder of her. The few pieces he contributed when they met have slowly been replaced with eclectic ones that Anna has either recycled from flea markets or bought via online auctions. Will she ever do that again?

He calls Rob, the only friend he can truly be himself with. "I'm so fucking frustrated," he says, not just referring to the failed login to Anna's laptop but to everything that has just happened. "I feel so lost. I don't know what's going on. Will she get better? Why can't someone answer that simple question? And the police... I don't know, they expect me to tell them stuff but... but then they don't tell me shit!"

Spitting the words down the phone makes him realise how true they are. How can they exclude him like that? They are married; he is her next of kin.

"I'm sorry, man," Rob says. "I know that sucks but you've got to keep faith. Anna is strong. And maybe the police have been really busy. I read in the paper this morning that someone was murdered in the city."

"And that's more important, you mean? Anna is still alive so why should they keep writing about her in the papers?"

He knows he's pushing it too far but it feels good to take his frustration out on someone else.

"Look, Erik," Rob says. "Perhaps it's just that this other case has left Anna lost within the pages. It doesn't mean no one cares."

Erik rocks back and forth in the chair. The plastic creaks. Another thing he hates about this chair. It's irrelevant, though. Is Anna going to wake up? That's the important question.

Rob clears his throat. "It's really tough, Erik. I know. I mean, obviously I have no idea, but I can imagine. Anna is a gem... I really wish I could help." He stops rambling and sighs before starting again. "Hey, why don't you call that policewoman I dated last year? Big hair, bad breath? Eh… Tina. I'm sure she could, you know, give you some info, tell you what's going on."

Erik starts to listen. He has no idea who Rob is talking about but it gives him hope.

"I don't want to get pulled into something messy though," he says. "Why did you break up?"

Rob coughs. "It's totally cool," he says. "I mean, it wasn't like that. She agreed that I wasn't the one for her. She needed too much attention, you know, always creating drama."

"Well, I prefer drama to no info," Erik says and makes a note of her number.

As soon as he's put the phone down, he calls this Tina.

"Erik? Rob's friend?" She doesn't sound impressed but the moment he tells her about Anna, she changes her tone. "That's your wife? I'm so sorry. Look, from what I can tell, there's not really anything new."

"I see." He starts to cry but he doesn't mind that she can hear him. He wants sympathy.

"Look," she says more quietly. "I'm not supposed to tell you this. They spoke to her colleagues and rumour is she was very close with one teacher in particular… Kent."

"Yes, I know." Because of course he knows. But her tone… is she insinuating something else? He pictures Kent, his greying beard and hawk-like nose pressed against Anna's, the two of them kissing. He laughs through the tears. What a ridiculous idea! Plus there's Märta. Anna has mentioned what a great marriage they have. He does listen sometimes.

"He's happily married," he says even though she hasn't asked.

"Well, they're going to talk to him again. Now, I have to go."

"That's it?"

"Look, I don't have to tell you anything."

Fine. He needs her. "Thanks," he says. "I mean it. I appreciate your help."

*

He walks upstairs and surveys Anna's desk. If he can't get into her laptop, then what else can he look through? The next time he talks to the police, he wants to have something useful to say, and if he can't find anything, perhaps he will have no choice but to give them the computer.

The old IKEA unit from Anna's student days is constantly cluttered with papers; there must be something he can go on, something the police have missed? He imagines them searching her desk in a rush. The house wasn't particularly messy when he arrived home, but then Anna is only a small-town teacher, not an important politician or businesswoman. Mum thinks he's cynical but he's just realistic. This isn't a big city; it's a claustrophobic little town where no one gives a shit about anyone else. Anything out of the ordinary turns to gossip. He imagines the whispers that must be going around about Anna and it makes him ill.

Erik pulls out the wooden swivel chair in front of Anna's desk and sits down. There are a couple of books and he picks them up, thumbing through them. It's mostly fiction. He recognises a few of the authors' names, such as Selma Lagerlöf, August Strindberg and Karin Boye. Anna would be proud of him for knowing his Swedish literature, but unfortunately nothing is hidden inside the hard covers. Not that he had really expected there to be.

Under the books are a number of notepads with scribbled

sentences. *War and Peace intriguing enough? Presenta-tions – Monday – book projector. Renaissance essays? Kent and Märta – Strindberg play Saturday.* He remembers not wanting to go to the play and feels bad.

He tosses the notepad to the side and picks up a stack of papers instead. It's mainly bills, which makes him realise he has to pay them. It's always been Anna who logs in to the Internet bank to pay their bills. He has no idea how it's done. Maybe Mum can do it for him? Another realisation: they have many bills. Electricity, water, waste, phone, broadband, TV... His salary as a house painter doesn't stretch far. They need Anna's income. What will happen now that she can't work? Will she still get paid? He realises he can't ask that question. It will seem insensitive.

He flicks through the bills, his heart growing heavier with each one. Then a note. He finds himself holding a personally written note, not a bill.

That was a nasty thing to do, Anna. You know I'm smarter than that.

It's so small, no wonder no one has seen it. Erik looks closely at the words. The handwriting is tiny and neat. He reads it a few times, trying to understand if there is a hidden message. Who wrote this? A colleague? A student? Her sister? Anna has had her dramas through the years. She's firm with people around her, but fair. At least that's what she used to say. He's not sure anymore. He stopped listening a long time ago.

4

Iris

1983

*B*illie Jean is not my lover, Michael Jackson belted out, making the crowd go crazy.

Bille Jean is not my lover.

But are you?

Iris watched as a woman with red hair navigated her way through the dance floor. She looked older, late twenties perhaps, tall and voluptuous, a cheeky fringe above green eyes. Iris parted her lips, raised her glass and slowly drank the cold white wine, conveying sophistication.

"I'm Hanna."

The woman brought an air of perfume with her and gracefully stretched a hand out. Iris took it. It was soft but firm and she held it slightly longer than was customary for a handshake.

"Iris," she said.

"Are you here alone?"

She was tempted to make up a story about a date

abandoning her but Rolf wouldn't have approved. *Stay as close to the truth as possible.* Their arrangement was so new, she didn't want to let him down.

"Yes. And you?"

"I'm here with friends." Hanna nodded in the direction she had just come from. "They're about to leave though. So... what do you do, Iris?"

The casualness of the question was an emotional U-turn.

"I work in a library," she said drily, anticipating a yawn from Hanna. That was generally the reaction her profession generated. Instead, Hanna's eyes lit up.

"A lover of books!" Her smile broadened. "I'm an actress and also a lover of books."

"Really? What are you reading at the moment?"

"A play I'm rehearsing, *No Exit.*"

"By Jean-Paul Sartre?"

Hanna tilted her head slightly. "You know it?"

"Of course. Who are you playing?"

"Inez."

They looked at each other knowingly: Inez, the woman who ended up in hell for seducing her cousin's wife.

*

Walking down a cobbled street with multi-coloured buildings on either side, they talked about the play; leaving the comforting, smoky buzz of the club behind.

"Inez sings as well," Hanna told her. "*They've set trestles in a row, with a scaffold and a knife...*"

Her voice was beautiful and the intimacy it brought made Iris slip her hand into Hanna's. Warmth spread through her palm. It was a crisp summer evening and still light outside. Iris loved the months of the year when it never grew dark; the optimism that filled the air, the love, the hope…

"… *Come, good folks, to Whitefriars Lane, come to see the merry show!*"

Iris clapped while still holding Hanna's hand, not wanting to withdraw it. Hanna bowed.

"Thank you," she said. "It's always been my dream to be on stage."

They walked past a small harbour and a row of shoreline restaurants that were busy closing for the night. Iris let Hanna lead the way, not knowing where they were heading. She had travelled to another city, wanting to remain anonymous, and no street felt familiar. It was frightening but mostly thrilling.

"What about you?" Hanna asked. "Are you living your dream?"

"I'm happy." She didn't want Hanna to know that this was her first job out of university. "I love literature and now I'm surrounded by it every day."

"Good for you."

Hanna started singing again and soon they reached a modern, whitewashed apartment building, each window frame displaying potted St Paulias, hydrangeas or orchids. One day, Iris was hoping to have a large garden filled with flowers. Hanna fished out a key from her handbag.

"*So here we are, for ever,*" she said dramatically, opening the door. "Inez's famous last words."

The apartment on the third floor was a contrast of white furniture and colourful cushions, drapes and curtains. Vibrant and inviting, the open plan space was covered with candleholders: on tables, dressers and shelves. Hanna slipped out of her heels and retrieved a lighter. Barefooted, she elegantly leaned over furniture to light candles, gradually making the room glow. Iris silently watched her while taking her own heels off. Hanna was so graceful.

"Nice moves," Iris said but the words came out all wrong. They sounded like Rolf's. Cheesy. It wasn't a line for her, she meant it. The words needed to be her own to sound authentic. "I mean, did you train as a dancer?"

Hanna nodded and kissed her. Just for a second, their lips touched, before Hanna removed Iris's coat from her shoulders.

"Here, let me take that," she said, her cheeks rosy. "Red or white wine?"

"Red, please." She liked variety.

Iris stepped into the area designated as kitchen. It consisted of a small oven and a cooker, a fridge and a microwave. Hanna pulled out the cork from an already opened bottle on the counter, and poured two glasses. The wine felt like a formality, their eyes observing each other over the rim of the glass as they took a couple of sips. Iris slipped her arm around Hanna's waist, pulling her close. *Quickly take charge.* She pressed herself against Hanna's soft lips, their tongues meeting in a playful kiss. Then Iris pulled away.

"Let's slow down," she said.

Hanna smiled but instead of releasing Iris, she pulled her closer. This was really happening. *Go with the flow.* Iris's hands travelled over Hanna's curves, caressing the firm behind, stroking her muscular back and shoulders, grabbing a handful of the long hair, pulling it back. Hanna moaned as Iris's lips brushed her neck.

"Turn around," Iris said as she moved the glossy, red hair out of the way, hooking her finger around the zip in Hanna's short, patterned dress. She pulled it down, revealing pale, smooth skin and gently slipped the dress off the shoulders. Hanna wasn't wearing a bra and Iris stretched her hands around her front, cupping the generous breasts, gently tugging at the hardened nipples. Pressed against Hanna's back, her own breasts tingled at the warmth of another body. She felt her insides contract.

"I want you," she said.

5

Anna

September 2015

D aniel didn't call her "Miss", he insisted on calling her
Anna. She normally preferred it, but the way he pro-
nounced her name, long and drawn out, was uncomfortable.
Aaaa-nnn-a.

He was in the teachers' lounge after school hours yet again,
wearing the same well-worn clothes, shoelaces undone; his
gangly frame hardened by the muscles of adolescence. It was
the second time in a week that he had appeared uninvited.
Last time, Kent had turned up to fetch his keys and Daniel
had bolted before she got a chance to speak to him. Now she
seized the opportunity.

"How did you get in?" she asked.

Perhaps he had managed to sneak in when Kent left?
The door did take a while to close. Or had he been hiding
in the shadows since the bell rang, eavesdropping on their
conversation?

Daniel's smirk unsettled her. Had she revealed something
to Kent she shouldn't have? She was happy that she hadn't

mentioned the letters even though she had received another one.

His gaze was intense. "I just did," he said casually and threw himself on the couch, resting his muddy trainers on the table.

She made no comment; she had to choose her battles.

"How can I help you?" she asked, trying to sound upbeat.

Daniel studied the floor, a bored look on his face, and wiped his nose with the back of his fist. His dirty blond hair always appeared messy, even though a large amount of gel was probably involved.

"There's no one at home," he said, as if the teacher's lounge was the most natural place to be instead.

"And you don't want to be alone?"

He didn't respond, his eyes wandering around the room, seemingly soaking in every detail: the shared hot desks, the out-dated computer, the grey monster copying machine, the hat rack with a number of multi-coloured caps on it, the umbrellas next to the door.

Eventually he turned towards her.

"You haven't responded to my letters," he said, the words hard yet lined with a slight vulnerability.

The last handwritten note, like the others, had been short and to the point.

Homework is a waste of time. I'm not learning. Do you actually want to teach me something?

He was obviously trying to provoke her into responding. Choosing her words carefully, she said: "I'm really happy that you express yourself in writing." The fact that he had used a pen to write, instead of throwing it through the room like an arrow, did please her. "Although I'm not as good at writing as you are. I prefer to talk."

This wasn't entirely true but conversations couldn't be used against you the way letters could. She still wasn't sure it was appropriate to write back.

"I'm not interested in talking," he said. "No one listens."

"Try me."

Normally, she had everything under control. Discipline had never been an issue in her classroom, but Daniel was different. One minute he was an insolent child, the next he expressed depth. She often caught him reading between classes.

"I could kick your head in," he said, jolting her out of her thoughts.

Her spine straightened, her eyes trying to gauge if he was serious. His clenched fists suggested that he was. She wondered if the janitor was still in the building. Although he was notoriously unreliable, he was someone, an obstruction, a witness.

Dread mixed with uncertainty. Did she know what she was doing?

"Daniel," she said, trying to sound calm. *He's only a teenager.* "You have the potential to do really well." She cleared her throat: "If you just apply yourself."

He seemed to relax his hands.

"Who cares?" he said.

"I do," she said, too quickly. She needed to be more constructive; no student was going to learn for her sake.

"Did your parents care?"

Again, he turned the tables, making it about anyone but

himself. At least it was easier to handle it here, where it was just the two of them, as opposed to the classroom where another twenty students were watching.

"It was important to me to have an education," she said.

It felt too personal to divulge that her parents barely noticed when she moved out to go to university.

"My brother beats people up," he said.

Already, they were onto a new topic. His way of jumping from subject to subject unnerved her, as much as his obsession with violence. Not a week went by without him being involved in a major fight. Perhaps he did have a diagnosis. Could she force the counsellor to get involved?

"That doesn't sound nice," she said.

"My mum couldn't care less." He shrugged. "Can I just stay here, while you work?"

There was the child again. She could deal with him.

"You should go home," she said gently and although she made an effort to sound kind, her words seemed to bring back the callous Daniel. His eyes grew dark and he didn't move. He just stared at her, leaving her no choice but to start packing up: papers neatly slid into her bag, pens and pencils went back in their case, her laptop zipped up in its cover.

"Right," she said, standing up. "I'm going home now."

He didn't get up immediately but she could feel him watching her. To distract herself, she fussed with her jacket, putting it on slowly to give him time, changing her shoes; taking the ballet flats off, stepping into her boots. She needed to get out.

"Anna..." he said then and inwardly she sighed. Not only had she missed her precious preparation time, he was making her feel uncomfortable. He needed to understand that while at school, she was in charge. Not him.

She turned to him, her strict teacher's face plastered on. "Yes, Daniel?"

Standing up, he was bigger than her. His face was symmetrical, the cheekbones high and the forehead tall. She could easily picture girls falling for him. Daniel's eyes were firmly on his trainers, as if he was mounting up the courage to say something. She waited patiently, cautious.

Then he raised his head and looked at her. She couldn't quite read his facial expression.

"I have decided..." he started.

"Yes?"

"...that you're going to be my new mum."

6

Erik

March 2016

"Has your wife got any enemies?"

Erik has been asked to the police station in the city to assist with the investigation. Or to be questioned? Either way, the female police officer gains his full attention with her compassionate eyes. The policeman at her side, on the other hand, looks less sympathetic. Erik appreciates that he's asked about enemies, not his alibi. Perhaps that's because the policewoman, who's introduced herself as Linda Johansson, is new. She looks young. Or maybe he's told them already? He has a vague recollection of someone at the hospital asking of his whereabouts. He can't remember what he answered.

"I don't know," he says. "Did you talk to the people at her school?"

Did you talk to Kent?

"Yes, we talked to her colleagues," Officer Johansson says, but she doesn't mention any names.

It irritates him. They should tell him every single lead they might have. He needs to remain calm though. Otherwise he will achieve nothing.

"Why do you ask?" says the policeman whose name he can't remember.

Erik debates whether he should mention Kent, but if he does, they will wonder why. All he knows is that Anna really respected the guy. That's it. He can't imagine the two of them together.

He shrugs. "Just want to make sure no stone is unturned," he says.

"Were you aware of any conflicts at school? Difficult students?"

Erik shakes his head, although there's a nagging feeling he might have missed something during all those daily conversations about school. The note he found on Anna's desk comes to mind but would it make him sound paranoid? It could be completely irrelevant.

"You sure?" asks Officer Johansson. "Nothing that was bothering her?"

Anna has an annoying habit of rattling off every event of her day, he thinks, every single evening, and with time he has learned to nod and say the appropriate amounts of okays and a-has to get through it. Now he wishes he had paid more attention.

"Well," he says, taking a chance. He'd rather share the note than give up the laptop. Tina has explained that electronics are put in storage, labelled as "evidence" and then pretty much forgotten about. "I'm not sure if it will help, but I found this."

He puts the handwritten note in front of Officer Johansson whose interest peaks.

That was a nasty thing to do, Anna. You know I'm smarter than that.

"Could be a student," she says. "Someone who wanted a better grade?"

"Sure, I mean, of course."

"We will look into it."

The note is bagged and he imagines it being tested for fingerprints. What will they find?

"How has Anna been lately?"

Officer Johansson leans back in her chair and he tries to look equally comfortable. He's just not sure what to tell them. If only he had something tangible to share. The last couple of months Anna didn't really talk about school anymore. She didn't talk about anything.

"She was always busy," he says honestly.

"On Tuesday, did you speak to her in the afternoon?"

He nods. "Yes, she called and asked me to pick up the children from day care, even though it was her turn."

"Is that unusual?"

"Not exactly."

He remembers the phone conversation well; has had that same talk many times over in different versions.

"What if I'm busy?" he said, tired of being taken for granted.

"You don't have a paint job today."

She was always so aware of his schedule. No, he didn't have a job that day, but Rob had the day off and they were jamming in his garage.

"Are you with Rob?" she asked.

"No," he lied, signalling to Rob to stop tuning his guitar.

"I'll see you later then. I need more time to plan my lessons for tomorrow."

If it wasn't lessons she needed to prepare for, then it was exam papers, photocopying or whatever boring stuff it was she had to do.

"Or she needs to drop a student home who's missed the bus," he complained to Rob. "As if that's even her responsibility."

"She cares, man," said Rob. "If I had a wife like Anna, I'm sure I would change underwear more often. You know what I'm saying? I would make an effort."

"What do you know?"

"Nothing. Can we play now?"

"No," he tells Officer Johansson. "It wasn't unusual."

"Did anyone see you pick up the children?"

Ah, there it is: his alibi.

"Pernilla Arvidsson saw me."

Officer Johansson makes a note and he realises someone will contact Pernilla. What will she say?

"How is your marriage?"

How is their marriage? Erik looks at the male police officer. Is he that transparent?

"What's that got to do with anything?"

"Were you happy?" Officer Johansson's voice is softer.

"I see what you're doing," Erik says despite himself. "You're playing good cop, bad cop."

He wants to laugh but he can't. How would that look? His wife may never wake up. This is real life. The policeman scoffs but Officer Johansson leans in closer and asks: "Was Anna happy?"

"Yes, she was happy." What kind of a question is that?

"She was frustrated at work and she would get annoyed with me, just like any other wife would, but she was happy."

He slumps back into his chair, feeling tired.

"Coffee?"

He nods. "Yes, please."

"I understand it's hard," Officer Johansson says.

Erik looks at her, suppressing the urge to shout: "Do you really?" It wouldn't help. He knows that. Instead he sips the hot coffee, burning his tongue.

"We haven't been able to locate Anna's laptop or mobile phone," the policeman says. "They weren't in the car, at the school, or at your house. Have you seen those items or do you know where she would keep them?"

Erik doesn't appreciate his tone. He doesn't have her phone.

"She would have had the phone with her," he says.

"There was no phone in her handbag or in the car."

"Right." *Well, you're the police, you figure it out: prove your worth to the taxpayers who pay your salaries.*

"Where were you that evening?" asks the policeman. He's annoyingly arrogant, as if he wants to catch Erik lying.

"I'm sure someone has asked me that already," Erik says. "After we arrived home from day care, the boys and I were home all afternoon and evening. No, wait." Erik thinks back to that afternoon. They were out of milk. "I went to the supermarket when Anna got home." Maybe he left that out last time.

"Anna was at home?"

They both lean forward, as if this is really interesting. Except it's not.

"Yes, she came home briefly," he says. "Cooked dinner and then she had to go back to school."

"Why?"

"No idea. To prepare something or pick something up maybe?"

"And while she was at school, you were home alone with the boys?"

Erik nods. "There was no one else to watch them," he says. Isn't that obvious?

"They would be sleeping by what? Eight o'clock?" the policeman asks.

"Yes, that's about right."

"And around ten o'clock, where were you?"

"Getting ready for bed probably."

"So you didn't step out of the house?"

"I might have been in the garden briefly, but that's it. You can't leave sleeping children home alone," Erik says. Stupid man probably doesn't have children of his own.

"Can anyone else verify that you were at home?"

The policeman grins. He wants blood.

"We have to ask," Officer Johansson says.

"Rob," Erik says, at once grateful that Rob decided to come by that evening. "My mate, Rob. He knows I was at home."

They make a note and the policeman leaves the room to check this new fact out, returning within minutes. Rob has confirmed via phone that he did see Erik. He exhales. Finally, this is over. Erik gets up to leave.

"I need to get back to the hospital," he says.

7

Anna

September 2015

The boys were already in bed when she got home. Disappointed to have missed them, she tiptoed into their bedroom to kiss them goodnight. Every time she saw them sprawled across their beds, carefree and peacefully asleep, her heart felt warmer.

"Little rascals," she whispered, quietly kissing their soft cheeks.

How amazing that she and Erik had been part of their creation. That thought always astonished her, that they were their children. Before she left the room, she lingered by the door for a few seconds, watching them. Snoring mouths and blond tousled hair. Miniature versions of Erik.

"It took forever to get them to sleep," he complained when she returned downstairs.

She sighed. He didn't enforce any rules, so what did he expect? She bit her tongue though, but the spell of love she had just felt was broken.

"I'm going to Rob's." Erik grabbed his jacket and headed for the door.

"I only just got home." She couldn't help herself. "What about dinner?"

"Leftover sausages in the fridge."

She heard the front door open.

"Wait, Erik. Please." She ran after him. Couldn't he spend at least five minutes with her? "Please don't leave me alone."

Not tonight. He was already halfway out when he turned around.

"What's going on?"

"I just... There's this student..."

She sat down on the chair next to the hall table. Maybe she could talk to him about Daniel. Erik was a child at heart, perhaps he would understand and provide some insight.

"Right." His face tightened. "It's about work. Not: how were the boys today? Did they get up to anything fun at day care, did they behave, do we need to send extra clothes?" He was really going for it and she let him. He clearly needed to vent. "You care more about your students than your own children."

A clear violation. She wanted to fight back but chose not to. It would only escalate; she had learned that the hard way.

"Come on, Erik," she said.

"Students and parents call you twenty-four hours a day, Anna. How the hell do they even have the right to have your number?"

"Let's not do this."

He was jealous. She had a purpose in life and he didn't. He busied himself painting houses while dreaming of a music career. They could be stuck in this argument for ages. She needed to distract him.

"Kent and Märta are going to the theatre next weekend. Should we join them?"

"I won't sit through another four-hour *Hamlet*, if that's what you think?"

"I have apologised for that enough times, Erik. I didn't realise it was going to be so long. This is a Strindberg play…"

"How great. No thanks."

"Come on."

"Unless it's bloody sex on stage I'm not going."

Where did that come from?

"Not everything is about sex, Erik."

"Don't I know it?"

She didn't want to discuss it. He knew she felt insecure about her weight gain, but it was also something else, something she couldn't explain. She just didn't feel *that way* when she looked at him. A painful truth that she needed to deal with. But how? His behaviour didn't exactly encourage her.

"What happened to us?" she said, depleted.

He came back in and stood in front of her, still angry but calmer. Then he put his hands on her shoulders, the physical contact almost making her cry. She reciprocated by wrapping her arm around his leg, resting her forehead on his thigh.

"I have no life," she whispered.

"What does that even mean, Anna?"

He sounded exasperated and her instinct was to get annoyed. He didn't understand anything! Her arm squeezed his leg tighter but she felt him back away.

"I work hard to provide a good life for us. But sometimes I feel like no one really cares about me, Erik."

"Anna, stop it."

"I mean it." She looked up at him. *See me.* "The boys prefer you. You're the fun dad and I'm the mean mum. My boss no longer appreciates my efforts, he takes them for granted. The students... they're sucking me dry."

She was specifically thinking of Daniel, who had opened up a whole new problem for her to solve.

"You just need validation," he said. "Reality check, Anna, you were Teacher of the Year last year." He spat it out as if it was an accusation. "I hate to break it to you but everywhere we go, you receive praise."

She knew this bothered him; parents and previous students telling her how wonderful she was. This was superficial though: comments said in passing. And she hadn't asked to be named Teacher of the Year. It was one of the principal's new incentives that was supposed to make her feel valued instead of underpaid. The truth was, she felt empty. Erik needed to know. To understand.

"Everyone thinks I'm a terrible mother and that you're a great father."

"That's not true."

"Really?" she said. "If I were to leave early to pick up the children, my boss thinks I'm a bad employee. If one of my male colleagues on the other hand has to pick up his children, he's a good dad. You see? Even though we supposedly live in a modern society, there are still these preconceived ideas. I'm sick of it. I can never win..."

"I don't agree." He broke away from her, forcing her to let go. "Anyway, if that's all, I'm off to Rob's."

She looked at him, perplexed. How could he be so callous?

"Erik."

"Yes?"

It was pointless. She grabbed her bag and the car keys

and shot out the door before he got the chance. That would teach him.

"Anna!"

He followed her out to the carport but only caught up with her when she had already slammed the car door shut and locked it.

"Anna! I have to go." He was knocking on the window. She ignored him, started the car and sped off. He wanted her to join him in a screaming match but she wouldn't. In the rear-view mirror she saw him standing in the road, arms up in the air. A mixture of triumph and sadness hit her.

Her phone rang almost immediately. Erik's name flashed on the screen. She didn't pick up. Nothing either of them had to say would be constructive now.

She needed to get away from him. From everything. If only she had made an effort to make friends, she would have somewhere to go. Apart from university friends who were now all over the country, she didn't really know anyone well enough to call in an hour of need. No shoulders to cry on. A fleeting image of Kent. Could she? No. Their friendship seemed to be put on hold when they left the school building for the day, to be reignited when the next day began. Her mother wasn't a viable alternative either. They hadn't spoken for months and when they did talk, her father's grunts and demands in the background kept her mother distracted.

*

Anna drove around for a while, wasting petrol, passing green sprawling woods interlinked with horse paddocks and vast fields, the sea revealed in the distance, the moon sparkling on its dark surface. When they first arrived in

Skåne County, she had found the southern countryside breathtaking. They had moved down in summer, when everywhere you looked was lush and green; the lavender blooming, bumblebees hovering, the ice cream kiosks busy, and families biking to the beach. That first Midsummer had been precious, the tradition from the Middle Ages brought to life in a nearby meadow, celebrated with a few hundred people from Mörna, their new town. Children and their parents had clad the maypole in birch leaves and brightly coloured flowers, a man played folk songs on an accordion while they danced around the pole. It was before Sebastian and Lukas were born and she had made a mental note to bring her future children there. They had continued to celebrate each Midsummer in that same meadow but other than that one time every year, they didn't make use of their beautiful surroundings. She couldn't even remember the last time they had gone for a walk. *There's a life outside of school*. There was indeed.

Erik kept calling. She could imagine his words: "For fuck's sake, Anna! Come back!" He definitely wouldn't be calling to say sorry because he wouldn't know what to apologise for. He didn't understand her, couldn't read her emotional barometer. She kept ignoring him.

When she had met Erik on holiday in Gran Canaria, he was the tall, handsome bartender from the north of Sweden doing a gap year in the sun. She had fallen for his gentle ways, how he was charming but neither pushy nor arrogant. His golden hair glowing, his lips plump. Kissable. She remembered her friends quarrelling because she chose to spend a large part of the holiday with Erik. "We came to have fun, not hang out with boys!" It was true, the purpose had been to get away from their studies. But she had been too exhilarated and had shrugged it off, thinking they were just jealous.

After she had returned to Stockholm, Erik had also moved back and soon they lived together. They had been madly in love and so it hadn't felt rushed. Plus they had their own circles of friends and would sometimes party separately and at other times, together. Since moving to the south, however, they had become overly dependent on each other. It felt like they were this one compact unit, which at first had felt exciting (it was them against the world) but then she had started to feel that every time she broke away from him, she was made to feel guilty.

She drove back into Mörna but the imminent darkness and dimly lit streets didn't welcome her. Instead, she kept driving past their house, along the main street, Mörnavägen, which sliced the town in two: the "right side" meaning the part that was closest to the sea, and the "wrong side", where they lived. She exited the town, passing a long stretch of dense fir forest followed by more farms and fields. After a few kilometres, the next town's lights and rows of houses appeared. She felt herself exhale. It was good to create distance between herself and the town that her whole life seemed to revolve around. She drove down to the sea, passed a small harbour and thought of going for a walk, but it felt chilly and in her rush to get out, she hadn't brought a jacket.

Aimlessly, she drove up and down the small windy Hågarp roads with their doll-sized houses. It was getting dark and most homes were equally submerged in darkness, the majority of the residents being summer guests only.

She managed to get back to the main road and was surprised to see there was a library. How could it possibly survive in such an underpopulated place when most small-town libraries in the county were closing down? It was an old dilapidated building in red brick that had probably been grandiose once upon a time. The word LIBRARY hung precariously above a glass door, glowing like a vintage cinema sign. She stopped the car, welcoming the distraction. Without a plan, she got out and walked up the steps towards the sign. The notion of reading spurred her on. Memories as a child of escaping reality through adventure stories.

Next to the door was a notice with the opening hours: the library would be open until nine that evening. In fact, it was open late two nights a week. She made a mental note as she pushed the heavy glass door. There was a muffled sound of a bell as she stepped into the otherwise quiet hallway. A couple of students were typing on computers, a man was reading a newspaper. She moved inside, sucked into the centre where rows upon rows of books welcomed her.

"Hi there, can I help you?"

A lady behind the counter eyed her up and down. She was chic-looking, in a French sort of way, with a dark bob, pale skin and bright lipstick.

"I'm not sure," Anna said.

The woman viewed her quizzically over the red-rimmed reading glasses, before resuming her typing. Anna noted how slender her fingers were, like a pianist's. She was wearing a black jersey dress, a big arty necklace in silver decorating her neckline. How simple it could be to make an effort. Her own jeans and stretchy jumper could have done with some adornments. When had she stopped caring about her looks?

"Actually," she said. "I do know. I'm in need of some escapism but I don't know where to begin."

The woman looked up, a broad smile on her face.

"You've come to the right place then," she said and stretched out a hand. "I'm Iris."

8

Daniel

September 2015

Dan loved writing. His mother knew this but his brother would tease the shit out of him if he knew. At night, he would compose stories with the aid of a flashlight, hiding the unfinished work at the bottom of his box of comics. It felt childish but satisfying, the blue ink on lined paper, stories created out of nothing, the sense of accomplishment. *She* liked that he wrote. Lying on his back he stared up into the cracked ceiling, following the lines like it was a treasure map. *I'm really happy that you have expressed yourself in writing.* He had memorised Anna's words.

He turned on his side and picked up his phone. No messages, which was no surprise. This was bullshit, moving from town to town.

"I have to follow the work," Frida said, like she was some important businesswoman whose services were indispensable.

"You follow the fucking men, Fri-i-i-da," he said. He couldn't bring himself to call her Mother or even Mum.

"Shut your mouth."

His name had been Emil. Ten years her junior. Martin had beaten the crap out of him after catching them fucking on the couch and that had ended that. The police had picked both Martin and Emil up and Dan hadn't seen either of them since.

Dan missed him. Martin hadn't been the best brother but he had protected him. Now he had to fend for himself and that included keeping Frida in check.

"She needs a good beating from time to time, to keep her head clear," Martin would say. "Or she will be getting up to some dumb shit, start drinking again or smoking weed or worse…"

Dan understood, had seen her at her worst. Memories of no food, uninvited guests, the smell of smoke and vomit, no space sacred. He would sleep on the cold stairs of whatever apartment block they lived in at the time, his backpack filled with books, pens and paper. When the noise got too much, he would hide between the pages and create his own world.

At one point they had been dangerously close to being handed over to a foster family, but Martin had taken charge. At fifteen he had started going to the gym, which had made the junkies an easy win for him. Then he had locked Frida up in her bedroom after first beating her up. Once detoxed, she had tried to start over, moved them to a new town, and secured herself a job. She was scared of Martin but she kept looking for a new man and they followed whomever she had caught in her net, thinking he would bring money, stability, a home somewhere.

Martin's father was dead but Dan's own father had left. He had never even known Frida was pregnant. At least that was the story she told.

"We are the men of the house," Martin would say. "The

others are just temporary." He was right. It turned out none of them wanted to play daddy, they were only interested in getting Frida's knickers off. Early on, Dan had realised that men liked his mother. If she had stayed away from mind-altering substances, she would be truly beautiful. His late grandmother had given him a picture of her as a teenager, showing a striking girl with long blonde hair, a cheeky grin and a slender, tanned body. He kept the photo in his box as a reminder of her youthful innocence.

Emil was gone but Frida would meet someone else of course. That's why Dan had been forced to make a plan. He had formulated it with great ease and it was now as clear in his head as it was on his lined paper. While executing it, he made sure Frida behaved. She needed to stay off the booze and she needed to stay employed.

He hoped she would hook up with a man at the factory. That would mean they could stay for a while. It was a small town and there wasn't much to do, but it wasn't like the shithole they lived in before. Here, they rented a one-storey house with a miniature garden. The rooms were damp and draughty and freezing cold but that didn't bother him much. At least they didn't have to share walls with another family and the area was peaceful. He could walk through the woods, down to the sea, or cycle around in the countryside. Not many arseholes hassled him and the ones who had at school, he had already shut up. They stayed out of his way now.

It felt gratifying getting into fights. He wasn't likely to get kicked out of school for it but he knew he couldn't keep it up without social services getting on his case. He just needed to do it long enough to get Anna's attention.

9

Iris

September 2015

"I guess it's just the two of us, then?"

As the heads of the municipality and county librarians left, Lena Blom, chairman of the social welfare committee, made herself comfortable. Leaning against the reception counter in the middle of the library, she kicked her shoes off and let the silk Hermès scarf slide to the floor.

"I'm opening up to the public again after lunch," Iris said.

"I know."

Iris loaded the coffee cups on a tray and wiped the white, circular sixties' table clean, before heading to the kitchen. Lena quickly followed, her bare feet running up behind Iris, soft on the wooden floor.

"It was a good meeting," Lena said. "You like Britt, don't you?"

"I think she's someone who will deliver on her promises," Iris said. "That's what we need. We need to create a hunger or our local libraries will have to shut down."

"Not yours."

"You never know. Who knows who our anonymous beneficiary is? He or she might run out of money."

"I don't think so."

Iris didn't respond. Lena didn't understand the value of money. Born into a rich family, she lived an affluent lifestyle many would envy. Despite this, she was, however, dedicated to her government job and Iris did respect that.

"How much do you really like Britt?" Lena asked. "Just so I know."

The insecurity wasn't becoming and Iris chose not to reply. Instead, she unloaded the cups and washed them in the sink, handing them one by one to Lena.

Lena dried them, somewhat reluctantly.

"I thought..."

"Not today," Iris said. "It's... we work together."

"We have done for a long time."

Iris handed her the last cup and rinsed out the sink, watching the foam disappear into the minuscule plughole. She needed more time.

"That's exactly it," she said eventually, turning to Lena.

Lena awkwardly held the dishtowel between her hands, as if she might drop it. She looked adorable and out of place, her sparkly jewellery a sharp contrast to the old kitchen décor. Iris found herself losing her thread.

"We will just..." she started, but before she could finish, Lena's mouth was on hers and Iris gave in. She grabbed Lena's waist and pushed her up against the wall, expertly unbuttoning her trousers. Her skilful hand slipped inside Lena's knickers with ease, reaching a rich wetness. Her fingers circulated and played. Lena's moans echoed into the kitchen, spurring her on and Iris quickened her movement, going faster and faster until her fingers almost cramped. They met in a stormy kiss; Lena's hand travelled up Iris's dress, then inside her tights. Lace stretched, the right buttons were pressed; their breathing heightened, their bodies pushed together, the friction intensifying. Groans exploded off their lips as they climaxed. Lena leaned into Iris, panting. Satisfied, Iris held on tight, wrapping her arms around Lena. Just for a moment. Then a brief kiss followed by disentanglement.

Iris felt that although she deeply cared about Lena, their meetings had become a rehearsed routine, it was too familiar. This needed to be the last time, Iris thought. The relationship needed to go back to being a professional one, or perhaps even a friendship if possible.

"Wow," Lena said.

She buttoned up her trousers, grinning.

"I have to go back to work," Iris said.

"I know." Lena combed her hair and checked her make-up in the kitchen mirror. "By the way, I went to your husband's exhibition last weekend."

Iris felt herself tense. "Really?"

Pride mixed with dread; she was immensely proud of him but she wanted him as far away from her colleagues as possible.

"The paintings were extremely dark," Lena continued. "Mysterious."

"I'll pass on the message," Iris said and opened the back door.

"See you next week."

Lena skipped down the steps like an adolescent girl and then she was gone.

*

Iris unlocked the main door, noticing a slight drizzle, which made the newly laid asphalt in the parking lot glisten. One of her regular visitors, Tore, had already pulled up. She waited for him by the door as his eighty-year-old body and accompanying umbrella shuffled up the stairs.

"It's cold," he said, sneezing.

"It's a glorious day though," Iris said.

From the top of the stairs, she could just about see the ocean. It was chilly and windy but fresh, the waves foaming, the seagulls squawking.

"Just come to read the newspaper," Tore said, reaching her.

"You're always welcome here."

While Tore settled in, Iris relaxed back into her day. This was her library, her domain. She breathed in the smell of paper and started to push the trolley down an aisle, returning books to their rightful places.

Then two hands, hugging her from behind. She was about to turn around when she spotted the familiar pair of Converse on the floor. "Excuse me..." said the voice, hands sliding up her stomach, cupping her weightless breasts. She closed her eyes, enjoying the touch for just a moment. "... I'm looking for my wife."

Rolf pressed himself against her back, nibbling her ear, an erection against her spine. Back in the day, she would have giggled.

"I want to fuck you," he hissed into her ear.

"Not here," she said, pulling away.

"Come on, Iris. Where's your sense of adventure?"

When she didn't respond, he released her.

"So..." he said grumpily. "How was your meeting?"

"It was fine, thank you." She turned to face him. "What are you doing here?"

"I wanted to see you."

"I thought you disliked this non-creative environment. I believe you called it 'conventional and uninspiring' the last time you were here." It had upset her and she wanted to get him back. This was her home away from home.

"Iris..."

"Perhaps you don't like it because it's not displaying your art?"

"Anyway..." He stroked her hair. "Who was that woman I just saw leaving?"

He had seen Lena even though she had left through the back door? Was he spying on her?

"Lena," she said. "She's part of the council meetings."

"Right. She's hot. Available?"

"No."

"That doesn't normally stop you," he said, stroking her cheek.

She gave him a disapproving look. "Rolf, don't."

"Right, you don't talk about it anymore, I remember."

He scratched the Jimi Hendrix moustache, sulking, and she pulled his ponytail to lighten the mood, just like she would have in the old days.

"Get out of here," she said playfully. "I've got a group of second graders coming any minute."

"Oh, baby." He kissed her intensely; his relentless desire for her was still arousing. "If only people could see you like this... this wild thing. Everyone thinks you're so fucking polished."

She laughed.

"Let's not tell anyone."

"So this Lena…?"

"She's a colleague. You're not getting jealous with old age, are you?"

He winked at her. "Just making sure everyone appreciates you as much as I do."

She picked up a book and demonstratively placed it on a shelf. *I have a job to do.*

"Okay, I will leave you to it," he said. "I'm sure you have your reasons."

The mood changed as he backed away. He was upset about being rejected, but she knew he wouldn't want to fight. No matter how much he loved starting debates in the media, he despised conflict with her.

"I should mind my own business," he muttered.

"You should."

She glanced at him as he left, the flamboyant shirt disappearing around the corner, acknowledging that she still loved the man she had married over twenty years ago. Her mother hadn't been quite so thrilled at the time.

"I give you one year," she had said. "He's too elusive."

It gave Iris immense pleasure to prove her mother wrong. At the time, however, she had felt disappointed and upset, especially since her mother had been a rebel herself. Brought up in Ireland, she had run off with a Swedish sailor at a young age and her family had never forgiven her.

Iris hadn't intended to live an alternative life with Rolf. It was just that with Rolf, you had to take it or leave it. And so she had agreed to take it.

Erik

March 2016

An agonising week and a half has gone past without Anna's condition changing. She's not better but she's also not worse; Erik is supposed to seek comfort in this. Only the colour on her face has changed, from a bruised purple to a yellowy green.

She's in the same ward, the same room, the same bed. Everything is unchanged, even the depressing view of the two-storey parking garage, the dreary cement cold and uninviting. Every time he looks outside, it's as if the world is grey, even the clouds look like they're mocking him with their greyness.

Anna also remains in the same position. Don't they move her?

Her still frame unnerves him. If only she could wake up and argue with him. Anything but this silence.

"She looks kind of weird, Daddy. When is she going to wake up?"

The doctors keep saying "if" but the boys stick to "when".

It worries him, because no one knows for sure. Despite this, he tries to remain optimistic in front of the boys.

"Her body just needs to heal, buddy."

Sebastian kisses her cheek and tells her to please get better soon.

"We need you at home," he whispers in his mum's ear.

How will Sebastian cope if Anna doesn't make it? Lukas, on the other hand, is handling it better. He seems more oblivious, driving a car down Anna's leg, pretending it's a road, her knee a mountain. At least until his grandmother tells him to stop. Mum's big cuddly arms can be deceiving, her wagging finger turning her into a total killjoy. Give Lukas a break, he wants to say, but he doesn't. He is too tired to argue. Being in the hospital with the children is exhausting.

*

When they arrive back home, the white postbox with daintily painted flowers on it is filled with "get well soon" cards from people in the town, mainly parents, students and colleagues.

"People prefer to send a card than to come over," he comments.

While he thinks people are cowards for hiding behind their precious wooden doors, he's secretly happy. If someone did visit, he wouldn't know what to say. Even the short conversation with the neighbour was awkward.

"Well, maybe they don't know how to express themselves," Mum says. "That's understandable after all. At least a card is better than nothing, it shows they care."

He shrugs. "Sure."

The boys ask to watch TV and Mum lets them without asking his opinion. It's okay, he doesn't mind too much. He's used to Anna calling the shots and making up the rules.

Mum has more or less moved in and handles Sebastian and Lukas. Out of the hospital, the boys and Mum are good at sticking with the program of "business as usual". The counsellor has suggested this approach. Erik tries to adopt it himself but he feels a constant unease, an unreachable scratch under his skin. The continuity that surrounds him helps though. The day care hours remain the same, everybody must treat the boys as they did before, and at home... well, Erik probably hugs them more than normal.

He does that now, even though they are heavily invested in Tom chasing Jerry. Competing with the cat versus mouse race, Erik kneels down and holds Lukas. "I'm here for you," he says.

"Mm," Lukas responds, his eyes on the screen.

Erik inhales the scent of his son, a mixture of washing powder and dried ketchup. Then he lets him go. Time to switch. The never-ending battle with twins: giving the children the exact same amount of attention.

"Come here, Sebastian," he says.

Sebastian hugs him hard, burrowing his head into Erik's chest. His hair smells of baby shampoo. Anna hasn't wanted to upgrade to adult hair products yet.

This is my life, he thinks. *These children. I am never letting them go.*

But in that moment, he has to, because Lukas is laughing so hard that Sebastian withdraws from Erik's embrace to see what's so funny. It's comforting to see that they're still able to be carefree children.

Erik leaves them to it and joins Mum in the kitchen. She's busy making coffee.

"I can't compete with cartoons," he complains.

"They'll grow out of it," she says, amused.

Outside the window, a few boys are making their way home from ice hockey training, their sticks slung over their shoulders as they cycle down the road. It looks unsafe but also very normal. It's as if nothing has changed out there. The world continues as if Anna wasn't attacked.

In that moment, Erik decides not to go back to the hospital. The band has a gig this evening. He hasn't told Mum and the guys aren't exactly counting on him but maybe he could go? Be normal for one night.

Mum puts two cups of coffee on a tray together with a plate of rye bread covered in soft prawn cheese. His favourite. Mum knows how to look after him. She carries the tray into the living room where they both slump into a Poäng armchair each, rocking back and forth a couple of times. They're both feeling drained.

The police interviewed Mum today. Apparently she told them she couldn't think of anyone who would want to harm someone as "truly wonderful" as Anna.

"It won't be easy for the police," Erik agrees. "Everyone loves her."

"I know," Mum says gravely. "I really don't understand what could have happened. How could someone like Anna be attacked? I mean... I don't know. I just..."

"You don't have to understand everything," he says.

"But it's such a small town," she continues. "This isn't Malmö or Stockholm. Surely everybody knows everything about everybody? I mean, someone must know who did this. And why. She's so caring, Erik. It doesn't make any sense."

"I know." But he doesn't know about everybody knowing everything.

He puts the bread in his mouth, chews and looks out over the garden. The hedge bordering onto the road and the neighbours' plots needs cutting. Normally Anna would remind him of this.

"This is Mörna," Mum says. "Only what... ten thousand people live here?"

"It's a sleepy town," Erik agrees. "But we're not particularly friendly with anyone. Maybe because of Anna's job we've been quite private."

He's always hated the weekend trips to the supermarket, when they would have to stop every five minutes, bumping into parents who would want to discuss their child's progress. Anna didn't mind and would happily chat while he disappeared down an aisle. Even though he also worked locally, few people seemed to recognise the guy who painted their house.

"The police will find the person who did this," Mum says confidently. "They have to."

"Maybe it was just a random act, a criminal travelling through town who happened to see her alone?"

Have the police thought of that possibility?

"I'm sure they are looking into it, Erik. You need to let them get on with their job."

Linda Johansson hasn't revealed any possible results related to the note he provided them with. There's a need for "confidentiality during the preliminary investigation" apparently but she "thanks him for his cooperation". Fucking fantastic. So he must just sit here and do what exactly? He can't stand it.

"Mum, tonight..."

"You're going to the hospital?"

He drinks up his coffee and wipes his mouth on a flower-clad napkin.

"I thought maybe I would hang out with Rob... I feel like I'm going nuts."

Mum raises her eyebrows and he can tell what she's thinking.

"Sure, whatever," she says and gets up to do the dishes, her back to him.

"I mean, I think it would be good to..."

"Fine."

She doesn't sound "fine" and so he doesn't go. He doesn't want to deal with Mum's disapproval. Not now. Until he's found a new routine, he needs her. Should he drive back to the hospital? The thought of Anna being there alone makes him feel guilty, and what if she wakes up and he's not there? It's unsettling. But at night, when the ward is eerily quiet and only the disheartening sound of machines can be heard, it scares him, the tense white walls and the stretched over-washed linen adding to the intimidation. Everything around Anna has been set up to look perfect, masking her frailty.

When the boys are bathed and in bed, he stays in his room and flicks through the TV channels. He ends up watching an old war movie, *Where Eagles Dare*. Anna used to like it, especially Clint Eastwood's performance. She would fall asleep of course; she rarely made it through an entire film. He imagines Anna next to him, her head resting on the pillow, gently snoring. But all he can see is her swollen eye, the cut lip, the cheeks covered in a gradient of yellow and green.

He turns to face the wall and goes to sleep.

*

In the morning, while Mum and the boys go about "business as usual", he drives to the hospital. There, he sits in Anna's room, on a stiff wooden chair, watching his wife. He would feel better if he could do something, help in any way. Everyone treads so damn carefully around him. They feed him coffee regularly but then they go about their day while he simply sits there, his eyes darting from Anna, to the muted TV, to the window. Green city buses and yellow long-distance buses pick people up and drop them off. That's the most exciting event there is. Cars drive past too. Mostly Volvos. Sometimes he counts them.

Mum pops in to see him, which breaks the monotony. She has a habit of disturbing the staff however, asking them a million questions about the respirator, Anna's position in the bed, her brain activity, the bruising, her ribs – are they healing? – and her hair. Is someone washing her hair? Mum has also inquired about the security measures at the hospital.

"What if her attacker comes back to finish the job?"

"We're taking it seriously," they were told, but there's no guard outside Anna's room.

"Maybe that only happens in the movies?" he tells Mum.

When Mum leaves, the nurses sigh with relief, and so does Erik but he does have a few questions of his own.

He asks the nurse: "What's the security really like here?"

"People can't just come and go," she says. "We have tight controls."

That sounds true. Thinking about his own visits, he realises that no one can enter the ward without buzzing the door first. A nurse needs to tick your name of a list before he or she can let you in.

"What if someone asks for her, someone who isn't on the approved list?"

"That's unlikely to happen. No one should know where exactly she is," the nurse says. "She's been registered as an anonymous patient." She smiles faintly. "Just like a famous person would be."

"Right," he says. Comparing his wife to a celebrity doesn't feel particularly appropriate. Still, he's content. He's asked and has received an answer. That's responsible.

Perhaps as a result of Mum's constant nagging, the nurse is washing Anna today, revealing the bruises on her body. It's the first time he witnesses these.

"I'm sorry," she says, looking up at him. "Maybe you should wait outside."

"It's okay, I just…" He can't finish the sentence.

He's thinking: it's just that I haven't seen her naked in so long. The skin is so white, creating a sharp contrast with the vast, blood-filled patches where she was beaten. He wants to turn away but he can't. He forces himself to look, to follow the lines of the veins as they merge with the discolorations. His eyes linger by the scar from where the twins were born. Under her navel, close to the dark pubic hair. He closes his eyes, remembers the birth. The failed epidural, Anna's discomfort at the doctor's tugging hands. Her pain but then also their joy. Two healthy boys. He loves his sons.

He opens his eyes and watches the nurse's caring hand sweep up and down Anna's legs with a sponge, the flesh melting into the mattress.

"Can she… feel anything?" he asks. "I don't want her to feel any pain."

"I'm very gentle," the nurse assures him.

Gentle. He was a gentle lover. Anna appreciated that; it made her feel safe and adventurous. She often made him blush. Not that he would ever admit it, not even to Rob, but he was pretty straight-laced. Anna, however, wanted to try everything "at least once". It made them grow closer and stronger, and when she returned to Sweden from her week's holiday in Spain, he quit his job and followed her. He told her his contract was up even though it wasn't. He was in fact giving up the opportunity to join a local band. He just couldn't let her get away.

After the C-section, they waited two months to have sex, as per the doctor's recommendation. Then another month and yet another. Anna wanted to lose the weight first. She was worried it was going to hurt and she didn't want to risk another pregnancy, yet she no longer favoured birth control. Abstinence seemed to be her new preference.

"You would be a really good nun," he said once, a joke she didn't appreciate.

Perhaps he didn't try hard enough or he didn't compliment her enough. All he knows is that the few times they did have sex, she didn't let go as fully as the girl he married. He hasn't been able to discuss it with anyone.

The nurse moves up to wash Anna's chest. *She has amazing breasts.* It's wrong. He can't stare. Sitting quietly, he glares at the walls instead. He doesn't feel like getting up, just wants to sit here, in the same room as his naked wife. Him and his thoughts, the splashing of sponge in water, sponge on skin, sponge back in the water, soothing him.

"I love her," he says to the room.

"Of course you do," the nurse says. "I'm really sorry about what happened."

He doesn't want to think about it. Instead he concentrates on the landscape someone has carelessly framed and stuck on one of the walls. It's completely uninspiring. Not a person in sight. Just grass and water, a cloudy sky. He squints, looking for life. A bird even? But no. The painter obviously had a bad day. Just like he is right now.

When the nurse finally leaves, the overpowering respirator takes over the room again. The sound of the machine gets on his nerves. He stands up and paces around the room, the plain décor not stimulating in the least.

Everyone tells him he must be patient, that he must wait for a sign of improvement. They don't understand shit. Erik's eyes rest on Anna's motionless face.

"Are you in there?" he says, his voice breaking. "Can you hear me?"

It's torture. He needs to talk to someone who won't just give him the standard "hopefully she will wake up soon". He picks up the phone to call Rob, but notices he has a missed call from Tina. He immediately phones her back. Maybe she has more information?

She answers on the second ring. "They spoke to Pernilla Arvidsson," she says so quickly the words fall on top of each other and he struggles to understand. Pernilla? "She says you're together."

"Together?" He thinks for a second. "I only see her when I drop the children at day care."

"According to her it extends to outside of day care."

"I'm sure we see each other at the supermarket from time to time."

"She says it's more than that."

"It's not." What the hell?

It was only the one time, but he's not keen to tell Tina or anyone else about it.

Rob had begged him to go out and he had agreed, a boys' night was probably not such a bad idea. Except it had been. They had drunk far too much and when he went to the bathroom to piss, Pernilla had been in line to the ladies.

"Hey there." Blue eyes, sparkling along with her smile. "Fancy seeing you here."

"Hi."

It felt good. To be looked at that way.

"Do you want to have a drink?" she asked.

"Sure, I just..." he pointed to the bathroom.

She smiled and giggled. "Me too."

They reunited in the bar. He looked for Rob but couldn't find him. Knowing him, he had probably left with someone already. Another night, another girl, he laughed. The joke was getting old. He knew it. Erik knew it too but sometimes he felt jealous. Of the attention Rob got, the variety, the excitement of flirting and sealing the deal.

"So what's the occasion?" she asked.

"Boys' night out."

"You're such a good dad," she said and punched him gently on the arm.

She was drunk, her words slightly slurred.

"Thanks. I guess."

"So sweet."

They spoke about the children, about the town, the weather. Anything really. Soon the eyelids that had batted at him seductively, started to move at a slower pace, as if she was about to close them altogether and fall asleep.

"Are you okay?" he asked.

"I'm tired. I want to go home."

"Where are your friends? Should I get them for you?"

"They've gone home," she said, now leaning her nose on his shoulder. He felt her go heavy, her head sinking into his arm, her body closing in, pressing against his chest.

"Don't fall asleep!" he said. "I'll put you in a taxi."

"I can't afford that," she mumbled.

"I'll pay for it."

He couldn't just leave her. After hailing a taxi and placing her in the backseat, she pulled him in.

"Please stay, I think I'm going to be sick."

The taxi driver refused to drive. "Get out, I don't want puke in my cab."

"Are you sure your friends aren't still around?" Erik asked desperately. If he took her out of the taxi, where would he leave her?

She didn't reply; she was leaning against the headrest, fast asleep. He needed to get her home.

"Look," he said to the taxi driver. "Please just get her home. She hasn't had that much to drink," he lied. "She's just tired. Been working a lot."

The driver didn't look convinced but he too needed to get her out of the car and agreed to drive if Erik joined them. Luckily, he had managed to get her address before she started snoring.

When they arrived at her apartment block, he had to pay the taxi driver and get out to assist her. She could barely get the key in the lock. He could have asked the driver to wait. He could have… but he didn't.

Tina clears her throat, alerting him to the present.

"Pernilla says that you are," she tells him.

He hates the excitement in her voice and wants to tell her to fuck off. But right now, she is the only link he has to the latest news and he needs to maintain it. It's what's keeping him sane.

"She's mistaken," he says. "I mean, we get on really well and we always talk when we see each other but that's it…

I'm married," he adds even though he realises that isn't a foolproof defence.

"Okay," she says.

Okay? That's it?

"Not sure where she got that idea then," Tina says and he imagines her twining her hair, biting it between pink lips, enjoying pushing him into the corner just a little bit further. Then he remembers Rob's comment about her bad breath and that makes it easier: now she's a frog barfing down the phone and he almost laughs. Almost.

"Look," he says, thinking hard. "We've got a good rapport. We talk when I'm picking the children up. Have I bumped into her outside of day care? I'm sure I have."

Why does Pernilla have to complicate matters? He hasn't seen her since Anna was hospitalised. Mum is like a taxi driver, taking the children back and forth. While he sits with Anna, Mum does the shopping, cleaning, washing, ironing and cooking. Sooner or later, Dad will need her back of course.

"They might want to question you again."

"What? Why?"

If you were seeing someone else, you could have a motive for hurting her. Is that what they're thinking? He tries not to panic.

"Someone is going to call you," she says.

"Wait, please... Tina." She can't hang up just yet. "What about the note I gave Linda Johansson? Do you know if it's led to anything?"

"Eh, hang on." It sounds as if she's ruffling through some papers.

"No, sorry. I don't know."

"Oh..." That's disappointing.

"Well, it's not your fault. Thank you."

As soon as he puts the phone down it buzzes, alerting him to a new message. Pernilla's name appears and two perfectly shaped, round breasts fill his screen. What on earth is she doing? He doesn't respond.

He sits down and moves his chair closer to Anna's bed. Her translucent skin is fresh from the sponge bath, which makes her look somewhat thinner, paler, camouflaged in the sheets. He leans forward and whispers in her ear:

"I'm sorry."

11

Anna

September 2015

Spit was hanging from the ceiling in Anna's classroom. The girls were pretending to vomit while the boys broke out laughing. Daniel just looked at her, his light-brown eyes defiant and intense.

"Daniel, please can you step outside with me?"

Anna detected a faint smile, which annoyed her. This wasn't meant to be a reward. She just couldn't deal with him in front of the others, ignoring her every request. He stood up and she was glad that at least he was doing as he was told. The boys whistled as he made his way to the door, papers went flying. Chaos was breaking out in her orderly environment. It had to stop.

"The rest of you read from page twenty-five. If you don't settle down, you will all get detention." At least it worked with the majority of the class.

As she followed Daniel out of the classroom, she thought of his latest letter, which could be likened more to a note, only containing one line: *I need a mum, okay?* No threats.

And her heart did ache for him. At the same time, she wasn't sure if she could trust it. Was it just a game for him? It was also the way he chose to communicate: she still wasn't sure how he managed to get the letters into the teachers' lounge.

In the corridor, she pushed her hair back, folded her arms and applied her serious voice.

"This can't go on, Daniel," she said. "If you don't stop disrupting my lessons I will request that you are moved to another class."

This wasn't as easy as it sounded but hopefully he wouldn't know about school procedures. She wasn't sure how his last school had operated and despite numerous attempts, hadn't been able to speak to a former teacher.

"You can't do that," he said.

"I can," she said. "The principal trusts my judgement and if I suggest you're better off in another class, he will consider it."

Now he didn't look so sure anymore. He was biting his lip, shuffling his feet from side to side, hands deep in his pockets.

She had spoken to the principal, not about moving Daniel to another class but about additional support.

"I don't understand," Johan had said while vigorously looking through a pile of papers. "What is the issue exactly?"

"You know Daniel is the reason for the fire alarms going off and all the fights?"

Johan had nodded, his greasy hair and penguin-decorated tie making it difficult for her to take him seriously. He kept searching for something and his eyes lit up as he found it. With a piece of paper in his hand, he quickly glanced up at Anna – as if to check whether she was still there – and said: "Anna, you're the best person to deal with a boy like that."

He might as well have added: "there, there, off you go now."

Johan had only been in the position for a year and during that time he hadn't managed to gain the teachers' confidence. His focus seemed to be on his bosses at the council office. MÖRNA SCHOOL SAVES MONEY UNDER NEW LEADERSHIP read the headline in the local paper, except nowhere did the article mention that new books hadn't been ordered, that the courtyard was in desperate need of repair, or that staff training was on the backburner. Anna had kept an open mind, not wanting to judge too soon, but she felt her patience weaken.

"Daniel needs help," she had explained. *I need help dealing with him.*

"Speak to the parents."

The oblivious look on Johan's face, his hands up in the air. She had stood up and excused herself, realising that she would have to sort this out on her own.

Now standing in the corridor, Daniel whisked his growing fringe out of his eyes. In the fluorescent light, the reflection of emerging stubble was just about visible on his upper lip. It made him look older.

"You know what I want," he said. "And if I get what I want, you get what you want."

"I don't really understand. You want a mum? You already have one."

"She doesn't give a shit about me or my brother. She's a total slacker. Martin was arrested last week and she did nothing about it."

"Maybe she's giving him tough love?" she suggested.

You're way out on a limb, Kent would say. *Keep it real, Anna. The students respond to that.*

"Okay, so what do you want? You want to talk to me?"

He hesitated.

"I want to live in your house," he said.

The words didn't sound like a naïve boy's wishful thinking. She braced herself. "Daniel, it doesn't work like that."

"I know you like me," he said.

"I think…" she started, sighing. What could she possibly say?

"Don't," he said then, his eyes narrowing. "Don't give me sympathy, that's not what I want."

"We can't always have what we want."

She took a deep breath. There had to be a solution, a middle ground.

"Let's talk to your mum, together? In the meantime, please can you wipe off the ceiling, then sit down and listen?"

A compromise.

He shook his shoulders, either he couldn't care less, or he was agreeing. Then he nodded and headed back towards the classroom. Hopefully his mum would profess her undying love for her son. Hopefully. If not, she would talk to Kent and ask his advice.

*

At the end of the school day, she sat in the teachers' lounge with a couple of other teachers. They all had their heads down, working away. Kent had left early and she wished there was someone she could call, just to talk. These days, it felt like phone calls with old friends had to be scheduled. When they were younger, her sister Helen would phone her regularly with various issues, but she wasn't someone Anna in turn could call for support. Now they hardly ever spoke; Helen was wrapped up in her new family.

Erik had a close family. That had added to the attraction when they first met. He seemed so secure and she was sure it was as a result of all the love he had been surrounded by growing up. Her own parents had been strict and controlling, at least in some ways. If she started eating before everyone was served, forgot to put something back in its place, or didn't say "thank you", then she would be shouted at, but if she was out late with her friends, no one seemed to miss her. Helen had rebelled as a teenager but Anna had kept her head down and counted the days until she could leave.

She wished that her family had been closer. Although she had read that once you passed the age of thirty-five you could no longer blame your parents for the mistakes that you made. She had two years to go.

She wondered about Daniel's family. Did he know his father? What little she had found out had revealed that he lived with his mother, Frida, and his brother, Martin. There were no notes about the father. It was a sad situation and she just knew she couldn't turn her back on him. Too many children were left disappointed by adults in their lives, whether it was parents, teachers or government officials, and they tended to end up in a downward spiral of criminality. Daniel's brother was a perfect example of that and she didn't want Daniel to follow in his footsteps. Although he obviously could not move in with her. She felt relieved to have found a line that could not be crossed.

She left work early to spend the rest of the afternoon with Sebastian and Lukas. Erik was working and she decided to bake something with the boys. They loved getting messy in the kitchen and she tolerated that better than Erik, even though he wasn't exactly a neat freak.

"We had muffins at day care today," Sebastian told her.

"Really? I didn't think parents were allowed to bring cake?"

She was sure a health-consciousness note had been sent out proclaiming that only fruit would be served at children's birthdays.

"Pernilla brought it."

"Oh."

The young day care teacher with the long eyelashes. Anna had only met her a few times but it was as if the teacher was assessing her every time, eyeing her from top to toe.

"Is she nice?" she asked.

Lukas shrugged his shoulders. "I like her," he said.

"Good, that's the most important thing," she said.

Twenty-four chocolate muffins later she made spaghetti Bolognese and then rounded the children's evening off with a massive apple-flavoured bubble bath. Sebastian and Lukas put white foam on their chins, pretending to be Santas, singing Christmas songs even though it was only September. Anna joined in, both in the singing and the Santa look-alike competition.

"Mine is better."

"No, mine is."

"No," Anna said. "I believe mine is best."

There were bubbles everywhere, even on the ceiling, but it wasn't a big deal. It could easily be washed off. Listening to the boys' laughter was more important.

Being with her children, Anna could think of nothing else. Not work, not Erik, not even the latest book she had devoured, *Affinity*, which had been recommended by the librarian. Time with Sebastian and Lukas was like a soothing tonic much appreciated after a long day at work.

When the children were in bed, she went downstairs and

waited for Erik. He was late even though he had promised to be home in time for her to go out. She had planned to go to the library, which was open late that evening. He didn't answer his phone so she called Rob.

"Is Erik there?" she asked.

"Sure, do you want to talk to him?"

Bingo.

"Yes, please."

"Anna?" Erik's voice. She said nothing. Would he figure it out by himself?

"Oh, sorry," he said and she felt relief. That meant she wouldn't have to sound like a nagging wife. "I completely forgot. You had something on?"

"That's right."

"On my way."

"Thanks."

While she waited for him, she opened her wardrobe to get changed. Did she own anything that didn't scream "teacher"? Perhaps something that would flatter her figure? Erik always used to compliment her breasts and so she picked out a black V-neck jumper and added a pair of dark grey figure-hugging trousers. It didn't look too shabby. She stood in front of the mirror, deciding which necklace to use. The white moonstone pendant or the silver Bismarck chain? She opted for the moonstone. What about shoes? She mainly wore trainers, boots or ballet flats. There were only a few heels in her wardrobe since she felt awkward increasing her height. She opted for a pair of leather boots with a low heel and sprayed Calvin Klein One on her wrists.

"Fancy."

Erik stood in the bedroom door, his eyes taking her in. He was dressed in loose hanging, low-cut jeans and a dark green hoody, a classic staple Erik outfit that most likely consisted of famous brands. When they first started dating, she found his style to be cool and stylish. At that time he had a wide collection of trainers as well. It was casual but fashionable. She walked across to him and planted her lips on his. He tasted of beer.

"So where are you going, looking so dressed up?" he said, grabbing her waist.

"Work do," she said.

He wouldn't be talking to her colleagues anyway and he didn't need to know about Hågarp's library; he wouldn't appreciate that she yearned to go back for more books. Books were apparently boring, unlike movies.

"You smell so good," Erik said, burying his nose in her hair.

He kissed her ear, her cheeks, her neck; his hands slid down over her curves and she tensed.

"Not now, Erik," she said but he didn't stop and so she stretched her hand out and flicked the lights off.

She tried to think about the tanned, muscular bartender, lovemaking under a whirring fan, his laughter, their bodies sticky between warm sheets; flamenco music from a nearby bar, tourists laughing, the slight breeze from the open window.

His tongue pushed into her mouth and the bitter taste of alcohol made the visualisation more difficult.

She took a step back. Her body wasn't able to cooperate.

"Another time," she said. "Please."

She switched the lights back on.

"There never is another time." He sighed. "I have needs, okay?"

"So do I," she said.

They stood quietly for a while, their bodies no longer touching.

"Can we just cuddle?" she asked.

She could sense his annoyance but it was a decent compromise.

"I'm not..." he started. She waited and eventually he succumbed, sounding defeated: "Sure, why not?"

She would have to visit the library another time. Peace at home came first. She didn't take her boots off, just laid down on her side of the bed. Erik did the same and then they moved closer to each other, eventually embracing. Erik had a way of making her feel protected, the way he held his arm around her. Anna focused on the closeness, the warmth, the feeling of being loved; evoking that tingling feeling you felt on a date.

In the dark, he could be anyone. But it scared her that she wished just that: for him to be anyone but Erik. If only there was someone she could confide in.

12

Iris

September 2015

The sun was up, yet cold winds were banging on the library windows. Iris was unpacking her latest book delivery – a source of joy every time – when the phone rang.

"Hi Mum, it's me."

"Karin?"

She was about to say "you don't usually call me at work" but her daughter started crying before she got the chance.

"What's wrong?" she asked.

Since her daughter had started university she only ever cried if she had failed an exam but Iris suspected it could also be boyfriend trouble. Iris pushed the new book delivery to the side and sat down while Karin blew her nose on the other end of the line.

"I don't know, maybe I shouldn't say it," Karin said.

Iris waited patiently, wondering why Karin hadn't called her father. He was normally the one she turned to. Rolf and Karin had always been close, often leaving Iris feeling like a distant aunt. She wasn't bitter about it but she tried to keep an open door for her daughter, their only child. Karin continued to cry and Iris didn't want to frighten her away by being pushy. She absentmindedly picked up a book, attracted by the dramatic cover, a red title stretched across it like a colourful tattoo, and started reading the blurb.

"Mum..."

She could tell that Karin was mustering up courage to tell her something, and she recognised that she needed to be more receptive.

"I'm listening."

She loved Karin and wished that she could tell her that more often. Her own parents had never told her they loved her. Not once. She sometimes caught herself wondering why they hadn't. Rolf's theory was that their own parents hadn't said those magic words, that they were simply repeating the pattern. It made sense but Iris was intent on breaking that trend.

"I spoke to Granddad," her daughter said.

She could tell where this was going. Her father had been in a home for a few years now and was growing increasingly bitter.

"He said that you're a whore," Karin said. "He said it over and over again. I couldn't stand it."

A whore? Surely her father didn't know about her lifestyle? Not that it made her a whore but in her father's old-fashioned world perhaps it did. She and Rolf had always been discreet, even more so after Karin was born.

"He's... don't listen to him," Iris tried. "His dementia is getting worse, you know that."

Karin started crying again.

"He said that you and Dad don't take your marriage vows seriously. What does that even mean?"

Iris sank back into her chair. So he knew.

"Is it true?" Karin asked, her voice weak.

Iris tried to construct a sensible sentence. They were silent for a while, the seriousness of the revelation sinking in. If Karin were to ask Rolf, she knew he would tell her the truth.

"It's not as simple as that," she said. "We just don't believe in owning each other."

"So, what, you have *affairs*?" The last word was spoken with such distaste. Iris chose to ignore Karin's bitter tone. She had to remind herself that her daughter was only nineteen. An adult by law but still a child in her eyes; not old enough to judge her own mother.

It was hard to admit, but: "Yes, that sometimes happens. I can't speak for your dad but not very often for me."

"Mum..." Karin said. "It's like... it's like I don't know you."

Karin sounded sad rather than accusing and Iris felt compassion for her daughter.

"Are you seeing someone at the moment?" Karin asked.

Iris squirmed in her seat, glad that she hadn't opened for the day.

"No," she said eventually.

She was going to end it with Lena anyway so it wasn't exactly a lie. Getting involved with someone so intricately linked to her work had been a mistake.

"No more secrets," Karin said. "Please."

"Of course," Iris said, feeling like the child. "Those days are sort of over anyway. It was more... when we were younger."

She had still been the model mother, attending parent evenings and football games, taught her daughter how to cook and had spent countless hours supervising her driving. There were just certain compromises involved in her marriage.

Just then, the alarm on her phone went off. It was ten o'clock, time to open for the day.

"I love you but I'm sorry, I have to go," she told Karin. "Why don't you call your dad and speak to him about it? Really though, it's no big deal. We were young and free and now we're getting older and more... sensible."

She sighed when she put the phone down. They had spoken about this, her and Rolf.

"What if Karin finds out?" she had said.

"Then we explain to her that it's fair to let someone be who they are."

"Shouldn't we promote monogamy to our daughter?"

"Why?"

He had a point. It wasn't for everyone. She hadn't even realised she would consider a no-strings-attached marriage until Rolf proposed it. She had been offended at first (was she not good enough in bed?) but when he had explained that he loved only her, that no one could ever replace her, she had opened up. They had agreed on set rules and she had found it to be liberating. At least at first.

Now, with Karin knowing, those memories became tainted. It felt like being exposed while masturbating. For the first time, her choices didn't make her feel quite so open-minded and progressive.

She continued to unpack her new books, pushing the phone call with Karin to the back of her mind. She would discuss it with Rolf later and they would solve it together.

Iris concentrated on reading each blurb even though she had carefully handpicked the newly purchased books herself.

These were her babies, her trusted companions. Once she received a new order, she would read all the books to be able to recommend every one of them.

The first title that took her fancy had been chosen by none other than Lena. It had been a bit of an inside joke, but she had still ordered it. *Delta of Venus* by the avant-garde writer Anaïs Nin was not a recent release but it was an erotic classic. Lena could wait for it. This was the perfect book for Iris to get past her daughter's judgement and to re-engage with her true, sexual self. She slipped it into her bag.

The bell above the door sounded, notifying her of a new visitor. She looked up and saw a curvaceous woman with long dark hair walk towards her. She recognised her from the other day. Already? She smiled to herself. She remembered her name. Anna.

13

Anna

September 2015

It was Saturday morning, the sun had broken through the grey clouds, and Anna had successfully built the tallest Lego tower with Sebastian and Lukas.

"It's as tall as me, Mummy," Sebastian announced proudly, standing next to it.

Lukas quickly got to his feet.

"Me too!"

Erik appeared, looking equally excited, although it wasn't related to the multi-coloured creation on the floor.

"We have a gig," he said. "It's small, but it's in a bar in the city, so it's good. Really good."

"Good for you," she said.

His childish excitement was almost contagious. She wanted to get up and hug him the way she used to, assure him that it was truly amazing, but that closeness seemed to be gone, and she held back.

"I know you've got something on this morning," he said, his voice soft. "I'll rehearse with Rob later."

"Yes, thanks. I'm going to the library."

He scrunched his face up, in that characteristically annoyed way.

"Not to work," she added quickly. "For myself. I just finished a really good book and need a new one." He still looked doubtful so she tried to open up: "I miss reading for pleasure as opposed to what is in line with the curriculum. I guess you could say that I have rekindled an old passion."

He looked like he was going to refer to another old passion they should rekindle. Thankfully he knew not to say anything in front of the boys, who were now busy destroying their tower, Lego pieces flying across the room.

"I wonder who they get their destructive behaviour from," Erik said and left the room.

She detested his way of dropping a grenade and then leaving. Why was she always to blame? He gave her no credit for anything. Who did all the cleaning, the washing, the ironing? She was the mother of their children, the breadwinner and also his maid! If anyone was destroying it all, it wasn't her. But looking at her watch, she realised there was no time for pointless arguments.

"Bye, boys." She leaned down and kissed them both, making exaggerated smacking noises, which often made them giggle.

"Come on, Mum," Lukas said, pushing her away.

They didn't have time for her affection, they were already in the middle of a new creation: a space station. Once upon a time, she had been creative too. What happened to people when they grew up? Why did they lose their sense of fun and adventure?

"I'll see you later. Have fun!"

She slipped out and drove towards Daniel's house. If she had time, she would still go to the library but she couldn't tell Erik the truth. Between her need to borrow books and visiting a student on a Saturday, he was less likely to understand the latter.

*

The house was only a ten-minute drive from Anna's house, straight through town along Mörnavägen, past the sprawling school area on the right and then down a hill towards the seaside. This area used to be taken up by multiple summerhouses, the gardens overflowing with wild flowers. The last few years, people had built larger family homes on these plots but the odd red-painted summerhouse was still visible here and there. Daniel's house was one of those exceptions. A small, quaint-looking shack that had seen better days and most likely lacked insulation.

Daniel's mother, Frida, opened the door; untidy blonde hair, no make-up and dressed in a pair of baggy sweatpants and a top without a bra. She seemed sleepy.

"I'm sorry," Anna said. "Did I wake you up?"

"No, I just forgot that you were coming."

Anna had sent her a text message as a reminder but she must have missed it.

"Is Daniel home?"

"Dan!" Frida screamed, rather than called, into the house. A minute later he appeared, looking newly showered but dressed in the same clothes as the day before. With his hair wet, he looked sleek and less rebellious.

"Come in," Frida said. "Sorry, it's a bit messy."

Anna stepped into the living room, which indeed was a

mess and reeked of something unidentifiable. Bags of crisps, drinking glasses, Coke bottles, scraps of paper and videos were strewn across the table and the floor. No sign of alcohol though.

She found a space on the denim-covered sofa and sat down. Frida flopped down on a swivelling chair on the other side of the table, looking like an exhausted teenager who was about to be reprimanded by her mother.

Except Frida was older than Anna. She was at least forty, the lines on her face reflecting a hard life. With a little effort, however, she would be pretty.

"Thanks for coming on a Saturday," Frida said and Anna appreciated the acknowledgement.

"No problem," she said. "I know you're working a lot during the week."

"Have to do extra shifts where I can."

Frida worked at a local factory, sewing bags, if Anna had understood it correctly. On paper, she didn't sound like a "slacker".

"Daniel, why don't you join us?" Anna said and he motioned closer but didn't sit down.

"Is he in trouble?" Frida asked. She looked fatigued rather than angry.

"Daniel is very bright," Anna said, avoiding the question since she didn't want to lie. "Although I feel he could use more support."

"Can't the school sort that out?"

Daniel grimaced behind his mother's back as if to say "see, I told you".

"I mean from home."

"Look, honey." Frida leaned forward in her chair, assuming

a condescending look. "I'm sure you mean well but I have to work and his father isn't exactly around."

"Where is his father?"

Frida threw her arms in the air, finally showing some energy. "With another woman, God knows where."

"Right." Anna nodded knowingly. "Anyway, if you could perhaps..." *Take an interest in his education.* "Work with him to get his assignments done."

"He's not five," she snapped.

"Oh, I know," Anna said. "He can do it by himself. But perhaps you could acknowledge that he's done it."

Behind Frida, Daniel sighed and Anna couldn't help herself. She turned to him and said: "You don't have to like the work, you just need to get it done."

"*You know what I need*," Daniel mouthed quietly.

Frida cut in: "Wait, what?" she said. "You want me to pat him on the head like a dog and say 'bloody well done'?"

The way the conversation was going, it would have been better for Daniel not to be there. Then Anna could have been tougher, more forceful, to make the mother see that Daniel needed her badly. Now she had to tiptoe around the issue.

"Encouragement goes a long way," she said, ignoring Frida's sarcastic tone.

Frida turned to her son. "Dan, can you please make your teacher a cup of tea?"

He reluctantly disappeared into the kitchen and Anna was relieved. Now she would take the bull by the horns, except Frida leaned forward, revealing a large, oval bruise on her left arm. Frida must have seen the shock in her eyes because she quickly pulled her sleeve down and whispered:

"Look," she said before Anna could think of anything to

say. "I don't understand the stuff Dan is studying. It's going to make me look stupid."

Frida's tone had changed. It was softer. Anna forced herself to shake off the deep purple image on Frida's arm. It could be work-related. A machine gone wild.

She cleared her throat. "Frida, if you could just ask him a few questions, such as 'what are you studying at the moment?' or 'have you got any tests this week', then that would be encouraging in its own way."

"He will lie."

Anna nodded.

"Possibly. Look, he's really bright, he just needs motivation. If he thinks you're going to be proud of him, he's likely to pay more attention."

Show him you care! That he needs you.

Just then, Daniel turned up with only one cup of tea and Anna drank it self-consciously while they watched her. She tried to keep the conversation going but it was hard work; Frida mostly answered "yes" or "no" to her questions. Daniel seemed pleased though.

*

Anna felt lighter as she drove out of town towards Hågarp. She tried to enjoy the scenery along the road, cast in glorious sunlight. Autumn colours were slowly making their appearance in the midst of the greenery; the cool deep-blue ocean on her right making her feel free. Daniel and his mother soon became distant characters. Finally, she would be going back to the library. She was determined to leave work and Mörna behind. It bothered her that most people knew who she was there. It made it difficult to get close to anyone, in case they should gossip.

When she parked, her phone alerted her to two new messages from an unknown number.

You see? She doesn't give a shit.

The sender's face took shape in her mind. Messy blond hair, upturned nose and intense brown eyes. A disparaging message from a lost young man. Her heart heavy, she read the second message.

You turned up. That's what someone who cares would do.

She leaned against the headrest and took a deep breath. It seemed she could do nothing right. He chose to misunderstand. She should notify someone. She should but she wouldn't. The new principal had clearly shown he wasn't interested in problematic issues, he was too green for that, and Kent would try to talk to Daniel, which would make the situation worse. She had toyed with the idea of speaking directly to the counsellor but her hippie style put Anna off; she was too aloof, someone who wanted to be the students' buddy. Daniel wouldn't respond to that. Erik was right about one thing: she cared too much. That was the problem. But how could she not?

She needed a breather, to recharge and come up with a new solution. That's why she was here. She looked up at the library as Iris flipped the "Closed" sign to "Open". *Time to escape*, she thought, and got out of the car.

*

No one else had arrived by the time Anna stepped through the door. She felt transported into a capsule, the air warm and inviting, the rows upon rows of books giving off a sense of culture and history. She walked straight to the counter where Iris had her hands in a large cardboard box.

"Hi," Anna said.

Iris was removing a pile of books. Perhaps she was disturbing her. Should she browse on her own first?

"Hello," Iris said then, putting the books down. "You're back already?"

She remembered her.

"I finished *Affinity*," Anna explained.

Iris's lips curled. "That was fast. What did you think?"

"It was great," she said, immediately trying to think of something deeper to add. "It took me by surprise." That's all she could come up with? She groaned, but any standard interpretation she was used to sounded too pompous, too rigid and boring. *A linear story with a feminist heroine.*

"Would you be interested in another book by Sarah Waters?" Iris asked and Anna nodded.

"Sure."

She followed Iris as she steered the way, feeling like a kid, walking behind her. The ancient bookcases gave the place character and the soft glow from the overhead lights made it feel like someone's living room.

"By the way," Iris said, turning to her. "We're starting up a book club. Would you like to join?"

Her instinct was to say "yes" but insecurity overcame her.

"I'm not sure," Anna said honestly. "I probably won't be able to add much value."

"Don't worry about that. The other women aren't literary geniuses."

Without the reading glasses on, Iris looked younger. She was probably in her late forties or early fifties. It was hard to tell. She was wearing another stylish ensemble, a tight black knitted dress, oversized silver bangles and fashionable ankle boots.

"I'll think about it," Anna said.

"Please do. We start on Wednesday at seven."

Iris stopped and eyed the uneven row of spines.

"Ah, here it is." Pulling out a book, she said: "*Tipping the Velvet*."

Anna held her hand out but Iris didn't give her the book at first. Instead, she looked at her seriously.

"This book," she said. "It's a bit… erotic. Just so you know."

Anna broke into a smile and then a giggle. It sounded like Iris was reading out a health warning. MAY CAUSE HEARTBURN. Although Iris didn't seem to get the joke.

"No problem." Anna composed herself. "I think I can handle it."

"More books?" Iris asked and Anna nodded.

"Yes, please."

*

When they had compiled a stack of books and were ready to scan them, the library was still quiet. It had a wonderfully calm atmosphere, making Anna feel completely stress-free.

"Does your husband read?" Iris asked.

It was an odd question. Anna had enjoyed not thinking about Erik, to just *be*. Yet there seemed to be an expectation of her to say something.

"Not really," Anna said. "He's a painter," she added as if that would explain his lack of interest in books. The truth was, he didn't have the patience.

"So is mine," Iris said and Anna was relieved to meet someone else who wasn't married to a doctor, lawyer or schoolteacher for that matter. "Maybe Rolf knows him. What's his name?"

"Erik..." Anna started before she caught on. Iris's husband was an actual artist and she thought Erik was as well, because obviously, there was no way someone like Iris would be married to a house painter. "... but he paints houses." Her cheeks reddened.

"Well, that's being an artist in a way too."

It was kind of her. "What about your husband?" Anna asked to deflect from herself and Erik.

"He's Rolf Sören."

"Oh, I've heard of him..." She stopped herself.

Now Iris smiled, even showing her teeth.

"That's all right, I know what you were going to say. The troublemaker."

Anna smiled. Rolf Sören didn't do anything conventional according to the papers. His reviews varied but he seemed to thrive on attention. There had even been rumours about him using body parts in his artwork.

"He only used fingernails," Iris said. She grimaced as if to say "what can I do?".

"Didn't they detect blood in one of his paintings?"

Anna regretted her words immediately. Being nosy was no way to make friends and it wasn't like her to pry. It was just that Iris fascinated her and this information added a new dimension.

"That was pure PR," Iris said. "Most rumours are spread

by Rolf himself. It makes sales go up, not that I agree with it."

"But you obviously support him?"

"I do. I adore him."

She *adored* him? If only she could say the same about Erik. In that moment, Anna truly wished that she could. At the same time, Iris didn't seem like the type of woman who would adore anyone. She came across as independent and headstrong, someone to *be* adored.

"Can I help you with anything else?" Iris asked.

Anna tried to think of new topics of conversation to stay a bit longer, but a woman had made her way over and the moment was lost.

"I hope you will be back soon," Iris said. "I would love to hear what you think of *Tipping the Velvet*. And don't forget. Wednesday, seven o'clock."

14

Erik

March 2016

"She wasn't raped," Erik tells Mum.

"Oh, thank God."

"Although…"

Mum puts her coffee cup down. "Although what?"

"This could mean nothing but her shirt had been pulled out and her fly was undone. It's possible that someone… that someone started…" He doesn't continue the sentence.

"Poor Anna."

Mum stretches a hand across the table, comforting him.

"I just get so mad," he says. He clenches his fists, bangs them on the table. "Nobody gives me the full picture. Are the police twiddling their thumbs?"

"They're busy, Erik. There have been two murders in the city, just in the last fortnight," Mum says. "That's highly unusual for this part of the country, isn't it? That must be draining their resources."

Mum always has an explanation for everything.

"I'm still upset," he says.

"I know, honey. I know. But right now we need to focus on Anna getting better."

"There's no improvement."

"Have you spoken to the doctors?"

Of course he has. Every day. "Nothing is better."

"Something must have improved, Erik, even if it's minor. Her bruises, for example, they were better when I last saw her." She moves closer, takes both his hands in hers. "Honey, do you remember when you were kids, you and Jonna? When you had trouble with friends, we used to focus on one good thing?"

"Please don't talk about Jonna, Mum. Not now."

"We can't just pretend she never existed."

"Mum, I can't lose a sister and a wife before I'm forty. That would be cruel. I will stop going to church. I will."

He knows this will upset her and she doesn't need to know that he already stopped going. What kind of God would make his sister fall off a cliff and die at the mere age of twenty-three?

"She died doing something she loved to do," Mum says calmly.

"Why do you have to be so damn accepting all the time?"

He gets up, his hands slipping out of hers, the chair falling back onto the tiled floor. He stomps his feet.

"My wife might die, Mum!"

His body feels heavy and drained. Mum gets up, waddles over to him in her indoor slippers and wraps her arms around him, embracing him properly. He bends over to reach her shoulders, leans in. She strokes his hair and as if he's a little boy again, she starts to sing: "*When I find myself in times of trouble, Mother Mary comes to me. Speaking words of wisdom, let it be, let it be...*"

"I'm not a baby, Mum," he sniffles half-heartedly.

She keeps singing and it feels good, soothing. He inhales the musky scent of her cardigan.

*

When Erik is back at the hospital, holding Anna's soft, pale hand, Rob calls him.

"Just checking in, man," he says. "The gig went well. Thought you'd want to know."

Great. Now they're having success. Without him.

"I'll join you soon, I promise. Once this… this mess is sorted out."

"Of course, no pressure. We all know you're going through a tough time."

Do you? Do you really know? He stops himself. Rob's his mate, he's been supportive.

"The police came to my house," Rob says. "To ask about that night."

"I know. Sorry about that," Erik says. "They're just doing their job."

He hates that his friends are pulled into this.

"Of course, Erik. But they asked how long I was at your house for and I wasn't sure. You know me and time."

Why does Rob sound so nervous? Did he say something he shouldn't have? Did he mention the laptop? No one has been in touch with him about it, so probably not. Come to think of it, Rob might not know that Anna's laptop was in that bag. It's probably better not to bring it up. Anyway, Erik just needs to try and access it a few more times.

"It's okay," Erik says supportively. "They're obviously happy with whatever you said. Also, I owe you for putting me in touch with your ex, Tina. She's been helpful."

"Oh, good. Maybe she still has the hots for me? Tell her I said 'Hi'. No wait, don't do that, she might get ideas. Don't say anything."

"You done?"

"Yes, and Erik... I know I haven't been around and haven't said much but I'm really sorry." He takes a breather, collecting his thoughts perhaps, which undoubtedly would be a first for Rob. "You know I have a soft spot for Anna. If there's anything I can do, let me know."

Erik knows how much this means, coming from Rob.

"Thanks," he says.

He should call Tina. The police haven't contacted him regarding Pernilla and although that should bring relief, it makes him feel worse.

He takes a deep breath, pours a glass of water from the jug on Anna's bedside table, psyching himself up to call.

Tina picks up almost immediately.

"Hi, Tina, it's me. Erik."

"Hi, Erik."

She sounds happy to hear from him, which makes him relax. He fiddles with his paper, the questions he has written down.

"I'm sorry to bother you again, but have you... um... heard anything more about Pernilla?" He has to ask.

"Sorry, no."

He decides not to push it.

"Okay," he says casually. "What about Kent? I haven't heard anything."

"This is between us," she says in a hushed tone and then there's what Anna would call "a theatrical pause" before she continues: "They were definitely close."

Right. That could mean many things though. Kent has tried to get in touch with Erik but he hasn't called him back yet. It seems easier not to.

"He also mentioned a difficult student," Tina continues in her hushed voice. He wonders where she's calling from. A quiet corner in the police headquarters? "I'm sure she must have talked about it at home?"

Quite possibly, he thinks and ransacks his brain. Nope, there's nothing apart from the note that really could mean anything. It might not even be from a student.

"Anyway," Tina says, now sounding bored. "I don't know much more."

He can sense she is about to hang up and he can't blame her. At the end of the day, why should she tell him anything?

*

That evening he opens Anna's laptop again. What is her password? He needs to work it out, or at least try to. Her computer must contain emails about the student Tina mentioned. In what way was he difficult? Would he have a reason to hurt Anna? If he can find a possible suspect, then the police will understand that he's helping them and perhaps include him more. It would make him feel less isolated. They will probably be upset about the laptop being withheld but he will come up with a reasonable explanation. It was at a friend's house and he only just received it. Something like that.

Mum is proud of him for being proactive but she thinks he should leave it to the experts.

"But I want to do my bit," he says. "They might be missing something."

Mum is doing the dishes downstairs when he tries the first password combination. This time he is better prepared and has written down a list of possible options. The children's names, their surname, birthdays, anniversaries. He starts to type them in, one after the other, together and apart. Try again. Forgotten your password?

He's about to give up when Mum pops her head into the bedroom.

"Erik, I have to go home for a couple of days. I need to make sure your dad is taking his medication. Will you be all right?"

"Sure." He has to be.

Mum hovers in the doorway. "Is that Anna's computer?"

He nods, feeling like he's been caught. "I'm just, you know... looking."

"Is that wise?" she asks. "Shouldn't you hand it over to the police?"

She clearly disapproves, but what else can he do?

"I know what I'm doing. They're not prioritising Anna because she's still alive."

"I'm not sure about that, Erik."

That really frustrates him. She needs to be on *his* side.

"Have they caught anyone yet?" he says. "No, they haven't. I will give them the laptop if I find anything, okay? Goodnight, Mum."

She leaves him to it but he puts the laptop away, out of guilt. To keep himself occupied, he brushes his teeth, flosses, gargles with mouthwash – all the things that would make Anna proud – before returning to the bedroom to put a pair of pyjamas on. But the laptop beckons to him and he yields to its invisible powers and picks it up again. Like an addict, he just can't stay away. Three more tries and he's going to bed, he tells himself. First one. The year the twins were born. SebastianLukas2010.

Try again.

The place and year Anna was born. Gothenburg1982.

Try again.

The place they got married. Lund2009.

The computer kicks into action. Astonished he watches as the screen changes colour. He's in!

Where to look first? He feels like he's entered a maze. He opens Outlook and goes through the folders, clicking on the one labelled "School". There are a few messages from Kent but they are all of a practical nature.

Are you booking the restaurant for Anne's leaving do? There will be fifteen of us...

I think *War and Peace* is a bit advanced for the students but I know you like to try new methods so I will bring the book tomorrow...

If you need me to assist during the test, I will be available from 10-11am. Does that work?

Hands-on and friendly. He should call Kent; he's obviously been a good support for Anna. The guy has just always made him feel awkward. Like he's not a good enough husband for Anna.

There is no mention of a difficult student, though. Only one email could be interpreted as possibly being related.

Anna, I'm here if you need me. Don't take too much on by yourself.

It could also refer to her workload.

He goes back to the list of folders. Nothing looks all that interesting. Instead he clicks on "Deleted". Perhaps she didn't want to keep certain emails, especially if they were related to problematic students? He stops himself. No. If that were the case she would want to keep them. She would be collecting evidence. Anna is sensible. He's about to leave the deleted folder when an email address catches his eye, only because she has deleted numerous emails from that same address: blackadam4321@hotmail.com. Is it junk? He opens one of them at random.

Hi Anna, it has to be you. No one else.

The sender has mentioned her name. Surely that can't be junk? There is no mention of a company at the bottom. There is no signature at all. This could be anything. Erik opens another one.

Hi Anna, I need someone who listens to me.

Huh. Erik leans back in the chair. What is this? He opens one more.

Hi Anna, I'm sick of this. How about the basement?

The basement? Which basement? The one under their house? He reads it again. It sounds like a response to another email but there is no message from Anna further down. What did Anna say to this person for him or her to send this? He looks in the "Sent" folder and scrolls down but can't find a single one from Anna to this blackadam4321.

He goes back to the deleted folder and opens one more.

Hi Anna, I can't take it anymore. Fucking agree, will you?

He feels as if he's stumbled onto something significant, he's just not sure what it is. Can he bring this to the police?

He calls Officer Johansson and tells her he might have found something.

"I would prefer to meet in person," he says.

He wants to form a connection with her. The police and him should be a team. They can't keep leaving him in the dark.

15

Iris

September 2015

Iris watched as Lena pulled her fingers through her blonde, highlighted hair, and applied the same pink lip-gloss she had used for the last five years. Eventually, Lena picked up her handbag and slid it over her shoulder.

"See you next week," she said, planting a kiss on Iris's cheek.

"Maybe."

Lena turned to Iris, her smile dead. "What do you mean, *maybe*?"

"I mean that all good things must come to an end."

Her words were friendly but firm. This was unavoidable. She had been sucked in once more but it ended here. Lena had become too persistent, calling unnecessary meetings, which could jeopardise her position.

"Must they now?" Lena crossed her arms defiantly, her tone sharp. "And why is that?"

"I will see you at the next meeting," Iris said, heading out of the kitchen, away from the sweet smell of sweat and sex, away from drama.

Lena hurried after her, her heels *clip-clopping* on the hardwood floor.

"When we have our monthly meetings, am I supposed to act like nothing happened?"

Iris was upset with herself. Why had she become involved with someone so close to home?

"Lena," she said, the sweetness in her voice perhaps a tad too exaggerated. "That's what we have done so far. Because we're professionals."

She kept walking, but Lena caught up with her.

"That's because it's been exciting, Iris, knowing we share this… bond. I don't want it to end."

"I care about you," Iris said. "But you have always known I have a husband."

"And I'm sure he would love to know what you have been up to!"

"As I'm sure your husband would," countered Iris calmly.

Lena stormed out; the bells above the door dangerously close to smashing onto the floor.

Iris didn't wish to hurt Lena but there seemed to be no other option. They couldn't keep seeing each other. Lena would hopefully calm down.

Iris wiped evidence of the meeting off the table, crumbs from cinnamon rolls and ginger biscuits falling into her hand. When she had restored order, she went to the bathroom and reapplied her lipstick. It was important to remain professional. She needed to go back to being Iris, the reliable librarian. The task for the day: to discard long-forgotten books that had lost their shelf appeal.

Shaking off images of Lena's gym-trimmed body and her dramatic exit, Iris commenced the much needed weeding out process. In order to make space for new additions, some books unfortunately had to go.

She picked up a short novel that only one person had ever borrowed. Stefan. He had asked her to order the book two years previously. Even in a small town, known for being desolate during wintertime, her customers did have refined literary tastes. Stefan had just moved to Hågarp with his young family. "A fresh start" he had called it, and had quickly become one of her most frequent customers. Keeping her on her toes, they had discussed her favourite authors: Leo Tolstoy, William Trevor, Doris Lessing and Virginia Woolf. Many regarded Woolf's books as women's literature but not Stefan. Gender was irrelevant, he had said and the meeting of their minds had been the foundation of a wonderful but short-lived friendship.

Stefan's new start had ended in divorce and he and his wife had moved away. No one else had borrowed the book since. Iris had read it of course: a story about an older woman in a home for the elderly who became sexually involved with a young male carer. A controversial subject and well worth reading.

Just as she decided to keep the book, a group of teenagers arrived and parked themselves by the computers. They greeted her politely.

"Let me know if you need any help," she said but before she had a chance to strike up a conversation, her phone rang. She normally didn't answer it during working hours, but it was Karin and after the last phone call, she felt she should.

"Hi, Mum. I spoke to Dad."

"Oh." Iris felt anxious. What had Rolf actually said? Had he explained that their arrangement was his idea? That she had been reluctant but had gone along with it to avoid losing him?

"He said the same, Mum. That it was when you were younger, that he loves you and that it's just the two of you now."

Did he now? Perhaps he wasn't so honest after all.

"Great. I'm glad we're all on the same page," Iris said, putting on a cheerful tone. "I have to go now, lots of people here."

"Yes, I can hear that," Karin laughed and they hung up.

More teenagers arrived and while the library got swamped with young voices and laughter, she could feel the phone in her hand vibrate, alerting her to a new message. Lena's name appeared on the screen. Iris would have preferred no contact for a while but they did work together. She opened the text message.

Dear Iris, I thought you would enjoy the first lines from this poem by Natasha Trethewey. Heard of her? I'm guessing you haven't.

The lies I could tell,
when I was growing up
light-bright, near-white,
high-yellow, red-boned
in a black place,
were just white lies.

If I don't hear back from you, I will contact Rolf.

Angry and revenge-seeking. Iris hadn't expected Lena to take the break-up quite so badly. She had assumed they were both fairly casual about it, but she realised now that Lena thought this was a one-off, worthy of telling Rolf if she didn't get what she wanted. Iris clicked "Delete".

Lena was right about one thing. It was white lies. Not real lies.

16

Daniel

September 2015

Dan was busy writing his own story. It had a happy ending.

"Where are the bottles?"

Frida was banging on his door, disturbing his creative process. He ignored her, continuing to form words, transfixed by the paper absorbing ink. But her furious knocking didn't stop, which resulted in a Stephen King inspired moment: suddenly a woman died in his story, buried alive in the foundation of a construction site, her screams muffled by the wet cement. He decided to call her Frida. If she ever read it, that would teach her.

Dan liked that every door in their house had a key. Locking his room made him feel safe. No matter whom she brought home, he was untouchable. And it also kept his mother out when necessary.

"You little shit!" she shouted. "She didn't suspect a thing, so bring them out."

"I poured them down the sink," he said calmly.

He hadn't. Instead, he was going to sell every bottle. Vodka could fetch a good price, he reckoned. Better than beer. There were plenty of under-aged buyers around. Every town had them, even this seemingly perfect one. There was nothing else to do but get together with your friends and drink illegally. That was considered "cool".

The door vibrated as she kicked it. Screaming.

"Focus on your bloody job, Frida," he shouted back.

He remembered the last town they had lived in. His mother at the central square that had become her home away from home, where all the drunks hung out together, making it feel okay to drink a beer at nine in the morning. He had tried to bring her home several times. She had screamed but he had pulled at her top, told her to shut the fuck up and be a mother for once. Everyone had heard them. Her newfound buddies had laughed. It had been humiliating every time but he couldn't give up on her, could he? Then nothing would improve.

He and Martin confiscated her booze regularly. This time, with Anna visiting, it had been different. She had willingly agreed to hide the bottles.

"Why the hell is your teacher coming over anyway?" she had asked. "As if I don't have enough fucking problems!"

He had calmed her down, told her Anna was cool.

"Then why are we getting a home visit?"

"It's a sort of welcome to the school thing," he had said.

On the other side of the door, she continued her pleading.

"Just one fucking bottle, Dan! One!"

She hadn't known that he had hidden the other bottles too, the ones she kept at the bottom of the ironing pile, behind the cleaning products under the sink, in the shed, under the seat in her car. Martin had always been one step ahead of her and with him locked up, Dan had to act the detective.

The best thing about this town was that Frida had to drive to the liquor store. *Systembolaget* was too far away for a walk or even a bike ride. He was hoping that would make the binges less frequent. She really needed to keep this job until he had Anna wrapped around his finger.

Luckily, Anna had witnessed the unbearable living conditions. He had added to the mess, but so what? No one cleaned up around here, it wasn't that far from reality. It would have looked even better with the frosted vodka bottles lined up on the table, but he wasn't stupid. Then she definitely would have contacted social services.

"Dan!"

He continued to ignore her and after a while the kicking stopped. Sobs could be heard through the thin door.

"Fuck off, will you?" he said, feeling like his big brother.

"What's happened to yo-u?" she stuttered between the cries. "My ba-a-by."

"I'm not your fucking baby," he muttered.

I'm somebody else's baby.

17

Anna

October 2015

A nna had decided to stay late to prepare the next day's classes but she kept checking the time. She had to be at the library in Hågarp at seven.

"Everything okay with Daniel?" Kent asked.

"I spoke to the mother," she said.

"Good. How did you approach it?"

Kent already had his coat on but he didn't seem to be in a rush. The teachers' lounge was unusually busy for this time of day but thankfully no one was sitting in their corner. She didn't want to discuss Daniel openly. No other teacher seemed to have any real issues with him, and she didn't want them to start looking for problems if there weren't any.

"I wanted Daniel to be there," she explained quietly. "I wanted him to hear that she cares, because she must do. All mothers who stick by their children and raise them care to some level."

Not the right choice of words, she realised, but it was too late. Kent already looked concerned.

"Aren't you letting this get too personal? Daniel is not your son."

"You would have done the same."

He nodded contemplatively. "Perhaps."

"It didn't go well," she revealed. "She seemed distant. I can't explain it."

"Depression? Drugs? Alcohol?"

"Not sure." Anna hadn't seen any evidence of drugs or alcohol. Maybe she was depressed? It would make sense, with Daniel's father leaving, her sons getting into trouble, the responsibility to make ends meet.

"Anyway, I'm sure you're expected at home," she said. "We can talk some more another time."

She valued Kent's advice but something about this situation made her feel weary. Kent followed the rulebook and she wasn't sure that was the way to get through to Daniel.

"Don't stay too late," he said.

*

It was already dark when Anna headed out of Mörna. Dim streetlights guided her out of town as she followed the windy road to Hågarp. Reindeer were known for making an appearance in these parts and so she held the steering wheel in a tight grip, her eyes constantly darting from left to right.

Eager to get to Hågarp, she also felt uneasy and slightly guilty. As a mother she felt that she should be at home with her children, that every moment away from work should be spent with Sebastian and Lukas. That was the reason she hadn't picked up a hobby since they were born, to always be there for them. But by the time she walked up the stone steps to the library, she had convinced herself that she deserved this, that a book club would in fact make her a better mother.

Through the glass she could see that the library was deserted. She pushed the door open and stepped inside, drawing in the welcoming smell of books and perfume, which seemed to linger in the air. Once again she moved into the centre, the hub where all the borrowing and returning activity took place. Iris was behind the counter, crouched over a plastic crate.

"Hello," Anna said.

"I'm just busy closing," Iris said and Anna thought that perhaps she had got the date or the time wrong.

"Sorry, I thought... book club?"

"Oh, yes. That's still on. I just need to get this delivery packed and lock up. Do you mind getting the coffee ready?"

Iris was just as stylish as she had been the last couple of times and Anna was pleased that she herself had made an effort. She was wearing a matching black outfit with a multi-coloured scarf loosely wrapped around her neck.

Anna followed Iris as she showed her to a small kitchen at the back. There was a sink, a coffee maker, a fridge, a small table with two chairs and an ugly photocopier, not unlike the one they used at school. Still, it was cosy.

Iris directed Anna to the coffee filters and Zoegas beans.

"How many people am I making it for?"

Iris took the reading glasses off and paused for a moment.

"Let's see," she said. "There were going to be four of us but one is working late and the other one just called about some car trouble."

"Oh." Anna felt disappointed. "So you want to cancel?"

"No. We can still have a chat. You've come all this way and you've read the book, haven't you?"

Anna blushed. She had and she had to admit she was

petrified of discussing an erotic, lesbian relationship set in the 1800s. Although perhaps it would be easier without other people there?

"I'm sure you have better things to do," she said. "I can come back next week."

"I need a cup of coffee," Iris insisted. "I've been on my feet all day."

"All right then. I'll just stay a short while."

Anna got to work straight away: she put the filter and beans in, added water and switched the coffee maker on. While she waited for it to brew, she located a couple of mugs and some biscuits in a tin that she placed on a plate. Once ready, she loaded everything on a tray and carried it into the library.

Where should they sit? It wasn't a large space but there were a number of reading chairs and low tables around.

"Over there," Iris called and pointed to a couple of comfortable-looking orange reading chairs. Next to the chairs stood a wide, square pillar that had an old-fashioned, ceramic fireplace in it.

Anna placed the tray on a small table and sat down. The ceiling in this room, the main hall, was exceptionally tall and when Iris turned the lights off, only leaving a couple of floor lamps on, it almost felt spooky.

"This is how we switch out of work mode." Iris said as she lit the tea candles on the table and the mantelpiece.

"So this doesn't feel like work to you?"

"Not really. I may work with literature but it would be sad if I couldn't also enjoy it for what it is."

Anna found herself wishing that Iris would smile. Was she disappointed to be left with only one person to discuss the book with? *You just need validation.* Erik's words hurt.

"Thank you for inviting me," she said.

"Thank you for coming." Iris slipped her shoes off and pulled her feet into the chair. "We don't have to discuss the book if you don't want to?"

Iris eyed her quizzically over the red, moon-shaped glasses.

"It was just very different to the books that I normally read. Similar to *Affinity* of course but well... different all the same."

"Different how?"

"I think, because of being a teacher, I have been stuck on the classics. Shakespeare, Sartre, Austen, Tolstoy..."

"Wow, I had no idea." Iris did a dramatic bow to Anna and it made her laugh.

"Oh, no. I'm not... I mean it's basic stuff. I'm completely hopeless when it comes to contemporary fiction."

Iris seemed to view her with new eyes and although it felt good, Anna wanted to lower the expectations. Everything she covered at school *was* basic; she never had the time to delve too deeply as she tried to cover a broad spectrum of time periods.

"You mean you're not used to reading such explicit books? You don't cover D. H. Lawrence's *Lady Chatterley's Lover*?"

"I don't." She smiled. "I have to admit, the sex scenes in *Tipping the Velvet* made me feel slightly uncomfortable."

She had never been promiscuous. Erik was only her third sexual partner but when they first met he had made her feel that it was safe to explore.

"That's good," Iris said. "Makes you feel something."

Anna picked up a biscuit, which crumbled dryly in her mouth.

"Do you often feel uncomfortable?" Iris asked.

Anna coughed. She certainly couldn't accuse Iris of being predictable.

"You obviously don't," she said, finding her voice.

"Of course I do," Iris said. "I hate large groups of people, for example."

"Me too. I don't understand the politics and the games. I thought getting older would make that easier but often I just can't break the code."

"Too many personalities in the mix, I think. Equally though, I don't like being the centre of attention," Iris continued. "It makes me feel self-conscious. I couldn't be Nan or Kitty in *Tipping the Velvet*, on stage."

"I agree," Anna said. But then there were a lot of things Nan and Kitty did together that she couldn't imagine doing.

They sipped the coffee, the sudden silence feeling comfortable at first but then Anna had to fill it with words. If only to maintain interest. She wanted to be invited back.

"They had a tough life, Nan and Kitty," Anna said.

"The past shapes us, just like it shaped them."

"I know what you mean," Anna said. Her past had definitely shaped her and perhaps she wished they were talking about that.

Iris looked at her deeply then, as if she understood. "People, both in literature and real life, have all sorts of drama in their lives," she said. "Everyone has had a dysfunctional upbringing to some extent."

Anna nodded.

"Although it's what you do with your baggage that really matters," Iris continued.

"That's true."

Iris took her glasses off and wiped a tired-looking eye, a black mascara smudge appearing underneath. Anna felt that perhaps she should be heading off and not overstay her welcome.

"So what are we supposed to read for the next meeting?" she asked.

"I was thinking," Iris said. "That perhaps we should meet weekly? A month seems too long. Don't you think?"

Anna agreed. A month felt like a long time. It felt good to sit there; like inhabiting a warm cocoon.

"What about the others?" Anna asked. "Won't they mind?"

"I'll just inform them. They're easygoing."

Iris put her glasses back on and pulled out a book from a basket on the floor.

"So," she said. "This book will be uncomfortable on a whole other level. This author caused a representative of the Nobel Prize academy to resign, stating her work was 'unenjoyable public pornography'."

Anna wasn't sure in which direction this book club was heading but she felt strangely excited.

"I'm always happy to try something new," she said.

18

Erik

March 2016

Mum has gone home and Erik is relieved for about five minutes. It's nice to have the house back. No pretending that everything is A-okay, no looks of disapproval, no dissecting what could have happened. With Mum gone, he will also be able to look at Anna's emails more closely. Having slept on it, he feels he needs to get his head around them, one way or another.

The day before, he had sat in front of Linda Johansson at the swanky police headquarters, on a blue upholstered chair with wooden armrests, trying to connect with her. Except he struggled. She looked tired and uninterested and he wanted to ask what her problem was? He didn't though. He reasoned she could have a number of issues that were unrelated to him and Anna. Perhaps she was distracted by another case or it could be personal problems?

"I want to help," he said. "For the sake of my children."

She looked pleased. "Good," she said and in a softer voice, she added: "How are the children coping?"

And there it was: her compassion, and... some sort of connection.

He rested his arms on the table between them, to change position – he seemed to be sitting an awful lot lately – but also to be closer to her.

"They're dealing with it the best that they can," he said. "Thank you for asking. It's not easy."

"I'm sure it's not."

She put a pad and a pen in front of her and said: "We talked to Pernilla again, the day care teacher."

He should have expected that but he still felt himself grow hot.

"She verified that you were at day care Tuesday afternoon."

He nodded, waiting for her to continue, but she didn't say anything else. *That's it? She wasn't going to ask if they were an item?* Although it would be uncomfortable to talk about, he wondered why she was holding back. They obviously suspected that he was seeing her. Should he deny it even though she hadn't asked?

"Did you find out who wrote that note?" he asked. A new topic felt safer.

"I can't discuss that with you, Erik."

"Come on." They had to give him something.

She appeared to think. "Fine. We know who wrote it but it appears to have been work-related and is of no further interest."

He sighed. Right. Okay.

"Does Anna have a student called Adam?" he asked instead.

Officer Johansson made a note.

"Why do you ask?"

He hesitated for a second. Shifted in his seat.

"Did you speak to the people at her school again?" he asked.

Are you going to tell me if you spoke to Kent?

"Yes, we have spoken to her colleagues."

She insisted on keeping it vague.

"And no one said anything about an Adam?" he asked.

"I will have to check. What do you know about him?"

"Anna might have mentioned someone with that name," he lied. What else could he do?

He could have shared the email address with them, he had the printout in his pocket, but he held back. They would want the laptop and he wasn't done with it yet. They obviously wouldn't reveal their full hand, so why should he leave the police with all the cards? He decided to email Black Adam himself. To take control, collect more evidence and make sure it got done. Then he would hand any findings over to the police.

"Can I just ask you something?" Officer Johansson said.

"Sure..."

"In your opinion, is Anna a good mother?"

"Of course." Aren't all mothers viewed as the superior parent?

"So you don't feel like she was working too much?"

He shook his head before answering. "No, of course not. She was doing that for her family."

He felt satisfied with his answer. Soon, Linda Johansson would surely have new evidence to deal with and would stop questioning his wife's mothering skills. Why would they even care about that?

*

Erik emailed blackadam4321 when he got home but he is yet to receive a response. For now, he hasn't used Anna's email address in case this person knows that Anna is in the hospital. Instead, he has set up a new, vague email account. He wrote:

Hi Adam, Anna has told me about you. Let me know if I can help in any way?

He toyed with the idea of signing it as Kent but that felt naughty and could become messy. Instead, he signed it as

someone who cares

He will give the guy two more days to respond before he sends a new message.

Right now he is busy. The downside of Mum being gone is that he has to take on the responsibilities she has shouldered for him.

First stop: day care. Having managed to get the boys dressed, a harder task than he remembers, especially with emotions running high, they buckle up in the V70.

Mörnavägen is lined with cycling children so Erik maintains the thirty km per hour speed limit that applies during school hours. They could have cycled themselves, or even walked, but he doesn't want to be forced into any conversations. What do you say when you know your family is the target of gossip?

"When is Grandma coming back?"

Erik glances at Sebastian in the rear-view mirror.

"Hopefully end of the week, buddy."

The boys have sour faces and the drive feels like an eternity, even though it's only a few minutes away.

"So what's new at day care?" Erik asks, trying to sound cheerful.

"We have a new teacher," Sebastian says.

Could this new teacher be a replacement for Pernilla? Not having to face her again would be magic.

"So Pernilla... is she still there?"

"Yes," Lukas says. "I don't like her though."

"Really?" This is a surprise. "I thought you loved her?"

"She's kind of mean," adds Sebastian.

Erik immediately pulls the car over to the side of the road, stops and turns to face them. Fear. He feels fear.

"What has she done?" he asks.

They look at each other, in that twins sort of way. *Should you tell him, or should I?*

"She says Mummy is going to die," Sebastian says and looks down. He can hear the tears in his voice.

What the hell? "She doesn't know anything," Erik bursts out. "Don't listen to her!" Fuck.

"Is she going to die, Daddy?"

Lukas looks at Erik, his eyes big and hurt. He doesn't cry as much as Sebastian but he looks so defeated.

"No, buddy, she's going to be fine," he assures him. "She just needs time. We don't know how long it's going to take, that's all."

He collapses onto the horn, accidentally hooting at a passer-by who starts gesturing rudely towards him. He doesn't care.

"She's doing fine," he tells them. "She's just sleeping. I'm there every day, checking on her."

"Grandma says you have to start working soon," Lukas says. "Who's going to watch her then?"

This astounds him. They know about work and they worry about that?

"Are you sure you're only five?" he jokes, his face not

quite looking as jokey as he would have liked. How did they grow up so fast?

"We're almost six," they say in unison.

"That's right, in three months. How could I forget?"

He turns and smiles at them.

"Boys," he says, choosing his words carefully. "We're the three musketeers. We stick together, sending Mummy love every day."

They nod. "One for all, all for one." He's taught them well.

He gets back onto the road, thoughts of Pernilla now filling his head. What is he going to do? He just doesn't understand what's got into her.

He could speak to her supervisor but what if she tells her about their night together? Then he will be asked to move the boys elsewhere. It's almost impossible to get a new place anywhere nowadays, let alone two. He must talk to her, try and fix things.

When they arrive, a teenager on a bike is cycling around the parking lot, doing tricks. He's got a denim jacket with a faded print on the back and his shoelaces are undone. *They could get caught in the wheels*, Erik thinks, *make him crash*. That's living on the edge, being cool. Erik remembers what that was like, how carefree he himself used to be. Life was uncomplicated back then.

"Nice jacket," he says to the boy as they pass him.

He looks at them intently, then cycles off without a reply.

"Who was that?" Lukas asks.

"No idea, but I used to have a jacket like that when I was growing up." They look impressed. "It made me feel like a rock star. Like on *Idol*."

He wishes there had been programmes like that on TV when he grew up. Stardom within his grasp.

"Maybe you should sing to Mummy?" Lukas says and Sebastian agrees: "That would make her feel better."

They look so sweet. Anna would hate a rock or eighties repertoire but she does love the good old 'Hotel California'. He could sing that.

"Maybe."

He follows them inside, hoping to catch Pernilla. Maybe he can gain her sympathy, make her back away at such a difficult time in his life?

Other parents are also heading towards the door. He has always hated this part of the drop-off and pick-up: the chit-chat. The mums are the worst, with their sympathetic glances and parrot-like comments: "Anna working late again?" Now, with Anna in hospital it's intolerable, as if he's going to break out in a rash there and then.

A man taps his shoulder and Erik freezes.

"I'm Sophie's dad," Sophie's dad says. "My wife tells me Sebastian has a crush on our daughter?"

Erik stops, grateful for how normal the words sound. No mention of Anna, no mention of coma.

"Really?" Good boy.

"Keep him away from her," the dad jokes, hitting Erik's arm with his fist, a little too hard, before bouncing ahead of him, through the door.

Erik shakes his head. Bloody idiot.

"Sophie is really funny," Sebastian says.

"Good for you, son." Even though her father is a prick.

Erik's phone starts to vibrate. It's Mum.

"Hi, Erik," she says. "Are you coping okay?"

"You only just left."

"I know but I worry about you."

"We're okay." *Apart from Sebastian and Lukas's teacher*

telling them that their mum is about to die. "I've got to go, I'll call you later."

"I was just reading the paper on the train," Mum says, ignoring him. "About the police being criticised."

He stops in the day care playground, at once concerned.

"About Anna's case?"

"No, it was just a general attack on the police's operations in rural areas."

"Oh."

His interest wanes but Mum reads out loud from the article: "*We might need to look at changing the lighting in some areas.*" She pauses. "That probably would have helped Anna. It's awfully dark in that parking lot."

That's useful, Mum. "It's too late now."

"It also says that they don't have enough staff and that they can only do so much."

"So?"

"I just mean that they're doing the best that they can."

The boys are about to go inside and he's spotted Pernilla through the open door.

"Thanks, Mum, for that very helpful information... got to go."

He doesn't wait for her to say goodbye.

Pernilla is in the cloakroom, helping another child hang his jacket up.

"Hi," he says nervously as he enters.

Her eyes meet his, glossy lips turned at the corners.

"Hi," she says.

"Go on, boys," he says. "Put your bags away and off you go."

He pats their heads and they run off. With the boys out of sight, he asks Pernilla if they can talk.

"Sure."

"Somewhere private."

She opens the door to a storage room and they squeeze in between brooms and buckets. Before he's had a chance to speak, she's wrapped her arms around him, pushing those lush lips against his. At first he lets it happen, soaks up the affection and feels comforted, welcoming the feeling of being close to another person's body. Then, a couple of seconds later, he resurfaces and pushes her away.

"No, Pernilla. Please. Stop."

Blue, wounded eyes.

"What do you want from me?" she asks, arms folded.

He sighs. *I could ask you the same.*

"Pernilla," he starts. He's older, he needs to explain maturely. "Anna is in a coma. My *wife* is in a coma."

"I know. I'm not stupid. But she's not likely to wake up though, is she?"

"She might." For the love of God, why does she have to make it so difficult? "Stop telling the boys their mum is going to die. It's not fucking okay."

"But what if she doesn't make it?" she says. "You're going to need someone to help you look after the boys. I know them, Erik. They're practically like my own."

He stares at her, the words alarming.

"And you," she continues, her hands caressing his hips. "You will need a lot of love and attention." A hand strokes the front of his trousers and he's torn, wanting to get out, to get back to life, another part wanting to escape into nothingness, to forget, to stay here, away from it all, postponing reality. His cock wants him to stay. She snuggles closer, kissing his neck and it's so soothing. He lets her hold him, leans into her body, hands himself over. Just for a short while. He's going to leave. Soon. Then, his brain poking him: he has something else to say, something important.

"Erm, Pernilla... you told the police we were seeing each other," he says, trying not to smell her newly washed hair. It's still wet, she must have rushed to work after showering. Lavender?

"I just..." she whispers. "I want us to be seeing each other."

"I know, but we can't."

"Just one last time. Please. I'll take care of you."

A loud bang outside the door and he pulls away.

"I have to go," he says. "Don't say anything stupid to the police, Pernilla."

"If we can just... talk. Can we talk, Erik?"

He nods. Sure. If that's what it's going to take.

"I'll come over to your house this week," she says. "Before your mum comes back."

She knows Mum's plans? Of course she does. Mum speaks to her every day.

"Do you know where I live?" he asks.

She nods and he wonders, what doesn't she know?

19

Iris

October 2015

Iris cracked four eggs into a ceramic bowl and whisked them absentmindedly. In the background of her country kitchen, Ella Fitzgerald encouraged Iris to fall in love. *Let's do it, let's fall in love.* Outside the window, the overgrown garden reminded her of how long they had lived in this house, with its white-stained walls and red window frames. Far away from any affairs. Just the two of them, surrounded by serenity, the garden bordering onto kilometres of farmland.

It had been their first house after years of being cooped up with Rolf's paints and canvases in a sparsely furnished Linköping apartment. A big step, but then, her new job had also been a huge leap. Heading up a library had been her dream and it didn't matter that it was a quaint library in the middle of nowhere. Rolf had supported her; he had told her he could work anywhere, as long as they were together.

"It's picturesque," she had told her mother, in an attempt to get her to visit, and just as she thought that, Ella's voice appropriately filled the kitchen with *Heaven, I'm in heaven.*

Iris smiled and pulled out a frying pan. She felt a sense of peace as she melted butter on the cream-coloured AGA cooker, pouring in the eggs, adding fresh thyme and basil from the pots in her kitchen window.

"... *dance with me, I want my arm around you...*" she sang along.

"Of course I will," a voice said behind her and she felt Rolf's arms wrap around her waist, holding her tight. He nuzzled her neck. "You making enough for two?"

"Might do," she said and turned to kiss him.

He had paint on his cheeks and she rubbed it with her thumb in an attempt to remove it. She had felt him slip out of bed early that morning, which wasn't uncommon. When inspiration struck, it didn't matter what time it was, he would be outside, in the red-painted wooden extension that housed his studio.

Rolf slipped his hands inside her robe; he found her breasts with ease, his erection poking her stomach.

"Right here?" she said.

"It's nice and warm by the cooker," he said and pushed her back.

He smelt of turpentine, a smell she had come to associate with lust, and she pulled him close. Their tongues sought each other out; kissing Rolf made her feel like a teenager. His passion shot through her and she was wet before his hand even cupped her sex. He knew how to touch her, knew exactly which buttons to press. She shivered under his touch, reciprocating through his open robe, his naked body moving closer to hers. He painted in the nude, at least when no one was around. When she was ready for him, she spread her legs and he pushed himself inside, the AGA hard behind her back. She wanted him; her hands grabbed his behind and pulled him in deeper. Behind them the eggs were burning.

"You're mine!" Rolf cried out as he came. "Mine! Mine! Mine!"

Afterwards, when their bodies relaxed into the aftermath of the great orgasm, Iris tightened her robe and cracked four new eggs into a bowl.

Rolf had never been domesticated but he did value mealtimes. He would always eat with her if she was at home. They had shared many treasured moments as a family around the kitchen table, the three of them. The house felt empty without Karin.

"Will you join me for a gallery opening this evening?" Rolf asked when they sat down to eat.

"Are any of your pieces showing?" she asked.

Although her support for Rolf was unwavering, the older she got, the further removed she felt from his circus.

"Not exactly," he said. "But we should go. The owner is interested in my religious series."

They exchanged a glance over the near empty plates. He knew that she strongly opposed his latest creative efforts. They were both atheists, so why play with fire?

"I'm sure you will be fine without me," she said.

She wanted to avoid lecturing him about cultural sensitivities. Her dislike would only spur him on. When she had opposed a series of art projects that incorporated human blood, she had spoken up. Except, instead of backing down, he had become more excited than ever.

"If that's your reaction, Iris, imagine the world's reaction!"

He wasn't known across the world but she hadn't pointed that out.

"I need you there," he begged.

"I have book club this evening."

He stopped eating. "Book club?" A cheeky grin. "Since when?"

"We have our second meeting tonight," she said, maintaining a serious look. "You were away last Wednesday. Out of town, remember?"

To see a woman? The less she knew, the better.

"I thought you wanted to keep your distance from the public?"

"Just trying something new."

"This Lena involved?"

"No." Thank goodness.

Lena had sent her another text.

Dear Iris, you're familiar with the poet Karin Boye but I'm 100% sure you haven't read this poem: "From a bad girl".

I hope you're having a rotten time.
I hope you're lying awake like I am,
and feeling strangely glad and stirred
and dizzy and anxious and very disturbed,
and suddenly you'll hurry up
to settle down and sleep like a top.
I hope it takes you longer than you think...
I hope you don't even get a wink!

Why couldn't Lena move on? For now, Iris opted for silence. It was the tried and tested method.

"You spoke to Karin?" she asked.

"I told her I love you," he said.

"That's all?"

"That's all she needs to know." He started singing. "*I can't give you anything but love.*"

131

He pulled her up and they moved slowly to the music; Iris rested her head on his shoulder. The floor creaked, birds sang outside and in the distance a tractor was pulling a plough through a field. It felt peaceful. Until Rolf stopped dancing. Holding her in a firm grip, he asked:

"Do you remember our rules?"

"Of course," she said.

"No matter what, nothing or no one comes between us," he said. She nodded, not sure if it was a statement or a threat.

20

Daniel

October 2015

While Frida was engrossed in a strenuous fuck aerobics session with a long-haired man with a ridiculous moustache, Dan started to pack. The walls transported every moan into his bedroom, and he furiously threw his few belongings into a backpack. Books, comics, paper, pens, the school folder, clothes and a toothbrush were all the things he needed. He just about managed to pull the zip closed in his inherited Fjällräven backpack.

When he walked through the living room, Frida looked up from the tattered old couch, only a blanket covering her naked body.

"Where are you going, hun?"

"As far away as fucking possible."

The man pulled her back down, as if shielding himself. Fucking loser.

Dan slammed the door shut, not bothering to wait for her to protest.

Martin would have thrown the guy to the kerb by now.

They hadn't visited him in prison. It wasn't exactly Dan's fault. He had no idea where he was held and Frida refused to tell him.

Martin was due to get out soon and would probably deal with Frida's moustache-dude then. Except Frida had said he wasn't welcome back home.

"He's old enough to get his own place. I may have done some stupid shit but I have never been arrested."

"We have forgiven you plenty, Frida," Dan had said but she didn't seem to get it.

He kept asking her if she had spoken to the lawyer but she couldn't get her facts straight. Dan wasn't even clear about why his brother was locked up. Surely it wasn't just because of that stupid fight? The rumour at school was that Martin had been busted for drugs, but Dan refused to believe that.

Tears stung, but he clenched his jaws and made them go away. He was resilient; maybe not a superhero but he could make a decent villain. Nekron or Eclipso. Someone tough. He knew it was childish to still read comics but no one needed to know. Superheroes had been his trustworthy buddies for a long time; they made him feel invincible, like there was nothing he couldn't get through. For Anna, he could be Black Adam, a reformed villain.

Dan unlocked his bike and rolled down the hill towards school. It was past six o'clock but Anna was most likely still there. When she realised he had no intention of going back home she would have no choice but to let him stay. "Just one night," she would say and then it would be another and yet another. He envisioned dinners around their wooden table. Her family, soon to be his. There was a chance she would notify someone, but so what? Nothing ventured, nothing gained. He had to at least try.

Except through the windows of the teachers' lounge, he could see that it was empty. Where was she? He cycled down to the parking lot when her car pulled out. Shit! His feet trampled hard, pushing his bike forward with such speed, his lungs ached from the cold air. At the top of the road he expected her to turn left, to go home, but instead she turned right, exiting town. He tried to follow her but she was too fast and he had to give up. How could she? She was meant to go home, to receive him.

He took out his notebook and read through the story he had written earlier, in amongst the secret pages at the back. It was never out of his sight, it was sacred.

She greeted him with open arms.

"Come in, let me take your bag."

"What about your husband?"

"Dan, let me tell you a secret." She lowered her voice. "I don't love him."

"You don't? So what, you're going to leave him?"

"Yes. For you."

She held him close. He could feel her heart beating through the sheer fabric of her blouse.

Dan looked up, still feeling the smooth silk. It had seemed so real. What was he going to do now?

21

Anna

October 2015

The book on the coffee table sat between them, the letters in red pulsating from the cover: *Greed*. They were waiting for the other members of the book club. Anna tried to think of something to talk about. Small talk. Why was it so hard?

"Do you have children?" she asked.

After the twins were born, Anna had discovered that this was a great ice-breaker, provided the other person answered "yes".

"A daughter," Iris said. "She's at university already, she wants to be a graphic designer, much to her father's delight. He's constantly visiting her."

"That's good. My husband is also a very involved dad. He's good at playing with the children." She thought for a moment. "I probably don't tell him that often enough. I don't know, we tend to get stuck on the small things, argue about who's picking them up or putting them to bed, who's turn it is to cook dinner."

Iris seemed to contemplate this. "I don't think we have ever argued about that," she said. "We have been very clear about our roles from the beginning."

Anna watched as Iris poured the coffee into two yellow Höganäs Keramik cups. They were sitting in the same spot as the last time, their feet free of shoes, legs pulled underneath them. The room was glowing in the candlelight, the sky dark outside. In the distance, she could hear the gentle rise and fall of the ocean.

"I guess I thought we were clear about our roles," Anna said. "But then, when the boys were born... I don't know, they're my life and being a mother is everything I expected it to be, but we don't seem to have found a rhythm since. It's like we're constantly chasing our tails."

Iris added a dash of milk to her coffee.

"Having children isn't easy on any relationship," Iris said. "Our world was completely turned upside down after Karin was born. It gets easier." She stirred her cup. "The trick is to focus on the good parts. Those are the things you end up remembering."

Iris was right. It was just that something had changed. Was it Erik? Or was it herself? Parenthood had definitely altered the dynamic between them.

"So, what did you think of the book?" Iris asked.

She picked it up from the table, as if to remind Anna which one they had read.

Anna hesitated: "What about the others?"

It was only the second book club meeting but no one else had turned up this time either. Anna didn't mind. It made it easier for her to express her opinions, especially when she felt out of her depth. "A Nobel prize-winning author is pressure," she had told Kent, who had chuckled, not

knowing who Elfriede Jelinek was. "You know your literature," Kent had said. "You'll be fine."

"They're a bit unreliable," Iris said. "They probably won't
make it."

She reached for one of the cinnamon rolls Anna had
bought from the local bakery and Anna took one too. According to Kent, his wife's circle "read, discussed, drank coffee
and ate pastries" and so after last week's dry biscuits, Anna
had wanted to bring something more inspiring. Next time,
she would perhaps even bake.

"I wish this smell could be bottled," Iris said between
bites. "Cinnamon, dark roasted coffee and books. It would
be a bestseller."

Anna nodded in agreement. It was a pleasant thought.

"Of course, you would have to add sweaty feet to make
it realistic," Iris added and wriggled her toes, the red lacquer
on her nails glowing.

She chuckled and Anna joined in, relaxing into the large
chair. Iris's dimples deepened, making her look youthful,
girlish almost.

A couple of weeks earlier, Anna never would have imagined herself sitting here, at the library in Hågarp, laughing
and enjoying herself. It was as if a new window had opened
in her life, fresh air streaming in.

"So," Iris said. "What did you think of *Greed*?"

Anna sipped her coffee. Where to start?

"It's quite sad... depressing even," she said. "I mean, a
man who exploits women is not uplifting."

"Although he's described as pathetic," Iris retorted. "That's
vindicating, don't you think?"

"I guess so," Anna said, tugging at her floral maxi skirt.
"But the women are so vulnerable, so... I don't know, sad?"

She regretted having used the word "sad" twice in such a short space of time and quickly added: "These women, they're constantly seeking approval by men. I wish they would be stronger."

Iris nodded.

"And what about the violence?" Anna continued, daring herself to take charge. "One of the women asks the man to avoid hitting her in the face. As if she accepts the abuse as long as the world can't witness it. I mean, she asks him, almost politely!"

She was getting too emotional; she should hold back. This wasn't about her, although she had a brief vision of her mother, running away, over and over, always returning. Hiding behind a heavy green curtain, Anna would sit on the cold wooden floor and watch her parents argue. She was not going to have that type of marriage. Ever.

"It's supposed to be ironic," Iris said.

"But he really hates women."

"The narrator hates him," Iris corrected her.

"I just wish the women were stronger," Anna said and to her horror, she started to cry. "I'm sorry," she said, embarrassed, wiping the tears away. "I'm not sure what came over me."

"You're passionate about the book," Iris said. "Or the subject at least."

She stretched a hand across the table and took Anna's in hers.

"It's okay," she said. "Every feeling is allowed in this library."

"I'm just..." Anna started but was interrupted by a loud knocking.

Even though they were in the heart of the library, away from the door, the banging couldn't be ignored.

"Is it the other members of the book club?" Anna asked.

She wiped her face with the sleeve of her top, her fingers tracing under the eyes, clearing the skin of smeared mascara.

Iris shook her head and got up. "I don't think so, but I should check to see who it is."

She stood up and made her way towards the door. Anna decided to join her. She couldn't just let Iris go alone, what if someone was trying to break in? Bringing her phone, she followed a few paces behind, wiping her face once again, making sure she looked presentable.

When they had passed the reception, Anna could make out a woman through the glass. She felt as if she recognised her, but was distracted the moment Iris opened the door and the woman started shouting.

"I called Rolf!" she said, her high-pitched voice piercing through the evening. "He said you were here. It's a bloody book club and I'm not invited?"

Anna decided to hang back, the situation feeling personal, as if she were intruding. Except the woman had seen her and barged in.

"Who's this?"

"This is Anna," Iris said calmly. "She's borrowing books for her class. She's a teacher in Mörna."

"Lena?" Anna asked, now realising who she was. "Lena Blom? I think you know my colleague, Kent."

Lena eyed her. She appeared to be collecting herself. "Why aren't you borrowing books from Tania Svensson in Mörna?"

"Because she's not as familiar with Karin Boye," Iris interjected.

"You're teaching Boye?" Lena asked, looking suspicious.

Anna had no idea why Iris would say that because they

hadn't discussed the twentieth century Swedish author once, but she quickly found herself. Reciting the beginning of a Boye poem, she said: "*Yes, of course it hurts when buds are breaking. Why else would the springtime falter?* That's my favourite."

Lena fiddled with the strap on her handbag, the atmosphere in the room feeling awkward.

"I see," Lena said. "Well, Iris is the perfect person to help you. She loves Boye's poems. Especially 'From a bad girl'. That's *her* favourite."

She turned to Iris, who showed no reaction to Lena's bizarre outburst. Lena smacked her glossy lips, her feet moving around like a boxer about to take the next swing. "So, Iris, should I wait until you two are finished?"

"No, Lena, I think it will take a while. We have only just started."

"So you're saying I have to share you now?"

Lena glared at Anna.

"Lena," Iris said firmly. "You better leave."

Anna wasn't quite sure what was happening but she was impressed that Iris managed to keep her cool. Lena didn't move at first but eventually she opened the door, letting the cold October air seep through. "Say 'Hi' to Kent," she said in Anna's direction.

"Oh, sure." She nodded, perhaps a bit too enthusiastically. "I will."

Iris closed the door and turned the key.

"I'm really sorry about that," she said. "We work together and recently had a disagreement that involved Boye. I didn't want her to join us."

"There's no need to apologise."

Lena's presence wasn't welcomed by her either.

22

Iris

October 2015

After the unfortunate drama with Lena, Anna asked for the bathroom and Iris worried that perhaps she felt the need to escape.

"This way," she said and escorted Anna back through the hall of books, past the central counter that was submerged in darkness, all the way to where the small kitchen was. "Right through there," she showed Anna.

This part of the library had been an apartment once. A small one-bedroom that was now merged with the large hall. The kitchen and the bathroom had been left intact, however. Charming but in need of an update.

Iris remained outside the bathroom door, invisible in the unlit room, allowing her thoughts to form. She felt dizzy, as if she had been drinking a few glasses of wine. What was she doing?

For some reason, she thought of Hanna, who had been one of the very first women in her life. Everything had been easy, from start to finish. When she had left Hanna, no numbers had been exchanged; they had been happy to meet but equally happy to go their separate ways. Through the years, she had floated around, like a ghost, from bed to bed, withdrawing satisfied. The women: artistic, rebellious, passionate and living life to the full. She wanted no regrets, for either party. Anna was different altogether. Nurturing rather than adventurous, reserved, clearly inexperienced, young, a wife and mother.

When Anna opened the door, she walked straight into Iris.

"I'm sorry," Iris said as she took a step back. "I didn't mean to scare you."

She should shut down the book club, withdraw. Old age had obviously blurred her sense of realism.

Anna didn't respond. They were simply standing in the dark, aware of each other's presence but barely able to make each other out.

Then Iris made a decision. She took a cautious step towards Anna, drawing in the scent of soap and cardamom, wrapped her arms around Anna's back, bringing her into a hug. Anna moulded into her embrace. She was taller; Iris could feel her heart beating on her shoulder. The thought of not wanting to let go was intense and frightening. Closing her eyes, she tapped into her instincts and immediately felt her heart jolt. This wasn't lust.

At the realisation, she withdrew, opened her eyes and held Anna at arm's length. She cleared her throat.

"I just wanted to make sure you were okay," she said.

A streetlight switched on outside the window, stretching its glum fingers into the room. Iris observed Anna's face, soft and serious.

"I'm sorry," Anna said. "I don't normally cry, at least not in front of people I have only just met."

143

"Don't worry. I prefer emotions to no emotions." *She's strong, yet vulnerable*, Iris thought. *I need to lighten the mood, make her feel comfortable.* "Now we'd better read Karin Boye," she said.

Anna laughed. "I guess so. In case I bump into Lena!"

"Which I sincerely hope you don't," Iris said quietly, as she led Anna down one of the aisles.

Together, they located the dystopian Boye novel *Kallocain*.

"It was her last novel and I dare say the most read one," Iris said. "It's dark, a mixture of sci-fi, horror and drama."

No sex or intimate relations, but Iris did enjoy the experimental premise in Boye's novel.

23

Erik

March 2016

Shaking his arms out, Erik wakes himself up. He's spent hours going through the documents on Anna's laptop. It's tedious and hasn't been fruitful so far, and as much as it is an intrusion into his wife's private life, he feels he is entitled to do it. They're married, right?

Tina has told him there was no Adam in any of Anna's classes. Yet he feels this Adam could be important. It's his tone of voice, his outbursts. Erik feels he needs to find him.

Almost everything on Anna's laptop seems to be related to her job. His eyes have scanned through files as mundane as tests to passages from books. Literature. Her newfound love.

"I'm a teacher, Erik. I am expected to read."

"You always read."

"I stopped reading fiction for pleasure, Erik," she said, as if that was his fault. "Now I have found my way back."

"I wish you could find your way back to my bed."

"Everything isn't about sex," she said.

He doesn't want to think about his wife's rejections.

It's easier to think about the early days, when she had no inhibitions.

He's had enough of her boring documents. He clicks back to Outlook. Maybe there will be a new email from blackadam4321? There isn't, but he goes to the "Deleted" folder, opens the emails from Black Adam and reads all twenty-six of them. Every single one starts with **Hi Anna**. Most of them are one-liners (**This is bullshit, I'm going to quit**). Most of them are demanding (**You need to listen, you need to talk to me**). Only a couple of them are longer (**You know what it's like. You have seen it. Please will you just help me? I want to be like everyone else. Normal, you know?**). And one is truly revealing (**I wish I had done better in the test, I wish I had made you proud. You deserve that.**) He refers to a test. So it definitely must be a student, except his name can't be Adam since Tina hasn't seen him listed in Anna's file. Who is he then?

Erik has made some notes and has almost picked up the phone to call Kent several times. Instead he tries to think of other teachers he could contact. Anna invited a bunch of them to the house once. End of year drinks. It was totally lame. Someone pulled out a guitar and encouraged Erik to play along to their folk songs. It was like sticking rusty needles in his eyes. And he can't remember anyone's name.

He decides to write another email to blackadam4321 instead. Time is ticking; the police seem sidetracked and he needs to move them back to the real issues. He needs to help. He writes: **I know you cared about Anna.** The guy wanted to make her proud so he must have cared? **I cared about her too,** he continues. **I did well in her tests. She appreciated that.** Would that rile him? Get him to respond? Knowing there was someone else who wanted to be her top student? Or would it be viewed as entrapment? He looks at his words. Entrapment is awesome in the movies but very illegal in Sweden. Boring square Swedish Government doesn't think it's fair. He erases the last two sentences and writes: Please can we talk? I need to talk to someone else who cared about her. I feel so alone.

He feels fairly pleased with the words. Writing was never his strength but this isn't bad. Erik clicks "Send".

He's so engrossed in the email that he's almost late for pick-up at day care. At least the teachers don't raise their eyebrows now. He has a reason not to follow the rules. His wife is in a coma. Thankfully, no one wants to talk about it. One must maintain a cheerful attitude: "the boys were so good today" or "the boys ate really well". Even though Sebastian and Lukas have a tendency to fight when surrounded by other children. They are also fussy eaters. Therefore, he can't trust anything they say. It's all bull.

*

The boys are missing Grandma and so is he. Although he is trying to stay on top of it, the house is already a picture of total chaos. He hasn't had time to do any dishes so the sink is now full. Clothes, toys, mail... He will deal with it. Later.

"Did you sing to Mummy today?" Sebastian asks.

Shit, he forgot. He only spent a couple of hours at the hospital this morning before heading home to Anna's computer. No one can blame him. It would drive anyone insane to wait by a hospital bed. Sometimes it feels like a wake, she's so still.

"I will take my acoustic guitar to the hospital tomorrow," he promises. "I don't think the nurses will like the sound of my Gretsch."

Sebastian giggles. "She will love it," he says confidently, although Erik isn't sure that Anna will enjoy it as much as the boys would. She never attended any of his gigs anymore. Only a few months ago she promised to be there but then something came up. As usual. Stupid book meeting probably.

*

That evening, when the boys are finally sleeping, Erik attempts to clean up the kitchen. Filling up the dishwasher seems to be the best use of his time. Then a knock on the door and the dishes remain in the sink.

His heart sinks when he opens it... Pernilla.

"Now is not a good time," he says but either she's deaf or she's ignorant because she's already on her way in, pushing him to the side, sliding her leather jacket off her shoulders.

"Seb and Lukas in bed?"

Seb? They hardly ever call him that.

"Yes, Seb*astian* and Lukas are sleeping," he says.

"Good."

She walks into the kitchen as if she's been there before, opens the fridge and pulls out two Pripps Blå.

"Opener?"

He can't believe it. What is she doing? He is about to tell her to leave but the sight of the cold beer makes his taste buds stir; let's face it, no one likes to drink alone.

"Just one beer," he says and digs out the opener from a drawer.

"Sure," she says and hands him one.

He expertly opens it, takes a swig and closes his eyes, relishing the cold bubbles, the dark malt slipping down his throat. Sighing, he opens his eyes again, slightly more relaxed than a second ago. Pernilla holds her own beer out, still unopened.

"Oh, shit. Sorry," he says.

She doesn't seem the least offended. While he opens her beer and hands it back to her, she keeps smiling. She doesn't even comment on the visible mess. They clink their bottles and take a couple of sips.

He has to talk to her about the police. Their suspicions are creating an unnecessary stress. Pernilla twirls her curly hair with one finger, a cheeky grin on her face. She's wearing a white summer dress even though it's only just spring and still chilly outside. No bra, he notices. Just two straps holding her large bosom up. It was only the one time, he reminds himself. One time. One beer. That's all.

"Let's sit down," he says. He'll think more clearly then.

"I'm here for you," she says as soon as they're parked on the much too comfortable navy linen couch. Her fingers rest on the sleeve of his shirt.

"Thank you." He clears his throat. "I appreciate it, but Pernilla, you're making it difficult…"

Her eyes, wide like a reindeer's.

"I don't understand," she says.

"You can't tell the police that we're seeing each other." He feels himself getting worked up. "I mean, it's not even true. And I need to focus on Anna, on her getting better. And the boys."

"Like I said," Pernilla says calmly. "I'm here for you and I won't say anything." She hesitates. "If…"

"If what?"

"If we, you know… keep meeting up. No strings attached if that's what's bothering you."

"I don't want to cheat on my wife."

"Too late."

Touché. He leans back, takes another swig, swallows, gaining time. Her fingers are squeezing his arm, moving up towards his shoulder.

"Pernilla…"

"Yes?" Her other hand is now working his crotch; she's leaning in, her warm breath on his throat. Soft lips against his. *I should throw her out.* He's just so tired; he closes his eyes, lets her playful tongue into his mouth. Then her body moves in, straddling him, her breasts in his face, her perfume intoxicating.

The doorbell. Somewhere in the background he can hear it, the annoying tune like a cheesy song.

"Just ignore it," she whispers, but it's persistent.

He can't block it out; he sits up and pushes her off.

"Have to get that," he says, rushing to the door, hoping it's Mum. She won't approve of him getting cosy – or even just sharing a beer – with the boys' teacher but he doesn't care.

"Hey, man."

"Rob?"

His mate is looking dishevelled; spiky hair held down by a well-worn Arsenal cap.

"Sorry to just come over without calling first. It's just, well… there's a football game on…"

"Come the hell in!" Erik grabs his arm and pulls him in.

"Okay, okay," he laughs. "I'm coming. Have one of those for me?" He points to the beer.

"Of course."

"Hi there." Pernilla is standing in the doorway, seductively leaning against the door frame. Is she hitting on Rob? He can't be jealous. He has no right to be.

"Hi." Rob's tentacles are out.

"Pernilla was just leaving," Erik says. "She's the boys' teacher. We were just discussing... the boys."

He takes her jacket from the hallway and hands it to her.

"Another time," she says.

Then she's out the door, leaving it open, the cold evening air washing over Erik, finally waking him up.

"That's the boys' teacher?" Rob's eyes follow her down the street. "I need to get some children, man."

*

Six beers and a football victory later, Rob leaves. Erik feels restless. Perhaps it's the beer or it's Pernilla's fingers, still etched on his cock. Going to sleep is out of the question. He needs to do something, perhaps watch a movie? The TV is still on and he zaps through the channels. Except he can't hear anything. The mouths on the screen are moving but it feels as if he's accidentally pressed the "Mute" button. Nothing registers.

He switches the TV off and opens Anna's laptop instead; clicks on Safari and logs in to his new Gmail account. There are still no emails from blackadam4321. Anna's Outlook folder doesn't contain anything new either, not counting irrelevant junk mail. He clicks back to her folders and scrolls down the list. He's looked at most of them already. It's all pretty dull apart from the emails from blackadam4321. There are a couple near the bottom of the screen, which he hasn't seen yet. One is called "House" and another one simply "Other". The first one is full of bills and maintenance issues, everything predictably related to their house. He opens "Other" instead, expecting it to contain random messages that don't fit anywhere else. Except it only contains messages from one sender xeroxwed@gmail.com. Nothing about the name is familiar. He opens the first email.

I can't wait to see you this week. To be near you, to taste you. I miss you.

An uncomfortable feeling takes hold of his body. It's a total body freeze. He doesn't want to read this. He closes it down. Then opens it again.

What is Xeroxwed?

Despite himself, he clicks through to another message at random.

Your fingers clasped around my nipple, tugging. I can still smell you on my fingers. What have you done to me?

He stares at the screen. Then shuts it down. All of it. Power off.

PART TWO

24

Rolf

November 2015

A naked woman was strapped to the bed. Pale arms above her head, heavy breasts with mole-like nipples; dark-blue nails harsh against the skin. Another woman, dressed in a PVC corset, a stereotypical German bun on her head, bore down on the first woman, a leather whip entrusted to her strong hand. Muffled sounds of lashes hitting bare flesh; slivers of red across thighs, stomach and breasts. Rolf watched the two women, their perfectly shaped bodies and immaculately made-up faces, making the right noises, their aim to arouse him. Finally, the dominant woman pleasured the submissive with a dildo, bringing her to a climax that was restricted due to the straps holding her down.

"How original," he said.

He felt bored, his erection separated from his mind.

"Well, I'm turned on," Måna said. She mischievously took the remote control out of his hand and clicked "Pause".

He turned to Måna, her bronze-coloured cheeks, abnormally plump lips, the brown ringlets of hair reaching her full bosom. She was a goddess and there was no way he wouldn't finish what he had started.

He tied her up, her bed the perfect set-up: a black wrought-iron four-poster with leopard print throws and pillows. The scarves were strong and Måna agreeable.

Once his work of art was complete, Rolf admired his own skills along with her spread-eagle position. Grabbing her long hair, holding it in a firm grip, he bore into her. She gasped, laughed and moaned, but after a while he felt like it was merely skin rubbing against skin, rather than fucking. He couldn't climax.

Måna was loud when she came, a trait he loved in a woman, but he had to focus, close his eyes and think of... Iris. Pressed up against Lena in the library kitchen, their bodies barely visible from the street. That did it. He groaned and exploded into the condom.

Climbing out of bed, he felt hot and sticky and quickly started to get dressed.

"You're not staying the night?"

He smiled sweetly, leaned down towards Måna's rosy face and kissed her long and hard (leaving a lasting Rolf impression). Then he stood back and studied her intently, taking a mental picture. He wanted to remember them all.

"Your hair is incredibly shiny," he said. "Would you let me cut a lock off to remember you by?"

It wasn't unusual for women to appear in his work in one form or another, each piece a sample of DNA. Måna chuckled, so obviously comfortable in her nakedness, her glistening body crumpling the bed linen.

"If anyone else had said that, it would sound creepy," she said. "But I know your work so I will agree."

This threw him. He never told anyone his real identity.

He was Fredrik, the journalist, or Niklas, the art critic. There had been a time when he had chased the fame to pay the bills, but then he had chased the fame for fame. Iris had warned him about the added exposure, how it could compromise their lifestyle, but he had told her she was paranoid. Should the papers get hold of his personal affairs, then well... bad press was also good press. As long as it was all legal. Kinky was legal. For the most part.

"Don't worry," Måna said. "Your secret is safe with me."

"Scissors?" he asked.

She nodded her head towards a desk in the far corner, and he walked across the carpeted room, opening the drawers until he found a large pair, probably meant for sewing. Her eyes were gleaming with excitement as he cut into the brown hair.

Then he kissed her one last time and made to leave.

"Are you not going to untie me?"

Her smile faded.

"You got yourself into this," he said. "I'm sure you can get yourself out of it."

*

Rolf walked through the streets, making his way back to the car. He would tell Iris that his meeting with a gallery owner had gone well and she would congratulate him. Or he would be honest. He wasn't sure yet. Perhaps it was old age but he felt jaded after a life of sexual exploration. He had tried everything except monogamy: having Iris all to himself.

The air was cold, the pavements lined with drunk youngsters, beers in their hands, shrieks of laughter, open jackets revealing skimpy outfits. He walked past them, not even noticing the young breasts on display.

He stopped at a bar and ordered a whiskey on the rocks and downed it.

"Tough night?" the bartender asked, a tattooed snake wrapped around his muscled arm.

If only you knew, Rolf thought. *You would be jealous as hell.*

"I miss my wife," he said instead.

"Gotcha."

Tattoo man poured him another whiskey. "On the house, mate."

"Thanks." Kindness offered by strangers always surprised him.

"So, you're on a business trip?"

"Something like that," Rolf said distractedly, the fingers in his pocket wrapped around the silky smooth hair.

"Your wife couldn't join you?"

He imagined Iris standing next to him, the two of them on a weekend trip. No more women. No more extramarital sex. Was that really what he wanted? He nodded to himself: yes.

Rolf looked up; the guy's eyes were a bit too inquisitive for his liking.

He was tempted to say that his wife was dead, to make him squirm. Except he couldn't say the words "Iris" and "dead" in the same sentence.

"I've got to go," he said.

25

Anna

November 2015

Anna parked on the dusty gravel and walked up to Iris's house. It was fairly large, with an extension to the left, three doors facing the courtyard she was standing in. She stepped up to what she assumed was the main entrance but couldn't find a doorbell. Instead she knocked hard, small flecks of red paint peeling off, landing by her feet.

After their last meeting had been interrupted by Lena and her adolescent attitude, Anna's excitement about book club had been dampened slightly. She had passed on Lena's greeting to Kent and his reaction had confirmed her gut feeling: "She's a nutcase," he had said. "Don't involve yourself with her unless you have to."

Iris had called Anna, which at first had surprised her since they had never swapped numbers, but then she had remembered that her contact details – much to Erik's annoyance – were publicly listed.

"Would you mind if we meet at my house next week

instead?" she had asked. "The vents are being cleaned at the library."

Anna's enthusiasm had immediately been resurrected. She would have the opportunity to soak in Iris's home atmosphere, to learn more about her, and that was exciting. Although she had to admit she was nervous about potentially meeting Iris's husband. Rolf Sören had featured in the newspaper over the weekend after it was discovered that one of the paintings in his "Red Series" was painted with one hundred per cent pig's blood. He had claimed it was from a local butcher's shop but the art critics had had a field day, claiming he had killed the pig himself.

Iris was barefoot when she opened the door, wearing a multi-coloured kaftan. It was the first time Anna had seen her in anything other than black.

"There you are," Iris said, opening up her arms. "I hope you didn't get lost."

They embraced in a typical greeting. It was genuine but quick.

"I almost did," Anna said. "It's so dark out here without streetlights."

"That's what I like," Iris said. "It's almost as if we don't exist, it's so deserted and tranquil."

Anna held up a golden-brown sponge creation. "I baked a banana cake," she said.

"Lovely. Come on in."

Inside, there were a number of lanterns and tea-lights, creating a truly wonderful ambiance.

"I simply love candles," Iris said. "Don't you?"

They sat down in the living room, the walls made up of unpainted terracotta-coloured bricks, the furniture random, the sofas covered in blankets. Books were everywhere: stacked on the coffee table, lined up on shelves, in piles on the floor. Various paintings were either hanging or leaning up against the walls. Anna didn't understand what most of them portrayed, but then she wasn't that interested in Rolf Sören's art.

"Welcome to our creative chaos," Iris said.

They sat down, sinking into a couple of deep armchairs with batik-patterned cushions. Anna was about to ask one of her pre-prepared small-talk questions (*How was your week? Have you read* War and Peace? *Can you recommend any new Swedish authors?*) when Iris said: "You look amazing."

"Oh..." She looked down on her grey shirtdress. "This old thing?" she said, even though it was brand new. It looked so plain in Iris's vibrant living room.

Iris wasn't wearing her reading glasses this evening, only a hint of mascara framing her green eyes.

"I really enjoyed *Kallocain*," Anna said.

Iris poured the coffee and handed Anna a knife and plates for the cake.

"What did you like about it?"

Anna felt self-conscious, as if her role as a teacher had been exchanged with that of a student. At the same time, she couldn't help wanting to perform well.

"It was scary how the state really controlled the people in the book," she said. "How they couldn't think for themselves."

"I think the idea of the truth serum is fascinating," Iris said. "How Leo Kall uses it on his wife because he thinks she will reveal that she's in love with someone else."

"Only he finds out she fantasises about killing him," Anna said.

"Exactly. It works against him."

"Can you imagine?" Anna said, sitting back. "Living with someone who wants to kill you?"

"This is delicious!" Iris exclaimed as she bit into the cake. "Leo and Linda's marriage isn't real of course," she continued, wiping her mouth on a small square napkin. "The purpose of the marriages in the book is to produce children, nothing else."

"I know. It's a strange set-up," Anna agreed.

"Not all marriages are the same," Iris said, chewing on the cake. "I wouldn't want to harm Rolf but he's not enough for me."

He wasn't enough for Iris? But she *adored* him? Anna processed the new information, shocked but intrigued. She took a piece of cake and sipped her coffee, not quite sure how to respond.

"I'm going to make more coffee," Iris said and stood up. "This is cold."

Anna moved in her seat, pulling at her dress. She wanted to be friends with Iris and that meant communicating.

"What do you mean exactly?" Anna said. "About him not being enough?"

"I mean," Iris said, picking up the thermos. "I mean that I'm not monogamous."

It sounded so matter of fact; Iris's face open, the personal divulgence like a trap released.

Anna's heart beat fast.

"You're not?" she said. "What about your husband?"

"Neither of us is," Iris said simply. "Not that we broadcast it."

Anna nodded. "Wow."

"Anyway, that's not for everyone. Do you want more coffee?"

Iris made her way to the kitchen and Anna quickly got up

to join her, a feeling of wanting to normalise the environment in which the bomb had landed.

"I don't think Boye was monogamous either," Anna said, catching up to Iris. *Let's talk literature.*

"Actually, I think she was," Iris said. "Just because she lived with a woman doesn't mean she cheated."

"Maybe, I don't know."

Working in tandem, Iris pulled out a new filter and filled it with coffee while Anna measured the water.

"Boye was modern that way," Anna said. "Living with a woman even though it was against the law. I admire that. Everyone should be brave enough to be who they are."

Iris nodded, pouring the water into the coffee maker.

Contemplatively, and without thinking, Anna continued: "And you're not monogamous."

For a moment, Iris looked unsure. She switched the machine on and as it kicked into gear, water started spluttering out. They both turned their attention to the glass pot, filling up with the tar-like liquid.

"Does that mean you see other people?" Anna asked.

They didn't look at each other; still transfixed by the fresh brew.

"It does," Iris said eventually.

"I shouldn't pry," Anna said, apologising. She rinsed out their mugs and put them on the sink, next to an amazing AGA cooker. "I can't remember, do you take milk?"

"It's fine," Iris said, resting a hand on Anna's arm. "Don't worry about it. I never talk about it because, well, it's a small town and I don't want people to judge me."

"I won't tell anyone."

"I know you won't. And yes, I do take milk."

26

Iris

November 2015

After a deep but lively discussion about the permeated darkness in *Kallocain*, Anna made to leave. She started stacking the plates and the coffee cups and Iris had to stop her.

"I'll do it later," she said.

She didn't want the ordinary to overshadow the mystery too much.

Anna put her coat on, a warm woolly creation, and leaned in for their farewell hug. Iris couldn't resist closing her eyes, feeling Anna's curves, assured that the thick fabric wouldn't give her away. Anna lingered longer than normal, her ear warm on Iris's cheek.

Iris knew that she had opened the door of possibilities. All she needed to do now was invite Anna in. *Always follow your instincts*. And so she did. Leaving the warmth of the embrace, she pulled back and faced Anna. Their eyes locked and Iris could sense her uncertainty. Then, very gently so as not to scare Anna away, she put her hands around Anna's glowing face and leaned in.

Soft. Her lips were soft.

Anna seemed puzzled yet she didn't pull away so Iris brought her closer. Their bodies were touching now, the kiss growing intense; lips explored, strong flavours of dark roasted beans mixed with longing. Anna wrapped her arms around Iris, showing an enthusiasm Iris hadn't expected, which made her heart beat stronger. The minutes got lost; Iris wanted Anna to stay. For a long, long time.

"Wait," Anna said, breaking away. There was panic in her voice. "Rolf?"

"He's not home," Iris said. "He will be back very late."

"You're sure?"

Iris held Anna's face in her hands. "Anna, I have never brought anyone to my home before."

Anna's face relaxed.

"What happens here, is no one else's business," Iris continued. "It's just between you and me."

She removed Anna's coat, then kissed her neck, her cheeks, her nose, her forehead. Her lips.

Anna looked down. "I'm nervous," she said quietly.

So fragile. Iris would need to be gentle.

She opened the buttons in Anna's dress, one by one; her breasts warm against Iris's own body. She could sense Anna handing herself over, her body weightless, lithe and willing.

They moved smoothly from the hallway to the living room, transporting their bodies from up against the wall, to the couch, to the floor, like two characters in a silent movie, their bodies entwined. As they moaned, caressed and kissed, clothing began to fall to the floor.

27

Erik

March 2016

When Erik married Anna he never imagined she might die before him. They never signed a pre-nup, nor did they draw up wills. Naïve perhaps but they never even discussed it. Only when they bought the house, did they arrange life insurance. That way the mortgage would be paid off, should one of them die. It felt morbid, signing those papers. Although necessary of course. Mature. It made him feel responsible.

Anna isn't dead. She's still in this limbo-land where she might wake up or she might not. When people ask him about her condition, he gets annoyed, and to deal with it better, he's come up with a standard reply: "All we can do is wait."

He has learned not to show too much emotion. Sometimes his emotions can be beneficial of course. Like when he called the council office about new day care placements for the children. He's still in a queue but someone now cares enough to work on it. Soon, it will be resolved – "to give Sebastian and Lukas a fresh start" – and he will never have to see Pernilla again.

Anna once insinuated that he had cheated. It was the night he had been out with Rob. For weeks, he felt nervous every time Anna dropped or picked up the children at day care but at the time, Pernilla seemed to regard it as what it was: a one-night stand.

Erik cheated. Only once. It barely counts but he recognises that he did. With Anna it is different. He never expected her to be unfaithful. Especially since she no longer seemed interested in sex. Yet she did cheat. He knows this. The question is, how does he notify the police? He could show the emails Anna was sent from Xeroxwed, but they could be viewed as harmless. Internet chats done in the comfort of your own home, without the exchange of bodily fluids.

That's when he has a "light bulb" moment.

*

As soon as Rob steps over the threshold, Erik lashes out: "Did you fuck my wife?"

He slams the door shut behind Rob, locks it. Now there's no escape.

"Dude, what are you talking about?"

The offended look on Rob's face.

"Took you by surprise, did I? Thought I wouldn't find out? You have to have all the girls, don't you?" Erik grabs Rob's collar and shoves him up against the wall. Coats and bags come crashing down, landing in a heap on the wooden floor. "Including Anna."

He's spitting and Rob angrily wipes his face.

"Get off me!" Rob shouts.

He takes hold of Erik's shirt. A button pops.

"Just bloody admit it, will you?" Erik shouts back.

"You're one to talk. Having a beer with the boys' sexy teacher while your wife is in a coma."

That does it. The pain goes deep into Erik's stomach and he wants Rob to feel that same throbbing soreness. He lunges at him and Rob buckles and ends up flattened on the floor. There's a distinct look of contempt on Rob's face as he gathers his limbs. Erik's anger subsides momentarily but he can't stop now. He grabs hold of Rob's shoulders to headbutt him when Rob shakes him off, sweat running down his furrowed brow.

"Get the fuck away from me!"

"Just admit it..." Erik starts, his voice trailing off.

Once again, the fury makes room for something else. Rob is his best friend... Fuck. Tears push against his eyelids but he won't cry in front of Rob. He leans forward but instead of hitting Rob, he embraces him. Hard.

"What the hell is going on?"

Rob's voice is angry but it also sounds concerned.

"Did you sleep with her?" Erik asks.

"Of course not! Who do you think I am?"

"A womaniser?"

Erik is half-serious, half-joking but Rob is clearly beyond offended.

"Your best pal's wife is off limits, man."

"I'm just so confused right now," Erik says.

"Then talk to me. Don't fucking attack me."

"Sorry. Come here, I need to show you something."

He pulls Rob into the kitchen.

"Whatever you say," Rob says, following him. "I know

you're upset but don't ever do that again."

Instead of answering, Erik opens Anna's laptop and logs in. He opens the "Other" folder and picks an email at random. "Read this."

Just thinking about you makes me wet. Your moans. Tender, passionate, wild. You're insatiable. And I love it.

Erik studies Rob's contorting face.

"What *is* this?"

"An email."

"I can see that. Who's it from? Your little teacher friend?"

"What? No! It was sent to Anna."

Rob's eyes widen, his mouth a big dark hole. "Anna?"

Erik relaxes, his own feelings justified.

"Wait," Rob says. "You thought I sent these? That's why you just accused me of...?"

"I'm sorry, I just don't know what to think anymore. This has completely thrown me."

"I'm impressed," Rob says, smiling and looking like his old self. "You thought I had written this? That is way too poetic for me. I would be like 'you make me wanna come'. Straight to the point, you know?"

"Rob, we're talking about my wife."

"Sorry, but how could you possibly think I wrote that?"

Rob scratches his head and they both stare at the screen.

"So who sent it?" Rob asks. "Are there more?"

Erik nods. "There are loads. I have no idea who sent them. It must be some sick joke, or... I don't know. We weren't, you know..." He squirms but clears his throat and says it: "... having sex all that often."

Although he's allowed himself to be vulnerable, Rob

doesn't seem to notice. He's busy clicking back to the folder to open another email.

"Have you shown this to the police?"

Erik shakes his head. "Not yet. They're sort of accusing me of cheating so I don't want them to think that I made this up."

"It's evidence, though. Black and white. This could be a motive. Jealous lover attacks... or something. It's just that I can't believe that Anna would cheat. She's so... perfect. But it definitely seems that way." He looks at Erik with compassion. "I'm sorry, man."

"Thanks. I'm just... Maybe you could mention it to the police?"

"Me?" Rob looks like it's a crazy idea. "I would have to tell them you showed it to me and then they would wonder why you're not telling them yourself."

"No, I thought that perhaps..." Erik thinks carefully about what he says next. "... that perhaps you could tell them you suspected she was cheating."

"But they will ask who with and I won't know. I mean, I want to help but I... Oh, wait a minute..." Rob stands up straight, his hand is in the air as if he's asking for permission to speak.

"What?"

"What I said earlier, about the emails being poetic," Rob says. "Do you think a teacher could write something like that?"

"I'm not sure..." Where is he going with this?

"Maybe what's-his-name, her colleague, wrote it? Kent?"

Erik nods slowly even though he doesn't agree.

"Maybe you need to pay him a visit," Rob says.

"If I do, will you go to the police?"

"Let's see what you find out first."

Rob looks like he's playing a part in a soap opera but Erik isn't stupid. He knows what he has to do.

*

Kent and Märta live in an art deco house at the outskirts of town, accompanied by an unruly garden. Erik navigates through the tall grass, where there used to be a tiled path.

The moment Märta opens the door he thinks: *I would cheat with Anna if I were Kent.* He would need a bit of fun on the side. It's not that Märta is ugly, she's just tense, the lines in her face deep, making her look grouchy. That would put them in the same boat. Him and Märta, bobbing on the ocean of adultery victims.

"I'm here to see Kent," he says.

She shakes his hand. "I'm so sorry about Anna." Her lines soften, a sympathetic smile appears.

"Thanks. And… thank you for the flowers you sent."

Kent and Märta sent white lilies to the hospital. Kent obviously knew they were Anna's favourite.

"There you are." Kent shows up, giving him a manly, albeit uncomfortable, hug. "I've been trying to call you. How is she?"

"The same." Erik clears his throat. "All we can do is wait."

"She's strong, Erik. She will get better."

Erik nods. *What do you know?*

"Come in, sit down."

They draw him into their home, filled with old-fashioned farm cupboards, flower-patterned cushions and figurines, making him feel like he's in his mother's house. A cup of coffee is placed in his hand, accompanied by a Vanilla Heart on a plate. He takes a bite, the sweet custard filling his mouth.

"How are the boys?"

He swallows and takes a gulp of the coffee. They need to get through the pleasantries so that they can get down to business.

"They're okay," he says. "Dealing with it, you know. They're brave. Sleeping right now. My mate, Rob, is at the house."

The words seem to disappear into space, like puffs of smoke. He felt more sure of this when he left home. Confrontation is never comfortable, especially not with someone like Kent. Erik reminds himself that Kent may have been Anna's support pillar at work but he did not father Anna's children. *He* did. He is the man.

Kent stands up and pours Erik a whiskey.

"You look like you need one."

Erik agrees and takes a sip as soon as it's placed in his hand. It's strong and smooth.

"So, I just need to ask you some questions," he finally says, mounting up the courage. "Was Anna... happy at school?" Let's start there.

"You know she loves her job."

"Yeah, I know. But were there any problems?"

Kent seems to think about this.

"She had a tough start to the year," Kent says. "I'm sure she's told you about the new boy. He had some issues and Anna wanted to help him."

Erik racks his brain, searching for a point of reference? Did she talk about having problems with a student?

"What kind of issues did he have?" he asks.

"He was getting himself into fights."

"Right, had no problem beating people up, did he?"

"Erik." Kent seems to understand what he's getting at. "We can't jump to conclusions."

"Why not?"

"Erik, she did her best and he did calm down. Anna definitely had something to do with that, which is exactly what I told the police. He respected her and wouldn't have attacked her, is my opinion."

"His name isn't Adam, is it?"

"No, and you really shouldn't go chasing after her students, Erik."

"Okay, what about you then? Were you a support to Anna?"

"Of course, we talked about it regularly."

"After hours."

"Sometimes."

"Right."

Silence descends on them. They look at each other, tension prevalent in the air. Until Märta speaks: "Are you insinuating something here?" She looks intrigued rather than upset.

"Is that so strange?" Erik defends himself. "Anna fucking loves Kent. It's always 'Kent this' and 'Kent that'."

Kent looks baffled. "We are very good friends, Erik."

The way he says it makes Erik feel dirty. As if he has dragged something pure and beautiful through the mud that will never be completely clean again. He's already crossed the line though. No point turning back.

"That's it? You sure?"

"Erik, I am one hundred per cent sure. I'm flattered that

you think she would be interested in an old bloke like me, but I am not on the market." He exchanges a smile with Märta. They're so textbook. Happily ever after.

"So who do you think attacked Anna?"

"I honestly don't know," Kent says. He's resting a hand on Märta's knee, as if he needs to reassure her that he is there for her, no one else. "I feel like Anna has been so happy lately. A bit withdrawn perhaps but radiant, I would say."

Radiant? Erik nods. "So you think she was cheating on me?"

Kent looks perplexed. "Not at all."

Shit. Why doesn't anyone cooperate?

"But it's possible?" Erik probes.

Kent shakes his head. "I think she would have told me."

Do you now? What else would she have told you? Erik imagines Anna and Kent after work, heads close together, her soft voice complaining about her husband, gaining Kent's sympathy. It burns his ego as much as his heart.

"Have you been helping the police?" Erik asks.

Kent takes an annoyingly long sip of his whiskey. "As I already explained, I have spoken to them, yes. But I don't think I have been all that helpful." He looks Erik in the eye. "I can't think of anyone who would want to harm Anna."

28

Daniel

November 2015

Dan cycled around town, past Anna's two-storey house and its empty driveway. The lights were on and he could make out her husband and their two small boys at the kitchen table. A white ceramic lamp dangled from the ceiling, lighting up their plates of meatballs and mashed potatoes. "Lingonberry?" he imagined their father asking them as he passed them the red jar. They shook their little heads, stretching their hands out to the bottle of ketchup instead. Anna had probably hand-rolled the meatballs and made the mashed potatoes from scratch, or maybe her husband had. Frida only ever bought the supermarket's readymade super-savers pack. She would eat the meatballs with her fingers, often dressed in only her underwear. Occasionally, if she was sober and her payday didn't end up at the liquor store, she would actually cook. His favourite meal was *fläskpannkaka*, a thick oven pancake made with pork.

A car came driving down the road and he quickly hid

behind a bush. A station wagon passed him; it wasn't Anna's black Volvo but a navy-blue Volkswagen Passat. He felt like throwing a stone at it but thought better of it. He didn't want to draw attention to himself. Inside the house, dinner seemed to be over. While the boys ran out of the kitchen, their father took care of the dishes. Dan promised himself to help clear the table when he lived there. Anna would smile and thank him for being so helpful.

Except Anna wasn't there. Where was she? He waited for another hour, then cycled down to the town centre where he bought a hot dog. He was starving after seeing Anna's family eat. With the hot dog in his hand, he continued on to the church. Not only was it clad in scaffolding while it was being painted, making it easy to hide; it was also strategically placed between two roads, both acting as entrances into Mörna. From here, he would be able to see Anna's car. But it didn't show.

An hour later, he went back to Anna's house. Now the lights were out and goodnight stories most likely read. A faint blue flicker, perhaps from a TV, could be seen from the room next to the dark kitchen. Nothing else. He toyed with the idea of ringing the doorbell.

"When will Anna be home?" he would ask. "I have a question about an assignment."

But what if her husband looked at him with disgust, a misplaced nobody who interrupted his evening? He couldn't take that risk.

In the end he had no choice but to go back to Frida. She was snoring on the couch but at least the dickhead was gone. He preferred it when her shags didn't stay the night. No smug or guilty face eyeing him up in the morning. Both scenarios were equally excruciating.

He went into Martin's room. Soon it would be packed up. Not that his brother had many belongings. Next to the wardrobe there was an old hockey stick and his second-hand ice skates. They hadn't been skating in a while. His brother had outgrown most of their regular activities. Dan wondered why his brother hadn't moved out sooner. *Because of me.* He had stayed to protect his little brother. The realisation made him head for the door. He felt guilty, the weak sibling in need of babying. Dan would make it easy for Martin. He would move out and create his own future.

Back in his room, he flopped down on his bed, his shoes still on, and stared at the now familiar ceiling. He had thought about sneaking back inside the teachers' lounge but he wasn't sure. That first time, Kent had unfortunately snuck up on them and he had been forced to escape into a closet down the corridor before running outside. The second time he had had Anna to himself but she had been on edge and that wasn't the way he liked her. He wanted her to hug him and stuff, tell him everything was okay, that she loved him.

In his notebook, he continued his story.

"Where do you want me to sleep?" he asked.

"In the basement, so that my husband doesn't get suspicious."

"Does he... touch you?"

She looked alarmed.

"No, we never have sex anymore," she said. "I'm leaving him. Plus we have young children so that wouldn't be appropriate."

He felt pleased.

"I'm going to take care of you," he said.

"Oh Dan!" she said, her eyes happy.

She seductively undressed in front of him, revealing an

hourglass figure. Pulling him close, her hand started knea-
ding the growing bulge between his legs.

Dan stopped writing, his cock hard, his mind filled with
confidence. Now he knew what he needed to do. He had to
either catch Anna outside of school or her home, where there
was no one else; just the two of them. The next evening he
would be better prepared. If Frida's car was back from the
shop, he would drive. He might not have a licence but he
knew how to get around. Otherwise, he would "borrow" the
neighbour's moped. That way she wouldn't escape.

29

Iris

November 2015

Anna was on Iris's mind the moment she woke up. She dared to admit she felt happy. Anna on the other hand, would probably be feeling guilty right now. *Love them but leave them*, Rolf would have said. He had always offered so much advice. Too much. There had been times when she had toyed with the idea of leaving Rolf, but she felt she owed him too much. They had met at a time when her confidence was at rock bottom, and he had made her feel worthy. Would she ever feel like she had repaid him?

With Anna, Iris felt she had achieved the impossible. Anna was so unlike anyone she had ever wanted, so unpretentious and real. There was nothing remotely flaky about her. The fact that they had made love amazed her. If Rolf knew, he would have felt proud, pulled her close and wanted her, right there. He got off on her affairs, had encouraged them from the moment they met. But he didn't know about Anna and neither would he.

Iris felt she needed to get to know Anna better, explore...

She sighed and shook her head. Anna was much younger. She had a family. It was most likely already over.

"Coffee?" Rolf handed her a cup and sat down on the bed. "Fun night last night?"

"I should be asking you."

She had smelt perfume on him as he crept into bed. He used to think that turned her on: "It's a reminder that although others find me attractive, I'm still yours at the end of the night."

"Last night was actually quite boring," Rolf said and gently stroked her cheek.

Then he got back into bed and spooned her. It was the last thing she had expected.

"You're going to make me spill my coffee," she said.

"Sorry." His right hand was cradling her breast, the left hand playing with her hair.

"Are you okay?" she asked.

"I missed you last night, and I was thinking... perhaps we should, I don't know, renew our vows?"

He stroked her nipple through the sheer fabric of her nightie. She tensed even though she enjoyed the sensation his touch caused her body.

"Why now?" she asked.

"Because I want to start over."

At that, she gently pushed his arm away, rejecting his words.

"I want us to be exclusive," he said. "Not see other women anymore."

She laughed. "Is it April Fool's Day?"

He pulled himself up on one elbow and looked at her. "I mean it." His facial expression looked hurt and for a moment she felt sympathy for her husband of twenty-two years, a sporadic sense of pity. That was until the bleaker memories of their marriage resurfaced, the feelings of inadequacy, of being shared.

"But it was your idea," she said.

"I've had enough, Iris. You're the one I want to spend my life with."

"You must have had a bad evening, Rolf. What did she do? Did she talk too much? Did she criticise your art? Did she turn out to be male?" She forced a laugh, trying to be overly humorous to distract from her own emotional evening. *Anna on the floor, her eyes filled with affection.*

"No, Iris, it wasn't like that. Anyway, you don't want to know."

"Normally I don't, but I can make an exception since this one seems to have given you some sort of an epiphany."

"It wasn't her. She was fine, attractive, great hair." He pulled out a brown, shiny lock from his bedside table and showed it to her.

"That's disgusting."

"She gave it to me willingly."

She sipped her hot coffee.

"Lena called me to tell me about your affair," he said.

That didn't surprise her. Lena had been mad.

"I thought as much," Iris said. "Did you at least pretend to be upset?"

"Of course. She wants to meet me to tell me all about it."

She felt calm although it was clearly a problem that needed to be solved. Lena was part of her work life.

"Maybe," she said and turned to Rolf. "You could... I don't know. Pay her some attention? So that we can end this."

"Really? What about being exclusive?"

She stroked his chest. "You know you don't really want

that. Anyway, you think she's hot, don't you? And this one time, I don't mind sharing."

"Why not?"

She wasn't sure exactly but most likely because there was someone else, a woman who made her feel something new entirely.

"I stayed with her for too long," Iris said. "She's all yours."

He seemed to contemplate this. "She *is* a knock-out," he said. "Want to fuck?"

He looked so excited, she felt she needed to reward him for agreeing to her plan, and so she embraced him and fucked away, her closed eyes imagining someone else. A woman who quite possibly would break her heart.

30

Erik

March 2016

When Erik returns home from Märta and Kent's house, Rob is asleep on the couch. He opens a beer and sits down next to his mate. To clear his head. He wishes he could put electrodes on either side of his brain and flick a switch, go back in time. Then he would have been a better listener, more attentive; he would have been a musician, not just a wannabe doing gigs at near-empty bars. He would have kept his dick in his pants, been an amazing husband. Fatherhood should have made him grow up. He worked that out too late.

"Isn't life a bitch?" he says to Rob. "When you finally realise what you have, it's gone?"

Rob snores and Erik takes another sip. The beer goes down with ease. He gets another bottle, then another. He switches the TV on, zaps through the channels. It's all so boring, so far removed from reality.

Rob wakes up. "Sorry, did I fall asleep?"

"Yeah."

He sits up, rubs his eyes and yawns.

"So, what did he say?"

"Not much." Erik leans back. "Something about a bratty student."

"What about him and her? I mean Anna and Kent?"

"Nah. Don't think so."

"Look, I've been thinking," Rob says.

"Really? Hurt your head?"

Rob does an uppercut under Erik's arm.

"Careful!" He laughs. "No, but seriously. I could call Tina. Maybe tell her that Anna was cheating?"

"Maybe."

Erik thinks. Actually, that might be a brilliant idea.

"She can pass the info on to whoever is dealing with the case," Rob says.

"Won't she say it came from you?"

"She loves me, man. She's been calling me and stuff. I'm sure she will be cool with it."

"That would be great. Thanks."

Rob doesn't even wait. He takes out his phone and calls Tina straight away.

*

The next day, Pernilla sends several explicit photos. Erik keeps the phone far away from the boys these days and clears it of anything inappropriate. Pernilla isn't just satisfied with pictures. She also sends many, many messages:

When can we meet up? Let's have some fun. You and me = forever.

He responds to none of these. Although it makes it particularly awkward to drop the children at day care.

Today, however, the boy with the denim jacket and untied shoes is outside the day care gate. He cycles towards them.

"My dad used to have a jacket like yours," Sebastian says.

"Anna is my teacher," he says. This time he speaks. "I hope she's getting better."

"Thanks, pal. I appreciate it."

The boy nods his head and cycles off but Erik spots an opportunity.

"Hey," he calls after the boy. "What's your name?"

"Da... David," he stutters.

"Can I ask you something?" Erik says. "Please."

The boy stops his bike and looks at them. His hair is dishevelled and although his jacket is still cool, Erik can now see that it's in need of a wash, the denim no longer blue.

Erik takes a leap of faith.

"Is there a boy in Anna's class called Adam?"

Erik thinks of the emails from Black Adam. Unstable. Possessive. Direct. Does this boy know who Black Adam is?

The boy looks puzzled. "Eh, no," he says.

Erik takes a couple of steps towards him. "You sure? What about in another class at your school, is someone, anyone, called Adam?"

"Maybe," the boy says. He adjusts the folded sleeves on his jacket. "It's not an unusual name." He pauses. "Why do you want to know?"

"Nothing really. I just thought that perhaps she had talked about someone called Adam."

"Oh. Like, what did she say?" The boy is holding onto the handlebars again, ready to cycle off. "I mean, maybe I can help?"

"No, that's okay," Erik says. This was perhaps not the best move. "Anyway, nice to meet you. I'd better get the boys inside."

"Sure."

Erik watches his back swerve around a corner.

"He's cool," Lukas says, awe in his voice.

"Yeah," Erik says.

Inside the day care building, the cloakroom is almost empty. Thank goodness. The boys put their backpacks away, hang up their coats and put their shoes on the rack.

"Good job," he says to them, sounding like Anna.

"There's Sophie!" exclaims Sebastian and he's off, running inside to the action, where children and teachers sing and play instruments. Lukas joins him and Erik is sure he's rolling his eyes at his brother.

He sighs with relief. He can't see Pernilla.

Back in the Volvo, he calls Linda Johansson for an update. Hopefully Tina's news has reached her fast, but she seems rushed off her feet and doesn't mention anything.

"I'm sorry," she says. "I know this is very difficult for you and your family but unfortunately we can't share information about the investigation with you. We'll be in touch."

"Trust Tina," Rob said. He hopes his mate is right.

31

Rolf

November 2015

Rolf put his heart and soul into fucking Lena. He hadn't
expected any bells or whistles but anger could apparently
be converted into the wildest passion. She really wanted to get
back at Iris.

"You're not Iris, but you're pretty good," she said, her
hair sweaty, perfectly round, fake breasts resting above a
trim stomach.

Iris's ongoing affair with Lena had endured for too long
and he emptied himself into her, marking his territory. Then
he stood to leave. He didn't ask for any hair, didn't clip one
of her nails or ask for a drop of saliva. It was a revenge fuck,
not a piece of art.

Exiting the motel room, leaving a satisfied Lena in bed, he
got into his car and called Iris.

"It's taken care of," he said.

It seemed to take a while for her to register what he meant.

"Oh, good. Thanks."

"See you later?"

"I think so."

"Have something better to do?"

"Don't start, Rolf."

It was obvious that she didn't want to change their arrangement and although that frustrated him, he couldn't blame her. He still remembered having to convince her to have an open marriage in the first place. Just because it didn't suit him anymore, he couldn't realistically expect her to flick a switch. At the same time, he didn't like taking no for an answer.

"If you change your mind, I'll be in the studio," he said.

They hung up and he started the car.

Driving out of the city, down the familiar roads to their house in the countryside, his headspace was occupied with images. Iris and that woman, together. Normally, such a sighting would have meant a heightened sexual experience for the two of them later, or at least for him when he was on his own. There were times when he would go back to his car and pleasure himself, his eyes closed, his mind on Iris and her passing partner. Not last night. He had opened the door, seen the fireplace lit up (which in itself was unusual), the glow reflected on their naked bodies. It had been a shock. He recognised that perhaps it shouldn't have been but this was their home, which meant Iris had broken the rules and that had stunned him, then momentarily mesmerised him. *I like rule-breakers.* He had silently moved closer until he had seen them. Really seen them. The tenderness, Iris's hands caressing the other woman's face, her eyes glowing with desire; the other woman tentative, fully under Iris's spell. Jealousy had hit him, quite possibly for the first time, his gut on fire, his heart bruised.

At that point he had backed out of the room, an immediate

need to block out their moans, urgently escaping. He had stayed in the studio. He had tried to paint. He had tried to drink. He had tried to listen out for that woman's car leaving.

Who was she? Her ridiculously common Volvo V70 parked in their courtyard.

He had waited. And waited. He had poured the wine down the sink, the taste bitter and off. He had grabbed the car keys and left. A need to curb his boredom had made him call Frida. She was wild and a lot of fun. The way Måna had been. Although Måna had been a one-off, he had met Frida twice already. It wasn't forbidden but it was against their set principles that Frida was single and wanted him, not only as a lover, but all out. That wasn't allowed. You couldn't "complete a transaction" under those circumstances because then you would risk hurting someone. He distinctly remembered this being Iris's one and only request. But she seemed to have rewritten the rulebook since then, so what did it matter?

He had felt a strong need to get back on the horse, so to speak, to ride someone hard. And so what if Frida wanted him? At least someone did.

32

Erik

April 2016

At the hospital, a new bunch of flowers sits on the table next to Anna.

"They arrived this morning."

The nurse's words startle him. Erik turns around, he doesn't remember her name. He should know them all by now. Should recognise their faces. At the same time, he doesn't want to get too familiar.

"Maybe they're sent out of guilt," he says.

"You think whoever put her here sent her flowers and added his or her name on the card?"

She's mocking him. He turns away. There are too many thoughts in his head, crowding his frail brain. He wants to punch something. Hard. He waits until the nurse is gone and then he packs one into Anna's mattress. Her body barely moves but he still feels guilty.

The red roses are squashed together in the vase, there are so many of them. He reaches across and reads the card.

Your husband needs me. P.

He rips it out from the bouquet. Stares at it for another second to make sure he's read it correctly. Has anyone else read it? He rips it into miniature pieces and sprinkles them into the bin. Only he gets paranoid and starts to pick them out again.

"Lose something?"

The nurse is back in the room, watching him bent over the wired basket attached to the wall.

"My ring slipped off," he says.

"Oh, dear, can I help you?"

She's already standing next to him and he blocks her by grabbing hold of the basket with both hands, pretending to retch. "I'm going to be sick."

"But your ring?"

"I'll get it…" Pretend retching. "Later."

"Let me get you something else to vomit in," she says and she's off.

He manages to get the plastic bag out from the bin and ties a knot around it in time for her to return.

"I just need some fresh air," he says and shoots out of there.

*

Erik fires up the car engine and heads back home, although "home" is a loose term these days. It's where he used to live with his wife and children. Now it feels like a temporary place. Maybe they should move? He feels like they're stuck in time. Apart from the police having moved through the house like phantoms that first day when he was still at the hospital, everything is the way Anna left it, yet she's not there. The white-and-blue furniture runs through the house like a pulsating vein about to explode in his brain. If he moves anything or paints a wall, she might get upset if she comes back home. If he doesn't change anything, he might go crazy.

Inside the house he takes his shoes off and goes straight to the laptop, which he now keeps in a kitchen cupboard. He checks the emails regularly. He has composed at least twenty more emails to Black Adam but he hasn't sent them. He has also done some research on Kent to understand him better. After their meeting, he doesn't want the guy to think he's paranoid. He wants them to be cool, which means he might need to see him again, strike up a form of friendship. Not that he could find much out about Kent. From the Internet, he has learned that Kent attends theatre premieres and council meetings from time to time and that he has worked at the same school forever. Boring stuff. They don't have much in common.

Now he looks Pernilla up. Sometimes you need to know your enemies and she's obviously got it in for him. She's extremely active on social media, which doesn't surprise him. They're not friends on Facebook but he can still view her profile. Privacy doesn't seem to bother her. There are photos of Pernilla wearing sunglasses, Pernilla dancing, Pernilla drinking shots, Pernilla with her arms wrapped around friends in bikinis. Posing, her lips kissing the camera. He lingers a bit too long. It's like porn though, once you look, you can't stop.

It's harmless voyeurism but it makes him feel he can deal with her. Eventually he forces himself away from Pernilla's photo gallery to check Anna's emails. It's become a habit, to make sure he doesn't miss anything. Her inbox still receives subscription mail but no longer messages from her personal contacts. People obviously know about her coma by now. Does Black Adam also know?

It's a tedious task, checking emails all the time, but it keeps him sane to have a routine. Today, however, he notices a new email and it's not from Black Adam. He opens it, the feeling of surprise quickly replaced by total disbelief: it's from Anna's own mother and she most definitely knows that her daughter is in hospital with only a fifty per cent chance of survival.

> Hi Anna, when you're back on your feet, I hope you will read this. Please know that I wanted to visit you but you know what your father is like. There's not much going on here. Helen's daughter is almost two now and she's such a little chatterbox. She has a real bond with her granddad and I think she has softened him somehow. Anyway, I hope the boys are well.
>
> I miss you, Mum.

Apart from being completely disgusted, Erik isn't sure whether to also be utterly pissed off or if he should laugh. *Back on your feet?*

"She doesn't have flu, Gerda."

He feels a sudden loyalty to Anna, the way he used to when they first started dating, the two of them conquering the world.

"Just stay where you are," he says to the email. "That makes my life easier."

He feels angry and unsettled. What he would give to let

rip on his guitar with the band. Lately, they have excluded him from any jamming sessions. At first, it felt respectful but now it's infuriating. He's even heard rumours about some guy replacing him. He picks up the phone and calls Rob.

"Any gigs coming up?" he asks. No point wrapping it in cotton wool.

"Ehm, no."

"Are you jamming?"

"We know you're busy, Erik."

"Don't shut me out, I need to play." He realises he sounds too desperate but the words are flowing. "Come on, Rob. Please. It's the one thing I'm..."

No, he stops himself. He can't say it. *The one thing I'm good at.* He needs to sound less whiny. There's no need to alienate Rob. He needs his friend and music buddy.

"Did you speak to Tina?" he asks instead. "Did she deliver the information about Anna?"

"She's here," Rob says cheerfully.

"Really, you're what, back together?" That's a shocker. Erik has a bad feeling about it.

"Yeah, sort of," Rob says.

Thinking about it, Erik isn't sure he cares. Having Tina even closer might be good. He still has to ask: "I thought you said it was too much drama?"

There's giggling in the background and absentmindedly, Erik logs into his new email account. This is another routine. He does it every day, sometimes several times: opens and closes the inbox. Occasionally he receives emails about money he is supposed to have won or about penis extensions, the usual junk.

Rob resurfaces. "It's all good," he says. "Why don't you come over and meet her?"

"Wait…"

There's an email from Black Adam.

"I'll talk to you later, Rob."

Excited but nervous, he puts the phone down and opens the email.

Hi there, thank you for caring (whoever you are). I loved Anna. I still love her. Whatever I can do, please tell me. I will do anything.

Anything?

"How about revealing who you really are?"

And he "loved" her? Was it really a student? Erik had assumed so because of the mention of a test but perhaps it had been a different type of test? The thought makes his muscles tense.

Then he gets an idea.

Thank you. That's very kind of you. Do you know Xeroxwed?

If he doesn't get a response, then it's possible that Black Adam and Xeroxwed are one and the same. He's searched for emails that Anna might have sent to this Xeroxwed but hasn't found any. Maybe she deleted them. Or did she not reply at all?

It's such a mess. He rests his head in his hands, closes his eyes and wishes he were somewhere else, the emotions tearing him in different directions. Nothing means anything.

But then again, anything means something. Like a Rubik's cube, he twists and turns, hoping it will all come together. He needs to get everything back to normal.

33

Anna

November 2015

The road lay deserted in front of Anna as her old running shoes hit the asphalted pavement. The air was chilly and her lungs sore. Her body already wanted to give up but she kept going. The aim: to eliminate intrusive thoughts. Thinking would mean taking responsibility for her actions. It would mean entering reality where she was a wife and a mother and... a lesbian?

She stumbled, a tree root protruding through the cracked tarmac, briefly making her think of marriage. She shook her head at the absurdity and kept putting one foot in front of the other. Moving forward.

What had she done?

As she ran past the closed-down flower shop, the memory of Iris's feminine scent hit her, strong and sensual. That feeling of longing wrapping its arms around her chest. Desire.

Her run slowed to a walk. It wasn't just the way Iris smelt or how safe she made Anna feel, there seemed to be invisible ties pulling them close. They were so strong they scared her.

Her sex had been entrusted to Iris whose fingers had been soft but firm. Anna recognised that she had reciprocated, the arousal making her brave. All the way home, she had lifted her right hand from the steering wheel to smell her fingers, to remind herself of what had actually happened.

She picked up her pace again. Her heart was aching. Never in her life had she imagined doing what she had done. It had just felt so natural, like something she couldn't have stopped from happening. But she had cheated on Erik.

She ran faster.

The darkness closed in on her. Only a few lights were on in the town's houses. Most people were asleep. Her feet moved forward while her brain raced at an even faster speed. She ran past the small supermarket that was now closed, signalling that everything had shut down for the day. It was like a ghost town, eerily quiet without the sound of traffic.

Then a car came from behind. She could hear its wheels slowing down and braced herself, waiting for it to pass. Out of the corner of her eye, she noticed a dented bumper and paint peeling off. The car didn't pass by, instead it stopped and a dirty window was rolled down.

"Excuse me, is there a petrol station around here?"

A man in his fifties or sixties, sporting a moustache. A familiar face that she couldn't quite place. A student's parent?

"You need to turn around and go back," she said. "Then take the first road to your right. About fifty metres down you'll find a self-service station."

She started running again, feeling vulnerable. Most likely she was being paranoid but she wanted to keep moving. The car followed her and soon it was level with her again.

"Do you live around here?"

The question was unnerving and so she ignored him. She kept looking straight ahead as her feet ran forward but he kept driving next to her. Why hadn't she brought her phone? Her heart was beating double beats. Could she cut through the bushes to her right or run into someone's garden and ring a doorbell? While she was debating what to do, he sped off.

Had he really left? She waited for him to turn around and head towards the petrol station but instead he drove straight ahead as if exiting the town.

After a hundred metres or so, she stopped, out of breath. She looked over her shoulder but there was no one there. Yet she couldn't shake the feeling of unease and pushed herself to keep running no matter how much her throat hurt.

When she returned home, she needed a few minutes in the hallway to digest what had just happened. Was it just a weirdo trying his luck? She wanted to tell Erik about the man and the car but he was engrossed in an action movie and barely looked up. She hesitated for a moment, hoping he would turn to her and ask about her run. He didn't and so she decided not to bother him. He would probably tell her she was paranoid anyway.

In the bathroom, she undressed. Her pulse slowed down and she felt calmer, her focus now elsewhere: on Iris and their night together. Her fingers tracing Anna's curves, making her feel beautiful.

Anna viewed herself in the mirror. Her body felt different, it felt new. Her skin was glowing instead of looking loose and flabby and her breasts appeared shapely as opposed to sagging. As she stepped into the shower, hot water warming her up, she closed her eyes and stroked her arms, her hips, her waist, the same way Iris had done. She transported herself to Iris's living room, imagining her fingers were Iris's, following the line of her breasts and belly, down between her legs. Opening her eyes with a jolt, guilt overshadowed the sensation of lust: could she really see Iris again?

Then again, how could she not?

34

Rolf

November 2015

Frida's moody kid had just arrived home and Rolf wanted to smash his head in. The way he spoke to Frida was completely unacceptable. Except he didn't want to get involved. As soon as Dan slammed his door shut, Rolf got out of Frida's bed to dress.

"See you soon, lover boy," Frida said.

Her limbs were spread out on the flimsy duvet cover, her long, blonde hair floating around her head. She resembled an angel but she sure as hell wasn't one. He knew all about her financial difficulties as well as the liquor induced ones. It didn't worry him. She had never asked him for a single krona – he actually thought she genuinely wanted him to love her – and the booze… well, it made her one hell of a spirited lay, so no complaints there.

"Not sure when," he said because he worried that perhaps it was becoming a bit too regular.

The feeling of being with a woman who was in love with him was attractive and gave him comfort, but he wasn't going to throw his marriage away. Iris was his. At home, he had a rare painting with actual human blood in it, his and Iris's. The red blotches he had managed to squeeze out of their fingers on their wedding day had quickly dried to a dark brown on the canvas, but it served as a reminder of their eternal union.

Rolf left Frida's converted summerhouse and drove through Mörna. It was completely deserted, as most small towns after ten o'clock tended to be. That's why he was surprised to see a woman jogging along the pavement. It was always worth slowing down, especially when a woman was alone.

He rolled down his window and asked for a petrol station even though his tank was almost full. When she leaned down and peered at him, he couldn't come up with another single line. It was *her*. The woman who had screwed his wife on the Turkish rug in his living room. She gave him some directions to which he didn't listen and then she kept running. He couldn't just let her go and so he followed her. Did she live around here, a town that was only twenty minutes from his and Iris's home? He had to know if this woman, who made his wife irresponsible, lived so treacherously close to them. And perhaps not too tactfully, he asked her this directly.

"Do you live around here?"

She ignored him and he had no choice but to drive off and leave her and his resentment behind. He had to go home and reclaim his wife.

35

Anna

December 2015

The temperature had dropped below zero and the road was perilously icy, but Anna had to see Iris. She drove carefully to the library, and by the time she got there, it was almost closing time. She hurried inside and walked towards the counter, where Iris normally was; her heart racing, nerves and excitement making it difficult to concentrate.

Just then, Iris appeared from the back although she didn't seem to show any signs of recognition and that made Anna even more nervous. When Iris reached her, Anna had no idea what to say but Iris beat her to it.

"It's not Wednesday," she said, eyeing Anna over the reading glasses. "Did you finish the book already?"

The book? She couldn't remember what it was called. Had Iris even given her a new one?

"Jodi Picoult?" Iris clarified. "*Sing You Home?*"

Now she remembered. She had agreed to read a book in English, since the book was yet to be translated into Swedish.

"I haven't started it," she said truthfully.

Of course, she should have. She was at a library, meeting her librarian. Whether it was book club or not, she should be there because of books.

Disappointed, she made to leave. In the time they had been apart, she had obviously attached more importance to each and every little word that had been said in Iris's house, every touch, every moan. She had got it all wrong.

As she opened the door, the sky heavy with snow, she heard Iris's voice behind her.

"Wait."

Anna took a deep breath and turned back to face Iris, bracing herself for her words: "I think you misunderstood", "it was a mistake" or "it can't happen again".

"Why don't you make some coffee while I lock up?"

It was impossible to interpret Iris's gaze but a sense of relief still established itself in Anna's heart, making it lighter.

"Are you sure?" she asked.

"Yes. I'll just be a minute."

Anna walked through the familiar library, hoping everyone had already left so that they could be alone. No matter what was to come.

*

When Iris finally entered the kitchen, Anna was leaning on the counter, waiting for the coffee to brew. They faced each other and although Anna had spent the last ten minutes telling herself that she had no expectations, the moment she saw Iris, her sleek black jersey dress and silver bangles, she realised that she did.

Iris opened her mouth. "I..." she started and in sheer panic, Anna took a step forward, reached her arms out and pulled

Iris towards her, resting her chin on her shoulder blade. She closed her eyes and felt the softness of Iris's velvety dark hair, the droopy earrings shaped like black rain drops cold against her face, arms plaited into a tight embrace.

Then Iris pulled away. She was still holding onto Anna's arms as she raised her head. She had removed the glasses, her green eyes deep and naked. Butterfly wings touched the delicate lining of Anna's stomach. Iris parted her lips slightly, as if to say something, but instead she leaned forward and kissed Anna.

Iris's tongue was warm and eager and Anna's insecurities vanished, confusion laid to rest. Iris clearly wanted her. With her hands firmly on Iris's waist, she pulled her close. Anna could feel Iris's fingers stroking her back, nestling their way in between the lining of her skirt and her jumper, touching the bare skin. More. She wanted more. She wanted to feel Iris's hands all over. Should she remove her clothes? Or undress Iris? Her inexperienced hands pulled at Iris's dress when she took Anna's hands in hers and whispered: "Slowly".

"Sorry, I just…"

Iris's lips silenced her, the soothing sensation making her close her eyes and hand herself over. She leaned backwards and hit something hard. Turning her head around, she realised it was the photocopier.

"It's okay," Iris said. "It won't break."

From the moment they had met, Iris had been in charge and it was comforting in a way. Anna would go with the flow and not force it. At least there was no rushed kneading of the breasts and wham-bam-thank-you-maam, as was the case with Erik these days. Iris seemed to treasure every part of Anna's body, her hands gliding over her waist, her bottom, her hips. Lips nuzzled Anna's neck, kissing it tenderly. Through her clothes, Anna felt the outline of Iris's small round breasts, the hard nipples pressed against her body.

"Spread your legs," Iris commanded.

Without hesitation, Anna moved her feet, sensing the vacuum between her thighs as they parted, filled with feverish anticipation. Iris intimately touched her belly button, caressing the soft skin on Anna's stomach, taking her time before gently nudging the skirt down. Her hand slipped inside the lining of Anna's carefully chosen black lace knickers, softly stroking the pubic hair before moving further down.

Their eyes exchanged a silent agreement, saying this was okay. This was good. This was better than good. Anna nodded her approval and Iris was on her knees, caressing the inside of Anna's thighs, her lips soft between her legs. Still leaning against the photocopier, Anna rested her hands on Iris's head, wrapping the short hairs around her index fingers, enjoying the sensation of Iris making her way inside of her. Anna groaned as Iris's tongue and fingers expertly tipped her over the edge.

Afterwards, even though Iris had done all the work, Anna felt exhausted as she slid onto the floor. She held Iris's face in her hands and kissed her hard.

"Thank you," she said. She really meant it.

"You have amazing breasts," Iris said and burrowed her nose in Anna's cleavage.

Anna felt euphoric but also unexpectedly shy: she wanted to make Iris feel equally ecstatic but didn't know how to start. As if sensing this, Iris took Anna's hands in hers, showing her the way, under the hem of her dress. Anna's fingers fumbled but she learned to follow Iris's moans and used them as a guide. Her confidence growing, Anna leaned down and pressed her lips against Iris's sex. A taste of earth on her tongue, in her mouth. Iris came fast, a rattling in her throat confirming her climax, bringing on an even deeper satisfaction than Anna's own orgasm had.

Later, when they were lying on the floor together, Anna leaning her head on Iris's outstretched arm, Anna's mobile started to ring. Dull signals vibrated in her bag, reminding her that there was a world out there. She shuffled across the floor and fished out her phone.

Erik's name appeared on the screen. "When will you be home?" His voice sounded tired.

"Not sure... eh, in an hour?"

"Sebastian won't go to sleep. He wants you."

She sat up, her mummy autopilot on. "Is he okay?"

"I think he might have a fever."

"Might have? Did you check?"

Iris moved behind her and Anna stopped herself. She had no right to be upset with Erik even though he clearly should have checked Sebastian's temperature.

"I'm on my way," she said instead.

After she put her phone back, she turned to Iris.

"You have to go," Iris said simply.

Anna nodded. "I'm sorry." She hurriedly got dressed.

"Before you go..." Iris said, the words trailing off as her mouth met Anna's, the kiss deep. Anna's steps were unsteady as she backed away, reeling.

"I'll be back next week," she promised.

36

Iris

December 2015

Iris wanted Anna. Not just for a few hours or a day. She wanted her for an entire week, a month or more. To discover each other and to talk and make love. Anna was so pure, so inexperienced and sweet, yet also intelligent and passionate. There was so much she wanted to teach her, the way she had once been taught. A holiday together would be incredible.

Iris had only ever taken a woman on holiday once before. Rolf had thought she was scouring the stands of a foreign book fair when in actual fact she had been walking down the streets of Berlin, hand in hand with a woman. They had enjoyed art museums, bratwursts, beer, an operetta and sex shops in between long sessions in their hotel room. It had been love.

Back home, however, the woman had chosen her husband and had ended the relationship. From then on, Iris had never disclosed any of her affairs to Rolf. It was as if she had crossed a forbidden bridge that had then collapsed behind her. There was no way of going back.

Iris realised that Anna had a life. A life that she would most likely go back to after she had experimented with Iris. A holiday would perhaps be too much to ask for? Also, Anna had children.

Iris had never planned to have any. She had been on the pill when she accidentally fell pregnant. Rolf had wanted a child, a protégée of sorts. Now, she couldn't imagine her life without Karin but at the time it had brought up too many bad memories: the pregnancy at sixteen and the miscarriage, which had turned out to be a blessing in disguise since her mother had refused the abortion, but traumatising nonetheless. Just thinking about it put her on edge. Her mother would have preferred to throw her out on the street than be humiliated. The fact that Iris later wanted a university degree hadn't gone down well either, but thankfully university was free and didn't require her parents' consent. She had been a very different type of mother to Karin. She encouraged her to dream big.

Rolf's advice would have been to end it with Anna immediately. *If you start to invest your heart, pull out.* But she couldn't end it. Anna was unique. Rolf would have laughed at that. *What a cliché!* She had to smile. It was perhaps ridiculous but, with or without children, she was determined to have Anna. And, she thought, if that meant losing Rolf, then it had been a long time coming and would be worth the sacrifice.

Anna had a different life, with children and a husband and an important job. She wasn't like Lena, rich and bored, seeking excitement wherever she could find it. Anna was a good person and sooner or later she would have to make a choice. A good girl's choice. How could Iris convince Anna that this was real, that she was worth it?

37

Daniel

December 2015

Dan recognised the dude's car as soon as he arrived back home. An old and bashed-up Nissan was parked dangerously close to the row of leaning trees by their driveway. What if one of them fell on his car? That would be funny. With that awful car, the dude obviously wouldn't be bringing them money anyway. It didn't matter. He kept Frida busy and that wasn't so bad. Dan couldn't stand it when Frida turned needy. *Sit on my lap, Danny boy. Bring me a beer, will you? Let me hug you. Just for a second.*

He went straight to his room. Frida's car was still in the shop since she couldn't afford the repairs and the moped next door hadn't been parked in its normal spot for three days. He had taken a chance and had waited for Anna outside the school building on his bike but both afternoons she had walked to her car with Kent. The guy was creepy. Dan had tried to cycle after her but she hadn't headed straight home. Maybe she had gone food shopping or to visit friends? It was possible. He didn't know much about her life. At least not yet. They needed something to talk about over Sunday dinners.

It was almost five o'clock and Anna would be leaving school soon. Perhaps he could borrow the dude's car? With an ear to the wall, Dan tried to listen to any sounds. Were they fucking? He could hear voices. Perhaps it was some sort of foreplay? He sneaked out to the living room to see if the keys were there. He looked through the pockets of a worn leather jacket but apart from chewing gum wrappers they were empty.

He went outside. You never knew, maybe the dumb fuck had left the keys in the ignition? It was a pretty safe area where people were known to leave their houses unlocked. Nope, not there either.

Back inside, he grabbed a snack. Cheese crackers without cheese. That fucking summed up his life. He sat down and poured himself a Coke Zero (Frida lived on the stuff, usually mixed with vodka of course).

That's when he saw the dude's jeans, thrown over the side of the couch. They had obviously started out here. Not as eager as last time then, when they hadn't even made it to the bedroom.

The car key was in the pocket.

*

Dan swerved into the school parking lot. Anna's Volvo was there. Score! He parked on the other side, behind a bus. Out of sight. Then he waited. Every now and then he would check her status on WhatsApp. Had she been online recently? She rarely was but he had nothing better to do. He didn't want to contact her via WhatsApp anyway. He preferred to send emails from a nondescript email address. Although she had only responded to a couple of his initial emails, then she had stopped. That needed to change. He needed to make her listen.

Black Adam wanted to rule the world and, like his super-hero, Dan had been patient. He might not have spent five thousand years travelling to earth, but he had waited three whole days and this was his chance. Together with his superpower: a trashy old car. He laughed because it was kind of crazy. But according to some ancient writer, all was fair in love and war. Anna would be pleased if she knew that he listened during her classes.

After about half an hour, she emerged from the school building (alone!) and started walking towards her car. He waited a few seconds before he followed her.

38

Anna

December 2015

Daniel had stopped leaving Anna notes, which was just as well, since she had started to discard his handwritten scribbles. She did not want to be caught in a compromising position. Except now he had turned to email, and the ease of sending an email, compared to delivering a note into the teachers' lounge, meant the volume of messages had risen considerably. His email address was blackadam4321@hotmail. com and curiosity won her over. She emailed him back asking about the name. Perhaps she would better understand him if she asked questions he could actually answer.

Hi Anna, he was someone bad who turned out to be good.

Every email started that same way. Hi Anna. He not only loved saying her name, he loved writing it.

Hi Anna, I need someone who listens to me.

She sighed. It wasn't an unrealistic request. Once again, she tried to direct him to a counsellor but that only angered him.

Hi Anna, I don't need a fucking professional. I need you. I want to live with you. I need a family.

She deleted the message immediately, even going as far as emptying it from the trash folder. It was better to pretend he hadn't written that, but still, he kept writing.

Hi Anna, I'm sick of this. How about the basement?

The basement? Even if he knew her address, he would have had to see her house to know she had a basement. It was unsettling and she debated whether she should go as far as to report this. But once again she reasoned that he needed her help, not authorities treating him like a criminal.

She shut down the emails and switched to Google. After much hesitation, she keyed in l followed by e s b i a n. It had happened twice, sex with Iris, and she needed to understand.

On the screen, a number of words flashed at her like a red-light district: lesbians, fuck, porn, sex novels. She had the urge to erase them, wanting to resist their harshness. They didn't represent her experience. She added the keyword l o v e. It looked oddly surreal on the screen but she clicked "Search".

Sexual how-to books and pages and pages about lesbian women's sexual habits stared at her, as if to say: is this what you need? It wasn't.

She had never been with a woman before, so why did she feel this way? Would she be forced to make a choice? Leave

Erik and be with Iris? How would that affect the boys? Would they hate her? Would Iris even want to be with her so permanently? She too was married.

She longed for Kent's straightforward advice but there was no way she could confide in him.

She examined the options on the screen again, then changed the search. Sex wasn't the goal, only a consequence. In Google, she added the words y o u n g e r and o l d e r. News about discrimination against lesbians and reading tips about forbidden and unrequited love in black and white. A sign?

She really wanted to talk to someone and speaking to Iris about what had just happened felt like ruining the magic. To Iris everything seemed so simple and obvious.

What would her friends from university say if she told them? *I've slept with a woman.* Most likely, every single one of them would feel the need to share such yummy gossip. This wasn't just any news, it was dynamite. She couldn't take that risk. Anyway, how could she expect someone else to understand when she didn't even understand it herself?

Her mobile notified her of a message and she picked it up, both dreading and hoping that it was a message from Iris.

It was from Kent.

Didn't see you today. Daniel's last school called.
Please call Maria Bergman.

The woman's contact details popped up on her screen.

Daniel. A headache came on. Reality had a way of penetrating her fantasy world. Except Iris wasn't a fantasy. She was real.

At least the school had finally called.

*

Maria Bergman sounded strict. That was a good sign. It would mean no nonsense and Anna liked that.

"I was Daniel's humanities teacher," Maria Bergman explained. "The principal told me you had enquired about him."

"That's right. I just..." Where to start? "I'm worried about him."

"Really, why? Has something happened?" Maria Bergman asked but Anna didn't pick up on any real concern in her tone.

"Well, a few things," she said. "He likes fighting a bit too much, as I'm sure you know."

She tried to laugh but it sounded stiff.

"Fighting? The Daniel I taught was always sitting quietly at the back of the classroom. Clever boy though, always did well in exams."

Now it was Anna's turn to be puzzled.

"Daniel Persson? Tall, blond, could do with a haircut and seems to have a dislike for tying his shoelaces."

"Yes, sounds about right. And you said he's getting into fights? Are the other students picking on him?"

"Not exactly. It's more... the other way around."

Maria Bergman was quiet, as if she pondered this. "That sounds odd. I mean, he's had it tough. His brother was known for getting into trouble with the law and his mother... well, she drank apparently."

"Are you sure about that?" Anna asked. "About his mother? I'm only asking because I've been to his house and didn't see any signs of that."

"Well, that was the rumour."

Rumour? Anna felt she needed to push this teacher a bit more. "Did you find out for sure?"

"No, I didn't..." She sighed. "Look, I have many students."

Didn't they all? Anna was speechless.

"I wish you the best of luck," Maria Bergman said, sounding as if she had had enough. "I wouldn't want him getting into trouble."

"Why not?" Anna quickly added: "I mean, did you become attached to him?"

"He made no trouble for me. Always love students like that, don't you?"

I love all my students, Anna wanted to say, but for an easy way out, she said: "Sure."

She wanted to get off this call. This woman clearly didn't know the Daniel she knew. Whether that was good or not, she wasn't sure. Something had made him change though and she couldn't quite figure out what.

*

Anna wanted to see Iris. It was more than an escape, she was that friend she had missed, someone to talk to. So far, Anna hadn't spoken about work but perhaps it was time to open up. Knowing the library closed early on Tuesdays, Anna hurried out of the school building.

It was just past five o'clock and the roads were busy with people heading home from work. That was probably why she didn't notice the car behind her, at least not until she was about to turn into Hågarp. She had to look twice to realise it was the same sedan that had stopped her when she was jogging. Was it a coincidence?

She looked in the rear-view mirror to catch sight of the driver. Did the guy have a moustache? It was too dark and therefore impossible to make him out but it was such a wreck of a car (with the bumper knocked, paint coming off) that surely there couldn't be two of the same?

She turned into Hågarp as planned but instead of going straight to the library, she turned right. The car behind her also turned right. She turned left and drove down a residential street. Again, the car behind her went down the same road. Why was he following her? She stopped her car and got out, feeling safe amongst all the houses, ready to confront him.

He drove past her, an arm in front of his face, clearly wanting to shield himself from her. It was odd. Who was he? She got in her car again and drove back to the road she had come from but he was soon on her tail again. That's it, she thought, I have to lose him. She drove up and down, turning left and right, then she exited Hågarp and drove to the next town, where she did the same manoeuvre: up and down the streets, oblivious to parents and children in ski suits building poor snowmen from the wet snow about to melt away. Finally, she noticed he was gone. She was on her own and she could drive back to the library. Except by the time she arrived, it was too late. The door was locked and Iris most likely already at home. With her husband.

39

Rolf

January 2016

Christmas was over.

"Thank fucking goodness for that!"

Rolf had always hated traditions. Iris went through the motions every year for Karin's sake but even Karin had felt that the last Christmas had been lame. She had kept asking her mother if she was okay and Rolf had whispered in Iris's ear: "Missing your fuck buddy?"

She hadn't taken the bait. That was the most unnerving thing about his wife. She could ride any argument out through silence, her eyes calm but serious, her back straight, her lips always perfectly painted.

"Someone seems to have forgotten about our rules," he said through clenched teeth. "No one comes between us."

She stared at him, looking fascinated by his outburst.

"How many women have *you* fucked through the years?" she asked.

She rarely used the f-word but he didn't let that throw him off.

"A gentleman doesn't count," he said.

"Well, I have never butted into your affairs," she said. "So stay out of mine."

Then she walked off. He resented arguing with her. The whole situation was frustrating. There had been limited action in the bedroom. Needless to say, it hadn't been enough. He had seen Frida a couple of times. She was Iris's polar opposite, screaming and threatening him but also fucking him with a heated passion. He knew it would end, but he needed her. At least for the time being. There was no pretence with her. She turned herself inside out, she was raw and vulnerable and real.

"I also hate Christmas," Frida said.

They were still lying in bed.

"That's because you make no fucking effort," the kid shouted.

"Stop eavesdropping!"

"Where's his father?" Rolf asked. Couldn't he buzz off to his dad for a couple of weeks?

The sun was up, causing water to drip from the icicles by the window. Rolf should be heading home.

"I don't know," she said. "He ran off and I've never heard from him since."

To be fair, the kid had been away a lot. Rolf wasn't sure where he spent his time, with friends most likely, but it was a bloody godsend when he wasn't there. He was negative energy.

"He's writing a book," Frida whispered in his ear.

"Oh, really. What's it about?"

"Some girl. I think he's in love. I don't know."

This was good news. That was obviously who he was spending his time with.

"Have you met her?" he asked.

That seemed to crack her up: "Do you honestly think he would bring her home to meet me?"

"But aren't you curious about who she is, what she looks like?" If she's got firm breasts, a thin waist, long hair?

"I've looked for photos but I couldn't find any. He's only got photos of his teacher, printouts from the Internet, loads of them. I think he's kind of obsessed with her."

Ha. The older woman crush. "Maybe that's who he's in love with?"

She shook her head. "I've met her and I don't think so. She's not exactly.... I mean, she's kind of average looking, plus she's like my age."

She pulled out a folded A4 from her side table, opened it and smoothed out the creases.

"Judge for yourself."

He sat up. "That's his teacher?"

She nodded. "Why? Is she an axe murderer or something?" Her laugh was raspy.

He shook his head. "Hopefully not." But it's *her*, he thought. Again. He got up. "I have to go."

Her lips pouted: "Already?"

"Gotta love you and leave you," he joked.

"You love me?"

Oh, shit. He looked at her, weighed his words. He needed her now, more than ever. In fact, he needed the kid.

"Sure," he said.

40

Daniel

January 2016

Thankfully, Frida's latest dude hadn't realised that Dan had used his car. If he had, he hadn't said anything. The problem was, Anna had realised she was being followed so after that fiasco he needed to find another way.

A couple of weeks later, the moped next door had been replaced by a new one, quite possibly a Christmas present, judging by how spoilt those children were. It was perfect and if there was such a thing as a God, he was smiling at Dan right now, as he got down on his knees to hotwire it.

He wasn't likely to get caught by the police in a small town like this; he had never seen a single patrol car circulate Mörna, so he felt confident. This time he was going to corner Anna and talk some sense into her. She needed to understand that she couldn't turn her back on him, a young man in need, that he craved the stability of her home, her love and care, even her firm hand at times. She would see this, one way or another.

Dan stationed himself behind the school gym, at the outskirts of the school area next to the parking lot, and waited for Anna to emerge. He prayed that she would have ditched the creep and that she would be alone. She wasn't and he cursed silently. Kent and Anna strolled down past the basketball court, appearing to have a serious conversation. What were they talking about? Did they discuss Dan? His letters and emails? He bloody hoped not. He needed to trust Anna.

As luck would have it, Kent left before her. Anna stayed in her car, her head bowed down (over a phone maybe?) as Dan waited. If she were headed home, he would catch her in the garage and if she was going elsewhere, he would talk to her there, wherever it was.

When Anna drove out of the parking lot, he followed her at a distance. She turned right and then right again, heading out of town, the same direction as the other day. Although the moped had been suped, it still couldn't quite keep up. At least Dan had an idea of where she was heading this time. He was going to drive up and down every street in the two towns she had been to the last time if he had to. He was as determined as determined could be.

Was she going to someone's house or a shop? He felt like a secret agent, sweeping the assigned territory for Anna's car. Every now and then he stopped and looked for her. Many times, he felt furious; stuck in new housing areas with slow-growing hedges and white flagpoles. How could she just go off like that? Vanish into nothing? Yet he couldn't give up. This was quite possibly the only time he would be able to use the moped. If they realised the petrol tank was low, they would most likely lock it up.

So he kept going. He needed to live with her, to get away

from Frida without ending up in some fucking foster care or youth facility.

"It's just one more year," Martin had said. "Then we'll get a place together."

Martin had said that right before he ended up in prison. He would be out soon, but while Martin had been away, Dan had worked a few things out: his brother was caring but he wasn't the brightest, he would keep breaking and entering rather than getting a nine-to-five job. He surrounded himself with losers. "Only because no one else will have me," he had said. It was a pretty lame excuse. Dan wanted "normal". Before it was too late, he wanted what he deserved: rights. Anna was his and he was going to prove to her how true that was.

He decided to plead with her, cry if he had to.

Renewed with energy, he kept going. Luckily, there was still plenty of petrol in the tank. Another five minutes went past, ten, twenty. He couldn't stop. His life depended on this one night.

About thirty minutes later he found her car.

"Yes!" he shouted, his arms in the air. "Victory!"

The car was parked outside a red brick building. A library, apparently. He walked up the steps and pulled at the door but it was locked. He looked around. Where else could she have gone?

There was an old post office next door that still had the post office sign hanging outside but was clearly converted into a home. White crocheted curtains decorated the windows. He liked that. It was homely.

He walked around the library building. A light was on in one of the windows at the back. Was she there? Maybe some sort of a meeting? A séance or a Bible study group or a book circle. The last one obviously made the most sense.

He walked up to the door, a brown wooden one with a heavy handle. Should he try to open it? Or knock? He hesitated. What would she say if she was actually in there? She would think he was crazy. He pulled his hand back. He needed to see what was going on through the window first. How many were they? The parking lot only had two cars in it so he suspected there weren't many of them but people could have walked or cycled there. There was a bike parked up front.

He walked over to a lamppost and climbed onto the rock wall behind it. From there, he had a pretty good view. There was Anna and another woman. They were talking. Could he interrupt them? She would know he had followed her and that would look bad. There was no good explanation why he had accidentally ended up by the back door of a library in the next town, was there? Maybe he should wait until her meeting was over and corner her then?

He was about to jump down from his viewing spot when something changed. The woman leaned forward and... kissed Anna? He strained his eyes to see better. Had he been mistaken? But no, Anna was kissing the woman back. Not just a friendly kiss. A full-on snog. Both jealousy and excitement hit him like a force. How could this be happening? He imagined Anna's arms wrapped around him instead, her soft hair against his face.

Then he emerged from the dream. This was a fucking pain in the arse. A mega-bump in his road to happiness. He started laughing. This was ridiculous. How could someone as innocent as Anna end up in the claws of some woman?

Ah. That's when he saw it: *the opportunity*. Now she would have no choice but to move him in. If he had to blackmail her, then so be it. He could totally do that.

41

Erik

April 2016

Black Adam is now corresponding with Erik. He is extremely direct and he causes Erik some concern:

Who the fuck is Xeroxwed? You know, you should get out every now and then, let someone babysit the children. Take care of yourself.

It is signed **someone who cares**. Erik isn't sure if that is supposed to be sarcasm? Is he making fun of Erik's first email, which was signed in that same way? And how does he know they have children? That's a worry. He is debating whether this is worth pursuing but then he thinks about Tina.

He met her at Rob's and she wasn't exactly what he had expected. Just like Rob had said, she was a whole lot of big hair. When she leaned in to hug him, she smelt of spearmint chewing gum and strong perfume. She wore gold bracelets and many rings and had an excess of make-up. He couldn't imagine her patrolling the streets, dealing with criminals or even working on a high-level investigation. Then again, one shouldn't judge.

"So, what's your role at the police station?" he asked, his thoughts becoming unprocessed words.

She looked surprised. "I'm a police woman," she said, while tickling and kissing Rob, which was distracting.

"Did you, eh, tell the team about… you know, that Anna might have cheated?"

This was hard.

"Yes, of course," she said.

Oh, great. He felt lighter. "Is it being taken seriously?"

"Totally."

Her hands were under Rob's shirt, her long nails scratching his back. He purred like a kitten. Erik had never seen him this ridiculous before.

"Right," he said. "So are they looking into it?"

"I can't really tell you that."

He needed more information. Flattery? That usually worked.

"You must be really good at your job." Too much? "I mean, your job must be fascinating."

"Oh, it is!"

That got her going. She told them about a murder investigation in the city, the "slippery eel" suspect, an mc gang bust where stacks of money and guns were found, and the large supermarket fire that had featured in the papers recently.

"It could be arson," she said.

"Should you really be telling us this?" Erik asked. "Isn't that, like, classified information?"

"I completely trust you," she said, an offended look on her face. "You won't tell anyone, will you? I know Robbie won't."

A smile and a shower of kisses on Rob's blushing cheeks.

"Of course not," Erik said. *But what are you telling people about Anna's case?*

He felt nervous and no reassurance from Rob could make him feel at peace.

"She won't talk about your case," Rob said later on the phone.

"You don't know that. You heard her, she was telling us way too much. Inside stuff."

"Come on, don't be like that. She's helped you, hasn't she?"

"I know."

Yet he can't stop feeling anxious, which is why he needs to keep the correspondence with Black Adam up. He needs alternatives. He writes:

Thanks for the concern. I will take that into consideration. Were you Anna's student?

Right down to business. Black Adam's response is immediate:

Anna had many students. Your question should be: was I special? The answer to that would be YES. She loved me.

This annoys the hell out of Erik and he wants to send this to the police faster than fast. Instead he calms down and composes another email. He needs Black Adam to keep talking.

I'm sure she did love you. The question is, in what way? She was, and still is, married.

So far, it's been as if Black Adam is sitting by the computer, waiting for Erik's emails. But this last email is like hitting a wall. There are no more responses.

*

That evening Erik sits with the boys at the dinner table, imagining that this is going to be their life going forward. Can he do this on his own?

"Everything okay today?" he asks the boys as they tuck into the ready-made ravioli. It's been luxuriously poured from a can and heated in the microwave.

"How's Mummy?" Sebastian asks, picking at his food with a fork.

"She's getting better, I think."

Mum would give him a blasting for that one. We don't know, Erik, she would tell him.

"Really?" Lukas looks up. "When is she coming home?"

"Oh, I don't know yet. She has to rest."

Even though he wants to move, maybe they're not ready just yet. Mum has promised to help him with the mortgage if needed, so he can't use that as an excuse. Something needs to happen though.

"How would you feel about going away for a few days?"

Sebastian scrunches his face up. "And leave Mummy?" He shakes his head.

Shit. "You miss her." He says it more as a statement than a question but they both nod.

His pocket vibrates and he takes his phone out. Unknown number.

"Erik?" A vaguely familiar voice.

"Yes?"

"Linda Johansson here. We need you to come down to the police station."

Her words are abrupt which alarms him.

"Why? What's happened? Did you find the attacker?"

Or did they finally find out who Anna was sleeping with?

"We have a few questions."

His chest starts to burn. She offers no further information and he's afraid to ask. She hangs up and he has to go into the other room, dread filling him.

Shaking, he keys in Tina's number. Rob was right. She's been helpful, he shouldn't be ungrateful.

"I'm sorry to call you but I'm scared, Tina. Why do they need to see me? I haven't done anything."

Tina takes a second to catch up. "Slow down," she says. "I'm sure no one is accusing you of anything."

"But you've heard something?"

"Shit, Erik, don't do this to me. I can't..." she pauses. "They know about the baby."

"What baby?" Then he understands. "Anna was pregnant?" But they hadn't... not in months. The punch in his gut. He can't breathe.

"Anna isn't pregnant," Tina whispers down the line. "But Pernilla Arvidsson is. With your baby."

PART THREE

42

Rolf

January 2016

The kid's favourite food was kebab pizza, so Rolf had ordered two large ones. The kid could eat and Rolf needed him to open up. What were his vulnerabilities?

Rolf and Frida sat on the couch like a united team while the kid was draped over an armchair, the pizza boxes balancing on a pile of crap on the coffee table.

"What's your job?" the kid asked, drenching his first slice in garlic sauce.

Look who's talking already?

"I'm an existentialist," Rolf said. He took a small slice of pizza even though he didn't normally eat such vulgar food but he wanted them to feel like he was one of them. "I believe that we are all individuals," he explained. "And that each person is responsible for giving meaning to his or her own life."

"Are you a fucking philosopher?"

"Language…" Frida said half-heartedly, kebab meat spilling out of her mouth.

"So how do you make money?" the kid asked.

"Dan!" Frida looked horrified.

"It's fine, babe." Rolf turned to the kid. "I make money by interpreting life and making it accessible to others, or sometimes, I guess I end up doing the opposite. I love to shock people. That's the truth."

"And this turns into cash?" The kid didn't look convinced. "Your car looks kind of cheap."

Rolf started laughing. "I'm not into material things," he said. "What about you, kid. What's your purpose? What do you want out of life?"

The kid shrugged. "What's *your* fucking purpose? To be a creative loser?"

"Dan!" Frida hissed. "That's enough!"

"Leave him," Rolf said. "This is a good conversation."

The kid actually smiled, which was a huge step.

"You know, I had a great teacher at school," Rolf said, now that they were getting somewhere. "She helped me find my purpose. That one person changed my life. For once, someone believed in me."

He studied the kid's frozen smile, trying to interpret what was going through his young cranium. The kid didn't give anything away; he simply wiped his mouth with the back of his hand and drank his Coke.

"School is good that way," Rolf continued. "The special teachers stay with you for the rest of your life."

"Please don't." Frida seemed to cotton on. "Rolf, don't." She pulled at his shirt but he yanked his arm back. Why did she have to spoil it?

"Just having a conversation about life, babe."

The teacher's name was Anna. Frida had been helpful but her knowledge didn't stretch very far. He needed more.

"Have any teachers like that?" Rolf asked.

The kid looked down, shook his head and put the rest of his slice away. He stood up. "Thanks for the pizza." And then he was out the door.

"Leave him alone," Frida begged. "He hasn't done anything."

Rolf smiled and grabbed hold of her arm, twisting it upwards. "If I leave him alone, I will also leave you alone."

"I'm sorry," she said, cowering under his touch. "I'm really sorry. I'll find out more, I promise."

43

Anna

January 2016

Anna finished reading *Sing You Home*, a book about two women falling in love and wanting a baby. She wondered if Iris was trying to send her a message. Perhaps not the baby part, even though she clearly loved her daughter, but the two women, one a lesbian and the other one previously married to a man, had fallen in love.

Was it love?

She had only just come to terms with living in the moment and not put too much pressure on herself.

"So what did Daniel's old teacher have to say?"

Anna looked up from her desk as Kent handed her a cup of coffee. The book slipped into her bag.

For once, Anna didn't want to talk about work. She wanted to discuss her complex feelings, the tigress trapped inside her body. She wanted to discuss the meaning of love, lust and the two combined. Was there such a thing?

Kent looked at her expectantly.

"Actually, I feel more relaxed now," Anna said, packing up

the remainder of her belongings: pens and papers, her laptop and phone. "He was apparently quiet and fairly studious at his last school."

"Oh." Kent sat down, making himself comfortable. "That's odd. Isn't it?"

She glanced at her watch. Book club started at seven but she wanted to have dinner with the children at home first. At least, she assumed there would be book club. There had been no messages from Iris.

"Ehm," she said. She looked at Kent, focused on his blue eyes. He was always there for her; she needed to be more generous with her time. "It's probably just a case of him struggling to fit in. I mean, this place is so homogenous."

Kent nodded.

"Maybe."

"I'm sure he will calm down," she rattled on. "At least now I know that he wasn't always like this."

Kent understandably looked doubtful. She just didn't have time to discuss it right now.

*

At home, Anna was watching Erik over the dinner table. He was engrossed in his tablet, a headphone hanging loose around his neck, the other one in his ear. Instinctively, she wanted to tell him he was setting a bad example for the children but who was she to talk? *Thoughts of Iris's hands.* She closed her eyes as if to reboot and then she opened them again, thinking: *Iris is a woman, a female friend whom I am simply very close with.*

Perhaps that's all it was? There had been no time to talk the last time they had seen each other since Anna had rushed home to Sebastian. Only, he hadn't been ill. As soon as she had arrived home that night, Erik had announced he was going to Rob's.

"You're using your own son to make me come home?" she had asked.

"I need to rehearse," he had said. "Not that you would know that."

He had been upset because she had missed his last gig.

"We didn't have a babysitter that night," she had defended herself yet again.

"You could have sorted that out, if you really wanted to be there."

"Why couldn't *you* arrange the babysitting for once?"

And just like that, they had been back on the treadmill of arguments. Anna had felt she needed to hit the stop button but Erik had beaten her to it by slamming the door in her face. It didn't matter. And yet it did. This wasn't how life was supposed to be. You got married, had children, worked, spent time with friends and family. And you were happy. Weren't you?

"Found it," Erik said and gave the boys an earphone each. "What do you think?"

"They're five," she muttered. How refined did Erik think their music tastes were? She realised she was being grumpy. The look on Lukas and Sebastian's faces, bums happily dancing in their seats to the beat. They were having fun. If they weren't going to invite her to join, she would have to crash the party.

"Let me hear that," she said and stretched a hand out but neither one of them was willing to share their earphone.

She sat back, accepting the defeat but feeling left out nonetheless. A dull sound on her phone signalled that she had an email and she picked up the phone to keep herself occupied. She opened her inbox, and found a new message, not from Daniel aka Black Adam, but from a cryptic address. Her stomach tightened. Was it yet another trick? Was it another one of his personas? Apprehensively, she opened it.

I can't wait to see you this week. To be near you, to taste you. I miss you.

She stared at the screen, her mood sunnier. That could only be from one person. Reading the email address again, Xeroxwed, it made sense. Book club had initially been on a Wednesday and the photocopier she had leaned on that time in the library kitchen, Iris's tongue between her legs, was most likely a Xerox. She would check next time.

"Okay, Mummy, you can listen now."

She felt caught, and as she looked up and Sebastian gave her his headphone, she quickly switched back to being Mummy again. Her ear filled with Taylor Swift's girly voice singing 'Bad Blood'.

"It's pretty good," she admitted, humming along to *Now we've got bad blood, it used to be mad love.* She looked at Erik to see if he remembered the mad love they had once shared but he seemed distant. She danced with the boys as they did their moves and she wondered how long this innocence would last. In a few years they would surely find their parents embarrassing and boring. Time would fly by and the boys would leave. What would remain? Herself and Erik, sleeping as far away from each other as possible?

When the song ended, the boys left the table. "Can we go and play?"

"Sure," Erik said and pretended to chase them out of the kitchen.

She was about to remind them to take their plates away but she stopped herself. They needed to view her as the fun mum from time to time. She was going to say to Erik: let's put some music on the speakers so that we can both listen, but with the boys out of the room, Erik was back on his tablet, playing Candy Crush.

She stacked the dishwasher in silence and once she had switched it on, it was Sebastian and Lukas's bedtime.

The boys were in the living room, building a train set in a dinosaur park. She knelt down and picked up what she thought was a T-rex, and with a dinosaur voice, she said: "Time to go to sleep."

Unwillingly, they tore themselves away if she promised to read an entire dinosaur book, and after struggling to pronounce Carcharodontosaurus, Euoplocephalus and Deinonychus, with the children falling over with laughter, she finally tucked them in and kissed them goodnight.

"I love you. Sweet dreams."

Downstairs, she picked up her bag and her library books.

"Book club again?" Erik said back in the kitchen. "Seems a bit frequent."

She stood still for a moment and stared at him.

Hold me. Hug me. Kiss me. Tell me you love me and I will stay.

Her eyes obviously did a lousy job communicating her feelings. Erik put his feet up on one of the new chairs and kept swiping colourful candy across the screen.

"Reading keeps me sane," she said and then she left.

44

Iris

January 2016

O nce Anna sat down with her, the smell of freshly brewed coffee in the air, candles lit, Iris felt at peace. Their last meeting had been too brief. This would be different.

"So, how have you been?" Iris asked.

Anna was wearing another maxi skirt and Iris allowed herself to brush her bare feet against Anna's stockings, sliding underneath the floral fabric. A bit of human contact, that's all she wanted.

Anna seemed tense, however. "Were there ever any other members of this book club?" she asked, pulling her legs up and onto the chair.

"Oh." Iris had half expected that question. "Well, yes. Initially there were going to be two more but they dropped out. And to be honest with you... I was pleased to have you to myself."

Anna looked at her intensely. Iris wasn't sure if she was trying to assess whether she was being truthful or if she was searching for something else. Then she finally spoke: "I'm not sure I can do this."

"Right." She couldn't pretend to be unaffected. "That's unfortunate. I mean, I had anticipated that you might not, but I…"

She took the reading glasses off and rubbed her nose.

"Did you read *Sing You Home?*" she asked.

Anna nodded.

"So, then you know how Vanessa felt, how she worried that Zoe would leave her, that perhaps it wasn't real for her?"

"Yes…"

"That's how I have felt since you came to my house," Iris said. Her eyes met Anna's; she wanted the sincerity of her words to hit Anna straight in the heart.

"But you're not faithful to anyone," Anna said.

She sounded calm but her words were tinged with something else. Hurt? Worry? Or was it judgement?

"I can be," Iris said.

Anna picked at something on her skirt. She looked beautiful. Wavy hair, minimal make-up, the natural features pure.

"I'm married," Anna said, as if disclosing this for the first time. "I have children. Having an affair, I just can't…"

"An affair? This is not an affair."

Anna looked up. "It's not?"

"Perhaps it was at first," Iris said.

She felt herself gravitate towards Anna as she got out of her seat and sat down on the floor next to Anna's chair. Uncharacteristically, she rested her head in Anna's lap. It wasn't necessarily a conscious action, to give Anna the power while she exposed her feelings.

"I need to be close to you," Iris said.

Anna's hands stroked Iris's head, her fingers softly combing through the hair. Iris closed her eyes, pacified by the touch. They sat in silence for a long time before Anna spoke.

"I feel confused," she said.

Her words sounded genuine but not exasperated, and Iris lifted her head to meet Anna's gaze. She smiled to show that she understood before leaning forward. Their lips met halfway.

It was a long and sensual kiss.

"Maybe we could go somewhere," Iris said, their mouths withdrawing for air. "A holiday, just the two of us."

Anna shook her head. "I'm not sure," she said. "My children..." She looked away, her eyes watery. "Anyway, we would just be back where we are now."

"What do you mean?"

Iris stroked the back of Anna's hands with her thumbs, the skin young and supple.

"I know I would have a lovely time," Anna said. "It's not that. But I would be back here, in this library, feeling equally guilty and confused. Perhaps even more so."

Iris placed her hands on Anna's cheeks, forcing their eyes to meet.

"I want only you," Iris said. "No one else."

"Why me?"

Iris pictured Lena's face together with the text she had sent after Rolf supposedly had "taken care of her".

I fucked your husband but I have a feeling you don't care, so I will make you care. My final words to you by Emily Dickinson: "Mine Enemy is growing old, I have at last Revenge." Revenge, such a sweet word.

Iris looked at Anna. "You're different," she wanted to say. Instead, she stood up and squeezed herself into Anna's chair.

Anna was larger and so she had to make do with resting one buttock cheek on Anna's thigh. She just needed to be as physically close to Anna as possible.

"Anna," she started. "I feel as if you're going to question me over and over. I can't change my past but you need to know this." She fiddled with the silver pendant around her neck. "Anna. The way I feel about you, this is new for me. In fact, it's astonishingly complex and incredible and absolutely terrifyingly wonderful." She hesitated before saying the crucial words: "I have fallen in love with you."

Right then, Anna seemed to have given in. Her shoulders relaxed, her face looked almost sad, as if she had lost an internal battle.

"What about your husband?" she asked.

"I'm going to leave Rolf."

45

Anna

January 2016

When Anna woke up in the morning she felt a stab of excitement at the thought of the previous evening, the intense moments with Iris in the small kitchen; their conversation trailing off, the physical taking over. She felt guilty however as she lifted her body off the mattress – the very body that Iris had caressed and nurtured with her touch – and turned to the other side.

Erik's face was squashed on the pillow, his mouth partly open, a gentle snore escaping his throat. It was surreal. This was her life. This was reality. It was as if she had been airlifted into another world the night before, into a delicious vacuum where she had been allowed to just be Anna. What she shared with Iris couldn't be real. Despite Iris's declaration of love, their relationship felt fake as soon as she was back home.

Yet Erik looked like a foreign object in her bed. She always woke up before him and when they had first got together, she would lay quietly, stroking his cheeks, his bare arms, his chest. A feeling of being truly happy made a momentary comeback. The way she felt with Iris, could she once again feel like that with Erik? She lifted up her hand, ready to touch him, to make the memories real, but put it back down again. She couldn't face the rejection. If she touched him, he would probably flick her hand away.

The house was quiet, the boys were either still sleeping or they had switched the TV on, making sure the volume was on mute. They were smart.

She let Erik sleep while she went downstairs to organise breakfast and sure enough, the boys were submerged into their beanbags in front of *Pippi Longstocking*.

"Let's leave Pippi for now and have some breakfast. Otherwise we will be late for day care and I'm sure you want to see Sophie?"

Sebastian was up and out of his beanbag within a second, on his way into the kitchen. She could hear him opening the fridge.

"Lukas, cheese or ham?" he yelled.

Lukas was grumpy when she switched the TV off.

"Come on," she said and kissed his head. "Cheese or ham?"

"Ham."

While they were making open sandwiches for breakfast, Sebastian asked about her evening meeting. "Did you bring cake?"

Her stomach clenched. "Not this time," she said. "But I will bake another one with you soon. I promise."

Lukas stopped drinking his milk. "Chocolate cake?" he asked.

"Absolutely," she said.

She did treasure their time in the kitchen. It was important to teach your sons to cook and bake. Erik wasn't too bad as long as it was basics he had learned from domestic science at school.

"Did the others like the last one we made?" Sebastian asked thoughtfully.

"They loved it."

He nodded, obviously happy about this, wiping his mouth on the back of his pyjama sleeve. Guilt held her back from reprimanding him, aware that she needed to create good memories.

"Is Daddy driving us?"

"No, we will let Daddy sleep."

"Will he pick us up?"

"No, I will."

It wasn't just good memories that she needed to create. She needed to take back control of her life. Only then, would she decide what to do about Iris.

*

That evening Anna was relieved that Erik had gone out. Unless the band was playing, which seemed to be less frequently these days, he tended to stay at home in front of the TV. She cherished having the house to herself. The children were sleeping after a precious moment of bedtime stories. Reading to Sebastian and Lukas had always been her job and every time she did, she thought, I must do this more often.

The tranquillity of the silent house was liberating. She poured a glass of red wine and sat on the couch with the latest book on her lap. Iris had opened up about her own private library, full of English titles that she was campaigning to have translated into Swedish. The collection was stored in a room behind the library reception.

"I haven't been too successful," Iris had explained. "I think the publishers are tired of my emails and phone calls, but at least I can share these books with people who are comfortable enough reading in English."

Anna opened the book: *Loving Her* by Ann Allen Shockley. The title wasn't lost on her and she found herself reading until she fell asleep, the book resting on her stomach, her glass empty on the coffee table.

She woke up when Erik came home, banging into the railing like he was drunk. Instinctively, she looked at her watch: four thirty a.m. That was late even for him. He went straight to the bathroom and showered, which she found odd. Had he been smoking? He knew that she hated that. She would find out the next morning. These days, bars didn't allow smoking so clothes no longer shrieked of smoke after a night out, unless you had actually smoked yourself.

She went upstairs and decided to go straight to bed instead of popping into the bathroom to ask about his evening. If he were drunk, he would be argumentative.

When he came to bed he kept to his side, wrapping his duvet tightly around his body, as if he were upset. Perhaps he had had a fight with Rob?

"Are you okay?" she asked.

"Had a bit too much to drink," he said.

"Fun night?"

"Not bad. Really need to sleep. G'night."

He didn't turn to her for a goodnight kiss. Was he trying to hide his nicotine breath?

The next morning, she pulled out his clothes from the wash basket. They smelled of grimy bar and stale beer, but not smoke. His shirt, a black short-sleeved one from a medium-range clothing chain, had a stain on the collar however, which she tried to brush off with her thumb. Greasy red paint, or... lipstick?

A million thoughts went through her head. Did he know about Iris? Was he trying to get her back? But how could he possibly know? They had been so careful, there was no way he would know, she reasoned.

"Erik?" She went into the bedroom where he was still nursing his hangover. "Erik? I was just going to do the laundry and found this."

He squinted as she held the shirt up to his face.

"It seems to have a lipstick stain on it. Kind of clichéd, don't you think?"

"Oh," he said, looking away. "Yeah, well I bumped into what's-her-name... a teacher from day care. She gave me a hug. That must be it."

"Kerstin?" Anna asked even though she couldn't imagine the fifty-plus teacher in a bar with red lipstick.

"No, oh... I can't remember her name. Starts with a P, I think."

"Pernilla?"

"That's the one."

"So you had a good time?"

"Yeah, I mean. With Rob. Not with her. Felt a bit awkward chatting to her, you know. She's young and hip and must think I'm like ancient."

"So you chatted to her?"

"She really likes Lukas and Sebastian. Had lots of nice things to say about them."

"I heard that she is the daughter of what's-his-name, the owner of that big coffee company. Apparently she only got the job as a favour, she's not even a trained teacher."

"I wouldn't know."

Right. "So you're sure that's it?"

"Of course." A pained look on his face. "Actually, Anna... honey, please can you get me some Ibuprofen. My head is killing me."

Honey? As she went down to fetch the painkillers, she thought about Iris's suggestion to go away for a couple of days. Perhaps she shouldn't feel too guilty after all?

46

Rolf

February 2016

Rolf wanted to paint Frida; a bottle of vodka in one hand, legs spread to the wind. The cross around her neck prominent above the small tits. She was raw and unpolished and not like his other objects. Hair and red nails didn't have a place in this painting. Instead he would sample drool out of her mouth, skin off of her heels, and pubic hair. Lots of it, protruding through the smooth acrylic paint. It would be a large canvas, his central piece in the next collection.

"Dan's teacher is married with two children," she said, visibly excited to have some new information. "She's known for being a fucking Mother Teresa who's generous with her time. She's strict though, doesn't take any shit from her students."

He sat up, not bothering to cover himself with the blanket. The kid wasn't there.

"Want a drink?"

He shook his head but she got up, pulled out a large

packet of washing powder from a cupboard and fished out two beers.

"Keeping the beer clean?" he joked.

"It's my son. He keeps confiscating everything."

She was being dramatic. That could be good or it could be bad.

"So, who did you ask?" he said. "People at work? Other parents? Your kid?"

She took a gulp of the beer, then another. Lost in another world, she started dancing even though there was no music. He needed to reel her back in. Did she need another round of the Rolf gun? He laughed. Iris had found that funny once. His Rolf gun.

"Frida? I'm talking to you."

"I just know," she said.

At that moment, he'd had enough. Forget the painting. Fucking and leaving was better than this pretending to have a relationship shit.

"That's not fucking good enough," he said. "I'm off."

Loneliness was her enemy and he shamelessly abused it.

"Please don't go," she predictably begged him.

Her beer breath was upon him, her wet lips on his.

"You just don't take me seriously," he sulked.

Violence didn't seem to work on her, guilt worked better.

"I do," she said but he didn't budge, and so she sat down and lit a cigarette. "I read about it... in Dan's story."

"Right."

"He's deep," she said. "Writes all kinds of shit. Poems, stories, even comics that he draws pictures for."

"Yes, yes, you've told me already. But maybe what he wrote about his teacher is just fiction."

"It's not a story. He also writes in a special notebook."

"And he just left that out for you to read?"

"Of course not! He keeps notes and shit in a box under his bed but this notebook is always in that stupid backpack. Someone gave it to him, way back. It's got holes and everything but he won't give it up. Anyway, he was sleeping when I sneaked into his bedroom. I didn't have time to read the whole thing, he started stirring, but I think he wants me to be like her. So whatever you can do to get her off my back, do it."

47

Daniel

January 2016

Dan was exhilarated. Excited. Pumped. He wrote the adjectives down in his notebook, wanting to remember this moment. Lying on his bed, a big fat grin on his face, he closed his eyes and imagined Anna. Her lips on his, holding him just the way she had held that woman, in a tight I-will-never-let-you-go grip. She smelt of summer, freshly cut grass and yellow buttercups. "Oh, Dan," she would whisper and hand herself over, her large breasts pushed into his face, his erection hard. Her expert hands would undress him, one layer at a time, until he was completely naked. She would view his body, impressed by his biceps, the almost six-pack and how hard he was. Then she would dig her nails into his back, spread her legs and ask him to fill her up.

He wanked. And instead of the usual guilt that followed his release, he felt happier than in a long time.

"Where have you been?"

Frida had opened the door and was standing at the foot of his bed. He looked at his hand, covered in a sticky white liquid.

"Get out!" he shouted. He quickly pulled a blanket over himself.

"Thinking about your girlfriend?"

"I don't have one." He got off the bed, drying his hand on the rough fabric before he pushed her out of the room. "Get out, I said."

Frida fell backwards but she was quickly back up on her feet.

"Get the fuck away from me!" He shoved her hard.

This time, she slipped on the rug and hit her head on the wall. Her body descended to the floor. A sad pile of bones.

"Leave me alone," she cried.

He was too worked up and had no intention of listening to her pleas. He raised his leg and kicked her, his bare foot hitting the sharp outline of a rib. It hurt but he lifted his foot up again. This time he aimed at her stomach and his foot sank into the fat, the elasticity of her skin accommodating. No one would see the bruises apart from the Nissan dude and he didn't seem like someone who would care.

When Dan grew tired of her whimpering, he stepped over her and went into the kitchen, opened the fridge and took out a snack. The selection was fantastic: plain yoghurt, a dried piece of cheese and half a leftover sausage. He felt hungry and ate all of it, washing it down with Coke Zero, which he drank straight from the bottle. Then he returned to his room. Frida was crying on the floor outside.

"You need to go food shopping," he told her. "I want bananas."

All sports people seemed to eat bananas to keep their energy levels up. He would need that.

He slammed the door shut and pulled out his book and wrote a to-do list:

Step 1 – blackmail

Step 2 – move into Anna's house

Step 3 – become best mates with her kids

Step 4 – fuck her/she dumps the husband

Her husband was clearly not man enough for her. This would be easy.

*

Outside, in the corridor, Frida was quietening down. All he could hear was a muffled groan as she tried to stand up. She would be heading straight for a bottle, if there was one – he'd done a raid earlier in the week and had confiscated three six-packs of beer and two bottles of home brew. If she had been to *Systembolaget* since then, she would soon be passed out on her bed, her limbs floppy and unresponsive, drool trickling out of her mouth. For once, he didn't mind. It would mean peace and quiet and he needed that for two important reasons: to create a detailed plan and to write about his new life. He needed to visualise it. That way he wouldn't lose faith.

I'm really happy that you have expressed yourself in writing.

In his last assignment, Anna had told him he had a poetic streak. He had circled her observation with a red pen and he now kept the paper in the box with his other sacred stuff.

Bang!

He sat up and faced the door. Frida had swung it open

and was swiftly taking the key from the inside lock. What the...? He got to his feet to stop her but she had already shut it. He grabbed the handle but the door wouldn't open. It was already locked.

"Gotcha!" Frida shouted gleefully outside.

Fuck. The key was meant to lock her out, not the other way around.

He banged on the door as hard as he could.

"Open it right now or I will beat the crap out of you!"

"Haven't you done that already?" she said, her tone acidic.

He went over to the window but it was jammed. The owners had painted the house before they moved in and the window had been stuck ever since. The small panes wouldn't be able to let him out, even if he smashed them one by one. He was stuck. Shit, shit, shit.

"Frida... I'm sorry," he said, changing tactic. "I don't know why I did that. Are you okay?"

He leaned on the door and stroked its wooden surface, imagining it was Anna's skin. Soft and cool.

"I'm not fucking okay," Frida said.

She hit the door which made his head bounce. He hit it back.

"Let me the fuck out of here!"

"No. Game over, son."

48

Anna

February 2016

Anna was going to spend the afternoon talking about family, war and death, with *War and Peace* featuring at the centre of the class discussion. But to quote her late grandmother, "the young are not how they used to be." Her grandmother had had a point: the students' attention span was limited. The use of multiple electronic devices was partly to blame and they wouldn't read an extensive piece of work such as Tolstoy's classic masterpiece. She had therefore decided to bring Shakespeare into the mix. Although it had been four hundred years since his death, his work still seemed to resonate with her students.

"*Othello* is about love and revenge," she said and that immediately got their attention. The drama of teenage life meant that everyone could relate. Young love, whether seemingly true or unrequited, was something they all had experienced. Except perhaps Daniel, who didn't seem interested even though there were plenty of girls mooning over the "bad boy".

Daniel hadn't turned up for school that morning. She had received no emails from him and no one had picked up the phone when she had tried to call his house. It didn't exactly worry her, it just seemed unusual. He didn't ordinarily skip school. So where was he? If he was ill then why hadn't the school been notified? Lately he had appeared to be a better listener in class and he was causing less drama. There were still fights outside of the classroom from time to time, but he seemed to have settled in. Apart from his obsessive messages, which she ignored for the most part, things were looking up.

"Othello is a black soldier who falls in love with an Italian woman called Desdemona," she explained. "But her father doesn't want her to marry a black man." She paused to make sure they were listening. "Yet she does marry him behind her father's back. That's how strong Desdemona's love for Othello is."

Many of them smiled, as was expected. To marry for love, that was romantic. She herself had married for love. In the past, Erik had even bought her flowers.

But Erik had changed.

Then again, Othello had also changed.

Anna let the class read the passage where Othello passed Iago over for lieutenant, in favour of the less-experienced Cassio.

"Iago was upset and wanted to seek revenge," she explained. "To hurt Othello, Iago claimed that Desdemona had cheated with Cassio. In fact, Iago was so persuasive that he pushed Othello into insanity. Eventually Othello started to doubt Desdemona's fidelity, and to protect his honour, he killed her."

She looked out at the class, their attention completely on her and Shakespeare's dramatic plot. It was a fantastic feeling, to capture them like this; one of the many perks of being a teacher.

"When the truth finally came out and Iago was exposed as a liar," she said, "Othello couldn't live with himself and took his own life."

"What an idiot," someone said.

"What happened to Iago?" someone else asked. "Did someone kill him?"

Anna thrived. "No," she said. "Iago lived."

That got the discussion going. Everyone was talking at the same time and she had to structure it, divide them into groups and hand out specific discussion points. She loved the energy, how passionate they felt as they tackled anything from fairness, inequality, death and gender roles to racism, love and revenge. While they talked, she glanced at the open book in front of her and caught sight of two lines.

But that our loves and comforts should increase,

Even as our days do grow!

The group's heated debate became a distant murmur as she lost herself in her own world, just for a moment. Loves and comforts, even as our days do grow. As our days grow. The future, what would it bring?

*

As the school day drew to a close, Anna packed up swiftly. There would be no staying behind to mark papers or plan future lessons today.

"Happy weekend," Kent said as she stepped out of her new lightweight heels and pulled the winter boots on. There was a gentle sprinkling of snowflakes outside the window.

"Thanks," she said. "You too."

She had revealed part of her weekend plans, saying it was a book club outing, but hadn't provided too much detail. Kent knew her too well; he might detect holes in her story. He was happy for her, though. Not like Erik.

"An author's visit?" he had said, as if she was going to a sect meeting.

"Yes," she had confirmed. "She's travelling from the UK to do a talk and my book club is going. We thought we would make a weekend of it."

"Yes, but Lund? That's an hour away. What if I need the car?"

"I don't have to drive. I can either take the train, or I'm sure I can catch a ride with someone from the book club."

He had looked unsure. Was it the prospect of being left alone with the children over the weekend that bothered him, or that she was breaking away from him, like a piece of furniture out of place?

"It's good that I've made some friends, isn't it?" she had tried.

"I guess."

She had walked up to him and given him a hug. A friendly cuddle. He had hugged her back, his customary annoyance filling the air, but he had given in.

*

Anna headed home to pick up her overnight bag and to drop the car off for Erik. He would use it to pick the boys up after he arrived home from work.

"Another day, another house to paint," he had said unenthusiastically that morning, but perhaps because of her own weekend ahead, she had tried to show an interest.

"Are the owners nice?"

"They're okay. Bankers."

"Interesting colour?"

She really couldn't think of anything better to ask.

"Grey. Unfortunately it's still very popular."

"At least you're an expert on grey."

He had actually smiled at that.

She had dropped Sebastian and Lukas off at day care that morning and had said goodbye then. They weren't used to her being away overnight and she could tell they had been anxious. She felt guilty but Erik did love them. He might not be the disciplinarian that she had hoped he would be, but he did genuinely care about his children. They would be fine.

*

Iris picked her up at five o'clock sharp, despite the slush that was now sadly prevalent on the roads. The above-zero temperature wasn't giving the snow a fighting chance, which would disappoint the boys. Every morning, they were hoping for an opportunity to have a snowball fight.

They needed to get going. The author's event would start at seven and they had agreed to check into their hotel before then. Anna put her overnight bag in the boot of Iris's Golf and got into the passenger seat.

"Everything okay?" Iris asked, nodding towards the house.

It felt peculiar, to have Iris literally so close to home.

"Erik's at work."

"And what about you?" Iris asked. "Are you all right?"

Anna nodded. "Let's do this," she said confidentially.

Before Iris left Rolf. Before she made such a life-altering

decision, they had agreed to do this. A whole weekend. Just the two of them, together. A trial of sorts.

Loves and comforts, even as our days do grow. What did the future hold?

Could she leave Erik?

49

Iris

February 2016

"It wasn't a holiday but it was close. A weekend with Anna. Iris had signed them up for a talk by the Welsh young adult writer Gwenhwyfar Dunne, an up and coming novelist who she had wanted to listen to anyway. The fact that it was in Lund, an hour away – not too far from Hågarp, but not too close – was an added bonus.

All we have is each other
each other, each other, each other

Iris thought of these few but significant words by the poet Lars Forssell, as she guided them out of Mörna and onto the E4 motorway. The weather was abysmal and at first, small talk filled the silence. Then Anna became braver. She opened up about her work, about the students and her desire to at least help one student better him – or herself every year.

"Hopefully more!" she said.

"You're passionate about your job."

Iris liked that about Anna. That she cared.

"How do you like Mörna?" Iris asked. "Would you ever consider living anywhere else?"

If we actually do this, if we are going to be together, would you be able to do that in a small-town mentality? Or would you move somewhere else with me?

"I find it peaceful," Anna said.

"But life is so transient," Iris said. "Like the poet Theodore Roethke said, 'I learn by going where I have to go.' I think that sums me up at least."

The comfortable silence in between, Anna's hand resting by the gear box, her pinkie almost touching Iris's leg. It was exhilarating, sharing this ride, heading towards an unexpected future.

Love didn't come easily for Iris. To say it out loud to Anna, 'I have fallen in love with you,' had been momentous and out of character for her.

Iris thought about the first time she had fallen in love. She had been sixteen, more than three decades ago. Her mother's strict, religious upbringing combined with Iris being an only child, had created a sheltered life. When she thought back to it now, her own naivety always got her.

*

"Big Mac?" Svenne asked her.

She nodded even though she had no idea what it was, not wanting to admit that she had never been to a McDonald's before.

"American burgers," he had said and that had somehow convinced her.

They sat on opposite sides of a small table, the fake leather chairs hot and slippery. He was everything her mother would hate: long hair, unshaven face and a brand-new tattoo. A black swan. It clashed with his overall look, the beautiful bird so unlike his torn jeans and crumpled shirt.

She picked at the skinny fries.

"Not hungry?" he asked as he shovelled his own burger down. A few bites and it was gone. She offered him hers, not able to eat anyway. The smell made her nauseous.

"My mum wants to meet you," she said and he looked at her, those grey eyes that had met hers at the local video store. He had been renting foreign movies with subtitles. He was deep and different and she liked that.

"You think that's a good idea?" he asked.

That was another thing she liked: his self-awareness. He knew he wasn't everyone's cup of tea.

"It's going to happen sooner or later anyway," she said.

A raised eyebrow. "Is it?" A smile she couldn't quite read.

"Well... I mean..." They had done it. Surely that meant they were serious.

"I've harvested some new weed," he said. "Want to smoke some after?"

He was creative. He wasn't just a dealer like the other boys on the housing estate, he grew his own, trying out new plants, combining them.

"Sure."

She liked the sensation of being someone else when she smoked, of floating, the weightlessness. Except lately she couldn't stand the smell, it brought on that feeling of wanting to hug a toilet bowl.

"Iris," he said and looked at her. "Never compromise who you are."

That made her feel good. She walked him home, smoked

even though it made her feel sick, and made love to him, feeling like she was the only person in the world for him.

The following Saturday, she went back to McDonald's to try that Big Mac after all, to remember that precious time of just the two of them. He hadn't returned her calls.

"Never compromise who you are."

The words made something flutter in her stomach and she turned around, happy to hear his voice. But those grey eyes were not on her; the words formed by the lips that had tenderly kissed her were aimed at someone else. A young girl with pretty blonde hair in braids. Iris ran out, holding her stomach, the pregnancy test glowing in her handbag.

*

She cringed at the memory. Love had been so complicated after that. Then Rolf had swooped in and her perspective had changed. Was it time for it to change again?

In the corner of her eye, she caught Anna fiddling with her rings. A sparkling diamond set in gold, next to a plain gold band. Was she thinking of her husband and the betrayal that lay ahead?

Iris was glad that she had offered to drive them. Should Anna suddenly have second thoughts, she couldn't just drive off; they would be able to give this a proper chance.

"Have you read Gwenhwyfar Dunne's book?" Iris asked her.

Anna shook her head. "Not yet, but I'm hoping to this weekend. I know it would have been better to do it before the talk but I haven't had a chance. Busy at work and with the boys at home."

"That's fine. I can always fill you in."

They exchanged a smile.

"Tell me about Erik," Iris said then and she sensed Anna flinching slightly. She realised it was an unexpected request but it was better to get the elephant out of the room.

"I've told you about Rolf," Iris continued. "So I would like to hear about Erik. I just want us to be honest with each other. Let's talk about everything, even our dirty laundry, our doubts and concerns."

In the corner of her eye, she could sense Anna studying her, and it felt good, to have her undivided attention. To be with Anna was easy. Not only did they share a love of literature, Anna was a kind and thoughtful woman who made her heart expand. She made Iris feel like she cared again, not just for herself, but also for humankind. She could easily do this. The two of them together. Forever.

"So, what do you think? Should we air the dirty laundry?"

50

Anna

February 2016

I do like the sound of that," Anna said.

It was true, her mind did like the notion of complete honesty, but what could she possibly tell Iris about Erik?

"As you already know, he paints houses," she said. "But he likes to play the guitar. They've got a band, him and his friend Rob and a couple of others. People come and go in that band but Rob and Erik always remain." She was blabbering. "He's a great dad," she added. "Not strict enough, but fun and loving and well, without him, I wouldn't have my beautiful boys."

"And is he a good husband?"

The question was loaded and very personal. How should she respond?

"We were obviously in love when we got married," Anna said. "And in those early days he was very attentive. Then…" she felt like she had already explained this to Iris a long time ago but she told her anyway. "Then we got a mortgage, had children and bought a Volvo. I guess it wasn't what we had expected."

"Have you tried counselling?"

Anna shook her head. Although she urged her students to seek help, she couldn't imagine sitting in front of a therapist with Erik. He would make a mockery of it.

Iris didn't ask any more questions about Erik and Anna felt happy to leave it behind.

*

They were going to share a room. Iris had asked her permission before booking the hotel. It felt completely natural. Like platonic friends, they unpacked, went to the bathroom and got changed for the evening's book talk. Only when they were leaving the room, did Iris take hold of Anna's waist, their hips touching.

"Thank you," Iris said. "For coming here."

She leaned in and kissed Anna, who felt the heat spread from her mouth to her body. If Iris had asked her to stay in this room and not go, she would have. Anything, for this feeling to last. But Iris withdrew her lips.

"Come on," she said and playfully smacked Anna's behind. "Or we will be late."

*

The author was enigmatic. She talked with confidence about her book, a story about telepathic gypsy twins fighting an ancient magic. Even though Anna hadn't read the novel, based on the presentation, she could imagine her students loving it. It sounded like it would transport them to another world filled with drama, intrigue and adventure. There was no limit to the imagination and that's what students needed, to be swept off their feet by books as opposed to video games, computers, apps and all the rest of it. Having said that, the book would most likely become a video or computer game or even an app if it became a hit.

Anna bought thirty books to have them signed. The sales assistant thought she heard wrong.

"Did you say thirty books? I'm just worried we won't have enough for everyone else."

The author, who was signing at a table nearby, heard this.

"Don't worry," she said, catching Anna's eye. She seemed warm and friendly; a beautiful tattoo of a gypsy woman displayed on the arm signing books. "If they don't have enough, they can order more. Just out of interest though, why do you want to buy so many?" She flicked her short, silver-blonde hair. "Not that I'm complaining!"

"It's for one of my classes, they've done really well this year," Anna said.

"I thought students were supposed to buy the teachers presents, not the other way around?"

Erik had asked that same question every single year. Normally, she only bought something small, a bookmark or an Ernest Hemingway or Selma Lagerlöf keyring. She took out her debit card.

"I just want to inspire them to read," she said.

"That's just like her," Iris said. She had appeared next to Anna, holding a book of her own. "She really cares."

"Here, let me sign them for you," Gwenhwyfar, said. She reached out her hands to take Anna's load of books.

"But the queue...?" the sales woman said.

"Why don't we offer them some coffee while they wait?"

Gwenhwyfar said. "Or better yet, wine!" She turned to Anna. "What are your students' names?"

Anna rattled off their names one by one. It took about half an hour, the queue not sighing and muttering as much as she had expected. Drinks had magically appeared and everyone seemed to be chatting and having a lovely time.

"I wish there were more teachers like you," Gwenhwyfar said, as she handed the last book to Anna.

When they left, Iris helped her carry her purchases.

"She was lovely!" Iris said. "One of the nicest authors I've met. And I've met many. So charismatic as well and did you see those grey-blue eyes? Beautiful."

She couldn't explain it, but Anna felt odd. Was this how Iris normally talked about other women? How would she tackle this?

"And she let you pass the whole queue," Iris continued. "She definitely liked *you*!"

This confused Anna even further. She reminded herself that this weekend was about discovery: there was so much she needed to learn about Iris.

They walked in silence to a nearby restaurant where they were generously provided with space for the bags of books.

Tables covered in white linen, candles and subtle tones of jazz in the background made it an intimate setting.

"This is romantic," Iris said as she smoothed out a napkin on her lap.

Anna felt that in order to carry the conversation forward, she needed a few answers. There was no point waiting.

"What did you mean back there?" she asked.

Iris looked curious. "I don't understand?" She tucked her short hair behind her ears, the candlelight reflected in her shiny red lipstick.

"That author might have liked me for buying thirty books," Anna said. "But did you like, *like* her?"

She realised she sounded like a twelve-year-old as the shape of Iris's face changed.

"Oh," Iris said. "No. I just thought she was nice." Her words were stale, which made Anna feel insecure. Had she made a mistake talking about this?

"There's just so much I don't know about you," Anna said honestly. "You're not monogamous, remember. Would you want to…" *do it with her?*

"Anna." Iris placed her hands over Anna's across the table. "I already told you it's different now that I have met you."

Her face softened, her words tinged with colour.

"But can you just change like that?" Anna said. "Overnight?" Surely she didn't have that effect on people; that they could just alter their way of living?

"Anna," Iris said and Anna involuntarily pulled her hands back. The way Iris said her name reminded her of Daniel and he was the last person she wanted to think about. Iris didn't look offended however. She just leaned back in her chair and said: "I love you."

Love. That word, which Anna hadn't repeated back. She looked at the white tablecloth, the uneven threads, the faint stains of spilt red wine. Iris waited. Anna had to give her credit for that. There was no pushing her up against a wall and making her say or do anything. Anna looked up.

"Iris, I don't know how I feel right now."

"I know," she said. "But I'm still leaving Rolf." She paused. "Not for you. For me."

She seemed to leave space for Anna to inject her thoughts on the matter but she had nothing to say.

"I do adore him," Iris said. "I think he's brilliant in so

many ways, but we should be friends, not lovers anymore. Lately, I have found myself switching off. I think he's sensed that because he's become… not suffocating exactly, but close enough for someone like Rolf. He's never been like that before and I can feel myself being tied down."

"I have children," Anna said. "Responsibilities."

"You do. I don't know how we would work it out but I don't feel like that's important right now. We wouldn't even have to live together." Iris leaned forward and Anna found herself stretching her hands out once again. She wanted to touch Iris, to feel the comfort of her warm skin. "But we can't stay married, that wouldn't be fair," Iris said.

"You have slept with married women before."

Iris nodded. "I have, but affairs are brief," she said. "This isn't."

Their eyes met, their hands touching. *This wasn't brief.* Anna affectionately squeezed Iris's fingers, trying to convey her own feelings, the outside world no longer existing.

"Are you ready to order?" A waiter stood next to their table, pen and pad in hand.

They simultaneously turned to him and Anna was about to say, "Can't you see we're in the middle of something?" when Iris patiently said, "I'll have the salmon. What about you, Anna?"

*

They shared a bottle of Sauvignon Blanc and left the relationship and serious questions. They spoke about books and holidays and dreams, realising they were both lucky enough to have jobs they loved.

"Whenever I have a class coming in to the library, I always

feel such admiration for the teacher. How do you cope with so many of them, day in and day out?"

For the hundredth time in her life, Anna found herself explaining that: "Discipline should be dealt with at home." Although she quickly added that her students, for the most part, were well behaved.

Again, Daniel came to mind but she didn't want to tell Iris about him. Two more years and he would either be working or moving on to university, which at the moment didn't seem likely. He was clever, though. That was the frustrating part.

When they walked back to the hotel, Anna carried a plastic bag in one hand, the other hand dangling suggestively close to Iris's. She wanted so badly to hold it, but what if they bumped into someone they knew?

Would it always be like that, if they were an actual couple? Or was it acceptable if it was out in the open?

Just then, Iris grabbed hold of Anna's hand and pulled her into an alleyway. A dark, moist wall behind her back, Iris's lips on hers. Anna giggled, the bags falling to the ground; their hands caressing, stroking, loving. She didn't care that it was cold. Anna had dreamed of being taken like this, with such passionate unexpected force, but she had never thought it would happen in this lifetime. She no longer cared if anyone passed by or if she would know someone here. It wasn't the alcohol, it was Iris, the way she made her feel, like fire on her skin, inside her heart, a longing to stay with this woman at any cost.

Iris hoisted up Anna's dress, her hands expertly inside her knickers, finding a sensitive spot, circulating, applying the right amount of pressure. Anna moaned into Iris's ear as she neared a climax. She wanted to reciprocate but her limbs went numb with pleasure and any feeble attempts to satisfy

Iris were brushed aside. "Later," Iris said. "Later."

She came hard into Iris's hand. Shocked by the strength of her orgasm and slightly embarrassed by the loud sound coming out of her mouth, she adjusted her knickers and pulled her dress down.

"That was incredible," Iris said, kissing her. A soft, intense meeting of lips. "You're so hot."

Anna laughed nervously.

"You make me *feel* hot," she admitted.

They held hands the rest of the way, and once they arrived at the hotel, there were no inhibitions. If she could have an orgasm in a public, albeit hidden, place, then she could do anything.

Clothes fell to the floor, the covers of the bed pulled away. Limbs stretched, backs arched, wet lips searched and discovered new territory. Iris's body became her own; her erogenous zones Anna's, her nakedness less awkward. Lights on or off, it didn't matter.

"Who are you?" Iris asked at one point, laughter bubbling out of her.

Anna laughed as well. This was new. Laughing while having sex. Who knew that could be so good? So comfortable.

No more shyness, no more self-consciousness. Anna could feel how much Iris worshipped her body, including her dimpled behind, round thighs and chunky toes. In fact Iris sucked them. One by one, she pulled Anna's toes into her mouth, her warm tongue circling, causing a tickling but sensual feeling that made her tingle between her thighs.

Iris had taught Anna to tease and delay and to avoid reaching an early climax. This ran through their every meeting, whether it was sexual or not. They seemed to linger in every moment, making the most of it.

Feeling adventurous, Anna pushed Iris off of her and pinned her to the bed.

"Now it's my turn," she said laughing, and she could tell Iris was excited by the changing roles.

Anna separated Iris's slender legs and for a few seconds, she just watched Iris: her perky breasts, hardened nipples, slim waist and tanned arms that were now resting comfortably under her head. Her lipstick had worn off but her eyes were like emeralds, emphasised by the black eyeliner.

"Your body is so young," Anna said. "What is your secret?"

"Lots of sex," Iris said, grinning.

It was a joy to be with Iris. She made Anna feel as if she had the whole future ahead of her. Iris tried to sit up to kiss Anna, but Anna pinned her down again.

"Hey, I wasn't done with you," she said and this time she acted quickly, opening up Iris's sex, resting her tongue in the opening, boring it into Iris. She let out a gasp and grabbed hold of Anna's hair. Anna's tongue slipped out, over Iris's parted lips, wetting them. The satisfaction Anna felt from Iris's moans egged her on. *I can do more.* She had looked at handbooks online that freely showed sample pages and felt spurred on.

Kissing a woman between her legs was like kissing her mouth. Anna's tongue licked and circled and sucked, her hand simultaneously moving up to Iris's breast, tugging at the nipple.

"Oh…" Iris gasped, her breath uneven, her hips rocking back and forth.

Anna lifted her head up briefly. She wanted to witness Iris's pleasure, her relaxed face, widened nostrils, her closed but fluttering eyelids. It was exhilarating to know she could stimulate Iris this way. Encouraged, she placed two fingers on Iris's dark, trimmed pubic hair, moving it up and out of the way, stretching the skin to expose the vulva. A bare rose, pink petals blooming just for her. Her tongue ran over the delicate lining, the skin smooth and silky. Iris's moans intensified. With growing comfort, Anna let her right-hand index finger play with Iris for a while, slipping it over the wetness, licking and rubbing, before slipping it inside of her. She was warm and tight, and Anna was turned on by the confined wetness. She pushed another finger in, slipping them both in and out, watching Iris's body react, the contracting stomach muscles, the upper body almost floating over the bed, the spread legs taut and toes stretched out. It was time to let her come and Anna moved the fingers in and out faster, her eager tongue kissing Iris's vaginal lips. She screamed out her orgasm, sweat (or was it tears?) on her face.

Afterwards, Iris lay motionless, not speaking a word and having felt on top of the world for making Iris's release so intense, Anna now felt concerned. Had she done it all wrong?

Then Iris spoke. "That was... a-m-azing," she said.

She opened her eyes and pulled Anna down next to her, kissing her gently but passionately. At once, Anna felt both exhausted and thrilled. She rested her hand on Iris, caressing her stomach. *I think I am falling in love with you.*

They lay in each other's arms for a long time, Iris's heartbeat comforting, and once they had recovered, they started over. Their bodies moved from one position to the next, the orgasms woven into one another's. With plenty of playfulness and versatility, Anna's body tried new positions: she was on her back, on top of Iris, sitting up, on her knees, in front of, behind.

The minutes went past, the hours; darkness became day, daylight turned to night. They talked, they made love, they showered, they talked some more, they ate, made love again, came and went.

When it was time to go home, Anna had decided. She would need to have a difficult conversation with Erik.

51

Erik

April 2016

It's Walpurgis Night, marking the arrival of spring, and Erik's happy to have Mum back, if only she didn't insist they attend the annual bonfire by the beach. He doesn't want to. Having to see Anna's colleagues, students and their families, Sebastian and Lukas's friends with parents... what if everyone knows about Pernilla? Then he won't just be a sad fuck whose wife is in a coma, he will be a fucking scumbag.

"Don't be selfish," Mum says. "Think of the children."

Her words are sharp and uncompromising and he wants to please her, he just can't face the humiliation.

"I *am* thinking of the children," he says. "I don't want to embarrass them."

"Erik, I have just had enough!"

He shrinks in his seat as he watches her eyes widen, the way they did when he was young and got into trouble.

"You're a grown man," she continues. "I have been quiet long enough. Anna has been more of a mother to you than a wife." She pauses as if grounding herself. "Tradition is important. You grew up in a small town so you should know."

"My wife wasn't in a coma then, was she?"

"And your girlfriend wasn't pregnant, you mean?"

She twists the dagger in his chest.

When he spoke to the police they didn't mention Pernilla and that freaks him out. After first calling him to request that he comes down to the police station, they cancelled the meeting because of "other priorities". Mum reads out loud from the paper every morning, highlighting more severe crimes, which obviously are more urgent than a small-town teacher who is still alive and has no obvious threat to her. When they finally managed to fit him in, it was a brief meeting, the questions hitting him one after the other.

"You haven't come across her phone or her laptop?"

"No." He was too annoyed with them to admit that he had the laptop, and too much time seemed to have passed. What if he got into trouble?

"How long did Rob stay at your house that night? Did you watch anything particular on TV, what did you talk about?"

He tried to answer as best he could.

Then the rough punch: "Were you faithful to Anna?"

"Yes," he said.

He had really thought about it, should the subject arise. If they were going to accuse him of sleeping with someone, he was going to confess, but in the seriousness of the moment, he just couldn't. After all, what proof did they have, other than Pernilla's words? Even if they found the taxi driver, he didn't see them have sex. Quite possibly, the baby wasn't even his. Pernilla most probably slept around. He decided that it was his word against hers.

"Do you have any reason to believe that Anna might not have been faithful to you?"

There it was, finally. "No," he said, because it couldn't come from him. Someone else needed to verify it. Not him.

"Did she mention any particular students?"

"No." She really hadn't.

"Did any students call the house? Was anyone upset with her?"

"Plenty of people called her and who knows if anyone was upset? She was pretty strict."

It was an unsatisfying interview and he really wishes they had asked him about Pernilla straight out. Why play games with him? Are they waiting for a DNA test to see if the baby is his?

The situation is too stressful and he just can't handle Mum's judgement right now.

"I'm not the only one," he tells her. "Anna was also cheating."

"No wonder. A woman needs a man, not a boy."

He can't believe it. "You're defending her?"

"It's time to grow up and start taking responsibility. We're going tonight, whether you like it or not. Otherwise I'm going back home."

Their eyes duel for a few seconds but he knows he can't win.

"Fine," he sulks and heads up to shower.

"Great," Mum says from the bottom of the stairs, back to her old spirited tone of voice. "We leave in ten minutes."

*

They walk even though he would have preferred to drive

to avoid the customary greetings along the way. The town's population turns into pilgrims, walking in clusters, a strong current pulling them down to the sea. He puts his head down and pretends to be in an animated conversation with Mum but she greets every person they walk past, even though she barely knows anyone. Sebastian and Lukas wave to their friends and Erik is forced to raise his hand a few times.

Luckily, it only takes five minutes and when they arrive they stay at the outskirts of the crowd. In the middle is a pile of trees and bushes that the community has scraped together from their gardens and outer farms. There is even the odd Christmas tree, dry and ready to be burnt to a crisp.

"Can we go and play?"

He hesitates, Anna wouldn't have been comfortable with the boys roaming around unattended.

"I'm not sure," he begins.

"Of course you can," Mum interrupts and turns to him. "Let them have some fun."

"Mum, the times have changed." What was it Anna used to say? "It's not like when I was young." *They could be kidnapped.*

He used to accuse Anna of being paranoid but now that Mum is the liberal one, the boot has ended up on the other foot.

"It's about to start," Mum says and the matter is dismissed.

He looks to the stage, a temporary wooden platform, where the traditional speech will be held and everyone quietens down: no more small talk about the latest house project or school gossip.

A man in a ponytail and a ridiculous moustache starts to talk into a microphone. He welcomes the spring and launches into the history of the bonfire, the farmers letting the animals out this time of the year and explaining that the fires were used to scare vultures away. He talks about the intricate hide of an animal and of blood. Blood? Erik looks at Mum and whispers:

"What is this rubbish?"

"He's an artist, Erik. I read about him in the paper. He's famous – or infamous is perhaps a better word – for adding blood to his artwork."

"That's fucked up."

"Language."

"The boys can't even hear me!"

Sebastian and Lukas have found a couple of friends and are playing nearby. They seem to be having fun, which makes him feel slightly better.

On stage, the artist drones on about individuality instead of spring and his eyes wander, bored. He scans the crowd, wondering if Pernilla is there. He's going to have to talk to her at some point. Mum has already discussed it with him.

"Don't ask her if the baby is yours," was her advice.

"Why the hell not? Maybe she has had multiple one-night stands?"

"Erik, you will come across as a heartless man."

"Who cares?"

But he realises he needs to think about what he's going to say. At the moment, anger and the notion of child support payments are preventing him from thinking clearly.

People start to clap as the speech finally comes to an end, and two men begin the job of lighting the fire.

"I hope it doesn't rain," Mum says.

Erik wishes it would. Then the fire would be out and they could head home. A couple of people have cracked open cans of beer and his taste buds are longing for one.

"Mum, did you bring…"

"Hi there," someone says and stretches out a hand. It's the artist who did the speech. "You must be Erik?"

"Yes…" He better not be related to Pernilla. Instinctively, Erik takes a step back. "Do I know you?"

Behind them, the fire grows, the heat tickling his back.

"I'm really sorry about your wife. How is she?"

"She's been better." He can't help it, he gets defensive. Who the hell is this dude, turning up asking about his wife?

"My wife knew Anna."

"Right…"

"Anyway, I wish her a speedy recovery."

The dodgy looking artist presses his palm into Erik's before walking off.

"How weird was that?" he says to Mum.

"You can't be upset with people for being friendly."

He looks around, aware that he hasn't seen the boys for some time.

"Can you see Sebastian and Lukas?"

Mum looks around. "They were just here…"

Were they now? *If only you hadn't let them run off!* His pulse is quickening as he looks left and right but there's no sign of them. He searches through the crowd, which at that moment starts to sing about spring, backed by the local church choir.

"They're probably off playing with their friends," Mum says.

"They're only five!"

"You ran around at five," she says but she doesn't understand. *I can't lose them too.*

"What if they're too close to the fire?" he says to get Mum to react.

"Then someone will pull them back."

People are either busy singing or drinking, he doubts they would notice the children. He circles the outskirts of the crowd, words of fresh, playful winds and streams following him around. Every time he sees a little boy he thinks it's Sebastian or Lukas but it's not. They're wearing matching, bright green jackets, bought by Anna during the sales season. They should be visible.

When he's rushed around the fire and pushed his way through the people, no longer caring who knows what about him, he returns to Mum.

"I can't find them," he says, out of breath.

Was Pernilla there after all? He realises that she quite possibly could have taken his children to deliberately piss him off. They trust her and would absolutely follow her if she asked them to.

"They must be here somewhere," Mum says. "Go and look behind the trees. Maybe they're playing hide and seek?"

"Why do you have to be so fucking calm?!"

He storms off.

Where are my boys?

52

Erik

April 2016

Erik runs over the grassy sand dunes, the cold grabbing hold of him as the distance from the fire grows. There are other children around and he asks them if they've seen two boys in green jackets. They shake their heads and run off. Frustrated, Erik starts running too, like a mad man, he looks behind, even under, every single pine tree in sight.

"Sebastian! Lukas! Where are you?"

Someone offers to help him look and then there are more of them. He doesn't have time to thank them, he just keeps going, and then he hears a voice out of nowhere that sounds familiar.

"That's cool!"

"Sebastian?"

His heart is beating so fast, it could very well be an upcoming heart attack, he thinks, and calls again: "Sebastian? Lukas?" Please.

"We're here."

They brush past a tree branch, grinning mischievously.

"Bloody hell, where have you been? You scared me!" He gets down on his knees and hugs them tightly. "Don't ever run away from me again, okay?"

"Don't worry, Daddy. We were with the boy with the cool jacket."

"Who?"

The boy who was cycling outside day care, the one who knows Mum."

"Oh. Is he here?"

The boy appears from behind a branch and steps in front of Erik and the boys.

"We were just playing. Sorry if you got scared."

"They just don't normally run off like that."

"Well, we were having fun. Weren't we?"

"Your name is David, right?"

The boy nods.

"Thanks for looking after them."

"No problem, if you ever need a babysitter, I would be happy to help."

Erik vaguely remembers someone else suggesting he should get a babysitter. Black Adam? Why are people so obsessed with him getting out?

"That's okay," he starts but Lukas is pulling at his jacket. "Please, Daddy," he whispers. "David loves Lego and he's promised to build a really cool ship with us. You know, for all our Lego people?"

Right. "Why don't you come over and hang out with the boys sometime?"

Maybe he can tell Erik about school, what Anna was up to. He needs to catch up on everything she's told him that he hasn't listened to.

"Sure."

"How about this weekend? Saturday at ten?"

The boy smiles. He high fives the boys and is off.

*

They head back to the fire when Erik's phone starts to ring. He expects it to be Mum, wondering if he's found the boys, but it's the hospital.

"You'd better come," someone says.

This is the call he's been waiting for.

"Has she stopped breathing?"

He tells the boys to quickly get Grandma, his life with Anna passing by like a silent movie.

"I don't want you to get too excited because it's still early..."

Has Anna moved? "Is she okay? Can she talk?"

"We're not quite sure yet."

"You've got to give me something," he shouts. "I can't drive for twenty minutes wondering? Don't you get that?"

"Erik." Mum has appeared at his side, her hand resting on his arm. "Calm down."

But he can't. He's shaking with built-up anger.

"Tell me!" he spits. "Tell me now!"

The person on the other side of the line hesitates. Is it a nurse? A doctor? An administrator? He wants someone with authority, someone who can offer a confident explanation.

Eventually the person on the line speaks: "She is awake."

53

Rolf

February 2016

Frida had become increasingly demanding and Rolf wasn't sure how long he could keep it up. Daily texts and phone calls, often in the middle of the night, was normally the reminder he needed – affairs should be brief – but Iris had gone away for the weekend and although she hadn't confirmed it, he was sure the teacher was involved.

He went over to Frida's to see if the kid knew about his teacher's whereabouts but it turned out he was locked up in his room like some five-year-old being punished for a temper tantrum. Not that he was complaining, it was nice having him out of the way.

"*Hej*, babe."

The place was damp and chilly, as if the heating wasn't working properly, but Frida didn't seem to notice. She was tipsy. And badly bruised. She always did have a few black marks here and there. That was apparently part of working at a factory, but it was worse than normal.

"Get into a fight?" he asked, pulling her close.

"Something like that."

"Looks pretty bad."

"Nothing a bit of love can't heal."

Her manipulation worked. He needed a shag to take his mind off things, and to warm up.

This time he tied her up. She was drunk enough to agree to anything, so it was easy. She was loud though. Louder than normal, and the kid kept banging on the wall. There was a lot of "shut the fuck up" and at one point, Rolf had to really focus to remember that he was having sex with Frida only, because at times it felt like a sick threesome.

He realised that he must be a masochist to put up with this. Frida was useless at getting information out of the kid – all he knew was where Anna lived, that she was married with two children, and that she had been voted Teacher of the Year the previous year. All very ordinary, non-juicy stuff.

"You're leaving already?"

"Gotta go."

The problem with the kid being locked up was that he couldn't talk to him. It would seem desperate to communicate through a door. He needed to come up with another idea.

"Will you come over later?" she asked.

"Sorry," he said. "I have to see my daughter."

It was true, he had planned to go to Gothenburg for a couple of days while Iris was away. If nothing else worked, he wouldn't hesitate to use Karin, who definitely wouldn't want to see her parents apart.

*

When he arrived home, he planned to pack, but first he had

to write an email from Xeroxwed. He would send it to Anna after the weekend. Even though Anna hadn't responded to his earlier emails, he had to assume she was reading them. She would definitely think they were from Iris. Wednesday book club meetings and fucking up against the Xerox copying machine – who else would know about that other than Iris? And should she mention the emails to Iris, which he didn't think she would, but if she did, then he knew Iris well enough: she would keep a straight face and realise how serious he was about hanging on to her.

Xeroxwed wrote:

After this weekend, the sex... well, I'm not sure you're up for this. I don't want to see you again.

54

Daniel

February 2016

While locked up in his room for a whole fucking weekend without a phone or even toilet breaks, Dan had spent his time shitting in a bag. He had tried to break the door down several times but despite his strong arms it wouldn't budge. It was freezing cold as well, the windows specked with ice, the air in his room stale.

Frida would be lucky to be alive by the time he got out. Apart from sinister murder plans which involved poisoning her vodka, he had also put some careful thought into his next move with Anna.

He didn't want to threaten Anna via email, SMS or a handwritten note. That was too much evidence. He would have to see her in person. The temporary school parking lot seemed to be the best place. Mörna School didn't have a sophisticated surveillance system, and there were no cameras in the gravel-filled plot serving as parking while the new canteen was being built.

After having to endure Frida's sexual circus next door

over the weekend and being driven crazy by the smell of shit, she had eventually let him out. On one condition: he would have to agree to hug her for two whole minutes. She would time it with her phone. It had seemed ridiculous and even though he had imagined hugging her so tight she would be strangled, it was still too stupid. He was not a child.

"I don't want your saggy tits on my chest," he had said.

That hadn't gone down too well. She hadn't spoken to him for half an hour. Then she must have got lonely because she had given him a second chance. She was all for second and third and fourth chances, Frida. God knew they had given *her* many.

"Okay, fine." What choice did he have? Soon the saggy tits would be replaced with Anna's full bosom. Her breasts were large. Firm.

"I have one more condition," she had said.

"What is it now?"

"I want to know about your teacher. Anna. The one who came to our house."

Anna's name coming from his mother's mouth had made him feel cold. What the hell did she want to know about Anna for? Had she rummaged through the papers under his bed? The violation of his privacy. Had he mentioned Anna's name there? He believed he had been discreet enough not to. Oh. The photos! She would have seen the photos. Fuck.

He had taken a deep breath to sound calm. "What do you want to know?"

"Is she nice?"

"Yes."

"So you like her?"

"Yes."

She had paused.

"Are you..." She had sounded as if she were about to cry. "Are you in love with her?"

What? No. Please. It had seemed so unbelievable when verbalised. Made up.

"Of course not."

"Are you sure? You just seem to really, really like her."

"Come on, *Mum*." Not Frida this time. Anything was fair in love and war. "You know I like to write and she's very supportive of that in her class."

She had cried then. The word "Mum" had that affect on her.

"Is she messing with your head?" she had said in between sobs.

"No! She's just a cool teacher."

She had opened the door to let him out and she had clung to him as if he were saving her life and for a tiny second he had felt guilty about his plan. What would happen to her when he left? Would the Nissan dude move in? Would they shack up and have more children? Most likely she wouldn't want more mouths to feed. He pushed the image away. From now on, it was her life and she could do whatever she wanted to. He was heading somewhere. Onward and upward, as they said.

"Got to go," he said and peeled her arms off.

*

He waited on his bike. If he was lucky, Kent the creep wouldn't be with Anna and he could cycle right up to her and deliver his blackmail message. Plan B was to go to her house and ring the doorbell. He would ask to speak to her privately and she would have to step outside. Plan C was to take Frida's dude's car and go to the library and deliver the message there. He didn't much care if the other woman saw him. He was in control now.

As he waited, he wondered how Anna would react. He didn't want to anger her after all; his wholesome, down to earth, sexy Anna. But would she cry? Would she beg him not to tell anyone? Would she embrace him, agree to anything as long as he left the matter alone? He had a feeling she wouldn't. She was feisty.

After about twenty minutes, Anna appeared. She had a serious look on her face and her steps were determined, which made him hesitate. Was she already upset with him? Did she know that he had been spying on her? He had missed school and hadn't been able to send any emails. For a brief second he wondered if she was upset because he *hadn't* emailed her.

Less sure of himself, he wheeled his bike towards her. She looked up but kept walking.

"Hi," he said.

"Hi, Daniel."

"Ehm…" Shit, this was not how it was supposed to go. It had sounded so good in his head, so easy. *I saw you.*

She opened the car door and hauled her bags in. As she was about to get in herself, he said: "Wait, I need to talk to you."

She turned to him and said: "Not now, Daniel. I have something important…"

"No," he said. Please don't do this. Why was she being so rude?

The stern look on her face. "I'm sorry," she said. "It's just that I have to go."

But she couldn't go. Not when he finally had her attention.

"Do you like it when I send you emails?" he asked.

"What?" She looked at him quizzically. "I don't understand."

It was as if she was waiting for an explanation. Would he give her one? No.

"I don't exactly mind," she said then. "It's just that you send so many, which can be stressful. It would be good if you slowed down the traffic."

"Okay," he said. "I will do that." Except, no. He realised he wouldn't. "I need your help, Anna. To have a normal life, you know."

"Yes, I do know," she said. "You have written that many times, but I can't help you with that. Not even if I wanted to."

She wanted to?

"So, you mean... you want to help me?"

"Of course."

He straightened up, felt the acceptance, the feeling of a warm comforting blanket, Christmas with a real tree, newly baked gingerbread biscuits.

"Does that mean I can move in?"

She sighed and her expression drastically shattered his illusion: the blanket suddenly with holes, the tree made of plastic, the biscuits stale. And that angered him. Was she trying to fool him?

"Is that a 'no'?" he said, his teeth clenched even though he had meant to portray a calm and mature attitude.

"Daniel, why don't we meet and talk about it tomorrow?" she suggested. "I have to leave, I have an important..."

"Yeah, I know," he interrupted. "Something important." *That doesn't include me.* Before she said anything else – he didn't want to hear her excuses – he said what he had come to say, because there was clearly no other way.

"I saw you," he said. "And now you will do what I say."

"What?" she said. "What are you talking about?"

"You belong to me now!" he said, his words forceful. He needed to make her understand that he was in charge. Not her. Perhaps it had been unrealistic to expect her to shout "Oh, Dan. Fuck me!" at that point but he had at least hoped she would break down in tears and make herself vulnerable.

"Dan," she said firmly, placing a hand on his arm and he looked at her fingers, the light-pink nail polish, the bent knuckles, squeezing his bicep. Maybe he hadn't been too unrealistic after all? But her tone didn't sound loving. The battle within him; the confusion she caused. He wanted to flick her hand away to show her that he was the boss, but he also wanted to move closer, to smell her hair, burrow his nose in it, let her hold him. Could he do that? Would she let him? He leaned his head forward and rested it on her shoulder. Shut his eyes and let her feminine scent soothe him.

He felt her move closer, felt her arms wrapped around his back, holding him. This feeling, he needed to savour it, to mentally lock it in his memory. Then she grabbed his arms and pushed him away.

"Daniel," she said. "I really care about you, but…"

He didn't want to hear "but", and without thinking, he just acted to stop her from speaking. His lips landed on hers and he kissed her. He decided to let his tongue loose, to taste her, really taste her, but she pressed her hands into his chest and shoved him back. Not as gently as before. This was rough. The pressure made her fall back onto her car door while he tripped over his bike and landed on the ground.

They looked at each other. She seemed paralysed, she just

stood there. He could feel her "I care for you" evaporate, her disgust for him taking over.

He wanted to get back at her. He wanted revenge. "I saw you and that woman," he said, spitting the words out.

The horror in her eyes. He enjoyed it as much as the kiss.

"What woman?" she asked.

She clearly tried to remain composed. It wasn't good enough. He needed her to sweat, to understand that this was some real shit.

He said: "I saw you with that woman, at the library in Hågarp."

Her face dropped, her cheeks red. And so he kept going, feeling more self-assured by the second.

"Yes, that's right," he said. "I know you're a lesbo. And if you don't want anyone else to know, you will do as I say."

55

Erik

April 2016

On the way to the hospital, Erik takes out his phone to call Tina.

"You shouldn't use your phone while driving," Mum says.

"I'm calling Tina, to see what she knows."

"We will find out when we get there. Anna is awake, that's what's important."

"You don't understand," he says. "I need to talk to her, to get more information." He hesitates. "It's nice to have someone on your side."

"I'm on your side." Mum's words are sharp and critical. After what's happened with Pernilla, he understands how pathetic he must sound.

"It's not like that," he says but he's too tired to explain.

He scrolls down to Tina's number and presses "Call". She picks up almost immediately and before he's had a chance to say anything, she says: "Have you heard?"

"About Anna waking up..."

"Exactly."

"I'm on my way to the hospital," Erik says. "Do you know anything else?"

"No." Tina pauses. "I guess you won't need me anymore, then?"

Her choice of words combined with her tone makes him feel like shit. She's Rob's girlfriend now, isn't she? How many policemen or women would willingly share information the way she has? He reckons not many.

"Of course not, Tina," he says. "You're a gem. I'll call you later."

"You will?" She seems relieved. "That's great."

He's about to hang up when she adds: "Actually, Erik..."

"Yes?"

"There's one thing I could tell you. About Pernilla."

Really? He looks at Mum. Can she hear the conversation? She's staring out the window so he has to assume that she can't.

"Did you warn her about talking to the police about your relationship?"

Fuck. "We don't have a relationship." He glances towards Mum again but there is no reaction.

"But you slept with her," Tina says.

Once. It was once! "No!"

"Well, she claims that she spoke to you the day of your wife's attack and that you were very upset."

"Ehm..." He needs to think. Did he speak to her at day care that day? Maybe about Anna taking him for granted, that he had to pick the children up even though it was her turn? Shit. He might have talked to Pernilla about that. It was possible. His verbal filter wasn't always switched on.

"Well, now there's a new rumour..."

Not another one! What is it now? Is he fathering more

children? He waits for her to continue, glancing in the rear-view mirror. The boys are fast asleep in the back.

"Yes?" he asks after a few seconds.

"Apparently a colleague of Anna's..." she starts, and there's an excited urgency in her voice that puts him on edge. A minute ago she didn't have anything to tell him but now the information is flowing. "Well... anyway... now there's a rumour that maybe you tried to kill your wife."

He swerves and Mum shrieks, grabbing the phone from his hand.

"That's enough talking," she says.

"No!" he shouts. "I need my phone back!"

He pulls over and stops the car. "Happy now? Give me my phone."

Mum looks at him grimly. In the back, the boys are stirring.

"Please?" he tries.

Mum hands it to him with a condemning frown, but it's too late. Tina is gone and she's not answering when he tries to call her back. He tries three times before he decides it's stalker behaviour. She must be tending to an urgent case. It's just that he doesn't get it. What the hell did she mean? *He* is a suspect? And a colleague of Anna's said what? Did she mean Kent? Or has Pernilla concocted something out of a desire for revenge? He leans his head on the steering wheel and takes a few deep breaths.

"I thought we were in a hurry?" Mum says.

He turns and stares at her, wanting to convey his annoyance, because right now he is a mess. "I know," he says. Anna is awake. A part of him can't wait to get to the hospital, to hold her. Another part is worried. Will she be a vegetable? Or will she be the woman he married?

*

They drive in silence. Erik thinks about Anna, when they first met. The dimples when she smiled at him, the hair loose and wavy, her lips a soft red. How she caught his eye despite the busy crowd in the bar, how he unashamedly called in sick almost every day after that. When she was on a plane back to Sweden and he was still behind the bar, a job he had just about managed to hang onto, the joy of being a bartender at a resort quickly disappeared. The party was no more.

"I've been such a fool," he says more to himself than anyone else but Mum says: "Yes, you have." Although she squeezes his arm gently and in that moment he feels her unconditional love. Despite his faults, she's still there for him.

They park in the parking garage and half-run, half-walk into the hospital, taking the elevator up to the third floor. Mum tries to chat to the boys but Erik is too tense. He just holds Sebastian's hand and tries to focus on each step he has to take, the grey linoleum floor sticky under his feet.

*

Inside the room, the first thing he notices is Anna's head. The bed has been raised, and her head is resting on a pillow, her hair flowing over her shoulders. They've let it out of the ponytail. She must hear the commotion as they enter because she turns to them, her eyes open. He gasps. Her brown eyes are looking straight at him. Time stands still, he can't move and doesn't notice the boys running up to the bed, shouting "Mummy!"

When they jump up to her, her eyes are averted, moving

away from him and onto the boys, with an almost terrified look.

"Boys, take it easy." Erik's Mum is there, gently moving the boys down from the bed. "Mummy only just woke up."

"Mu-u-u-mmy?" Anna slurs.

The doctor appears.

"Sorry, I was hoping to speak to you before..."

"Before we barged in?" Mum asks.

He smiles self-consciously and continues: "Well, yes. You see, Anna might be experiencing some initial memory loss."

Erik finally moves, as if he's been released from a stranglehold. He walks up to Anna and leans down to kiss her, closing his eyes to feel the full softness of her lips. *My wife.* But all he can feel is a cold cheek, and when he opens his eyes he realises she has turned her face; her eyes, harrowing.

"Who ar-r-r-e yo-ou?" she says, as if she's only just learned to speak, and her words hit him right in the chest. She doesn't recognise him either?

He feels someone's hand on his arm, pulling him back.

"You don't know who I am?" he asks lamely.

"I'm sorry," the doctor says. "Most likely she will regain her memory. Her head was badly injured, so this is not uncommon."

The boys are crying and Mum ushers them out of the room, her words soothing them along the way: "Mummy needs to rest, she has a headache. We will come back later."

With Mum and the boys out of the room, the doctor asks in a hushed tone if Erik can perhaps bring some family photo albums to help jog Anna's memory.

"She has called for her mother," he explains. "If she recognises her photo, it might be a good idea for her mother to come and visit."

Erik feels the pressure on his chest tighten.

"Right now she is frightened," the doctor continues, his wiry nose hair moving as he speaks. Erik struggles to concentrate. "She needs someone by her side who she remembers."

"I'm sorry, I don't understand," Erik says, meeting the doctor's tired eyes. "She doesn't remember me?"

"Unfortunately, she doesn't seem to recall everyone who was in her life before the attack," the doctor says. "Once she is stable enough, she can go home and hopefully her memory will come back when she is surrounded by her own belongings."

"Come home?"

"Not yet, but hopefully soon."

The doctor smiles, the typical smoker's lines around his mouth deepening. Erik feels terrified. He glances at Anna, who has closed her eyes and looks like she's sleeping, as if she's back in the coma.

"Is she...?" he asks.

"Just resting. This is very traumatic for her."

He says they mustn't rush anything, they must take it slowly so as not to stress her out.

"It might take months to get her back on her feet."

"And her memory?"

"We will have to wait and see."

Erik picks Anna's hand up, puts it to his lips and kisses it.

"I love you," he says.

PART FOUR

56

Anna

February 2016

After her weekend with Iris, Anna planned to speak to Erik immediately. As soon as she stepped inside the house, she put her bag down and called his name. There was no time like the present.

"Erik?"

There was no response. Where was he? She needed to tackle this now, before the guilt overpowered her. Resolutely, she walked inside, only to find him fast asleep on the living room couch. She watched him, debating whether to wake him up or not. He looked so innocent; could she really be so cruel as to rouse him from a dream, only to tell him she loved someone else? She couldn't.

Yet there was so much to talk about. They needed to discuss the children, how they would alternate the weeks that they cared for Sebastian and Lukas. She dreaded being separated from them for seven whole days at a time, but it was only fair. Erik was a great father and he hadn't really done anything wrong. They had simply stopped loving each other. That's what she would tell him.

*

The next morning was buzzing like all other mornings, children needed to be fed, clothed and chauffeured to day care. There was no time to talk. The only line Erik threw her way was: "You must have arrived late last night."

He didn't ask any questions about her weekend.

"I had a great time, thank you," she said, trying to make a point.

It was lost on him.

All day, she struggled to concentrate at work and to make matters worse, she had a meeting after school. Kent was there too, and during a short coffee break, he sat down next to her.

"You look tired," he said. He graciously handed her a cup of coffee, for which she was very grateful. "Did you have fun with the book club?"

"Yes, it was good. Thank you."

He looked disappointed. "That's it? No literary scandals? Didn't anyone get drunk and do something embarrassing?"

"If you're trying to live out your wild fantasies through me..." *then you have come to the right person.* "Then I'm sorry to let you down." She was tempted to tell him about Iris, to share something original for once. "*Actually, Kent, I have met someone and I'm going to leave Erik.*" It would sound too ridiculous; could she really do this without discussing it with someone else first?

"Kent," she said, lowering her voice. "Do you and Märta ever have any problems or are you always happy?"

He moved his chair closer. The teachers' lounge was

unusually busy because of the meeting, with a number of discussions going on.

"You need to nurture your marriage," he said and she couldn't deny that it stung. When had she given up? Then again, Erik didn't try either. Not that it was an excuse. "I've been lucky," Kent said. "We are compatible and have fun together almost daily but sometimes I think people need to accept that they will be happier without each other. Look at our students for example. A number of them have divorced parents but everyone gets along and shares the responsibilities. Then you have parents who stay together 'for the children'..." Kent did quotation marks in the air. "... who have toxic relationships which the children end up suffering from."

She nodded. "Do you think my marriage is toxic?"

She had never allowed herself to get this personal with Kent but he was the closest to a friend that she had. He hesitated, she could tell.

"It's okay," she said. "I appreciate your honesty, you know that."

"Fine," he said. "I don't necessarily think it's toxic but I have always wondered why you're married to him."

She hadn't expected that response, and she wished they were sitting in a wine bar having this discussion instead of a busy teachers' lounge.

"Why?"

Kent put a hand through his hair, looking pressured.

"You seem to have different interests and goals in life," he said.

She nodded. "What if I told you I'm planning to leave him?"

"Then I'd say I'm not surprised. You need to follow your

gut, Anna." He placed a hand on her shoulder. "I'll be here for you if you need me."

She was grateful for his support but she also felt embarrassed about the state of her marriage. Perhaps she shouldn't have opened up quite so much?

"Sorry to drag you into this," she said.

"Anna," he said seriously. "Whatever you tell me, I will not share with anyone, not under any circumstances. You have my word."

His loyalty made her feel better.

"Thank you."

*

Anna just about got through the rest of the afternoon meeting and as soon as she could, she packed to get home.

On her way to the car, her mind was preoccupied with what she was going to say. "We've had problems for a while", "Something has happened, Erik", "I've fallen in love", "This isn't just a fling, it's real", "I'm really sorry".

She could sense someone cycling up to her but she didn't want her practised monologue to be interrupted, so she kept walking.

"Hi."

It was Daniel.

"Hi, Daniel."

She wasn't in the mood for him today, the conversation with his previous teacher reminding her that he was playing her. *But why me?* Why not Maria Bergman? What made them so different?

Before she had a chance to question his motives he ambushed her, and perhaps out of compassion, or perhaps to do the opposite of what he was expecting, she hugged him. He wanted a mother and so she gave him exactly what a son would need. Comfort.

Except he then took it one step further and kissed her. In that moment, for the first time, she realised what was actually going on. He had a *crush* on her? She pushed him away, shoving him harder than intended. They both fell backwards.

"I saw you and that woman," he said.

She froze. Iris? But how? When? It wasn't something he could have made up or even have guessed, which meant he was telling the truth. But how could he possibly have seen her and Iris together? She wanted to defend herself but didn't get a chance, the words now leaving his mouth like a machine gun, one after the other, quick and forceful: "I know you're a lesbo. And if you don't want anyone else to know, you will do as I say. I don't want anyone else fucking you. Do you hear me?"

Panic rose in her. She had completely misjudged him. She was such a fool. When he finally rode off on his bike, he left her with the words: "I move in tomorrow."

*

She drove straight to the library. She hadn't planned to see Iris this evening but there was no one else she could talk to. She called Erik and said she would be slightly late.

"Rob and I need to leave at eight," he said.

She had forgotten that he had a gig. She needed to speak to him but she also needed to talk to Iris first. Daniel had spooked her.

"I will be back by then, I promise," she said, a tremor in her voice.

Could he tell how shaken up she was?

"Okay," he said and hung up. Obviously he wasn't that perceptive.

It didn't matter. Her attention was on the road. Her mind, however, was on Daniel. His glistening eyes, the looming body, exerting his best efforts to be overpowering and intimidating. His words. *You belong to me now.* How could he have crossed the line without her noticing? How naïve she had been. Distracted by the jittery new sensations of love for Iris.

She barged through the library door, the bells clanging together, drawing Iris out from one of the aisles.

"Anna? What's going on? Are you okay?"

"We need to talk," Anna said. Her determined steps reached Iris within seconds. "In the kitchen, please."

"I can't leave the library unattended, it's still open."

"Then close it."

"I can't. There are people…"

"Just two minutes." She sighed. "Please."

"Okay." Iris nodded. "Give me a minute. I'll see you back there."

Anna paced back and forth in the kitchen. She had felt so safe in this small seaside town, like it was just the two of them in the world. The fact that Daniel had spied on them tarnished everything.

Iris entered the kitchen and closed the door behind her.

"Do we need coffee for this?"

Anna shook her head and then she hugged Iris and cried.

"What is it, Anna?" Iris stroked her hair. "Did you tell Erik?"

Erik's name sounded foreign in Iris's mouth. She didn't even know him. *Don't talk about him.*

"Someone saw us together," Anna said. "A student of mine. And now he's blackmailing me."

"What?"

Iris grabbed Anna's shoulders, pushed her back so that they faced each other.

"Who is he?"

"It doesn't matter, just a student." Her voice felt weak. Tired, she slumped down onto the floor, leaning up against the cold photocopier, resting her head on its plastic surface.

"So tell me about him," Iris said.

"Where to start?" She thought for a moment. "He moved to Hågarp during the summer. He has moved around a lot."

She told Iris about his increasing obsession with her, his wish for her to be his mother, but she didn't mention the kiss or his comment about her not being allowed to *fuck* anyone else. She couldn't.

"Why didn't you report him?"

"It's not that simple, Iris. You can't just shuffle children around the system. It has to end somewhere, someone along their journey has to care."

"But does that have to be you?"

Those words were all too familiar. "You sound like my husband," she said.

"Sorry." Iris looked genuinely concerned. "I'm just worried about you."

"So what do we do?" Anna said. This was surely a joint problem?

"You could tell Erik and I will tell Rolf. That way no one is in the dark and there is no one to blackmail."

Iris made it sound so simple.

"I guess that would suit you," Anna said.

She felt angry, not necessarily with Iris, but with the whole situation and she wouldn't be in this mess if she hadn't met Iris.

Iris withdrew, looking as if Anna had physically hit her.

"I'm sorry," Anna said, wishing she had kept her mouth shut. "I'm just stressed out."

She stretched her arms out, reached for Iris. They would find a way.

"You make me sound like a predator," Iris said, staying where she was.

"It's just," Anna said, trying to find a way to explain herself, "there have been so many others for you. I mean, Lena? She was with you as well, wasn't she?"

She realised that this was actually part of the problem, that perhaps she was going through this pain only to lose Iris down the line. Would she be able to overcome her insecurities about Iris's past?

"The important thing for you to know, Anna, is that it's just you now. You and me."

She looked sincere and Anna leaned into her arms, wanting to believe that Iris meant it.

57

Erik

May 2016

Anna is awake but doesn't remember Erik or her children. The police have already been to see her but it appears that she can't remember anything about the night she was attacked.

Erik spends limited time in her hospital room, needing to keep the children away from her. It's a battle: she might remember more if she sees them but it's too upsetting for the boys.

On top of that, Mum has announced that she is going home at this most critical time. And when he thinks it can't get worse, Linda Johansson calls and says she is on her way to see him. He begs Mum to at least stay for that. If he really is a suspect like Tina said, then he will need Mum's support.

"Okay," she says. "I'm sure there is no need to worry but I will stay and see the officer with you. Then I have to go home. Dad needs me."

Apparently his father cut himself the day before; he was

bleeding profusely and Mum feels that something worse could happen if she's not there.

"At least Anna is awake now," Mum says. "Things will only get better from now on."

"Anna's mother is on her way," he says. There is nothing *better* about that. But he realises he needs to be grateful that his wife is awake even if she doesn't recall that she has a husband.

"That's good," Mum says.

"Yeah, great. Her husband agreed to grant her a week's freedom."

"Surely it's not that bad?"

He looks at her, with total disbelief. "I'm sorry, were you not at the wedding?"

Mum nods. "They're just old-fashioned," she says. "At least he's not coming along."

"But, Mum. She's not going to be any help. I'm going to have to babysit her!"

Speaking of babysitting, he needs to talk to Pernilla about her – their – baby. She has stopped sending him messages now that he actually needs to be in contact with her. With Anna being awake, it's essential that he's viewed as someone who takes responsibility for his mistakes. He will tell Pernilla that he can't leave his wife but if she could perhaps move elsewhere, he can visit her and the baby regularly. Not seeing his child would be devastating but he also has a reputation to think about. He will agree to pay child support. If only the jobs were more frequent. Recently, people have been complaining about him being distracted.

Unfortunately, Tina has also disappeared. Not even Rob has heard from her.

"She's probably busy with some investigation," Rob says.

Or she doesn't want to be in touch with a suspect, Erik thinks.

When the doorbell rings, Erik expects it to be Linda Johansson and he puts his best smile on. Except it's that boy…

"David?"

"You said to come by?"

"Oh, yeah. Sorry, I completely forgot."

Shit. He should send him away.

"I've really looked forward to seeing Sebastian and Lukas," David says. "I only have an older brother so it's like they're my little brothers."

Maybe he could let him play with the boys while he talks to Linda Johansson? It would be better if Mum doesn't tend to the children when the police arrive, she could be by his side one hundred per cent.

"The boys are in the basement," he says. "They're playing with their train set. Maybe you could hang out with them for a while? If you could just you know… keep them occupied. I have an important meeting."

"Sure, no problem."

David takes his shoes off, something Anna would appreciate.

"If you wouldn't mind closing the door," Erik says. "I'll get you all some cordial and buns when we're done up here."

"Sounds great."

Is it odd that a teenage boy wants to hang out with two five year olds? No. He shakes it off. He remembers playing with his younger sister, how great it was that he could use her as an excuse to still play.

*

When Officer Johansson arrives, Mum is overly friendly, offering coffee and newly baked cinnamon buns. He just wants to get it over and done with.

"We have tried to interview Anna but her memory loss has made it difficult," she says.

"I know."

He's fidgeting with a napkin and tries to stop.

"A witness has stepped forward," Officer Johansson says.

"Really?"

Someone saw something at the school? It amazes Erik that the inhabitants of their town have been talking to the police, sharing their sightings of her, as if they were spies. He wants to move away so badly in that moment, go far away from this small-town nonsense.

"Does that mean you know who attacked her?" Mum asks.

"We're not sure. If we arrest him, we only have four days to charge him." Officer Johansson looks at Erik intently. "Did Anna really never mention being frightened of anyone?"

He thinks hard, wishing there was someone he could mention, but Anna wasn't easily intimidated by anyone.

"No. I don't think so," he says.

"Did Anna ever have any guest speakers at work?"

He has no idea. "Maybe. You would have to check with the principal."

"Okay." She makes a note. "I also need to ask you... was Anna interested in art or did she do any art modelling?"

"What?" He racks his brain for anything that could vaguely be relevant but comes up with absolutely nothing. "No."

Who are they talking to? Is it based on actual suspicion? Especially after Tina's comments about the police now suspecting him, he would really like to know.

"I know you can't tell me who it is," he says. "But do you think he or she is guilty?"

"We'll see. Anything you can think of would help."

"He's an artist?" Mum asks.

Officer Johansson looks at her apologetically. "I have already said too much," she says.

"Fuck, that's sick," Erik says. He can't wrap his head around this news.

Mum strokes his back. "At least they've found him."

"I guess that means I'm no longer a suspect," Erik says.

"I'm sorry?"

"Yeah, I heard you might have it in for me," he says, forcing himself to laugh.

Officer Johansson arches her eyebrows.

"Why would you think that?" she asks.

"Just someone…"

"It's that woman, Tina," Mum says, her voice shrill.

He looks at Mum and tries to kill her with his eyes, his lips a whisper: "She's put her job on the line for me, Mum. You can't expose her."

"Who's Tina?" Officer Johansson asks.

He shakes his head to Mum. "No one," he says.

"For God's sake, Erik. She can't tell you things like that without any evidence!"

"Who are you talking about?"

Officer Johansson looks as if she's demanding an answer and Mum is all too willing to provide one.

"Tina something. She's with the police. One of your colleagues."

Officer Johansson shakes her head. "I don't know of any Tina and I'm familiar with most staff."

Mum sighs. "Erik?"

He gives up. "I don't know. Tina. Big hair, green eyes, very pink lipstick although perhaps not when she's on duty." Officer Johansson still looks like a question mark. "I've only met her once... eh... small gap between her front teeth." That's all he's got.

"Tina Olsson?"

That sounds familiar. "Think so."

The officer gets her phone out and scrolls through some pictures before she shows him a Facebook photo of Tina. It appears to be from a party and Tina has her arm around a man, a drink in the other hand. "Yes, that's her," he says, relieved. For a second, he thought she was some psycho pretending to be someone she's not.

"She's not a police officer," Officer Johansson says. "She's a cleaner at the police station."

"Oh..."

There's brief eye contact with Mum who seems to be saying "I told you not to trust her" but he's too busy racking his brains. What did Tina actually tell him? She knew about Pernilla and she mentioned Anna's student, and also Kent. She insinuated that Anna had an affair with Kent? Was it all lies?

"This is very serious," Officer Johansson says as she makes a few notes in her notepad. "What exactly did she tell...?"

"Did you ever speak to Anna's colleague, Kent?"

He knows it's rude to interrupt but he has his own thought process and he needs to go back to the beginning.

"I don't understand how that's relevant."

"It's just... I need to know if she was telling me the truth."

"I'm more concerned about her telling you anything."

Right. He needs to play this differently.

"I understand but she... Did you speak to Kent? Did he seem to like Anna a bit too much?"

"Look, she's had no insight into our investigation. It's possible that she has seen some paperwork on someone's desk but..." Officer Johansson rubs her temples. "This is very serious."

She's clearly not going to tell him anything.

"At least you seem to have found the attacker," Mum says. "Just one question. Is there a motive?"

58

Rolf

March 2016

Rolf usually got what he wanted. He wanted a wife who accepted that he slept with other women and he found someone who didn't value herself highly enough. He wanted a baby and he replaced the birth-control pills with sugar pills. He wanted press attention and he stirred up a storm. He wanted a woman and he read her like a book and found her weak spot.

Now, he wanted Anna gone. He had tried talking to Iris but she had built a wall around herself.

Instead, he went to see Frida, bringing a couple of bottles of cheap red wine.

"Where's the party?" he asked and held up the bag.

"Babe!" She was all over him, hungry for his attention.

"I need to see your kid," he said.

"Dan?"

"Unless the other one is out of prison?"

She didn't find that amusing.

"He's out in a couple of months," she said.

Rolf would be gone by then; that one was even more trouble than the young one.

"He's in his room," she said. "Happy as can be. Don't ask me why!"

She too was in an excellent mood.

"Be a dear and open the wine and I'll be right back," he said.

He knocked on the kid's door before he opened it. It was sparsely furnished with only a bed, a chair and a badly built wardrobe. Frida wasn't exactly an interior designer.

"Get out," the kid said, not even giving him a chance.

As much as that pissed Rolf off, he maintained a friendly tone.

"Hang on," he said. "I have something that you want."

The kid, who had been lying down on his unmade bed, sat up.

"I've got everything I need," he said.

He looked a bit too cheerful. "Are you on drugs?" Rolf asked.

"Fuck off, I'm not stupid."

"Sorry," Rolf said, holding his hands up like a bad guy caught by the police. He entered the room while talking. "You know your teacher friend?"

That zapped the good mood right out of him. "What about her?"

"I know you want to fuck her."

"What? No!"

He was a useless liar. Rolf inched closer to the kid's bed and sat down.

"You see, your desire will solve a problem of mine. I need

you to tell social services that she made advances on you."

"No way." He laughed at Rolf. "You're insane. She will never talk to me after that."

Rolf leaned against the wall, making himself comfortable despite the room's overpowering smell of dirt and sweat. It really needed to be aired out. He picked up a book, a notebook of sorts with a hard cover, and threw it at the window. A small windowpane popped.

"What the hell are you doing?"

"You love your mother, don't you?"

"What's going on?" Frida was at the door. She looked at the window. "What happened?"

"Just an accident, babe. I was talking to Dan here about you, and how much he must love you."

Her face contorted into a grimace. "What?" A second later, Rolf got up and held her by the neck, pushing her up against the wall. His life was falling apart, his perfect marriage of over twenty years was coming to an end, and he needed these lowlifes to help him restore it.

"You love your mother, don't you, Dan?" he said. "She's all you've got. That teacher friend of yours couldn't care less about you. You know that, right?"

The conflict within the boy was obvious. He would pick his mother though, all boys did. If Rolf's mother were still alive, he would pick her any day.

"Your teacher is fucking someone else," Rolf said. "My wife, to be precise."

The kid didn't look as shocked as he thought he would, or perhaps he was used to keeping a straight face. Frida was more upset.

"You're married?" she asked, letting out a sob.

"If only you read the papers, babe, you would know that."

The kid stood up. He didn't even try to reach for Frida. He simply stared at Rolf.

"Get the fuck out of our house," he said.

Rolf tightened his grip on Frida's neck.

"If you honour your part of the deal."

59

Erik

May 2016

David is back. He puts his trainers next to the door and hangs his denim jacket on one of the hooks in the narrow entrance hall. Erik notices his jeans are short and his T-shirt has seen better days. Perhaps he can dig out a few old shirts for the guy? Unless that would offend him? Or perhaps it's just the fashion? He wishes Anna was there to clarify.

"The boys are in there somewhere," Erik says.

Erik isn't quite sure why David is here. Did they agree for him to come back and play with the kids? Or is he babysitting? Is he supposed to pay him?

"You've got a really nice house," David says.

"Thanks. It still needs quite a bit of work."

It really does. They had underestimated how much maintenance it needed, a source of endless arguments since Anna didn't favour his DIY skills.

"If you need help with anything, let me know," David says. "I'm good at carpentry."

"Good to know."

Anna must like this student, he's polite.

They locate Sebastian and Lukas. Always together: different but inseparable. They're building a puzzle but the pieces are not quite sticking together the way they want them to.

"Careful," Erik says. "Or you'll break them."

"Here, let me help you," David says.

He patiently shows them what goes where.

"Boys," Erik says. "We're leaving for the hospital in half an hour."

Hopefully David understands that he will need to leave by then.

Thumbs up from the boys. Great. Erik goes back to the kitchen and pulls out Anna's laptop. He hasn't received any emails from Black Adam in about two weeks. He looks at the last email he sent. I'm sure she did love you. The question is, in what way? She was, and still is, married. Why had that upset him so much? Was he harbouring feelings for Anna?

His phone rings. It's Rob.

"Hey, I heard Anna woke up?"

"Yes, it's great." He says that to everyone. Great. Fantastic. What a miracle. No one understands that it's not his wife who's woken up. It's a woman who looks like his wife.

"Look, Erik. I'm calling because… I mean, I know you have a lot going on, especially with Anna being awake and everything but I don't want you to feel excluded, so… would you be up for a gig?"

"We haven't practised in ages."

"It's like cycling! There's an opening tonight. Lead singer of the other band is ill and they refuse to do it without him. Total amateurs, obviously!"

He laughs and Erik can't deny he feels a stir of excitement.

It would feel good to bring the guitar out, to be a musician for the night.

"What about the others?"

"They're in as well."

But. "Shit. I don't have a babysitter. Mum just left."

"Oh." Rob is obviously disappointed.

"Do you have any girlfriends who can babysit?" Erik asks. Joking about Tina makes it less painful. He called Rob as soon as he found out that Tina was a cleaner, not a police officer. Why would Tina even do that? To get back with Rob? Or to stir up someone's life? Rob, however, seemed more worried about Tina being exposed than about Erik.

"I'm sorry about Tina," he says.

"I know. You were just trying to help," Erik says sarcastically.

"That's right, and now Anna is awake so it's all good, right?"

Erik ignores him. Rob still feels bruised about Tina.

"Can't you find someone else?" Rob says. "A neighbour's kid or something?"

Erik does want to play, so he racks his brain. Who could he reach out to? Just then, the boys – all three of them – come rushing into the kitchen, cars on the floor, racing. *That could work.*

"Hey, David? Are you free tonight?"

*

Erik isn't planning to get drunk, it just happens. No one can blame him though; he's been through a lot. He enjoys the pumping music, the smell of beer, the feeling of being "one of the gang", swigging the beers back mixed with a few shots. Not too many. He keeps saying "no more" but drinks anyway, reality breaking away at the seams.

The women crowd around him and the band as they dance, sprinkling compliments about the set they played. He notices that the average age of the audience is older than it used to be. When did he become old?

Someone grabs his arms and he turns around.

"*Hej*, Erik."

Pernilla? She seems like a drunken vision.

"I've never heard you play before," she says. "You were great!"

"Thanks." He reminds himself that she's carrying his baby. This is awkward. He should say something. "What are you doing here?"

"I heard you were playing so I thought I would check it out."

"But I haven't heard from you in ages."

"Right." She studies the floor briefly before fixing him with her blue, blue eyes again. "I wanted to see if you would chase me if I played hard to get."

"Oh." They should talk. "Can I get you a drink?"

"Sure."

They make their way to the bar and he notices that she has slipped her hand into his. He will let that one slide for now.

"What can I get you?" he says. "Coke, water, juice?"

"Vodka tonic, please."

"Vodka?" He attempts to shake the fuzzy drunken feeling. "Shouldn't you drink soft drinks only?"

She laughs. "I'm not an alcoholic."

"But... you're pregnant."

"What?" She's not laughing anymore. "Are you saying I look fat?"

"No, of course not, but you told the police you're carrying my baby…"

Her face distorts. "What the hell are you talking about? I'm not pregnant."

"You're not?"

"No!"

Wow. He looks at her stomach and it doesn't look swollen at all. Why *did* he think she was pregnant? He needs to sober up.

"A vodka tonic for the lady and a Coke for me, please."

"Party pooper." Her palms are on his chest, stroking his shirt. "So, you thought we were having a baby together." She snuggles up to him. "Were you excited?"

The drinks arrive and he pays before downing his Coke.

"Shit," he says, ignoring her question. "You're definitely not pregnant?"

She shakes her head. "No, but we could make a baby if that's what you want?"

It's not what he wants. Not at all.

"I'm mad," he says.

He really is mad as hell. It was Tina who told him Pernilla was pregnant. This whole time, he's felt like shit because of it. He should leave and go home to calm down, but instead he heads back to the dance floor.

Pernilla runs after him. "Hey, wait up."

But he's heading for Rob. He grabs his mate's shoulder and turns him around. "Remember how your girlfriend said Pernilla was pregnant?" he says loudly, talking over the music. "Look, she's right here and guess what? NOT pregnant." He gestures to Pernilla who's clearly not sure how to react.

"Maybe she's lying?" Rob shouts. "Maybe she did tell

the police and now she's getting cold feet?" He throws an unimpressed look at Pernilla.

Erik looks at her. "Did you?"

"Of course not."

She seems genuine and considering that Tina has lied before that seems the best bet. It's all Rob's fault. He's responsible for bringing Tina into Erik's life. At that moment, Erik shuts down his friendly feelings for Rob and activates his fists.

"What the fuck!"

Rob ducks but is quickly back up, throwing him a punch of his own. Erik's face hurts. He will not stand for this. He gathers all his strength and rams into Rob, flooring him. But Rob is quick; he wraps his legs around Erik and they end up wrestling, rolling around on the sticky floor, sweat dripping, strong arms pulling and punching. Erik isn't sure how long they fight. He's just so angry, his hands hungry for blood.

Someone breaks them apart. Erik is accused of being the instigator and he's thrown out, but Pernilla is immediately on hand with a napkin, wiping the blood off.

"You did that for me?" she asks, her body too close, her lips almost on his. He pushes her off.

"Get off me," he says. "I don't know if you lied or not. I was angry about something else."

She stares at him with hurt eyes.

"You will regret that," she says, and storms off.

60

Daniel

March 2016

What a douche bag.

Rolf was pinning Frida against the wall, making threats.

"There is no deal," Dan muttered as he grabbed his brother's hockey stick and swung it into the Nissan dude's back. Both he and Frida fell to the floor like an old set of dominos, Frida clutching her neck, breathing hard, and the dude holding his hands to his back.

"Getting a bit old for fighting, grandpa," Dan said and swung it again.

"Stop it!" Frida begged. "Don't kill him."

"Just teaching him a lesson."

When Dan was satisfied that the dude no longer posed a threat, he let the hockey stick slide out of his hand. It landed on the floor with a *bang*. The dude was groaning and Frida crying.

Dan quickly filled up the Fjällräven backpack and threw

his toiletries into an ICA supermarket bag. He was out of there.

In the hallway, Frida was trying to comfort her lover but he didn't seem into it. Dan stepped over the sad twosome and bent down to the dude's level: "Nice try, you dumb fuck, but I fucking hate my whore mother."

He avoided looking at Frida's face; the tears rapidly turning her into a hopeless mess of a victim. *I'm doing this to protect you, Mother.* He was confident the dude wouldn't be back after this. But it was a worry that he had it in for Anna. Dan needed to protect her now.

"When you're with me, no one will hurt you."

"Oh, Dan. You make me feel so safe."

She leaned into him and he held her in a firm grip.

"I will never let you go."

Outside the air was cool. He put his jacket on and unlocked his bike. Frida hadn't asked him where he was going. She hadn't even asked if he was okay. Instead she had been huddled over that loser. The choices she made. He spat on the ground. He was over it.

Getting on his bike, he headed over to Anna's.

61

Rolf

March 2016

Despite his best violent efforts, the kid didn't scare Rolf. He was messing with the wrong artist. If he didn't watch it, his life would be portrayed in a series of paintings: "A sad little shit's life" – an epic, dark story told by the world-renowned artist, Rolf Sören. He would happily let everyone see how pathetic the kid's life was: drunken mum, jailbird brother, a childish crush on a teacher. It was depressing as hell.

Rolf decided to end it with Frida. Apart from being beaten up by her son, the final straw was the downward spiral that had become their sex life. He had been on top, deep inside of her, when her body had become unnaturally still, almost lifeless. His concern had barely had time to register. She had been snoring! Asleep in the middle of his winning, circular cock-movement.

He no longer had a use for her, anyway. He had all the information he needed. But Frida had no one, her son's affections elsewhere, and so she incessantly texted and called him.

When he arrived home, he planned to tell Iris about Frida. It would feel good to share, cleansing, and a good way to start over. But before he got the chance, she said: "I'm leaving you."

Iris sat in the kitchen, a cup of tea and an open book in front of her. It was as if she had been waiting for him. Next to her were two suitcases. She had already packed.

"Where are you going?" he asked. "Moving in with your teacher friend?"

"How do you know she's a teacher?"

Ah. She got him. How was he supposed to know that?

"She was Teacher of the Year. I read about her somewhere."

"Right, and you just happened to know that's the same person I'm seeing because there aren't many teachers around?"

"I know what she looks like, Iris, and it matched the photo in the article."

Iris stopped fiddling with her tea cup.

"You know what she looks like?"

"I fucking saw you, Iris. In our own home!" God, that felt good. Like he was justified in his anger. Her face was priceless too. "That's right, Iris, I came home early because I was having a boring evening, because other women just can't give me what you can, Iris."

She stood up but instead of picking her bags up, she gently touched the cut on his face.

"What happened to you, Rolf?"

"Oh." He touched her hand. "Nothing, just a mindless fight."

"Since when do you fight?"

337

He shrugged, not in the mood to share.

"I'm sorry," she said. She composed herself, kissed his cheek and made to leave. "I'll tell Karin we're taking a break."

"Is that all it is?" he asked. "A break? Because I don't want to die alone."

"You still have plenty of years in you," Iris said, looking amused. "And there's always Frida. She called. She's hot for you, but you should tell her to stop beating you up. You're more of a 'make love, not war' kind of man."

"Frida called you?"

"I've had enough of the drama, Rolf. I'm out. I have rented an apartment and ... well, I will always love you. We have Karin and we will behave in a civilised way."

It was as if she spoke for the both of them, and when he heard her car roll out of the courtyard and onto the asphalted single lane road, he didn't think. He just acted, got into his car and drove to that teacher's school for a heart to heart.

*

Frida had been useful to some extent. She had read the kid's journal and had found Anna's routine written down. That's how he knew she often stayed late at work. He had also found out that her husband was a house painter named Erik. Rolf had seen a photo of him on the painting company's website and he was an attractive man, in a rugged kind of way: blond with a slight stubble. Anna's life seemed perfect. What could she possibly be thinking, wanting to give that up for an adventure with Iris? Even if they thought it was the real deal – love – it wouldn't last. Iris was a free spirit, she wouldn't want to become a stepmother to two young boys. The very thought was ridiculous. Had Iris made any promises to Anna? He needed to know if she really was the reason his marriage was over.

He had printed off a photo of Anna from a school event, thanks to Google Images, just in case. He had obviously seen her but the first time it had been, well... without clothes and the second time she had been sweaty while jogging. She had brown, glossy hair that reached her shoulders, she was larger than Iris's women used to be, and although she dressed like a teacher in rather ordinary clothes, there was an element of pretty to her. He had to admit that. She was shaggable.

When Rolf arrived at the school he wasn't sure whether to barge into the teacher's area or whether to wait for her in the parking lot. Her black Volvo V70 was there, poking him in the eye: hello-I-have-been-to-your-house-before.

Being back at a school was strangely intimidating. Memories of bullies teasing him about his hippie clothes and his cheating, lowlife father and his mother who tried to cover for her husband's mistakes. He found he couldn't go into the school building. He would wait for her here, in the school courtyard.

62

Anna

March 2016

The day after Daniel threatened Anna, she bumped into Kent several times, and every time she was about to say "I have an issue with Daniel." But then what? "He wants to move into my house. I know it's crazy. Well, he wants me to be his mother but he also kissed me, so I'm not sure what his intentions are. Why haven't I reported it? Well, he's seen me kiss, and perhaps even make love to, another woman even though I am married. Yes, I have decided to leave my husband, so who cares about that? It would tarnish my reputation but I could possibly, possibly live with that. But Daniel also stopped me in the corridor today, whispering that he will kill himself if I report him or stop him from moving in. So I'm kind of stuck."

Daniel had slowed down as he approached her, smirking. She refused to turn around, choosing to show no fear. But the moment he leaned in with his threat, she couldn't help it, she let out an involuntary gasp. This couldn't go on. She immediately went to see the principal but Johan was at a conference and could only fit her in the following day.

She felt trapped. Daniel had played her well. It was a classic case of manipulation and she kicked herself for allowing it to become so personal. But then again, that's who she was. Her Teacher of the Year accolade had been a result of her "creativity, pedagogical approach and going that extra mile for her students".

Anna called Erik to ask if he could please pick the children up from day care, blaming lessons she needed to plan. He was off work that day anyway but he was jamming with Rob and got annoyed. Still, he grudgingly agreed. In the meantime, Anna headed to the counsellor but she was off sick. She felt let down, even though she blamed herself. Her idealistic views had allowed this to go on for too long. She decided to leave and instead deal with her situation at home first. Erik had rushed to his gig the night before and not given her a chance to speak.

*

By the time she got home, she felt ready to discuss their marriage but Erik had his jacket on.

"We're out of milk," he said. "I'll just go and pick up some groceries. The boys are watching a movie."

"Okay…" She was so focused on the conversation she was finally going to have with Erik that she couldn't really think of anything else to say.

She went into the living room where Sebastian and Lukas were slumped into their beanbags.

"How was your day?"

She kissed their heads but they were non-responsive, *The Lion King* clearly more captivating. Her heart felt heavy watching the two of them, but it didn't change anything. She loved them.

She returned to the kitchen to start dinner. Twenty minutes later, when the sausages were fried and the potatoes were boiling, she laid the table and finally sat down to wait for Erik. He should be home soon. She checked her emails to make the time go by faster. Thankfully there were no emails from Daniel but there was a new one from Xeroxwed. Excitement quickly turned to shock as she read it.

> After this weekend, the sex... well, I'm not sure you're up for this. I don't want to see you again.

Her stomach started cramping and her heart was squeezed so hard that she thought she might be having a heart attack. Had it meant nothing to Iris? Had it really only been about sex and due to Anna's inexperience, she was now going to end it? She hadn't mentioned anything the night before so why this sudden realisation? Anna picked up the phone to call Iris when there was a knock on the door.

Daniel. She had almost forgotten about him. Thankfully the children were still watching TV.

"Is my room ready?" he asked, his backpack slung over one shoulder and a plastic bag in one hand.

He was about to step over the threshold when she physically had to stop him.

"Daniel," she said. "You can't live here."

"Sure I can."

He was in a spirited mood.

"Daniel, I have a family."

"I know," he said. "I want that too and I'm here to protect both you and your family."

He took another step towards her and once again, she had to put her hands up to keep him out.

"I don't want to call the police," she said. "But I will if I have to."

"So? I couldn't care less. By the time they arrive, I will already have established myself in the basement."

That didn't even make sense. "Then they will remove you," she said.

"I have a knife and if they come anywhere near me, I will kill myself."

It was too much. Was he even serious? She wasn't sure how she had ended up in this situation. All she had tried to do was show compassion.

"This is not appropriate," she said. "You need to leave and we will have to talk tomorrow at school." *And at that point, I will have talked to Kent, the principal and social services.* There was no other way.

Just then, she heard the Volvo pulling in to the carport. That would be Erik returning from the supermarket. Daniel wouldn't be able to push past her husband.

"That's my husband," Anna said.

"I'm sure he would love to hear about your woman," he said and made no attempt to leave.

"Don't blackmail me," she said. It wasn't going to matter if he did even though Iris had obviously changed her mind. She would still talk to Erik but she needed to be in control of the communication. It shouldn't come from a student of hers. "That's not what I would expect from someone who wants to move into my house," she continued.

His facial expression changed then, from arrogant to almost sweet.

"So I can move in?"

"Tomorrow," she lied. "I need time to prepare your room."

She could hear Erik opening and closing the car door. He would be there any minute and she needed Daniel out of the way. Otherwise the conversation she was going to have with him would start on the wrong foot. He couldn't stand students turning up unannounced.

Daniel looked at her as if he were assessing her. "Don't mess with me," he said. He grabbed hold of her shirt and when they were face to face, he said through gritted teeth. "I will live here, I will eat at your dinner table and I will fuck you when you're ready to accept that."

His words slapped her in the face and she instinctively pushed him.

"I'll be back," he said and walked off.

When Erik turned up at the door, her pulse was still racing.

"What's up?" he asked.

She felt fear. *I will fuck you when you're ready to accept that.*

"Nothing," she said, her heart beating fast. "It's nothing. I just thought I heard someone."

"No burglars," he said. "Just me."

She sat down, attempting to regulate her breathing, and told Erik she needed to speak to him.

"Sounds ominous," he said. "What's it about?"

He seemed annoyed and a panic attack washed over her. She couldn't do this now. "Let's talk later." She needed fresh air.

"What?"

"I'll just be an hour. Please feed the boys. I need to dash down to the school to collect something."

"School? Now?"

Where else could she go? If she went outside, Daniel might

follow her. She needed to go to her safe haven, where she could unlock a door with her access card and then lock the door behind her. Where no one else would be at this hour. She needed solitude.

She grabbed the car keys and headed out before Erik could say anything further. Driving normally soothed her but she kept looking left and right for signs of Daniel on his bike.

Like someone on the run, she rushed from her car to the school building, quickly swiping her card and entering the building, then pulling the door closed behind her.

But even though she was alone at a desk, with only a dim light on, she couldn't find a sense of peace. She tried to call Kent but he didn't pick up. Should she call Iris? While debating whether she wanted to talk to her, the words in the email still raw and hurtful, Iris called her. Her name flashed on the screen and Anna felt her protective wall give way. She answered.

"Hi Anna, sorry to disturb you. Can you talk?"

"Sure."

"Did you speak to Erik? I don't want to put any pressure on you, I just thought that perhaps you wanted to talk about it?"

"What does it matter?"

"What do you mean? I thought this weekend..." Iris paused and Anna felt the tears on her cheeks. She was already mourning Iris. "I thought," Iris continued. "I guess I thought I was Terry in *Loving Her* and that you were Renay but instead of moving in with your daughter you would be bringing Sebastian and Lukas. Was that naïve?"

Iris's way of sending mixed messages angered Anna.

"Do you always interpret life through novels?" she asked.

"Great novels are a reflection of life," Iris replied.

"Are they?" That wasn't Anna's experience. "Everything seems so much easier in novels."

"Anna, what's going on? Did he take it badly... or did you not tell him?"

Anna scoffed. "Why would I tell him anything?"

Iris was quiet. Did she feel bad about the email? Because she should, especially after such a magical time together.

"Did you have a bet with someone?" Anna asked. "Your husband perhaps. To see if you could make a straight woman love you? Oh no, silly me, you've obviously had sex with married women before, so that can't be it. So why do it?"

"Anna... are you saying that you love me?"

That's what Iris picked up from her outburst? "You're so fickle," Anna said frustrated. "So what if I'm not good enough in bed?"

That's when the dam completely broke and the tears started flooding for real. She grabbed a tissue from a packet on the desk.

"Anna," Iris said. "What are you talking about?"

Iris just didn't get it. Anna blew her nose and said: "Iris, let me translate this into your own language, namely literature. I'm like Anna Karenina to you. You toy with me but when I'm about to ask my husband for a divorce you change your mind, and I'm the one who will be scorned by society. Or perhaps you thought I was Madame Bovary? Well, let me tell you that I am not as desperate as her. I was not just seeking an adventure." She paused and took a deep breath but she wasn't finished. "The fact that both of these women die is perhaps an indication of where this is heading."

"Anna, stop," Iris said. "Please, just stop. I have no idea what you're talking about. I love you and I have left Rolf. I was simply calling to see how your conversation with Erik went. If you're trying to tell me that you changed your mind, then just say so. I'm a big girl."

"*Me* changing my mind? You're the one who… oh, wait let me just…" She scrolled through her emails. "Oh, here it is. 'After this weekend, the sex… well, I'm not sure you're up for this. I don't want to see you again.' That's a pretty clear message so there is really no need to call me to see how I'm doing."

She wanted to hang up but couldn't. Deep down she wanted Iris to apologise and say that she hadn't meant it like that.

"Anna, I haven't sent you an email," Iris said. "I don't think I even know what your email address is."

Denial was worse.

"Really," Anna said. "So xeroxwed@gmail.com just happens to be someone who knows about us having sex up against the library photocopier."

"Oh, dear God."

"Exactly."

It was supposed to feel good, to feel justified, but she just felt a permeating sadness.

"Anna, please trust me. That was not from me. I am fully committed to you."

Was that possible? Anna tried to piece it together. If it hadn't been sent by Iris, could it have been from Daniel? Was it one of his other games?

"I've got to go," she said. She needed to call Kent again.

"Anna, wait. Where are you? You sound really upset. I'm coming to see you right now."

"No, don't. I'm at school but I need to go home and talk to Erik, to get it over with."

"Okay. And Anna…"

"Yes?"

"I really do love you."

Anna still felt bruised, and also confused. Had Iris really not sent that email? She wanted to believe that it was from anyone but Iris. She needed to move on. Finding the courage to be true to herself, she said: "I love you too."

Anna wiped her tears and called Kent but there was still no reply. She sent him a text message Call me when you get a chance please. She needed to talk to him about Daniel and brainstorm what she was going to tell the principal the next day.

She stood up to leave. The deserted teachers' lounge felt foreign. Perhaps she wouldn't be coming back here? Maybe she would have to move and start over somewhere else? The thought made her sad.

She went to the bathroom and checked her make-up. Her face was swollen and her hair a mess, and she wanted to look approachable when she faced Erik. She combed through her hair and pulled out a lip-balm from her handbag.

When she left the building and walked towards her car, she heard footsteps behind her. She turned around and saw someone she recognised.

63

Iris

March 2016

Leaving Rolf had been easy. Despite their many years together, Iris had always felt that the time spent with others had meant less time cementing their own foundation. Obviously, she would always care for him; he had taught her so much, most importantly, confidence.

Jealousy hadn't really been an issue when she was married to Rolf, at least not after the first couple of years. By then she had adjusted to the marriage set-up. Now, however, Iris felt an irrational jealousy towards Erik, a man she hadn't even met. She felt threatened by the fact that he was Anna's age and at one point he had obviously made her feel loved enough to want marriage and children.

Niggling at the back of her mind was the fact that Anna hadn't been in touch since the previous evening, when she called her from the school. Despite Anna finally declaring her love, it had seemed under duress. Had she changed her mind since? Had the callous email about the sex not being good enough scared her away? She hadn't explained to Anna that

Rolf was the likely sender; it would have revealed too much about her complicated marriage. At least now Iris was free of her soon to be ex-husband's twisted ways.

To stop herself from worrying, Iris thought about their weekend away. Anna's inquisitive eyes, the mounting passion and how adventurous she had become. There was a never-ending sense of exploration between them.

She hadn't imagined it. They had a connection. Surely Anna would get a divorce? Iris couldn't imagine Anna going back to her loveless marriage, and the student threatening her had actually done Iris a favour. There would be no more secrecy.

Even if Anna didn't leave Erik, it wouldn't change anything with Rolf. She had made her decision, and Rolf would come round. They would be friends, she was sure. No more sex though and she was okay with that.

"Your father and I are taking a break," she told Karin.

"Are you getting divorced?" She sounded unexpectedly unemotional about it.

"Probably."

"At least you won't have to fight over custody," Karin said.

Iris ignored the sarcasm. She wanted Karin on board.

"We're still friends," she explained. "We will spend your birthday together."

"Really? I spoke to Dad and I think you have some making-up to do."

He had beaten her to it then. "I guess."

"I mean, come on, Mum. Are you a lesbian now?" Her tone was growing harder. "Plus she's like half your age. Are you having a mid-life crisis?"

"It's not like that."

"Of course not. It's different, isn't it? Everything is always different with you and Dad."

"We love you."

"Really? But you don't give a shit about my reputation? It's bad enough having a father who is controversial for the sake of it. At least he used to have a message. 'Save the planet, love each other.' But now every painting is a bloody mess! No pun intended. And now you..."

Finally Karin stopped for air and Iris gasped. She had never heard Karin speak badly about her father and although it probably should have upset her, it made her feel slightly better. She needed to capitalise on this new-found neutralisation of their relationship before it tipped over.

"I'm just following my heart," Iris paused. "Her name is Anna. Even if I hadn't met her, I still would have left. Our relationship was once built on a mutual understanding..."

"Of sleeping with others, yeah, I know."

Iris pretended not to hear. "But then it became cheap."

The word "cheap" hung between them like a tattered old T-shirt on a laundry line. They sat in silence but at least Karin didn't hang up.

"I'm happy," Iris said.

"So it's going to be you and her?"

"I don't know."

They promised to speak again the next day. Despite Karin's belligerence, Iris felt closer to her daughter. Rolf could no longer monopolise the time with Karin. Now Iris would form her own bond with her.

Iris had Googled the phone number for the painting company Erik worked for. It was incredible how easily accessible everything was these days.

"I need my apartment painted," she said. "By Erik Berg. I hear he's the best."

The apartment did need painting and someone had to do it.

"I'm sorry, he's on leave at the moment."

"Oh." Anna had never mentioned a holiday. Could she really go from one get-away to another so effortlessly, as if the first one didn't mean anything? Or was it an emergency trip to fix the marriage?

"When will he be back?" Iris asked.

"We're not sure."

"Right... well, how long did he ask to be on leave for?"

"He didn't exactly..."

"I see. Erm... I'm a friend of his wife's and I promised I would only ask for him." A white lie was like a companion, a trusted friend.

She needed to have met Erik, to see whether they would all be able to get along. Even though Rolf was upset at the moment, she knew he would come round. Would Erik?

"Look, I'm really sorry," the man on the phone said. "Anna is in the hospital... she's been attacked."

64

Rolf

March 2016

R olf brought Iris lunch but she didn't eat, the fork playing with the spaghetti, moving it around like a picky
child. She wasn't sulking, she was just calm and composed
and he realised this wasn't about Lena or Frida or even
about them anymore. Iris was really through with him. The
realisation was a major blow.

"I don't know what to tell the police," she said. "Should I
call them and tell them I knew her? Would that help?"

He didn't like the idea of her getting involved with the
police.

"If you don't have to, I wouldn't," Rolf said. "I mean, you
can't help them anyway."

Her facial expression was pained.

"There was this... thing she told me about, someone threatening her. I should tell them."

Rolf had a different opinion: he wanted them to forget
that this woman had ever existed.

"I don't know, Iris. In my experience, you stay away from the police unless they contact you."

"No one knew that we were friends, I don't think they will contact me."

"That's good, Iris. Hopefully that means you won't have to get involved."

"But Rolf," she said. "I want to help."

"I know you do and I'm sorry about her being in the hospital," he said. "But you need to face reality... even if she wakes up, she might not leave him."

At first she didn't say anything but when he reached a hand across to touch hers, she withdrew her hand, saying: "I'm more concerned about her recovering."

"I'm sure she will, she seems like a healthy and strong woman." He paused for effect. "I mean up close."

She looked up and loosened her grip on the fork, which bounced off of the plate and onto the floor. He leaned down to pick it up, letting her wait for an explanation, a strong need to torture her.

"How exactly do you know that?" she asked, her words barely audible.

"I'm just joking," he said.

"Rolf?" She looked as if she was going to attack him, the lines on her face deep, her body tensing. "Where were you that night?"

"Now hold on..."

He realised that it was only now that it occurred to her, that he might have something to do with her lover's attack.

"You had a cut on your face. Was that the night?" she shrieked. "You obviously hate her! Was it you?"

She scared him: he'd never seen her so tortuously unhappy.

354

"Of course not," he said. "How could you possibly think that?"

She screwed her eyes shut and brought her hands to her face, hiding. Rolf noticed she was still wearing her wedding ring. That was a good sign.

"I don't know what to believe anymore," she said and walked off.

He suspected she was crying and he knew she preferred to do this alone. Yet he followed her, couldn't leave it like this. He needed her. She kept walking down a corridor and into a bedroom. It felt odd, this being her apartment, but he couldn't leave.

She was sitting on a bed, a white quilted bedspread he'd never seen before, pulling under her weight. Her body slumped, his heart ached. Could he enter her private space to comfort her? He cautiously remained in the doorway.

"You gave me your word," she said, as if speaking to the wall. "That you wouldn't tie me down, that you would allow me to be free. That was our agreement. In fact, it was *your* agreement and I adapted."

"I know and I'm sorry," he said. "It's just that we had rules, Iris, and you broke them."

"She didn't deserve this."

PART FIVE

June 2016

65

Erik

Anna's mother is sitting next to her daughter's bed, holding her hand. The sight is astonishing in itself but even stranger is the fact that Anna is talking in a mild manner to her mother. Like an outsider, Erik stands by the door, watching the two women. It feels like a TV set where a director will call "cut" at any time. But so far, the show is rolling on. Erik feels he needs subtitles for the bullshit. "I've been so worried about you" should be translated into "I haven't really cared until now" and "I hope I can help you remember" should be "a week is all I've got, honey, so you better hurry up."

"*Hej*, Erik."

It's the doctor, his coat unbuttoned, revealing a tight, white shirt and pink tie. He looks smart, Erik thinks. He is starting to grow fond of him, not because of his fashion sense but because of how he treats Erik. He is always respectful of his feelings.

"I hear someone has been arrested," he says. "That must be a relief."

"It is," Erik says. "But I don't think he's been charged yet."

Linda Johansson had the courtesy to notify him of the arrest but he doesn't know much more. All he can do is read what's in the papers, which isn't much. Who is it? Can they all relax now? He's desperate enough to call Tina but her phone has been disconnected. Maybe she's been fired? He won't feel guilty about it. She brought this on herself.

"Well, Anna's memory has been getting better," the doctor says. "She may not remember what happened yet but the prospects are good."

"Has she remembered anything specific?" *Like her husband?*

"Not exactly, but it has helped having her mother here. Also, she has spoken of leaving the hospital, which is a good sign. I think that perhaps it's time to start transitioning her back home. Would you be able to cope?"

"Sure..."

"E-e-erik?"

The sound is coming from the bed and they all look at Anna. Did she just say his name? She says it again, with more conviction this time.

"Erik?"

"Anna!"

Erik runs to her bed and holds her hands. He wants to kiss her but he's worried she will turn her head away like the last time.

"Do you remember me?" he says, his words so soft he's not even sure she can hear him. He starts to cry. This is so unexpected.

Anna looks bewildered, as if she's woken up from a bad dream. "I think so," she says.

He turns to the doctor. "I need to take her home."

"I guess I'll go back, then?" her mother says.

Gerda, with her rat-coloured hair tucked behind her ears, the thick glasses making her eyes look comic-like, actually speaks to him. *Yes*, he wants to say, *you can go back to your wife-beating motherfucker of a husband.* But he cordially, albeit sarcastically, says: "I guess your job is done."

He studies Anna: will she react to the exchange between him and her mother? Will she roll her eyes and share a conspiratorial smile with him? Does she remember what her mother is really like, or are they now best buddies? But there is nothing. Just confusion. Still, she's coming home.

*

In the car, his phone rings and it's a woman from the police. Not Linda Johansson unfortunately.

"We would like to talk to you about Tina Olsson," the woman on the phone says.

And he was having such a good day.

"What do you want to know?"

"We need to know everything she told you."

Apparently her information might have compromised their investigation. He wants to yell: what investigation? *You have already arrested someone.* Or haven't they? He should be more helpful.

"I will come down and tell you everything," he says.

*

Erik is excited to pick the children up from day care. They will be happy about Anna coming home. She still may not remember them, but at the moment, they have to take one step at a time.

He used to wonder if Anna would still love him when she woke up. He's been holding her hands, massaging them to keep the blood flowing, etching his touch into her skin so that when she opened her eyes, she would remember his loving touch. And yet when she did wake up, she didn't remember him at all, at least not until now. The question is: does she still love him?

When he arrives at day care and opens the door, he hears someone laughing. He turns his head just as the door to the broom cupboard opens and Pernilla tumbles out. Her hair is messy and she's not alone. She's with... Sophie's dad? Erik stares at the two of them giggling. Although the moment they realise that Erik is there, their faces straighten and they go their separate ways, like two tree branches stretching away from each other. Sophie's dad, whose name Erik doesn't know, has opened and shut the door in less than a second without a glance at Erik. Pernilla makes her way towards the group singing inside, ignoring him. It's almost as if he's invisible.

"Pernilla!" he calls.

She keeps walking and at first, it hurts. Then a feeling of liberation. He might be off the hook. For the first time in a while, he feels what can only be described as hope. Anna is coming home, the police have a suspect for her attack, and he's free of Pernilla.

Just then, Pernilla turns around and winks, before running up to him. She grabs his arm and drags him into the broom cupboard. It feels awkward, especially since she was just here with Sophie's dad.

"I just wanted to get back at you by making you jealous," she whispers. "Did it work?"

Her hands are holding his buttocks in a firm grip.

"No," he says even though he must admit he did feel slightly sidelined.

"Come on, Erik."

"Anna is awake," he says. "I can't do this."

She backs off.

"Unless you kiss me right now, I will make your life very difficult for you."

He hesitates. A kiss is just a kiss, right? He leans in and plants one on her pouty lips. Flash. He opens his eyes and realises she's taken a picture.

"What the hell was that for?"

"Facebook," she says.

"What? Give me that!"

He tries to take the phone off of her but she wriggles out of his grip, laughing. Enough is enough. He takes a firm grip of her body and pushes it up against the wall. "That's enough, Pernilla. Delete that photo now or I will..."

"You will what?"

She seems more turned on than scared.

"What do you want from me?" he says. "You want this?"

He pushes her against the wall, snogs her hard and feels up her boobs, pushing a hand between her legs. He's rough and he's hoping she will cry and tell him she's sorry, but she moans, she bloody moans!

"Fuck this," he says and backs off.

"Come on, that was amazing."

"Just delete that photo, please."

"Fine." She takes out her phone and deletes it in front of him. "But if we don't get together soon, trust me, I will fuck you over."

He leaves the cupboard and goes into the assembly room to collect the boys. If only he had never slept with her. If only he had walked away.

"Sebastian, Lukas…" He's lost his thread. "I have some news."

*

Back at the house, David is waiting for them in the driveway. Erik can't remember asking him to babysit but his life is so chaotic at the moment. Perhaps he planned to jam with Rob? Except they haven't spoken since the incident at the bar. Anyway, the boy has proven himself to be a fantastic babysitter and the children look up to him. He's helpful too, laying the table for dinner and stacking and unloading the dishwasher.

"Our mummy is coming home," Sebastian tells him as soon as he's out of the car.

"Really?"

David seems as happy as Sebastian and Lukas, so Erik feels he can't turn him away. Instead he invites him in for a *fika*. Some defrosted cinnamon buns and cordial never hurt anyone, and the children really do like David being there, even though Erik still doesn't understand what David gets out of this.

The boys talk nonstop about what they're going to do when Mummy comes home.

"Do you think she can bake a cake with us?" Sebastian asks.

"Yeah, for our birthday," Lukas adds.

Shit, they're turning six in a week and he hasn't prepared anything.

"She might not be quite ready for that," Erik says.

"I can bake something," David says.

"You know how to bake?" Erik asks. He just doesn't look the part.

"Sure," he says. "You just need to follow a recipe."

Erik laughs. "You're on."

"Oh, and one more thing," David says. "This is kind of awkward but our house is being fumigated, the owner insists on it, so I was wondering... could I crash here for just one night?"

Oh. It's not that he doesn't like David, he seems like a good kid, but staying overnight? What does he actually know about him?

"Mummy would have said 'yes'," Sebastian says seriously and Erik nods. She would have. How do the boys know about Anna's charitable nature?

"Okay, one night," Erik says.

"Yay, it's like a sleepover!" Lukas says.

"You can sleep in the basement," Erik says. "We have a sleeper couch there." Then he's separated from the rest of them. One whole floor between them.

"What about our room?" Sebastian asks.

"It's fine, buddy," David says. He looks elated. "The basement will be awesome."

"Will Mummy be home for our birthday?" Lukas asks.

"I think so," Erik says. "But no birthday party this year. It will be too much for her."

"What about Grandma?"

"Grandpa can't travel at the moment and she needs to stay

with him, so probably not. She will Facetime you, though."

"And... Gerda?"

"Who's that?" David asks. He picks up another bun and tucks into it with great appetite.

"Anna's mother," Erik explains. They call her by her first name because... well, they have only met her twice."

"Oh, how come?"

It's not really David's business but Erik finds himself telling him anyway. Talking to David is like being friends with your younger self.

"Anna isn't close to her parents," Erik mouths quietly. Sebastian and Lukas don't need to know about this. "Her parents aren't... particularly pleasant."

"Oh, but Anna is so... nice."

"She's worked hard not to be like them I guess."

David nods. "Yeah, that makes a whole lot of sense."

The boys leave the table and run into the living room where Erik can hear them pulling their Lego out. Soon, Sebastian pops his head into the kitchen to ask if David will join them.

"Soon," he says. "Just going to finish this bun." It's his third one.

"My mum isn't nice either," David says to Erik when they're alone again. "I mean, she sort of means well sometimes, but she's..." It looks like he's about to cry and Erik feels panic. He can't deal with any more drama. "Anyway." David seems to pull himself together. "With my brother travelling, he's in Australia right now, she's all I've got. My dad is dead."

"Oh."

Does that mean David sees him as a father figure? He straightens his back, at once feeling respected.

"Where's your mum staying tonight?" he asks.

"She's got a boyfriend," David says. "She's at his place most of the time. I'm usually home alone."

"And your brother, when will he be back from Australia?"

"In about three months or so. It was extended due to... another place he wanted to visit first."

"Sounds amazing," Erik says. "To be so free."

"I guess so. Anyway, I'd better go home and pack."

David puts his shoes on without tying the shoelaces and runs outside. Erik can hear the wheels of his bike skidding on the gravel. He sips his coffee, an unsettling feeling in his stomach; perhaps he's been a bit too generous, agreeing to let the boy stay?

66

Daniel

When Dan unpacks his bags in the basement of Anna's house, it's the same bags he packed only three months earlier before cycling here. Except, that time he wasn't allowed in. Now he's here.

The house smells like a home. He takes out his notebook and writes the scents down: washing powder, coffee, vanilla candles and air-dried sheets. Then he places a tick next to *Step 2 – move into Anna's house*. He's halfway there.

Step 3 – become best mates with her kids

They're getting on quite well already.

Step 4 – fuck her/she dumps the husband

Her husband, Erik, has helped him pull out the sofa bed and provided him with a pile of bed linen, a pillow and a duvet. When Erik is back upstairs, Dan sinks his nose into the sheets and takes a deep breath. At Frida's house, the smell of booze and cigarettes overpowers everything else. This is paradise.

While Dan makes the bed, he can hear the commotions of a family above him. Children playing, fighting and laughing. A father reprimanding them from time to time. The sound of a washing machine whirring in the background together with soft eighties' music.

No sounds of a mother but she's on her way home. He needs to find a way to stay here until then. He's desperate to see the look on Anna's face when she first lays eyes on him. Will she be happy or won't she recognise him? Erik has explained that she's struggling with her memory. Maybe that's good. She won't remember pushing him or that he tried to blackmail her. He can simply be the family friend staying at her house, someone she grows to love. He will be sympathetic and take such good care of her that she will feel as if she can't survive without him. It's an ideal scenario really, her being so vulnerable. It almost feels too simple.

"You're such a special person, David."

He will have to accept that for now, he is David.

"I'm doing this for you," he says.

"Please won't you stay home from school and keep me company?"

"Of course I will."

"Can you lie here next to me, please? I feel so lonely."

He crawls up into her bed and lies on his side, facing her. They lie there together, looking deeply into each other's eyes. She strokes his cheek and that's when he leans in to kiss her. He's a gentleman, he will take things slowly. They kiss for a long time but eventually he grows restless. His hands start to wonder, touch and squeeze. He's so hard now, he needs to get some action.

"Everything okay?"

Dan looks up and sees Erik on the stairs. Couldn't he bloody knock? He quickly puts the notebook on his lap, covering his stiffy.

"Yeah, sure. It's fine."

"Do you want me to help you make the bed?"

"No, that's okay."

"Come on, let's do it together. It will be quicker."

Fuck. He thinks of cold running water, yellow pimples and wonky teeth. That works.

"Sure," he says and gets up.

They work in silence but Dan's mind is in overdrive. He's not sure how he should convince Erik that he must stay. Then again, he hadn't expected the fumigation story to work at all. Erik practically invited him with open arms. Maybe he should make Erik feel like he needs him? That's the one good thing Frida has taught him. "People like to feel needed," she says. The problem is, she's the one needing everyone else. No one needs *her.*

"If you need help with anything around the house, just ask," Dan says.

"Thanks."

Erik smiles and Dan reckons that's a good sign. They tackle the duvet, with Erik holding the cover and Dan feeding the feather-filled comforter into it.

"I mean, with anything," Dan clarifies. "Babysitting, cleaning or food shopping. I'm used to doing housework at home."

"That's nice of you," Erik says and he seems to genuinely consider it. "I might take you up on that. It's been busy here lately."

"I can imagine. It must have been hard... I mean, Anna being attacked."

He glances at Erik, wanting to see his reaction. How much does he love his wife? How hard will it be to eliminate him from her life?

"Yeah," Erik says absentmindedly and they smooth the duvet out over the bed. "That's all done then."

Why can't Erik just open up to him? Should he push it?

"I know you must love her very much," Dan says, hoping to sound like an adult, an equal.

"Mm," Erik says and it looks as if he might cry. "Anyway, I better start dinner."

He turns and walks up the stairs and Dan calls after him.

"Thanks for helping me with the bed!"

When Erik is gone, Dan sits down and thinks about his next move. It's time to stop daydreaming; he needs to make things happen. Frida is a worry. What if she interferes? He wonders if she will miss him when he doesn't come home this evening. Will she call the police? He doubts it. Someone like Frida doesn't trust the police. They came to the school after the attack and before he knew it, he was asked to the police station to answer questions about a note. Since he was a minor, a shaking Frida had to come along. They put the note in front of them.

That was a nasty thing to do, Anna. You know I'm smarter than that.

Dan confessed immediately. There was no point lying.

"Yeah, I wrote that. I regret it now but I was just so upset with my exam results. It was really nasty of her to fail me when I had actually done an okay job. I mean..." He almost started crying here, for effect. "I was trying really hard."

He told them what a great teacher Anna was and that everyone loved her.

"Anyone will back me up on that," he said. "But she was tough, man, and when I first arrived I just wasn't used to that. That's why I wrote the note. I'm sorry. I really hope she gets better soon so that I can tell her that in person."

Frida stayed quiet the entire time, not even mentioning Anna's personal visit to their home. Afterwards, she was hysterical, asking him: "Did you have anything to do with that teacher's attack?"

"I swear, I didn't," he said. "You know I really like her."

She nodded. Yes, she did know that. But she didn't seem happy about it, not even when the exam in question was submitted to the police, and he was in the clear. For now, he just needs to stay out of her way.

He needs to be careful though. Erik and the boys think his name is David. Someone might call him Daniel or Dan but it might be similar enough?

What he needs to do now is make himself indispensable. Luckily, Sebastian and Lukas are already eating out of his hand. They're sweet actually. When they're finally together, himself and Anna, she will obviously want the children to live with them (because that's the kind of mother she is) so he needs them on his side. That's okay though; he really likes Sebastian and Lukas. He could easily be their dad.

That evening he places a tick next to *Step 3 – become best mates with her kids*. He feels he has covered that after just one full day with them.

Now he needs to tackle Erik. What are his weaknesses?

67

Iris

An "Unknown" number flashes on Iris's phone, and she quickly answers it, hoping it's a fully recovered Anna.

"I've been arrested!" a stressed voice says instead. Rolf? "Can you believe it?" he continues. "They're going to search through our house and my studio."

"Really?" she says. What is he up to now? Rolf has been desperately needy lately, constantly calling her. Most likely, the police have simply warned him about his inflammatory art, but she does relish him feeling cornered for once. "And you always think you can get away with anything?"

"Seriously, Iris?" he sulks. "Don't you care?"

"Rolf, what's actually happening?"

She's not in the mood for his theatrics.

"It's true, Iris. I really have been arrested. They're just trying to find evidence to charge me for Anna's attack."

Anna's attack?

"Why?" she says.

"I don't know." He sighs. "They seem to think I had some-thing to do with it."

She doesn't know where to start, what to say. He unequivocally blames Anna for their marriage break-up but would he go to such lengths to get rid of her? She can't believe that he's capable of such a monstrous act but he's Rolf and he can be an enigma. There was that cut on his face. *Did she fight back?*

"Did you have anything to do with it?"

"Of course not!"

Then why would they suspect him? She needs to think. He's the father of her child, the man she has shared her life with for so long. She has to process the information and sort it in her head, go through it step by step.

"Do you have anything to hide?"

"Not really," he says. "Apart from the painting with Anna's hair in it."

"What painting?" *There's a painting?* "With Anna's hair in it?"

This shocks her more than Rolf being arrested. He always sleeps with the women he incorporates into his art. Anna would never...

"I guess they'll charge you in no time," she says, her voice hard.

She's staring out the window, at the lush greenery that's supposed to symbolise summer and love and dreams come true. Why is her world crashing down on her? Anna in a coma, Karin hostile and Rolf... he's somehow involved. How?

"Don't be like that, Iris," he says. It sounds as if he's cry-ing. That would be typical, Rolf making himself the victim. "You make it sound as if you want me to go to prison."

"Perhaps you deserve it," she says. "And just out of curiosity, did you pick a strand of hair off the rug after she had been to the house?"

That would make sense, to get back at Iris.

"No, I didn't."

"Then please do tell me, how come you had her hair in your possession?"

She tries to sound calm but her blood is nearing boiling point.

"I may have met with her to obtain it..." he says.

He what? "You said that you didn't, that it was a joke, a bad one but still, a joke." She had believed him. How stupid of her. He had actually met with her!

"You scared me that time, Iris. I was going to tell you but you were so upset."

"When?" she asks, the anger seeping through.

"It doesn't matter. I've already told them she gave it to me willingly, that plenty of people do, and so far she's not really been in a position to argue about that, has she? Anyway... perhaps *you* should be worried. The police don't seem to know about your relationship with Anna, but maybe they will after going through our house."

"She was only there one time, Rolf, and anyway, so what if they find out?"

"Maybe they feel you should have come forward?"

She is done with this conversation. They may have spent years together but if he gets charged, he only has himself to blame. Still, she has to protect Anna.

"You know that would just upset her husband and anyway, I haven't done anything wrong."

If Iris is forced to speak to the police, she won't reveal the nature of her relationship with Anna. If Anna dies, she doesn't want her husband to know she cheated. She owes Anna that. If anyone asks, they are simply "friends".

"No," says Rolf. "In your eyes you have done nothing wrong."

He always thinks he's better than her, trying to manipulate her into his twisted web.

"Anyway... I heard she might be awake," Rolf says.

Her heart stops beating. "She is?" Or is he just trying to get attention?

"Well, it's a rumour," he says. "I'm sure they don't want me to know."

Iris hasn't heard anything, so Rolf might be lying. She needs to find out for herself. If Anna is awake, it will be the best news. Will she want to see Iris? Especially after the email that Rolf sent her, who knows?

"Why did you send her an email?" she asks.

She expects him to at least try to wriggle his way out of answering but he comes clean immediately. "It wasn't just one email," he says. "I sent many."

"Why?"

"I had to get her to trust me, to believe they were from you. Then I ended it on your behalf."

She wishes she were standing in front of him so that she could hit him with something, or squeeze his neck. "If you weren't the father of my child, I would never speak to you again," she says.

"For fuck's sake, Iris. Listen to me, I did you a favour. Don't you see? She's young enough to be your daughter. It would never have lasted anyway!"

Iris wants to hang up but can't give him the satisfaction of losing her temper. To calm herself down, she thinks back to the first night she met Rolf, how she admired him. It was at a gallery opening where he was the centre of attention, telling stories about a warped reality and being able to exist in the present. She was instantly drawn to him; their eyes met across the room and she probably looked away momentarily, intimidated by his stare.

"You no longer intimidate me," she says.

The words seem to stump him. In a friendlier voice, he says: "I'm just telling you to be prepared, Iris. The police will obviously question you since you're my wife."

"I will tell them the truth," she lies.

He seems to hesitate before he answers. "You will?"

"I have nothing to hide."

"If you tell them the truth you will put me in a very difficult position, Iris. They might think I was jealous and wanted her out of the way."

"That's possible."

"Fucking hell! You see, Iris, what I don't understand is this: if they don't know about your relationship with Anna already, then why would they even suspect me?"

68

Daniel

Dan is reading the paper at breakfast, like a proper grown-up. It's going to be sunny today. Maybe he can take the boys to the beach this afternoon? There's a long stretch of sand with shallow water close by. Every now and then he tickles Sebastian and Lukas and they laugh. It's amazing how they look up to him. He imagines what it will be like to drop them off at day care after breakfast (in a year he will have an actual driving licence if he can work out how to pay for it – maybe Anna will?). Afterwards, he will come back home. Anna will be newly showered and even if she isn't, he will still fuck the shit out of her. She will giggle, then moan until she screams with excitement and comes.

He looks across the table at Erik, who will be long gone by then. Maybe he was cool once but he's a nerd, someone who thinks he is younger than he actually is.

"When is your next gig?" Dan asks. "I would love to hear you play."

Erik laps it right up. "That would be awesome but it will

be in a bar. You're not eighteen yet, are you?"

"Next year," Dan says. *But I doubt you'll be around then.* "I could babysit while you're playing?"

Both Sebastian and Lukas think that's a great idea.

"Please, Daddy!"

"But I'm not playing tonight," Erik says.

Dan ignores him. "What's your favourite movie?" he asks the boys.

"The *Lego Movie.*"

"Maybe we could watch it together?"

"Yes, please! Tonight?"

Dan looks expectantly at Erik. "Would that be okay?"

Sebastian and Lukas are doing such funny faces: "pretty please we promise to be so very good." Dan laughs. He's noticed that Erik struggles to say "No" to them and has entered this as a weakness in his notebook.

"Fine," Erik says. "But David, your house is ready to move back into, right?"

"Actually, my mum sent me a message late last night. They recommended another night. Apparently they had to spray twice." Lying is easy. All those years he watched Frida lie has taught him how not to do it. She is always annoyingly obvious and adds too much detail, as if that's supposed to make him believe her. *I didn't drink, I promise. I had no money so I couldn't have gone to the liquor store even if I had wanted to. They cut my salary this month, those buggers, some story about me being late too often. Plus I don't need to drink, you know that. I don't really feel like it tonight actually.*

Dan can tell that Erik is thinking about what to do.

"Does your mum know where you are?" he asks.

"Of course. Anna came to visit my house once and my

mum really liked her... so she's totally happy about me being here." He stops himself. That's already too much.

"Anna came to visit your house, did she?"

Dan can immediately tell that Erik doesn't like this.

"Well, Anna was actually trying to do me a favour because my mum doesn't care about school. She would prefer that I work and make some money."

"And did your mum come round?"

Both Sebastian and Lukas are listening too, their little mouths full of cereal.

"Yeah," Dan says. "Anna's a great teacher."

"Okay, well... as long as your mum is okay with it."

"Awesome," Dan says and high fives Sebastian and Lukas. "Shouldn't you two be getting dressed now? But don't forget to clear the table." That's what an adult would say. Frida would tell him to *fucking* clear the table but Dan actually knows his manners when he wants to. Erik looks at him appreciatively over the table. *See, I'm helping. You need me. We're cool*, Dan thinks. But just in case, he has prepared another speech.

"I was planning to learn guitar," he says. "If you have time, would you be able to teach me? I read about your band and it has awesome reviews."

It's true, he has read old reviews online and they did say "okay" and "pretty good" in-between a number of less favourable statements such as "inconsistent" and "all over the place".

Erik's face brightens. His music is definitely another weakness.

"Sure thing. What kind of music are you into?"

"Eh... mainly eighties. My mum plays it all the time. 'Should I Stay or Should I Go' by the Clash and 'Don't You

Forget About Me' by Simple Minds are my favourites."

Both of them were mentioned in the last article about the band.

"Wow, you know your stuff. It would be an honour to teach you. Do you have a guitar yet? If not, don't worry, I have a spare one."

They talk about music for a while and when Dan has exhausted his knowledge of eighties music and guitars, he demonstratively turns over a page in the newspaper.

"I need to keep track of the news for school," he explains.

Erik is now in a great mood and Dan sits back and relaxes. He's so easy to read, that man. This will be a piece of cake.

Dan quickly locates an article about Anna's attack. The papers generally provide a short update, especially now that a suspect has emerged. He reads it with great interest. The suspect isn't named but it says that he's a local artist, and to Dan's great pleasure, a character witness has come forward saying he is a "sadistic swine".

When Dan called the police with the anonymous tip, he told them Rolf was obsessed with Anna and that Rolf's car had been seen following Anna in Hågarp one night. It was risky but he didn't think anyone could have seen him behind the wheel. It was dark and the dude's windows were tinted.

"How do you know all this?" they asked.

He told them he knew Rolf and that he had heard him talk about Anna in a very fixated way, as if he had to have her at all cost. He claimed to be afraid for his own safety and therefore wouldn't be able to come forward as a witness.

"We will look into it," they said but he felt they didn't think it was enough. He needed to tell them more.

"He's into some grisly art," Dan said. "Blood and body parts and shit."

He had been smart enough to do a bit of research on the guy. For someone who was in the paper so much, he should have more money, but maybe no one wanted to buy his sicko art.

"I've heard he's violent too. He's rumoured to have murdered people to display them in his paintings," Dan said. "But I don't know, that's just what I've heard."

He didn't want to sound too confident, or they might think he was framing the guy.

Nothing happened at first. There were no news articles, so he kept busy with other strategies. If truly desperate, he would involve Frida. The anonymous phone call was the seed, however, that would hopefully grow. Now the article says that a school janitor, who had been on holiday since the incident, has stepped forward. "The said artist was talking to Anna in what looked like a heated conversation," he told the journalist, clearly clamouring for a moment of fame. Rolf's name isn't mentioned but it's him, for sure.

The fact that someone has also labelled him "sadistic" is pretty awesome. More people digging the Nissan dude's grave is a good thing. No more poking his dick into Frida and, more importantly, no more trash talking Anna with Frida.

He might have to remove Frida if she stands in his way. It will be easy; he's daydreamed about it enough times. It's just that Anna is not herself at the moment and that's a gamble. He needs Frida as a back-up. No foster care for him.

"David, hello?"

Erik is waving a hand in front of his face.

"Don't you have school to go to?"

"Oh, yes. Of course, I'll just shower and get ready."

"Can I just ask you something?" Erik says and Dan nods.

Go ahead. "Have you heard any rumours at school about me?"

"Eh, no." But this is interesting. "What kind of rumours?"

"No, it's nothing. I just thought, well, people talk, you know, in a small place like this."

"I could listen a bit extra," Dan offers. "And if I hear anything, I'll tell you."

Erik looks pleased about this. "That would be great."

Another weakness. Erik cares what other people think. That could come in handy. He needs to make Erik think they're aligned, that Dan is his buffer from the world outside. That would bring awesome power.

"I won't let anyone talk badly about your family," he says. "I really care about you all."

"Thanks, David. I appreciate that."

Feeling like he's scored, Dan whistles as he showers and gets dressed. Although he realises he will need to do some washing later; he's running out of clothes. Or he could buy new clothes with the money he made from his last beer sale, maybe before Anna comes back? He wants to look presentable so that she sees the potential in him.

She saw him across the room and immediately felt an attraction.

He looks at the line. It's shit. The words are just not flowing. Perhaps he's read too many of his mother's romance novels? It makes him sound like a pussy. He sighs. He needs to decide what he wants. It's so complicated. She has to love him but she also needs to understand that he has a raw urge to stick his cock inside of her. Repeatedly. He's running out of patience. She better come home and spread her legs soon.

69

Erik

Officer Johansson and a young policeman Erik hasn't seen before are sitting on the other side of the table. He doesn't have time for this, but they haven't given him a choice.

"How did you get in touch with Tina Olsson?"

He's not keen to involve Rob but what to do?

"It was my mate, he used to date her. Really, she was just trying to help me." *That one's for you, Rob.*

"Help you how?" Officer Johansson looks at him sternly. "Why would you need help?"

Okay, maybe he shouldn't have chosen those words. He looks back at her, his eyes trying to convey: *remember how you used to think this was hard for me, how you felt sorry for my family?*

"I just felt like you weren't involving me," he says. "That's all."

"Our focus is to find Anna's attacker," Officer Johansson says. "Not to keep you informed."

Wow, that hurts.

"I have an alibi," he says.

"You could have hired someone."

It's the new face sitting next to Linda Johansson. His self-satisfied mug and shaven head makes him look more like a thug than a professional member of the police establishment. Erik feels a violent dislike for him. But he's an adult, so he politely says: "My wife means everything to me."

"Well, we'll see," the new face says.

What does that mean? Erik stares at him, the wide, penetrating eyes uncomfortable. Are they... investigating him?

"You have already arrested someone," he says. "I don't have to listen to this."

"Getting a bit defensive," the new face says.

"I have nothing to hide," Erik says. He holds up his hands. "You want my phone?"

They will find messages from Pernilla but he no longer cares. So what if he made a mistake? *One* mistake. Just because he isn't perfect, doesn't mean he beat Anna up.

"Speaking of phones," Officer Johansson says. "How many times did you talk to Tina Olsson?"

"I don't know, a few times."

"Did you call her or did she contact you?"

He needs to think. "I think I called her."

Even though there's a recording device on the table, they note down everything he says.

"What information did she give you?"

He leans back in the chair to try and feel more comfortable.

"She said that Anna and Kent were very close," he says. "Too close perhaps. Also... something about a student of Anna's being difficult."

"And you never mentioned any of this to us?"

He can't believe it. "I assumed the information was coming from you and that you were checking it out," he says. *God, they're annoying.*

Linda Johansson scribbles something down. "What else?"

"She said that you possibly suspected me…" He's told her that already anyway. But what about Pernilla? Should he tell them? "She also lied to me."

"About?"

"She claimed that I had made someone pregnant."

Linda Johansson's face says it all. She didn't know, which means that Tina made that up, not Pernilla. Stupid cow. Why would she do that? Did Tina get some deep, perverse sense of satisfaction, thinking about Erik's life unravelling? *Kick me when I'm down, won't you?*

"Who?" Of course they want to know with whom he was supposed to have fathered a child but it feels like a test, as if they already know and want to see if he will tell them the truth.

"A day care teacher," he says. "It was just a one-off, a *mistake*." He emphasises the last word to show them that he only has eyes for his wife.

The officer's pen is writing furiously now. It sounds like nails on chalk. He wants to leave.

"You told us you were faithful to Anna," Officer Johansson says.

"Sorry," he says. "I forgot. It was just one time. One!"

The silence is the room is suffocating.

Eventually the new face says: "Did Tina say anything else?"

"No." Erik shakes his head, feeling drained. "That's it."

"Thank you," Officer Johansson says. "We will call you if we need anything else."

"Sure, call me any time." He stands to leave, and to show

them what his life is really like, he adds: "It's my children's birthday today and I have to bring their mother home."

*

Sebastian and Lukas have picked flowers from the garden for their mum, and numerous drinking glasses, turned vases, decorate the home. The best birthday present for the boys is not only Anna being home, but more importantly, that she remembers them.

"Sebastian and Lukas?" she says tentatively and they throw themselves around her neck.

"All right, calm down," Erik says.

He pushes the wheelchair into the living room where he has placed a guest bed for her. She won't be able to climb any stairs just yet.

"Happy birthday," Gerda says.

She hasn't bought them any gifts and stands awkwardly next to Erik, looking at Sebastian and Lukas. The boys' eyes seem to ask the question "why is she here?".

"Gerda is going to stay here for one night only," Erik explains.

Anna panicked when her mother said she was leaving and they agreed that Gerda would stay in order for Anna to settle in. Then she will leave. Tomorrow or the day after, at the latest. Not soon enough.

A nurse will be coming to check on Anna regularly and help monitor her medication. Erik barely listened to her orders. Anna is home and they will be able to get by just fine. He's going to right any wrongs by taking care of her.

He does need to work, however. Summer time is when people want the exterior of their house painted and apparently his boss is desperate enough to need him. It's good. He needs a distraction. Seeing Anna like this other person is distressing. Also, he needs to contribute to their bills. He still has to figure out what's happening to Anna's salary. Is she receiving sick pay and if so, how much is it? Surely it's lower than her normal salary? Finding out means sitting in those phone queues that take forever.

Gerda just exists. She makes no attempt to ask the children any questions and doesn't talk to Erik. All she does is sit on Anna's bed, holding her hand, not talking or engaging with any of them. Considering how she waits on her husband at home, Erik is perplexed. Couldn't she at least make herself useful and clean a bit?

"I've put a mattress in the children's room for you," he says.

Anna looks concerned.

"Don't we have a sofa bed somewhere?" she says. "I thought we did."

Yes, but it's currently occupied by your student, David. He imagines saying it out loud to Anna: "I didn't think it was a good idea at first, but it's great actually. The boy is useful. Not only can he babysit from time to time, but he's also listening out for news about our family. Plus, he just told me his mother had to go on a business trip so she's happy that he has somewhere to stay. It's all good."

The doctor would have disagreed – "don't overwhelm her" – but what does he know?

"We do have a sofa bed," Erik says. "But we have a house guest at the moment, a family friend. You can meet him later."

Before anyone asks any further questions, Erik tells them he needs to go to the supermarket to buy ingredients for the children's favourite dish.

"Lasagne," Anna says.

She remembers. Yet she has a vacant stare when she looks at her husband. Every time he goes near her, she holds on to her mother for dear life and he wants to yell: "Your mother was never there for you, remember that? You used to hate her."

"Will you be okay with the boys or do you want me to take them with me?" The question is aimed at Gerda.

"Of course, but I need to be here for Anna first and foremost," she says and smiles at her daughter, who lovingly returns the smile.

Is Gerda hoping for a second shot at being a good mother? Or is she trying to manipulate Anna's memory loss so that she will appear to be a nice, loving person? Either way, she's a body and she's there when no one else is. David will be home from school later and he's promised the boys to join them for dinner. Hopefully, Anna won't mind.

When Erik is in the car, Rob calls him. He hesitates before he answers. They still haven't spoken since the fight in the bar, but he misses his mate. Maybe he should just answer? He could use a friendly ear with everything being so intense at home.

"Hey, how are you doing?" Rob says. He sounds nervous and Erik finds himself being annoyed all over. Why did Rob bring that ghastly woman into his life?

"I'm fine," Erik says even though he isn't.

"Look," Rob says. "Let's forget about that night. We were both drunk. I'm just calling because, well... have you heard from Tina?"

Tina has apparently split from Rob. Normally, he's the one doing the splitting but her rejection appears to have turned him on.

"I don't ever want to talk about her," Erik says. "Especially now that Anna is at home. Plus, it's the boys' birthday. If you really were my best friend, you would know that."

"Whoa, happy birthday, boys! But Erik, that's great, you should be happy. Your wife is home."

"I'm just so sick of you. Maybe I should find a new band that actually takes music seriously. You're just in the band to attract the chicks anyway."

Erik parks the car but leaves the engine running. Has he gone too far? He's just so pissed off with Rob and the world right now.

"Oh, man. You're on a roll!"

"I'm sorry," Erik says. "It's just... Anna looks at me like I'm a fucking stranger."

"But she remembers your name, right. That's a start."

"I know, you're right." He feels bad now. What's got into him? "Sorry about all that. I didn't mean it."

"It's okay," Rob says but Erik can detect a hurt tone. He really needs to care more about his friend.

"You've always been there for me," he says to assure Rob that he truly is sorry.

"You're right though," Rob says, "I *am* in the band because of the chicks."

They laugh and Erik feels better. "If you're really my friend," Erik says, "then stay away from Tina. She really messed with me."

"Come on, she helped a little bit too. Maybe she didn't have the authority but she meant well."

Erik isn't so sure about that. He felt like she was more interested in placing a bomb in Erik's life, waiting for it to explode, than to assist him.

"Still not coming to your wedding," he says.

He puts the phone down and notices a new message. It's from Pernilla.

I'm waiting to hear from you. I'll give you one day.

He's not sure what to reply and can't exactly give her any further ammunition, so he simply writes: Let's catch up tomorrow. He has no plans to do so but hopefully it will sustain her. He can't deal with her now, not tonight. The rest of the messages, he ignores.

*

When he's back home, Sebastian and Lukas are in front of the TV watching a movie. Anna is watching too, from her bed. Gerda is asleep.

Erik cooks dinner and when David arrives, he bakes a cake as promised.

"Is she here?" he asks in a hushed tone.

Erik can tell he's excited.

"She is but her memory is still a bit shaky," he explains.

"Okay," David says. He leans on the door into the living room so that it slightly opens. He smiles and Erik is about to tell him to leave her for the time being, when he closes it again and says: "If I upset her I'll just go downstairs."

That's considerate of him. "Thanks, buddy. I'm sorry but that's just the way it's going to have to be."

"No worries."

Erik puts the lasagne in the oven. "How was school?"

David shrugs. "Okay. Not the same without Anna, of course."

"I'm sure." Erik clears his throat. "Are people talking about her?"

"Sometimes. People are worried that she's not coming back."

391

Erik watches David stir the melted butter into his cake mix. Even though he's following a recipe from the Internet, it looks as if he's done it before.

"What about her attack?" Erik says. "I mean, it happened at school. Didn't anyone see anything apart from that janitor?"

He's wanted to ask David this question for a while. Surely people talk?

"Nope," David says. "And there are no cameras in the parking lot."

"I know, the police told me."

David stops in the middle of opening the oven to put the cake in.

"What else did the police say?" he asks.

Erik shakes his head. "Not much."

David proceeds to put the cake in and sets the timer. That's where the conversation ends. Erik doesn't want to talk about it anymore. His attention needs to be on the evening ahead.

When dinner and the cake are ready, Erik puts Anna in the wheelchair and the boys wake Gerda up. Together, they make their way to the kitchen where David is standing by the table like a waiter, his back straight and his hair combed to one side. He's quickly got changed and it looks like he's wearing new clothes. Instead of the ripped jeans and much too small T-shirt, he's wearing a white shirt and blue chinos. Very smart indeed. Someone wants to impress.

"Anna," Erik says. "This is one of your students. Do you remember him?"

70

Iris

Ever since Iris found out about Anna's attack, her life has become suffocatingly small. She avoids seeing people when she's not at work, electing to stay at home. It feels too cruel, to have fallen in love with someone only to have that person taken away from you.

When she's alone at home, she spends her time reading user manuals for the new dishwasher and washing machine, determined to install them herself to keep her mind occupied. She can't concentrate on reading fiction. Everything seems banal compared to reality.

Iris managed to visit Anna in the hospital. The sight of her was painful and her instinct was to gently kiss her while talking to her as if she were awake. Anna's face looked serene on the hospital pillow, but her body looked uncomfortable, the stretched duvet holding her down as if it were a straitjacket. Iris pulled it out, making it fluffier.

At first, she wasn't sure where Anna was. When she called the different hospitals in the region, no one could confirm her presence. It would make sense, however, if Anna had been taken to the one closest to Mörna. Iris predicted that security around her room would be tight but how could she live with herself if she didn't at least try to access it? The security guard would surely need the bathroom at some point? There was also Erik to consider, of course, and so Iris drove around the hospital car park, up through the parking garage, to scan it for Erik and Anna's car. Everyone seemed to be driving a Volvo these days but she knew that the twins' baby shoes adorned the rear-view mirror in Anna's car, which made it easy to recognise. Finally seeing the car on the second floor was a huge relief; it confirmed that this was the correct hospital. Iris parked and waited for Erik to leave.

Iris had never actually seen Erik, not counting the blurred photo on the painting company's website, and when he arrived, she felt guilty. This man was married to Anna. He was the father of her children. His hair was a bit too long for Iris's liking but he wasn't bad looking either.

Once he left, Iris stepped out of her car and walked into the building to ask for Anna Berg. No one with that name was registered. Frustrated but not deterred, she ventured up in one of the many elevators. On each floor she would stop and read the signs outside the wards. It was a case of elimination. Anna wasn't likely to be in the psychiatric or the OB-gyn wards, and so Iris narrowed it down to the third floor. On that level, only one ward was locked, therefore signalling that this was the one. There was a seating area outside and Iris sat down, waiting for someone to exit. Twenty minutes later, she was able to sneak inside.

There was neither security by the entrance, nor down the hallway, and Iris walked in with an air of confidence, as if she knew where she was going. That's how she managed to find Anna's room, the door slightly ajar.

After loosening the duvet cover, Iris sat by Anna's bed and held her hand. At least she wasn't in any visible pain, but her skin was pale and her lips dry. Iris dug out a lip balm from her bag and applied it to Anna's lips. The skin felt rough under her touch but after a few applications the smoothness under her finger made Anna's lips more recognisable. By that point the one-sided dialogue had dried up and instead Iris started to read out loud from *Loving Her*, hoping the words would filter into Anna's inner world.

*

Today is a new day, however, a day filled with hope. Although Iris has lost her job (Lena got her revenge in the end, as promised), she has no need for user manuals. After speaking to Rolf, she went to the hospital and found Anna's room positively empty. That could only mean one thing – she was awake. Any other outcome would have been reported in the newspaper. It wasn't just a rumour. She leaned against the wall in the hallway around the corner from the nurses' station, pretending to be absorbed by her phone, as most people these days were. From there she picked up snippets of a conversation that she assumed was about Anna. Words such as "home" and "awake" lifted her spirits but did they also say "amnesia"?

What's important is that she's on the mend. She's awake! It feels better than a thousand book deliveries combined.

Iris paces up and down in her new living room. Can she visit Anna at her home? She needs to see her, speak to her.

Nothing else seems to matter. Her marriage is over and she's got nowhere she needs to be.

When Rolf calls her, she reluctantly answers.

"One more day or they have to let me go," he happily informs her.

Apparently there is not enough evidence yet. Iris has been questioned but is confident that she didn't speak out of turn or compromise anyone. She and Anna were friends but they hadn't known each other for very long, she told the police.

Should she tell Rolf that Anna is indeed awake? She doesn't particularly want to, but who else can she talk to? No close friendships have formed over the years, unless they involved work.

"I heard about Lena," Rolf says. "Who would have thought she was the anonymous benefactor? She seemed like somebody who would have screamed that from the roof tops, someone who would want to feel important."

"You don't know her," Iris says.

Rolf scoffs. "She fucked you over and you're defending her?"

"I clearly played with her emotions," Iris says. "I have to take responsibility for that."

"So will there be no more library or just no more Iris?"

Iris doesn't actually know. She was simply told that funds were low and that they could no longer afford her salary. Lena will pay her until the end of the month but she was asked to leave immediately.

"Who knows?" Iris says. "She has no interest in keeping it going, especially not for my sake."

"Sorry, I really thought I had made things right with her."

"Well, you didn't."

She can't really blame him but she does.

"Come on!" he says. "Many things are my fault, but not *that*."

There is no point arguing. "I guess you did your best," she says.

For Karin's sake, she's trying to bury the hatchet.

"Anyway, there's something else I want to tell you." She pauses. "She's awake, Rolf."

Her heart is beating fast as she says it. She's excited but she also wonders how he will react. Will he be upset? Worried? Now that Anna is able to speak to the police, what will she say? Iris wants to believe that he's innocent, but he's acted irrationally since their separation.

"Right," Rolf says. "Well, I guess that's good. I mean, good... for her."

"A witness saw you, Rolf," she says. "It was in the paper."

"I know, but he didn't see me in the parking lot, Iris. He only saw me in the courtyard. Then he left."

"That doesn't really mean anything, Rolf. Why were you even there?"

She tries to supress her anger, has promised herself to keep it amicable.

"I don't want to talk about it, Iris."

If he doesn't want to talk, he won't. She can imagine how frustrating it must be for the police to question him. At least she will no longer be married to him. It's amazing how accepting you become when you spend over twenty years with someone. She obviously needed to meet Anna to break free. Anna has a big heart, she's considerate of other people; she's someone who doesn't need to be the centre of attention. She's also generous with her time and her affections. Iris has never met anyone like her. She wants to wrap her arms around her at night, share her inner thoughts and just be with her.

"I'm going to see her," she says.

"I thought you might say that."

He sounds more tired than worried and she decides to hang up. She never tells him what she's really worried about. That Anna might be suffering from memory loss. What if she doesn't remember her?

71

Rolf

Rolf is having the best day. Well, it would be better if Iris was sharing it with him but he's spending it with Karin, which is just as good. Despite her sometimes cynical views on life, he respects and admires his daughter. She is her own person, which is exactly how they raised her.

"We're celebrating," he says. "I'm a free man."

Karin has taken him to a trendy café in the heart of Gothenburg, where they're drinking café lattes in large white mugs and sharing a giant chocolate ball.

"Did you even know that teacher?" she asks him.

"Not really," he says. "She provided some hair for one of my paintings but that's all. Anyway, I'm off the hook. Not enough evidence!"

Karin crosses her arms and views him quizzically.

"Why aren't you more upset about this?"

She's got that "I'm deep and serious at university" look. Black hair and clothes, red lipstick like her mother but no tattoos or piercings. Apparently that's for "losers".

"I don't know," he says. He wants to move on, they should focus on happy subjects, and he vigorously stirs sugar into his coffee. "I can never be…"

"… sweet enough," she finishes his sentence.

"I guess I've said that before."

She nods and he feels ancient.

"I just don't understand," she says. "My dad hates any kind of injustice. And you were treated very unfairly, wouldn't you say? I mean, you were arrested and almost charged!"

"That's the point though. *Almost.*"

Karin shakes her head. He knows that she has never understood his desire to experience life to the fullest, whether for better or worse. She once accused him of being "attention-seeking". That hurt.

"Another thing I find odd," Karin says and he braces himself. Why isn't he scared of critics but terrified of his daughter? "That teacher wasn't the type of woman you normally include in your art."

"Oh, so I have a type now, do I?" He laughs. "How do you even know about the women in my art?"

"They've been pretty forthcoming in the press."

Oh, yes. That's right. The accusations have been great for publicity.

"It just doesn't add up for me," Karin says.

"Well, as long as it adds up for the police, that's all that matters."

Karin sips her coffee but her phone rings and she gets up to answer it. The whispered talking suggests it's an intimate conversation, so Rolf leans back and enjoys his freedom, which is now so much more enjoyable than just a few days ago.

It went too far. He shouldn't have allowed himself to get

so emotional. Iris will never come back to him, even without Anna, he realises that now. He has decided that if that means they will only be friends, then he will take Iris's friendship over nothing at all.

He told Iris about his run-in with Anna. There was no longer a reason to hold back. He explained that he did go to the teacher's school the night of her attack, filled with anger after Iris had packed her bags and left.

"I just wanted to talk to her," he said.

He stressed that he was there before her attack and that he in no way was responsible. It was just a coincidence that he was there that particular night. She didn't sound convinced.

"Tell me exactly what happened," she demanded.

"I parked at the school because her Volvo was still there," he told her. "Then I walked up to the school building just as she was leaving."

He left out that Anna recognised him from that night she was jogging.

"What do you want?" she asked.

"I'm Iris's husband."

"Oh."

"She let down her guard when she realised I was connected to you."

"What did you tell her?"

"I said you were mine and that she better not mess with our marriage. She apologised and said she hadn't intended for anything to happen but apparently she's dumb enough to love you."

"Did you leave her alone after that or did you…?"

"Iris! You can't possibly think I would do anything stupid."

"Let me think, my husband, Rolf Sören, doing something stupid? No, not at all."

"Okay, there's no need for that."

He had known it would be a tough conversation but now he needed to get it over and done with.

"Iris, I love you. I was simply trying to scare her off."

"And how exactly did you 'scare' her?"

"I might have reached out and grabbed a handful of her hair, but then I left," he said. "That's the truth."

"Sorry, Dad."

Karin is back at the table, her cheeks flushed.

"Good talk?" he asks, winking at her.

"Don't," she says. "Let's focus on you. So, you were arrested. I guess it was just a matter of time before you got into trouble."

"But they let me go, remember."

Karin nods and finishes off the chocolate ball.

"It's odd though, isn't it?" she says, swallowing. "A woman you took hair from was attacked the very same night you saw her?"

72

Erik

Erik looks for signs of recognition on Anna's face.

"David?" Erik says. "Do you remember him?"

"Da..." she says before stopping.

Erik can tell she's working her brain muscles hard. She badly wants to remember, her expression pained.

"You're my favourite teacher," David says, his face lit up.

"What is he doing here?" Gerda whispers to Erik.

"He's been very concerned about Anna," Erik whispers back. "And he's been a great support for the boys."

It's a slight exaggeration but he wants to shut her up. Who he invites into this house is not her business.

"David?" Anna says, studying the boy.

He nods. "That's right."

It's painful to see his wife, Teacher of the Year, not recollect a student.

"Let's eat," Erik says, to avoid any further awkwardness.

He wheels Anna up to the table which has been laid out with blue Höganäs Keramik plates and blue-and-yellow napkins, portraying the Swedish flag. He places one on Anna's lap, and Gerda sits down next to her as if she's Anna's carer. She doesn't offer to help but expectantly waits for her glass to be filled, holding it up to no one in particular. Erik is pleased to see David take charge: he pours Fanta and Coke for everyone while Erik dishes up the lasagne. He can't say it's his best work but at least it's not burnt and no one complains, not even Gerda.

They mainly eat in silence. Sebastian and Lukas chime in every now and then, telling their mum about day care, Sophie, Lego and pirate ships. She nods and says "a-ha" and "wow" which spurs them on. Erik wonders how much she actually understands. Is her brain intact? Can she comprehend what's being said and turn words into something meaningful, something that relates to her old life?

She's different. Milder and more contemplative. Obviously she has no work to stress about, but still. She simply exists. There's grumpiness, which is probably due to her not remembering everything, but she doesn't ask as many questions as he had expected. It's as if she observes them all, which at times can be unnerving. She's also not able to get around by herself just yet. She can walk but her body is slow and quickly gets tired.

Will he need to hire someone to care for her full time? Mum has promised to come down for a few days but not for another week at least. He doesn't want Gerda there and quite honestly he can tell she would rather get back to her heartless husband than stay with her daughter in need. She's constantly on the phone to him, listening rather than talking.

Will the government provide a full-time carer? He probably should have asked. If he needs to hire someone himself, he needs more cash. Maybe he can do more evening and weekend shifts when the pay is better? Would David be able to watch the boys and Anna? Is it even fair to expect that of a seventeen-year-old? Having said that, if he was Sebastian and Lukas's brother, he would have to do his bit. Except he isn't, of course. Living far away from family is difficult when you have young children. That was one of his objections when Anna wanted to move here.

"We have to share the responsibility," she said back then, but her job obviously became more important than his.

Anyway, he can't dwell on that now.

"David says school isn't the same without you," Erik says.

Anna doesn't respond, she just stares at him for a few seconds as if she can't understand what he's saying, before looking down at her food. Erik notices that she avoids looking at David throughout dinner. There is something unsettling about it. Even though David tries his best to make polite conversation, Anna doesn't seem to register his existence. Perhaps he should have kept this meal to family only? Maybe she doesn't want to be reminded of her work life, especially since she has to recover fully before she can return. He should have thought of that.

At one point, David puts his knife and fork down, sighs and says with a dejected look on his face to Anna: "Do you not remember me at all?"

Erik feels his muscles tense. *You shouldn't have said that. Lay low please.* But it's too late. Anna is stirring in her seat. Everyone looks at her, even Sebastian and Lukas. What will she say? Will she be annoyed?

She nods and briefly meets David's eyes. "I do," she says. "At least, I think I do."

"That's great," Erik says, trying to sound positive. "I thought that perhaps you didn't—"

"No," she interrupts. "I remember something about him."
She looks down at her plate again where she's moving pieces
of lasagne around. "I just can't... I'm not sure."

"That's good, though," David says. "A toast to that."

He raises his glass.

"Yes, a toast to that," Erik says, ignoring the fact that
Anna is rejecting his food, and they all say "cheers", clink
their glasses and sing a spontaneous happy birthday to the
children.

Despite drinking only water, Anna seems drunk. It's probably the medication. She's distant, except for when she looks
at Sebastian and Lukas. Then a new energy surges through
her. Apart from fighting about who gets to sit next to her –
if only Gerda would move and let them sit on either side of
their mother – they seem to be having an okay birthday.

"Do you want me to read to you tonight?" Anna asks.

"YES!"

"Are you sure?" Erik says. "You don't want to overexert
yourself."

What if she finds she can no longer read?

"Of course I will," she says and hugs them tightly.

He should be fully content. His wife is back and his
children are happy. He needs to chill.

*

That evening, when the children are in bed and Gerda is in
the bathroom, Anna calls Erik. He sits on her bed, not sure
whether to touch her or not.

"Are you okay?" he asks. "Was dinner a bit too much?"

"It was a lovely birthday dinner," she says. "Thank you for

organising it. But why was he here? Da... David?"

She's already struggling to remember his name. Maybe she won't fully recover her memory?

"I understand that you feel uncomfortable," Erik says, because the doctor has told him to validate Anna's feelings to make her feel heard. "It probably reminds you that you can't teach for a while, but he's staying here, only temporarily, of course." He pauses as he watches her reaction. Will she be happy that he's housing a student of hers, or not? It's hard to tell. She looks puzzled. "He needed somewhere to stay," he explains. "So I offered him a bed for a night or two. I thought you would be happy that I was helping one of your students?" She doesn't react. Maybe she doesn't remember the countless arguments they have had about her work?

She turns on her side and a strand of hair falls over her face. He leans in, brushes it away. "He'll be out of here soon," he says.

Anna puts a finger in her mouth, biting her nail. He's never seen her do that before.

"How many days has he been here now?" she asks, not looking at him, making him feel like a failure. He's just never good enough.

"A week," he admits.

She scrunches up her face. "I may not remember him, Erik," she says. "But there is something about him... I don't want him here."

"Well, I have asked him to leave several times," Erik defends himself. "But he always has a new excuse and, well, I feel bad. I was trying to think what you would do, and I thought you would let him stay."

The latter is a lie but a hugely satisfying one.

"For God's sake, Erik," she says then and in that explosive moment she is his old Anna, the fiery woman he fell in love with. "Talk to Kent if you need help."

"Kent? You remember Kent?"

"Yes," she says. "We work together."

73

Iris

The next morning, Iris knocks on the door of Anna's house. It's a relatively small home, which now has a rather neglected garden. Still, it's cute. The straight panel curtains have a maritime look about them; she can picture Anna choosing them. *Anna has decorated this home for her family.* Iris quickly flicks the thought away and knocks on the door one more time.

Finally, an older woman with grey hair weaved into a plait, answers it.

"Hi," Iris says, not sure who the woman is. "I'm Iris, a friend of Anna's."

"Come on in. I'm Gerda, Anna's mum."

They shake hands. "Nice to meet you." It's a relief that it's not the husband opening the door. He might not know about their relationship but it would still feel awkward. She would be torn between being polite for Anna's sake while also demonstrating to him that she plays an important role in Anna's life. A very important one.

Gerda shows Iris into a living room with wooden floors and tasteful navy and white furniture. Anna is lying in a bed next to a sofa and Iris walks over to her, full of nerves. She has no idea what to expect.

"Anna?" she says.

At first Anna looks as if she doesn't know who Iris is but then her expression changes. Her body softens, her lips part. She smoothens her hair out and gestures for Iris to sit down next to her.

"You came to see me?" she says.

Iris takes Anna's hands in hers. "Of course. I've been so worried about you. I visited you in the hospital but... well, you were asleep but... still so beautiful."

She can't take her eyes of Anna. *She remembers me.*

"Would you like some coffee, Iris?" Gerda asks.

"Yes, please," Iris says, only so that Anna's mum will leave them alone.

"That's my mother," Anna says when Gerda goes into the kitchen. "I can tell that Erik doesn't like her."

"She's not his mother," Iris says.

Even though she has no right to, Iris doesn't like Erik. From the few stories Anna has told her he seems childish with a chip on his shoulder. But he also seems like a good father and, no matter what happens in the future, he will always be a part of Anna's children's lives. They need to get on.

"My husband was accused of your attack," Iris says. She has debated whether to tell Anna but has decided that it's better that the news comes from her.

"I'm sorry," she says.

She can't tell from Anna's expression if she knew about this already.

"Don't be," Iris says. "They don't seem interested in him anymore."

"The police showed me some pictures of a man with a dark moustache and a ponytail."

Iris nods. "That would be him."

Does Anna remember meeting him at the school? Does she recall how he pulled at her hair? Iris feels a knot in her stomach at the thought. Should she remind Anna, to help her with her memory?

"I told them I didn't recognise him," Anna says. "But I also said I wasn't one hundred per cent sure, that maybe I had seen him, I just didn't know when."

Iris feels torn.

"You might have seen him," she says. "I think the two of you met at some point."

"Oh," Anna says. "When was that?"

"He wanted to tell you to stay away from me but you said you loved me and he backed off."

That's his version of the event. Maybe Anna's will be different, should she ever remember, but Iris wants to remind her: *you said you loved me.*

Anna doesn't respond and Iris quickly says: "Anyway, the police interviewing him was a reality check. He needed it."

She kisses Anna's hand. She smells the same.

"It's just that I don't remember what happened that night," Anna says.

"So what have you told the police?"

"I haven't been able to tell them much."

"That's terrifying," Iris says, at once feeling both outraged and alarmed. "That means the attacker is still out there?"

Anna nods and Iris can feel the heat in her veins. Whoever he or she is, she wants to grab that person by the neck.

"What if you're not safe here?" she says. "What if that person comes back for you?"

"The police check in on me regularly. Anyway, it might just have been a random act, Iris. There is no apparent threat. Also, Erik is here," Anna adds, and Iris feels more than jealous in that moment. She wants to be the one protecting Anna.

Gerda brings them coffee and Iris lets go of Anna's hands.

"I will leave you to it," Gerda says. "I need to pack anyway." She heads upstairs and Iris is thankful that she doesn't stay to make trite conversation. It's Anna's mother and she should make an effort. But not today.

"So how much do you remember?" Iris asks.

If you can't recall who attacked you, do you remember that you were going to leave your husband?

Anna doesn't seem to like the question. She sips her water and Iris picks up a coffee cup to give her time.

"I remember a lot," she says eventually, avoiding eye contact.

Has she forgotten about their weekend away? Their intense lovemaking, the laughs, the intimate conversations. The love.

"Do you remember how we met?" Iris asks tentatively.

Anna lies back on her pillow. She looks frail. Maybe she shouldn't probe her with questions?

"You wore a black outfit and silver jewellery," Anna says. "Red reading glasses and matching lipstick. I didn't think you would be approachable at first, but then we became friends..." She pauses, before adding: "More than friends."

Iris's heart beats hard, swelling with emotion for this woman, and when Anna looks up at her, all she wants to do is plant a kiss on her soft lips. Yet she's afraid to.

"I fell in love with you," Anna says and Iris sighs. This is what she had hoped to hear.

"I love you very much," she says to Anna.

Anna closes her eyes and after a while, Iris worries that she might have fallen asleep. Is she okay? She gently strokes her cheek.

"Things are different now," Anna says. She opens her eyes but avoids looking at Iris.

Iris feels herself grow cold. She fears asking but she has to know.

"Different how?"

Anna's breathing is laboured as she tries to talk, and it takes her a while to get the words out: "I need my husband and my children."

Iris wants to scream. Anna is finally awake and talking to her, and this is what she wants?

"So what are you saying?" When Anna doesn't respond, Iris eventually forces the words out: "It's over?"

Anna pats her hand and Iris can't decide if she's being caring, because it feels patronising.

"It has to be," Anna says.

74

Daniel

Dan is happy. Anna is at home and he was included in her first family dinner. It's a miracle that she has woken up. It's a sign. He is where he is meant to be. What's even better, is that Erik went to sleep on the first floor, Anna on the ground floor and Dan in the basement. He's one step closer...

This morning, he woke up in a house with two parents, two younger siblings and a grumpy grandmother. It felt like something out of a storybook. If people woke up like this every morning, they would definitely want to go into the world, making it a better place.

After breakfast, Erik gets ready to drive the children to day care. Then he will do some errands before coming back to pick Gerda up. He's going to drop her at the bus stop, he says. Dan listens carefully to keep track of Erik's schedule. He needs to be alone with Anna. If he can hide away in the basement until Gerda leaves, then he figures he will have the opportunity he's been looking for.

"Erik, can't you drive me to the train station instead?" Gerda asks. "I don't feel comfortable taking first a bus, then a train."

She's an odd lady; spaced out most of the time and when she does talk, she complains a lot. Dan is happy that she's leaving. He does try to be nice to her though, for Anna's sake.

"I wish I could drive you," he tells her ingratiatingly. "But I don't have a licence yet."

"Thanks, young man," she says. She almost smiles and that's great.

They will obviously have to spend time together in the future. Although, if he's going to cut his mother out of his life, perhaps Anna can cut hers out too. That would be better.

"Do you want me to drop you at school?" Erik asks.

"No, that's okay. I've got my bike."

When they are out of the house, the children in the car and Erik about to get in, Dan pretends to have forgotten something inside.

"See you later," Erik says and Dan waves goodbye to the boys as they leave.

He does plan to go to school later because it isn't worth getting into trouble. The principal might call Frida and that's to be avoided. But he plans to be late. He will say that he had an emergency appointment at the doctors, or that he simply overslept.

Dan can hear Gerda talking to Anna, so he takes the opportunity to slip down to the basement unnoticed. He's lying on his bed, waiting for Gerda to leave, when he hears the doorbell ring. Who the hell is that? More visitors? A nurse? He really doesn't need that today.

A woman is being greeted by Gerda, she says she's a friend of Anna's, and then there is muffled conversation. He strains his ears to hear what is going on but it's impossible now. They must be in the living room. He has to be patient and wait this one out. Sooner or later Erik will be back for Gerda anyway.

While he's waiting, Dan gets off the bed and checks himself out in the floor-length mirror. He's wearing a new T-shirt and jeans and has washed his hair. He checks his breath as well and it isn't bad.

It seems to take forever before he finally hears the door close. First, the friend leaves, then Gerda is picked up by Erik.

Dan counts to a hundred before he tentatively makes his way upstairs. He needs to make sure Gerda won't rush back for something she's forgotten.

The house is quiet when he reaches the top of the stairs. Leaving the dark basement with its wood-clad walls behind, it's like stepping into the sun, being up here. It's warm, light and airy. He heads towards the living room, his moves now quick and alert. Dan doesn't know how much time he has before Erik comes back. Hopefully Gerda will manage to convince Erik to drive her all the way into the city to the train station.

The parquet floor creaks under Dan's sock-clad feet. He looks down, trying to soften his steps. The fishbone pattern on the floor is beautiful. The whole house is. Erik claims it's small but it's a mansion compared to what Dan is used to. He hopes they can stay living here.

Anna looks like she's sleeping, the duvet only half covering her body. She's wearing a thigh-high nightie with a Mickey Mouse print on the front. Gerda brought it for her. Erik thought it was ridiculous. "She's thirty-four!" he said. "Not fucking five." But Dan likes it. It makes her look youthful.

He carefully sits down next to her, which causes her to stir, but she doesn't wake up. Maybe she's just taken her medication? Her face looks relaxed. He places a hand on hers and squeezes it gently. This feels so right. He looks at her heaving chest as she inhales. Transfixed, he feels a deep desire to touch her upper body. He's sure she won't mind. Letting go of her hand, he excitedly places his hands on Anna's round breasts. They're heavy and warm. He strokes them and watches the nipples harden. They actually stiffen under his touch! He feels himself grow hard. She's responding to him. Excited, he leans down and tugs at a nipple with his mouth, the cotton fabric growing damp in his mouth. His heart beats fast, the thrill of being this close to her overshadowing anything he has ever experienced. This is what he's wanted. He's fooled around with girls before but this is different. His whole body wants Anna. It's like he's on fire, his cock is throbbing. He needs to be even closer, this isn't enough; he lies down next to her. She smells of hospital but he doesn't mind, her flowery perfume is still detectable underneath. He snuggles closely, burrowing his nose into her neck, his hands stroking her stomach, sliding down between her legs. She's warm there and he wants to undress her so badly, to feel her skin against his, but first, he opens his fly and lets the hard-on out. It springs into position, leaning against Anna's leg. He looks at it almost in awe: his cock on Anna's leg. If only he had a camera to document this.

Just then he hears Erik's car pulling into the driveway. *Fucking hell!* Why couldn't he stay in the town centre a bit longer? It makes him angry, he's not ready to leave yet. Dan quickly thinks of possible options. Beat the crap out of Erik and go back to Anna? That's what his body wants but his mind is smarter than that. He can't be caught, then he'll be sent packing, and he's not done here yet.

Panicked, he sits up but Anna starts to move and he quickly stands up and forces his fly shut, which isn't an easy task. He should run but he needs to gaze at her for just another second. That's when she opens her eyes, and looks straight at him. *Fuck!*

"Eh, hi," he says, his voice trembling. "How are you feeling?"

Her eyes look alarmed and she scrambles into a sitting position, hiding her body.

"Get away from me!"

He stalls but he hears a key in the door and grabs his bag. Using the patio door, he runs outside. He doesn't stop until he's far away from the house. The anger subsides and is replaced by excitement. He was just lying next to her! He can't believe how close he got, and how incredible that he now lives in the same house as Anna. He's achieved a lot in a short space of time.

*

Several times during the day, Dan locks himself in a bathroom to think about Anna's body and how it reacted. Over and over, he fantasises about what could have happened if Erik hadn't arrived.

He slips his hand inside her knickers and touches her.

She wakes up and looks at him, grateful that someone is making her feel good. She smiles and lets out a contented sigh. "Please don't stop, Dan. That feels amazing."

And with his limited experience he does the best that he

can because that's what she deserves, the best. At least until he's so hard he's worried he might come. He mounts her and with her encouragement, he thrusts himself inside of her. It feels so bloody good!

After school, he wants to rush home to Anna but a nasty surprise is waiting for him in the courtyard. Frida.

"I'm not some fucking toddler you need to pick up," he says.

He walks off but she runs after him. "Dan, where have you been? I need to talk to you."

He keeps walking but slows down. It's not worth causing a scene. He finally has people's respect; he doesn't need them to see this.

"Okay," he says and turns to her. "Not here though. Over there."

He shows her to a quiet area, a meadow with trees and a pond. This is by far the nicest school he has ever gone to. He wants to do his final year here before... before what? Anna will expect him to go to university, she already mentioned that, but he also needs to work to take care of her. Once she recovers fully, they will have to discuss it and plan their future together. A mental flash of her body again, warm and willing.

"I'm not coming back home," he says.

Frida studies her feet: sparkly sandals and chipped nail polish.

"Where are you staying?" she asks after a while.

"None of your business."

"Dan!" Her eyes stare at him in disbelief. How can she not understand that he's fed up with her being such a mess? Her arms hang by her sides like a ragdoll, her hair is uncombed and her make-up smeared. "I'm your mum. I... need you."

"You need the bottle," he says.

He revels in her hurt eyes. *That's right, I fucking hate you.*

"Is this to do with your teacher, Anna?" she says quietly. "Do you miss her or... did..." She takes a visibly deep breath. "Did you hurt her?"

"We've already been over this," he says. "You obviously think I'm capable of such violence."

Maybe she finally realises he's not a little baby anymore.

"Maybe it was you," he says. "Maybe you were sick of being compared to her and you attacked her?"

"I didn't like her, Dan," she admits. "She was trying to take my son away from me, but I'm not a monster!"

"Maybe your boyfriend did it to impress you? It said in the papers that an artist was suspected of her attack."

"He w-wouldn't harm a fly," she stutters.

"Really? Remember how he had your head in a headlock or all the times when he fucked you hard, tying you up and shit?"

He's enjoying this. Her world falling apart, like she has destroyed his over and over.

"That's different, that was harmless fun..."

"You think that's appropriate, especially with your son in the house? It's fucked up, that's what it is."

She starts to cry. "Dan, please! You're my son."

"But I'm never your number-one priority."

"And for her you are? She's only a teacher, Dan. She has loads of other students. You're not fucking special!" She's raising her voice and he can tell where this is going. He needs to exit now, to get away. Back home.

"I'll call you later," he says even though he has no credit on his phone.

"I spoke to the police," she says as he walks off.

He stops and turns to her. "You did what?"

"They had questions about Rolf, about his alibi."

"And what did you say, I mean, about me? Did you mention me at all?"

She bites her lip, delaying, as if she wants to get back at him. He won't take the bait; he will wait a hundred years for her to respond if he has to.

"Rolf didn't do it, Dan," she says. "They let him go."

Fuck, they did?

"That means nothing," he says.

"You need to give him a break."

"What about me?" he says. "Don't I fucking get a break?"

"I told them that Anna was your favourite teacher. They remembered me. Dan, I don't want anything bad to happen to you. You're all I've got!"

He scoffs. Sure. But the dude is off the hook? That's a bummer. He will have to fix this, and he will, because he deserves Anna. He closes his eyes, thinking of her hard nipple on his tongue. No one can take that away from him. No one.

He walks off, leaving Frida behind, and in that moment he decides that when he gets home, he will get rid of Erik. No more games. Forget the guitar lessons. There's no time to scheme and act out a whole plan. He needs to take him out the old-fashioned way.

75

Erik

Erik feels a strong desire for his wife. He likes this calm version of Anna. It reminds him of their younger days. She's not rushing around, trying to do a million things; she doesn't care about colleagues or students or tests. She's also lost weight, which means that, physically, she resembles the old Anna. Now, for the first time since she arrived home from the hospital, they're going to be alone together, and he's looking forward to that.

This morning, he was a dutiful husband; he dropped the children off at day care, picked up a parcel with gear for an amplifier that he probably won't get to use, did the grocery shopping and dropped the mother-in-law-from-hell off. The self-righteous Gerda is finally gone, but only after first declaring herself indispensable.

"How will you cope without me? Who will open the door? Anna had a visitor earlier." She said it as if the queen herself had called on her daughter.

"Who was it?" Another supposedly concerned teacher or parent?

"Her name was Iris," she said.

He had no idea who that was.

"She was a bit older than Anna," Gerda said. "Very sophisticated."

"Must have been a colleague. She has many," he said drily.

He doesn't know half the people who want to see her. All he is there to do is serve them coffee and cake. Ahead of him stretches months of Anna recovering. He is expected to focus on nothing else.

"When is the bus leaving? Do I have to *wait*?" she asked, at which point Erik had enough.

"Would you ever speak to your husband that way?" She looked baffled. "What I mean," he continued, "is that you let your husband walk all over you but when he's not around, you speak to people like they're shit."

"Not to my Anna!" she exclaimed.

"Well, you used to. Her coma has obviously made you nicer, but only to her. You still look at me like I'm dirt on your shoe."

"Not at all!"

"What was it you said on our wedding day? 'He might be a looker but how will he provide for you?' Like we're living in the Stone Age."

"Well, she wouldn't be working so hard if it wasn't for you and if she hadn't been working late she wouldn't have been attacked!"

She started to cry and it was the first time he had witnessed that. Normally, her husband's boot in her arse wouldn't even make her flinch.

Erik still doesn't feel bad. He can't hide that he doesn't like the woman and it bothers him a great deal that she pretends to now care about her daughter's welfare.

Gerda is gone, however, and there are no unexpected visitors, which means they're alone. He takes a moment to deliberate on his next move. Should he be ashamed about his feelings of desire?

He wonders how Anna feels right now. She just about remembers who he is, will she want to get undressed and receive him with open arms? He's not sure. Yet he wants her. Badly. A part of him feels an animalistic need to repossess her after she cheated, even though he pretends not to know. Another part wants to keep the peace until she fully recovers. *If* she recovers. There is still a chance she could get worse.

He walks into the living room, deciding to play it by ear.

"*Hej*," he says jovially.

She's sitting up, cradling her knees.

"What's going on?" he asks. "Are you okay?"

Is she upset about her mum leaving? At least she's not crying but he sits down and hugs her. She hugs him back. That's a good start. Then he kisses her cheek, her forehead, her lips. She doesn't exactly kiss him back but she doesn't pull away.

"I've missed you," he says.

He strokes her back and moves his hands to the front, over her breasts. She closes her eyes so he pushes her down onto the bed, pulling at her knickers.

"Wait, Erik," she says, opening her eyes again and perhaps he's moving a bit fast but at that moment his fingers reach her magic spot and it sounds as if she's letting out a moan, which spurs him on. He rubs and circles for a few seconds before he yanks his trousers down.

"Erik, I'm not..." she starts but he's already hard, she's his wife, and he's waited patiently. Surely he can't be expected to stop now? This will be good for her memory, it will bring them back to the beginning when they were newly married and couldn't keep their hands off each other. He separates her legs and she doesn't stop him, so he quickly pushes himself into her, moving in and out.

"I'm your husband!" he pants but at that moment, she starts to bang her hands on his shoulders, begging him to stop.

"Stop Erik, just STOP..."

But he can't. He's so close, he just needs to...

"Argh!"

He comes hard, releasing his long-suppressed spunk into her. He lies on top of her for a short while, realising that he's heavy and she's still in recovery; he should move. She lies underneath him like a dead person, completely motionless, when he pulls out of her and sits up.

"I'll get some tissues," he says.

He can't look at her right now.

When he comes back with a roll of toilet paper, Anna is sitting at the end of the bed, the wet spot gleaming in the sunlight. He wipes at the bed linen, grateful that his mum isn't there to do the laundry.

"Anna," he says. "I'm sorry if that was too soon."

"You've missed me," she says.

He looks at her, surprised.

"I *have* missed you," he says.

"There's something I need to talk to you about."

She's got an apathetic look on her face and he tenses.

"I need your help," she says. "That boy, Da... David. He needs to go."

"Sure..."

"He was here, Erik." Her shoulders slump. "Just before you came home, he was here. He was *looking* at me."

"What do you mean?"

Didn't David leave for school earlier? Had he come back?

"I woke up and he was standing right in front of me, looking at me. I felt scared."

A protective instinct hits Erik but he also needs to defend David since he's the one who brought him into their house.

"He seems to think you're the greatest teacher on earth," Erik says. "He's a fan. You have a lot of them, remember?"

"I don't care, Erik. It was creepy. I need him gone."

It bothers him that she's ordering him around but perhaps he can let this one go.

"Did you speak to Kent?" she asks.

He shakes his head. "No, but I will do."

"When?" she demands.

He sighs. "I guess, right now."

*

Erik isn't looking forward to seeing Kent after accusing him of being a bit too chummy with Anna, but he does need his help. Apart from Anna's comments just now, he has to admit that David has overstepped the boundaries. He's made himself a little too comfortable. The night before, he even gave Anna a kiss on the cheek before going to bed. Erik witnessed her recoil at his touch but assumed it was because she didn't want anyone to touch her. Now he's not sure. He just wanted to be seen to do the right thing.

"Come on in, Erik."

Kent is always so sickeningly pleasant, it makes it hard to hate him.

"Hi there, sorry to disturb you."

"No problem. How is Anna settling in at home? You must be ecstatic!"

"I know, it's just... she's still recovering."

Kent shows him into the living room and they sit down. No coffee or whiskey like last time, Erik notes. Maybe that's because Märta is absent, or he just wants Erik out of there as soon as possible.

"When do you think she'll be back at work?" Kent asks.

That's all you fucking care about, isn't it? "Not for a while. Anyway, I came to talk to you about one of Anna's students, David." He realises he has no idea what David's surname is. "He's been helping me with the children, babysitting and stuff, but he's, well..." It sounds so embarrassing. "... he ended up staying the night when his place was being fumigated and now he keeps delaying moving back home."

"Did you ask him to leave?"

"Of course! He's just... he's a smooth operator, comes up with excuses."

"Erik, you're the adult."

Erik stares at Kent with contempt. It takes all of his mental strength not to hit him. Through gritted teeth, Erik explains that he is aware of this.

"Right," Kent says. "So, what do you want from me?"

He's so different, Kent, when it's just the two of them. Maybe he does secretly fancy Anna, or he just thinks that Erik is a piece of shit.

"Do you know anything about him?" Erik says, swallowing his anger. "Where he lives? I might need to speak to his mother."

"David?" Kent leans back on the flower-patterned sofa. "I'm not sure I know who that is. I know most of Anna's students, but not all of them of course."

Erik takes out his phone. "I took some photos last night when we were celebrating the boys' birthday."

"Oh, are they six already? Please wish them a happy birthday from me. They must be thrilled to have their mum back."

Erik nods. *That's kind of obvious, don't you think?* "Here." He moves across to the other side of the coffee table and sits next to Kent. He points to David.

Kent looks at him, his eyes growing. "Erik, that boy's name isn't David. That's Daniel, the boy who was giving Anna a difficult time at the beginning of the year."

"What?" *Fuck. He's been taken for a ride?* "Are you sure?"

"Yes, that's definitely Daniel."

76

Daniel

When Dan gets back to Anna's house he knocks on the door but no one answers. He knocks again. Same result. Even though they have agreed not to ring the doorbell in case Anna is sleeping, he pushes the black button outside the main entrance just the same. But nothing. He knows she's in there, so why isn't she opening the door? Perhaps she's in bed, unable to get up. He should have insisted on having his own key.

He walks around the house and looks in through the windows. Anna is lying in her bed in the living room and Erik is sitting next to her, talking. He tries to open the patio door but someone has locked it since he left. Can they not see him? He bangs on the window.

"Hello! Can you please let me in?"

Erik looks up, then he looks at Anna and they nod to each other. What the hell was that about? Erik picks up his phone and talks to someone, and Dan automatically takes a step back. Should he walk away? Are they on to him? Did Anna understand what happened this morning and has she told Erik? Is that what this is about?

Before Dan has made a decision about leaving, Erik looks at him, smiling and waving. Dan relaxes. Maybe Erik had to speak to the hospital about something urgent. Is Anna okay?

Erik gets up and walks across the floor to the patio door. It feels like it takes him a million years. Dan places his hand on the handle, eager to get in.

"What's wrong?" he says when Erik opens the door. "How is Anna?"

"She's fine," Erik says. "Just tired."

"I was ringing the doorbell. I thought you couldn't hear me?"

Erik doesn't respond. Instead he says: "Are you hungry, David?"

Dan looks over to Anna but she's lying down now, facing away from him, the duvet covering her.

"I could eat," he says.

They walk into the kitchen where Erik opens the fridge and pulls out leftovers from the previous night.

He sits down while Erik puts lasagne on a plate and heats it in the microwave. Why is he doing this? Is he just being nice? His body language seems stiff. He gets the feeling he has upset Erik somehow.

"So, you're ready to teach me the guitar later?" he says.

If he can get Erik into the basement, he should be able to overpower him there. Erik is fairly well built but so is Dan, plus he's found a set of golf clubs in the wardrobe downstairs that he can use.

"Maybe not today," Erik says.

"Oh, that's a shame. I was looking forward to it."

He starts to hum "Should I Stay or Should I Go" by The

Clash, but quickly stops. The lyrics don't feel appropriate: he's not going anywhere.

When the microwave pings, Erik puts the plate in front of Dan without a word. He hands him a knife and fork and a glass of water. It feels odd, being waited on like this, but perhaps that's what normal families do? They feed their family and friends.

"Where are Sebastian and Lukas?" Dan asks.

"At a friend's house."

"Right."

Erik keeps glancing towards the door. Is he expecting someone?

"I think Anna had a visitor this morning," Dan says.

"Really?"

Just then, the doorbell rings and Erik runs over, seemingly relieved. Who is it?

With his mouth full of pasta, Dan looks up when two people approach him. It's a woman and a man in police uniforms.

"*Daniel*," they say. "You'd better come with us."

*

It's all very confusing and it feels more serious this time. He's allocated a lawyer of some sort and suddenly, Frida is in the room. She sobs hysterically, lashing out at the police from time to time. "It wasn't him! You have it all wrong! Leave him alone!"

It feels like an action movie or a deranged comic, where the innocent are captured and tortured. They have his notebook. That fucking stinks. It's private. At first he just stares at it across the table.

They expect him to talk, but so far it's mostly Frida's voice that can be heard. He can't stand her pleading but eventually it becomes clear to her that nobody is taking any notice. She changes tack, predictable that she is, bringing out her round sad eyes and her smarmy voice: "I may be a bit stupid and not understand, so could you explain why we're here exactly?"

That's what she said to Anna as well. "I don't understand the stuff Dan is studying. It's going to make me look stupid." It's such bullshit. He already knows she's stupid. All she cares about is men who are prepared to fuck her. They always come first.

"So here we are again," they say.

He doesn't respond. What is it about this time?

"We have found a bracelet of Anna's amongst Daniel's belongings. It has blood on it. She was wearing it the night of the attack. There are also a number of compromising statements about Anna in his notebook." The policeman clears his throat and adds. "According to his own notes, Daniel has also associated himself with someone called Black Adam. It turns out that Anna received a large number of emails from someone calling himself that very same name."

"Bah!" Frida exclaims. "Who cares about emails? Anyone can claim to be someone and send an email these days."

Dan straightens his back. It's just occurred to him that Frida is defending him. He moves his chair closer to hers and she puts an arm around him. That feels good, not demanding but comforting.

"It's not just emails—" the policeman starts, but Frida interrupts him.

"Look," she says. "I think Dan has harboured some very loving feelings for Anna because, well, I probably haven't been the best mother and she is very... I mean, I can see why he would like her."

Hearing Frida speak like that about Anna makes him feel even better. Maybe sitting here, in this room, isn't so bad after all.

"I love Anna," he says, spurred on by Frida's words. "She sees me, she acknowledges me and despite some stupid shit I have pulled on her, she hasn't reported me to anyone."

Frida removes her arm. Maybe he got a bit carried away? Nevertheless, it saddens him that she lets her pride get in the way. She should be happy that someone has made her son feel like this. He can't stop, however. They need to understand how wonderful he thinks Anna is; that he wouldn't hurt her.

"Anna isn't like other teachers," he says. "They take their phone out as soon as a class is over, but I've never even seen Anna with a phone. Her attention is always on the students, on me..." He stops and looks at Frida, but she's avoiding eye contact. "We have moved a lot," he continues. "I mean a lot! And I have tried everything from being the quiet student who makes no fuss to being a troublemaker. And guess what?" He looks directly at the policewoman sitting opposite him whose eyes seem to care. "It makes no bloody difference! When you move, everyone forgets you. This time, I did want to draw attention to myself because I wanted Anna to notice me, and yes, I did email her and I did threaten her but I didn't do anything. I love her."

"You threatened her?"

He buries his head in his hands. He shouldn't have said that. Now what? He's not sure he wants to betray Anna and tell them about her and that woman, kissing. If she finds out he snitched, she will be upset with him.

"I wanted to move in with her family," he says.

Frida bursts out crying and he glances at her pathetic form, make-up running down her face. He feels no compassion. This woman fed him crisps for breakfast and made him clean up the vomit of strangers; she made a fool out of him in front of his friends until he realised it wasn't worth having any. He feels the rage accumulate at the memories of his failed childhood.

"You can't blame me," he says. "I wanted a normal fucking family."

"I'm your mother!"

"Don't even start!" he shouts. He doesn't care where he is; he can't control himself any longer. "Since when do you act like a mother?"

"Since now," the policewoman interjects. "She's here, isn't she?"

They both fall silent.

"Tell me about this bracelet," the policeman says, holding up a picture of a silver chain with two hearts on it.

Dan recognises it. "Anna used to wear that every day."

"Not when she was brought to the hospital," the policeman says.

"Maybe she dropped it somewhere?" Dan suggests.

"Or the attacker wanted a memory of her."

"It wasn't me," he says. "I didn't take that bracelet."

"And yet we found it hidden in your notebook."

His brain explodes. Did he take that bracelet? He remembers being upset with Anna in the parking lot, how she pushed him off and he fell to the ground like a stupid little kid. All he wanted was to rip her clothes off but she wanted nothing to do with him. Yet she hugged him. She grabbed his arm in a loving way and pulled him close. Surely he didn't misunderstand that?

He closes his eyes and pictures Anna naked.

Her expression is calm, her hair falling freely around her face. She smiles at him and stretches out a hand.

He takes it and together they walk into the woods behind the school. She's leaning against a tree and he lifts her up—

"Daniel?"

He looks at them.

"I didn't do it," he says. "I wouldn't hurt Anna."

The policewoman leans over the table.

"Daniel, where were you the evening of March the eighth?"

"I don't know."

"Maybe your mum knows?"

Dan looks at Frida. Why would they trust her? She's a mess.

"He was at home doing his homework," she says.

Frida cries and Dan knows why. She was most likely too pissed to know where he was. The question is: will she still confirm it to save her son? Dan needs to get out of this joint. He has unfinished business he needs to take care of.

Apparently Frida isn't a watertight alibi. Did anyone else see him at home? Did they have a pizza delivered? Frida looks as if she's thinking while Dan slowly feels the hope run out. It seems like he will have to stay here for a long time.

77

Rolf

Rolf is living every day as if it's his last. Mistakes change your life. He's learned that the hard way. No more messy affairs, no more controversy, no more media attention. He would also like to say "no more women" but that would be like cutting off his balls. There are limits.

His bags are packed and the moving van in the courtyard is full.

"Are you running away?" Karin asks over the phone.

His daughter's inherited directness always cheers him up.

"I'm not running away from anything," he says. "The police let me go, remember? It's just time to sell the house and create a life elsewhere."

"What about my childhood memories?"

"They're documented in a photo album somewhere."

"Seriously, Dad? Don't you think it's mean to let me suffer just because the two of you fucked up?"

"Hey," he says. "You might be of age but we're still your parents."

She laughs. "I'm just messing with you. Anyway, I would like to see you soon."

"Really? You don't need money, do you?"

She scoffs. "Since when do I ask for money? You know that I take care of myself."

He does. She has a monthly student grant, a generous loan that the state provides, and on top of that she works in a café on the weekends.

"It's just that I hear parents from your old class complain about their kids needing money."

"I'm not like other kids, and you're not like other parents. Anyway," she says. "You might have guessed that I've met someone and I want him to meet you and Mum."

His little girl with a boy in her life.

"Just bring him to your mother's place," he says. "I'm allowed to visit."

"But first, there's something you should know. He's not my boyfriend... He's my fiancé."

What the hell? Rolf wishes he were drinking so that he could get something caught in his throat and cough loudly. Instead he gasps silently.

"You're too young! Who is he? Did he get you pregnant? Is that why he asked you to marry him? And why didn't you tell us?"

"You done?" she asks calmly.

He sighs. "Yeah." Fuck, he really is losing everyone at the same time.

"Look, Dad. I'm not pregnant and he didn't ask me. I asked him."

She's taking charge of her life and this shouldn't exactly surprise him.

"Congratulations," he says. "I hope I'll like him..."

"Thanks, Dad. You will. And I'm sure Mum will too. So... the million-dollar question... what is Mum going to do now?"

The movers are packing up his paintings, revealing one at the back that he hasn't seen for years. It's of Iris. She's holding a book in her hand but she's gazing out over the garden; a shawl is draped over her legs and there's something sorrowful about her posture. Did he ever make her happy?

"Have you asked her?" he says.

"Of course," Karin says. "You know what she's like, though, she's like a clam. She won't tell me anything. I heard she woke up though, that woman."

"Yes, she did." He pauses as they pack up the painting of Iris. A part of him doesn't want to keep it, but at the same time, he can't bear to lose it. "Look, Karin... I have made a lot of mistakes in my life, I mean, I have seen them as learning experiences of course, not mistakes, but... your Mum, she's a much better person than I am. That woman might not want your mum anymore, so who knows what the future holds. Know what I'm saying?"

"Sure, I mean, my life already consists of an interesting brocade of people, so I'll support you both. So, where are you moving to?"

He's moving to a farmhouse, east of Gothenburg. At least for now, until he decides what he wants to do with the rest of his life.

"Gothenburg," he says. "So that I can keep an eye on you."

"That's cool as long as you don't interfere with my life too much," she laughs.

Rolf is standing in his bare studio, watching the movers pack the last pieces.

"I'm changing my style anyway," he says. "I'm going to paint something I feel passionate about. Nudes."

She chortles. "How original! But I mean, good for you."

He imagines the women lining up, willingly losing their clothes for him. Maybe some of them will be comfortable with him painting in the nude, maybe others won't. Either way, he will live an authentic life, filled with art, sex and strong family ties.

"So you're sure you're not escaping Hågarp?" Karin says.

"Not exactly," he says. "My new motto is simply 'if you find yourself in a hot seat... move seats'."

78

Erik

Officer Johansson has arrived at Erik's house with one of her male colleagues. They're sitting at the kitchen table but have turned down his offer of coffee.

"We appreciate that Anna can't come to the station right now," Officer Johansson says. "So we thought we would come here instead."

Erik wonders if everyone on the police force is as accommodating.

"She still doesn't remember anything about that night," he says.

"If she doesn't," Officer Johansson says, "then we need to assess whether to involve a therapist."

A therapist? More people coming and going in this house?

"Of course," he says. He needs to be agreeable.

"But first, we wanted to talk to you."

"Is this about Daniel?"

Officer Johansson nods. "We had to let him go."

What? No! "Why?"

"He's got an alibi," Officer Johansson says. "He can't have been at the school parking lot at the time of the attack."

"But he's creepy."

"Maybe so, but he can't have attacked Anna."

"What if he's bought his alibi? Kent told me his brother is a criminal."

"Erik," Officer Johansson says, making him feel like a child. "We are following all leads."

He finds himself missing Tina. They're so vague and diplomatic, but he mustn't show too much emotion. The iPhone on the table that is about to capture Anna's conversation might already be recording. He's not the enemy. Can't they see how much he cares about his wife?

"Everyone talks about Anna being dedicated to her work and not having any interests outside of school. She doesn't seem very tight with anyone around here. That must mean you're very close?"

"We are," he says.

"We have also spoken to her family..."

"I bet her father could have something to do with this," Erik interrupts. "He's a violent man." Why hasn't he thought of that before?

"He was at an auto convention with his wife. Anyway, there are people who don't seem to think you had such a great marriage."

Oh. "We do," he says. "I mean, of course we don't always see eye to eye but we love each other."

He starts to cry. It can't be helped. His marriage is under attack and David or Daniel or whatever his name is, has been released. What now?

"We appreciate how stressful it must be to care for your wife at home while she recovers," Officer Johansson says.

"Thank you for saying that," he says sincerely. Thank you. "Just find the person who attacked her," he pleads.

"I think we're ready to see Anna now."

*

Erik brings Anna into the kitchen. She walks by herself now, steadied by his hand. They greet each other and Officer Johansson apologises for the intrusion but Anna says she's grateful for the work they're doing.

"We don't want to bother you," Officer Johansson says. "We just have a few questions."

Anna nods. "Okay."

They look up at Erik and he realises he's expected to leave.

Why do they always make him feel like he can't be trusted? But he backs away. He has no choice.

"I guess I'll leave you to it."

He closes the door and walks up the stairs with heavy feet to signal that he is out of the way. Except he immediately sneaks back down again. The kitchen door is thin enough for him to hear what's going on. Anna is vulnerable; he can't leave her alone. That would be irresponsible.

"Do you know Pernilla Arvidsson?" they ask her.

Wow, straight in his gut. No small talk.

Anna doesn't say anything at first. He presses his ear against the white MDF door.

"The name is familiar," she says eventually.

Erik's had enough of Pernilla. Can't she run off with Sophie's dad and be done with him?

"If you think of anything, let us know," Officer Johansson can be heard saying.

"Okay."

Anna sounds so eager to please and he knows she's frustrated that she can't offer more help.

"We need to ask you something else." The policeman clears his throat. "Did you see your husband at the school parking lot the night you were attacked?"

Pernilla! That lying bitch. He wants to scream through the door. It must be her.

"Erik?" Anna says. "No, why would he have been there?"

"We have to ask."

"No," Anna says. "That doesn't make any sense."

There's muffled conversation and he can't hear them. When it sounds like they're about to pack up, he quickly runs upstairs to avoid getting caught. Then he waits until his name is called.

"Erik?" It's Officer Johansson. Anna's voice isn't strong enough.

He walks downstairs at a leisurely pace. *See, I've been busy up here.*

*

When they have left, Anna turns to Erik.

"They asked if I saw you in the parking lot. It sounds like someone might have seen you there." She looks as if she's trying to remember. "No, hang on, they said that someone *did* see you but that the person isn't necessarily trustworthy. That's why they needed to talk to me."

He leans his head back, sighs. *Shit.*

"Maybe someone is making it up," he says.

"Who?"

"I don't know."

"Erik, this isn't a time for secrets." She looks so helpless. "I need to remember. Please."

"I know," he says and places his hands over hers on the table. "But it's got nothing to do with you."

"Nothing to do with me?"

"I'm sorry, I didn't mean…" Maybe it's better to come clean? She will find out sooner or later anyway. "There's this girl who's been really into me and I think she might have said something to the police to piss me off."

Anna nods. "Right. Why would she want to get you in trouble?"

"Because I'm not into her."

"Anymore?"

It's like an alarm going off in his body. Does she know about Pernilla?

"I guess," he says.

"I'm trying to remember, Erik. No guesses, please."

The mild woman who was wheeled into the house a week ago seems to have gained some strength. He wants to lash out at her, tell her how hard these last three months have been, but how would that help? They would argue and he would be labelled the bad guy.

"Erik, I can't do this. I feel like I don't know you."

"What do you mean?"

Every moment since she came home feels like a test. He's not sure what's right or wrong, how to act, what to say.

"Who is she?" she asks.

He won't get into this. What he will do, however, is hold up a mirror and reflect Pernilla's pettiness right back at her.

"Perhaps she was so jealous she decided to get rid of the competition?"

The shocked look on Anna's face makes him regret his words.

"I'm sorry," he says. "I shouldn't have said that."

Pernilla was so sweet initially. Caring. The way Anna used to be. She listened and laughed and joked with Sebastian and Lukas. The way a mother should. Anyway, he obviously misjudged her. *You also misjudged Anna.*

"Why did we get married?" she asks. "I just don't feel... in love with you."

"Please don't say that," he says, injured. "After everything we have gone through, don't say that. You will feel it, I'm sure."

She pulls away and shakes her head.

"No," she says. "I want a divorce, Erik."

79

Anna

The following morning, Anna tells Erik to go to work. She needs to be alone, to think.

"I don't need a babysitter," she says.

"I'm not sure…"

"Please," she begs. "I need to rest and it would be nice to have some peace and quiet so that I can sleep, watch a bit of TV and perhaps even read."

He hesitates and she understands it's because of the previous evening's conversation. Erik hasn't agreed to the divorce yet. He told her that he married her for life.

"We are meant to be together, Anna," he said but nothing about his body language mimicked the passion or conviction that Iris had shown.

She appreciates everything Erik has done and she has tried, but her request for divorce slipped out and when it did, she found it more liberating than terrifying.

Anna remembers Iris. Their bodies entwined, pleasuring each other, moaning and giggling. How effortless it was. She wants to feel that way again but she needs to be on her own now, to get back to her old self. It's pointless telling Erik about Iris; until she has regained her full memory, she can't be with anyone. Anna hoped that Erik would help her fill in the gaps but every day she's annoyed with him. She's not sure why.

"What is it about me that you love?" she asked him.

She felt she had asked that question before, she just couldn't remember when. Nor could she remember his response.

"We have two children together," he said.

"Is that enough?" she asked, deciding to put pressure on him. "What is it about *me* that you love? Help me remember."

She wanted him to tell her that she was the only woman for him, that he loved her laugh, her eyes or her hair. Anything that she could hang onto.

He looked teary-eyed. "I don't know," he admitted. "I just feel like my life has gone down the toilet except for those two boys and I can't be without them, not even every other week if we share custody."

"That will be hard for me too," she admitted.

"I won't do it."

And there it was again. A flickering memory. He had said that before. *I won't do it.* Her memory was still fitting together like a puzzle, the pieces finding their place one at a time. Was it when she was offered the job in Mörna and she asked him to move with her? Or was it when she suggested they have children or when she asked him to take paternity leave? Nothing was ever straightforward with him.

"You have to take some responsibility," she said. "If you're not satisfied with your life…"

"Oh, here we go again," he said. "No, I'm not bloody satisfied with my life, especially not having a wife who wants to divorce me, and oh, I have a dead-end career. So apart from my boys, I pretty much have nothing."

"I didn't tell you to give up your music ambitions," Anna said.

At that point he stormed out of the kitchen and left her alone.

*

By half-past eight, Erik has agreed to leave but there is a knock on the door. It's two police officers.

"We just want to check that everything is okay," they say.

Erik is impatient and tells them he needs to take the children to day care.

"Can we come inside and talk to Anna?"

Erik looks at her and she nods. Of course they can.

"You go," she says to him but he lingers while they step into the hallway.

"We just want to make sure you're all right."

"Thanks," Anna says. She appreciates their concern. "But really, I don't think you need to worry. There still have been no threats."

This has slightly surprised her. If someone so violently attacked her, then he or she must have really hated her. Does that person feel satisfied, just knowing she was hurt? Is that enough? She hopes so.

She promises to call if anything seems suspicious and Erik assures them that Anna is only left alone for very short periods of time. They also show the police their new burglar alarm, with a panic button for Anna.

After they leave, Erik hugs her.

"You see," he says. "You need me to stick around to protect you."

"You're going to be late," she says, withdrawing from his embrace.

She kneels down to hug the boys, pulling them both close.

"Mum, you're hurting us," Lukas laughs.

"I love you so much," she says, breathing in their scent, remembering the baby stage when she tried to nurse them both at the same time. It made her feel like a cow! The sudden memory makes her smile.

"Mummy needs to rest," she explains. "But when you come home, I want you to tell me all about your adventures."

"We will," Sebastian promises.

When Erik and the boys have left, the house is completely quiet. She thinks of her beautiful boys playing at day care today and although she will miss them, she knows they will have fun. They have so much energy. Every time she sees them, she feels abundantly cheerful. That's an emotion she remembers.

She lies down on her bed, to rest and let her mind wander. All she can hear are the trees blowing in the wind outside, birds chirping; the stillness makes her feel content. At least until the previous evening's conversation repeats itself in her head. She's leaving her husband. That's big.

She shuts the thought down. It's too much for her brain to cope with right now. Her thoughts drift to the police instead. Why do they keep checking up on her? If only she could remember that night.

Daniel threatened her. She remembers that. She remembers *him*. He wrote her letters and emails and he was there, in the parking lot. Was it the same night as the attack?

That's the tricky part. She doesn't know. *You will do as I say.* He wanted to live under her roof and somehow he had managed to do that without her knowledge. Was that his plan all along? To attack her, get her out of the way and then wriggle his way in? He kissed her and she rejected him. Had he punished her?

She gets out of bed and walks through the house, to spark those final memories. This is her home but she feels like a houseguest. As soon as she feels better, she will move somewhere else. Maybe even sooner if she can arrange it. She decides to start upstairs. It takes her a while; she must stop on every other step and take a couple of breaths before she can move on. With each step, however, she feels her strength returning and it's a good feeling. She needs to be strong.

Sebastian and Lukas's room is a mess. She smells their pillows, her insides pulling so hard at her, she must steady herself. They are both incredibly pure. What must it have been like for them, seeing her in the hospital, not knowing if she would ever wake up again? The recurring guilt pains her. What could she have done differently? How could she have prevented this from happening? She feels very strongly that she had something to do with it, that it somehow was her fault.

She makes the boys' beds and moves onto the landing and into her and Erik's bedroom. The desk is still a mess and there are clothes all over the floor. She's been upset about this chaos many times before. She can hear her own voice: "Can you please, please pick up after yourself?" Sounding like a mother.

She feels an urge to tidy up. If she can clear up a part of the house perhaps she can also find some peace. She gathers up all the clothes and separates them into the two laundry baskets in the bathroom: white clothes in one and all the rest in the other. Exhausted, she sits down by the desk and stares at the paper pile towering like a pyramid in the middle. She picks one at random. An electricity bill. She puts it to the side. There are a number of bills and she wonders if Erik has paid them.

She knows she should be resting and not worry about mindless matters such as this but maybe something will trigger a recollection of an event that evening. Books always talk about an item or a phrase or a song bringing back a memory.

Seeing Iris made her happy. Nothing had changed. Her body might be bashed-up but her feelings are intact. Has she ever told Iris that she loves her? She can't remember. Yet she ended it because she felt she owed it to Erik to stay. He took care of her, sat by her hospital bed, willing her to wake up. His mother told her on the phone, how he was there every day.

She clears the desk, organising everything into piles. It's cleansing.

Then she makes the bed and lies on top of it. It feels odd, as if this has always been temporary. Her bedside table, a flea market bargain, is empty apart from her alarm clock. Erik's is another story. It's overflowing with glasses, beer bottles and crisp packets. She clears it all away, to make it look like an adult's bedroom, and then she pulls out the drawer in his bedside table.

Ever since Anna returned home from the hospital, Erik has felt like a stranger to her. She remembers their wedding day but the man she has come home to seems different. It's strange, to remember a day filled with laughter and love many years ago, but not being able to remember recent events. He just seems preoccupied. She remembers him as funny, charming and safe. What happened to him? Is it her fault? Has the incident crushed him? She wants to find proof of his love for her, love letters or photos of the two of them together during happy times. Even though she has decided to move on, she needs those full memories to tell her children one day.

There is a neat stack of papers in the drawer and she takes them out: birthday and anniversary cards, a notepad and a white envelope that has been torn open. All the cards are either from herself or the children. She opens all the cards to see what she's written. Most of them are pre-printed with only a line by her: *I love you, hugs from Anna.* The letter is the life insurance paper they signed when they bought the house. It strikes her that Erik thought she might die. That must have been awful. Maybe she should go easy on him? He's been through a lot.

She opens the notepad and finds a list of items with figures next to them. *Deposit for an apartment... new guitar... leasing of a recording studio.* The list is long and at the bottom, there is the total price tag, 2.5 million kronor. That's the value of their house. The value of their life insurance. Has Erik already spent the money he would have earned from her death?

It feels like a stab wound. He's already imagined a life without her.

It seems as if he has done it with ease as well, with enthusiasm even. He was planning to make his music dream come true, and leave this house for an apartment. How could he possibly think that would be better for the boys? Sebastian and Lukas don't even seem to factor into the list. Also, if he is so happy to have a life without her, then why is he against a divorce? It doesn't make sense. She looks at the list again. It's like a shopping list for a new life and it stings.

She puts everything back in its place when a folded page falls out of the pad. It's a different colour to the rest. Pastel green, like the paper provided in the school library. She picks it up and unfolds it. It's got printed text on it and as she starts to read it, she feels sickened.

ANNA IS CHEATING ON YOU WITH A WOMAN WHO LIVES OR WORKS IN HÅGARP. IF YOU WONDER HOW I KNOW THIS IT'S BECAUSE I SAW THEM TOGETHER, KISSING. NOT JUST IN A FRIENDLY WAY BUT PASSIONATELY, WITH TONGUES. YOU SHOULD LEAVE HER. SHE DOESN'T LOVE YOU. SHE WILL NEVER LOVE YOU AGAIN.

Her heart almost stops. Daniel went through with his threat. Erik knows about Iris. Or perhaps he didn't believe the accusations? After all, he wouldn't have known who the note was from. It could have been from anybody; it could have been made up. Erik must have thought it was a lie. There was no proof. No pictures. He wouldn't have paid any attention to it. Maybe he was going to show it to her but then she was assaulted and it was forgotten about?

What should she do now? Tell him that she found the note and explain to him what it was actually about? The very thought makes her sweat. She doesn't feel strong enough; they might argue. She will leave it for now. Having made a decision makes her feel better but her hand is shaking as she closes the drawer.

*

That evening, Erik brings home pizza from the local pizzeria. They eat with their hands. The boys are bubbly but Anna finds it difficult to keep up. All the time, she keeps thinking of the note and the list. *Calvin Klein underwear... Armani jeans... Trips to New York and Los Angeles – visit music studios.* So much detail. And Daniel. He had purposefully tried to sabotage her marriage.

"Not hungry?"

"It's probably the medication," she says.

"So how was your day today?" Erik asks while chewing. He quickly polishes off a slice and picks up another one.

"Fine," she says. "I tidied up a bit."

"Why?"

"I wanted to keep busy."

*

She sleeps badly. Every now and then she switches on a light and tries to read to avoid obsessing. She needs the hours to go faster until morning when the boys will be awake. They are the best remedy for negative thoughts. Her book lies open on her lap. She struggles to absorb the words, thoughts making their way through her head like it's a complicated labyrinth.

When Erik comes down in the morning, he kisses her before heading into the kitchen. The boys jump on her bed. They cuddle and giggle and she feels joyful. There is so much love when they're in the room.

"Time to eat," Erik calls and they all walk in to find the breakfast table loaded with bread, butter, ham, cheese, sliced cucumber and tomatoes, eggs, cereal, milk, juice and coffee. There's even mustard herring, her favourite.

"Wow," Anna says. He has gone all out. She hadn't expected a *smörgåsbord*. Is he trying to prove that he does love her and that he wants her to stay? Either way, she should enjoy this time with her family.

She drinks her coffee, careful not to spill. Her movements are still shaky plus Sebastian and Lukas are taking turns sitting on her lap, wriggling around as they stretch their little bodies to pick up a glass or a cereal bowl. The coffee tastes bitter. It's like it's corroding her tongue. Maybe she's forgotten what it's supposed to taste like? She tries to eat but halfway through breakfast the sleepless night catches up with her. She's so tired she can barely spread butter on the bread.

"Are you okay?" Erik asks.

"I slept really badly last night," she explains.

"Do you want to lie down?"

She nods. Her eyelids are getting heavier. Erik helps her to the bed while the boys finish eating.

Erik tucks her in and when her head comfortably rests on the pillow and the duvet is pulled up to her chin, he leans in and whispers: "Why did you go through my bedside table?"

Her body stiffens within the sheets, her mind hazy. "I'm not..."

"That was very naughty," he says, his hand bearing down on her, slapping her cheek.

The burning sensation momentarily clears the fog, bringing with it a memory.

*

She is outside the school building. It's *that* night. Iris's husband is there. There is something unnerving about him, not only because he has followed her twice but also because of his reputation and his obvious possessiveness of Iris. His being there also annoys her. Who does he think he is, demanding that she leave his wife alone, as if Iris doesn't have a mind of her own? She feels manipulated but her conviction remains strong. Fortunately, Rolf eventually sees that and she manages to make him leave. She heads towards her car, to drive home to Erik. She is going to end her marriage.

Unlocking her car, she leans in to put her bag on the back seat. That's when she hears footsteps on the gravel behind her. She prays it isn't Rolf again. It's pitch black in the parking lot and the encounter was unpleasant enough, leaving her feeling guilty and dirty.

"Hey, wait up."

"Erik?"

She looks up, thankful that it's him. But what is he doing there?

"Are the children okay?" she asks. She holds up her phone, looking for missed calls but finds none.

"They're fine," he says. "Sleeping."

Incredulously, she asks him: "You left them home alone? They're only five…"

"I needed to talk to you."

"Couldn't it wait until I got home? I'm just on my way now…"

"It couldn't wait, Anna." His face looks hard as he continues. "Because as usual I have no idea of knowing when you will be back, since you practically live at this fucking school. And I need to speak to you right now, away from the children because I can't account for my actions."

Her throat tightens.

"Okay, what's up?" she says, trying to ignore the dread she feels. Does he know about Iris?

"I know," he says.

His eyes are so intense, she takes a step back. With the car door supporting her, she asks: "What do you know?" Perhaps he saw Rolf and wondered who that was or maybe he has found out that Daniel is blackmailing her. Anything is possible. And anything is easier to talk about than Iris.

"I know about your affair."

He takes a couple of steps towards her until they are only a few centimetres apart. She can smell his coffee breath.

"I'm really sorry," she says. "I was going to talk to you about it this evening, I just didn't know what to say or how to say it." She buries her head in her hands. "I'm so sorry, I never meant to hurt you."

"I find that hard to believe," he says. He moves even closer now, their chests touching. She feels the edge of the car door press into her back. He is upset, which is understandable. "There will have been a moment when you could have pulled back and said 'you know what, I have a husband who I promised to love until death do us part'. But you didn't."

She looks up at him, at once resenting his threatening composure.

"Erik, I am leaving you," she says, as calmly as possible.

"No, you're not," he says.

"Yes, I am."

"And the children?"

"We can share custody. You're a great dad."

"I want full custody."

"Erik, come on. We need to sit down and talk about this in a constructive manner."

But he doesn't back off. "I've been your puppet ever since

we moved here," he says. "While you have dedicated yourself to the youth of Mörna, I have put my own life on hold."

"Erik, no one has asked you to do that."

"And now you do this to me? With a *woman*?" He spits the word out and she feels a need to defend her relationship.

"At first we were just friends," she tells him. "But then it became something else."

"When people find out I will be a laughing stock!"

"I'm sorry, Erik. I love her."

That's when the first blow hits her.

She staggers backwards, her back ramming into the car door. There is no sense of time. Instinctively, she puts her hand to her head. There's blood on her fingers. She stares at the dripping redness, amazed. *Erik did this?* Bewildered, she looks around. *Did anyone see?* She hopes not, that would be embarrassing: teacher beaten by her husband.

She looks at Erik, expecting to see remorse but his fists are still tight; the vicious stare alarming her. She's about to speak when another blow strikes her head. Her back bangs into the door again and this time she falls over. She immediately tries to get back up but a boot explodes into her stomach and she screams, or at least she thinks she does; nothing comes out as she gasps. She needs to make him stop.

"Erik." She strains to find her voice. "Please... don't!"

She cries and she senses him getting down on his knees next to her. He brushes the hair out of her face and wipes her tears, almost gently. She relaxes. This was obviously just a freak accident, his temper getting the better of him.

He helps her up, holding her arm just above the elbow.

"Thank you..."

"So, you're not going to see her again?" he asks.

It feels more like an order than a question.

"Ehm..." Not seeing Iris is not an option but maybe she needs to make him think that. It's just... it's ridiculous. This is Erik, her husband for over six years. She knows him; she must be able to reason with him.

"Erik, we need to go home." She catches her breath. "To talk, properly."

"I'm sorry?" he says. "I didn't hear you? Are you going to stop seeing her?"

His tone frightens her.

"Maybe it was a rash decision," she agrees. "I will rethink it."

He laughs.

"Are you saying that because I just punched you in the face?"

He's so obnoxious, and no matter how scary this side of him is, the anger bursts out of her, the words flying out of her mouth.

"Who the hell do you think you are, using violence to control me?"

He grabs her belt and pulls her to him.

"No need for violence," he says. "You need sex? Then how about with me, right now?"

He unzips her fly.

"Erik, please don't," she says, trying to fight him off but he's wearing a big hoody and gloves, she can't scratch him or really hurt him. Instead she pleads with him. "It's me. Your wife."

"Apparently not anymore."

Now he grabs her by the lapels of her coat, and pulls her face so close, spit hits her lips. "You fucking disgust me," he says and then he rams her head into the door. Over and over, she feels the thunderous pain. She tries to fight back but he's stronger, and eventually she realises that no matter what she says or does, he will keep going.

She feels dizzy, her eyes won't focus; they're getting increasingly damp and sticky and she wipes them, only to see her hands covered in even more red. It looks like paint.

"I have nothing!" Erik shouts at her. "You have taken everything from me!"

Another boot and it sounds like something breaks. She hopes it's a tree branch and not her ribs but the agony is unbearable. Despite the pain, she clambers on to her hands and knees. A blur of movement and her head smashes against cold metal. Then everything turns eerily quiet.

80

Iris

Iris has spent the morning in bed. There is no longer a library to go to. Lena has stopped paying the rent and a group of men have cleared out the books to give them to charity. Luckily, Iris managed to save her own private English book library before Lena pettily changed the locks. Iris bought those books with her own money so they are rightfully hers, and she will keep fighting for them to be translated into Swedish. Perhaps this will be her new sole focus?

When Rolf makes his daily morning phone call, he enquires about Anna. She's still upset with him but she recognises that he's trying.

"There has been no contact," she admits.

"I'm not sure if I should say this Iris, but I will: I told you so."

"I'm not in the mood, Rolf."

"Seriously? I'm only joking," he says. "Well, half-joking anyway." He laughs. "Have a sense of humour!"

"I'm just…" She can't do this. "I don't want to talk about it."

"To be honest, I don't either. I'm sick of Anna. If you work it out, great, let me know. If you don't, even better."

"Rolf!"

This was a mistake, but then she thinks of Karin. She can't alienate herself, and so she moves the conversation along to their daughter.

"Have you spoken to Karin?"

"Yes, she has a fiancé."

"I know," she says, pleased that Karin chose to tell her first.

"You do? But we haven't even met him? Well… I guess I hadn't met your mum when I popped the question either."

"We have to let her go," Iris says.

Rolf sighs. "So, what's going on this weekend? Should we go and see your delightfully demented father?"

She's grateful that she won't have to deal with her father on her own, but she doesn't feel ready for a road trip with Rolf. Not yet.

"Not this weekend, Rolf. I'll let you know when I'm ready."

"No problem. Anyway, I have plans so I gotta go… I haven't been laid in a while."

She suspects he wants to make her jealous but he should know better.

"What about that single mother who called me?" she says.

"Actually… her son was brought in by the police because of your teacher friend. He was apparently her student."

The anger comes back.

"I swear I had no idea about his connection to her," Rolf assures her.

Is he telling the truth? Rolf does spread his oats far and wide with little thought for anything but his own satisfaction. Unless... could he have been that calculating? She's not sure anymore.

She opts for silence, not wanting to be pulled into his world.

"I ended it anyway," he tells her. "It's time for a fresh start."

She couldn't agree more and hangs up, feeling a new fire inside of her. There is no longer a "Rolf and Iris". It's only "Iris" now. She's strong and stubborn and she won't go down without a fight.

She drags herself out of bed, showers and puts clothes on. Dressed in the same outfit she wore the day Anna entered her library for the first time, she applies her signature red lipstick, and reviews the result in the mirror. What does Anna see when she looks at her? Does she see an older woman or does she see a contemporary? Does she see someone who's in love with her or who is preying on her? Does she see a woman or a librarian? A woman to be taken seriously or a hippie? She kisses herself in the mirror.

"I don't care," she says out loud. "It doesn't matter."

She heads out to the Golf. Even if Anna's husband is at home, Iris will insist on seeing Anna. She is still a friend of hers; she has rights.

81

Anna

I can hear them talking about me and feel a tingling sensation on my leg. Something light is being moved up and down my calves. It tickles.

"Be careful, Lukas. Play with the cars on the floor, not her leg." I pick up Erik's voice. It's uncharacteristically brittle.

"Daddy? Is she sleeping?"

Lukas's words make my chest tighten. I badly want to scoop him up. I'm right here, baby. I can hear you. *But however much I try, my lips won't move. I'm so tired. A tiny finger pokes my stomach and I imagine it leaves a dent in my foamy skin.*

"I want Mummy," says Sebastian and I can feel his warm breath on my face. "I want to hug her."

My baby boy squeezes me and as much as I relish the skin-to-skin contact, it also makes me want to cry. My cheek is burning. That was very naughty. *The look in his eyes, like the man he became that night in the parking lot; pent-up rage exploding out of him, repeatedly slamming my head against the car, his callous words matching his forceful hands.*

Who is he?

Sebastian hugs me even tighter and the love he shows me makes me scared. I can't live without my boys. What has Erik done to me? I try to wriggle my fingers. Maybe I can reach the panic button? But my fingers won't move. Is this how it feels to be near the end?

Sebastian is Mummy's boy, always seeking comfort in my arms whenever he's hurt. If I don't wake up, who's going to hug him and tell him it's going to be okay? He's not like Lukas, who dusts himself off and keeps going.

Sebastian's small body squashes my aching lungs, but I don't care about the pain; I care about my boys, now that I remember them. The labour of bringing them into this world, the failed epidural but the immense joy at seeing them one by one: first Sebastian and then Lukas a minute later. Tears well up. Can they see my tears? Do they slide under my eyelids and down my cheeks? Are they real?

"*Get off!*"

Erik's cry alarms me. He sounds frustrated rather than angry but soon the weight is lifted off me and my chest is once again hollow. Give him back to me. Please.

"*You have to be careful with her.*" *Erik's voice breaks.*

"*Daddy, don't cry.*"

Erik is crying? You fake bastard! *Enough with the acting. If you hated me so much you could have just left me.*

There's a piercing sound. Over and over, it echoes in my head. I want to know what it is but succumb to the heavy tiredness swaddling me like a tight blanket. In the distance, I hear someone say: "*I came to see Anna.*"

I know that voice and immediately, I fight the sleep. She came back! Despite my efforts to push her away, she came back. Please dear God don't make me fall asleep just yet. Please. Iris, I can hear you.

"Get out."

No, Erik! I want to jump up from the bed, grab him and tell him that it's not her fault. But darkness stretches its arms around me, pulls me in.

Am I dying?

82

Erik

"Will you play with us, Daddy?"

"In a minute," he says.

Anna is lying on her bed. She looks like she's fast asleep and he can't decide whether he wants to be near her until the end, or whether he should just take the boys and leave the house.

He thinks back to the night when he received the note about Anna's alleged indiscretion. Rob had briefly popped in after Anna left for school that evening, and shortly after he went home, someone slipped the piece of paper under the door. At first, Erik thought it was Rob who had put it there, but it seemed too far-fetched. Rob would have told him something like that face to face anyway. He was a simple guy, he didn't play games. Also, the person who slipped it under the door had alerted Erik to it by incessantly ringing the doorbell like it was a fire alarm. Rob had strict instructions from Anna not to ring the doorbell, to avoid waking the children up, and he wouldn't have violated that. Erik stepped into the street to see if he could catch the delivery guy or girl, but there was no one there.

He walked back inside and unfolded the note. He read it a few times, the first time laughing, the second time inquisitively and the third time with concern. Surely it was a lie? But who would want to hurt him like this, was it someone trying to upend his marriage? Pernilla?

ANNA IS CHEATING ON YOU WITH A WOMAN WHO LIVES OR WORKS IN HÅGARP. IF YOU WONDER HOW I KNOW THIS IT'S BECAUSE I SAW THEM TOGETHER, KISSING. NOT JUST IN A FRIENDLY WAY BUT PASSIONATELY, WITH TONGUES. YOU SHOULD LEAVE HER. SHE DOESN'T LOVE YOU. SHE WILL NEVER LOVE YOU AGAIN.

It just didn't sound like Pernilla's words and she didn't know that Anna had been going to Hågarp regularly. Who would know that? Maybe Kent. It was possible, but if he knew anything about Anna he wouldn't tell Erik, especially not in this mysterious way. He was too boring.

Reading the words again, Erik realised that Anna had been different lately. She had been happy, smiling to herself when she didn't think he was watching, and he knew it wasn't because of him. There was something to this note, and he couldn't ignore it.

The sensible thing to do would have been to confront her when she got home but after pacing up and down the kitchen several times, he realised he couldn't wait. The thought of another person's hands on his wife – a woman at that – was disgusting. It was like someone was laughing in his face and he couldn't take it. He had to see her immediately.

Phoning was pointless, he needed to see her reaction when he confronted her.

If she had made a mistake, he would need to punish her, but they could work it out. She had told him she was going down to the school and so he put on a dark jacket with a hood, just like the old days when someone needed to be corrected. He didn't want anyone to recognise him – he couldn't have people thinking he was irresponsible, leaving his children unattended at home. He jogged down past the supermarket and the one-storey school building, which didn't take long. She was already in the parking lot when he arrived and when he saw her he felt better. At least she had told him the truth. She was at school, not with some woman. But he hadn't expected her to confess not only to having an affair with a woman, but that she was planning to *be* with her.

"Erik, I am leaving you," she said.

Her words were so calm and his first reaction was denial. She couldn't leave. She wouldn't leave.

"I'm sorry, Erik," she said. "I love her."

That's when the brain cables overheated. It was a physical reaction. He had never hit her before, but no words could convey how truly enraged he felt. He had lost a sister once, a person who loved him unconditionally, and now he was losing his wife, a person he was supposed to spend the rest of his life with. It wasn't just the loss of his marriage that upset him; he would lose his house and the car and, more importantly, his last hope of being in the music business. She would leave him with nothing. He didn't have a penny to his name. He had dropped out of college when Jonna died and his career had been off-track ever since. Without Anna, he was a nonentity. His name wasn't on anything; he hadn't been approved for a mortgage or a car loan. For each loss that popped up in his head, he banged her head against the car door again. It made him feel better. She deserved this. She was a liar. When they bought the house and the car, she had said that, in the eyes of the law, he owned half of everything but now he was sure she must have scammed him.

"I have nothing!" he said. "I have nothing!"

She didn't respond, which was just as well. The blood made him think of life and death and that's when the life insurance came to mind. Signing it had been smart. It had felt unnecessary at the time but now he saw himself standing in the spotlight on stage. It could help him start over. With that thought on his mind, his blind anger turned to focused bashing and when she finally fell to the ground he stood back and looked at the bloodied mess that had been his wife. It felt surreal, that he could have caused this, but then he corrected himself: she had caused this herself. She hadn't even fought very hard, as if she knew her own guilt.

He went into practical mode. Did he need to worry about evidence? There were no cameras. Anna had repeatedly complained about this after computers had once again been stolen from a classroom. They needed CCTV footage of which there wasn't any. He had still scanned the area when he walked up to her, just in case. DNA wouldn't be under her fingernails or anywhere else, other than where a husband's DNA would be expected. Who knew that TV shows could be so educational? *CSI* and *Dexter* had proven their worth. He wasn't sure whether he should move her body or whether that would be too difficult? He was worried he would leave evidence behind if he did. Thankfully, the parking lot was dark and no houses had been built at the back of the school due to the adjacent land being protected. Maybe she could remain where she was? There was no one around. Finally, there was a perk with the town being deserted by ten o'clock at night. The only sound was the murmur of the ocean in the distance, his only companion.

He decided to leave her there. That's when he noticed her bracelet on the ground, the silver one with the two hearts, one for Sebastian and one for Lukas. It must have come off her wrist. He leaned down to pick it up and tucked it in his pocket, not able to leave it behind.

Her phone was another matter; he couldn't hang onto that, but leaving it was too risky. There could be compromising messages and no one should know that his wife had cheated on him with a woman. He destroyed the phone with the back of his heel, ensuring the sim card was sufficiently damaged, and took the items with him to discard of them later.

He could have told the police about the message under the door but then he would have been suspect number one. He didn't have any other proof of her infidelity anyway, other than Anna's own confirmation. It wasn't until he found the Xeroxwed emails, the shockingly graphic emails that had made it even more real, that he had had some sort of evidence. But even then, he couldn't tie them to this woman whose name he didn't know. She most likely lived or worked in Hågarp, that was all he knew, and he couldn't exactly knock on people's doors and ask them if they had fucked his wife.

He thought about going to the library in Hågarp, where Anna had supposedly been meeting with a book club, if that was even what she was doing and where she was going. He's thought about going to the library many times since but he's been too afraid of what he will find. Plus, he hasn't wanted to draw attention to himself. The moment someone realises that he understands the truth about Anna's affair, it will be trouble. He has no problem with people knowing she cheated – it helps him play the victim – but they must think he only just found out. He had needed someone else to come forward about her infidelity. If only he had better friends.

Erik kept the note in Anna's workbag together with the life insurance papers but conveniently removed the bag from the house, telling Rob he had grabbed it in haste in case Anna should need it. He expected the police to search the house within the first twenty-four hours. Once she was back home, he moved the papers to the bedside table where it should have been safe. Why did she have to spoil it by snooping around?

He had been so careful. The clothes he wore that night had never made it into the house. He stripped down in the garden, grateful for the wild and lush bushes and trees that he was yet to trim, and after getting dressed in new clothes, he put them in a black bag. He almost put the bracelet in as well but he couldn't part with it. Using the gloves he had worn earlier, he put it in a ziplock bag, which he later kept with her laptop. The rest he discarded in a bin in another road. It was his lucky night; the bins were already lining the streets, ready to be emptied by noisy trucks early the next morning, before Anna was found. No one would be out walking behind the school at that time of night and he would wait until the morning to report her missing. He wasn't stupid.

The children were an issue. When he locked the door that night, believing that Anna would never return, his heart ached for them. But they have coped better than expected.

Sure, they're happy that she's home but they also recognise that she's different which makes them wary. He can tell. That makes him confident that the three of them will be just fine.

He's been on edge for months. It unnerves Erik that someone knows about Anna and that woman, but now it's finally about to come to an end. Anna will not be around to remember that night.

He can't let her live. Now that she wants to divorce him, as soon as her memory comes back, she will tell everyone that he confronted her that night. She already knows about the note.

When the doorbell rings, Erik ignores it.

"Why aren't you opening the door, Daddy?" Sebastian asks.

"It's a Jehovah's Witness," Erik says. "Leave it."

But Lukas has already opened the door and let a woman inside.

"She says she's a friend of Mummy's," Lukas says.

Erik gets up from his chair and walks across to a woman.

"I don't think we've met," he says apprehensively.

"I'm Iris," she says, extending a hand. "Anna's *very* good friend."

She looks deeply into his eyes as she says "very" and that's when he understands. What's worse is, she wants him to understand. *This is her?* She's so much older than Anna. He wants to laugh. This is the woman she was going to leave him for? But it's not funny.

"I came to see Anna," she says.

"Get out!" He gestures towards the door. "You're not welcome here. She is *my* wife."

"I know she is. I'm just a friend visiting a friend. How is she today?"

"She's sleeping," Sebastian tells her. Then he turns to Erik. "Is she back in a coma again, Daddy?"

"No," Erik says. "Say goodbye to the lady, she's about to leave."

"But I only just arrived. I would love a cup of coffee." Iris smiles sweetly at him and he wishes the boys weren't there so that he could show this woman who the boss of this house is.

"Why don't you boys go upstairs and get dressed," Erik says. "Let Mummy's friend visit and when she leaves, which will be soon, we can do something fun, okay?"

While Sebastian and Lukas walk upstairs, Erik needs to make a decision. This woman – Iris – is not Anna; he doesn't care enough about her to put his freedom at risk.

When he confronted Anna, he didn't think. Not at first. He was just so mad, and she didn't seem remorseful enough, which made him even angrier. Now it's different. He's already tasted life without Anna and since she's not willing to stay with him, he's decided that being a widower suits him. Especially one with life insurance money.

The sleeping pills he has crushed into her coffee should be enough to kill her. If it isn't, he will simply try again, but according to his research he's given her a deadly dose. He almost killed her once and that wasn't even planned, which caused a great deal of stress. This time he's calmer and more together. This time he will succeed.

"I heard a boy from school was in custody for her attack," Iris says.

Erik nods even though they've let him go, the fools. When

he hid Anna's bloodied bracelet in Daniel's notebook, he *did* think. He needed the boy out and he needed someone to take the blame after the police released the artist. As long as Anna couldn't remember that night, it would work.

"She told me about him," she says. "That he was threatening her."

Did she now? "Then why didn't you tell the police?"

She looks him up and down as if she's in charge.

"I didn't want to hurt you," she says. "But judging by your reaction when I arrived just now, I'm guessing you already knew about us?"

Shit.

Iris walks up to Anna's bed and sits down next to her, resting a hand on Anna's.

"I'll just make some coffee," he says.

Should he crush up more of the sleeping tablets? He just doesn't know. What's the right thing to do? This is not a decision he can call a friend about, not some fifty/fifty choice. He needs to be sure. Does he even have enough left to knock Iris out as well? He might not. Also, two dead bodies will be impossible to explain. The nurse won't be back until after the weekend. By that time, Anna will have died of "natural causes" due to her recent injuries, but Iris can't. He needs to get her out of here.

He pours a cup of coffee for Iris. Later, after Anna's body has been removed from the house, he will need Iris to explain that he was polite and not in any way acting odd.

"I'm sorry about before," he says, stepping into the living room. "I'm sure you can understand that this has been a stressful..." He stops, coffee spilling over his hands, burning. "What are you doing?"

Iris is leaning over Anna's face. Is she kissing her?

"I'm not sure she's breathing," Iris says in a stressed voice. "I've called an ambulance."

"What?" *No.* "I'm sure she's fine. She sleeps very deeply these days."

He walks across to Iris and attempts to hand the coffee over but she pushes him away. "She needs medical attention. Now!"

"Call them back and cancel that ambulance," he says. "You're overreacting. This is *my* wife we're talking about, not *your* fucking girlfriend."

He grabs her by the collar and pulls her back.

"Back the fuck off!" she says and manages to get out of his grip. She's petite and slippery.

This is not good, he thinks. I need to get her out, not bash her head in.

"Please just leave," he says. "I've got this covered." He picks up his phone to call 112 to cancel the ambulance but she snatches the phone out of his hand.

"I don't think you have your priorities right," she says. "That ambulance is taking Anna back to the hospital."

"Who the hell do you think you are, thinking you can dictate what goes on in my house?"

"I love Anna," she says.

He's so close to losing it, to ripping her head off. "Don't say those words about my wife, you predatory old lesbian."

He wants to hurt her with his words instead of his fists but Sebastian and Lukas, who must have heard the commotion, are making their way downstairs. He needs the boys to love him. *I'm a sensible man, I can control myself.*

"I'm so glad you're here," Iris says to them. "An ambulance

is coming for Mummy. Can you please keep an eye out through the window for me?"

They're visibly distressed by the sound of "ambulance" and Sebastian is immediately by his mother's side. Lukas, however, does as he's told, taking up his position by the window. Erik feels the blood heating up again. This woman cannot order his children around.

"Don't talk to my children! Don't you fucking dare. Just get out!"

"Or what?"

She's not afraid of him. At school he preferred to bully than to be bullied, but Iris seems immune to his scare tactics. She's right, though. What can he do to her? Then he realises what will hurt her.

"It's too late for an ambulance," he says.

83

Daniel

There's an ambulance outside Anna's house. Dan gets off his bike and runs through the crowd that's starting to gather around. People are so nosy.

"Anna!"

There's an argument going on at the back of the ambulance. Erik and that woman from the library are trying to push each other out of the way. The boys are there too, crying. Dan walks up to them.

"I'm going in the ambulance," the woman says.

"She's *my* wife. So clearly I'm going."

"You don't give a damn about her. Get away from her."

"*No one* goes with her," the paramedic says and closes the door. "You can drive to the hospital separately but I suggest you set aside your differences before you get there."

"What's happening?" Dan asks the guy. "Is she okay?"

But there seems to be no time to answer his questions. The paramedic gets into the passenger seat and they drive off.

"What's happening, Erik?" Dan asks.

Erik's eyes are burning into him. So he lied about his name, big deal. Surely they can make up?

"Stay the fuck away from us, creep."

Apparently they can't. But the boys, they must still like him?

"Sebastian, Lukas?"

Lukas runs up to him but Sebastian is holding onto his dad's leg.

"Mummy is really sick," Lukas cries.

Dan picks him up and hugs him.

"Come on, buddy, everything is going to be fine."

"Don't touch him," Erik says. "David, I mean Daniel, hurt Mummy."

"I didn't."

The Nissan dude came to Dan's rescue. He had apparently passed by their house that night and he verified that Dan was there. Frida had been Rolf's alibi and now Rolf was his. It was like a full circle of bullshitters helping each other but so what? He was in the clear.

The woman marches across to a red car and Dan runs after her, still holding on to Lukas.

"Are you going to the hospital?" he asks. "Can I go with you?"

She stops and surveys him. "Who are you?"

"Daniel."

"Are you the student who tried to blackmail Anna?"

Oh, shit. "Sorry, yeah, but I didn't mean any harm."

"Really? Well, I have no space for you."

The woman drives off but Erik is still there. He's picked Sebastian up now and he clings to his father like a koala bear.

"What's wrong with Anna?" Dan asks.

"Don't know."

Then why isn't he driving like a madman to the hospital to find out? Erik seems paralysed. Is he in shock?

"Let's go," Dan says. "You drive and I'll go with you."

"Sorry, pal, not happening."

"Okay, how about we all go inside and calm down then?"

"You're not coming into my house." Erik turns to Lukas. "Come here, son."

Lukas shakes his head sullenly. "Don't want to."

"Lukas. Here. Now!"

Erik's face is stern but Lukas refuses. Eventually Erik comes up to Dan and tries to take Lukas from him but it's not easy with Sebastian still clinging to him.

"He doesn't want to," Dan says. "Leave him be. He's okay. I can hold him."

"I want you to go."

Dan doesn't. They stand on the street for ages, both holding a child, trying to stare each other down. No one interferes but at some point a car pulls up next to them.

"It must be here to get you," Erik says. "After you escaped the last time."

Dan wants to run but he can't leave Lukas. Equally, he can't bring him. That would be kidnapping.

"Erik." It's Gerda, Anna's mother. Her hair swept back in a bun, the glasses heavy on her nose. "Anna called me last night and she didn't sound happy so I have driven *all* the way here."

"Hello," Dan says.

"This is *Daniel*," Erik says. "Not David. Daniel is the student who made Anna's life hell."

What? He didn't do that.

Gerda steps up to them and asks the children to join her.

"Come," she says. "Why don't we get some juice inside with Mummy."

"She's not there," Sebastian says. "The ambulance took her to the hospital."

Gerda looks at Erik. "What happened?"

"Just go inside," he says. "I'll explain in a minute. Everything is fine. I just need to take care of something first."

It's not fine, but the boys do as they're told and Dan is left feeling naked without the warmth of Lukas's little body holding onto him.

"I didn't make Anna's life hell," he tells Erik. "I love her."

"You love her?" Erik scoffs. "That's ridiculous. She would never be interested in a nobody like you!"

That's when Dan loses it, even if it's in plain view of the neighbours. He needs to eliminate this man from earth, this man who stands in his way of happiness, and now also mocks him.

He throws himself onto Erik, but Erik grabs hold of his neck and flings him onto the ground like he's made of paper. Dan is completely shocked; what the hell happened? He can't move. His legs are kicking and his hands are trying to push himself back up but Erik is strong, his grip firm. He struggles to breathe.

"Please..." Dan says. "Help..."

"Leave him alone," a woman shouts and a man grabs hold of Erik's shoulders, but he's strong and easily shakes the man off.

Erik continues what he's started: a knee pushes into Dan's back; a fist comes slamming down on the side of his head. Once, twice, three times.

Someone cries out that they've called the police, but are they bluffing? Erik appears unaffected, and Dan tries his best to get to Erik using his elbows. *Please stop!*

"You are never going to see her again," Erik shouts.

"I won't," Dan says, but he's not sure Erik hears him.

The blows continue and pinned to the ground, Dan starts to give up. *What's the point? Nobody loves me anyway.* He closes his eyes and imagines what it will be like to be dead. Will anyone attend his funeral? That's when screeching tyres bring him back to the present, a murmur running through the crowd. The pressure on his body lightens and the air flows back into his lungs. Freed, Dan quickly turns around to blue flashing lights and tries to stand up. His legs just won't cooperate. At least Erik is finally being pulled away from him, two police officers handcuffing his hands behind his back.

"Erik Berg, you are under arrest for the attack on your wife, Anna Berg."

Erik tries to break free, grunting, the rage out of control. Like a bear struggling against the restraints.

"I read your disgusting journal," Erik yells at Dan. "But guess what? She's dead."

Epilogue

"Apparently Pernilla writes to him every week. She's not working at day care anymore though. Thank goodness."

"Have the children visited their father in prison?"

"Yes."

"How are they coping?"

"They have to get used to seeing him incarcerated. On a good note, they're excited about moving to a new house and having their own bedrooms, although they're fighting about who should have the bigger room!"

"Have you spoken to him?"

"Well... yes. I felt it was the right thing to do, for the children."

"What did he say?"

"Believe it or not, he felt insulted that the police had been watching him! They told me he had been making enquiries at the insurance company recently, asking about 'what-if' scenarios. The day he drugged the coffee, he also called day care about report cards for the children, should they move abroad. Abroad? Can you believe it? Anyway, he was starting to get overly confident I think, with first Rolf, then Daniel, being arrested. The important thing for me is, that they never completely trusted him. I wish other people had felt that way too, including myself."

"Speaking of Daniel, how is he? Has anyone spoken to him?"

"Yes, he's moving to a small town south of Malmö. His mother is in AA and has a new job. This time, he says, he actually wants to move."

"That's good. What about you?"

"The children are my priority."

"And you?"

"I'm glad to be alive, thanks to you."

A man enters the room.

"Are you both ready to sign?"

The two women nod. Together they say: "One mortgage, no life insurance and no regrets."

"We intend to live our lives to the fullest," Iris says to the man.

"Ehm, good for you," he says. "But I really just need your signatures."

They sign and leave the bank, holding hands. Outside the sun is shining.

"It's good to be outside, but we need to pick the children up."

"I'd better get used to that," Iris says. "When you're running late, I guess I'll be picking them up."

Anna plans to go back to school after the summer. "Don't fix what isn't broken," as Kent rightly pointed out. "You love your job."

"What if your bookshop is busy?" she asks Iris.

"That's the pleasure of owning it. I can close it for thirty minutes!"

Anna stops in the middle of the crowded street. She looks at this woman who makes her feel alive, and kisses her for all to see. Love overshadows pain. She's able to walk, she's able to talk, she's able to think and read and raise her children.

Anything is possible.

Acknowledgements

There are so many people I would like to thank. First of all, my incredibly charismatic agent Luigi Bonomi whose enthusiasm and creative genius never ceases to amaze me. To the very best editor a girl could hope for: the wonderfully talented Sarah Ritherdon who is fabulous to work with. Copy editor Paul King, for his attention to detail – thank you!

I would also like to thank the Emirates Airline Festival of Literature (EAFOL) and Montegrappa for creating the Montegrappa Prize for First Fiction. Thank you to Isobel Abulhoul, Yvette Judge and the whole team at EAFOL, as well as Charles Nahhas.

Thank you to Alison Bonomi, Angela Chadwick and Gwenhwyfar Dunne for reading my book and providing valuable feedback, and to Danielle Zigner for coming up with the brilliant title *When I Wake Up*.

Research for this book was made easier thanks to Jörgen Winberg, Carina Bonde, Camilla Kunstelj, Linda Schönbäck,

Maria Jalakas and Jennie Eng. Any mistakes or liberties with the truth have, however, been made or taken by the author!

Without the support of friends, this book wouldn't be possible. I would especially like to thank Lotta Lindman, Teresia Stedt, Katarina Fröberg, Margareta Lindberg, Anna Janson, Annika Roslund, Anna Bromley, Sara Berger, Tobias Schildfat, Nicola Gregory, Lulu Mahaini, Sigrid Combüchen, Thérèse Granwald, Brandy Scott, Mikaela Théssen, Erica Siri, Annabel Kantaria (and the Green Suitcase Book Club), Cheryl Murree, Göran and Kerstin Larsson, for believing that I could do this. Also, thank you to my parents and my brother and his family for cheering me on. If you're not mentioned but you're in my life, that means you inspire me and for that I am very grateful.

To my wonderful husband, Mark, who is always supportive of anything I take on, and to our beautiful children who I hope are inspired to go after their dreams. I love you all.

Finally, to Aria and Head of Zeus – I am so grateful that you believed in this book, and to all the readers out there! If it weren't for you, there most definitely wouldn't be a book. Thank you!

Jessica Jarlvi